READING THE CLUES

This Large Print Book carries the
Seal of Approval of N.A.V.H.

SECRETS OF MARY'S BOOKSHOP, BOOK 3

READING THE CLUES

CHARLOTTE CARTER

THORNDIKE PRESS
A part of Gale, Cengage Learning

GALE
CENGAGE Learning·

Detroit • New York • San Francisco • New Haven, Conn • Waterville, Maine • London

GALE
CENGAGE Learning

LIBRARY OF CONGRESS CATALOGING-IN-PUBLICATION DATA

Carter, Charlotte (Charlotte C.)
   Reading the clues : secrets of Mary's bookshop / by Charlotte Carter. — Large print edition.
      pages ; cm. — (Thorndike Press large print Christian mystery)
   ISBN 978-1-4104-5867-4 (hardcover) — ISBN 1-4104-5867-9 (hardcover) 1. Booksellers and bookselling—Fiction. 2. Women detectives—Fiction. 3. Cape Cod (Mass.)—Fiction. 4. Large type books. I. Title.
   PS3553.A7736R43 2013
   813'.54—dc23   2013018330

Published in 2013 by arrangement with Guideposts, a Church Corporation

Printed in Mexico
1 2 3 4 5 6 7 17 16 15 14 13

Dear Reader,

I hope you'll enjoy your third visit to Cape Cod in *Reading the Clues,* and further getting to know Mary Fisher and her sister Betty Emerson. Since I don't have a sister, it was fun to write about sisters who are so close and loving. And, of course, the beauty of the Cape Cod area is a great locale for any story with historical elements.

The Emerson gristmill plays a large role in this story. Somewhat to my surprise, a good number of my California friends were only familiar with the lumber mills that are scattered across the Sierra Nevada Mountains. One friend thought a gristmill might be something like a "gossip mill." Of course, gristmills were actually used to grind grain, and virtually every small town had one in the early years of our country.

I have to commend the other authors of Secrets of Mary's Bookshop for the fine work they've done to set up the series. I know you'll enjoy returning to Ivy Bay again and again.

Happy reading!
Charlotte Carter

ONE

From Mary Fisher's perspective, there was nothing more exciting than opening a carton of new books — like the one the UPS man had just delivered to her bookshop. She loved the scent and texture of the paper as she rifled through the pages. She supposed that was why she'd spent much of her working life as a librarian and now owned Mary's Mystery Bookshop in Ivy Bay on Cape Cod.

It was August, and the height of tourist season in Ivy Bay. During the summer, she'd become inspired by how history and mystery often collided, so she'd established a theme for the month of August at her store. Across her front window, she and her sister Betty had displayed a banner: Ivy Bay — History, Romance, Intrigue . . . Mystery. Ever since the sign had gone up, alongside Betty's seaside-themed window display, sales had been so brisk that she'd just this morning had to order more books.

The sweet scent of freshly baked cupcakes hung in the air. Mary tried not to sample treats from Sweet Susan's Bakery next door too often, but after smelling them all day, it was sometimes all she could do to resist. She distracted herself by shelving the books she'd received in their respective sections, leaving some for the display table in the front, and stepped back to admire her work.

"What do you think, Gus?" she asked her gray cat, who was snoozing near the front counter. He briefly opened one eye, then closed it again.

She decided that was a sign of approval.

The chime over the front door tinkled, and Betty rushed into the shop as though she was being chased by a rabid dog. Her cheeks were bright with exertion, she was breathing hard, and her lightweight cardigan flapped open. Even her blonde hair, the same shade it had been when she was a young woman, looked disheveled.

"What is it? What's wrong, Bets?" A trickle of fear slid down Mary's spine. Had someone been hurt? Was the house on fire?

Even Gus stood, arched his back, and stretched, his nap disrupted by Betty's arrival.

Betty scanned the shop as if making sure

the coast was clear. There were no customers in the shop, so Betty began. "It's terrible. I don't know what to do!" Betty's words spilled out in a staccato voice, which was very uncharacteristic of her typically calm, even dignified demeanor. "I called Evan at his office, but he was out in the field with a client looking over a building site."

"*Sh,* now, take it easy. I'm sure Evan will call you back as soon as he can." Mary's sister, who was two years older, wasn't usually so excitable and rarely called her son in a panic. And given her rheumatoid arthritis, she seldom ran anywhere. She clutched a large brown mailing envelope in her hand.

"Come sit down and catch your breath. Then tell me what has happened." Mary led her sister to the pair of overstuffed chairs in the back of the shop where customers could browse through books at their leisure. Once Betty was seated, Mary dashed to the nearby refreshment table to get her a glass of water and put on some water for tea.

"Now then . . ." Mary sat in the chair next to her sister. "Take a drink and tell me what happened."

Betty's hand shook as she took a sip. She swallowed and exhaled. "I'm being sued," she said, her voice calmer but no less anxious.

9

Mary sat back and blinked. "Sued? By whom? And why?"

"A process server came to the door no more than an hour ago. He served me these papers." She handed Mary the envelope. "Daniel Hopkins is the one suing me. He claims the Hopkins family owns —" She put her hand over her heart. "He says the gristmill belongs to the Hopkins family."

"The *Emerson* gristmill?" Mary tried to imagine why anyone would say such a thing about the mill that had stood on the edge of town since sometime in the 1600s. She and Betty had played there as children during summer visits to their grandparents, even before Betty had married Edward Emerson, a member of one of the founding families of Ivy Bay. Now the only Emersons left in town were Betty; Edward's sister Eleanor Blakely, the self-proclaimed family matriarch; and Betty's son Evan and his young family. All the other Emersons had moved away.

"I couldn't make sense of those papers the court sent me." She shook an arthritic finger at the envelope. "Edward told me the Emersons had owned the gristmill since the day it was built. Since Edward passed away, I've faithfully paid the property tax every year. And Evan has even been talking to a contractor about restoring the old place. A considerable expense, but we both think it's the right thing to do. Why would Daniel say it isn't ours?"

Mary recalled a passage in Leviticus 6 where the Lord warned Moses about people stealing or extorting others for their property and how they must make restitution in full plus a fifth more. Betty had certainly not stolen the gristmill from the Hopkins family, and she didn't believe Betty's late husband Edward had either.

Hearing the teakettle whistle, Mary went to fill the teapot in the back room. She put milk in a pitcher and carried that and cups out front to Betty.

While the tea was steeping, Mary pulled the thick sheaf of paper from the envelope, adjusted her glasses, and skimmed the contents. The suit claimed that, in 1792, Isaac Emerson sold the gristmill to James Hopkins for the price of five British pounds.

She lifted her head. Gracious, 1792! That was going a long way back in history. Why was the sale and ownership of the mill just now being disputed?

"Do you have any idea what five British pounds in 1792 would be worth today?"

Betty shook her head. Her breathing had slowed to normal, and she had regained control of herself. "Probably a lot more than it was then. Evan thinks the property itself is worth quite a lot even though the mill is in disrepair." Still agitated, Betty ran a fingertip along the fabric seam on the arm of the chair.

"Sounds like there may be greed at the bottom of this suit." Mary leaned back in her chair to read the legal papers more thoroughly. "Do you have the original deed for the property?"

"I suppose it's possible, but I don't know that there ever was a deed, per se. Edward's ancestors built the mill so long ago; the area was part of the royal charter given to the Massachusetts Bay Company."

Mary appreciated her sister's depth of knowledge about the history of Ivy Bay, but for the moment, she was more worried about Betty's very contemporary problem. "I'm trying to think how to counter this suit. Surely there must be some sort of a record *if* the mill was sold as Hopkins apparently claims." She poured tea into their cups.

"All I know is that I have records of paying property taxes for years and years. The county certainly believes we own the mill. As far as I know, there's nothing in the file Edward kept that gives any suggestion the mill was ever sold." She sounded offended by even the mere suggestion that the mill didn't belong to the Emersons. That was understandable. So what evidence was the suit based on?

From the paperwork, it looked like Marc Dougher, an attorney on the Cape, had filed the suit for Hopkins. Mary wondered what sort of a man he was.

The chime over the door announced the arrival of a customer, a youngish woman dressed in shorts, halter top, and flip-flops.

"Hello," Mary said. "Is there anything I can help you find?"

"No, I'll just browse, if that's okay."

"Of course. Let me know if I can help in any way."

Mary turned back to Betty and lowered her voice. "Tell you what, after dinner tonight, let's go through what records you do have. I'm sure there's a way to put this suit to rest in a hurry."

Betty squeezed Mary's hand. "I'm sure too. Being served with papers caught me totally by surprise."

"I can sure understand that. Speaking of which, what do you know about Daniel Hopkins?" Although Jill Sanderson was in her prayer group, Mary hadn't ever met the man who was Jill's grandfather-in-law. Jill had expressed concern about Daniel's temperament since he'd moved in with her and her husband.

"Not much. I see him occasionally around town, but the Emersons have never been friends with the Hopkinses. I do know that they're a family of commercial fishermen and they live on the other side of town." She pursed her lips together and her brows lowered. "I don't want to speak unkindly of anyone, but from what I've seen, Daniel Hopkins is an angry man. I've always avoided him."

Mary nodded, encouraging Betty to go on.

"Edward didn't have anything to do with the Hopkinses either. I do remember he mentioned a couple of times something about a feud between the two families."

"What was the feud about?"

"He didn't know or wouldn't say. And you know how these stories start up and get distorted over time. Edward believed in 'live and let live.' He had no interest in pursuing whatever it was that had come between the two families generations ago."

As Mary slipped the papers back into the envelope, she wondered if Betty's sister-in-law Eleanor knew more about the feud than Edward had. "Apparently, Daniel Hopkins isn't into 'live and let live.' "

"I really can't let him take the mill away from us, Mar. It's such a big part of the Emerson family history. Edward was so proud —"

"Bets, try not to worry. I'm sure we'll find a way to stop this ridiculous suit."

Forcing a brave smile, Betty nodded.

Taking a sip of tea, Mary considered the situation. She realized in order to defend against the suit, someone would have to prove Isaac Emerson did not sell the gristmill to James Hopkins or anyone else. No easy task considering the sale was supposed to have taken place more than 220 years ago.

And proving something didn't happen was far harder than proving it did.

The young woman who had been browsing waved goodbye and went out the door.

"Maybe we should go talk with Mr. Hopkins," Mary said. "At least to find out what he bases his claim of ownership on," she suggested, her voice filled with caring. Betty's face still looked troubled, but Mary could tell her sister was comforted to have Mary by her side.

Betty shook her head. "I'm so upset that I'm not sure I could even be civil to the man. Edward and his family were honor-

15

able people. How dare Hopkins accuse them of being anything but? As much as I want to know what's going on, I don't think I'd have anything productive to say to him. I'm sure Evan will hire an attorney to represent us. Let's wait to see what the attorney advises."

That might be wise, Mary mused. But she had learned that it was often possible to solve a problem by having an honest, open conversation in order to get to the crux of the matter.

"You know what?" She stood and put the tea things back on the tray. "It's a lovely day, and I could use some exercise. Let's take a walk. Maybe it will clear our heads."

"Take a walk?" Betty's forehead wrinkled. "I suppose I could use a breather."

Mary carried the tray into the back room and retrieved a light jacket. Despite the heat of the day, there was always a breeze blowing off the ocean.

"I haven't been out to see that old mill since I moved back to town," Mary said. "Maybe we'll see something that triggers an idea about how to prove you own the mill."

Betty stood. "That's a good idea. But I should warn you, it's really run-down. Evan thinks it's unsafe."

Even though Rebecca Mason, Mary's one

employee, was off for the day, Mary wasn't worried about closing the shop for a bit. That was the beauty of owning your own business, anyway. She flipped the antique Open/Shut sign on the door to SHUT. Letting Betty out first, she locked up behind them.

As they walked, a light breeze coming off the ocean fluttered Mary's gray curls. She reflected not for the first time on how much she loved the little town of Ivy Bay. On the north side of the Cape, it was separated from the mainland by a channel. Two bridges provided access to Ivy Bay, with its charming shops and Victorian homes, some of which were on the historical registry.

"Evan was looking at the mill recently. He wants to either restore the mill or tear it down because of its poor condition. In fact, the city may insist on us doing something soon. But you see" — Betty's voice caught — "this is all my fault. In one of my last conversations with Edward before he passed away, he told me he was sorry he hadn't done something with the mill. Made it something more that all his descendants could be proud of. You remember that we were at the mill when he proposed to me."

"Yes, I remember. I thought it was very romantic of him."

"And then when he was dying, I promised
—"

Mary rubbed her sister's back to soothe her. "It's all right, Bets. We'll make it all right."

They walked past Meeting House Grocers, which had recently become one of Mary's favorite places in town, and up Meeting House Road. Cars passed by on the street, and pedestrians were strolling along peeking in shop windows.

"Evan was going to get something started, and then he got so busy. I couldn't ask him to drop everything to take care of the gristmill. But I should have done something before now. Evan has asked a contractor to take a look at the mill and give him some cost estimates."

Evan, an architect, lived nearby and had a busy life with a wife and two daughters. Even so, he had taken over some of Edward's business interests after his father's death.

"Evan is doing the right thing, and so are you." Betty's emotional response to the lawsuit had surprised Mary until she'd learned of Edward's final comments about the mill, Betty's nostalgic memories, and the promise Betty had made. No wonder her sister didn't want to lose the mill and fail her late husband.

Betty exhaled and pulled herself together.

Once out of the business district, houses appeared, many of them separated by white picket fences. When the road came near the shallow end of a pond, Mary stopped and held up a finger to get Betty's attention. "Do you hear that? Sounds like we have some saltmarsh sparrows." One of the stocky gray birds flitted so fast from one low-growing plant to another that it was hard to see the yellow markings on its face.

"They are the busiest little birds. They wear me out just watching them flit around."

As they turned the corner, the mill came into sight. Water for the gristmill ran from a pretty pond down a raceway past the mill to turn the waterwheel. Unfortunately, the aging wheel was now tilted at an odd angle, which prevented it from turning on its axis.

Sturdy gray rocks quarried from the mainland formed the mill's foundation. Someone had chiseled "1667" into the cornerstone block.

Wood siding on the building, weathered gray by hundreds of years of sun and rain, showed signs of decay, and the shutters for the windows were missing.

The mill had been used for hundreds of

years, but it had stopped operating in the 1930s. Edward's father moved the grain production to the new commercial baking facility he opened in Provincetown after the worst of the Depression was over. From there, he began delivering bread daily to grocery stores on the Cape. The company eventually expanded to a broader market, distributing specialty breads and rolls throughout much of New England.

Edward had followed in his father's footsteps, becoming the CEO of the company when his father retired, but the family had always made their home in Ivy Bay, and the mill had always been a part of their family history.

They approached the mill slowly. Years ago, someone had placed two water-worn logs across the raceway for a bridge. Mary scurried across, and Betty followed more slowly.

"Seems to me, there was an easier way to get here when we were children," Betty commented.

"Or maybe we were both more agile back then."

"Speak for yourself, little sister."

"I fear age is going to creep up on us whether we want it to or not." Mary laughed and slipped her arm around Betty's waist, hugging her.

"You remember when we were kids and came back to stay with Grandma during the summer?" Betty asked. "The older boys would try to scare us about a ghost that haunted the old place. One time a boy made such a scary noise, you went running out of there screaming."

Mary twisted her lips into a wry smile. She had all but forgotten that embarrassing incident. She couldn't have been more than seven or eight. "A few months went by before I built up enough courage to go back to the mill."

"The boys swore there were snakes inside the mill and a buried treasure left there by pirates. And there was something about colonial soldiers hiding there while a whole regiment of redcoats marched by."

"What grand imaginations we all had as children," Mary said with a laugh. "I remember one time some of us used the mill as a fort. We piled up grass-and-dirt clods. When anyone approached, we'd bombard him or her through the windows."

Although the mill door was still in place, it hung crookedly from old metal hinges. They eased their way into the dim interior, the small windows admitting little light even on a sunny day. The huge four-thousand-pound buhrstone — Mary recalled hearing it was originally from France — looked just as it always had, ready for a load of corn to be brought in.

Mary remembered learning as a child that to make cornmeal, the miller would haul the corn up to the second level and pour it down a shoot. The two matching grinding stones, driven by the waterwheel in the race, would grind it into a gritty product, probably accompanied by a great deal of noise.

During the early years of America, almost every town had a gristmill. Local villagers would bring their corn to the mill to be ground for a fee. If the person didn't grow his own corn, he'd buy cornmeal from the miller. Everyone needed cornmeal, so the miller did business with just about everyone in town. The Emerson who had built this mill had been wise. It had provided the foundation for the family's later wealth.

"I should have brought a flashlight." Mary walked gingerly across the dusty wooden floor. "Be careful. Some of the floorboards look rotten to me."

Betty stepped slowly back toward the door. "I don't think it's safe to walk around in here, Mary. We've seen the place, now let's —"

Mary let out a cry as her foot broke

through an aged floorboard.

"Mary!"

"I'm all right." The end of the rotten wood next to the foundation had given way and scratched her leg, but she hadn't fallen more than six inches. Thank the good Lord.

Feeling foolish, since she was the one who had warned Betty to be careful, she shook her head. Hoping to release her foot from the grasp of the rotting wood, she grabbed hold of the end of the plank that had snared her and lifted. The board squeaked and groaned. Then the rotten wood snapped about three feet from where she was standing.

"This place really is rotting," she said. "No wonder Evan wants to either restore the mill or tear it down. It's a lawsuit waiting to happen." Which made Mary wonder why anyone would want to sue for the right to own a piece a property that would be a money pit.

"I hate the thought that some children might be playing in here and get hurt," Betty said.

"If that happened, you and Evan might want to agree that it's owned by Hopkins and let it be his problem."

Betty giggled. "Sometimes you can be very devious, Mary."

Maybe so, but right now Mary's shoe was caught by something under the floorboards. A rock, or perhaps some leftover construction material.

With one leg in the hole, she knelt on the other knee and reached down to feel for whatever was pressing on her ankle and foot. Her fingers brushed something slick.

She tensed. On second thought, she might not actually want to know what was under the floorboards. But her innate curiosity —

"Really, Mary, I think we ought to get out of here before one of us is seriously injured. Those overhead beams don't look all that sturdy to me."

Mary chose to ignore her sister as her hand closed around the slick object. It was not all that big. She felt what she believed was the spine of a slender book. Interesting . . .

Carefully, she pulled the package out of the hole.

"What's that?" Betty asked.

"Some kind of book, wrapped in oilskin." She set it down next to her and reached her hand back into the hole. "Give me a minute to see if there's anything else down here."

"You'd better hope it's not a bed of snakes."

Mary shuddered. Her sister would have to

mention snakes. Worst case, she might find a hognose snake under the mill. It was an ugly creature, but it was harmless, as were all the snakes on Cape Cod. Or so Mary had been told as a child.

Her hand closed around something hard and cold. Smooth like a bone. Oh dear . . .

Grimacing, she pulled her find out of the hole.

Not a snake, she thought gratefully. But whatever it was, it was covered in dirt and grime. She rubbed her finger over one end of the object. A white spot appeared.

Not a bone either, she realized, rubbing more dirt away.

"What have you got?"

"I'm not sure." Holding the white object, she struggled out of the hole and found more secure footing. Then she picked up the book. Interesting. As far as Mary knew, oilskin hadn't been used as a wrapping in many years. Her heart rate picked up. "These items are old."

"Old? Antique? Show me." Betty, an avid antiquer, took a few more tentative steps farther into the mill house.

"Let's go outside where we can see better."

"Good idea," Betty said with a relieved laugh.

Glad to be out of the gloom of the mill, Mary studied the unfamiliar object. Maybe six inches long, it weighed no more than six or eight ounces.

Betty peered at Mary's find, and Mary could see her anticipation rising at the possibility of having found an antique. "Let's wash all that dirt off in the pond. It's probably a piece of some old pottery."

It didn't feel like pottery to Mary, not quite heavy enough, but she agreed they needed to get rid of the dirt.

At the pond, she knelt and swished the thing in the water. Layers of dirt melted away, revealing a porcelain doll standing on a chipped porcelain base. Around the base were the words *Only the Very Best* painted in a bright blue script.

"What a pretty little girl," Betty said. "A sweet face and a charming bonnet. It could be a child's doll."

"Maybe." Looking for a maker's mark, Mary turned the doll upside down. The base and doll were hollow. But she couldn't see an indication of who had made the doll.

After handing the doll to Betty, Mary carefully unwrapped the oilskin package. It wasn't a book, exactly, but rather some sort of bookkeeping ledger with page after page filled with odd markings.

Standing, Mary said, "What do you make of this?"

"*Hmm,* it looks a lot like the record book Edward used to keep track of our expenses. Of course, he changed to using his computer years ago."

The oilskin had kept the binding and pages in good condition, but the notations were indecipherable as far as Mary could tell. Just from the flourishing handwriting on the title page, she thought the ledger must be old. On each page, there were rows and columns, symbols of some sort. On the left, there were tally marks and what looked to be box-shaped markings across the rows.

She wasn't sure what it meant. She would have to spend some time studying it to try and learn more about it.

But why had the ledger and the doll been left under the floorboards? Had they been hidden for some reason? Or simply tossed away?

Could they possibly lead to answers about the ownership of the mill?

Two

Betty went home to see if Evan had returned her phone call, while Mary returned to her shop. She turned the sign on the door to Open and carried her finds from the mill inside. Gus was still curled up in his favorite patch of sunlight and barely opened his eyes to greet her.

"I do so like a warm welcome home, Gus," she teased. "No need to overdo it, though. I know you need your rest."

She smiled as he appeared undisturbed. For a cat that had once been a stray, he'd certainly found a good home and a soft-hearted owner. In payment, he'd provided love and solace, particularly when she'd lost her husband John.

After putting the wrapped ledger on the counter, she took the doll into the back room to wash it more thoroughly. She used soap and a soft scrub brush to get rid of the remaining grime stuck in the creases. She wiped it dry with a paper towel and then held it up for examination.

"Well, you are a pretty little thing." The doll wore a bonnet and old-fashioned skirt and had puckered red lips. It didn't look like a child's toy. Maybe a knickknack a woman would display on a shelf, discarded because of the chip in its base. "I guess whoever made you thought you were 'Only the Very Best,' " Mary said, reading the inscription on the doll. Or perhaps that was a reference to whoever had received the doll as a gift.

Smiling to herself, Mary took the doll back into the shop and placed it near the cash register. Later, she might try to identify the maker by checking online. The slogan on the base, if that was what it was, could be a good lead. It still wasn't evident how the items she found had anything to do with the ownership of the mill, but she was curious about them nonetheless.

When she started to unwrap the ledger, Gus roused himself. He jumped up onto the counter and sniffed the oilskin, then the ledger that she'd placed next to the wrapper.

"What do you think, Gus?"

His answer was to lie down with his paws on the wrapping. It must have carried a scent that interested him. Plain old dirt was the best Mary could imagine, but maybe the oilskin itself had an odor only a cat could appreciate.

Carefully, she opened the ledger. The handwriting on the first page was so arcane and filled with swirls it was hard to make out. But she was pretty certain it was in English. She saw what could have been a date on the first page, but she couldn't even be sure about that.

As she turned the pages, she frowned. The handwriting went from swirly English to what looked like Chinese-style characters, followed by rows of symbols and tally marks. What could those odd characters mean? There weren't many Asians in Ivy Bay now, and she couldn't imagine an early Emerson able to write in Chinese, but who knew?

After closing the ledger, she slipped the oilskin out from under Gus's paw, wrapped the ledger again, and put it on a shelf behind the counter. It probably wasn't valuable in any way except its connection to the mill, but maybe it would help her figure out more about the mill's history.

Mary thought again about Betty's promise to her husband. This mill was important to Betty, even more so now that she might lose it. Mary knew she needed to help her sister.

She mentally put three chores on her list. First, she'd look through Betty's files and make sure there was no record of sale. Even though she was confident she wouldn't find such a record, she needed to at least double-check. Second, despite Betty's determination to avoid him, Mary would drop by Daniel Hopkins' home tomorrow, after she found out where he lived. With any luck, she might be able to get him to drop the suit, or at least discover the reason he claimed to be the owner.

If those efforts failed, she'd head for the county clerk's office. The clerk's archives contained records back to almost the founding of Ivy Bay. Surely she could find who were the original owners of the mill — the first Emersons in town, according to Betty. It shouldn't be that hard.

And then she could check to see if the property had ever changed hands. If it had, a bill of sale would have been recorded and the title to the land changed.

She suspected whatever Daniel Hopkins claimed, he was going to lose his suit. The mill had been owned by the Emerson family forever. Everyone in town seemed to acknowledge that. Unless Daniel Hopkins had incontrovertible proof otherwise, surely that wouldn't change.

The chime over the door announced the arrival of Henry Woodrow, longtime resident of Ivy Bay. Henry was a good friend of Mary's from back when they were youngsters, and when she moved back to Ivy Bay, they had reconnected. They'd become close friends again, and Henry often came into the shop to visit. His silver hair was windblown, and from his casual attire, nonslip shoes, and captain's cap, Mary assumed he'd been out on his boat *Misty Horizon*.

"Hi there, Henry. How was your boating adventure today?"

"How'd you — ?" He looked down at his outfit and chuckled. "It was very pleasant, thank you. I took a tour group over to Wellfleet. The bay was so smooth."

"Sounds perfect." Mary suspected his days on the boat helped him to maintain an optimistic outlook. He'd recently lost his wife Misty and, just as Mary filled her life with the bookshop, his boating business kept him very busy.

"Yep, it was a good outing. Caught a couple of nice striped bass after lunch." Henry wandered over to the shelves of mystery titles. "I finished the last book you sold me — kept me up way too late at night — and I'm ready for another of your killer recommendations."

"No pun intended," Mary said with a smile.

"Nice one," Henry said, then began perusing the shelves. While he browsed, Bob Hiller, longtime mailman for Ivy Bay, walked into the shop. He placed the day's mail on the counter and gave Mary a wave.

"Thanks, Bob," she called out, then returned her attention to Henry. "Just this week, I got copies of Archer James's new book." She joined him at the historical mysteries section. "I haven't had a chance to read this one yet, but he writes wonderful mysteries based in the Scottish isles." She plucked the hardcover from the shelf and handed it to him.

He briefly considered the cover, then flipped to the back where there was a photo of the gray-haired author holding a pipe.

"Distinguished-looking gentleman," Henry said.

"I understand he's a bit of a recluse, but a lot of authors are. There always seems to be a ruined castle and lots of fog in his books."

Henry laughed and his smile crinkled the corners of his eyes. "Sounds sufficiently spooky. I'll take it."

He handed her the book, which she carried to the cash register. While she rang up

33

the sale, Henry petted Gus.

"You have a pretty soft life, Gus. I hope you appreciate how well Mary takes care of you."

With his eyes squeezed shut in pleasure, Gus pushed up against Henry's hand to encourage more petting. Mary smiled at the sight of Henry cooing over Gus. A man who could love a cat was definitely a good man.

"I'm lucky to have Gus." She gave Henry the total, and he passed her his credit card. "I can talk to him and people don't think I've gone 'round the bend talking to myself."

"Sounds perfectly reasonable to me. I've been known to do a little muttering myself." He chuckled. "Well, I should get going."

"Big plans?"

"Dorothy Johnson stopped me at the Meeting House Grocers the other day. She asked me to drop by sometime and take a look at her house."

"Oh?" Dorothy, who was a member of Mary's prayer group, frequently expressed an interest in Henry, which tickled Mary. She thought for sure Dorothy had her eye on the town widower for something more than casual conversation.

"Yep. She says some of her windows don't open and close right, and a couple of doors get stuck now and then. Hopes maybe I can fix 'em without a whole lot of trouble."

"Nice of you to help her out."

"I'll do what I can. I'm a little worried the house needs more than a few minor repairs."

"Oh, I hope not. It's such a lovely place, and on the historical register."

"It being old might be at the root of the problem."

"Good point." Mary finished ringing up the sale, slipped the book into a bag, and handed it to Henry along with his credit card. "Receipt's inside. Let me know what you think of the book."

"I will." He tipped his hat to her. The chime tinkled again as he left the store.

"Well, what do you think, Gus? Should we call it a day?" Tomorrow was Friday. Weekenders would start arriving by noon, and business would pick up again. Rebecca would be in tomorrow, so Mary decided she'd spend the morning trying to track down Hopkins.

She got her jacket from the back room and put Gus in his cat carrier. "Let's go see if we can help Betty with dinner."

Betty and Mary's home was located on Shore Drive and had a lovely view of Little Neck Beach and Cape Cod Bay. A two-story Federal-style house, it was painted a light green with darker green shutters on the front windows. Betty had planted rhododendrons along the property line with her neighbors, low shrubs across the front of the house, and had beds of annuals that provided bright colors all summer long. Given her arthritis, Mary couldn't imagine how Betty managed so much planting and weeding, but she was definitely glad for it. Betty had a wonderful aesthetic style.

Inside, Mary discovered Betty on the phone. From the conversation, she knew her sister was talking to her son. She released Gus from his carrier, and he scampered upstairs to one of his favorite napping places.

A couple of chicken breasts were on the kitchen counter. Mary washed her hands and started to prepare the chicken for baking.

Betty was a wonderful cook, but sometimes her arthritis made it hard for her to stand at the counter for any length of time.

When she finished her phone conversation, Betty joined Mary in the kitchen. She wore a rose-colored cardigan over her pretty housedress and had changed into her comfortable slippers.

"Evan is going to send a messenger over tomorrow to get a copy of the lawsuit. As I suspected, he's going to hire an attorney. He has a college friend Robert Dunlap, who he thinks could handle the case. Apparently, Rob is very experienced in property disputes."

"That sounds perfect. Unless Daniel Hopkins has a change of heart and drops the whole thing." Mary thought of her plans to visit the man tomorrow but decided it would be better not to mention them.

"Wouldn't it be nice if Hopkins forgot the whole thing." Sighing, she rubbed the knuckles of her left hand as though holding the phone had caused them to ache.

"Would you like me to get your hand cream from your room?" Mary asked. Her sister had a special prescription cream to soothe the pain in her hands when it flared up.

"Oh no, I'm fine. Just worried, I guess." She sat down at the kitchen table. "Evan asked me if I had any idea of why Daniel would claim the mill was his. I told him about the feud, but that's about all I know."

After sprinkling on some spices, Mary put the chicken in the oven, set the timer, and sat down with Betty. An arrangement of iris and daisy mums Betty had picked from the yard served as a centerpiece and lent a light floral fragrance to the room.

"You know," Betty said, "after our visit to the mill, so many memories of the mill and the fun we had there came back to me. Of course, as I recall, neither Mother nor Gram were pleased with that grass-clod stunt you reminded me of. You and the neighbor boys got into a lot of trouble."

"True." But Billy Joe Nesbitt had been the leader of the gang, and Mary had had a childish crush on him at the time. "The Emersons probably weren't all that pleased with us playing in the mill either. I'm surprised they didn't run us off."

"My in-laws were dear people and loved children. I suppose they thought God would watch over us."

Mary wondered if they could have possibly anticipated, years later, that Daniel Hopkins would try to claim the gristmill as his own.

After dinner, Mary and Betty went into Betty's bedroom, where her files and financial records were kept in a tall filing cabinet.

Betty opened a drawer. "Edward always told me we only had to keep financial records, like receipts for tax purposes, for seven years. I confess I haven't cleaned out the files recently, so they probably go back a little further." She indicated a group of manila file folders all carefully dated by year.

38

"Does that include a receipt for your property taxes?" Mary asked.

"Oh my, yes. That's a big tax deduction." She pulled out the folder with the oldest date and placed it on her nearby desk. Opening the folder, she flicked through the stack of receipts. "Here it is."

Mary picked up the sheet of paper. Clearly it was the bill for the mill's property tax. "From the date, it looks like the county knew you owned the mill back ten years ago."

"They certainly did. And they still do. There's a property tax bill in every one of these files."

Mary continued to flip through the papers. "And you're sure you don't have a copy of the deed?"

Shaking her head, Betty said, "I really don't think so. I've never seen anything like that." Betty and Mary continued scanning through files, but they came up short.

"I guess since the Emersons were granted the land from the Massachusetts Bay Company, you'd have to check back to the 1600s."

"Now *that* would be some research project." Mary closed the file folder. "Let's hope we only have to check as far back as 1792."

"When Daniel claims his ancestors bought the mill." Betty made a dismissive sound. "This whole suit business is so annoying. And stressful. After all this time, why would Daniel start fussing about the mill now?"

That's what Mary hoped to find out when she spoke with him tomorrow.

First thing Friday morning, Mary dropped into the shop to leave Gus and make sure Rebecca was okay being alone for a while.

"Hi, Rebecca. Ashley, you're looking very summery with that blue bow in your hair." Rebecca's daughter was the quickest and nicest seven-year-old imaginable, which made her a big help to both Mary and Rebecca. Today, she'd pulled her ash-blonde hair back in a ponytail.

"Mom pinned the short hairs back for me." She tossed her head, making her hair swish back and forth.

"You look lovely," Mary said as she gave Ashley a light kiss on the head. She set Gus's cat carrier on the floor and released him. He went directly to Ashley and rubbed up against her legs. Ashley dutifully knelt to pet him.

"I have a couple of errands to run this morning," Mary told Rebecca. "If you need me, call me on my cell."

"No problem. I'll do a little dusting and sorting to keep me busy until some customers show up."

"Wonderful. I so appreciate you being here." She smiled at Ashley. "Both of you."

Mary had checked the church directory at home last night and found Jill Sanderson's address. Jill had been widowed for several years before marrying Harry Hopkins. When she remarried, she had kept her married name from her first marriage for the sake of her children. She had mentioned at prayer group that Daniel was her grandfather-in-law and now lived with them. It was a situation that apparently troubled her. Since Mary didn't want to alert Daniel by calling first, she decided it would be better to arrive unannounced.

She drove her car to Water Street, then turned left. She slowed as she drove past older, one-story houses with attics. Scattered among them were what amounted to mansions in comparison, new houses recently built by wealthy owners.

She pulled over to the curb across from what she believed was Jill Sanderson's house. It was one of the larger homes on the street.

Resolving to be honey sweet with Daniel Hopkins, she climbed out of the car and walked across the street. She stepped around a skateboard, no doubt belonging to one of Jill's two adorable sons, and knocked on the door.

A moment later, Jill opened the door. Dressed in jeans and a tank top, the young blonde woman gave Mary a puzzled look.

"Mary? I, ah . . ."

"Hi, Jill, nice to see you. I'm sorry to drop by without calling first, but you mentioned that Daniel Hopkins is living with you now. Does he happen to be home? I'd like very much to talk to him."

"Daniel's here, which is unusual. He gets too restless to stay around the house all day and would rather be outside."

"Would you mind letting him know I'm here?"

Looking unsure of herself, Jill glanced over her shoulder. "I know what this is about, Mary. I'm sorry, but I'm not sure he'll want to talk to you."

"It'll just take a few minutes," she pressed, keeping her voice as light as possible.

"Really, it might be better if —"

"Who's at the door?" a male voice bellowed from a back room. "If it's one of those fool salesmen, send him away."

Jill flinched. "I'm sorry."

Leaning into the door, Mary called out.

"Mr. Hopkins, my name is Mary Fisher. I just need a few minutes of your time. I won't keep you long."

The man marched down the hallway toward her. Tall and wiry and wearing a sailor's cap, he had to be in his eighties. As he drew closer, Mary noted that his wrinkled face resembled a topographical map and spoke of a life spent outdoors. The tiny veins in his cheeks and the reddened tip of his nose suggested an equal number of years of heavy drinking.

His expression seemed permanently frozen in a frown. "What is it? I'm busy."

Mary straightened her spine. "Mr. Hopkins, I'm Mary Fisher. My sister is Betty Emerson." She kept her tone level and calm. "I'd like to ask you about the suit you've filed against her."

He snorted. "You got questions, you talk to my lawyer." He started to turn away.

"Mr. Hopkins, please. I'd just like to know why you believe you own the mill. It's been in the Emerson family since 1667, when it was built."

"Lady, your sister's got a real surprise coming." Leaning into Mary's personal space, he lifted one corner of his lips in a sneer. She got a whiff of alcohol on his

43

breath. "I got the bill of sale that says otherwise."

Wrinkling her nose, Mary took a step back. "If you have such a piece of paper, I'd very much like to see it. If you don't mind."

"I do mind."

"Well, then, would you tell me why you've brought the suit now instead of years ago?"

"Because I hadn't found the evidence yet, that's why. Didn't find that piece of paper 'til I was packing up my stuff to move in here with my grandson." He stepped out of the door and spit off the side of the porch. "We'll be showing the bill of sale when my attorney says it's time, and not before. I wouldn't trust it to an Emerson for so much as two seconds." His face flushed, a muscle flexed in his jaw, and his hands balled into fists at his side.

Instinctively, Mary retreated another step. "Mr. Hopkins, I know very little of the history of your family. I understand the Hopkinses and Emersons have been feuding for years."

His salt-and-pepper eyebrows angled downward. "Yeah. With good reason too." His beady eyes arrowed into her with laser precision.

Mary swallowed hard and pressed on. "Would you mind telling me what caused

44

the feud?" She heard a tremor in her voice, though she hoped Mr. Hopkins wouldn't notice. Or become aware of the beads of the perspiration that had formed on her upper lip.

"Because all them Emersons are thieves and murderers."

He spoke the accusation so loudly, with spittle coming out of his mouth, Jill grabbed his arm. "Come back in the house, Grandpa. Doctor says you shouldn't get all in a fuss. High blood pressure is bad for you."

He shook her off. "What I'm saying is the truth. William Emerson murdered my great-great-grandpa Caleb Hopkins because he wouldn't give over the mill that was rightfully ours."

Stunned, Mary's mouth dropped open. *A man was murdered over the ownership of the gristmill?* She shuddered. Surely that wasn't possible.

"When . . . when did this . . ." Mary was so taken aback by such a wild statement that she seemed unable to get the words out.

"I'll tell you when. Was October 1841, that's when."

"That's over 170 years ago," Mary blurted out. "All these years —"

"It's like yesterday for us Hopkinses. We know what's right and what's not."

Mary lifted her chin, appalled that an angry feud could go on so long without resolution. As far as Betty knew, Edward was vaguely aware of a feud but had no idea how or why it had started, and he had no interest in finding out.

Whether someone had been murdered or not, people had clearly been hurt. "Mr. Hopkins," she said politely, "I will be searching county property records. If there is a deed of transfer or a title change, I believe that I will find it. And if there isn't —"

"The mill is ours; has been since 1792 when it was sold to our family. No county records or nothin' will change that."

We'll see about that, Mary thought. But rather than upsetting Hopkins any further, she smiled. "I'm sure your attorney will be hearing from my sister's attorney soon."

Jill, poor dear, gave Mary a weak smile, obviously not happy with the situation or Daniel's behavior.

Shaken by the encounter, Mary eased backward down the steps, then hurried across the street to her car. It appeared Daniel Hopkins wasn't in the mood for honey.

He wanted to fight. For him, the feud had never ended.

Back in her car, Mary wondered if Daniel's attorney would be any more forthcoming about the lawsuit, particularly the bill of sale, than Daniel had been.

She checked with Information to get Marc Dougher's phone number. When the receptionist at his office answered the phone, Mary introduced herself and asked to speak with the attorney about the Emerson case.

While the young woman placed Mary on hold, she watched Jill's house. The last thing she needed was for Daniel to come outside and catch her talking with his attorney.

Finally, the receptionist came back on the line. "I'm sorry, Mrs. Fisher. Mr. Dougher says he would be happy to talk to Mrs. Emerson's attorney, but any conversation with you regarding the case would be inappropriate."

Inappropriate? So much for her bright idea to talk to the attorney. But that wouldn't stop Mary from investigating Daniel's assertion that he had a valid bill of sale.

THREE

From Jill's house, Mary headed to the county clerk's office, still unsettled by her encounter with Daniel.

When she arrived, the uncomfortable feeling she had from her conversation with Daniel Hopkins was replaced by the strange comfort she felt in the office's musty corridor.

Beatrice Winslow, the county clerk, was a tiny woman with short, closely trimmed silver hair and reading glasses she wore perched on the end of her nose. A counter covered with copies of the *Ivy Bay Bugle,* flyers about Cape Cod activities, and the county selectmen's next meeting agenda separated her from visitors.

Since the old records had been shifted from what was now Mary's bookshop, Bea's work area was crowded with filing cabinets and cupboards and smelled distinctly of aging paper.

"Hi, Bea. How are you?"

She glanced away from her computer screen, looked over the top of her glasses at Mary, and smiled.

"Mary, hi! I'm great, thanks. Except for a knee I twisted training for the 5K race in Provincetown next month, I'm feeling quite fit. How about you?"

For a woman who had to be close to seventy, Bea was in admirable shape. Which reminded Mary she ought to make a point of taking long walks more often now to take advantage of the summer weather. If only she could find the time. A convenient excuse, she admitted.

"I'm good, thank you. I'm doing some research on the old gristmill for my sister." Mary didn't have any trouble revealing the situation to Bea. Not only did she need Bea's help, but she knew the clerk was the soul of discretion. She'd never reveal a word she heard or secret she learned as county clerk. Probably not even under the threat of torture. It was why she'd been reelected more times than Mary could count.

Bea raised her gray eyebrows. "Is there a problem?"

"We're hoping it's much ado about nothing. Daniel Hopkins is challenging the ownership of the mill. Claims it belongs to his family."

"Oh, stuff and nonsense." Chuckling, she waved her hand in front of her face as though shooing a fly away. "Daniel Hopkins is so crazy that he couldn't even find his own house, let alone the mill. Everyone knows that."

Mary would have laughed except for the seriousness of the situation. "Well, he actually filed suit against Betty, so he must have found his way to an attorney." Although some attorneys weren't entirely ethical — taking on a case they knew they couldn't win just to claim the fee from their hapless client. "I thought I'd check the county property records to see if there was ever a title change or a new deed recorded. I need to know if there's any merit to his claim. I'm sure Betty's attorney will be searching too."

"How far back do you want to check?"

"As far as possible. How far back do the records go?"

"Ivy Bay was founded in 1639, but the county wasn't established until 1685. The records were a bit sketchy back then."

"I'd like to take a look at whatever you have."

Glancing at her computer screen, Bea typed a few keystrokes. "There wasn't enough room for all our records up here, so we stored the oldest ones down in the basement."

She got up and plucked a light-blue duster from the coatrack to cover her dress. "I hope you don't mind getting your clothes a little dusty. There's enough dust and dirt on the oldest boxes of records to build a new sandbar. I was joking the other day with the selectmen that we ought to put in some big lights and start a hydroponic garden down there to raise tomatoes all year long."

"Sounds like a good fund-raising project for the county," Mary joked. She was wearing a pair of washable khaki slacks and a light sweater over a blouse, and she wasn't worried about a little dirt.

Bea led her down a flight of steep stairs that would be dangerous if they hadn't had a solid handrail. The dim overhead lighting barely provided enough illumination to read the labels on row after row of boxes stacked on shelves six feet high. Certainly not enough light to grow tomatoes.

"I really appreciate you letting me look at the old files," Mary said.

"All part of the job," she said cheerfully. "Walking up and down the stairs makes for good thigh muscles."

They'd reached the end of an aisle, and

51

she pointed to a sturdy cardboard box with a green label on the highest shelf above the others. "Looks like 1689 is the oldest we've got for property records."

"Then I'll start there."

Bea dragged a rolling ladder over, climbed up, and handed down the top box.

Taking the weight of the box, Mary grunted and sneezed. It was heavier than she'd expected, and just as dusty as Bea had promised. No wonder Bea was in such great shape if she moved these boxes around with any regularity. She carried the box to the table in the center of the room.

"You're all set now," Bea said. "This box contains lists of property records. Each list is dated and indicates the name of the property owner. You shouldn't have any trouble figuring it out. Let me know if you need anything else."

"I will. Thanks, Bea."

Bea left her to go back to work upstairs, and Mary sat down at the steel table. Though the room was dungeon-like, it admittedly was more spacious than the dungeons described in historical novels. Perhaps she could use a musty-smelling basement in the mystery novel she had been writing for a half dozen years. She intended to finish the story someday, but not with publication in mind. Really, her writing was a hobby for cold, wintry days.

When she lifted the lid off the box, she sneezed again. Gracious, she should have brought a dust mask to cover her mouth and nose, and a dust cloth.

She started with the first file, dated 1689; the record listed all the properties in the county, along with the respective owners.

Unfortunately, the paper was so fragile that Mary probably should have worn white gloves to avoid damaging the records with body oil. The once-flourishing handwriting had faded, making some of the entries hard to decipher.

She laboriously worked her way through page after page that listed specific properties, describing each plot of land, the size and use at that time, and the owner's name. Many of the plots included a large amount of acreage, probably claimed by early settlers and sold off over the years for a profit.

The county was larger and had more residents than she had realized, certainly more than she'd expected for the late 1600s. She searched several pages before she found the name of Emerson mentioned.

She squinted and fussed with her glasses to read the faded ink. The corners of the property were given in degrees, minutes, and seconds of latitude and longitude. "Usage: residence and gristmill. Owner: Ezra Emerson."

"Well, there you are," she said to herself. "That proves the Emersons owned the property and the mill as early as 1689." Given the timeline, Ezra, or perhaps his father, had built the mill, though that would have no bearing on Hopkins' suit and the current ownership of the mill.

She leaned back in the hard metal chair. That didn't, however, prove the owner hadn't sold it in 1792, almost a hundred years and generations of Emersons later.

She skimmed down the page and turned to the next. An Arnold Hopkins was listed as owning a residence in Ivy Bay, presumably Daniel Hopkins' ancestor and another original settler.

She made copies of the records she'd found and returned the originals to the file box. After hefting the heavy container into her arms, she carried it down the aisle and struggled to lift it back into its proper place. She sneezed again and waved the dust she stirred up away from her face.

Glancing at her watch, she realized she didn't have time to look for the 1792 records. She needed to get back to the bookshop to give Rebecca a break. In fact, since this was Friday, with a busy weekend coming for the bookshop, she wouldn't be able to check more records until Monday.

A little after lunchtime, Mary had just finished with a customer when Betty entered the bookshop carrying a potted rose. She wore jeans, a man's old shirt that used to be Edward's, and her gardening gloves.

"Hey, Bets. What are you up to?"

"I got tired of fretting about the lawsuit, so I decided to go to Tanaka Florist and Garden Center and buy some plants to spruce up the bookshop's backyard." Mary knew Betty had planned to work on the backyard, but it was a surprise to see her there this afternoon.

"That's wonderful," Rebecca said from behind the counter. "It certainly could use some landscaping and some bright color."

Ashley looked up from the book she'd been reading. She was in the small area Mary called the children's nook. The centerpiece was a porcelain pedestal bathtub lined with a light-blue rug that children loved to sit in while they read. It was a gift from Betty for the shop's grand opening.

"Can I help you garden?" Ashley asked. "Sometimes I help my mom."

Betty eyed the girl. "I'd love for you to

join me, but you have to get permission from your mom. You'll probably get dirt all over your pretty outfit."

"Eh, it's all washable," Rebecca said with a resigned smile. "It's fine with me."

With a big grin, Ashley popped up and joined Betty.

Mary was grateful for her sister's green thumb and that she'd found a diversion to take her mind off the lawsuit. Before Mary had bought the property, the county had used the building for archives. Although she'd always loved the structure and its history, the county had done little to the small plot of ground in the back, and it had grown up in weeds. Except for a wild raspberry bush, she'd had the yard cleaned out shortly after she bought the building. To have flowers growing there would be a delight. Something both she and her customers could enjoy.

"I don't want you to overdo it," Mary said.

"Don't worry. Digging a few holes won't hurt me if I'm careful, and it will get my mind off my troubles. I bought a chokeberry bush, one like I have in my yard, and two of these antique roses. The berries attract migratory songbirds."

"Sounds great, Betty. Thanks. Yell if you need any help with the planting, okay?"

Mary offered.

"Ashley will do just fine." She smiled down at the child. "Right now, I came in to get a glass of water. Gardening is thirsty business in the summer. Which reminds me, the plants will have to be watered every day for a few days. As soon as they're established, once a week should do it."

"I'd be happy to do that," Rebecca volunteered.

"Me too," Ashley echoed.

"Perfect. That will be wonderful." Betty moved to the refreshment table to get her drink of water, Ashley right with her.

"I bet you two had lots of fun and were close when you were young," Rebecca commented to Mary.

"I'd say so. Of course, we did our share of sisterly bickering. And as my *older* sister," Mary said with Betty still in earshot, "she used to boss me around whenever she thought she could get away with it."

"I did not!" Betty said. "Besides, sometimes you were a pest."

Stifling a laugh, Mary shook her head for Rebecca's benefit. "I was always a complete angel," she whispered for her employee's ears only.

The arrival of a middle-aged woman halted their teasing banter. Not one of

Mary's regulars, the woman was probably from the mainland for the weekend. The local hotels and bed-and-breakfasts often referred customers to her since she'd opened.

"May I help you find something?"

"Absolutely. Silly me — we're here for the weekend, and I forgot to pack anything to read."

"Well, it's the perfect excuse to visit a bookstore." Mary smiled. "Tell me what sort of books you like to read, and I'm sure we can find something you'd enjoy."

When she had found a book for the customer, Mary stepped out the back door to see what progress Betty was making. It looked like she and Ashley already had the chokeberry in the ground and were now working on the rosebushes.

"Everything all right?" Mary asked.

Betty wiped her forehead with her gloved hand, which left a streak of dirt. "We're fine. Ashley's a good little helper."

Mary smiled and slipped back into the shop.

As Mary had predicted, the shop had a small but steady stream of customers drop in to browse and buy books throughout the rest of the afternoon, enough to keep Mary busy answering questions and Rebecca ringing up sales.

After her gardening, Betty washed up and browsed in the shop until closing time. Rebecca and Ashley had already gone home when Mary closed the shop with her sister.

Once back home, Mary helped Betty put away her gardening tools. Betty warmed up some chicken-and-barley soup she'd made earlier in the week. They sat at the kitchen table.

Mary spooned some soup into her mouth and considered how to tactfully bring up the murder comment Daniel Hopkins had made. "So, I know you said Edward never mentioned why there was a feud with the Hopkinses. But do you remember *any* rumors that may have been brought up?"

"No, I haven't been able to think of anything. I'm not sure Edward knew."

"So there was nothing ever said about a murder?"

Betty visibly shuddered. "Dear me, no."

Mary sighed. "I figured as much. Seems like something Edward or someone in the family would have mentioned." Mary set her spoon down and looked squarely at Betty, who looked sufficiently confused. "I went to see Daniel Hopkins this morning, in the hope I could convince him to give up the suit, or at least hear his explanation for why he filed it."

Betty's eyes widened, but Mary continued. She told her sister about his accusation that William Emerson had murdered Caleb Hopkins in 1841, over the question of mill ownership.

"That's ridiculous! Certainly if Edward knew about it, he would have said something."

"If there was a murder back in the 1800s, it sounds as though the Emersons had forgotten all about it." Mary buttered a whole-grain cracker.

"Because no such thing ever happened. I'm sure of it."

Mary looked at her sister tenderly. "Of course, I agree with you. But Daniel Hopkins certainly thinks there was."

Betty bristled and put her spoon down. "Really, Mary, I would know, wouldn't I, if the family had some deep, dark secret like that?"

Not necessarily, but Mary didn't want to press the point. Her sister was already upset enough. But her defense of the Emersons, her pride in having married into the family, left her less than objective about their role in Ivy Bay history. In the case of her husband's family, she'd always been fiercely loyal. Mary would have to tiptoe gently not to offend her.

Pensive, Mary and Betty finished their soup in silence. Finally, Mary spoke. "I think it will be important to learn as much about the history of the mill as possible. According to Daniel, William Emerson must have at least thought he owned the mill in 1841. It should be easy to check the census records for 1840, which will show where the Emersons and Hopkinses lived at the time. I'll do that after I've searched the property records up through the 1790s, when the suit claims Isaac Emerson sold the mill to James Hopkins."

"You won't find any record of the mill being sold, Mary, I guarantee it. And there was never a murder either. Daniel Hopkins has simply made it up. He's probably jealous of how prosperous the Emersons have always been." In a huff, she stood and carried her bowl and spoon to the counter.

Mary had another thought. "I wonder if Eleanor knows more about the feud than Edward did. Women tend to keep their ears more in tune with what's going on."

"I have no idea. She's never talked to me about any feud, and I've never asked."

"Maybe we can catch her after church on Sunday. See if she has any thoughts on the subject."

Turning, Betty eyed her sister. "If you insist. But I know no Emerson was involved in any murder."

As Betty left the kitchen, Mary whispered one of her favorite Bible verses: "The end of a matter is better than its beginning, and patience is better than pride. Do not be quickly provoked in your spirit, for anger resides in the lap of fools" (Ecclesiastes 7:8–9).

Both she and her sister would have to be patient until they could prove Daniel Hopkins' assertion was false.

Before she could get her dirty dishes in the dishwasher, Mary's cell phone rang. Her daughter's name flashed across the screen.

"Hi, Lizzie!" she said. She was always pleased to hear from her. "How are you, darling?"

"We're good, Mom. Luke wanted to tell you about his soccer game this afternoon. I'll put him on."

After a pause, Luke said in an excited voice, "Grandma, I made a goal today!"

Mary grinned. Hearing Luke's voice was just the pick-me-up she needed. "Congratulations, young man. I'm so proud of you."

"Yeah, I'm proud of me too. Love you."

With that, Luke handed the phone back to his mother, which made Mary laugh.

Boys were so much less articulate than their sisters.

Since Emma, her granddaughter, was at a sleepover for the night, Mary and Lizzie talked awhile, catching up, but Mary didn't mention the gristmill and the latest mystery that had embroiled her. She didn't want her daughter fussing over her or worrying about Betty. Not yet, anyway.

Not unless the court case went very badly against the Emersons.

Saturday afternoon, Betty dropped into the bookshop.

"I'm going over to the park to check out the summer festival," she told Mary, who was straightening books on a shelf. "I want to take a look at the craft guild's booth. Do you have time to come along?"

Mary slid a book into place and glanced around. They'd had a steady but small stream of customers that afternoon.

"You okay on your own for a bit?" she asked Rebecca.

"Oh, sure. I'll be fine."

"Okay. Call me if you need me."

The Albert Paddington Park, named after an early settler who'd given a nice chunk of land to the town, wasn't far away. As Mary and Betty stepped out onto the sidewalk, they could hear the high school jazz band playing in the park gazebo.

A committee chaired by Dorothy Johnson arranged entertainment in the park for each Saturday afternoon during the peak summer weeks. There was always music of some sort, ranging from string to barbershop quartets. Food booths sponsored by local businesses or organizations were set up around the perimeter of the park. The youth group of Grace Church of Ivy Bay had a hot dog booth, Sweet Susan's Bakery was always represented, and so was the Baileys' shop, which sold ice-cream cones.

The festival drew not only local residents but also tourists and visitors from other towns on the Cape.

"Are you looking for anything in particular?" Mary asked her sister. The temperature was warm, but the air smelled clean and fresh as it blew in off the bay. And it felt good to be out walking.

"Oh, you know me. I like to browse, and if I see anything I like, I like to buy." Betty shot Mary a quick grin. "Edward never wanted to go shopping with me but was terrified to let me go out alone."

Mary laughed, knowing that Edward had been a generous husband who never would have denied his wife anything. For her part,

Betty was always on the lookout for decorative pieces that would sparkle up her house. Her taste had made her home a showcase for local artisans.

The music grew louder as they approached the park. Teenagers had put up a volleyball net on the grass and had a pickup game going. Several fathers and sons were playing catch, and toddlers were running around in bare feet, having a wonderful time. Families sat in the shade of maple and poplar trees that put on a spectacular leaf display in the fall.

Several booths were set up in the craft guild's area. Betty headed in that direction.

Mary reached out to stop her sister. "Isn't that Dorothy Johnson over in the corner?" She squinted to see what Dorothy was selling on her table.

"Yes. It looks like she's got a table full of antiques. Now why would she be selling those?"

"I don't know." But Mary did know Henry thought Dorothy's home was in need of some serious repairs. "Should we go say hello?"

"Maybe later. There's something else I want to see first." Betty stopped to visit with a local artist. While they chatted, Mary examined the watercolors displayed on easels. Lovely scenes of children playing on the sand dunes at sunset, and sailboats, spinnakers blooming, racing across the bay. Idyllic scenes around the Cape.

Mary wondered if she ought to buy one or two to display in her bookshop. She was sure Betty, who had a much better artistic eye than she did, would help her select something appropriate. When she'd first bought the shop, she'd found a couple of framed old photographs, one featuring her uncle George in front of the shop, and one of the back of the building. But after one of the photographs was stolen, and Mary learned of some unsavory history behind them, she decided they'd be better suited for storage than display.

They wandered past the various booths until Betty stopped again at a table filled with handblown-glass pieces.

"Oh my," Betty murmured. Carefully, she picked up a pulpit vase, the colors progressing from a dark green at the base to a pale shade of green around the fluted edge.

"Are you the artist?" she asked a bearded young man wearing shorts and T-shirt, who was slouching in a chair behind the table.

"I am," he said without standing.

Betty turned the vase over to check the markings. "JK?"

"Jack Kerns. I work out of what used to be a boat repair shop in Falmouth."

"This is an extraordinary piece." She set it back on the table and picked up another vase, examining it with equal care. She returned that to the table and pointed at the first vase. "I assume it's for sale?"

A cute grin brightened his expression and he stood. "Yes, ma'am."

Within a few minutes, Betty had become the proud owner of a Jack Kerns original vase.

As she and Mary walked away, Mary said, "That was a pretty expensive impulse buy."

"Sister, dear, mark my words. That young man is going to have pieces of his glass in museums within a few years. This one piece will double or triple in value. Besides" — she smiled — "it's going to look perfect in our living room."

Betty's uncanny sense of taste and artistic value always stunned Mary. Lucky for her, she'd married into a wealthy family, Mary thought without envy. The life Mary had led with John and their children had been all she could have asked for.

"Now then," Betty said. "I saw you eyeing some watercolors earlier."

A flush warmed Mary's cheeks. "I was just thinking about buying a couple for the shop.

You know, to give the walls some color. But I don't need to —"

"Of course you do." Betty hooked her arm through Mary's and marched her back toward the art display. "Buying art is not only good for starving artists, but it's therapy for those who buy and enjoy the artist's talents. Now then, let's take a closer look."

The two of them wandered around the displays of half a dozen different artists who worked in oil, watercolor, and even charcoal. Many of the paintings were of Cape Cod scenes, but Mary kept being drawn back to those first paintings she'd noticed.

The fully rigged sailboat was a traditional subject, but this painter had caught the wind in the sails with such accuracy, Mary could almost feel the wind in her face and hear the zip of the boat racing over the water.

The scene of the two young girls making castles in the sand took her back to her youth. She and her sister could have been models for the artist.

Betty engaged in a little bargaining, and in no time, Mary was the proud owner of two lovely watercolors perfect to display in her bookshop.

By the time they were ready to drop by

Dorothy's table, she appeared to have closed up shop for the day.

Mary wondered again what she was selling. And why?

After church on Sunday, Betty and Mary made their way through the departing crowd.

"Do you see Eleanor?" Mary asked, peering around. She hadn't seen Edward's sister during the service but knew Eleanor faithfully attended virtually every Sunday.

"There she is." Betty struck off across the patio area. Mary followed.

A striking woman of seventy-five years, Eleanor had a regal carriage and wore a stylish silk lavender suit with low pumps. Her hair was impeccably arranged in an upsweep.

"Eleanor," Betty called. "Do you have a minute?"

Holding a cup of coffee in her hand, Eleanor turned. She raised her finely shaped brows. "Of course, Betty. Did you need something?"

"Actually, we wanted to ask you a few questions," Mary said.

"You appear very serious, Betty. Is something wrong?"

"Yes." Glancing around, Betty gestured to

an area of the patio where no one was standing. "Let's step over there so we won't be overheard."

Straightening her spine, Eleanor stood even more erect than she had been. "If you insist."

When they were away from other members of the congregation, Eleanor, in a firm, tight voice said, "Now tell me what this is all about."

Betty took a deep breath. "Eleanor, I'm being sued. Daniel Hopkins claims he owns the gristmill."

For a long moment, Eleanor simply stared at Betty as though she'd spoken in some alien tongue. "That's impossible."

"We know that," Betty said.

"But we were wondering if you'd ever heard any claims of that sort," Mary said.

"Absolutely not!"

"Daniel claims he has a bill of sale," Mary added.

"Utter nonsense." She set her coffee on a low wall and folded her arms across her chest.

"He also says there's been a feud between the Emerson and Hopkins families since 1841. And that the feud was over the death of Caleb Hopkins."

Eleanor gave an unladylike snort. "Those

Hopkins people have created more difficulties for our family than I can even count. They made up some story about unrequited love between a Hopkins and an Emerson girl in the early 1800s. When she turned the boy down, he went to sea and drowned. Fishermen drown all the time, but they blamed the girl."

"That doesn't sound reasonable," Betty commented.

"It wasn't." Eleanor held up two fingers as though counting transgressions committed by the Hopkins families. "Then there was another story around World War I. A Hopkins girl claimed one of our ancestors got her pregnant. He denied it was true. We Emersons don't trifle with the Hopkinses."

Mary wondered if that applied to Jill Sanderson, who was now married to Harry Hopkins, Daniel's grandson. But Eleanor might not know that information.

"There were earlier stories too," Eleanor continued. "Thievery. Fighting. All sorts of skullduggery."

Betty had paled. "Edward never said a word to me."

Eleanor waved off the comment. "Men are not usually involved in the social life of the community in the same way we women are."

"What about a murder?" Mary ventured.

"The Hopkinses started a rumor blaming our family for the death of one of their clan years and years ago, but nothing ever came of the story. Purely fiction, I assure you." Eleanor sniffed. "I really must get home now, but please keep me informed about the ridiculous suit over the mill ownership."

"Just one more thing," Mary said. "Would you happen to have any old records related to the mill? Anything at all would help."

Eleanor hesitated, her nicely arched brows pulling together. "There are boxes and boxes of old family records in the attic, most of which I've never examined at all."

"There might be something in them that would be helpful to Betty's case," Mary said. "If you have time, could you please take a look?"

"Of course," Eleanor said. "I'm as anxious to defend against this frivolous suit as you are." She nodded an abrupt good-bye.

Eleanor walked with purpose and made her way through the crowd without acknowledging anyone.

Mary turned to her sister. "Do you think Daniel Hopkins has made up this whole story to somehow get even for past injustices?"

"I think Eleanor knows the history of the Emerson family better than anyone else."

Mary certainly agreed with that. "I do hope she can find something useful in those boxes in her attic."

Evan had arranged for Robert Dunlap, his college friend and the attorney he had hired, to meet him at Betty's house Monday morning.

A tall man in his forties, Rob had a receding hairline, a slight thickening around his waist, and an easy smile. After introductions, he sat on the chair opposite the sofa where Betty and Evan sat. Mary took the matching chair.

"I've read the suit," Rob said, his leather briefcase across his lap. "As near as I can tell, it rests entirely on the claim of a bill of sale from 1792."

"It's absurd. I just can't imagine where he would have gotten such a document," Betty said. "The mill has always been owned by the Emersons. The bill of sale Hopkins claims he has must be a forgery."

"That would be our hope," Rob agreed. "We'll just have to prove it."

"How?" Evan asked.

Rob raised his brows, acknowledging the problem. "*If* Daniel really does have that document — which his lawyer claims he does — then the first thing we'll need to do is authenticate the signature. If we had a sample of Isaac Emerson's signature, that would be helpful."

Mary leaned forward. "Perhaps there is something in the county clerk's office that has Isaac's signature on it."

"I'll have my assistant look into that," Rob said.

Mary thought she'd do some searching herself too. She owed Betty her best effort to clear up the mess as soon as she could.

"I should mention," Rob said, "that the opposing attorney is Marc Dougher. He doesn't have a sterling reputation, but he does win a good percentage of his cases."

Mary didn't think that was good news. "Is there anything we can do to help you? And Betty's case?"

Rob chuckled a bit. "If any of you can convince Mr. Hopkins to withdraw the lawsuit altogether, that would save everyone a lot of time and trouble."

Mary agreed. But based on her one brief meeting with Daniel, she didn't think that would be possible.

After the meeting with the attorney, Mary went directly to the county clerk's office.

"Good morning, Bea. How was your weekend?"

Looking up over the top of her glasses, Bea said, "Wonderful, thank you. I took in a play in Barnstable with some friends, and it was hysterically funny. Back for more research?"

"Yep!"

"Go on down," Bea said with a wave of her hand.

Mary headed downstairs, daunted by the task ahead of her. In all these files, where would she find a signature? But she squared her shoulders and got to work.

She started by looking through the 1792 property records she hadn't had time to look through last time, but she didn't find anything to indicate that property had changed hands. Then, she spent the next several hours flipping through files during the mid- to late 1700s and early 1800s — the time of Emerson's adulthood — only to come up short. There were no examples of Isaac's signature, let alone any indications that the mill had been sold.

When she left the clerk's office, she was surprised to see Daniel Hopkins leaning against the wall of Cape Cod Togs across the street. The store sold clothing Mary liked to think of as country club casual and had high-end prices to match the designer duds.

She frowned. Why would Daniel, wearing overalls and his captain's cap, be loitering around Cape Cod Togs? Navy blazers, white slacks, and loafers definitely did not seem his style.

She glanced up and down the sidewalk. No one was in sight, and Daniel was looking right at her.

A cool breeze raised the hair on the nape of her neck as she considered approaching him. But considering the menacing look on his face, and knowing how he'd reacted the last time they'd interacted, Mary thought it best to avoid him. She turned and hurried back to the bookshop.

FOUR

Mary reached the shop somewhat breathless, not from exertion but from a sudden
case of nerves. Daniel Hopkins had rattled
her simply by standing across the street. Her
skin was still crawling from the way he'd
stared at her. The fact that he seemed so
confident about his right of ownership to
the gristmill made her all the more uneasy
about him. Maybe she was just being silly.
Jill had told her Daniel liked to wander
around town.

"Are you all right?" Rebecca asked. "Your
cheeks are flushed."

Ashley came in from the backyard and
hopped up on the stool next to her mother.
A few splashes of water on her shoes suggested she'd been watering the new plants.
"You look like I do when I hold my breath
too long and my face turns all red."

"I'm fine, sweetie." Despite her anxiety,
she smiled at young Ashley and drew a set-

tling breath. "I guess I walked back from the clerk's office too fast."

Gus roused himself enough to greet Mary by rubbing up against her legs.

Feeling foolish that she'd reacted to Daniel's presence so strongly, Mary looked for a distraction. Her gaze fell on the old ledger from the mill, which she'd left on a shelf behind the counter.

"How are you at reading old-fashioned handwriting?" she asked Rebecca.

"How do you mean?"

Mary retrieved the ledger and placed it on the counter, then opened it to the first page. "I'm having a hard time reading this. Can you make anything of it?"

Rebecca took a look. "Artistic doodling?"

Peering around her mother, Ashley said, "A map of a river that's gone silly?"

Chuckling, Mary shook her head. "Artistic, I agree. But I don't think it's a river map or doodling."

"Oh, I see it now. At least I think this bit . . ." Rebecca pointed at a grouping of swirling lines. "Does this say 'Lord'?"

"Lord?" Mary took another look and a tingle of excitement skittered through her stomach. "I think you're right. But what about the rest of it?"

Slowly, Rebecca shook her head. "The

best I can guess is that it's the artist's idea of what God looks like. Sort of all swirly around the whole universe."

An interesting guess, but Mary didn't think it was the answer she was looking for. "Maybe it's a phrase that ends in the word *Lord*?"

She opened the ledger to one of the pages with peculiar marks. "Does this look like anything to you?"

Rebecca studied the page. "It almost looks like the marks I used to use in high school to keep score of a baseball game. You know, hits and runs and outs marked in little diamond shapes in the columns." Rebecca frowned. "But it looks like there were a lot of players on the team."

Eyeing the rows and columns, Mary supposed it could be a record of scores in some sort of game, although the shapes looked more like boxes than the diamonds John used to make when he was keeping score of a Red Sox game. She had never understood why he did that, since the score was posted right where everyone could see it, but he enjoyed it.

And why would a record of scores be hidden or thrown away under the gristmill's floorboards? That made little sense to Mary. Then again, maybe the ledger had fallen off of something and been forgotten. Over time, perhaps it had simply tumbled into a crack between the rock foundation and the floor of the gristmill. All she knew was that it was likely some kind of ledger, and she couldn't ignore the distant possibility that it might shed some light on the ownership of the mill.

"Well, whatever this is, we know that it's old," Rebecca said. "Maybe Rich or Jayne Tucker at the antique store could figure it out."

Mary lifted her head. "What a good idea! I should have thought of that myself." She wrapped the ledger in its oil-skin and picked up the porcelain doll. Might as well take that along as well. "I'll pop over there now to see if they can help me out."

She headed out across the street and waved to Jeremy Court, who was walking his dog down Main Street. Jeremy owned Meeting House Grocers with his wife Kaley and though they were young and could come across as aloof, they were actually quite warm and kind. Mary headed to Gems and Antiques, the store Jayne Tucker and her husband Rich had opened more than twenty years ago. Every winter the Tuckers closed up shop for up to a month and toured Europe in search of gems and antiques they could bring back to sell. During the rest of the year, one or the other of them would slip away to estate sales all over the Northeast.

Mary suspected they'd chosen the business in order to have an excuse to travel.

Mary had come to love the antique shop. It was a maze of New England heritage — antique quilts, desks and dressers hand-crafted in the 1800s, Paul Revere silver, wooden rocking horses, and old cradles. The European side of the maze featured silver, exquisite china, brooches, and jewelry chock-full of gemstones.

Just as some of the original buildings in town had their own stories, so did each of the antiques Jayne had on display.

Jayne, a vibrant woman with auburn hair to match her personality, was sitting on a stool behind the counter.

"Hey there, Mary. Haven't seen you in a while."

"Hi, Jayne. Good to see you. How's everything going?"

"All's well. Rich is just back from a Maryland estate sale, in fact. Amazing jewelry and stones, plus some original paintings from the 1700s. If you're in the market . . ."

"You're talking to the wrong sister," Mary

said with a smile. "But I'll be sure to tell Betty about your new stock. I just dropped in to see if you or Rich can tell me anything about a couple of items I've come across."

"Sure. What have you got?"

Mary placed the doll on the counter.

After picking it up, Jayne examined the doll, turning it around and checking the bottom much as Mary had when she found it. "There aren't any markings, which means there's no way to date it. I don't think it's worth much, but let me ask Rich."

Jayne vanished behind a curtain into the back room, and a moment later Rich appeared. In contrast to Jayne's incredibly beautiful hair, Rich's head was shaved bald. Fortunately, he had a well-shaped head and was somehow equally attractive in a masculine way, particularly with his intelligent blue eyes.

"Hello there, Mary. What brings you to our modest shop today?"

She smiled since there was nothing modest about the value of the antiques they sold. "Just doing a little research."

Jayne handed her husband the doll. "Does this speak to you?"

"Hmm." As he examined it, he shook his head. "Only the very best. But best what?"

"I have no idea," Mary said. "That's what

I'm trying to find out."

"Sorry. Can't help you."

"That's all right. Here's something else I'd like you two to take a look at and tell me what you think."

After unwrapping the ledger, she placed it on the counter beside the doll. Rich flipped open the pages. "Now this looks old; at least the handwriting on the front page does."

"I thought that too." Mary turned a page. "But what could all of this mean?"

Shoulder to shoulder, Jayne and her husband studied the ledger pages.

"Some kind of game? Like dominoes?" Jayne guessed.

"I suppose something like that." Rich rubbed his palm over the top of his head. "I know who could probably help you. A guy named Lincoln King. He's an expert on antiquities, though he's mostly retired now. But if you could entice him to take a look . . ." Rich rummaged around in a drawer and came up with Mr. King's card. His address was on the outskirts of town.

Excited to have the name of an expert, Mary expressed her appreciation and hurried back to the bookshop. She'd try to reach the gentleman right away.

To her delight, she reached the soft-spoken Mr. King in one call. He was currently working on a project with a tight deadline, but she arranged for the expert to visit her shop a week from Wednesday. Apparently, he had heard of her store and had been curious about it. That plus the situation she described — and the fact she volunteered to give him a selection of mystery books in exchange for his services — helped her to close the deal.

Glad to have arranged the appointment with Mr. King, she rolled her shoulders in an effort to relax the tension she'd been feeling.

Her gaze fell on the porcelain doll from beside the cash register. Picking it up, she weighed it in her hand. *Only the Very Best.* What could the doll, or the phrase, mean as they related to the mill? And where did the doll come from? She figured it was probably unrelated to the ownership of the mill, but she wasn't willing to entirely ignore the artifact either.

With a sigh, she put the doll down and went into the back room to get a stepladder. She hadn't had a chance yet to hang the paintings she'd bought at the festival. No one, including herself, could enjoy them if they weren't on display.

She found a hammer and some nails. She positioned the stepladder where she wanted it and climbed up.

The chime over the door sounded.

"What are you up to?" Henry strolled into the shop. "I saw you through the window. Need some help?"

Keeping herself steady on the ladder, she looked over her shoulder. "I'm hanging a couple of paintings. I think I've got it okay."

"She doesn't look too steady to me," Rebecca commented.

"I agree. It doesn't look like she's measured right either."

Mary scowled. "This isn't rocket science." She banged a nail into the wall, climbed down and picked up the painting.

"A painting that size needs two nails or it will hang lopsided. And you need to measure the distance between them and between the bottom of the crown molding and the top of the pictures to get it right."

She eyed Henry with a mock glare, yet felt nothing but warmth for his friendship. "I don't suppose you know any handyman who's really good at hanging paintings?"

He grinned broadly. "I thought you'd never ask."

Laughing, she stepped off the ladder and out of the way, so he could climb it. "Thank you, Sir Galahad."

■ ■ ■ ■

During the lunch hour, Mary was alone in the shop. Henry had finished hanging the paintings, which looked perfect on the wall. *Very Cape Coddish,* she thought with a smile.

Rebecca and Ashley had left to pick up some items they needed for dinner and had then gone home for a quick bite.

As Mary was reshelving some books, the chime sounded above the door. She turned to see Jill Sanderson glance up and down the sidewalk, then slip inside.

"Hello, Jill." The young woman's furtive manner and the way she stepped away from the front window troubled Mary. "What can I do to help you?"

"I just came by to apologize." She spoke in a low voice and glanced over her shoulder out the window. "My grandfather-in-law can be a little rude sometimes, but at heart, he's a good man."

A little rude was an understatement. "Thanks, Jill. But you have nothing to be sorry for. You certainly aren't responsible for your grandfather-in-law's behavior."

"I just . . . I can't get involved in the whole lawsuit thing. But I wanted you to know

86

that I felt bad about the other day when you came by the house. You've always been so kind and friendly to me, and I love our prayer group."

"It was not your fault, Jill. And I feel the same way about you."

Jill smiled weakly and started to leave.

"Jill, can I ask you something?" Mary said tentatively. She didn't want to push Jill, but she couldn't help asking this one question. "Have you seen the bill of sale Daniel claims he has?"

She quickly shook her head. "Like I said, Mary, I really can't get involved. I'm sorry." She ducked out the door and was gone without another word.

Mary puzzled over Jill's visit. She supposed Jill sympathized with Mary's quest for information but was afraid to say anything. Assuming she had any firsthand knowledge of the lawsuit.

Mary mentally tucked away her questions. There might come a time when she would need to test Jill's sympathies for more information. But she'd have to tread very lightly if the need occurred.

The following morning was the ladies' prayer group. This time, they were meeting for breakfast in the Grace Church chapel.

Mary had formed the women's prayer group shortly after she'd moved to Ivy Bay and found it a good respite from her everyday worries. Somehow an hour or so contemplating the Lord's message in the company of fellow believers and praying for others lifted her spirits.

Facing Water Street, the church was only a block from her shop. In typical New England style, the church was painted white and boasted a tall spire that could be seen for miles. The church and setting were so striking that during the tourist season, the sidewalk across the street was virtually lined with people taking photos of the church — especially true when the maple trees changed color.

Mary arrived for the meeting in the church's prayer chapel at the same time as Dorothy Johnson, one of the group members. Mary felt dowdy next to Dorothy, who wore a stylish navy dress that emphasized her slim figure, matching pumps, and her ever-present string of pearls.

Mary greeted her. "How are you this morning?"

"Quite well, thank you." Dorothy angled directly toward the coffeepot next to the serving plates filled with a selection of sweet rolls and a variety of fresh fruit.

Mary decided one roll and a slice of melon wouldn't hurt her. She took a plate and served herself.

"Henry came by yesterday," Dorothy said, her tone casual. "Such a sweet man. I'm just useless at house repairs. So he volunteered to fix a couple of my windows that have gotten stuck." She stirred some creamer into her coffee.

"Oh, that's so nice of him. I remember he mentioned something about you asking him to do that."

Dorothy's head snapped around so fast, her coffee nearly sloshed out of her cup, and she narrowed her eyes. "He mentioned it to you?"

Immediately, Mary regretted saying anything. She had no desire to compete with Dorothy. "Oh, it was no big deal. He dropped by the bookshop looking for a new mystery to read."

"So he was just shopping. I see. Does he come in often?"

Mary hesitated. She was good friends with Henry, and she didn't mind if Dorothy knew that. She just didn't want to hurt Dorothy's feelings. Still, there was no reason to pretend she and Henry weren't close. "He comes in fairly often. We were child-

hood friends, so it's been nice to recon-
nect."

"Oh." Dorothy's voice went to ice. "How
nice." Lifting her chin, she walked away as
though Mary had suddenly developed an
unpleasant odor.

Mary couldn't help but feel sympathy for
Dorothy. She didn't sense any attraction to
Dorothy from Henry, but it was clear how
Dorothy felt.

Mary sighed and checked the clock on the
wall. It was time for the prayer meeting,
which was a refreshing distraction from
both the mill case and Dorothy's unwarranted jealousy. "Ladies, I think it's time to
get started." They'd gathered around a
grouping of chairs and a soft glow from a
nearby stained-glass window illuminated the
small room.

Carrying her plate, Mary found a seat next
to Tricia Miles, the pastor's wife, who had
recently joined the group. A lovely woman
in her late forties, she was almost as soft-
spoken as her husband.

"Good morning, dear." Tricia squeezed
Mary's free hand. "I'm so glad to see you
this morning."

"You too." Mary squeezed back, then
found her notes for the meeting. "We have
quite a number of folks needing our prayers

this morning." She read off a list of church members or their relatives who were ill or struggling with problems — a gentleman recovering from a heart attack, a child with chicken pox, a woman who was trying to repair a breach in her family.

When she concluded the list, Mary invited those present to request prayers for themselves or for others in need of the Lord's help.

Tricia spoke up. "There's a teenage boy in town who has recently lost his father. He's having a hard time adjusting to his loss. I'd like you all to pray for him."

The ladies all nodded sympathetically, promising to pray for the unnamed boy.

Amy Stebble, who was the principal at the elementary school, asked for prayers to help her husband, who was an artist, through an advanced online course in Web site building. "It's really hard, but when he finishes, he might be able to do some freelance work."

Lynn Teagarden wanted to give praise that her husband had found a good-paying, steady job.

When everyone had expressed their prayer needs, Mary said, "We'll now have a few moments of silent prayer asking the Lord's help for our friends and families who are in need. By all means, pray for yourself and your loved ones as well."

Mary bowed her head and beseeched God's help for those in pain and those who were suffering in their personal lives. And then, during a lull in the prayer circle, she silently asked the Lord to protect her family and guide her as she tried to find the truth about the Emerson gristmill.

When everyone had finished praying, Mary concluded by quoting 2 Thessalonians 1:12: "We pray this so that the name of our Lord Jesus may be glorified in you, and you in him, according to the grace of our God and the Lord Jesus Christ."

She glanced around the room and at the group of women she was coming to know and love. "This morning, Millie Russell has agreed to present our Bible lesson." She nodded to the dear little lady who was fast approaching her ninetieth birthday.

Millie's lesson was about having grace in the Lord. Mary couldn't help but recognize how little grace she'd had in her heart dealing with Dorothy, and she vowed to do better. Sometimes doing the *right* thing, loving your neighbors, didn't come easily.

"That was a wonderful lesson, Millie," Mary said. "I know it reminded me to live with more of the Lord's grace in my everyday life. Now then" — she glanced around the room — "next week, do you want to meet here again or somewhere else?"

Lynn Teagarden, a tall, friendly woman with dark brown hair, raised her hand. "I'd like to have the group come to my house. I could prepare a buffet lunch for us all."

"That's a very generous offer, Lynn. Thank you. Do you all like that idea, or would you rather meet at another time or place?"

After a bit of discussion, the ladies agreed to meet at Lynn's house but insisted it be a potluck affair rather than imposing on Lynn's generosity.

After Mary closed the meeting, several members left to go about their days. Mary stayed to visit and help the cleanup committee. When she finally said her good-byes to the last of the helpers, she left the meeting, her heart lighter for companionship of the church ladies.

Once again, Mary stopped by the county clerk's office before going to the bookshop. After she made an appointment with Mr. King, she realized there was another angle, aside from signature comparisons, that she could pursue toward potentially proving that Daniel's so-called bill of sale was a forgery.

Bea smiled broadly when she saw Mary. "Hello again, Mary. Still on your search for information about the mill?"

Mary returned her smile. "I am getting to be a pest, aren't I?"

"Not at all. I love helping people search through our records. It means they're important to someone besides me."

"Well, this time I have a bit of a challenge. The attorney suspects whatever paperwork Hopkins has is a forgery, but since I wasn't able to find a sample signature, I'm wondering if an expert could tell something about the age of the paper and maybe even the ink that was used?"

"I've seen that on the *History Detectives* television show, so I guess it's possible."

She and Betty occasionally watched that program. "Do you think it would be possible for me to borrow a bill of sale from the same time period that Hopkins claims the mill was sold — 1790s? I have an expert coming next week and —"

"Oh, I'm so sorry, Mary. Your expert is welcome to come here to examine public records. But I cannot release any of the county's official documents."

Rules are rules and not to be broken. "I

understand. I'll ask my expert if he has time to take a look while he's in town. And if you do think of somewhere else Isaac Emerson's signature might appear —"

"I'll be sure to let you know."

Mary reached the bookshop in time to open for the day. Ashley had a dentist's appointment that morning so Rebecca was taking a few hours off.

Gus, whom she'd brought to the shop before going to the prayer meeting, jumped up on the counter. Automatically, Mary stroked him and scratched under his chin. She was rewarded by such loud purring, Gus sounded like a motorboat warming up at the marina. Because he traveled back and forth with her, Gus had a food dish and litter box in the back room of the shop as well as at home.

"I seem to be stuck." She continued to stroke and pet her big gray cat, musing out loud. "What records I've found indicated Isaac Emerson never sold the mill. But that makes me wonder why Daniel is in such a snit over this whole thing. I can't believe he actually has a bill of sale, but that's what he claims." He also refused to show it to anyone before a hearing, which made her even more suspicious.

95

The bell chimed over the door, admitting the first customer of the day.

"Good morning," Mary said. "Anything special you're looking for?"

The woman was probably in her thirties. She had lovely long blonde hair and perfect makeup, and wore expensive jewelry. She'd stopped in front of the special Ivy Bay display.

"I think I've found it already." Her accent was pure Southern sweet tea. "This is my first visit to Cape Cod, and I always try to learn something about the history of the areas I visit."

"Then you've come to the right place, although each of these books focuses on some of the mysteries and mysterious features of our town." Mary joined her at the display, pointing out and describing what each book offered, and telling her a little about each author. "In addition to these nonfiction books, we also have some mysteries written by local authors who include a lot of the flavor of the Cape in their stories."

The young woman nodded her head with interest. "These books all sound fascinating."

The woman browsed through several books, selecting three. She put those books on the counter, then wandered around the shop, a book lover enjoying herself.

Meanwhile, Mary returned to the front of the store to ring up the sale.

"I could stay here all day," the young woman said, "but my husband will be back from his run on the beach by now. We're going to do some sightseeing."

Mary bagged the books the young woman had purchased and handed them to her. "Well, then, have a good day and come back when you can. We love to have browsers drop by."

As she left, Mary contemplated what her next step should be to learn more about the gristmill's history.

With a spark of inspiration, she decided to do some research, in between serving customers, right here on her own computer.

FIVE

Two more customers dropped in before she could get to the computer. But then, selling books was her business. She wasn't going to complain when business was booming.

When she was finally able to sit on the tall stool behind the counter, she booted up the computer and Googled the US census from 1790. She was amazed to discover that these early records had been digitized, and she was actually able to pull up information from over two hundred years ago with the click of a few buttons. The first census the government had conducted was in 1790, which meant there would be no census record of the original settlers in Ivy Bay, like Ezra Emerson and Arnold Hopkins. But she wanted a better picture of who the Emersons were, as well as the Hopkins family.

When she pulled up the census for the county, she scanned down the names. A few of the first names caught her eye, including many biblical names, some of them quite unusual like Bezalel and Zepheniah. But the really special ones made her chuckle: Remember, Comfort, and Thankful. She imagined a mother standing on her front steps calling her children to dinner, and wondered what sort of nicknames they might have acquired. "Dinnertime, Memsy!"

Shaking her head, she got back to the question at hand. She found Isaac Emerson easily enough. Apparently, Isaac had been a prolific man. The record showed there were three males over the age of sixteen in the household, four younger males, and a total of six females. He'd been blessed with twelve children!

That was a lot of mouths to feed, but did that mean he'd had to sell the mill and his livelihood for five British pounds so the family could survive? After the five pounds had been spent, how did the family live if they no longer owned the mill?

"That doesn't seem reasonable, does it, Gus?" The cat had leaped onto her lap in search of attention. She dutifully scratched him under the chin. "Certainly Edward believed he and his family owned the mill. That makes me believe his father and grandfather held that belief as well. And, until now, apparently no one had claimed otherwise."

Balancing Gus on her lap, she searched further in the 1790 census report and found the listing for James Hopkins and his family. He'd had two boys and two girls.

Multiple generations would have been born, lived, and died by 1841 when William Emerson supposedly killed Caleb Hopkins.

Leaning back in her chair, she decided she hadn't learned much about the situation in 1790 except that both men had families. Hardly an earthshaking revelation.

Gus climbed up her chest and purred in her ear.

"You'd be a lot more helpful, Gus, if you'd been around in one of your nine lives way back in the 1790s. We'd have this mystery solved in no time."

Rebecca walked in the door. Gus jumped down to the floor and headed toward the back room to his feeding dish.

"Good morning, Mary. How has the day been so far?"

Mary turned away from the computer. "All's good. How did Ashley do at the dentist?"

"One little cavity in a baby tooth, but she behaved like a lady." A proud smile graced Rebecca's face. "I dropped her off at a friend's house for a playdate. The dentist gave her a stern lecture about brushing regularly. It was pretty cute."

"So much more effective coming from a doctor instead of a mom, I imagine."

Rebecca laughed, her brown eyes sparkling with amusement. "You're absolutely right, which is why I quietly asked him to do just that."

Slipping off her sweater, she said, "Anything I can help you with on the computer?"

"No, I don't think so." Mary told her about the census and that she was investigating the gristmill ownership. She didn't go into *why*. She wasn't hiding anything from Rebecca; she just didn't sense there was any reason to share Betty's troubles with her for the time being. "The census only gives the name of the head of household and the number of people living at that address. There's no other information."

Rebecca frowned. "Boy, for the last census, we had to fill out a huge form about ages, occupations, and I don't know what. It took forever."

"That's right, I remember. If I'd had a large family, it would have been a real bother." She turned back to the computer. Maybe a later census would include more information.

Rebecca went to work tidying up the display table, and Mary continued to work on her computer. With a few quick keystrokes, she brought up the 1840 census. If Daniel's story was right, Caleb Hopkins ought to appear among the names of those counted that year.

Sure enough, she found him right off. Caleb Hopkins, head of household, four children. Occupation: fisherman. Not miller, she noted. Apparently, the fishing occupation had been passed down from father to son through many generations of Hopkinses including to Daniel. Now his grandsons were in the same business.

That, at least, was new information. But she couldn't imagine what motive an owner of a gristmill would have to murder a fisherman. Certainly an argument over ownership of a mill wasn't reason enough to commit murder. Nothing was, Mary knew. Still, Mary couldn't help but wonder where Daniel's accusation had come from.

If it had any validity, Mary didn't think her sister would accept it at all well. It might be pride and loyalty to the Emersons that drove Betty's insistence that the mill had never been sold. But behind that insistence was a deep pool of emotion and the promise she'd made to Edward. She knew Betty wouldn't give up the gristmill easily.

She'd fight with all she had to save her family's legacy.

Late that afternoon, Betty called Mary at the shop.

"I don't feel much like cooking," she said. "How about after you get home, we'll drive down to Sam's Seafood? It's going to be a beautiful evening, and I'm in the mood for shrimp and chips."

"Sounds delicious." Mary's stomach rumbled in agreement, and she realized she hadn't taken time for lunch. "Maybe we can get outdoor seating on the deck." Sam's Seafood, right by the marina, was a bit of a dive but remained popular with both locals and tourists. Plus it was a great place to watch the boats come and go.

An hour later, Rebecca had tallied the sales for the day and gone to pick up Ashley on the way home. Mary straightened the counter and looked for Gus. He was not in his usual place, in a sunny spot in the front window, which meant he was hiding out to avoid the ride.

"Come on, Gus. I've got a dinner date." She looked under the display tables and then found him snoozing in one of the comfortable chairs at the back of the shop.

She squeezed the reluctant cat into his carrier and headed for home.

Only taking enough time upstairs in her room to freshen up, Mary was quickly ready to leave for Sam's.

"Was the shop busy today?" Betty asked as she backed out of the driveway.

"About the same as usual. And I've done some more research into the case."

"Any luck?"

"Not much, but I'm at least gathering some puzzle pieces. There is no record I can find of the property being sold, and there doesn't seem to be anywhere to find Isaac's signature."

Betty stopped momentarily at an intersection and waited for oncoming traffic to pass before turning right.

"Then there's no way Daniel can win the suit, right?"

Mary gnawed on her lower lip. "I certainly can't find any justification for the suit. But Daniel was able to find a lawyer willing to take on his case, and as Rob said, he's a lawyer who wins a lot."

Betty just shook her head in disgust.

Mary looked out the window. Could Daniel Hopkins be so mean-spirited and angry about ancient history and an old feud that he'd filed a suit without any merit as a way to get back at the Emersons? Make them run up attorney bills? That seemed crazy, considering none of the Emersons even remembered the original cause of the quarrel. Eleanor had related other incidents that wouldn't make for good neighbors, if they were true, but surely they weren't worth suing over.

The parking lot at Sam's was three-quarters full even at this early dinner hour. Betty found a place to park, and they walked to the restaurant, which was housed in an old, low cottage down by the marina. The building was one of the oldest in town and started its life as a fisherman's shack but had had many incarnations since then. The ceiling was low, and the walls of the vestibule where guests wait for a table were dark wood decorated with old black-and-white pictures of Ivy Bay. They were all scenes of the town — a swimsuit competition in the 1930s with the women covered from neck to toe, the commercial fishermen lounging on the dock near their boats, even a picture of the Emerson gristmill when it was in far better condition than it was now.

Mary inhaled deeply. It smelled like fried seafood. Her mouth watered. There were a few small mismatched tables scattered around the small dining room, but they were all occupied, and Mary waved to a couple of women she recognized from church as they made their way to the counter to order.

The menu was printed on chalkboards hung above the low counter. Mary studied the menu, but Betty knew what she wanted.

"Mary, Betty," Sam greeted them when it was their turn to order. Sam, the owner of the restaurant, was a fixture around Ivy Bay. Over eighty, he was still spry and sassy to his customers, and he still came to work at his restaurant every day. Sam started out doing all the cooking at the restaurant, but he preferred to chat with everyone who came in, so now he took orders and left the cooking to the help. The line moved slowly, as he chatted with each person who came to the counter, but Sam earned loyal customers.

"What'll you have?"

"Shrimp and chips for me," Betty said.

"Make that two," Mary said, glancing up at the menu one last time. The lobster roll was tempting, but she'd have that next time.

"Coming right up."

A few minutes later, they carried plastic trays out to the outdoor deck, which was lined with weather-worn wooden picnic tables. Mary spotted a couple of free seats available at one end of a table and threaded her way through the crowd toward it. Sam's wasn't fancy, but the food couldn't be beat, and the view out over the marina was stunning. Mary took in the panoramic view of the narrow rows of fishing shanties along the waterfront, as well as the small boat marina and the commercial fishing fleet.

While there were several people in the small boat marina washing the salt off their boats or loading up their gear, the commercial docks appeared deserted. Fishing trawlers rode easily on the shifting tide, leashed by heavy lines to the dock. Big piles of fishing nets sat at intervals on the dock like giant mounds of forgotten debris. Out in the bay, motorboats arced through the water, leaving a wake of V-shaped waves moving toward both shores of the bay.

As they ate, Mary looked out over the dock where the commercial fishing fleet was tied up. As usual, most of the boats had probably left the harbor as early as two in the morning, returning by noon with their day's catch.

Betty liberally sprinkled pepper over her meal and squirted ketchup from a plastic container onto her fries.

"I can't get the suit out of my mind," Betty admitted. "And I've been going over

107

and over what Daniel said to you. He seems to think his great-great-grandfather was murdered because he was trying to claim the mill from William Emerson."

"Right . . ." Mary wasn't sure what her sister was suggesting. She wiped her hands on a paper napkin that was somehow already coated in grease. No one ever claimed Sam's served health food.

"It seems to me that since there's no record of the sale, William Emerson wouldn't have had any reason to kill Caleb Hopkins." She sat back, content with her line of reasoning, and took another bite of bread.

She had a point. "Well, playing devil's advocate . . . Maybe the mill wasn't a motive. They could have just gotten into an argument." She thought of Daniel Hopkins and the chip he had on his shoulder. If Caleb had had the same volatile personality, perhaps that caused the rift between the two families. "If things got overheated, William Emerson could have accidentally —"

"Really, Mary." Betty set the ketchup bottle back down with a thud. "I don't know why you persist in thinking the worst about Edward's ancestors."

"Oh, Bets. I'm not thinking the worst of anyone, and I dearly loved Edward. But I

108

am trying to get to the bottom of this suit. Naturally, I have to consider all possibilities." And perhaps, since she was stumped in determining ownership of the mill, she should investigate Daniel's story about the murder of his ancestor.

Betty sniffed and turned away to look at the marina.

Mary's hand trembled slightly as she reached for a fried shrimp.

"I promise, Bets, I'll do what I can." She reached across the table and held her sister's hand. "I'll look into Daniel's story about the murder of Caleb Hopkins."

Betty gave a nod of acceptance. "Thanks, Mar. And when you're done, I'd love to be there when you tell Daniel Hopkins he'll have to stop maligning the Emersons' name or we'll . . . we'll . . ."

"I hate to be the voice of reason, but I do remember there's something in the book of Romans about not taking revenge but leaving room for God's wrath. Instead, we're supposed to feed our enemies."

"There are days, sister," Betty said good-naturedly, "that I'm sorry you've memorized so much of the Bible. There is no possible way I'm going to feed Daniel Hopkins a bite of food out of my cupboard."

With the tension between them eased,

Mary and Betty ate for a time in companionable silence, accompanied by the murmur of voices around them and the shrill call of seagulls soaring overhead.

Betty asked how the plants at the shop were doing, and Mary told her how eager Ashley was to care for them. Their conversation then touched on their respective grandchildren's accomplishments, news of mutual friends, and the county's proposal to widen the beach by dredging sand from the bay.

While they chatted, the sun dropped lower in the sky, the boat masts in the marina casting longer and longer shadows. Seagulls vied for a spot on top of the tallest masts with the best perch for spotting luckless fish for their evening meal.

When they'd finished eating, Mary stood and took one last look at the view. She scanned the commercial fishing fleet with its wide-beamed boats tied up to the dock. That made her wonder. . . .

"Sam!" The restaurant owner must have been taking advantage of a lull in business to come out and say hi to his patrons. Sam finished chatting with a woman holding a new baby and then leaned in to caress its cheeks before making his way over toward Mary and Betty. The light breeze ruffled his little gray tufts of hair at the back of his head.

"Did you enjoy your meal?" Sam noted the empty plastic baskets in front of them.

"It was delicious." Mary brushed the crumbs off her hands. "Clearly."

"Glad to hear it. It's a beautiful night." Sam smiled out over the marina. The sun was just starting to slip down below the horizon, casting a warm orange glow over the boats.

"It sure is." Mary paused, trying to figure out how to phrase her question. "We've loved looking out over the marina. There are some beautiful boats. But do you know if one of those fishing boats is owned by Daniel Hopkins?"

Sam glanced toward the boats. "Not by old man Hopkins. The family beached him some years ago after he fell off the boat and almost drowned. His son captains the *Queen Ann* now, with his sons as crew."

"Oh. I just wondered." For a moment, she imagined the hard life of the early fishermen on the Cape. Their struggles. The lives that were so often lost.

Suddenly, her throat tight with sympathy for generations of Hopkinses who had gone to sea, she took Betty's arm. "Let's go home."

Six

Friday morning, Mary headed to the library. Although she was on a serious errand, she couldn't help but reflect on how much she loved libraries and had ever since she was a child. She'd devoured books by the dozens, including the original *Doctor Dolittle* series and *Black Beauty* during her animal-lover stage. However, a visit to a working farm with horses and pigs and all manner of earthy smells quickly dissuaded her from a career as a large-animal veterinarian.

Although the Ivy Bay library was of modest size, it was perfect, in Mary's mind; she always found it comforting and familiar.

She walked in and immediately looked up and smiled at the library's skylights in the vaulted ceiling, which made the space feel light and airy. She also noted the small statue of her stepgrandfather Adam Franklin, who had once been the mayor of Ivy Bay. As she had several times before, she felt a stab of pride at the representation of the long history her family had in Ivy Bay.

She moved to the front desk, where Victoria Pickerton stood in front of four bronze sculptures lined up on the wall. The sculptures commemorated important men in Ivy Bay's history, including Franklin, who had been influential in preserving the library's historic building.

"Hi, Victoria. Good morning," Mary said with a smile. Mary had spent so much time at the library since she'd moved to Ivy Bay that Victoria was quickly becoming a good friend. The woman had an amazing memory for details — she could put her finger on the most obscure facts within minutes. Mary hoped to put that skill to good use today.

"Love the new glasses." An energetic woman in her forties, Victoria seemed to have an endless selection of cat's-eye glasses. Today's pair was a sparkling blue.

"Hi, Mary. Thanks! Haven't seen you in a little while. How are you?" She removed her glasses momentarily, looking at them as though she were surprised to see which pair she was wearing.

"Busy with the bookshop as always, and then these little mysteries keep popping up. I can't seem to stop trying to solve them."

Victoria clapped her hands. "Wonderful! I do love a mystery. How can I help you?"

She made sure no one was around, then told Victoria about the lawsuit and how that might be linked to a murder in 1841.

"A murder?" She gasped, her eyes widening.

"That's the accusation."

"Oh dear. Was there an arrest or trial?"

"I don't know, but it seems unlikely. According to Betty, Emerson family lore hasn't included any mention of someone sent to prison for murder. In fact, I don't know if there even was a murder. It could be nothing more than an old rumor passed down through the generations with no merit at all. Purely gossip or envy-based."

"*Hmm,* I suppose you could check court records." Victoria closed up the material on her desk that she'd been studying.

"Actually, I thought I might check for a newspaper account of the incident first, assuming there was one. What do you think?"

"Excellent idea. Archives, it is." She waved toward the room with a bow. "My lady."

Mary laughed. "Why, thank you."

Victoria led Mary into the humidity-controlled room where the most fragile archives were safely stored under lock and key. Several microfilm readers were set up at desks. The rolls of microfilm were stored in a bank of shallow drawers in a large cabinet.

"The *Ivy Bay Bugle* wasn't around then, but the *Ivy Bay Observer* was published weekly starting in 1839," Victoria said, "and all through the 1840s. I suppose by then, larger papers were being published and put the *Observer* out of business. But that's probably a good place to start."

Victoria ran her fingertip down the drawers marked with the relevant date. When she came to the appropriate drawer, she stopped and pulled it out.

Mary took the roll and sat down at one of the familiar machines and threaded the film through rollers. A front page headline appeared: Fleet Reports Record Catch. The subhead indicated record numbers of cod and haddock had filled the holds of returning fishing boats.

"Looks like exciting times," Mary commented.

"I'm sure it was to the fishermen who hauled in the catch." Victoria stood behind her, watching the screen change. "We have a very complete collection of the *Observer*. I believe the publisher's family passed them on to us."

"How generous." Mary loved the commitment citizens old and new had to Ivy Bay.

"I'll leave you to it," Victoria said. "But if you have any questions or problems, I'm right outside."

"Thanks, Vic."

The librarian hesitated before she walked out. Her eyes, magnified by her glasses, flashed with amusement. "I've always wanted to help catch a murderer."

Mary laughed. "If there is a murderer, I'm sure he's long dead. So at least we won't be in any danger." Not in danger from the deceased, anyway. Daniel Hopkins might be a different matter.

Daniel had claimed his ancestor had been killed in October 1841. Just to be safe, she started with issues dated in late September. She carried the drawer marked with those dates to the table and sat down to study the papers.

Each edition of the newspaper consisted of only four pages. The headline-making news appeared on the front page, often including some affront a politician or the state legislature had committed. Inside were more local stories of weddings and births, county affairs, fishing and harvesting reports. A few official government notices appeared on page three, as well as merchandise offered for sale — horses, pigs, hay, wagons, and the like.

She even found a small ad placed by the Emerson gristmill: Cornmeal half-barrel — $2.25.

In addition to identifying the effect of inflation between the 1790s and 1841, this showed the mill was still owned by the Emersons. At least the name hadn't changed.

Mary made a note on the yellow notepad she'd brought along.

She continued to browse. The issue of Wednesday, October 6, reported that a huge storm with the power of a hurricane had swept through the area, damaging the fishing fleet and destroying the saltworks. But there was no mention of the murder of Caleb Hopkins.

She moved on to the following week's edition, October 13. There, in the bottom right-hand corner of the front page, below the fold, the headline read: Ivy Bay Man Reported Missing.

Mary's heart jumped as she read the article: "Late on the afternoon of October 6, Mrs. Martha Hopkins reported that her husband, Caleb Hopkins, had been missing since the prior Saturday night, October 2, when he went to the Horse Head Tavern."

Apparently, Mrs. Hopkins' report to the constable had just missed the paper's deadline for the prior week.

"Constable Greenstock has been investigating the case. He determined that Mr. Hopkins was last seen outside the Horse Head Tavern arguing with William Emerson at approximately midnight Saturday."

Mary drew in a quick breath. "Oh goodness. Daniel could be telling the truth." But no, she immediately corrected herself, just because Emerson argued with the missing man didn't mean he had killed Caleb Hopkins.

And why, she wondered, if Caleb hadn't come home on October 3, had it taken until the sixth for Martha Hopkins to report her husband was missing? Was she used to him going off on his own for days at a time? Did she think he was out fishing on his boat? Or had she delayed the report for a more sinister reason?

Shaking her head, Mary studied that paragraph one more time. She'd never heard of the Horse Head Tavern.

As she mulled that over, she continued reading the article.

"Prior to this incident, the tavern barkeep Mountie Baker admitted throwing Hopkins out of the tavern for rowdy behavior and starting a fight with one of his patrons."

Mary wondered once again if Daniel's

cranky temperament had been passed down through the generations, going at least all the way back to Caleb.

The article went on to indicate the constable had questioned Mrs. Hopkins and her eldest son at length, and had discovered a bloodstained butcher knife in the Hopkinses' kitchen. Both Mrs. Hopkins and her son Peter claimed not to have seen or spoken to Caleb Hopkins since early on the day he went missing.

Mary stopped reading. Would a bloody knife in a kitchen be that unusual? They would have kept animals for food back then. There wasn't any way at the time to determine whether the blood was human or not. Yet the constable had taken special note of the knife. Interesting.

She resumed reading.

"Interviews by this reporter with the Hopkinses' neighbors suggest the constable was well acquainted with the Hopkinses' household, as he was frequently called to break up loud arguments between the husband and wife, sometimes involving injuries to Mrs. Hopkins.

"Other reports indicate Mr. Hopkins had a loud argument with Irving Smith, a fellow fisherman, earlier in the day. Mr. Hopkins had accused Mr. Smith of running through and destroying his nets on purpose.

"No arrests have been made, and the case is still being investigated. The Hopkinses' boat, though slightly damaged in the recent storm, remains moored at the Ivy Bay dock."

Mary pondered that last sentence. A big storm had damaged the fishing fleet, but apparently Caleb's boat had survived intact. She would presume, then, that Caleb hadn't been lost at sea in the storm.

Leaning back, Mary let out a long sigh. Based on the argument they'd had at the Horse Head Tavern, William Emerson was an obvious suspect for Caleb's murder. But Mrs. Hopkins, who might have tired of being abused, was a viable suspect as well. So was Irving Smith, who had possibly damaged Caleb's fishing gear on purpose, perhaps because of prior disagreements between the two men.

Mary tried to visualize a possible scenario — William Emerson left Caleb standing in front of the tavern and went home alone. Still angry, Caleb could have stormed back inside the tavern, started another fight and been somehow killed, perhaps accidentally, in the ensuing melee with the barkeep and his patrons.

A gruesome thought came to her then. If

Caleb wasn't popular among the locals who patronized the tavern, they might have disposed of the body and kept the secret of his death in order to avoid arrest. Yet surely, if there had been more than a few patrons in the tavern, one of them would have let slip something about Caleb's death. The truth would have leaked out.

In any event, how on earth could she prove that or any other possibility after so many years had passed?

She scanned through several more editions of the newspaper but found no update to the story and no further information regarding the whereabouts of Caleb Hopkins.

Still mulling the problem, she returned the microfilm to the file cabinet. She'd have to see what information she could discover about the Horse Head Tavern, and she still wanted to ask Victoria for suggestions where she could find a sample of Isaac Emerson's signature.

She also needed to get hold of a copy of the original police report for the case of Caleb Hopkins' death, if that still existed. Did they even do police reports back then? Mary wasn't sure, but she knew how to find out.

"Did you find what you were looking for?" Victoria asked as Mary stepped out of the archive room.

"I guess the answer is yes and no. I found an article that said Caleb Hopkins was reported missing and that he had last been seen with William Emerson."

"Is that the yes or no part?"

Mary laughed. "I'm not sure. The fact is, based on that one story, there seem to be four possible suspects."

"Well, I suppose the first thing you need to figure out is if you're trying to prove guilt or innocence?"

"Exactly." Mary straightened her spine and tried to determine how she should approach the problem. "I'm not looking for a guilty man. I just need to know once and for all that William Emerson is *not* a murderer."

"So you can begin by attempting to *eliminate* the suspects."

"My plan exactly."

"Anything else I can do to help?"

"I hope so. I'd like to find a sample of Isaac Emerson's signature or handwriting. He owned the gristmill in 1792."

"In 1792?" Laughing, Victoria placed her hand over her chest. "You're really trying to give me a challenge, aren't you?"

"Well, I can't think where I'd find his signature. I did check in the county records, but there was nothing. There might have been a signature on a bill of sale if a copy had been kept in the files. But there is no copy in the county records. And no transfer of title, that I can find. Thus no signature." Mary gave her an innocent smile. "Any thoughts?"

"*Hmm,* let me see if there's any mention of Isaac Emerson in my archives." She sat down in front of her computer. "We have some very old church records, including records of births, deaths, and marriages. The clerk's office only keeps public records, activities that involve the government in some way." As Victoria's fingers clicked away on the keyboard, her frown deepened. She shook her head. "I'm not finding any mention of Isaac except in the census reports." She looked up. "Sorry, Mary. There's not a thing in our archives that would contain his signature."

"Well, I do appreciate you checking. I think I'll use your computers to see what I can find out about William Emerson or his family while I'm here."

"Good luck!"

In the back of the library, there was a separate computer room, which had access to the Internet as well as an interlibrary loan system. Mary sat at one of the computers.

Maybe she could find a reference to an old journal. Anything that would hint that William did — or rather did not — kill a man.

As she browsed various sites, she found lots of mentions of the gristmill, including a reference to a birthday party held there in 1907. Hardly the information she needed. She worked on the computer for quite a while but found nothing of use.

The lack of results, however, meant there were no direct avenues to pursue William's guilt, or hopefully, his innocence. With no records, and no one in the Emerson family with any specific knowledge of the murder, she had quickly reached a dead end.

Once outside, Mary took out her cell phone, hoping to catch Benjamin McArthur, the police chief, in his office.

After talking with the clerk first, Mary waited on hold until the chief answered his phone. Mary briefly explained the situation about the mill and the Daniel Hopkins lawsuit.

"It sounds crazy to me that Daniel would be trying to claim the mill is his after all this time."

"I completely agree," Mary said. "That's why I called you. Do you store old police reports in your office?"

He paused a minute. "Yeah. What did you need?"

"The original constable's report about Caleb Hopkins going missing in October of 1841."

He snorted. "You've got to be kidding."

"They did police reports back then, right?"

"I'm not even sure."

"Would you mind looking? I know it's a lot to ask. But I've already checked with Victoria at the library and went through old newspaper accounts. The problem is Daniel Hopkins claims William Emerson murdered his great-great-whatever in 1841. Apparently, that was the start of a feud between the two families and, I suspect, somehow related to Daniel suing Betty and her family over the ownership of the gristmill. I'm having trouble getting to the truth instead of hand-me-down rumors. If you can come up with the police report, it could really help."

In the background, Mary heard the police chief's chair creak, and she pictured him adjusting his position. "It's possible the report is still around, but it's not going to be easy to find."

"Could someone in your office look? If that's too difficult, I could search for the record myself, if that would be easier," Mary volunteered.

"Let me talk to my clerk. Maybe it'll be easier to find than I expect. I'll get back to you."

"Thank you, Chief. I really appreciate your help." And just maybe the original report would help her get to the bottom of the mystery.

That evening, while Mary and Betty relaxed in the living room and watched the shadows lengthen across sand dunes, Mary brought Betty up to date about what she had learned.

"So Caleb Hopkins really was murdered?" The dejection in Betty's voice touched Mary's heart.

"I don't think we can jump directly to that conclusion, but according to the newspaper article, his absence was being investigated as suspicious."

"That's terrible. I can't even imagine any Emerson —"

"Remember there are other possible suspects as well. William Emerson is simply the last person who admitted being seen with Caleb before he went missing."

Betty brightened. "A murderer wouldn't have admitted that, would he?"

"That's what I'm thinking." *Unless he was*

trying to lead the constable off track or knew there had been witnesses, Mary considered.

"So which suspect do you think killed him?"

"I don't know. They all seem likely suspects with perfectly good motives. I'm thinking about trying to eliminate them one at a time."

"How are you going to do that?"

"I don't know that either," she said with a discouraged sigh.

Betty frowned, which was happening more frequently since she'd received the copy of Daniel's lawsuit. "You know, I have a vague memory of seeing some old photos of the gristmill around here somewhere. I wonder if they would hold any clues."

"Really? Where?" Mary asked.

"I think they were in a box in the attic."

Hope sparked in Mary's chest. "Let's go take a look. Maybe there's more in the box than photos."

They climbed the stairs to the second floor, then lowered the pull-down stairs to reach the attic.

Betty was breathing hard when they reached their destination. "I'd forgotten how hard it is on my arthritic knees to come up here."

"I had forgotten how much heat an attic

holds in. It must be a hundred degrees in here." Sweat beaded on Mary's forehead.

The attic was filled with cardboard boxes, children's toys, an old rocking chair. A metal sewing mannequin stood guard in one corner.

Betty made her way through a narrow path between boxes. "I think what I'm looking for is over here." She lifted one box out of the way. Groaning, she knelt in front of another and opened it.

"What have you got?" Mary asked.

"A few of Edward's books. An old tie. I have no idea why I saved that." Finding a manila envelope, she opened it. "And pictures."

Mary knelt beside her sister as she pulled a handful of black-and-white photos out of the envelope. An old town map came out with them.

"These pictures look like they were taken in the 1930s, before the mill was so run-down."

"Those will be useful if Evan decides to restore the mill." Mary opened the map, which was dated 1939. She recognized the layout of Ivy Bay, but there were also notations on the map regarding historical features. After turning the map over, she skimmed through the interesting details until her eyes fell on the words *Horse Head Tavern.* The caption read: "Originally, the tavern served as a popular spot for local fishermen and for overnight travelers passing through the Cape Cod area. The interior has been remodeled and is now a private home owned by the Stebble family."

"Look at this," Mary said. "The old Horse Head Tavern, where Caleb Hopkins and William Emerson were seen fighting, was converted to a house and was owned by the Stebble family in 1939. I think that's where Amy Stebble, who is in my prayer group, must live now."

"Really? Where is it?"

Mary flipped over the map. "Looks like it's just off Meeting House Road, quite close to the mill."

That was definitely a place Mary wanted to see.

SEVEN

After a restless night, Mary awoke especially groggy. She definitely needed a cup of coffee to get the day going.

She noticed she was moving a little slower than usual as she got ready to go to the bookshop. She chose comfort over speed, opting for a pair of dark-colored jeans instead of slacks and a slightly overlarge white cardigan over a seagreen boatneck tee. Carrying her laptop, she made her way to the kitchen and noticed that Betty was still sleeping. She moved quietly to not wake her sister; she knew that especially with her arthritis, Betty needed a healthy amount of sleep.

Mary made a small pot of coffee and sat at the kitchen table to enjoy her coffee and let the caffeine take effect. She was looking at another long day of running a bookshop and investigating a mystery.

She smiled. *Investigating a mystery.* She

knew she wasn't anything close to a real detective, but she still couldn't help but enjoy the feeling of being helpful in times like these. As she often had before, she thanked her grandmother for getting her hooked on mystery books, which seemed to have permeated her brain and given her the instincts of a sleuth.

After booting up her computer, she searched again for the 1840 census. It didn't take her long to discover the listing for Caleb Hopkins and his address, which looked to be in an older and poorer part of town. She jotted the address on a slip of paper.

She took a final sip of her coffee and glanced toward Gus, who had meandered his way into the kitchen. She'd leave Gus home so he could keep Betty company. Her sister pretended to be a curmudgeon when it came to cats, but the number of times Mary had caught Betty snuggling with Gus belied her claim.

"Sorry, Gus. Today, you'll be staying home," she said to the gray cat, who seemed to almost visibly shrug in indifference and then padded toward Betty's room.

Mary smiled, put the coffee mug in the sink, then made her way to her silver Impala and drove to the bookshop. Rebecca was already inside getting the store ready to open for the day.

"How is everything this morning?" she asked Rebecca.

"Quiet, for now. But I noticed we've sold several of the books you featured about Ivy Bay and Cape Cod, and we're entirely sold out of two of them. Again, if you can believe it."

"That's great news."

"Would you like me to make a list of those we need to reorder?" Rebecca asked.

"That would be perfect." Since Mary had been gallivanting around town so much lately trying to solve the mystery of the gristmill, she felt doubly blessed to have Rebecca working for her.

Ashley called from the children's area. "Mrs. Fisher, I really like this book about the mysteries of the *Mayflower.* I think you ought to include it in your history display."

"Why, thank you, Ashley. That's a good idea. I'll order a couple of extra copies too. Grandparents love to buy books for their grandchildren."

She winked at Rebecca, who rightfully looked proud of her daughter's suggestion.

Mary went back to the original town plot map and spread it out to examine. She checked the street address she'd found in the census record. She had decided to start with understanding Caleb's wife's role in his disappearance, if there had been one.

The address was within easy walking distance of where the commercial fishing fleet docked, and not too far from the location of the Horse Head Tavern. Caleb could have easily walked home in the dark of night. He could have still been angry about whatever had transpired between him and William Emerson when he arrived at his house. And he could have been drunk.

It was possible Caleb's wife knew more about what happened that night than she'd let on.

That evening, they ate a dinner of a delicate cold potato-and-leek soup and tuna sandwiches on toast. Betty took a bite of her sandwich and washed it down with a sip of iced tea. "Henry came by this afternoon. He caught me trying to replace the stake for the young poplar tree I planted last spring. Somehow the old one got broken."

"Oh? I hadn't even noticed." The garden was under Betty's purview, not Mary's.

"At any rate, Henry stopped to help me set the new stake properly and stayed for a cup of tea."

"He is the nicest man. Always volunteering to help others. Sometimes I worry that

133

we all take advantage of his good nature."

"He seems to thrive on being helpful," Betty said, and Mary tended to agree.

When dinner was finished and the kitchen cleaned up, Mary invited her sister to walk into town to get an ice-cream cone and stroll around a bit.

Betty raised her brows. "Where are we going?"

"I want to see how far the mill is from the Horse Head Tavern."

"Horse Head Tavern? You mean where Amy Stebble lives now?"

Mary ran her hand over her hair, hoping to smooth the flyaway ends. "Unfortunately, it's also where Caleb was last seen arguing with William Emerson."

They both grabbed light jackets and went out the door and up the block. They strolled along the sidewalk, cracked in places, and passed by well-tended yards bordered by white picket fences.

"After we check how far the mill is to the tavern, I want to do the same thing between the tavern and Caleb's house."

"Where did he live?"

"Quite near the docks. Probably one of those small shanties."

As they turned on Main Street, Mary explained the information about Caleb's wife, and how Mary was trying to figure out if she could have been responsible for his disappearance.

Tourists, most of them sunburned, filled Bailey's Ice Cream Shop, sitting at small tables or waiting to order a cone from Jamie, a daughter of the owners. Jamie's auburn hair was short, and she wore a white bib apron with the name of the shop embroidered in pink floss across the front.

When it was their turn, Mary ordered a vanilla chocolate chip, and Betty ordered Mary's special ice cream of the month, peach and pralines. It tickled Mary that Bailey's had latched on to her talent for making different flavored ice creams soon after she moved back to Ivy Bay and now featured a different flavor of hers every month.

They made their way out of the shop and headed for what was now the Stebble home. Enjoying the warm air and the cold ice cream, they took their time, checking out late-blooming roses in various gardens and watching the flight of birds in search of their evening meal.

"There it is." Mary stopped across the street from the Stebble house. Two stories, with wood siding, it had a straight, flat-sided look.

"Not exactly inspiring architecture," Betty commented.

"No, but look how close it is to the mill. And it's close enough to the docks that Caleb could easily have walked home." The three points of interest were virtually on a straight line with the old tavern in the center.

Mentally, Mary tried to picture what could have happened. "If Caleb walked home that night, mistreated his wife, who then, for the sake of argument, killed him, what would she have done with his body?"

"*Hmm.* Well, first of all, I don't imagine there were this many houses around in the 1840s."

"Good point. And since it was several days before she reported him missing, she would have had plenty of time to dispose of a body."

"Like digging a grave?"

Mary rubbed her chin and considered the possibility. "If the grave was only a few days old, you'd think the constable investigating Caleb's death would have noticed."

"Couldn't she have taken him down to the water?"

"I suppose it's possible. But could Mrs. Hopkins have carried or dragged Caleb that far? How would she have gotten him all the way to the bay?"

"I don't know. You're the professional."

"Hardly!" Mary laughed. "And anyway, a murder mystery is a whole new ball game." Just then, Mary noticed a curtain move in the upstairs window of the Stebble house.

Not wanting Amy or her family to think they were gawking at their home, Mary took Betty's arm and they walked toward the marsh that was between the mill and the center of town.

They turned left at the corner, and Mary continued to think out loud about Martha Hopkins' possible actions. "So if Martha had access to a carriage or wagon, she could have used the knife the constable found, probably in self-defense, then dragged him outside, lifted him into the wagon —"

"All by herself? I wouldn't have been able to drag Edward two feet, much less lift him into a wagon."

Her sister was right. The scenario she'd imagined simply didn't make sense.

She would love, for Betty's sake and her family's, to make the morbid conclusion that Martha Hopkins was guilty of murder just so she could exonerate William. But there simply weren't enough facts. Yet.

By Sunday morning, Mary was ready for a

quiet day and a chance to worship the Lord. After getting ready for church, she went downstairs, a Bible verse of grateful praise in her heart: *Shout for joy to the Lord, all the earth. Worship the Lord with gladness; come before him with joyful songs* (Psalm 100:1–2).

Betty, purse in hand, was waiting for her by the door. She wore a summery skirt with a border print and a lightweight sweater over a silk blouse with cap sleeves.

"Sorry to keep you waiting," Mary said.

"No problem. We have plenty of time."

They had no trouble finding a parking space in the lot outside Grace Church, and they leisurely strolled inside. As they stepped into the vestibule, organ music greeted them.

So did Dorothy Johnson. She looked striking in a turquoise dress topped with a cropped white jacket and pearls.

"Hello, you two. Lovely day, isn't it?"

"It is," Betty agreed. "And you're looking lovely yourself."

"Thank you." Dorothy flushed modestly. "Mary, you remember me telling you that Henry was going to do some repairs around the house for me?"

Mary admitted she did with a slight nod. Why Dorothy felt compelled to bring this up again made Mary feel a mix of irritation and amusement.

"Well, that dear man spent almost all Friday at my house." She beamed with feminine pleasure at relating her day with Henry. "He worked very hard to get my windows working again. He was so sweet I invited him to stay for dinner. I'm sure he doesn't get many homemade meals since his wife passed on."

"I'm sure Henry enjoyed your home cooking." Mary spoke softly, her lips tight. Dorothy acted as though she wanted to either make Mary jealous . . . or warn her to keep her hands off.

Mary forced herself to remember her vow to deal with Dorothy with God's grace and smiled. "And I'm glad he could fix your windows."

"Oh yes, he's a wonderful handyman."

Mary took Betty's arm. "We'd better get seated. I'll see you at the next prayer group." She hoped it wasn't obvious that she had practically dragged her sister into the sanctuary.

When they were halfway down the aisle, Betty whispered, "Poor Dorothy certainly has her eye on Henry. I hope he doesn't mind."

"I don't imagine so."

"He might not be so willing to help if she gets too pushy."

They slid into a pew and sat down. The high ceiling soared above the congregation. Tall windows down each side of the sanctuary admitted sunlight. Behind the pulpit, a stained-glass window depicted a scene of Jesus praying.

The choir took their places. A moment later the congregation stood to sing the first hymn, "When Morning Gilds the Skies."

While Mary wasn't blessed with vocal talent, she loved to blend her voice with those around her and with the choir and organ. The music lifted her spirits to the Lord and opened her heart to His salvation.

When the hymn concluded, Pastor Frank Miles led them in prayer.

Pastor Miles had been the pastor of Grace Church of Ivy Bay for quite some time, and Mary loved worshipping under his leadership. He had an uncanny way of making his sermons relevant to the lives of ordinary people and offering up solutions to problems.

This morning's sermon was typically profound and very timely. He spoke of asking the Lord to heal past hurts rather than letting them fester and grow.

The dispute over the ownership of the mill

certainly represented an injury that had occurred years ago, which had now festered in Daniel Hopkins' mind. Mary prayed for the Lord's help in resolving the issue so that the wound could be healed.

After the service, as they passed through the crowd of churchgoers enjoying cups of coffee or tea, Mary spotted Jill Sanderson and her husband, Harry. She started to speak to Jill, but the young woman turned away.

Mary got the disheartening feeling that Jill was avoiding her in order not to cause conflict within her family. Mary hated the thought that Daniel's suit had put a barrier between herself and Jill. She prayed she'd find a way to restore their budding friendship.

Her musings were interrupted by the voice of her nephew Evan. "Hello, Mother. Aunt Mary."

Betty turned and embraced her son. "How are you, dear?"

"We're good, Mom." He reached out to his wife Mindy, whom Betty hugged as well. "Beautiful day, isn't it?"

"Not quite as hot as it has been lately." In turn, Mary gave Evan and Mindy hugs.

"Where are the children?" Betty asked.

"They're around somewhere visiting with

their friends," Evan replied. Mary spotted ten-year-old Betsy in the middle of a group of girls standing by the doughnut table.

Betty glanced around, then spoke in a lowered voice. "How's the attorney coming along with our case?"

"Rob went out to the mill last week to look around. And his assistant has also been poring over old records at the county clerk's office."

"I hope she wore old clothes," Mary commented. "It's really dusty down in the basement."

"I don't know about that, but she doesn't seem to have had much luck finding Isaac's signature or any records that indicate the mill has ever changed hands."

Mary chuckled. "I could have told Rob that, and I wouldn't have charged him a penny."

Evan laughed. "I can believe that, but I'm sure Rob wants to make sure to cover every possibility and earn his fee."

"I'm confident Rob is doing a good job for us," Betty said.

Mary was sure that was the case. Still, she wished either she or Rob's assistant would come up with something concrete that would prove the Emerson mill rightfully belonged to Betty and her family.

For the rest of the day, Mary mulled over Martha Hopkins' potential guilt in the murder of Caleb Hopkins. How could she have disposed of his body without anyone being the wiser? It simply didn't seem possible. But, then again, some of those early pioneering women were pretty hefty. They certainly hadn't had a soft life, carrying buckets of water to wash and bathe with, chopping wood for the stove and fireplace. Perhaps Martha Hopkins was a lot bigger and stronger than Mary had imagined.

But how could she possibly find out?

Mary and Rebecca were in the process of opening the shop Monday morning when she happened to glance out the window. As though her thoughts about Martha Hopkins had conjured up the perfect answer, Jill Sanderson walked past on the sidewalk carrying a shopping bag.

Impulsively, Mary grabbed the latest book in the cupcake mystery series Jill enjoyed.

"I'm going to dash out for a minute," she told Rebecca. "I shouldn't be gone long."

Rebecca grinned. "I'm used to your coming and going by now, and it doesn't bother me one bit. That's what I'm here for. Take your time."

Mary thanked Rebecca, then hurried after Jill and spotted her going into the Black & White Diner. Perhaps she was stopping for a cup of coffee or breakfast.

As Mary opened the door, the smell of bacon sizzling and fresh-roasted coffee brewing drew her inside. Jill had settled on a vinyl-covered stool at the counter. Mary walked up next to her.

"Hi, Jill. I saw you walk by. May I join you?"

Startled, Jill looked up. "I, um, hi. Of course."

Mary slid onto the seat next to her and put the book on the counter. "I wanted to catch you. I just got copies of the latest cupcake mystery and thought you would like to know."

A smile brightened her face and she picked up the book, examining the cartoonish cover. "Oh, isn't that cute? I love her stories."

"I knew you'd like it." The waitress arrived to take their orders. "Let me buy you a cup of coffee and some breakfast, if you'd like."

"Oh no. You don't have to do that. I only want coffee and a sweet roll."

144

"Make mine the same," Mary told the waitress. "My treat."

Jill flipped over the book to read the back cover.

"I just wanted to reassure you," Mary said. "Despite the dispute about the mill, I don't blame you in the slightest. I know the suit is none of your doing."

"No, it's not. In fact —" Jill hesitated. "Never mind."

Mary could tell that Jill was close to confiding in her, so she pressed forward, treading lightly. "It's really okay, Jill. I know that it's complicated. You can trust me."

Jill's shoulders sank, and she began to talk. "I believe you, Mary. It's just that . . . my husband and his brother have tried to talk Grandpa out of this whole thing. Harry keeps asking Grandpa what on earth we would do with the mill if we owned it. It's pretty run-down. All the Hopkinses have been fishermen for as long as anyone can remember. We don't know anything about restoring an old mill."

"So what does Daniel say when your husband asks that question?"

"He blusters. A lot." She half laughed at that. "Then proceeds to tell Harry that the mill is going to make us wealthy."

"How?"

The waitress brought their coffee and sweet rolls. Jill stirred a teaspoon of sugar into her cup and added milk.

"He won't say." She swiveled to face Mary more directly. "The truth is, Grandpa Daniel has been getting more and more cantankerous since Grandma Judith passed on. And now his sons won't take him out any longer to fish because he's unsteady on his feet and not safe on the boat. Staying at home makes him restless and at loose ends, which makes him extra grumpy, so he goes out wandering a lot. I think that coming up with this mill business has made him feel important again. My boys are thrilled they're going to be rich if Grandpa is right."

Mary could understand the need to feel useful. But Daniel's claim on the mill would leave him feeling even worse when he lost the case. *If* he lost, she corrected herself.

Mary took a sip of her coffee, hot, rich, and creamy.

"I'm concerned about this feud for a lot of reasons, Jill, and one of them is Daniel's insistence that there was a murder involved. Do you know anything about that?"

"I know he doesn't have anything good to say about the Emersons. And I've heard him make the claim before, but he doesn't seem to say anything of substance about the matter. And Mary, really, I shouldn't be talking with you too much. I don't want to betray my grandfather-in-law, even if I disagree with him."

"I understand." She patted Jill's arm to reassure her. "I do need your help with one more thing, though, and this doesn't really have anything to do with the mill. By chance, do you know anything about Caleb Hopkins' wife, Martha?"

Jill thought for a moment, then shook her head. "I haven't been real interested in genealogy or anything like that. My mother-in-law did give me a box full of old family pictures and stuff, even a couple of tintypes and miniatures, but I've barely looked at them."

Possibility fluttered in Mary's chest. "Do you think there might be a picture of Martha Hopkins in that box?" Probably not a photograph. The 1840s were before the technology was in common use. But there could be a different kind of image.

"I don't know. I guess I could look."

"Only if it won't cause problems with your family. But I would definitely appreciate it."

"I can try." She used her fork to break off a bite of sweet roll. As she chewed, her eyes lit up. "These sweet rolls are so good; I'm tempted to have one every day. But that wouldn't do my weight much good, would it?"

"Oh, I think we should enjoy a special treat now and again without guilt."

Jill agreed by taking a hearty bite of the roll, and Mary laughed. They took the time to enjoy their sweet rolls and moved on to a conversation about the cupcake mysteries. Mary paid for their check and was glad she'd given the book as a gift to Jill. It seemed like the least Mary could do.

During the lunch hour, the flow of customers at the bookshop slowed. Since they weren't busy, Rebecca and Ashley decided to eat their lunch in the back room; they'd brought packed lunches and had stored them in the small refrigerator. They could sit and visit while they ate.

Mary, enjoying the brief quiet moment, picked up the porcelain doll beside the cash register and again weighed it in her hand, wondering where it had come from and how it had ended up at the gristmill. It still looked familiar, yet she hadn't the slightest idea why.

With a sigh, she put it aside and glanced at the ledger. *Loose ends.* She'd be so glad when Mr. King came to look at it. Hopefully she'd learn something worthwhile from him.

While she had a minute, she sat down at the computer and opened her Internet browser. Her home page was her store's Web site, and even though she saw it every time she logged on, she still got a thrill. She opened a search window and typed in "Only the Very Best slogan." A whole page of references to Hallmark cards popped up.

She doubted Hallmark had been around in the 1840s. Could the doll be a contemporary knickknack sold with greeting cards as a promotion or sales gimmick? Might it not be old, after all?

Continuing her pursuit, she did find a Hallmark porcelain doll Christmas ornament. It was lovely in a pink dress and bonnet, but it wasn't the doll she was searching for.

She tried including the words "family crest" when she Googled, and she got even less useful information.

Next, she searched "porcelain dolls" and found dozens of examples, but none that looked like the doll she'd found at the mill.

She still couldn't imagine what the doll would have to do with the ownership of the mill, let alone Caleb's presumed murder.

Discouraged, she sighed and looked for a

Web site to convert British pounds to US dollars in 1792. She found a site that came close. With a bit of math, she concluded five British pounds at that time would be worth about three hundred dollars. That's what Caleb Hopkins claimed his ancestor paid for the gristmill.

Add in the inflation rate after so many years, and the amount became quite substantial. Five pounds would have been a great investment. If Daniel's story was true.

She clicked off the Internet. Rather than waiting for Jill to produce a picture of Martha Hopkins, Mary decided she should try to investigate either one of the other suspects: Mountie Baker, the barkeep at the tavern, or Irving Smith, the fisherman accused of tearing up Caleb's nets.

Mary pondered where she might find information about a sea captain who lived in the 1840s.

Standing, she stretched, and then she strolled around the bookshop, touching a book here or there, picking up an odd scrap of paper. Just being near books often jogged her memory.

As she stood staring at a bookshelf of mysteries, her gaze landed on *The Seafarer's Wife,* a novel that had created a stir a few years ago when it was first released.

She started to reach for the book, and then it hit her. Down near the docks was a Seafarers' Hall. Originally, the hall had provided hot meals, showers, and cots for fishermen who were temporarily without ships. Now the hall could be rented for parties or special events, and the funds were used to help seamen who were down on their luck.

The octogenarian who ran the hall, Strom Engle, had a wealth of knowledge about the fishermen who had sailed from Ivy Bay.

When Rebecca finished her lunch, Mary told her she was going out again

Seafarers' Hall was a block off Route 6A. Built of red brick, it had stood in welcome to fishermen for more than hundred years. Mary walked to the side office entrance and knocked on the door.

"It's open!" came a reply from inside.

While Strom's office was shabby by most standards, the lean former fisherman stood straight and tall, his blue shirt spotless, his summer-weight slacks carefully pressed. He came around to her side of the desk.

"Why, Mrs. Fisher, haven't seen you in an age. How's your bookshop doing?" His voice was laced with the sea and the accent of a longtime New Englander.

"I do believe I've found my calling, and business is thriving."

"Would you be thinking of celebrating your success, then?"

"Not today." Her gaze skimmed around the room, where boxes were stacked haphazardly. "Today, I'm looking for information about an old sea captain. I couldn't thnk of anyone who would be better able to help me out than you."

"And who might this sea captain be?"

"His name is Irving Smith. He fished these waters around 1840."

Strom's white brows lowered. "That's a bit before my time." He clasped his hands behind his back and stared at the plank floor. "His name does ring a bell. Let me think. A cod fisherman, I think. Of course, most were at that time."

"I'm specifically looking for something that would tell me where he was on October 3 in 1841." She laughed. Of course, she didn't really expect him to know but was surprised when he lifted his head.

"During the October gale?"

Mary marveled at Strom's knowledge of the area's history. "I guess so. I read something about that in an edition of the old *Ivy Bay Observer.* It must have been quite a storm."

"Aye, it was a fierce one. Hurricane-force winds. Took out the old saltworks and wiped out half the fishing fleet, taking the men on-board to their watery graves."

"Do you know if Irving Smith died in that storm?" she asked. Depending on what time the storm came through, that might give Captain Smith a solid alibi for Caleb's murder.

"I actually know that he did not." He walked over to a wall and pointed to an old photograph, probably circa 1920. "There's a memorial monument out on the spit. It lists all the souls that were lost that day. Irving Smith is not listed."

She joined him to get a look at the memorial. Although the photo was a bit fuzzy, she could make out a large, probably brass anchor set on top of a concrete base. On a brass plate was a long list of names, which she couldn't make out.

"We lost eighty-one fishermen that day," Strom said in a low, respectful voice. He couldn't have been more grave if he'd known the men personally.

"What a tragedy." A wave of sadness welled in Mary. So many gone. Hardworking men who tried to harvest a life for themselves and their families from an unforgiving sea. She thought of the debris of broken ships that had washed ashore: planks that had once been the deck of a boat; masts snapped by nearly two-hundred-mile-an-hour winds; seat cushions, bedding, and waterproof boots that had floated above men who had drowned and slid beneath the waves. Those bits and pieces, the detritus of lives taken too soon, that came to rest on the shores of Cape Cod.

Perhaps even the remains of those who had died at sea had washed up on beaches along the Cape.

She pressed her lips together. "But Irving Smith wasn't among those lost?"

"Nope. His name would be up there with the others."

Sighing, she wondered what to do next. "Would there be a record anywhere of his life?"

"Well, now" — he jingled some change in his pants pocket — "used to be the old-timers who stayed here liked to read. We had a bunch of books, some of them old seafaring stories. Might be some old ships' logs in the group, but I don't recall a Smith."

"Would you mind if I took a look?" It seemed like a long shot, but she didn't want to give up too soon. Not when the Emerson mill was at stake.

Strom led her to a back storeroom, which was filled with boxes, old bed frames, broken lamps, and assorted items that had seen far better days.

The thought of searching through all the junk was daunting.

Strom pointed to a pile of boxes. "If we have what you're looking for, it would be in one of these boxes."

"Then I guess I'd better get started looking."

"I'll give you a hand." He lifted a couple of boxes down to the floor. They each opened one and started to search through the contents.

Some of the books had been attacked by bookworms that had gnawed their way through the pages. Almost all were damaged beyond repair. Still, Mary pressed on, checking each book title. When she finished with one box, she dragged out another.

The third box didn't contain published books but rather bound journals. She picked one up and read the cover: Captain's Log, *Good Hope.*

"Here's one," she said out loud.

"Let me see." Strom took the log from her and flipped through a few pages. "Aye, this is the sort of thing you're looking for. But your man Irving Smith was not the captain."

Disappointment tightened in her chest even as she checked another log. "*Princess II.* Would that be Smith's boat?"

"I have no idea, but I do have a list of all the ships that sailed from this port. I'll be right back." He got to his feet with amazing agility for a man his age.

Strom returned quickly. "I found him. Irving Smith, captain of the *Jolly Mae.*"

"The *Jolly Mae.* That must have been named for his wife." She eagerly sorted through the remaining contents of the box. Not finding the *Jolly Mae* log, she moved on to a fourth box.

Moments later, she announced, "I've found it!"

Excitement building, she sat back on her haunches, opened the log, and started to read.

It didn't take long for Mary to become engrossed in the log of the *Jolly Mae.* On each journey to sea, Captain Smith noted time of departure, destination, compass course, wind force, and the state of the sea. But most fascinating were the remarks. Sick crewmen. Tons of fish caught. Loss of nets. Even arguments among the crew.

She easily found the entries of early October 1841, which said they had set sail at 1900 hours, 7:00 PM, on the evening of October 3, 1841. But she couldn't stop reading. Although the entries were brief, she could clearly understand the hard life of those who went to sea to earn their living.

It occurred to her that even now, a century and more later, the life of a commercial fisherman was still both hard and dangerous. Suddenly, she felt a rush of sympathy for the long line of Hopkins family members who had gone to sea to fill their holds with fish for others to eat.

She also felt a bittersweet emotion, because she could now check a murder suspect off her list.

EIGHT

After closing the shop, Mary headed home to report her discovery to Betty. She found her sister kneeling on a rubber mat in front of a bed of colorful Johnny-jump-ups in the front yard. Betty appeared to be tidying up for the day. She paused to rub the small of her back.

"Hi, Betty," Mary greeted her, concerned about her sister's physical health. "Let me take over for you."

"Thanks," Betty said. "I'll let you this time. I've been feeling great, but I'm definitely ready to quit for the day."

"I know exactly what you mean." Searching for information on the Web and at the Seafarers' Hall might not be physically tiring, but it was wearing.

She picked up Betty's tools and placed them in her gardening basket.

"How about some leftovers and iced tea

for dinner?" Betty said, heading into the house.

The idea sounded perfect to Mary. She put the basket of gardening supplies in the garage and followed her sister into the house.

After they prepared their food, they took their dinner out to the sunroom, and as they sat, they almost simultaneously sighed with the satisfaction of finishing a busy day. Mary was about to tell Betty about her trip to the Seafarers' Hall, when Betty spoke up.

"I've been thinking about the shop's backyard and what to plant," she said.

Mary took a sip of her iced tea. "How exciting. The plants you've already put in are doing well. Rebecca has been so reliable about keeping them watered. Or rather Ashley has," Mary said with a smile.

"She is a sweetie, isn't she? But it has occurred to me that you don't want the yard to be too high maintenance. I'd thought of making flower beds along the back wall, but I've changed my mind."

"Oh?" In contrast to Mary's black thumb, Betty could grow almost anything and had a wonderful ability to design a garden to be beautiful all year long.

"What would you think of putting in a patio back there, probably brick to match the building? You could have an umbrella table with chairs where people could read comfortably. And you could even have readers' groups meet outside when the weather was good."

Mary brightened. "I love that idea."

"I'm glad." Pleased, Betty placed her hand on her chest as though she'd been afraid Mary would object to the concept. "I'll call Kip right away. And I thought for color, we could get a couple of big tubs and plant annuals in them. The nursery could deliver the tubs already planted, and I just have to keep the flowers trimmed. That would cut down on the amount of maintenance that would be needed."

"Sounds ideal. But are you sure you're not taking on too much — the shop's backyard plus your own gardening here at home?"

"I may be." Betty laughed. "But I love the work. I'll take it slow."

Mary nodded and left it at that. She knew she could trust Betty to know her own limits. "Well," she said, changing subjects, "I think I can eliminate one of our suspects."

"Oh?" Betty shot her a surprised look. "I do hope it's William Emerson."

"I'm afraid not yet." Mary ran her fingertips up and down the cold sweat on her glass of iced tea. "It's the ship's captain, Irving Smith. The man who'd had a fight with Caleb earlier on the day he went missing."

"How can you suddenly know he didn't kill Caleb?"

"I visited Seafarers' Hall today. Strom Engle has boxes and boxes of old books the fishermen read. He also had some old captains' logs, including Irving Smith's log for the *Jolly Mae*. It made fascinating reading. I felt almost like I was on the ship with him."

"Getting seasick?"

"Practically." Mary chuckled. "According to his log, the *Jolly Mae* set sail at 1900 hours, that's seven o'clock, on the evening of October 3, 1841."

"So? What does that prove?"

"The newspaper account said Caleb was last seen around midnight of that same night. Irving Smith had already set sail by then. Therefore, he couldn't possibly have killed Caleb. He had an iron-clad alibi."

"Although" — Betty considered that for a moment — "he may have lied in his log to give himself that iron-clad alibi."

"I suppose that's possible. But the log entries were very detailed. They left the harbor heading north-northeast to fish the outer banks around Nova Scotia. The seas were heavy, waves washing over the gunnels. The barometer falling fast. Seems hard to believe a captain would make that up in his log. It would be too easy to check. In fact, the newspaper reported a terrible storm had passed through Ivy Bay on October 3."

"That still sounds odd to me. The fishing fleet usually leaves around one or two o'clock in the morning, don't they? Then why did this Smith fellow leave at seven?"

"Good point." If Irving Smith had fabricated his logbook, that meant he could be guilty of murder. Mary looked at her sister with a weary smile. "For now, I'm too tired to think straight."

Betty took her sister's hand and squeezed gently. "Have I mentioned lately how much I love you?"

Chuckling, Mary said, "Probably, but I don't think we have to say the words. Just being here together speaks volumes."

Yes, Mary's decision to move in with her sister after John died had been good for them both. Neither of them had to rattle around in a house much too large for one, and they provided companionship for each other.

Smiling, Mary thought of her favorite old

adage: A sister is a forever friend.

The following morning, shortly after Mary opened the shop, Jill Sanderson walked in, a pleased smile on her face.

"Good morning, Jill!" Mary was genuinely pleased to see her.

Jill's smile grew wider and a little conspiratorial. "I found the picture you wanted."

A burst of adrenaline accelerated Mary's heart rate. "Caleb and his wife, Martha?" she almost whispered.

Jill nodded with a hint of accomplishment in her expression. Mary couldn't help but feel another tug of gratitude for the young woman. Of course she'd been hesitant to divulge any information about her family to Mary; familial politics were tricky, especially in this case. But Mary hoped Jill knew that she certainly understood Jill's lack of total allegiance to her grandfather-in-law, and would absolutely keep a tight lip about the help she had offered to Mary.

"I dug into that old box of photos in the attic, and I found a few things," Jill said. "I think it might be the same sea chest Daniel found the bill of sale in when he was storing his things in our attic. Fortunately, either my mother-in-law or someone else had labeled most of the pictures and even

163

dated some." She placed a small miniature painting in a gold frame on the counter. "It was kind of fun looking at my husband's ancestors. There's even a resemblance between him and Caleb."

Gingerly, Mary picked up the portrait. Martha stood next to a seated Caleb Hopkins. As was the custom of traveling portrait painters, the heads of the two subjects were proportionally larger than their bodies, their expressions somber. Mary couldn't be sure the painter had captured a good likeness of the couple, but they both looked to be in their thirties. Mary supposed the painter had purposefully made them look younger than they really were, though.

"This is wonderful to see what Caleb must have looked like," Mary said. "His wife too."

"I thought my Harry's resemblance to Caleb was mostly in the eyes."

Mary studied Caleb, then his wife. "How big a man do you think Caleb is?"

Tilting her head, Jill took another look. "Hard to tell with that funny perspective."

"Martha's head is only barely above Caleb's, and she's standing," Mary said. "She looks quite petite. But I guess it's possible the painter made her look that way on purpose."

"Yeah, she looks really tiny there." Jill

looked up at Mary. "But here, I found this as well. This may be more useful." She laid a small framed picture on the counter. It had a metal back and was covered with a thin sheet of glass. "I think it's a photograph of the family."

Mary leaned in to get a closer look and squinted against the glare in the glass. Caleb and Martha were standing, ramrod straight, staring at the camera. Two teenage boys and two young girls stood around them, with the same somber look on their faces.

"It's actually too early to be a photograph. It must be a daguerreotype," Mary said, touching the edge of the metal gently.

Jill looked at her blankly.

"It was an early kind of photography," Mary said. She'd recently read a historical mystery where a daguerreotype was a major clue, and the author had included lots of fascinating details about the process. "It was done by exposing a silver-surface copperplate to a lens and then exposing it to mercury."

Jill nodded, but she looked like she was trying to follow. "So it's old then?"

"Very. The process wasn't invented until the late 1830s. It would have been very new and not very common when Caleb died. It must have been done fairly soon before he disappeared."

Mary studied the photo. Caleb stood almost a full head taller than Martha, and he was thick. Martha was indeed much smaller than her husband, and Mary had the proof in the form of a photograph taken not long before he disappeared.

"So, does this help you?"

"Yes," Mary said. "Thank you so much." Considering Martha's small stature, Mary's question about her part in Caleb's death remained. If Martha had killed Caleb, how could she have disposed of his body? She didn't see how the tiny woman could have budged him — much less put him in a wagon to take the body somewhere else.

She thought about Jill's comment about Harry's bulk. "Jill, out of curiosity. If you had to pick up or drag Harry somewhere, could you manage?"

The young woman let out a guffaw. "Heavens, no. I'd need a block and tackle to even get him off the ground. He weighs a good two hundred pounds, and it's all muscle."

With the hard labor Caleb did as a fisherman, and the typical diet of the 1840s, Mary doubted he would have weighed quite that much. Still, given a muscular body, he'd be way too heavy for such a small woman as

Martha to manhandle into a wagon alone, no matter how many laborious chores she was responsible for herself.

With a sigh that was close to regret, Mary tentatively eliminated Martha Hopkins from the suspect list. The woman's size wasn't absolutely proof she wasn't involved, but nonetheless, it was telling. "Thank you for bringing these to me."

"Oh, it's no problem. I'm just glad I found them. They're family heirlooms I'm definitely going to hold on to for my children and grandchildren to enjoy. You're welcome to hold on to them for a while, if that will help you." Then she sobered. "Just . . . don't let Grandpa know I tried to help you. He'd be furious."

Mary touched Jill's shoulder and gave her a reassuring look. "My lips are sealed. I promise." At that, Jill left the shop and Mary returned to her post behind the counter.

Although Mary had now made some progress investigating the murder, she still couldn't see how the answers were getting her any closer to countering Daniel's lawsuit.

She hadn't been able to find any trace of a title change, despite Daniel's claim of a bill of sale. In fact, she'd found evidence that the Emersons had continually operated the gristmill from the earliest records until well past 1792.

She also hadn't found a signature or handwriting example of Isaac Emerson at the clerk's office or in the library archives. Neither had Rob's assistant.

For all intents and purposes, she'd hit a brick wall.

She laid the portrait and daguerreotype on the counter and tried to shake off her discouraged mood. Jill had found a valuable heirloom in that old chest. It would be a lovely way to pass family history to her children. And a daguerreotype that old was probably worth a fair amount, if she ever cared to sell it, though Mary was sure she wouldn't get rid of that piece of family history.

Mary was reminded of how she had traced her father's side of the family, the Nelsons, back as far as Plymouth, England, in the 1600s, although the name itself was originally from the Anglo-Saxon tribes in England. The Fishers, John's family, were originally Normans who arrived in England after the 1066 Norman Conquest. They had a long, proud history to pass on to her children and grandchildren.

The adrenaline Mary had felt at seeing the miniature of Caleb and Martha slowly drained away. She had no idea how to prove or disprove that the barkeep at Horse Head Tavern was involved in killing Caleb. And now that she'd pretty much eliminated Martha and Irving Smith. . . .

Gus jumped up on the counter right in front of Mary and bumped his head against her chest.

"You sense I'm discouraged, don't you?" She scratched the top of his head and smoothed the soft fur over his back. "I hate to think William was guilty, almost as much as Betty does. But I'm running out of ideas."

He bumped her again, harder this time.

"Augustine Fisher, what is it you want?"

He canted his head, gazing at her with blue eyes that suggested she was the thickest human he'd ever met.

"I'm not a mind reader, you know."

Tensing, he poked the daguerreotype with his paw.

She was about to shoo him off when she realized, as silly as she knew it was, that he was trying to tell her something. "You want me to look at that again?"

Nonchalantly, he began to wash his face with his paw.

"So we're going to play twenty questions, huh?" Maybe Gus simply felt a need for a face wash and decided —

She gasped as realization struck. "It's true that Martha couldn't have moved Caleb's body on her own. But she could have moved it with some help."

Lifting Gus, she put him on the floor, sat down on the stool in front of the counter, and stared at the picture. Of course. Maybe Martha had a helper right in her own household, a son who had witnessed Caleb hurting his mother one too many times. The newspaper article had mentioned Martha and her *son* had both been questioned at length.

The door chimed. She looked up to see Bob Hiller had arrived with the mail.

"Morning, Bob. How are you today?"

"All is well here, Mrs. Fisher. My granddaughter Isabella's T-ball team won their game last night, so that's given me an extra hop in my step, you might say."

Smiling, Mary clapped her hands. Isabella was in Ashley's grade, and so Mary had spent some time with the girl. "Here's to the win!"

Bob gave a deep nod. "You look busy. So I'll leave you to it."

"Thanks, Bob. See you soon."

She looked back down at the picture. The older boy looked to be in his late teens, maybe even early twenties.

"What do you think of that, Gus?" She looked around, but her cat had returned to his favorite napping spot by the window. Apparently, he'd done enough work for the day.

Leaning back, she imagined Caleb's oldest boy had already been to sea with his father as a member of the crew. He'd be a strong young man. Maybe even the second boy had developed a few muscles by working on the boat. Sons could be very protective of their mothers. And the way Caleb's children had grown up, watching and hearing Caleb mistreat his wife, all four of them could have had anger and resentment boiling in their hearts. Perhaps the boys had eventually gotten big enough to do something about protecting their mother.

In her mind's eye, she pictured Caleb staggering into the house, wet from the storm, drunk, and still angry because of the argument he'd had with William. As he had many times, she wondered if he had vented his fury on his wife. This time, however, perhaps Martha fought back. As Mary had imagined it before, perhaps Martha did, in fact, take the knife to Caleb's chest.

But Mary took the scenario further this time. By the time Martha had theoretically killed Caleb, her sons had perhaps been awake. They came into the kitchen and understood that what had happened was done in self-defense. They resolved to help their mother appear innocent.

Even on a stormy night, Mary realized it would have been possible, with the help of a strapping teenager or two, to cover Martha's tracks. Neighbors would have been hunkered down in their homes during the storm, not peering outside. Certainly after midnight, the townspeople would all be in bed.

Satisfied with the possibility of that scenario, Mary nodded her head.

"Well, then, Martha and now her sons go right back on the suspect list. Thank you, Gus."

In response, Gus stood, turned around as though taking his well-deserved bow, and curled up in his spot again.

"Don't get too proud of yourself yet, Gus. We still have one more problem to solve. How do I prove that's what actually happened?"

The phone rang, interrupting her train of thought. She answered with a cheerful greeting. "Mary's Mystery Bookshop, Mary speaking."

"Hi, Mary. It's Chief McArthur. My clerk found the police report you wanted."

Her spirits perked up. "That's wonderful, Chief. Thank her for me."

"I will. She's left them at the front desk for you. You can drop by anytime you'd like."

Mary glanced around the bookshop. Rebecca would arrive soon. "I'll be there as soon as I can get away."

NINE

The inside of the police station had sage-green walls and wide-plank floors. Sturdy wooden tables and chairs were arranged in the reception area.

The clerk handed Mary a brown folder that contained the old 1841 police file. Mary found a seat at a scarred table where she could study the contents. Instead of boxes in which to make entries, like the modern report Chief McArthur had filled out when her shop was broken into, this report simply had a blank area for the constable to fill in his report. The paper had yellowed with age, each sheet so fragile she feared it might crumble when she touched one.

Constable Greenstock's signature appeared on each report, as well as the date. His handwriting wasn't easy to read, but she managed to get the gist of what he'd done. The interview with Martha Hopkins and her son Peter. Another interview with Mountie Baker, the Horse Head Tavern barkeep, and witnesses to the argument between Caleb and William Emerson, with the notation that no blows had been struck during the dispute.

The interview with Emerson was apparently lengthy, worth several pages of handwritten notes, concluding there was no evidence that Emerson had killed Caleb, but that he was a primary suspect in the case.

Mary winced. Not a good sign for William. Or Betty.

As she read on, the report mentioned Irving Smith, the fisherman Mary had already cleared as a suspect with an iron-clad alibi.

Overall, the reports provided no new information beyond what she'd already discovered from the *Ivy Bay Observer.*

She returned the file to the clerk, thanking her and then walked back to the shop. The temperature had warmed again, and beads of perspiration formed on her forehead and under her arms. Hot summers might be fine for tourists, but she was already looking forward to fall.

Later that afternoon, Betty showed up at

the shop with Kip Hastings in tow.

"Hi, Bets. Hi, Kip!" Mary glanced past her sister to the man wearing overalls who was with her. "It's so nice to see you. How's married life?" Kip Hastings and his sweetheart Heather had just recently wed in the area, although Mary hadn't attended. She knew they had planned a very small wedding because Heather had wanted something intimate, and they also were pretty short on cash.

The beginning of Mary's and Kip's friendship had had a rocky start — he had stolen a framed photograph from Mary's store before her grand opening, as a favor to his grandmother-in-law, knowing what she didn't: that there was money hidden inside it. But within a short amount of time, the whole thing had been resolved, and Kip had even donated the money that was stolen to a local charity. He and Mary had worked closely together with the renovating of her building, and he was a very talented handyman. Especially knowing that he was just starting off and trying to build a nest egg, she was always happy to hire him for projects.

"Nice to see you too, Mrs. Fisher." Kip, whose overalls were streaked white with mortar, touched the brim of his cap and gave a modest smile. "Married life is great. It's nice to finally live in one place and get to share meals together without having to separate at the end of the day."

"I remember that feeling," Mary said. "It's such a relief to finally become official."

"You can say that again," Kip said and smiled. "Now, let's take a look at the back-yard." He spoke in the clipped tones of a New England native.

"Thank you, Kip. Betty's the one with the idea for a patio, but I fully approve."

The three of them went out the back door, leaving Rebecca to take care of the two customers browsing the bookshelves.

Betty described her concept for the patio. "We have the wild raspberry bush we're going to keep along this wall. And the choke-berry opposite that, plus the two rosebushes. The raspberry and chokeberry will attract birds. The roses will smell especially lovely in the spring."

Kip knelt and scooped up a handful of dirt. "First thing, you'll need good drainage so you don't have rainwater or snowmelt running in your back door." He glanced around the yard. "We'll have to grade the patio so the water runs off to the side there and out to the street in front of your shop."

That made sense to Mary, so she nodded

in agreement.

"I want to put a couple of tubs of flowers on the patio," Betty said. "And we'll have an umbrella table with chairs."

"That's no problem." Kip stood and paced off the breadth and width of the yard. "I'll need to spread sand around so I can get the bricks to seat good. Do you want them mortared or flush up against one another?"

Mary glanced to Betty for advice.

"Mortar always crumbles after a while. Will they stay flush, or will weeds grow up between them?"

"If it was me, I'd do them flush back here. Give you a nice, smooth surface to walk on. When I do it, bricks stick right together like they were glued that way."

Smiling at his self-confidence, Mary glanced down and found Ashley standing next to her, waiting patiently to interrupt.

"What is it, honey?" Mary asked.

"Mother asked me to tell you that Henry's here. She thought you'd want to say hello."

"Thank you, honey. I'll be right in." She turned to her sister. "You work out the details, and we'll talk about the cost later when Kip brings us the estimate."

She thanked Kip for his time and slipped inside right behind Ashley to find out if

Henry had enjoyed the latest book she'd sold him.

"Hi, Henry. How was that Scottish mystery?"

Wearing wash pants with frayed pockets and scuffed work boots, he grinned almost sheepishly. There were streaks of dirt on the shoulders of his cotton shirt. "I haven't quite finished it yet, but it's going well. All spooky fog and rattling noises down in the dungeon of the old castle. Although nothing's as scary as the crawl space I just saw this morning." He shook his head in dismay.

"Oh? Let me guess. . . . Dorothy's?"

"Yep, I'm afraid so." Henry looked at Mary hesitantly for a second, as if he didn't want to gossip. But then, clearly needing to vent, he continued. "The foundation seems to be settling. That's why her windows and doors aren't fitting well. I just feel so bad because it's not something I'm qualified to fix. I gave her the name of a contractor friend who I think she ought to call, but she seemed disappointed."

Mary knew there was more than one reason Dorothy would have been disappointed, but she simply said, "That sounds like a major project."

"It is. I've actually heard about several of the historic houses around the Cape that are having troubles like this. The foundations need shoring up, and the house needs to be releveled. Otherwise the house will fall down of its own weight."

"That would be terrible." She felt bad for Dorothy and also wondered if the gristmill had similar problems. No doubt that would have a major impact on the decision to restore or destroy the old place.

"Anyway, like I said, that's a job well beyond my pay grade. I wouldn't even know how to begin." While Henry was exceptionally good with his hands, he was a fisherman by trade and inclination.

As Mary contemplated Dorothy's problem, Henry gestured toward the back door. "What's Betty up to out there?"

"Oh, we're putting in a brick patio. We'll have tables and such for folks to sit and read or visit. I'm really excited."

"Sounds great to me. All those big bookstores in the city have coffee bars and lounge chairs for studying, so you'll be right up to date."

"I hadn't thought about it like that, but my goal has always been that this is a comfortable place where people can enjoy themselves."

Henry's eyes twinkled and he smiled. "With you around, it's sure to be."

Her cheeks warmed ever so slightly, and she laughed.

When Henry left, he got into his spiffy 1953 Chevy Bel Air, which was parked at the curb. Outside of his boat, Mary knew that the car was one of his favorite toys. He'd restored it to near-showroom condition and showed it at car clubs and other special events around the Cape.

By the time Mary closed the shop, clouds had crept in, bringing with them the first drops of rain that was predicted to last all night. She hoped the summer storm would cool the overheated air and reduce the humidity that had been plaguing the Cape for several days.

When she reached home, she parked and pulled her jacket up over her head to ward off the light shower and hustled inside with Gus in his carrier.

"Betty? You home?" she called.

"In my room."

Shrugging out of her jacket, Mary followed the sound of her sister's voice. Betty had converted her husband's former office on the first floor into a bedroom for herself so that she wouldn't have to climb stairs.

At the moment, Betty was sitting at her small desk, re-reading Daniel's lawsuit. She looked up. "Kip's going to bring us an

181

estimate by tomorrow or the next day."

"Good. Thanks, Bets." She walked across the plush carpet to the desk. "I have something that might interest you."

"About the mill?"

"Not directly. It's about Caleb's murder. I had pretty much written off Martha Hopkins as the culprit, but she's back on the suspect list."

"So you think Martha did it?" Betty said, her expression a mix of regret and hope.

"I think she's still a viable suspect, but at this point, I can't prove it one way or another."

"At least William isn't the only one left on the list."

"That's true. In fact, I read the official police report this morning at Chief McArthur's office, but it didn't provide any new information."

"This whole suit business is so troubling."

Mary rested her hand on Betty's shoulder as a gesture of support. She knew how strongly Betty felt about her family. Even so, Mary hadn't been able to eliminate William yet, and he had been the prime suspect.

Soon, she should take another walk over to the gristmill. Maybe she'd missed something, another lead, although she couldn't imagine what it might be.

Betty sighed. "My goodness, Mar. I feel like our lives have been taken over by this thing. I'm sorry it's been so crazy. But I'm also really thankful for your help."

"Don't mention it, Bets. It has been pretty intense, but hopefully soon, this whole lawsuit business will be resolved and we can return to our normal . . . What am I saying? Our lives are never exactly *normal.* But that's one of the things I love about living here with you."

"I couldn't agree more. For now, I'll take solace in the gardening — it's been such a nice distraction."

"Speaking of distractions . . . How's that quilting mystery I lent you?"

"Oh! I just started last night. And I'm pretty sure it was Jacob who stole Evelyn's quilt. Her own son. I'll bet you that's who it was."

Mary laughed. "I'm not saying a word." Although she was impressed; Betty was right.

They talked a little longer about the book, then Mary went to her room to clean up and get ready to prepare dinner. The rain was falling steadily now, drumming on a metal shed in the backyard. She hoped that the storm and the skies would clear for the prayer group.

■ ■ ■ ■

Lynn Teagarden had one of the nicest houses in Ivy Bay. Situated on a large lot surrounded by woods, the front had three dormer windows and a welcoming front porch.

Carrying a bowl of fresh fruit salad in a yogurt dressing, Mary walked up to the door and raised the brass knocker. Lynn quickly responded.

"Come in, come in, Mary." She gave Mary a polite kiss on the cheek. "I'm so glad to have a prayer meeting here."

Mary stepped into the foyer, which had a high ceiling and hardwood floor. "Oh, Lynn, what a beautiful home. You're so nice to invite us."

Lynn waved off the compliment as if her home was nothing special, then reached for the salad bowl. "Let me take that from you. Go on into the living room. Several ladies have already arrived."

As Mary headed toward the living room, she continued to take in the house. The light green carpet was so lush it was like walking across a field of spring grass. Original oil paintings of the area hung on the walls, and a grand piano sat on a raised portion of the living room. Tea and coffee had been set out on a cherry-wood credenza beneath the paintings.

Mary greeted the ladies already present. "This is a tiny bit fancier than the church chapel or the all-purpose room."

"It's a lot fancier than my *house,*" another woman said with mock envy.

They all echoed the same good-natured sentiment, including Tricia Miles, who lived in the parsonage provided by the church.

More members of the group arrived in twos and threes, all smiling and chatting, buoyed by the bright, sunny day. They helped themselves to coffee or tea and found chairs.

Dorothy Johnson seemed unusually quiet as she arrived and took a seat next to Mary.

"How are you, Dorothy?" Mary asked, genuinely concerned for Dorothy after hearing about the repairs her house needed. Of course, Mary wasn't planning to mention that she knew anything about it.

"Quite well, thank you." Her cryptic response suggested she was in no mood for idle conversation, and Mary didn't necessarily blame her. Still, this was their prayer group, a place where they could share their struggles. Mary wanted Dorothy to feel comfortable opening up. "How has Henry's handiwork gone?" Mary asked, hoping her question would encourage Dorothy to share.

Dorothy's face turned red and her lips narrowed. "I really don't want to talk about it, but if you must know, my house is a huge disaster. It's damaged to its very foundation." After she blurted out the words, she covered her mouth with her hand as if realizing that her comment may have been misinterpreted as a negative reflection on Henry. "Of course, Henry did a very fine job with what he could. It's just that my house is beyond the help of even someone as strong and skilled as him."

"I'm so sorry, Dorothy. If Henry can't fix the problem, it must be pretty major. Please let me know if there's anything I can do."

"Yes, it *is* major, and no, there's nothing you can do. I'm sorry. I'm simply not able to talk about it." Her spine ramrod straight, she lifted her chin and turned away from Mary.

All during the meeting, Dorothy never bent from her rigid posture. She neither spoke nor bowed her head in prayer. Her body language clearly said she was in pain of some sort.

As soon as the group adjourned for lunch, Dorothy left, not staying long enough to eat.

Lynn had noticed Dorothy's abrupt departure. "Is she okay?"

Mary didn't know how to respond. "I'm not sure," she finally said.

"Perhaps she wasn't feeling well," Lynn suggested, then went back to her hostess duties.

As the others went to help themselves to lunch, Mary turned to Tricia, the pastor's wife, and said quietly, "After lunch, could we chat?"

Her forehead furrowed in concern, Tricia nodded. "Of course."

Finally, after they had all enjoyed a delicious meal, and most of the others departed, Mary took a moment to talk with Tricia. "I know Dorothy is having some problems." Mary didn't want to gossip, but she decided this was a worthy conversation and that Tricia Miles was the right person to talk with. "From what I understand, her house is in pretty serious disrepair, including the foundation. I'm wondering if we can figure out a possible way to help her."

Tricia studied the last bite of strawberry pie on her plate. "I'm not sure Dorothy would want me to share this, but I do know that she's concerned about her finances. Apparently, her savings took a real tumble during the recession and haven't yet recovered."

"Oh my." Mary could understand why Dorothy has been so chilly lately.

"I suspect she's afraid she'll have to downsize and sell her house," Tricia went on.

"And with a foundation that's crumbling, she certainly won't get top dollar." Mary shook her head. "I just wish we could do something for her. It's a lovely, old historic house, and she's kept everything authentic over the years."

"I wish we could too, but I'm not sure what." Tricia's lopsided smile was both sad and wistful. "I guess we'll both have to pray about it."

"Let me know if anything comes to you," Mary said. "And I'll do the same. For now, Dorothy is officially a regular on my prayer list." *She should have been there long before now,* Mary realized with regret. She should have recognized Dorothy's attitude wasn't just because she was jealous, but because she was afraid for her own future.

Still pondering how she could help Dorothy, Mary headed for the bookshop.

"Everything all right?" she asked Rebecca, who was behind the counter, helping Ashley stamp the insides of new books with Mary's signature logo.

"Lots of browsers, but not many buyers,"

Rebecca said.

"It happens that way some days." Mary hung up her jacket in the back room and returned to the front of the store. "Speaking of buyers, riddle me this: If you needed a lot of money in a hurry, what would you do?" She was really asking, of course, about Dorothy's situation.

"*Mmm,* rob a bank?" Rebecca said with a playful smile.

"Mommy!" Ashley gasped. "That's against the law."

Mary coughed. "That's not quite what I had in mind, and I think your mother was teasing."

Then, with a tilt of her head, Rebecca looked at her with a frown of concern. "If you're running short —"

"No, no, it's not about me, although I appreciate your concern. I have a friend who is facing a serious financial expense, and I'd like to help her, but I don't know quite how to do that without offending her."

Rebecca blew out a sigh. "Well, I'm at least glad you're doing all right, but I'm sorry for your friend. I suppose . . . there's always a yard sale to raise a few dollars, or, maybe sell some jewelry?"

Interesting ideas, Mary thought, recalling Dorothy's table of antiques at the summer festival at the park. She was sure Dorothy would need more money than selling a few antiques or having a yard sale would generate.

The bell over the door chimed, interrupting Mary's thoughts and giving her pause as a stranger stepped into the shop.

Ten

The newcomer, an older man, his back hunched with osteoporosis, glanced around, surveying the shop. Despite the August weather, he wore a black raincoat that nearly touched the floor and a matching black rain hat. He lifted his hat, revealing a scant covering of silver hair. He peered through glasses so thick it was impossible to make out the actual shape of his eyes.

He acknowledged Mary and Rebecca with a nod.

"Ladies." Carrying an old-fashioned briefcase, he spoke in a voice far stronger than his physical appearance might suggest. "I'm looking for Mrs. Mary Fisher, the proprietor."

"You've found her. I'm Mary." More than a little curious, she stepped toward the gentleman.

"It's nice to meet you, Mrs. Fisher. I am Lincoln King."

"Oh, Mr. King. Good to see you. I wasn't quite sure what time you'd arrive." Smiling, she extended her hand. The document expert had finally arrived. His hand was smaller than hers and icy cold. No wonder he was all bundled up. He must not have any circulation at all. "I really appreciate you taking the time to come, Mr. King. This is Rebecca Mason."

"How do you do?" he said.

Rebecca nodded politely, then looked at Mary. "Unless you need me for anything else, I'll take off for the day."

"Go right ahead, Rebecca. See you tomorrow."

Rebecca smiled at the guest and went on her way.

"I'm so glad you could come, Mr. King."

"Just Lincoln. No mister required." His exceptionally narrow lips curled into what Mary took as a smile.

"Now then, I believe you have something you wanted me to examine, Mrs. Fisher."

"Mary, please. That's what everyone calls me." Their gazes met and they both smiled. Lincoln even chuckled a little.

She walked over to the counter to retrieve the ledger. "I found this at the Emerson gristmill, which is one of the oldest buildings in Ivy Bay, though it's in disrepair now.

I believe it is a ledger of some sort. It was wrapped in oilskin when I discovered it."

"It would be my pleasure to tell you what I can about your ledger." He bowed slightly and his narrow lips lifted again.

Anticipation rippled through her chest. Maybe the ledger could tell her something about the mill's history and the reason for the feud between the Hopkinses and the Emersons.

Not to mention the alleged murder of Caleb Hopkins.

"Let's sit over there where we can be more comfortable." She pointed toward the pair of upholstered chairs at the back of the shop.

Following her, Lincoln said, "You have a lovely little bookstore, Mary. I do love a mystery, and a whole shop full of mysteries is an extra bonus."

"I imagine your work has always been about solving puzzles." She waited for him to be seated.

"Indeed, it has been about puzzles and mysteries of one kind or another." After getting comfortable in his chair, he took the ledger and turned it carefully in his hands. He sniffed the cover. "This is definitely later than the 1700s. Mid-1800s, I would think."

Mary was immediately impressed, as she'd hoped she would be when she'd found out about Lincoln in the first place. "You know all that simply by looking at the cover?"

"I would be happy to substantiate my reasoning, if you'd like. But I will warn you, I can be quite enthusiastic and long-winded about these things."

Mary beamed at the man. "That is exactly why I reached out to you."

He nodded resolutely, took a deep breath, then began to explain. "Well, first, the binding is, of course, the primary clue. And if you smell it" — he sniffed the ledger again — "it is definitely glue utilized in the 1800s. There are other clues, if you'd like me to elaborate further." Mary nodded, and he continued to talk about the thickness of the cover, its coloring, and the size of the book in general.

As Lincoln spoke, Gus leaped up onto the arm of the chair, which startled the man. Mary picked up her cat and held him. "Sorry about that," she said. "You're not to bother Lincoln when he's working," she admonished Gus in a loving tone, then set him down on the floor.

Recognizing the cat was under control, Lincoln opened the ledger to the first page with the elaborate handwriting. "Ah, I was not far off. Clearly the author has identified the year for us: 'In the year of our Lord eighteen hundred forty-three.' "

How had he read that so quickly? Mary had stared at those words many times and couldn't come up with anything but "Lord," and that was all thanks to Rebecca. Then something hit her: 1843. *Two years after Caleb's death.* Hope stirred in her chest. Not only could the ledger ultimately be helpful in understanding the mill ownership, but it could also contain clues about the alleged murder. And maybe even the feud.

Mary leaned toward Lincoln to get a better look. "The only word I was able to make out of those squiggles was *Lord.*"

"Understandably. The scribe who penned this bit got somewhat carried away with her Spencerian ladies' hand."

"Spencerian?" *Ladies'?*

"The style of handwriting. It became popular in the mid- to late 1800s. But to have a sample of this sort, written by a woman on a business ledger, makes it quite unusual. Although, education for women was increasing in that day and age, typically it was only those from the wealthy class. Many ordinary people, such as farmworkers, fishermen, and laborers signed their name with an *X.* Or at the very most had a rough education no greater than third grade. This woman, on the other hand, was quite well trained."

Mary pondered that revelation for a moment. It meant Betty's husband had a female ancestor who was highly educated. She wondered if the writer was the wife of William Emerson.

"What about the notations on the inside?" she asked. "I haven't been able to make heads or tails out of them."

He carefully turned one page and then another. Then he retrieved his large magnifying glass from his briefcase and reexamined the first few pages of the ledger.

He lifted his head. "These marks were not made by the same woman who wrote the words on the title page. In fact, I would guess this person, probably a man, could not write at all. I suspect it was his own code."

"Any clue as to what the markings mean?"

He returned his magnifying glass to his briefcase. "I confess I do not know, and probably only the worker who made the marks could read and understand them."

Mary's shoulders slumped, though she hoped Lincoln couldn't see her disappointment. She'd been so hopeful he would provide her with answers to the meaning of the ledger entries. Unfortunately, that was not to be.

She pulled back her shoulders and gave Lincoln a grateful smile. "Well, I appreciate you taking a look at the book." She slipped the ledger back into its oilskin covering. "At least I know the year it was written. That's a start." But less than she'd hoped for.

She handed him the selection of books she'd handpicked for him. "As promised," she said. "I think you'll enjoy these. One of them centers around ancient diaries, another is a biography of a 1920s New England professor, and another is a fun collegiate mystery."

"Thank you very much, Mary. It's been a pleasure. As far as the ledger, you might try to find an expert in codes and hieroglyphics, which are definitely not my forte. I focus on actual handwriting, as well as paper and ink."

That reminded her. "Come to think of it, I wonder if you might have time to check out some old records at the county clerk's office? My sister, who owns the gristmill I mentioned, is being sued. The man claims to have a bill of sale from 1792, although I couldn't find any record of the property transfer."

"Then perhaps his claim isn't valid," Lincoln said.

"That's what we're hoping, of course."

She hesitated a moment, not wanting to take advantage of Lincoln's time but knowing his expertise could help Betty win the suit. "And when we get to actually see the presumed bill of sale, it would be enormously helpful if someone like you could evaluate the paper and even the ink to tell us whether it is a forgery or not. I figure, if you can evaluate paper from the same time and place as the plaintiff suggests the bill of sale was written, you could be an expert witness to deem whether the paper is authentic. And since you're in town. . . ."

"As a matter of fact, an attorney named Rob Dunlap has already contacted me. I believe it is regarding the same case you just described."

"Oh, that's perfect. Mr. Dunlap is my sister's attorney. Evidently he's one step ahead of me."

"It is reassuring to have an attorney who is working so diligently on your sister's behalf."

"I certainly agree." He stood and picked up the books and his briefcase. She walked him to the door. "Do drop by the shop again. I'm sure I can find other books you'd enjoy."

"It would be my pleasure, Mary."

They shook hands, and he slowly made

his way to his car, a pewter-silver 1957 Cadillac with huge shark fins. It looked brand-new, as though he had just driven it off of the showroom floor.

She smiled as she locked up the shop and headed to her own car, thinking how Henry would have loved to have seen Lincoln's car.

When Mary arrived home after work, Betty was resting in the living room, reading the quilting mystery. Mary let Gus out of his carrying case, and he immediately jumped onto Betty's lap. "Hey, little guy," Betty said, setting her book down and petting the cat. It tickled Mary that Betty and Gus had developed so much affection for each other.

"How's the book?" Mary said.

"It's going well. The author is trying to throw me off, but I'm still convinced." She continued to pet Gus, who purred loudly. "Kip gave me the estimate today for how much the brick patio would cost. The estimate is on the kitchen table." She set the cat down. Mary followed her into the kitchen and pulled out a chair.

The price was about as high as Mary had expected, but since she had some extra funds left over from her original budget, she was happy to spend them on something as valuable as a functional backyard.

"This looks fine to me, Betty. I'm so excited about it. Will you let Kip know that he can move forward? And please buy whatever supplies you need for your gardening."

"It will cost a bit to buy the tubs for the annuals, but it will be worth it."

"No problem. I'm just grateful you're taking care of everything for me," Mary said. "And now, in other news, I *have* to tell you about the character I met today." She went on to tell Betty about Lincoln, the date of the ledger, and the strange markings inside that even Lincoln couldn't discern.

"As it turns out, Rob Dunlap has already hired Lincoln to examine Daniel's bill of sale to authenticate the paper and ink. That's assuming we ever get to see the record."

"That's wonderful, Bets. I'm sure Rob knows what he's doing."

Mary could only hope Lincoln would discover that Daniel's bill of sale was a fake.

"Meanwhile, I'm going to keep digging into the whole thing about mill ownership and the presumed murder of Caleb Hopkins." Tomorrow, she was going to visit the gristmill again. Now that she knew more about the Emersons and Hopkinses, maybe she'd notice things she wouldn't have before. She was also going to see if she could find someone to help her decode the markings in the ledger. And she would to think through the murder suspects.

But for tonight, she intended to relax. She and Betty would eat out on the deck, enjoy the summer evening, and listen to the birds calling to one another across the expanse of neighborhood yards. She couldn't imagine a more perfect night.

The following morning, Mary rose earlier than usual. The late summer sun was up, promising a midday temperature in the high eighties. She wanted to be on her way as soon as she finished breakfast.

Dressed in her robe and slippers, Betty came into the kitchen. Her hair was mussed and she hadn't put on her makeup yet.

"Morning, sleepyhead," Mary said with a grin as she poured herself a cup of coffee from the pot. "Want some coffee?"

"Sure, but what are you doing up so early? Come to think of it, what am *I* doing up so early? Oh, that's right, that *cat* of yours woke me," Betty said in mock irritation.

"Sorry about that." Mary laughed and handed her sister a cup of coffee, with lots of milk and lots of sugar, as Betty preferred. "I'm going to go back to the gristmill and take another look before I go into the shop. I've been wondering if there's more to discover there."

Betty sat down at the table with her coffee. "I can't think what. At this point, it's just a dirty, dusty old building."

"You never know. Maybe I'll see something I didn't see before." After finishing the last bite of her toast, Mary washed it down with a sip of coffee. "I'll wait if you'd like to go with me."

"Thanks, but I can't today. This is my morning at the church library. Pastor Miles, Dorothy Johnson, and I are reviewing some possible books we may want to acquire. There are a couple of recent releases about raising children in a Christian family and ways to use family vacation time as an opportunity to help others and bear witness to your faith."

"They sound like worthwhile books." Mary carried her dishes to the sink, rinsed them, and put them in that dishwasher. "I may not learn anything new at the mill, but maybe something will strike a chord. I'll see you this evening."

"Be careful," Betty warned. "Keep away from those rotting boards."

"Trust me, I plan to." Mary grabbed the heavy-duty flashlight they kept for emergencies, like power failures, and was about to go out the door when she saw Gus waiting for her next to his carrier.

"Sorry, Gus. You'll have to stay here for now. I'll come back after I explore the gristmill."

At the mill, she parked and walked across the logs to the other side of the creek. The recent rain had raised the water level in the creek. It poured down the run to the mill, churning white over rocks that protruded above the surface of the water. She imagined in a serious storm, one like the October gale of 1841, the creek would be brimming over the top of its banks. Whatever had bridged the run could well have been washed away by the hurricane forces that night.

Reaching the door, her breath caught and she halted abruptly. Someone had shoved open the heavy door.

Probably just kids, she thought.

She eased past the open door with care. Compared to the morning sunlight outside, the room was dim and filled with shadows. The place smelled dusty and dank with hints of rotting wood and tobacco smoke in the air.

She wrinkled her nose. Someone must have been smoking in there. She'd have to talk to Evan about securing the mill more carefully. Having anyone, let alone a child, injured here would be bad news on any number of levels.

A single column of sunlight spilled through the window on the east side of the building. Dust motes floated like tiny fireflies that had lost their sparkle.

She heard a noise in the corner of the room. A shuffle of feet. Dirt being ground into the old wood. Animal? Or human?

Air stuttered in her lungs, and youthful tales of the gristmill ghost raced through her mind. *A ghost and hidden treasure.*

She raised her flashlight to take a look. Before she could switch it on, a figure appeared from out of the shadows behind the buhr stone. Tall. Sinewy. A cold cigar tucked in the corner of his mouth.

Mary screamed. She took a step back and lifted the heavy flashlight in defense. Her heart thundered in her chest.

"Why, if it isn't Mrs. Fisher, sister to that Emerson woman, who's gonna prove we Hopkinses don't own what's ours by rights."

"Mr. Hopkins! What are you doing here?" She glanced toward the door. She could make a run for it but hated to give ground to the man. Yet she knew, despite his age, after years of fishing the seas, he still had more strength than she'd be able to muster to protect herself. She wavered on the brink of indecision.

"I'm just visitin' the *Hopkinses'* gristmill. Lookin' at the view. It's my right, ya know." His snide tone sent shivers down her spine.

"No, it isn't." Despite shaking knees, she used her sternest librarian's voice, one that unfailingly silenced rowdy patrons. She wondered how often Daniel had been coming to the gristmill. It seemed too great a coincidence for him to arrive on the one day she'd come back. "You're trespassing until a court says otherwise." She pulled her cell phone from her pocket and flipped it open. It glowed in the dim light. "I'm afraid you'll have to leave, Mr. Hopkins, or I'll call Chief McArthur."

"I've been coming here for years, woman. You're not going to keep me out of my own building." He sauntered toward her, his menacing gait rolling like he was on the deck of a ship.

Trembling on the inside, she stepped aside, leaving plenty of room for him to get out the door without coming any closer to her. She mustered her most confident voice. "Leave, Daniel. Now."

"I'm leaving. But there's no use in you snooping around in here. Soon enough, the mill and everything in it will be legally mine." He placed his hand on the giant stone buhr, patting it almost affectionately. "You mark my words, woman. This place belongs to me."

His warning, along with her rapid breathing, echoed in the empty mill as he stormed out the door.

Leaning back against the wall, Mary tried to calm herself. Daniel was nothing but a braggart and bully, she told herself. All bluster and no bite.

He'd come here often? To look at the view? How very strange he should say that. Not that the view overlooking the town and the marina wasn't lovely. It was. But it was a view that could be seen from any number of places in town. Why did he specifically come here to the mill?

Slowly, her heart rate returned to normal. She wondered what on earth Daniel had meant that the mill and *everything in it* would be his.

The huge buhrstone? That couldn't be worth much, assuming anyone could move it. And why would anyone want it, anyway?

She shined the light around. The beam touched the far corners of the room. She pointed the light upward, where there was a loft area, perhaps a place to stand in order to repair or oil the grinding gears or to pour the corn.

Slowly, she circled the room. Evan, or someone, had nailed a plywood sheet over the flooring she'd broken through and over another spot that must have been rotten. She flashed her light over the grinding stones' surface and stepped closer. It looked like generations of young people had scratched their initials on the stone, some couples circling their initials with a heart. A romantic notion in a decidedly unromantic place.

Mary preferred the red roses John had given her on every one of their wedding anniversaries.

She scanned the walls with the beam of her light. More initials and some graffiti, but nothing of interest that she could see.

Then her light caught an irregularity in a section of the wall down low next to the floor. She knelt and ran her fingertips over the mismatched wood. A small space, less than a quarter-inch wide, separated the two sections. The unmatched wood formed a two-foot square.

Like it was a hatchway to another room.

She glanced over her shoulder. After getting to her feet, she went to the mill doorway to see if Daniel was still around.

With no one in sight, she went back to

examine the wall more carefully. Using the butt end of the flashlight, she tapped on what she thought might be a door and then on the undisturbed section.

The area behind the hatchway sounded hollow.

She ran her hand over the wood again. The edges seemed entirely flush with the rest of the wall. No knob or hinges were apparent.

Gnawing on her lip, she pushed on the top section. Nothing gave. She pressed on the bottom half. The wood gave a groan. She pushed harder.

Her hand shoved forward, which caused the top section to fall toward her.

"Oh my goodness!" She fell back. She hadn't really expected that.

Cautiously, she peered inside the empty space and discovered there was about an eighteen-inch gap between the interior wall and the exterior construction.

A false wall!

Eleven

Mary gaped at the hatch and the wall behind it.

Had this been a place for early settlers to hide in case of an Indian attack? Or a place to hide their valuables from those who might steal them? She'd heard of such things but had never expected to find a secret hiding place in the old mill.

She peered in a little farther. To the left of the opening, she spotted what looked like an old cornmeal bag covered with dust.

Excited and anxious at the same time, she poked at the bag with her flashlight. The contents compressed slightly like a pillow does when punched.

She took a deep breath. "You can't just leave it there, Mary. You have to find out what's in the sack." To give herself courage, she whispered a favorite Bible verse. "Though an army besiege me, my heart will not fear; though war break out against me, even then I will be confident" (Psalm 27:3).

"No army here today. Just a dirty old bag," she told herself. She reached for the sack and dragged it out onto the mill floor. Years of dust and dirt blew up into her face, and she sneezed.

A narrow length of leather tied the sack closed. She worked the stiff knot with her fingers, finally loosening the leather, which she pulled away. The fabric of the bag was so old she was afraid it would rip apart. Painstakingly, she opened the sack's neck.

To her amazement, she found some sort of dark red fabric with what appeared to be an old pewter button with a stamped number, forty-three, attached.

She stared at the fabric and button without understanding for several seconds, her head trying to make sense of what she was seeing.

Could it be, however impossible it seemed, a British military uniform? That of a red-coat?

She tugged on the material gently to remove it from the sack. As she did, she heard the distinct sound of metal clinking against metal.

Was this what Daniel Hopkins had been talking about? Had he spent years searching for the treasure in the mill, or even stranger, had he known it was there?

Too aware that Daniel might still be nearby, she decided not to dump out the contents here at the mill. She stuffed the uniform back inside the sack and retied the leather fastener.

With her flashlight, she took one last look into the cubbyhole.

Her throat tightened. Another, similar sack lay almost out of reach behind the false door.

Lying flat on her stomach, she eased past the hatchway and closed her hand around a corner of the sack. Slowly, she edged backward, pulling the bag along until she could get to her knees again.

This sack wasn't as full as the first and wasn't tied closed. Perhaps the contents had been hastily hidden behind the false wall. Folding back the opening, she let the sack fall open around the contents.

A boot? Leather. Twisted out of its shape as though it had been in the water a long time.

Why in the world would anyone hide a boot? A single boot, not even a pair?

Gingerly, she picked it up to examine the wear on the sole. An object fell out of the boot and clattered onto the floor. For a moment, she stared at what appeared to be a salt-encrusted pocket watch with a cracked face and a few links of broken chain attached.

One more look behind the wall revealed nothing more hidden there. She'd lingered at the mill long enough, risking Daniel's return or the appearance of someone else tempted to sneak past the No Trespassing sign.

Perhaps she should leave the items at the mill, she reasoned. But then, sympathetic thoughts for Betty and Evan and the Emerson family history made her change her mind. Daniel Hopkins was not going to bully them. And she certainly wasn't going to let Hopkins steal Emerson property.

It was time to get these treasures safely back home.

Mary restored the hatch to its proper place. Nervous about being observed, she carried the two sacks to her car and drove home. In the back mudroom, she spread newspapers on the floor, then carefully removed the contents of the first sack. She wished Betty was here to go through the bags with her, but Mary didn't want to wait for Betty to be finished at the church library.

She started by examining the red jacket she'd seen earlier. The wool fabric felt coarse between her fingers. Definitely not the kind of jacket you could buy at Cape Cod Togs in town. It was more like one you'd see in a museum of American history about the Revolutionary War.

Or one worn by reenactors. But in that case, there would be no reason to hide the uniform behind a false wall in a decidedly old cornmeal sack.

Gus strolled into the mudroom to see what she was up to. He sniffed at the jacket and pants.

"What do you think, Gus? Do you think this uniform dates back to the Revolutionary War?" Of course, the Revolutionary War was well before the date when Caleb went missing. But could Daniel have believed that these treasures were somewhere in the mill? It could certainly explain why he'd been so eager to claim ownership. Mary doubted he had enough money to restore the place, but perhaps he had planned to tear the building to shreds until he found the valuable treasures.

Gus began sniffing the second cornmeal sack.

"I'll get there, I'll get there," she said with a pat on Gus's head.

She spread out a white vest next to the jacket and matching white pants on the newspapers. Had the British really gone to war in white? She definitely wouldn't have let her son Jack out to play in the woods wearing white. She'd had enough trouble getting dirt stains out of his white Little League pants.

Finally, she pulled out a squashed tricornered hat with a feather on top.

She stared at the collection of clothing, wondering why someone would want to hide it. It was hard for her to believe there were many upstanding reasons for such a carefully masked hiding place. She supposed it could have been a deserter wanting to hide his identity. Or a British soldier who stayed in America after the war and wanted to keep his military days a secret. Or a worse scenario, a patriot who had killed a British soldier and didn't want anyone to know what he had done.

She shuddered at the thought.

The sound of her cell phone startled her, and she flinched. Taking a breath to settle her nerves, she pulled the cell from her pocket and said hello.

"Mary, are you okay?" Rebecca asked. "It's almost eleven."

"Oh, Rebecca, I'm so sorry." She glanced at her watch to verify the hour. "I, um, got so involved in something, I wasn't watching the time. I'll be there as soon as I can."

"No hurry, really. I was just worried about you."

"Thanks, Rebecca. I'll be in soon." Not for a minute could she have guessed what an engrossing treasure she would find at the mill.

After she got off the phone, Mary started to stuff the uniform back into the sack only to realize there was still something inside. Something relatively heavy compared to the uniform.

She held up the sack to let the contents slide out. A bag clunked to the floor.

Gingerly, she picked it up. A small leather pouch. The contents heavy in her hand. Untying the cord that closed the pouch, she poured the contents onto the newspaper.

Coins. More than a dozen of them spilled out, and the bag was still full. Not from the US mint.

She picked up a coin and turned it over. Given the uniform she'd found, she wasn't entirely surprised. Even so, she gawked at the profile of King George III and the date 1775 in amazement.

She began to think through what scenario would have brought this particular uniform to a random gristmill in a small town in Cape Cod. The image of British redcoats marching through the countryside. She pictured a soldier, a young man, who perhaps slipped away from his troop, hoping to escape the terrors of war, and found the gristmill as a temporary shelter.

An instant later, Mary frowned and the picture she'd created shattered into tiny pieces. As far as she could remember from her history books, there hadn't been any Revolutionary War battles on Cape Cod. Concord, Lexington, and Bunker Hill were a long march from the Cape.

Unless British troops passed through the area from Canada en route south to reinforce troops engaged elsewhere. Or perhaps simply a British patrol out scavenging for food. Still, they would have had to come a long way.

She shook her head. She didn't have time to worry about the source of the uniform now. She was ready to get to the bookshop and spend the day there.

Taking one coin, which she put in her pocket, she tied up the purse and put it, along with the uniform, back in the cornmeal sack.

Discovering the history of these items and determining if they had any connection to the ownership of the gristmill and how it related to the Emersons and Hopkinses in general would be quite a research project.

Particularly curious about the old watch, she dumped that out of the boot and looked at it again before putting it in her pocket along with the coin. She put the boot back in its sack.

She carried the sacks out to her car and put them in the trunk for safekeeping. If Daniel Hopkins really was after the coins, she didn't want to leave the telltale sacks laying around for him to find — or steal.

The sidewalks of Ivy Bay were busy with tourists wearing shorts, tank tops, and flip-flops, some women wearing floppy hats, when Mary arrived at the bookshop. A few of the tourists had wandered into the store to browse.

"Sorry I'm so late coming in," she said to Rebecca. Mary knelt to release Gus from her bag.

"It's fine. I was able to answer most of the questions, and with Ashley's help, we sold a bunch of children's books to one grand-mother. I hope her grandchildren appreci-ate how much time she took to select the right one for each child."

Sitting behind the cash register, Ashley grinned. "She told me how old her grand-children are and what they liked. Finding the right books was easy."

"Good for you, sweetie." She cupped the girl's cheek. "I'm going to have to put you on my payroll, after all."

Ashley seemed to like that idea, but her mother's quick shake of her head quashed the possibility. She glanced at Mary's slacks and lowered her voice. "*Umm,* Mary? The knees of your pants. . . ."

"Oh dear." Mary tried brushing away the dirt she'd picked up at the gristmill, but remnants remained. She'd washed her hands before she left for the shop but hadn't even thought of what a mess her pants had become. "I should've changed before I came in."

"It's all right. Nobody will notice if you stay behind the counter."

"I'm afraid that would limit the amount of help I could give customers."

Rebecca flushed. "I guess you're right."

Not wanting to run home to change, Mary said, "I'll try a damp cloth — see if I can make myself presentable."

As she went into the back room, she glanced out at the yard. Betty's plants were doing nicely, and she was anxious for Kip to get started on the patio.

Having done the best she could cleaning her slacks, she went back into the shop. Several people were browsing the shelves of mysteries. She put on her friendliest smile.

"Let me know if I can help you find something. We have both new releases and the old classics. Several local authors as well."

For the next few hours, she stayed busy helping customers and giving Rebecca a chance to take a lunch break.

By late afternoon, business had slowed and there were fewer people on the streets.

"Rebecca, I'm going to hop over to Gems and Antiques across the street. I have something I want Rich Tucker to take a look at."

"Sure. Go ahead. Almost time to close up anyway."

Mary knew that Rich was an ardent coin collector, and she wondered if he would have anything to say about these coins. She'd had other plans for the day, including trying to get in touch with someone who could potentially read the notations in the ledger, but she couldn't resist looking into the new treasure she'd found at the mill first.

At Gems and Antiques, she edged past an old footlocker decorated with ornate paintings of whales and ships at sea, and what looked to be a Tiffany table lamp.

Jayne was behind the counter. "Hey, Mary. Did you find out any more about that ledger?"

"I did, thank you for the recommendation."

"No problem. How can I help you today?"

"Actually, I dropped by to see your husband. I have a coin I'd like to show him."

"Oh, sure, he's in the back trying to restore the workings of an old clock. Just a sec."

Jayne let Rich know Mary was there, and he came out from the back room.

"What've you got, Mary?"

She placed the British coin on the counter. "I found this today," she said, careful not to mention where. "Any idea if it's authentic?"

His brows lifted. "Something you found around here?"

She nodded. "Nearby," she said, and she left it at that.

As Rich plucked a jeweler's eyepiece out of his pocket, Jayne joined him at the counter. He examined both sides of the coin.

"Interesting." He lifted his head. "A 1775 British farthing with dear ol' King George III on the front."

"Is it worth anything?"

"Indeed, yes. Although I don't recall any

British coins from this era found locally." He took a book down from a shelf behind the counter and flipped it open. "During the Revolutionary War, it was pretty quiet in our neck of the woods."

That's what Mary had suspected. "But you do think it's real?"

"*Hmm,* I do." He skimmed down a page with photos of various coins. "Not terribly rare, of course, but still valuable. I'd have to get the latest quotes, but from what I can tell, this coin would be worth at least twenty pounds sterling. That's something a bit over thirty US dollars."

Mary's mouth flew open in surprise. Thirty dollars for *one* of those coins. Who knew how many of them were in that pouch. All together, they could be worth a fortune. "Wow! That's good to know."

"That's quite a bit for a coin originally worth less than a penny," Rich commented.

Jayne, who'd been listening with interest asked, "Did you find more than just the one coin?"

"I did," Mary admitted. "There seemed to be several different size coins, but I just picked up the one so I could bring it to you to check."

Jayne hopped up onto the stool behind the counter. "Sounds like you may have found your pot of gold."

And a likely motive for Daniel to be prowling around the gristmill. But if he'd visited the mill often, as he had said, why hadn't he located the false wall? If Mary found it, surely he could have. Couldn't he?

Or what about the children who had played in the mill through many generations?

Perhaps only now, with aging, the foundation of the mill shifting and changes in the weather, had the seam of the hatch she'd spotted become apparent.

"The higher the initial value and the better the condition, the more a coin will be worth. Are you interested in selling the coins?" Rich asked.

"Not right now. But I may want you to assess them for Betty." From Mary's point of view, they rightfully belonged to Betty and the Emerson family.

Rich closed the book. "I'd be happy to, anytime you're ready."

"Thanks, Rich. But there's more." She retrieved the watch from her pocket. "What can you tell me about this?"

"That it's not worth much in that condition," Rich said without hesitation.

"I'm sure that's true. But can you tell me anything else, like how old it is?"

"Maybe. Let me see." He rubbed the back of the watch with a cloth, dislodging some of the crusty covering. "It wasn't a particularly expensive watch originally. Gold-plated, most of which has worn off. From the workings, I'd say it was made sometime in the mid-1800s, but I can't be sure without doing some research."

Mid-eighteen hundreds. Awfully close to the time of Caleb's death, Mary thought.

"There are some initials here." He got out his eyepiece again. "Looks like CAH. Does that help?"

Mary's stomach rose up into her throat. *CAH? Caleb Hopkins?*

"It may help, thank you." Not wanting to divulge how important these items might be to the lawsuit, she kept her tone calm. Rich handed her the watch and coin, and she returned them to her pocket. Even though she hadn't told him much, she still needed to rely on his discretion. "For now, I'd appreciate it if you didn't mention the coins to anyone else. There may be someone else who's searching for the same pot of gold."

"Our lips are sealed."

Mary started to leave, then turned back. "Are you able to authenticate things like old buttons?"

Rich's blue eyes twinkled. "I say, you must

have come upon a real cache of something. I'd love to take a look at whatever you have."

Mary left the shop with a simple thank-you.

Because of the warm day, Betty had set the table for dinner on the deck in the backyard. Trellises with climbing vines provided a privacy screen on one side of the deck, and a large umbrella could be adjusted to offer shade over the glass-top table.

Betty carried a bowl of chicken-apple-raisin salad out the door. Mary followed with a tray of lemonade, tumblers, and fruit salad.

"This heat wave is supposed to last for several days." Betty sat down at the table. "Personally, I'd rather have it cooler even if the tourists want it blazing hot."

"I hear you." Mary was anxious to tell Betty of her morning discovery at the mill. She said a brief prayer before the meal, then served her sister and herself a heaping spoonful of chicken salad, then took a bite.

"*Mmm.* This is delicious," she said, savoring the taste. "So, you'll never guess what I found this morning at the mill."

"*Ooh,*" said Betty. "Do tell."

Mary told her of Daniel's presence at the mill, the false wall, the disguised hatch, and what she discovered behind it. "I even took a coin and the watch to Rich Tucker today to see if he could determine any value for them. Turns out, the one coin I took him — which was worth about a penny back then — is worth something like thirty dollars now."

"Oh my goodness." Betty looked as surprised as Mary had been. "Where did you store everything? I have to see them."

"Everything's in the trunk of my car. I debated whether to leave them inside or in the car. I chose the car, because I figured that way if anyone — and mostly I just mean Daniel — had seen me with the bags, that he wouldn't try to break into our house." Mary twisted her lips in thought. "But I'm second-guessing it now. Even if I parked in the garage instead of the driveway like usual, I almost think it would be better to rely on our alarm system, should Daniel dare try to intrude."

Mary wondered if she was being paranoid with all this worrying about a break-in. On the other hand, if Daniel had gone to such lengths as to file a lawsuit and use apparent scare tactics of loitering around places Mary and Betty had visited, she certainly couldn't put it past him to try such measures as breaking and entering.

Betty looked thoughtful. "I think you're right. You should bring the bags inside." She smoothed the pleats in her khakis, then she looked up again. "You have to wonder if all the fuss Daniel is making about owning the mill is really about those coins."

"I've thought the same thing. Even with those stories we all heard when we were children, why would he be so determined to believe them *now*? That there was something valuable *inside* the mill, more valuable than the mill itself and the land?"

"I don't know, except that it has turned out there is, or was, a treasure of sorts." Pensive, Mary ate a few more bites of salad. "Oh, and the old watch has the initials CAH."

Betty slanted her a curious look. "Caleb Hopkins?"

"Right."

"Okay, but why would Caleb hide his things in there? And where'd he get a Revolutionary War uniform?" Betty covered her mouth with her fingertips. "You're thinking the mill could be where Caleb was killed. And that Caleb's things were hidden because they were evidence."

Mary nodded. She noticed how Betty hadn't mentioned William as the guilty party, but it's what they both were thinking.

The very thing they were afraid might be true.

Mary touched her sister's arm. "After we finish dinner, I'll bring the sacks with the uniform and coins and boot into the house. I'm going to see if Rich can tell us how much all the coins are worth. Perhaps he can even keep them in his safe."

"That's a good idea," Betty said. "I know Jayne puts her gemstones away every night. Their shop has great security."

"We'll both feel better knowing they are in a safe place."

Later that night, after Mary and Betty had pored over the treasures and continued to discuss the case, Mary went to bed with the coins and British uniform stashed in her closet.

Sometime during the night, after she'd long been asleep, a car alarm woke her. Occasionally that happened in the neighborhood. Someone would push the wrong button to lock their car. Knowing it would stop soon, she rolled over and went back to sleep.

While Betty and Mary were eating breakfast the next morning, there was a knock on the door.

Mary's eyebrows rose. "Early for visitors."

She pushed back from the table and went to the front door. Their neighbor Sherry was there, a single mother who worked at the high school as a secretary.

"I'm sorry to bother you so early," Sherry said. She was usually trim and well dressed, but this morning she looked and sounded rattled.

"What is it, Sherry? Come inside."

"No, no. I'm waiting for the police. Someone broke into my car last night."

"That's terrible. Did they take anything?" Suddenly Mary recalled the alarm she'd heard.

"It looks like they tried to take the car radio but ran off when I turned on my porch light."

Still in her blue terry-cloth robe, Betty joined them at the door. "Who could have done such an awful thing? Our neighborhood is usually —"

"While I was outside, I noticed your car, Mary. It looks like the same person tried to get into your trunk."

Mary's mouth dropped open. "The trunk of my car?"

"I'm afraid so. It's all scratched up." She glanced toward her house. "There's Chief McArthur's car now. I called 911 right away."

Sherry headed his way, quickly followed by Mary. She'd parked in the driveway last night. Thank goodness she'd brought the treasure inside.

Mary gaped at the rear of her Impala. It looked as though someone had taken a crowbar to one corner of her trunk lid, bending it up. Having failed to open the trunk, they dragged the sharp end of the crowbar across the lid, gouging into the paint.

She felt sick to her stomach.

"Looks like they got your car too." Chief McArthur strolled toward her. He thumbed his uniform cap up farther on his forehead and studied her car. "We had some vandals breaking into cars earlier this week in the parking lot at the Chadwick Inn. Probably bored kids out to do some mischief. They didn't take anything except some change in the glove boxes."

A large part of her strangely hoped that this was done by kids, but it seemed far too coincidental to Mary. "Chief McArthur, the person who did this might . . . not be a kid."

He turned, frowning. "Oh? What makes you think that?"

"Well, it's about the gristmill suit I mentioned. I have reason to suspect that Daniel

229

Hopkins could have tried to break into my car."

The chief frowned in disbelief. "You think old man Hopkins did this?"

"I think it's a strong possibility." Mary pursed her lips. "I was at the Emerson gristmill yesterday trying to help Betty by seeing if there were any clues that would point to ownership. Daniel was there when I arrived, and" — she shook her head at the memory of Daniel's rudeness — "after I told him he was trespassing and he had to leave, I found some items hidden behind a false wall. I thought he was gone by the time I carried what I'd found out to my car and put them in the trunk. He might have still been around and saw me."

Chief McArthur pulled out a notepad and took a few notes, though his expression was still dubious. "What did you find?"

She told him about the contents of the two cornmeal sacks and how she'd taken them inside last night.

"Interesting." He grew pensive for a moment and rubbed his chin with his fingertips. "You should come into the station and fill out a formal report. But first, I'll have to pay a visit to Daniel Hopkins and ask him a few questions."

TWELVE

Mary was already at the shop when Rebecca and Ashley arrived that morning.

"What in the world happened to your car?" A worried expression on her face, Rebecca shed her sweater. "I saw it parked outside. Did you have an accident? Are you hurt?"

Looking equally concerned, Ashley came over to be close to Mary.

Mary put a reassuring hand on the child's shoulder, then smoothed a loose curl of her hair back from her face. "No, I didn't have an accident. And I'm fine." Irritated. Even angry. But physically fine. "Just a little vandalism," she said, trying not to worry Rebecca any further.

"I'm sorry, Mary. Makes you wonder what this world is coming to when people don't respect the property of others."

That was all too true. Yet the possibility that Daniel Hopkins, as angry and grouchy as he was, would have the nerve to break into her car still boggled the mind.

Just then, Bob Hiller came in and placed the mail on the counter. He eyed the doll Mary still had beside the computer. "What are you doing with an old tap? I haven't seen one of those in a long time."

Mary spun around. Her gaze locked on the porcelain doll she'd found at the gristmill. "A tap?"

"Yeah, you know, like on a cask of beer. You can tell by its shape. They're collector items now. I saw one like it on that antiques TV show." Bob gave an easy shrug. "Too bad she's chipped, though."

"Yes, it is," Mary said, still floored by the news. She looked up at Bob. "Thanks so much."

"My pleasure." He tipped his hat and went out the door.

Mary slipped around the counter to get on the computer. Nothing of interest had turned up when she'd checked the slogan "Only the Very Best." Now she needed to expand her search parameters and include words like *collection, antique, beer* and *eighteen hundreds.*

She clicked through one Web site after another. Finally, she found a site dedicated to the history of beer and ale in the United

States. She read the part of the history that interested her: "For a brief period during the early to mid-1800s, Queen's Castle porcelain factory in England produced genteel dolls that fit over the spigots of kegs of ale, particularly specialty ales brewed in the United States. These dolls, which were stamped 'Only the Very Best,' became popular collector items and an early form of advertising."

"Yes!" Mary pumped her fist in the air.

"What is it?" Rebecca asked.

"I've found out what that little doll is all about." She explained briefly how the doll was used but didn't mention the Horse Head Tavern, which had to be the source of the doll she'd found.

Her forehead furrowed. But how would the doll have gotten to the mill, and why had it been hidden under the floorboards? Had William tossed it aside as trash? Or had the doll fallen out of Caleb's pocket during a fight with William?

Mary's stomach knotted on the fear the latter was the case. William could have been hiding the evidence that Caleb had been at the mill that night. He'd known there had been witnesses to the argument he'd had with Caleb.

Please, Lord, I don't want to have to tell

Betty that her husband's ancestor could be guilty of a serious crime.

Later that afternoon, after she'd filed her report with Chief McArthur at the sheriff's office, Mary went home to retrieve the coins and British uniform, leaving the boot and watch tucked away in her closet.

She wanted the uniform and coins in Jayne Tucker's safe as soon as possible. And she would ask Rich to give her an estimate of their value. Then she would return to the bookshop until closing time.

Daniel Hopkins could trash her car all he liked and threaten her, but he wasn't going to steal what was rightfully Betty's treasure.

Before she left the shop that evening, she sat down with a pad of paper and pencil to list all the information she still needed about the gristmill and Caleb Hopkins' death.

- Find someone to interpret the markings in the ledger.
- Brainstorm alternative causes for Caleb's death or prove that William was not guilty.

In her sister's mind, the latter would be the most important point. And the hardest

234

to produce.

In serious need of prayer and meditation in the presence of the Lord, Mary was eager to attend church Sunday morning. She drove Betty the short distance into town, only to find the parking lot nearly filled with summer visitors in addition to local church-goers.

Inside, the walnut pews, worn smooth over the years, were equally full. Betty and Mary squeezed into a row near the front. A whole phalanx of yellow and gold chrysan-themums stood in front of the pulpit and the choir. The faint floral scent drifted over the congregation.

As they sat down, Mary noticed Dorothy Johnson sitting at the opposite end of the pew, her head bent in prayer.

Guilt pierced Mary's conscience. She hadn't given any more thought to how she could help Dorothy with her financial problems. Not that it was her responsibility, but Mary felt for the woman. Dorothy simply looked troubled.

With the organ playing, Mary lowered her head. *Please, Lord, help me to find a way to lighten Dorothy's burdens. Use my hands and my heart to do Your work.*

As Pastor Miles began the service, Mary

opened her heart and mind to the will of God. If only she listened carefully enough, He would guide her.

Mary's mind began to drift during the sermon, when ideas began to stream in. Could she put donation jars in the shops in town, with the contributions going to restoring historic homes, houses like Dorothy's? She wondered if Dorothy would accept the charity. Clearly the woman was proud, and Mary didn't entirely blame her. It was hard for many people to admit when they're in trouble.

Mary thought again about the many historic buildings and houses in Ivy Bay, each of them a challenge to maintain, and each with its own story to tell. Even Grace Church had a history that went back to the 1800s. And there was her bookshop with its history as a depository of Ivy Bay archives and onetime auction house. The small houses that were once fishermen's homes and the lives they led were fascinating and the historic Emerson gristmill had a story to tell. Mary knew there were lots of historic places in Ivy Bay she hadn't even seen yet, stories she'd yet to hear. Then it hit her. . . .

"That's it!" she said out loud.

Betty looked at her, and so did the woman sitting in the pew in front of her.

Giving them each a weak smile, Mary's cheeks warmed in a blush and she slipped lower in the pew.

Despite her momentary embarrassment, she knew God had given her the answer. With the cooperation of downtown businesses and owners of historic homes, she was going to organize a walking tour of Ivy Bay. People would buy tickets, and there'd be volunteers at each location, usually the owner, who could tell visitors the narrative of their building or home.

And, if people would agree to it, the proceeds from the walking tour could go to Dorothy Johnson to defray the expense of restoring her home.

Smiling to herself, Mary relaxed.

Betty leaned toward her and whispered, "Are you all right?"

"I'm great, Bets. Thanks to the Lord's help."

After the service concluded and they were driving home, Mary was eager to share her revelation. When they got home, they prepared lunch together. Despite the late August heat, the table on the deck was shaded and a light breeze cooled the air, keeping the temperature comfortable.

Once they were seated and enjoying their

meal, Mary told Betty her plan.

"I think it's a wonderful idea," Betty said when Mary finished. "I've known a couple of the members of the board of selectmen for a very long time. I can talk to them and hopefully get them to help support the effort."

"That'd be great, Betty. I should have thought to include them in the planning and organizing."

"How about including Dorothy in the organizing as well? She's done a terrific job putting together the Summer in the Park Festival. This is right up her alley."

Mary popped a seedless grape into her mouth and pondered the idea. "You know, I think if she was part of the program, she'd feel like whatever money we're able to pass on to her is less charity and instead something she helped to earn."

"I agree. But I do worry that you have enough to do. Are you sure you want to put this together while helping me deal with Daniel Hopkins' suit *and* running the bookshop? Of course, you know I'm happy to help in any way I can, but it's still a lot to take on."

Her sister had a great point. But Mary knew Dorothy needed financial help soon or she might be forced to sell her house at a big loss.

"I'll figure it out," Mary said. "And speaking of the lawsuit, has Evan given you word yet on when the court date will be set?"

She shook her head. "I actually just spoke with him this morning. No date has been set yet, but preliminary meetings are being scheduled right now. Rob Dunlap told Evan we'd finally get to see the bill of sale at that meeting."

If only Mary could gather some solid evidence of who owned the gristmill before that meeting occurred. But she was far shorter of adequate answers than she had hoped.

Mary almost laughed. Betty was right — she was in over her head. Somewhere in the middle of all of this, she was running a business. And this was the busiest season of the year.

Lord, I'd appreciate Your help to get me through the next few weeks. I'm really going to need it.

On Monday, Mary arranged to take her car to the body shop and rented a compact car. Her insurance company assured her that the repairs and car rental would be covered except for her deductible.

During the next several days, Mary spent

much of her time organizing a committee for the historic tour of Ivy Bay. Among the businesses she visited, she went to Gems and Antiques to talk with Rich and Jayne.

Rich bounded out from the back room, a big grin on his face. "Mary, I was hoping you'd drop by. I've got great news."

"The coins?" She held her breath.

"The coins *and* the uniform. I'm used to dealing with valuable coins, but I had no idea there was such a market for authentic Revolutionary War uniforms. I checked online and then called a couple of guys I know who are in the business. It looks to me like that uniform could be museum quality."

Mary's mouth hung open for a moment before she could snap it closed. "What does that mean, exactly?"

"It means if you took it to the right auction house, you could make a bundle." He named an amount that made Mary's jaw drop again.

"Then when you add in the value of the coins" — he gave her a rough value — "you're going to come out with a tidy sum. Mind you, the coins aren't uncirculated, which would jack up their price considerably. But they're in better than average, even good condition for circulated coins from that time period. You found quite a treasure, Mary."

Her mouth went dry, and she swallowed hard. "I had no idea." It wasn't that Betty needed extra money. Edward had left her quite well-off. But to have that much "found" money to spend or save or give in any way Betty wanted would open up all sorts of possibilities.

Rich grinned even more broadly. "Looks like the cat's really got your tongue this time."

"I'm absolutely stunned." She frowned in thought. "How do you suppose that uniform and the coins made it to Cape Cod? There weren't any battles around here that I know about."

He eased himself onto the stool behind the counter. "I've been thinking about that too. The uniform belonged to an enlisted man, which means he probably came from the lower classes in Britain. If he didn't have much to go home to, maybe he deserted his company. Or when the British were retreating, he marched the other way planning to make a life for himself in this new country."

Mary had envisioned something like that herself. She wondered if the Emersons had helped the man get away.

She smiled a little. Maybe the British

soldier was hiding out at the mill and that's what started the story about the building being haunted. "Well, thank you, Rich. For the work you've done and for keeping the items in your safe."

"It's my pleasure, although I'll be anxious to know more about where you found the treasure and who it belongs to, once you're ready to tell me."

I'm anxious to know who they belong to as well, she thought. But she simply said, "Sounds good, Rich. Your discretion means a lot to me."

"It's my middle name," he said with a chuckle.

She turned and walked through the narrow aisle, past a child's rocking chair and chest of drawers made in the Federalist style, to the door, where she stopped.

She whirled around. "For pity's sake, I'd forgotten why I came to see you."

"Not about the coins?"

"No, not really," she said walking back to the counter. "I'm glad to know their value, of course, but I wanted to ask if you'd serve on the committee to organize an historic walking tour of Ivy Bay?"

He blinked and his tall forehead pleated. "You're going to have to tell me more, Mary. I've never heard of a walking tour around here."

*Yet another reason why it's such a good —
or rather, a God — idea,* she thought.

The street was nearly deserted as she
walked back to the shop and something
caught her eye. Two teenage boys skulking
around the parked cars. They'd duck down,
then pop up again.

Suddenly, one of them stood. He slammed
what looked like a big wrench against the
passenger window of an almost new Lexus.
The car alarm screamed. The boy with the
wrench reached inside and pulled out what
looked to be a laptop.

"Stop!" Mary cried. She hurried after
them, but the boys were too fast on their
feet for her to catch them.

After halting beside the damaged car, she
pulled out her cell and called the police station. "Chief McArthur, please," she said
when the operator answered.

A few moments later, the chief said hello.

"Chief McArthur, this is Mary Fisher. I
just witnessed two teenage boys breaking
into a car on Meeting House Road. They
stole what looked like a laptop."

By now, people had gathered on the
sidewalk, and the owner of the Lexus had
silenced the car alarm.

"We already got a 911 call on that," the

chief said. "Sounds like the teenagers we've been having trouble with. Probably the same kids who tried to get into your car trunk."

The act of vandalism that she'd blamed Daniel Hopkins for.

Unwarranted disappointment crept into Mary's heart and shame heated her cheeks. She'd jumped to a conclusion and accused Daniel without any evidence.

"So it wasn't Daniel who tried to get into my car," she said in a faint whisper.

"Doesn't seem like it." He paused for a moment. "Can you stick around there? The responding officer should be there by now. He'll take your statement."

"Of course." She ended the call. How had she let herself forget her Christian duty and judge a man so unjustly? *Forgive me, Father.*

When Mary arrived home that evening, Betty's air-conditioned house felt heavenly. She set her handbag on the floor and released Gus from his carrier. Sitting erect on the plush carpet, he looked at her as though insulted he had been trapped in the bag for even a few minutes.

"I'm just keeping you safe, Gus. Wild animals do sometimes come into our area. Don't look at me as though I were some ogre who cages you."

"Bets," she called, chuckling at her prideful cat. "Are you home?"

"In the bedroom."

Mary found her sister at her desk paying bills. "I've got good news for you."

Betty looked up. "Daniel has dropped his suit?"

"No, not that good, unfortunately. But you've come into some valuable property." She sat on the edge of the bed and related what Rich had told her.

Betty's eyes rounded and her mouth opened much like Mary's had when Rich had told her the value of the coins and uniform.

"My gracious." Betty put her pen down and shook her head in amazement. "I had no idea."

"I thought the coins would have some value, but I wouldn't have guessed so much for the uniform. Rich says he'll arrange things if you want to sell it at auction."

"How nice of him. I'll have to think what to do and talk to Evan."

Mary couldn't think of any reason to hold on to the uniform, but there was no rush to sell it either.

Overall, the day had turned out better

than she'd expected, considering it had started with a vandalized car.

THIRTEEN

Thanks to Eleanor Emerson Blakely, who was head of the chamber of commerce, the committee met in the chamber's renovated nineteenth-century carriage-house stable. The conference room had once been where the owner kept his tack.

Mary and Betty arrived early and set out a meeting agenda at each place, along with the names and contact information for the eleven members of the committee.

Several local businesses were represented, all of them housed in historic buildings. Dorothy Johnson had already lined up several owners of historic homes willing to open their houses to visitors and recruited two of them to serve on the committee. And, of course, Eleanor had agreed to serve on the committee as well.

Chief McArthur served as an ad hoc member of the committee to help with planning for traffic control and pedestrian safety, and his sister Cynthia, who had a strong interest in the history of Ivy Bay, was here as well.

By 8:10 AM, all the committee members had arrived. Mary asked them to introduce themselves, then briefed them on the concept of the walking tour. The members had agreed that the proceeds would go to Dorothy, but she'd only been told that the profits would be dedicated to the "preservation of historical homes and buildings." Mary was both excited and nervous to ultimately surprise her with the news that the money was for her.

Throughout the meeting, Mary's goal was to delegate some of the responsibilities: publicity, building and home selection, development of a brief description of the properties and a route map, and ticket sales.

Randy Overholt, an Ivy Bay selectman, would arrange for official sanction from the town leadership; Chief McArthur would work with the routing map subcommittee.

In just over an hour, Mary adjourned the meeting, pleased with everyone's enthusiasm.

As she was gathering her notes, the police chief lingered until everyone else had left.

"Mary, if you've got a couple of minutes, I'd like to talk to you about the teenagers you spotted. We caught them."

"I'm glad. I don't know what gets into youngsters like that. I hope they've learned their lesson."

He shoved his hands in his pockets. "I kind of doubt it. The parents didn't think it was a big deal. I wrote them up but had to let them go under their parents' supervision." He snorted. "Not that the parents have done such a great job of supervising them so far. They did say their insurance would cover the damages." He handed her a note with the parents' names and insurance carrier, which she could pass on to her insurance representative.

She gave him a reassuring pat on his shoulder. "You did what you could. Someday, their behavior will catch up with them. I just hope they don't hurt someone else in the process."

They walked out of the building together and then went their separate ways. After work, Mary drove to the garage to pick up her Impala and then went home ready for a restful weekend.

By the time Mary got to work on Monday, Kip was already in the backyard. He and a helper named Ian were grading the patio and laying a wooden border.

She unlocked the back door and stepped outside. "Good morning, Kip."

He tipped his hat and grinned. "Hope you don't mind we got started early. On these hot days, I like to get as much done as I can before it warms up."

"I can certainly understand that. I'll leave the door unlocked." She checked the progress they'd already made, pleased with the flowing shape of the patio as it was emerging. "You're welcome to come inside to get a drink of water or to cool off whenever you'd like."

"Thanks, Mrs. Fisher. We might just do that a time or two." Leaning on his shovel, he surveyed the patio area. "Do you want me to lay the bricks in any special way? Maybe a herringbone pattern?"

"That would look nice, I think."

"Good. Then that's what we'll do. The bricks are gonna be delivered tomorrow, early."

Definitely no moss growing under Kip's feet. "Sounds great. Just let me know if you need anything."

She stepped back inside and found Rebecca and Ashley had arrived. Ashley was already settled in the children's reading area, and Rebecca was in the process of checking the cash register.

"Patio going in?" she asked.

"Yes, indeed. I think Kip may have it all done by the end of the week."

"That's exciting. Maybe for the walking tour, we could serve punch and cookies on the patio. That would bring folks into the shop. If their interest was piqued by the tour, they might buy a book or two about Ivy Bay."

"What a good idea! I can order the cookies from Sweet Susan's." Although, Mary didn't want to treat herself to Susan's bakery goods *too* often or she'd have to buy all new clothes in a larger size.

"I know you're likely to be busy that night with all the organization of the walk, so I'll take care of the punch," Rebecca said. "I've got a couple of nice recipes with sherbet and sparkling soda."

"That'd be wonderful. You get whatever you need, and I'll reimburse you." Mary went behind the counter and sat at the computer. "But what about Ashley? I thought you were going to take her around on the tour."

"I talked to her about that. Turns out she'd rather come here to the bookshop and stamp the tickets of the visitors who drop by."

Mary chuckled and shook her head. "You

can never tell what's going to appeal to children, can you? Or how often they'll change their minds."

The punch and cookies at the bookshop sounded like a good plan. In fact, at next Friday's committee meeting, Mary would make the suggestion that the businesses on the tour route might want to do something similar.

Rebecca and her daughter set about re-arranging books to even out the shelf space, while Mary caught up with paperwork on the computer.

Idly, she picked up the ledger she'd found at the mill. Staring at the cover, she tried to picture what had happened on October 2 and 3, 1841. The storm must have been horrendous, blowing business signs down and toppling trees. Rain would have been coming down in cascades, to the accompaniment of thunder and lightning.

She wondered how Caleb Hopkins and William Emerson could even hear each other in the cacophony of noise. Surely they'd both wanted to get out of the rain and wind; William to the mill, and Caleb home or back to the tavern.

So how did the boot and watch end up hidden in the mill?

The chime over the door sounded. Mary

stopped her musings as Bob Hiller strolled into the shop. "Looks like you're doing some work around the old place." He put the mail, including a couple of catalogs, on the counter and picked up the outgoing mail.

Mary began sorting through the envelopes — mostly bills and advertisements. "We're putting in a brick patio. It'll be a quiet place to read or visit with friends."

"Sounds good. When you get it done, I'll slip out there one day and take myself a break." He shifted his weight from one foot to another. "These feet of mine are getting older by the day."

"I can imagine." There were days when Mary's feet hurt too, from standing most of the day. She glanced at the ledger again and thought about that long-ago fateful night. "As a child, I mostly visited Ivy Bay in the summer. But you've lived in Ivy Bay a long time. What's it like when a hurricane comes through here?"

His eyes widened. "Is there one coming our way? I hadn't heard anything —"

"No, Bob, it's okay. Don't panic," she said with a laugh. "I'm just doing some research. I'm wondering what the town would be like if several inches of rain fell in only a few hours."

"Well, now . . ." He removed his cap and ran his palm across the top of his receding hair. "When it gets real bad, the streets overflow their curbs. In fact, the streets that run down toward the marina turn into rivers, and some of the shop owners have to sandbag their doors so they don't get water inside."

"What about the pond and the race at the old gristmill? Does that usually overflow too?"

He paused again to contemplate her question. "I don't generally work the route out that direction. In fact, if there's a hurricane coming through, we don't deliver."

"None of this 'through rain and sleet' business for Ivy Bay mail carriers, huh?"

His cheeks darkened with a blush. "That old saying has sort of been replaced with safety first."

"Smart plan." She smiled to let him know she'd only been teasing. "Do you think the pond overflows in a heavy rainstorm?" she repeated.

"Oh yes, indeed. The pond breaks over its bank, and the race past the mill becomes a regular Mississippi River, covering a whole lot of land. When I was growing up, us kids would go over to take a look after the rain stopped. You didn't dare get too close to that river of water or you'd be washed right out to sea."

"Really?" During her summer visits, she recalled only a few times when it rained. She had never seen anything like what Bob had described.

"Absolutely. That rushing water would pick up anything in its way — garbage cans, bicycles. I saw a picnic table float away once. I heard it turned up a couple of days later on the beach at Provincetown. The owner went over to bring it back, but it was pretty well broken up."

If a storm could sweep a picnic table out to sea, would the power of a hurricane be enough to wash a full-grown man away? A man who was drunk?

"I'd best be on my way." With a grin, he touched his fingers to his cap and walked out the door.

Mary picked up the mail and started opening envelopes. An invoice from the wholesale book distributor. An electric bill, higher than usual because they'd been running the air conditioner a lot. A notice from her dentist that it was time for a checkup.

As if she had a lot of spare time for that, she thought with a sigh.

Frowning, she considered what Bob had told her. What if . . . A scenario began to form in her mind. What if Caleb had followed William Emerson back to the gristmill after their argument? It was raining hard. Caleb confronted William again, and they continued their argument. One of them threw a punch. Caleb fell or was pushed into the roaring water and was washed out to sea. His body, too, might have washed up on a nearby shore.

Later, after the storm had passed, William could have discovered Caleb's boot and his watch, which had been lost as Caleb battled in the rushing water to reach safety.

Of course, Caleb could have fallen into the race all on his own. William later found the evidence of Caleb's presence. Knowing he would be a suspect, he hid the boot and watch behind the false wall at the mill in order to protect himself and his family. That would explain why she'd found the porcelain doll too, because that also tied Caleb to being at the mill.

But why was the ledger hidden in the same place as the spigot for a keg of ale?

As Mary paused to consider those two possibilities, she realized there was yet another possibility. Not far from the gristmill, there were marshes; marshes that were quite close to where Caleb Hopkins lived.

With such a heavy rain, the marsh could

have overflowed just like the race at the gristmill.

What if Martha had stabbed Caleb with the bloodied butcher knife? She and her son could have dragged or carried Caleb to the marsh under the cover of darkness and the roaring noise of the storm. If they'd dumped him in the marsh, his body could have sunk to the bottom and still be there buried beneath the silt, mud, and goo. Or maybe his body had washed out to sea like the picnic table.

Washed all the way to Provincetown?

Gus leaped onto Mary's lap, startling her. "What is it, Gus? Do you think I'm on the right track now?"

He nudged his head under her chin.

"You're right. It's a lead I should at least follow."

But how? She couldn't go digging up the marsh looking for old bones in the mud. Nor did she want to.

Apparently, no one in Provincetown had reported finding Caleb's body. So maybe that wasn't what had happened.

Or perhaps it was, but the body had never been identified. Communication between the Cape and the mainland in the twenty-first century was far better than it had been in the 1800s.

A steady stream of customers began to drop into the shop, requiring Mary's attention. Kip and his helper came inside to cool off and eat their lunches. Rebecca and Ashley took a quick break as well.

Finally, when it was well after two o'clock, Mary decided to dash over to the library.

She made her way to Victoria, who was at her desk. "I seem to have become a bad penny that simply keeps on showing up."

Her friend laughed and her blue eyes sparkled behind her cat's-eye glasses. "I love pennies like you, Mary. Always so full of questions, you keep me on my toes."

"This one may be harder than most. Do you have old papers from Provincetown?"

She stood. "Are we going back to the 1840s again?"

"I'm afraid so," Mary admitted.

"I don't think I have a complete set, but let's see what I've got on microfilm."

Mary followed her into the room that held the microfilm records she'd read of back issues of the *Ivy Bay Observer*. Victoria went directly to a different cabinet.

"The Provincetown *Inquirer and Mirror* has been in publication since 1820, which is quite an accomplishment for a newspaper. Papers don't make a very large profit." She skimmed down the labels on the shallow drawers. "The records from that long ago are spotty. Lots of missing issues. But, let's see. . . . Here we go." She pulled out a drawer. "What date are you looking for?"

"Early October 1841."

"Oh yes, around the October gale disaster."

"That's right. I heard today, that in a big storm, the mill race can overflow. Whatever the water catches can wash out to sea."

"A big nor'easter storm can make a pretty big mess here on the Cape."

"I'm wondering if Caleb Hopkins might have fallen in and been washed out to sea."

"I suppose anything is possible." Victoria carefully searched through the microfilm rolls, checking dates. "I've got September 30, October 1 and 2. Then it jumps to October 4."

Mary leaned over Victoria's shoulder. "The storm came in on the third. They might not have been able to publish that day. Certainly distribution would have been nearly impossible."

"Okay, then." Victoria straightened and handed Mary the roll of film. "I leave you to it. Hope you find what you're looking for."

Mary hoped so too. She sat down and threaded the film through the machine. She found the October 4 edition and skimmed down the front page. It was filled with stories about the storm, the lost fishing boats, and the serious damage done to homes and businesses in Provincetown.

Carefully scanning the headlines, she read through several editions looking for a story about a body being washed up on the shore. Someone resembling Caleb. Although she didn't find anything right off, she still didn't give up and kept on reading.

Finally, a full week after the storm, a two-inch story reported an unidentified adult male had been discovered washed up in a rocky area north of town. The Provincetown constable suggested the man was likely a fisherman who had been lost at sea during the hurricane.

Her heart skipped a beat. She was guessing the deceased was a fisherman, all right, but he hadn't been out to sea. Either someone had killed him, or, drunk as he'd been, he'd fallen into fast-moving water and was dragged out to the ocean.

All she had to do now was determine if the man could actually have been Caleb. If so, she needed to know the cause of death — a stab wound, injuries that suggested a beating, or drowning — and she'd be one step closer to resolving that mystery.

But no closer to proving who owned the gristmill, she thought with a groan.

She made some quick notes about the report, returned the roll to its proper place, and thanked Victoria for her help. Then she hurried over to the police station. She wanted to catch Chief McArthur before he went home for the day.

Minutes later, Mary stood in front of the police chief, who was seated behind his steel desk, shaking his head.

"Now let me get this straight. You want me to call the police chief in Provincetown and ask him to find the medical examiner's records of an unidentified man who died in 1841."

"Exactly. I'd call myself, but I'm afraid he'd think I was a nut case." She ignored Chief McArthur's nod of agreement. "I assume you know the Provincetown police chief and have had dealings with him previously."

"I do. Chief Duncan and I meet a couple of times a year about the mutual-aid agreements between all the departments on the Cape and disaster planning for the area."

"Perfect." Mary slipped into the chair in front of his desk.

He leaned forward and gave her a hard stare. "You're not going to go away until I

261

make that call, are you?"

She grinned sheepishly. "Tenacity has always been one of my finer qualities."

He shook his head again and picked up the phone. "Tell me what you want to know."

She told him to ask if the man had sustained injuries from a knife or due to a fight, or if he had simply drowned. "One other thing. Ask if the man was missing one boot."

"Missing a boot?" Chief McArthur visibly did a double take before punching in the phone number. Mary sat back to listen to his side of the conversation. There were several pauses. Benjamin, the dear man, finally convinced an apparently reluctant fellow police chief to do this favor for him and said he'd reciprocate in kind in the future.

He disconnected the call and looked at Mary with weary eyes. "Duncan says he'll check but makes no promises. He'll get back to me when he can."

Mary wanted to do a little jig but restrained herself. With a bit of luck, she'd make real progress toward discovering what happened to Caleb.

"Thank you, Chief. I can't tell you how much I appreciate your help."

Standing, he grabbed his cap. "I'm on the

way home. Can I give you a lift to your shop?"

She thanked him but declined his offer. She suspected Police Chief McArthur had seen enough of her for one day.

FOURTEEN

"Look what Eleanor brought over." Betty thrust a bulky book into Mary's hand.

Mary had just come in the door after seeing Benjamin, and her head was still considering the possible cause of Caleb's death and what she might learn from the Provincetown police. She set Gus's carrier on the floor, released him, and stared dumbly at the book in her hand.

"What is it?"

"It's a Bible." Eleanor, who was seated on the living room couch, spoke up. "I finally had time to look through some of those boxes in the attic I mentioned. I had no idea I'd find a family Bible."

"How interesting." Mary flipped the book cover open and turned to the first page. There, in a Spencerian hand, someone had written the words: "For my dearest friend, Martha Hopkins, with eternal love, Elizabeth Emerson." It was dated January 1843.

The writing was lovely and seemed similar to the one on the ledger, even if it was less elaborately flourished.

Stunned, Mary sat down heavily in a nearby chair. "That's two years after Daniel claims William Emerson killed Caleb Hopkins."

Gus climbed up in Mary's lap to sniff the Bible.

"Yes, I know. That's why I brought the Bible over immediately." Sitting primly with her hands folded in her lap, Eleanor said, "Look at the signature. Those two women were obviously close friends. One probably the wife of William, and the other Caleb's widow, don't you think?"

Tilting her head, Mary continued to study the handwriting. "They could be. The census from that period doesn't list any names except the heads of households, virtually all of them males. I haven't come up with any genealogical records. The woman who wrote this must have been unusually well educated for the time. She writes a beautiful hand."

When Lincoln had examined the inscription on the ledger cover that Mary had found, he concluded the handwriting was that of a woman. Elizabeth Emerson? The miller's wife? Entirely possible. How many women in Ivy Bay in 1843 wrote such a fine hand?

Mary doubted there were many.

"If her husband's ancestor had sold the gristmill, it was likely his only means of supporting his family," Betty said. "I can't imagine Elizabeth Emerson would feel all that cordial toward the family who had bought the mill, which might well have made her and her family paupers."

"I quite agree," Eleanor said.

"Nor would Caleb's widow feel kindly toward the wife of the man who supposedly killed him," Mary added. She paused in thought, then continued. "The relationship between the two women does seem odd if either of those scenarios is true."

"Most certainly odd," Betty continued in a firm voice. "Which is one more reason we know Daniel is lying."

Eleanor nodded in agreement. "Lying because he is greedy and opportunistic."

Mary pursed her lips. "It's circumstantial evidence, I agree." But not proof. It would take much more than a signed Bible for a judge to agree that the two families were such close friends that one wouldn't buy property from the other. Business deals happen between friends all the time.

And more often than they should, turn

out badly.

She handed the Bible back to Betty. "You hold on to this. You'll want to give it to Rob Dunlap."

Betty gave a quick nod. "I know you're not totally convinced about any of this, but I am, Mary. And so is Eleanor. Think about it. We haven't found a single piece of evidence that Hopkins bought the mill or that William Emerson killed anyone, and we're not going to." She put her hand over her heart. "I believe that with every bit of faith I have in my husband's family."

Eleanor stood. "No Emerson would have ever murdered another soul. We are and always have been a good Christian family."

Mary sincerely hoped she was right.

Mary arrived at work the next morning to find a large truck in front of the shop, blocking several parking spaces. Kip and Ian were unloading bricks, using wheelbarrows to carry them to the backyard.

After unlocking the front door of the shop, Mary went inside and walked to the back door to observe the activity.

Ian was stacking the bricks alongside the chokeberry bush. A big pile of sand had been dumped in the center of what would soon be the brick patio.

"Good morning, Mrs. Fisher." Sweat already glistened on Kip's darkly tanned face, despite the comfortable temperature. "After getting the sand spread around, we can start laying the bricks. Then you'll be able to see how nice it'll look."

"I'm sure it will be a great improvement over what I have now." She stepped back into the shop to find that Rebecca and her daughter had arrived. "Good morning to you both."

Ashley skipped over to her. "My grandmother sent me a present!"

Mary knelt down to Ashley's level. As she did, she released Gus from his carrier. "What a nice grandmother. What did she send you?"

"A bookmark!" She thrust the bookmark at Mary. "She and Grandpa went to Yellowstone. That's a long way away, and they saw Old Faithful."

"They did?" Mary looked at the bookmark, which was a holographic-style picture of Old Faithful. As she turned the bookmark one way or the other, the geyser erupted and then retreated. "What a wonderful bookmark. You're a lucky girl."

After more conversation about the bookmark, all three of them went to work. Mary busied herself straightening books that patrons had left unshelved.

The chime over the door sounded. Mary smiled as Dorothy Johnson walked in the door, her stride determined, her head held high. Mary could hardly remember the last time the woman had visited her shop.

"Good morning, Dorothy. You're out early this morning."

"I simply couldn't wait until the Friday meeting. I've already lined up fifteen lovely, lovely homes for the walking tour."

"So quickly? You've definitely been working hard." Betty had told her that Dorothy was a good organizer, and Mary had known that was true.

"It's been fun." She placed a list of homes that she'd recruited on the counter. "And I've given some thought about showcasing my own house." She lifted her chin in a slightly defensive way. "I do have some nice things, one-of-a-kind handcrafted statuettes, fine china decorative pieces, not to mention some original paintings. Some of the smaller pieces I plan to put away. I also thought I'd put up some velvet ropes across doorways so the visitors can look but not go into certain rooms."

Mary was so glad Dorothy was on board. "That's an excellent idea."

"Yes, I thought so. It's what they do in

museums, you know." She eyed Mary. "I've suggested to the homeowners they consider something similar. I'd hate for anyone to have some priceless object stolen during the historic tour."

"Sounds perfect."

"I agree. That's why I've asked Henry to be at my house during the tour to help me keep an eye on things. He's such a close, good friend." A smile that looked more like a smirk tilted Dorothy's lips.

Mary forced herself to keep a straight face. "I'm sure Henry will be of great help to you, and you'll be able to rest easy while he's there."

"Yes, I am relieved he'll be there." She glanced toward the back door. "My goodness, what's going on back there?"

"I'm putting in a brick patio. Betty's already done some landscaping, and I plan to buy an umbrella table and some chairs so people can read or chat comfortably outdoors when the weather's good." Which reminded Mary she should start looking through catalogs and checking for sales for a suitable table. With the end of summer nearing, she might be able to pick up something for a good price. "For the walking tour, I plan to serve punch and cookies on the patio to anyone who drops by the shop."

Dorothy's shoulders straightened. "I hadn't heard anyone was planning to serve refreshments," she said.

"I'm going to mention the idea at our next committee meeting. It might help draw people to the businesses that are participating. The homes too. Purely optional, of course."

Dorothy huffed out a breath. "I'll be sure to inform the homeowners of that option, even though I hadn't previously been told about it."

A customer came in the door, and Mary felt as though she'd been rescued. "You're doing a wonderful job, Dorothy. I really appreciate all your efforts for the walking tour." She pointedly glanced toward the customer who was examining books in the cozy-mystery section. "I'll see you at the Friday meeting."

As Mary turned to greet her customer, she heard Dorothy promise to be at the meeting.

Please, Lord, help me to remember to be kind to Dorothy. As vexing as she can be at times, I know she mostly means well.

Later in the day, Mary picked up the ledger

and turned to the pages of symbols. When Lincoln had visited, he suggested an expert in code breaking or hieroglyphics could possibly help her. At this point, Mary wasn't sure deciphering the hieroglyphics in the ledger would make a difference. Still, if there was a chance to ensure the suit would come out in Betty's favor, she'd have to make the effort.

But the ledger, like a good many of the clues she'd found, could easily point the other direction.

Ashley came around to Mary's side of the counter. "You're frowning, Mrs. Fisher. Is something wrong?"

"Not exactly wrong." Mary smoothed Ashley's flyaway blonde hair. "More like a puzzle or a code I can't seem to figure out."

"I read a book about a code breaker the other day. It's a kids' story, but they said the author was a real code breaker in World War II."

"Really?" Mary's interest perked up. "Can you bring me the book? I'd like to take a look." She'd also love to find a code breaker to resolve her questions about the ledger.

Ashley dashed off to the children's section and returned quickly. "Here it is."

"Thank you, sweetie." Noticing the author's name, Arnold Binghamton, on the cover, she flipped to the back of the slender book to read about him. There was a photo of a very distinguished gentleman and notes about the work he'd done during the war. But the last part of his biography was what most interested her. "Major Binghamton currently resides on Cape Cod."

Knowing many World War II veterans had passed away, she quickly checked the date the book had been published. Only two years ago. So he was alive two years ago, at least. Maybe he still was.

"This is perfect, Ashley. Thank you."

It couldn't be that difficult to find one person on Cape Cod, could it? Mary sat down at her computer, her fingers resting on the keyboard, trying to think of where to start. A quick search turned up listings for his book, but no contact information. She pulled up the publisher's Web site. She found information about the book there, but nothing more about the author himself. She did find a link to a page where she could contact the publisher's authors, and she typed out a quick message and sent it in, but she had little faith that it would actually reach him.

If he was still on the Cape, where would he be likely to live? There were retired folks all over. But Mr. Binghamton would be quite elderly at this point, probably in his eighties. There was a good chance he'd be in a retirement community or nursing home now.

Mary typed in the phrase "nursing homes Cape Cod" and quickly pulled up a list of more than a dozen facilities.

There was no way to tell from his author biography which town on the Cape he lived in, so Mary decided to start at the top. She dialed the number listed for the Abingdon House assisted care facility in Hyannis. The woman who answered the phone was brisk and professional, and told Mary that she couldn't reveal whether someone by the name of Arnold Binghamton lived there or not. Mary had expected as much.

Next on the list was the Bay View retirement complex. Mary had been to Bay View. It was a nice facility right here in Ivy Bay. She dialed the number, and since the receptionist recognized her name, she told Mary that no one named Mr. Binghamton lived there.

Halfway down her list was the Roxbury retirement center in Chatham. After a few rings, someone picked up. Mary explained why she was calling, and she was put through to Mr. Binghamton, who sounded both pleasant and alert. He invited Mary to visit him on Sunday afternoon.

With any luck, Mr. Binghamton would provide the answers to this part of the gristmill mystery.

The Friday morning meeting of the walking tour committee went quite well. Even though the members were pressed for time, wanting to get to their businesses, Mary made sure Dorothy had ample opportunity to share her success with the historic homes portion of the tour.

The business side of the planning was going a little more slowly, but Rich Tucker from Gems and Antiques thought more businesses would sign on in the next day or two.

Cynthia McArthur had put together some information on the history of Ivy Bay's downtown shopping district for business owners to hand out during the tour, and she gave copies to everyone to look over.

Art Shirk presented a sample of the tickets for the event, which was approved by the committee. They'd be available for sale at the participating businesses in town.

As Mary picked up her notes and extra copies of the agenda, Chief McArthur hooked a hip over the meeting table next to her.

"Chief Duncan in Provincetown couldn't find what you were looking for. But he said the Forman Mortuary has been in business since the early 1800s, a family-run business. They've always had the contract for burying paupers and indigents." Benjamin handed her a slip of paper. "That's their phone number. He suggested they might have records back that far."

Disappointed the Provincetown police chief hadn't come up with what she needed, she looked at the phone number for the Forman Mortuary. "I'll give them a call and hope for the best."

"Good luck." Placing his cap on his head, Benjamin headed out the door.

Mary sat back down at the table. She needed to know if the unidentified body was Caleb before she'd be satisfied she could unravel the mystery of Caleb's death.

After picking up her cell phone, she punched in the number Benjamin had given her. "Forman Mortuary, Mildred Forman speaking," a professional-sounding female voice answered.

Mary introduced herself. "I'm looking into the death of a man who was washed ashore in 1841. I understand your mortuary handled burials for indigents at that time."

"Yes, we did. We have since the company was founded by my great-great-great-grandfather." Pride in her family's history was clear in her voice. "Are you working on your family's genealogy?"

"More like my sister's family, but it is important."

"Of course. Tell me exactly what you need to know. We have a strict policy of retaining our records. The oldest records like you're looking for have all been scanned and saved on CDs."

"That's wonderful." Mary explained what she needed and about the body that had washed ashore.

"May I e-mail you the records when I find them?"

"Yes, please do." Mary gave the woman her e-mail address. "I really appreciate your help."

"We're always glad to help those who come to us, whatever the reason."

Mary terminated the call, optimistic that she'd be receiving the information soon.

After picking up her committee materials, Mary walked back to the bookshop. Several customers were browsing the shelves, and Rebecca was at the cash register ringing up a sale.

Mary stepped into the back room to leave

her committee materials. She glanced out the back door. The patio was taking shape nicely, and she thought Kip would finish soon.

When she returned to the front, Rebecca asked, "How's the tour committee doing?"

"Things are nicely falling into place. I think it's going to be a wonderful event for the town." And Mary prayed it would raise enough money to give Dorothy a good start to cover the cost of repairs to her house.

Mary spent the next hour flipping through publishers' catalogs and making a list of books she'd include next time she placed an order. Then she turned back to her computer.

Although Mary couldn't imagine the woman at the mortuary could have responded this quickly to her request for information, she booted up the computer.

To her delight, she had an e-mail from the Forman Mortuary. She read the pleasant note from Mildred, then downloaded the attachment.

Mary stared in amazement at the scanned sheet of paper, a handwritten mortician's report. "Unidentified male, approx fifty years old, height five ten, weight 180 pounds. Except for minor contusions, no trauma visible. Cause of death — drowning.

Personal possessions included no identification; missing one boot. Deceased buried in pauper's grave #231."

Her heart jumped at the reference to the boot. And no visible trauma had to mean no stab marks on the body or signs of a fight.

Mary continued to puzzle over the report. If Caleb hadn't been stabbed, that meant the butcher knife with blood on it the constable found at the Hopkinses' house was not the murder weapon. Mary felt confident she could eliminate Caleb's wife Martha and her son as suspects.

She had been unable to prove the tavern keeper had any hand in Caleb's death. Nor did the police report or newspaper account indicate the tavern keeper was in any way a suspect. So only two other possibilities remained.

Either it was an accidental death, a result of the storm that caused him to fall into the fast-running race by the mill. Or William Emerson was a murderer who had thrown Caleb into the race and then hidden the evidence so his guilt wouldn't be discovered.

When Mary arrived home after work, Betty met her at the door and told her Evan had called.

"The lawyers have worked out a time for depositions," she said. "A week from next Wednesday at ten o'clock in the Ivy Bay county building."

"Finally." Mary released Gus from his travel carrier. "At least we won't have to drive to Boston." It was a congested drive on the best of days.

"Evan says Daniel's attorney will bring what Daniel purports is a bill of sale. In which case, your Mr. Lincoln will be able to show it's fake and a fraud."

Mary picked up the mail from the candle-stick end table by the entry. She immediately spotted a note from her granddaughter Daisy, her son's sixteen-year-old, who had been at summer camp all month. The quick note indicated she'd been riding a horse named Peaches all week and loved him. A friend of hers named Johnny hit his head diving into the pool. He was taken to the hospital. And finally, please send her some cookies. The food was terrible!

Chuckling, she brought her thoughts back to the upcoming depositions. "I wish I had more to say that would counter the bill of sale if Lincoln decides it could be legitimate."

"You can certainly say there's no evidence of the sale being recorded."

"Yes, I can do that." But would that be enough?

FIFTEEN

After church on Sunday, Mary hurried home to have a quick lunch before driving to Chatham.

"Are you sure you don't want to come with me?" she asked Betty as she put together two sliced turkey and cheese sandwiches on rye for their lunch.

"No, I promised I'd go with Sherry next door to a miniature show up in Plymouth. She says there's a seller who has some wonderfully detailed Victorian homes in one-inch-scale kits, including all the traditional furniture. They even have miniature wallpaper appropriate for the era, and hand-woven rugs."

"Sounds like you're about to apply your decorative skills to a dollhouse."

"Well, Christmas isn't all that far away, and I do have two lovely little granddaughters who are old enough to appreciate the finer things now."

Mary nodded in understanding. She always looked for something special to give to her grandchildren. That reminded her she'd have to bake some cookies tonight to send off to her granddaughter first thing tomorrow. "That would be a wonderful project for you."

"I'll have to decide *if* my poor old arthritic fingers wouldn't tire out too fast using those small tools." She flexed her hands for emphasis.

"Even if you decide not to buy, I'm sure it will be a fun outing for you and Sherry. Since she has two boys, she'd probably love to make something frilly and feminine for herself."

Betty chuckled. "As dear as her boys are, I do get the feeling she sometimes tires of robots, monster trucks, and alien war machines."

As soon as Mary finished her lunch, she changed into slacks and a loose cotton blouse for the drive to visit Arnold Binghamton. She tried not to be too optimistic. It seemed a long reach from German code breaking to deciphering an 1843 gristmill ledger.

Sunday traffic was heavy, and it took her almost an hour to reach her destination.

The main building of the Roxbury retirement complex was a one-story structure painted in blue and gray, echoing the colors of the independent-living duplexes scattered across a well-kept landscape. Attractive flower beds lined winding walkways that led to and from the central buildings.

Somewhere on the property, Mary was pretty confident there was an assisted-living facility and a central dining area.

With the ledger tucked under her arm, she walked toward the main building.

Inside, Mary found a comfortable lobby with conversational groupings of chairs and tables and potted plants strategically placed. The ambience of the lobby was what she would expect in a high-priced hotel. A grand piano sat quietly in one corner of the spacious room; two gentlemen were playing chess beside a window that looked out onto an outdoor patio.

Graceful living as we age, she thought, suspecting the cost was equally high-end.

A slender, gray-haired gentleman, who had been seated near the entrance, stood with the help of a walker. "Ms. Fisher?"

"Mr. Binghamton." She walked toward him with her hand extended. "Thank you for meeting with me." His handshake was firm. His light-blue eyes, although a little watery with age, sparkled with intelligence.

"I've been told by my loving children that my driving is hazardous to the lives of others, so I fear others must come to me."

"I was happy to come."

He gestured toward the chair next to his, and she sat down.

"Now tell me again how I can help you."

Briefly, she told him of the dispute over the gristmill and how she'd discovered the ledger. "This may or may not have anything to do with the ownership of the mill, but until I know what the symbols mean, it's a loose thread I'd like to tie up."

"I understand completely, my dear." He pulled a pair of glasses from his shirt pocket and slipped them on before taking the ledger from Mary. "I confess it's been a long time since I've attempted to decipher any notations as old as 1843, but I'm certainly willing to try. Good way to keep the synapses in the old brain working, don't you know."

Mary was immediately enamored with Arnold Binghamton. He might be well past ninety years, but he seemed as alert as a much younger man and had a good sense of humor as well.

"I assume these notations have something to do with selling cornmeal," he said.

"I'm assuming so. I don't know why else

the ledger would have been in the mill."

"Hmm." He ran his finger across the rows. "When decoding a message, you first look for repeated words or symbols. And then patterns begin to reveal themselves." He looked up from his study of the ledger and peered at her over the top of his glasses. "Most older codes, when you get down to it, are deceptively simple."

She nodded to show her interest, and he returned to his study of the ledger, turning to the next page and then the next.

Mary waited quietly, noting the people that passed through the lobby. Mostly well-dressed senior citizens, including a few who had apparently just returned from a round of golf. From a room behind the lobby, she heard laughter, and she had the feeling it must be happy hour at Roxbury.

Arnold removed his glasses. "I think I may be of some help. If you'll take a look."

Mary leaned toward him.

"The first pattern I see is these little squares that appear regularly. Sometimes there is one square inside the column, other times two or three. I take that to refer to the number of bags of cornmeal the author of the ledger sold to the individual involved."

Squinting, Mary followed his finger down

the columns. "Oh yes, wow. I see what you mean. That's very logical." Even though his comments made sense, she was sure she would have never been able to come up with his conclusion on her own.

"These things usually are quite logical," as if disagreeing with her thought. "Now then, notice there's a column of these squares followed, most often, by a column of hatch marks that are related in number to the squares."

Mary nodded. She'd never realized the pattern, but she could see it now.

"I can't be completely sure, of course, but my best guess at this point would be that the tally marks represent how much an individual paid for the cornmeal he purchased."

"Okay, I see. That makes sense." She was fascinated.

His smile broadened. "You're a perceptive student, my dear. You may also note that some tally marks are not preceded by what I believe represents bags of cornmeal. In that case, I suspect the individual in question bought cornmeal from the miller but had not raised the corn himself."

"Interesting. No wonder you were a code breaker."

"Simply a question of making assumptions and then testing them." He drew his finger from left to right across the page. "You'll notice there are gaps between the symbols over what has to be time. Two bags purchased and paid for here. . . . Another two bags possibly some days or weeks later here."

"Yes, I can see that now."

"Now, there are several things I can't yet discern. I can assume that the bags were of all equal weight. However, I don't know how much money each tally mark represents. There does appear to be some discrepancy in some instances."

"Why would that be?"

He shook his head. "I would need much more information about the particular situation to reach a conclusion about that. It seems in a case or two" — he pointed halfway down the page — "payment was not made for a sack of cornmeal. There are no tally marks. But we have an even more difficult problem."

Fearful that she'd come to another dead end, Mary pursed her lips and tugged at her earlobe. "I'm afraid to ask what the problem is."

"It may not be that dire, depending upon why you need this information." Reassuring her, he patted her hand. "The person who kept this ledger — I assume it was the miller — was apparently illiterate but quite intelligent. In this first column, he has identified his customers."

"Really?" She certainly hadn't gotten that out of looking at the ledger.

"Indeed. You see here what is clearly a cane." He pointed to the symbol halfway down the page. "It would be a reasonable guess that this customer used a cane."

Mary strained to see the figure he was referring to, which looked more like a candy cane to her rather than a walking cane.

"And here we see what amounts to a stick figure of a woman with, if I may be so unkind, wildly curly hair."

She laughed out loud, then quickly covered her mouth with her hand. She could only wonder what symbols William Emerson might have used to describe her and her sister.

"I do see what you mean there. Makes you want to let the woman borrow a comb from you."

"There are several reasonably clear signs or drawings, some less easily distinguished, but the difficulty is knowing who these people might be. Had we lived in the village in 1843, it would have made the task much easier. We'd know our neighbors and recognize their characteristics."

Leaning back, Mary contemplated how she could determine which Ivy Bay family had bought cornmeal at the mill and how that knowledge might help her regarding the mill's ownership.

"I am sorry I haven't been able to tell you more about your ledger," he said.

"No need to apologize. You've been very helpful." She took the ledger from him and stood. "You've certainly figured out more than I ever could have, and I appreciate your help."

With the help of his walker, he stood. "It's been my pleasure, my dear. I've enjoyed your company as well as the mental workout."

They parted on that note, and Mary walked to her car still wondering how she could use the information she'd been given. After driving back to Ivy Bay, she still hadn't come up with a plan.

Betty wasn't home from Plymouth when Mary returned, so she took the opportunity to whip up a double batch of chocolate-chip cookies, which she'd pack up and send to Daisy at camp tomorrow. She put the first cookie sheet into the oven.

Her grandmotherly duty under way, Mary poured herself some iced tea and refilled

Gus's water dish, which he'd apparently tipped over. The house phone rang, and she picked up the extension in the kitchen.

"Hi, Aunt Mary. How are you?"

She smiled at the sound of her nephew's voice. "I'm fine, Evan. How are you and your family?"

"The girls are good. I think Mindy is eager for school to start again."

Mary laughed. Summers could get long for a mother of two energetic girls. "If you're looking for your mother, she took a run up to Plymouth to look at miniature dollhouses." She took a sip of her tea, and Gus decided to brush up against her leg, asking for attention.

"Actually, I think you're the one I need to talk to. It's about the lawsuit."

"Oh dear. Has something happened?" She knelt to pet Gus.

"The arbitrator we're using has asked that we move up the deposition date to a week from Monday."

A ripple of panic raised her pulse rate. "Evan, I'm concerned about the hearing. I can testify there is no evidence in county records that the mill was ever sold, but if Daniel really does have a bill of sale, my statement won't be enough to invalidate his claim."

291

"You haven't been able to find a sample of Isaac's handwriting or signature?"

"No, there's simply no place else to look. I've searched all the property records that might apply. I was hoping Rob's assistant would turn up something."

"I'm afraid not," Evan said.

Thinking about the ledger, she frowned. "There is something that may help. I found a mill ledger dated 1843. The miller, who I'm quite sure was William Emerson, wasn't literate, although his wife was. Possibly the daughter of a minister or schoolteacher who insisted she learn to read and write. And I'd guess William's wife was busy raising their children and didn't take an active role in the workings of the mill. I think it's safe to say that Isaac was illiterate too. Which means that he probably wouldn't have signed his name anyway. He likely would have simply used an *X*."

The timer on the oven dinged. Still holding the phone, Mary pulled the cookie sheet out of the oven. The delicious smell of the cookies made her mouth water. She'd have to save a few cookies for her and Betty to enjoy.

"Sounds like if the bill of sale is signed with an *X,* we may be in trouble." Evan sounded discouraged.

"Exactly."

"Have you found anything else that could help our case?"

"Well, US census records show the Emersons consistently lived on the mill property as far back as 1790. If possession is nine-tenths of the law, we'd have that in our favor."

"I certainly hope so. Can you bring a copy of the census to the hearing?"

"Of course. I'll print out the records of the subsequent six or seven census periods. They all show an Emerson operating the gristmill."

"That's great, Aunt Mary. I know Rob's been working the case hard, but I'm really impressed by what you've been able to find."

She sipped her tea again to moisten her dry throat. "There is something else you should know."

"That sounds ominous."

"Not exactly ominous, however, Daniel has loudly claimed William Emerson killed Caleb Hopkins, his great-grandfather several times over."

"Yeah, Mom told me about that. Aunt Eleanor too. None of us believe it, though. We think Daniel's blowing smoke."

"Well, Daniel claims the reason why Caleb was murdered was about the mill ownership. I've been investigating, trying to disprove Daniel's statement. I've pretty well eliminated all the suspects I can, except William. That incident could have been what started the feud between the two families and what makes Daniel so determined to claim the gristmill." Although the two wives involved didn't seem to be feuding, she noted. In which case, the coins and uniform she'd found might well be an added incentive if Daniel believed in the old tales of hidden treasure at the mill. But if that were true, why hadn't he ransacked the mill years ago?

"You can't believe that guy's crazy story, can you?"

"I have no actual proof that there was a murder. It could have been an accident, for all I know. And I certainly hope that was the case. The report I received from the funeral home indicated an unidentified man, who I believe is Caleb, had drowned. But there is quite a bit of circumstantial evidence pointing to William. It's still possible William could have pushed Caleb into the flooded race."

Evan muttered something under his breath. "I don't think we ought to bring up this fake story of Daniel's. It has nothing to do with who owns the mill."

"Of course. I completely understand." Except she believed getting to the bottom of Caleb's death could shed a good deal of light on the situation. The wrong kind of light, if she proved William was indeed the murderer.

Evan thanked her for her help and asked her to pass on the change of date for the hearing to his mother. Mary said she would.

Troubled by the phone call and her inability to be of more help to save the mill for the Emerson family, she finished baking the rest of the cookies. She'd box them up for mailing after they cooled.

She took her tea and a sample cookie and went out to the deck. There was a light breeze blowing off the bay, keeping the summer temperature comfortable.

After pulling out a chair at the umbrella table, she sat down and opened the ledger. Because Arnold had shown her the patterns, they were now easier for her to identify. But that first column, the description of William's customers, was far harder to interpret.

Yes, there was a cane and a curly-haired woman. The outline of a fish in one square could easily mean the person in question was a fisherman. But Ivy Bay must have had dozens of fishermen that called the town their home in 1843. Besides, the squiggly line could instead be a bow tie. Whatever that might mean, Mary had no idea.

A small cross could be the local preacher; he was one who paid for cornmeal but hadn't brought William any corn to mill.

By the time Betty returned home, Mary's glass of iced tea was empty and she had stared at the ledger pages so long she felt like her eyes were permanently crossed.

"Yum," Betty said. "These cookies are delicious." She popped the last bite of one into her mouth.

"I'll mail them to Daisy in the morning. She says camp food is terrible." Smiling at her granddaughter's complaint, so common among kids off at a summer camp, Mary removed her glasses and rubbed her eyes.

"Assuming I can resist eating them all myself," Betty said with a teasing glint in her eye.

"Did you bring home a dollhouse?"

"I'm afraid not. They were quite lovely, but I think too delicate for the girls to play with, after all." Betty sat down next to her and stretched out her feet. "The unfinished kits take a great deal of work. In all honesty, I'm not sure either my patience or my hands would last long enough to get the job done." Betty glanced at the ledger in front of Mary.

"Did your code-breaking gentleman come up with any helpful revelations?"

"Enough that I understand the notations better. But I'm still trying to figure out who the marks in this first column represent." She showed her sister the symbols Arnold had identified. "I think I could get further if I knew what the residents here in 1843 looked like or their occupations. And the 1840 census didn't ask for that information."

Frowning, Betty skimmed down the page and pointed at one figure. "Is that a cow?"

Mary looked more closely. "It could be. You think he was a dairy farmer?"

"It'd be my guess, or maybe that's a pig instead of a cow, but who knows?"

A name instantly popped into Mary's head. "You know, I bet Bea could help me out. She certainly has a wealth of records. Property records might give me a hint about a person's occupation." Bea always welcomed her so warmly that Mary didn't think she'd mind yet another visit to the basement records.

"Excellent idea." Grimacing as if in pain, Betty stood up slowly. "I'm afraid I overdid at the miniature show. I got so engrossed I didn't want to miss anything."

"You go rest a bit. I'll fix us a light supper, and then we can both relax for the evening." Although Mary feared she'd be seeing strange symbols in her dreams tonight, which wouldn't make for a restful sleep. "Oh, I almost forgot. Evan called. The deposition meeting has been changed to a week from tomorrow."

"That soon? Are we ready to prove Daniel doesn't know what he's talking about?"

"Not entirely," Mary hedged. She was anxious to get a look at the bill of sale, but she only had a week to come up with more substantive evidence.

Suddenly, a week didn't seem like nearly enough time.

The week started with several local business owners dropping into the bookshop to see how plans were going for the historic walking tour. It seemed the idea was catching on and enthusiasm building. Even a couple of business owners who didn't operate out of a historic building wanted to know how they could help.

She referred those owners to Rich at Gems and Antiques.

Meanwhile, Kip had almost finished laying the bricks for the patio.

Mary realized she'd have to order a table for the patio soon. If she had to have it shipped, that might take a week or more. She didn't want to risk not having it here by the day of the walking tour.

When the flow of customers began to slow, she sat down at the computer. The first thing she needed to do was print out the census data she'd promised to Evan.

When she completed that task, she searched the Internet for the kind of table she wanted. She found the perfect one on sale at a big-box store that had an outlet in North Dartmouth. She could order it to be delivered to the store, but first she'd have to check with her sister. She didn't want to make a big design decision like this without Betty's approval.

She sent the link in an e-mail to Betty, then called her sister asking her to log on and have a look. She hung up the phone and began scanning a few invoices. A few minutes later, she got Betty's reply: "I love it. Your design eye is getting sharper, Mar, and believe me, I take all the credit." Then Betty had typed a smile emoticon. Mary smiled back at the e-mail, then she returned to the Internet browser and placed the order.

With that done, she glanced at her watch. Plenty of time left in the day to visit Bea at the clerk's office. Hopefully her records would provide some insight into who the townspeople were in 1843.

SIXTEEN

After so many visits to the basement of the county clerk's office, Mary was beginning to feel strangely at home. Which, in a way, was truly frightening. She didn't want to adjust to life in a dim, almost dank room with only stacks of files for company.

She found the box of property records that included 1843 easily enough. Hauling it over to the table, she settled down to see what information she could uncover.

She'd brought the ledger, her notepad, and the plot map from the shop so she could identify the location of property listings. Removing a handful of records, she studied them. Individual records identified the land use of the property — residential, business, or agricultural. Not as many specific land-use subdivisions as she would like, but it would have to do.

What a world of difference computers would have made in 1843.

Since cornmeal was such a staple in the diets of early Americans, for the moment she would assume all the residents of Ivy Bay at least bought cornmeal from William Emerson, even if they didn't raise any corn to be ground.

The first record read "Abmie, Frank," followed by a plot number with the notation "Residential."

She glanced at the ledger and the column of doodles she was supposed to decipher. How in the world could she pick out the symbol related to Mr. Abmie? He could be anything — the handlebar mustache William had drawn, the top hat, or any number of other symbols she couldn't interpret.

Setting that record aside, she found the next. "Adair, Mitchell," a plot number on the edge of town and described as a blacksmith. Slowly, she scanned the ledger symbols again.

A hammer. A neatly drawn sailing ship.

Her eye fell on a horseshoe. That had to be the blacksmith Mitchell Adair and his family.

Eagerly, she scanned across the horseshoe row. From what she could tell, the individual had purchased cornmeal at fairly regular intervals but had never sold corn to William Emerson.

Tentatively, she jotted down the row number and Mr. Adair's name. At this pace, it would take her days, if not weeks, to match names to the symbols for the gristmill's customers. And how did she think that information would get her closer to the cause of the Hopkins-Emerson feud or the ownership of the mill?

She removed her glasses and rubbed her eyes, which tired quickly in the dim light.

Deciding to take a different approach, she searched for the record of "Emerson, William," who was clearly noted as the owner of a plot identified as a business. And it looked as though he was all paid up on his taxes.

She found the Hopkinses' record next. This listed "Hopkins, Martha" as the owner of residential property. Caleb had been gone for two years; now a widow, the property belonged to her.

What would William have used for a symbol for a widow whose husband he may or may not have murdered?

She shuddered. "Don't even think about murder. Not in this dreary basement."

If she'd known how to translate the ledger when she'd been looking at the property records weeks ago, she could have checked for this detail as well.

She drew her finger down the column of symbols again. The woman with curly hair was drawn in simple lines. But several spaces below that was a woman drawn more carefully. She clearly wore a black skirt and a black bonnet.

A widow!

Forcing herself to take a breath, Mary checked the rest of the symbols all the way to the end. There was no other female figure dressed in black.

She turned back to the row of what she was almost sure was the record of Martha Hopkins' cornmeal purchases. What she found stunned her.

Periodically, William had drawn tiny *o*'s, or possibly zeros, where Mary would expect to see a tally mark indicating Martha had purchased a bag of cornmeal. But not a single tally mark appeared over a span of time that must be at least a year.

Did that mean William was giving Martha bags of cornmeal at no charge? If so, why? Out of charity, was he helping a widow faced with hard times?

Or was his generosity based on guilt for having killed her husband?

Walking back to the bookshop, the significance of all the evidence she had uncovered weighed heavily on her conscience.

All she could say for sure about the mill ownership was that she hadn't found any record of a sale to James Hopkins or anyone else.

But the cause of Caleb's death was still unclear. Yes, he could have accidentally drowned on the stormy night of October 3. Heavy drinking was likely a contributing factor to his end, no matter how it came about.

The argument he'd had with William could have equally as well become a fight. Without meaning to, William might have pushed Caleb into the overflowing race beside the mill. That, too, could have been an accident. Or in the worst case, manslaughter. Not first-degree murder.

If Martha Hopkins had believed her husband, abusive or not, had been killed by William, how could she have stayed such close friends with Elizabeth Emerson, as evidenced by the Bible that Eleanor had discovered? Was it because William had been so generous, giving her cornmeal to feed her family?

Evan wanted Mary to keep quiet about Caleb's death during the deposition meeting. She understood why. It would muddy the waters and divert attention from the issue of ownership.

But could she, in good conscience, keep silent if the issue of the feud came up? Or the cause of Caleb's death?

The Bible says: "So I strive always to keep my conscience clear before God and man" (Acts 24:16).

Whatever happened, Mary vowed to keep the word of God as she understood it.

She reached the bookshop and stepped inside. Ashley was playing a game of hopscotch in the aisle between the cozies and thrillers. She stopped. Standing on one foot, she grinned. Mary returned her smile. There were no customers around, so no harm done. The sweet girl was so good all day long, reading and actually helping customers, she needed a chance to use up some of her pent-up energy.

Rebecca was behind the counter, tidying up for the night.

"I wasn't sure you'd get back by closing time," Rebecca said.

"My errand didn't take quite as long as I had feared." But it had left Mary confused about her role in the lawsuit and how much she should reveal about her discoveries.

Returning the plot map to the map display, Mary said, "Why don't you go on home? I'll finish closing up."

"You're sure?"

"Yes." She waved Rebecca and Ashley to be on their way. "Go home and be with your family."

After they left, Mary lingered, deep in thought about the future and what would happen at the deposition.

Before she shut down her computer for the night, she checked her e-mail. The umbrella table she'd ordered that morning had already shipped and would be at the shop in a few days.

Over dinner on the back deck, Mary told Betty that the table would arrive shortly. Betty was glad it would be set up in time for the walking tour, and said she'd been back to Tanaka Florist and Garden Center and asked to have tubs of flowers delivered later in the week.

"And I had an idea about the tour," Betty said. "The gristmill isn't too far to walk from town for most people. Since it's one of the oldest structures in Ivy Bay, and one of the most important in its day, I've been thinking that it ought to be on the tour."

"No one would be able to go inside. It's too dangerous."

"I know. But I was talking to Evan about my idea. He thinks we can blow up old

307

photos of the mill I found up in the attic and mount them so visitors could see what it looked like before it got so run-down."

Mary nodded. "That sounds like it would work. Someone would have to be there to explain the mill's history."

She set her napkin aside. "If you have no objection, I'd like to do that. I can dress up in period costume. Even if Daniel wins his lawsuit" — her words drifted off — "it might be the last time I'll ever have a chance to tell the history of the Emerson gristmill," she finished weakly.

A lump filled Mary's throat, and she agonized for her sister and the vow she'd made to herself to restore the mill to honor Edward.

"I think that's a wonderful idea. Maybe we can even write up a brief history of the mill that could be handed to visitors who drop by."

"Good idea. I'll get started on that tomorrow."

Sleep did not come easily to Mary that night. She churned in bed trying to come up with what she had missed. What new avenue of research she could follow that would prove conclusively that the Emersons had always owned the gristmill.

She'd searched all the public records she could think of, and nowhere had she found any indication that an Emerson had ever sold the mill.

The connection between the Emersons and Ivy Bay, where their roots ran deep, was so strong it was impossible to believe any Emerson had even considered selling the mill.

Meanwhile, generations of Hopkinses had gone to sea, first in sailboats, then in trawlers where they were long-liners fishing from dories. More recently they went farther to sea in larger trawlers and brought home ever-larger catches of cod, redfish, flounder, and haddock. Then overexploitation caused the catches to shrink and the fishing fleets to slowly fade away.

Caleb Hopkins and his descendants continued to cling to their fishing tradition.

Why would Daniel Hopkins want to own a gristmill, particularly now in the twenty-first century?

Mary's eyes popped open, and she stared into the darkness. What would the gristmill land be worth if it was sold to a developer? Was simple greed really the crux of the lawsuit? And was Daniel not after the coins at all but rather something even more valuable?

What did they always say in murder mysteries? *Follow the money!*

Mary got up and dressed far earlier than usual and was downstairs drinking her morning cup of coffee when Betty strolled into the kitchen in her robe and slippers.

"My, you're up early. Is anything wrong?" Betty asked.

Without responding to her sister's question, Mary asked, "Have you had any offers to buy the mill property?"

Betty retrieved a mug from the cupboard and poured herself some coffee. "Not recently. Not since Edward passed away, that I can remember. He used to get queries from time to time, but he was never interested in selling. Why do you ask?"

"Last night I got to thinking this whole lawsuit thing might not have anything to do with Isaac selling the mill to James Hopkins. Or the accusation that William murdered Caleb Hopkins."

"Which he didn't do," Betty interjected as she sat down at the table.

"But the point is," Mary continued, "this could be a land grab, pure and simple. Daniel has almost admitted as much."

Betty peered at her over the top of her mug. "What do you mean?"

"Say, if Daniel had gotten wind of some

developer wanting to build condos or something on the mill property, he would use any ploy he could think of to get his hands on that land and make a killing selling it to a third party. Jill told me her children are all excited about the possibility of the family becoming really wealthy."

Wrapping both hands around her coffee mug as though she'd felt a sudden chill, Betty said, "Do you think that's really what is behind this lawsuit?"

"I don't know." Mary drank the last of her now-cold coffee and wrinkled her nose at the bitter taste, the same bitter taste Betty would experience if she lost the gristmill. "But I'm going to find time today to see Lori Stone."

"The Realtor?"

"Right. Lori always has her ear to the ground. She can tell me if there's been recent interest in the property and where that interest is coming from." Mary had been very impressed with Lori when she handled the purchase of the bookshop property for her. She was one sharp woman. Mary was sure she would have answers.

Mary had already opened the bookshop that morning when Rebecca arrived breathless, her hair mussed as though from sleep.

"Sorry I'm late." She stowed her lunch in the small refrigerator in the back room and waved hello to Kip, who was already working in the backyard. "Ashley and I finally got around to putting the snapshots of our trip to Boston into an album, and I lost track of the time. Anyway, I had a terrible time waking her up to get to work this morning. I finally decided to leave her with her dad. Russell didn't have to go to work today."

"No matter. Recalling good memories of family times is always important." Mary gave her employee an encouraging smile.

"Except when you're seven years old and are grumpy because you didn't get enough sleep."

"Oh dear. I remember days like that. When my son Jack was a teenager, it would take two alarm clocks and the threat of a bucket of ice water to get him up in the morning." Mary chuckled. "I have to talk to Kip to see how he's doing. I'll be out back."

She went out the back door and stood for a moment, amazed at how far the backyard had come. Once taken over by weeds, it was now an elegant space. The red-brick herringbone pattern of her new patio was gorgeous, and she loved how the surface was as smooth as a concrete floor but far more attractive. The contrasting green foliage of the chokeberry, raspberry and rosebushes seemed to make the bricks look even brighter and more cheerful.

"Hey, Mrs. Fisher." Kip, who was wearing stonewashed jeans and a light gray T-shirt, gave a wave around the garden. "What do you think?"

"Oh, Kip, I think it's perfect. What a lovely spot this will be to sit and read or talk with friends."

"That's what I've been thinking too. Heather will love this place."

"I'd love for her to visit," she said. "So when do you think it will be finished?"

"Should have it all cleaned up by tonight. I'm going to leave you a few extra bricks alongside the building in case some of these crack or get broken. That way, when we have to replace the old ones, the new ones will match just right."

"Sounds like a good idea." Although she hoped no one would drop anything on the patio heavy enough to break a brick. "Whenever you're all squared away, give me your invoice and I'll write you a check."

"Happy to, Mrs. Fisher." Mary and Kip shared a knowing smile. It wasn't too long ago that she had asked for an invoice for his work, only to have the request ignored. Of course, soon enough she'd learned that he hadn't charged her for the work he'd done because he'd broken into her store. She was so glad all of that was now water under the bridge.

Mary stepped back into the shop and noticed that there was little pedestrian traffic on the sidewalk out front and no customers had come into the bookshop yet. Midweek was usually quieter than the weekends when out-of-towners filled up the local bed-and-breakfasts and hotels.

"Rebecca, I need to run out to Stone Realty for a few minutes. It doesn't look like we'll be busy this morning."

Rebecca hitched herself up onto the stool behind the counter. "Sounds good, Mary. See you soon."

"I shouldn't be gone long."

Because Stone Realty was located on Route 6A just as the road entered Ivy Bay, Mary drove the few miles to see the Realtor.

A small Victorian home had been converted into a real estate office. It was painted dove-gray with white trim, and attractive landscaping and ample parking on a gravel lot welcomed visitors. Except for Lori's midsize SUV, there were no other cars in the lot. Mary pulled in beside it.

A buzzer sounded somewhere in the building when Mary opened the front door. In the entry, a large bouquet of fresh flowers rested on an early-American pine sideboard and flyers featuring homes and property for sale were displayed.

The click of high heels on the hardwood floor preceded Lori's appearance. She was carrying Bitsy, her adorable schnauzer in her arms.

"May I help . . . Mary! How nice to see you." Tall and quite slender, Lori wore her pecan-brown hair in a loose knot at the back of head. The warmth of her smile and the sparkle in her ginger-colored eyes embraced Mary with pleasure. "What can I do for you?"

"I need some real estate advice, so I thought I'd impose on your time and expertise."

"For you, it's no imposition at all. Come into my office."

Lori sat down in a swivel chair at her desk, which was cluttered with assorted escrow and appraisal forms and more flyers describing property for sale. Various awards and photos of the Little League team that Stone Realty supported decorated the walls.

Mary sat in the guest chair next to the desk.

Lori put Bitsy into her doggy bed, then turned back to Mary. "Now, tell me what kind of advice you need."

"I assume you're familiar with the Emerson gristmill and the property it's on."

"Of course. I've always hoped the Emersons would restore the mill. It would be a great tourist attraction. Some of the restored mills in New England have been turned into living-history exhibits, gift shops, and even restaurants."

"I think Betty's hoping that will become a reality one day."

"That would be so special, both for the Emerson family and the town."

"I was wondering if you have heard of anyone who wants to buy the land for development purposes?"

Her brows lowered as she considered Mary's question. "I haven't heard any rumors about a prospective buyer lately. But the fact is, I don't know what kind of development they'd be thinking of. Several years ago, the board of selectmen approved a long-range planning document. The mill and the land around it, including the mill pond, is zoned for open space and recreation."

Surprised, Mary sat back in her chair. "You mean no one could build condos or a big hotel on the property?"

"Only if they got the zoning changed or a waiver from the selectmen. As longtime owners, the Emerson family might be allowed to do something with the property, if it was consistent with the overall long-range plan. Like restoring it in a way visitors could learn about the mill's role in Ivy Bay history. But some big condo development or something like it?" She shook her head. "Getting approval for that would be a long shot."

Mary leaned her elbow on the arm of the chair and rubbed her temple with her fingertips. It sounded like she'd been way off track. She had started to believe that Daniel Hopkins was after the land because he's greedy, not because he really wanted to own an old, run-down gristmill.

"Well, I appreciate the information, Lori. If Betty does go ahead with plans to restore the mill, I do hope the selectmen will approve the proposal."

"I'm sure they will."

The two women stood and shook hands. "Let me know if there's anything else I can do for you," Lori said.

"I will." Mary walked back to her car. If Daniel couldn't develop the property, what made him so determined to own it? Was it possible Daniel believed the stories about buried treasure at the mill, after all? Treasure that Mary had actually found and stashed safely away?

SEVENTEEN

Friday morning, Mary called the meeting of the walking tour committee to order. Eleanor had seated herself at the head of the table, with Mary on her right-hand side.

"Good morning, everyone. Let's get started." Mary turned to Dorothy first.

"I have more than a dozen beautiful homes that will be on the tour." Dorothy passed copies of the list of homes and their addresses around the table. "I've suggested that owners be cautious about their possessions. All the tours will be on the main floors. For security reasons, no one will have access to the second or third floor of any house."

The members of the committee, including Eleanor, gave Dorothy a nod of approval.

"That's wonderful, Dorothy. Thanks," Mary concurred.

Mary turned to Rich Tucker. "How is the business community responding?"

"They've been terrific. We've got a dozen participating businesses, including your bookshop." He grinned in Mary's direction.

Betty raised her hand. "In addition to the homes and businesses, the Emerson gristmill will be on the tour. My son Evan and I will act as docents to explain the mill."

"As the principal member of the Emerson family," Eleanor said, "I will also share the docent honors."

"Yes, of course." Betty's face flushed. "Evan and I had planned to wear period costumes."

"An excellent idea," Eleanor agreed.

"What?" Dorothy's voice squeaked. "No one said anything about costumes."

"It's purely optional," Mary said hastily. "Betty simply thought it would add a little ambience to the mill site."

"Well, I never . . ." Bending over the table, Dorothy began scribbling on a notepad. "I'll have to get back to all my people again."

Not wanting to get bogged down about costumes, Mary turned to Jerry Avakian, who owned Meeting House Print and Copy and had volunteered to act as treasurer for the event. "What about publicity and tickets?"

"We've got the tickets printed." He passed samples to the other members of the committee. "And we're also planning to post flyers in the windows of every store in town plus make them available at hotels and bed-and-breakfasts." He placed several attractive 8 1/2″ × 11″ flyers on the table for everyone to pick up. "Jimmy volunteered to distribute the flyers and tickets to sell to local businesses and the visitor center next week." He gestured at Jimmy Shepard, owner of Jimmy's Hardware, who nodded.

"Jerry, sounds perfect. Thank you so much," Mary said. "And thanks to you too, Jimmy."

Despite Jerry's olive complexion, his face turned a deep shade of red. "It's for a good cause."

Pride in the committee's efforts, and building anticipation, pushed a broad smile to Mary's face. She rested her forearms on the table, her palms up as though encompassing everyone there. "It looks to me like we're going to have a wonderful event. All we need now are paying customers, and we'll have a nice chunk of money to help with" — she almost said Dorothy's house and stopped herself just in time — "restoration."

"Just over one week to go," Rich reminded them.

Just one week. Between now and the

walking tour, she and Betty still had to face Daniel Hopkins and the lawsuit deposition.

When the meeting finished, Mary hurried to the bookshop. The table had been delivered, and Tanaka Florist and Garden Center had promised they'd have the tubs of flowers delivered before eleven.

A young mother with two youngsters was looking over books in the children's nook. Ashley was talking with the customer's three-year-old daughter, introducing her to some of her favorite picture books. The three-year-old's older brother had far more interest in the pedestal bathtub. He'd climbed in and was making sounds like he was on a rocket ship.

Mary smiled. She knew just the right book that would catch the boy's interest.

The time passed quickly, and before she knew it, a big stake-bed truck pulled up in front, blocking two parked cars. The logo on the side read Tanaka Florist and Garden Center.

Mary went outside to greet the two husky young men who had exited the truck. At the same time, Betty showed up on the sidewalk.

"I didn't want to miss the big unveiling."

Only moments behind her, Henry appeared. "Looks like there's some excitement going on."

Mary greeted them both with a smile. "You're both just in time."

To the men, Betty said, "Everything goes around back. You can use the walkway along the side."

"No problem." The older of the two powered down the tailgate and hopped up into the truck. He wrestled the first tub of flowers — a rustic half-wooden barrel — onto a hand truck and wheeled it onto the tailgate, riding it down to the ground. There the younger of the two men took charge.

Mary went inside to meet the young man at the patio, Betty following closely behind her.

As the young man settled the first tub in place, Betty clapped her hands. "Look at that. Zinnias, dahlias, pansies. Marnie outdid herself this time. Just lovely." Marnie Reid was the head florist of the Tanaka center, and Mary knew she'd done an especially good job for Betty, but Mary also knew that Marnie had been given great direction.

Mary slipped her arm around Betty's waist. "You're the one who had the vision to make this yard a special place, Bets."

In no time, the two men had the tubs arranged on opposite sides of the patio and the table set up with the umbrella unfolded.

Rebecca had been watching the operation from the open back door. "That looks so great. In good weather, I'm going to eat my lunch out here."

Picturing herself taking a break to enjoy the fresh air and peaceful ambience, Mary agreed. *The patio would be a wonderful place to pray and give thanks,* she thought as she counted all the blessings the Lord had given her.

By Sunday, a heat wave had settled over the entire East Coast. Although the interior of Grace Church was a few degrees cooler than outside, many parishioners were using the morning programs to fan themselves.

During Pastor Miles's sermon, Betty stopped waving her program and leaned toward Mary. "I think we should pray for rain."

"A cold front would be just fine with me." Mary had noticed Betty fidgeting all during the service and thought her sister hadn't slept well last night. Worrying over the hearing tomorrow, she imagined.

Mary was doing her own worrying. Knowing there was not an official record of a sale might not be enough to save the gristmill.

And she had no idea what to say about the ledger showing William Emerson not charging Martha Hopkins for cornmeal. What would that have to do with the purported sale of the mill in 1792? Testifying about the ledger wouldn't do a bit of good.

Nor would mentioning her discovery of the British coins and military uniform. As for what could be Caleb Hopkins' boot and watch, she was almost sorry she'd found them.

Pastor Miles finished his sermon, and Mary realized with a spurt of guilt that she hadn't been paying any more attention to the minister than Betty had.

When they got home, they found Gus splayed out on the cool kitchen floor.

"Poor kitty." Mary bent down to give him a tummy rub. "This isn't a good day for a fur coat, is it?"

He squinted his eyes closed and stretched out his body even farther.

"A salad and then ice cream for dessert strikes me as a perfect lunch for a hot day."

"I think we still have some of your special peach and pralines ice cream."

Mary laughed. "I was hoping there was still a scoop or two left over."

Together, they made the salad, poured

some iced tea, and took their lunch out onto the deck. Only the faintest breeze crept past to cool them. When they'd finished their salads, Mary took their plates inside and served up two dishes of ice cream.

Betty sat staring off into the distance, toward a pair of seagulls swooping through the air.

"Are you as worried about tomorrow as I am?" she asked.

"Pretty much," Mary admitted. "We just have to have faith that the Lord knows what He's doing."

Betty took a bite of ice cream and let it melt in her mouth. "It's not always easy to let go, let God, is it?"

From the troubled look in Betty's eyes, Mary knew she was missing Edward and wishing he was here to deal with the problem. Mary could have used John's help about now too. He'd been a wonderful man to bounce ideas off of and help her resolve problems.

During the afternoon, Betty lay down for a rest before she had to dress to attend a lecture by an eminent historian at the Old State House in Boston. Eleanor, a longtime supporter of the historic organization, was on the foundation's board of directors. After the historian finished his presentation, Eleanor, Betty, and other members of the board would take him out to dinner. They'd very likely be late returning home. Because of that, Mary had begged off attending the lecture. She suspected Betty would just as soon stay home as well, but typically, when Eleanor invited her, Betty could not refuse.

Mary settled in the sunroom with a book written by a new mystery author. She was almost halfway through the delightful mystery featuring a handwriting expert as the amateur sleuth when the doorbell chimed.

"Can you let Eleanor in?" Betty called from her bedroom. "I'll be right there."

Marking her place, Mary went to the door.

Eleanor was dressed in an elegant, pale gray summer suit, accessorized with an exquisite gold necklace and earrings. She stepped inside as soon as Mary opened the door.

"Good. I'm glad you're here." Eleanor thrust a small, leather-covered book toward Mary. "I recalled my mother passed along a steamer trunk of family memorabilia years ago. I hadn't stored that in the attic. Instead, dear Richard stuffed it in the overhead storage area in the garage. I asked a neighbor to help me get it down. I knew you'd want to see this."

Betty walked into the entry. "I'm ready to

go if you are, Eleanor."

Mary looked at the book in her hand. "What is it?"

"I believe it's a diary of a young girl, but I really haven't had time to read it," Eleanor said.

Betty peered over Mary's shoulder. "Who was she?"

"An Emerson, of course." Eleanor reached back to open the door. "We really must leave now. You know how terrible Sunday traffic is going into Boston this time of day. We don't want to arrive late for our speaker."

Looking a little flustered, Betty told Mary good-bye and hurried out the door behind Eleanor.

Curious to know the contents of the book, Mary turned back the cover. On the first page, she read *Diary of Alice Emerson, In the Year of our Lord, 1843.*

She drew in a quick breath. The diary held firmly in her hands, she sat down in the nearest chair and continued to read.

My mama gave this diary to me for Christmas. She says I am to write down my thoughts and what happens each day and then I shall have a record of my life. I do not believe it will be a very interesting record. Today, it has rained all day, and I had to stay inside. Moses and Eldon teased me about the biscuits I burned for breakfast.

My mama's best friend is Martha Hopkins. Mother worries about her because she is a widow. Sometimes she takes an extra meat pie to Martha. I like to go with her because sometimes Peter is there, and he winks at me.

Mama told me often how she and Martha read the Bible together on rainy days in the mill loft. . . .

EIGHTEEN

The following morning, after Mary finished combing her hair and putting on a touch of makeup, she grabbed her purse and then hurried downstairs for breakfast.

"Good morning to you both." She greeted Betty and Evan; Evan had come by to drive them to the hearing. She slipped a piece of toast into the toaster. Betty had already cooked soft-boiled eggs for them and looked no worse for the wear after her night out in Boston.

"You look very professional in your suit, Aunt Mary. You must be planning to wow the opposition forces," Evan said.

With a troubled heart, she turned to look at her sister and nephew. She hadn't told Betty last night about the diary; it had been too late when Betty had arrived home. The truth was she hadn't known just what to say or how to reveal what she'd discovered. In fact, she'd been awake most of the night rereading sections of Alice's diary and praying about what she should do.

So I strive always to keep my conscience clear before God and man (Acts 24:16).

Those words had come to her a dozen times during the night. Before she gave her testimony today, she would swear to tell the truth, so help her God.

In so doing, she would deeply hurt her sister and the legacy of the Emerson name.

But how could she not tell the truth?

The toast popped up. Putting the toast on a plate, she spread it with butter. Her stomach roiled at the thought of eating anything. But going into the deposition on an empty stomach seemed like an invitation for disaster.

She poured herself a mug of coffee and carried that and the plate to the table.

"Don't you want an egg, Mary?" Betty had dressed in a lovely robin-egg silk suit that made her look very sophisticated.

"I'm too nervous to eat."

"No need to be nervous, Aunt Mary. Rob Dunlap is still hoping the so-called bill of sale will turn out to be a forgery."

Although the toast tasted like sand, Mary forced herself to eat and washed it down with coffee, grateful that she didn't gag.

A local Ivy Bay attorney had allowed them to use his conference room for the meeting. The large walnut table in the room was polished to such a high sheen that the overhead lights were reflected like it was a mirror.

In contrast to Rob Dunlap, the opposing attorney Marc Dougher was much younger. Blond and blue-eyed, with a quick smile, he looked more like a fraternity boy than an experienced attorney.

The Hopkinses were represented at the table by their attorney; Daniel, who wore a suit and a perpetual sneer; Jill Sanderson, who had found the old pictures of Martha Hopkins; and Jill's husband, Harry, a very sturdy-looking fisherman with massive hands roughened by years of hard work.

In addition to Rob, Mary, Evan, and Betty, Eleanor was seated on their side of the table.

Lincoln King arrived a little breathless, wearing his trademark black overcoat, completing the Emerson team.

Martin Goodhue, the arbitrator, sat at the head of the table, and a court reporter was seated to his right with her own chair and a stand for her stenotype.

"Good morning, ladies and gentlemen." Goodhue spoke with a tone of authority, yet his voice was calm, in control. "I'd like to start with a few ground rules. First, all of you will be sworn in and your depositions recorded by Ms. Stanley." He nodded toward the stenographer.

"When a person is testifying, no interruptions from the opposition will be permitted," he continued. "Attorneys may pose questions to their own clients but will restrain themselves from giving testimony. After an individual has completed his testimony, the opposing attorney may cross-examine."

Mary twisted her hands in her lap, fussing with the pearl ring John had given her as an anniversary present. Alice Emerson's diary was in her purse, the words the twelve-year-old had written in conflict with what Betty had believed about the gristmill.

Help me, Lord. What should I do?

"When this hearing is finished," Goodhue said, "I will make a ruling within thirty days. If either party objects to the ruling, you have the right to proceed to trial. If the parties can reach an amicable agreement prior to my ruling, the case will be concluded."

His ground rules completed, and everyone

sworn in, Goodhue turned his attention to Hopkins' attorney. "Mr. Dougher, your client has made a claim of ownership of the Emerson gristmill. You may proceed."

"Thank you, sir." Mr. Dougher began by asking Daniel some basic questions about himself, how long he'd lived in Ivy Bay, and his former occupation. "Now, Mr. Hopkins, I believe in the course of your usual activities, you discovered a bill of sale dated 1792 indicating one Isaac Emerson had sold the gristmill to your great-great-grandfather James Hopkins for the price of five British pounds. Is that correct?"

"It is," Daniel responded. Although his face was etched with the evidence of long years of heavy drinking, he sounded perfectly sober.

"Tell us how you came to be in the possession of this bill of sale."

"I was getting ready to move to my grandson's house." He nodded toward Harry. "I was cleaning out a closet filled with old junk. I came across a big sea chest someone had stuffed in there I don't know how many years ago. Stuck way down at the bottom, I found this here bill of sale. Clear as anything it proves that me and my kin have owned that mill since James bought it from Isaac."

Betty hissed under her breath.

"Would you please show us the bill of sale, Mr. Hopkins?" Mr. Dougher asked.

"Yes, sir, I have it right here." Hopkins slapped a clear plastic file folder with a letter inside on the table. "This ain't no forgery, neither." He glared across the table at Betty and Evan.

"Mr. Goodhue," Dunlap said. "Since we have not had an opportunity to examine the purported bill of sale, we'd like that opportunity now."

"Request granted." Goodhue indicated Hopkins should pass the folder to the Emerson side of the table.

Each of the members of the Emerson team took a look, then passed the folder along. When it was Mary's turn, she had to swallow a dispirited groan. Where Isaac Emerson's signature should be, there was a primitive drawing of a waterwheel much like the drawings in William Emerson's ledger that identified those who bought cornmeal from him. A technique no doubt passed down from father to son. A notary had carefully written Isaac's name beneath the symbol.

She thought for sure that this was indeed an authentic bill of sale for the gristmill.

Lincoln removed the bill of sale from the folder. He sniffed at it first, then studied every inch of the paper with his large magnifying glass.

Daniel began tapping his fingers on the table.

The knot in Mary's stomach tightened.

Betty's hand covered her mouth while she waited for Lincoln's conclusion.

Next to the arbitrator, Ms. Stanley waited patiently for Lincoln to speak.

He finally slipped the paper back into the folder and looked up. "The paper and ink used for this document appear appropriate for the period, most likely imported from Great Britain. However, I am not able to authenticate the signatures as I have no exemplars with which to compare them."

Betty exhaled and her shoulders relaxed. She gave Mary a tentative smile, but Mary was unable to return her expression. She was too sick at heart because she knew the truth.

Rob Dunlap spoke up. "My office has made an extensive search of records in an effort to discover any record of transfer of title to the property or the deed. We have found no such record. Mrs. Mary Fisher, the defendant's sister, has made an independent search for those records. Mary, were you able to find such a record?"

"No, sir." In response to Dunlap's further

questions, she related what she had done to establish the ownership history of the mill. "From what I researched, I concur with the findings of your office. It's clear the Emerson family has operated and been in sole possession of the gristmill since the earliest records were established."

"That's a lie!" Daniel pounded his fist on the table.

"Quiet, please," the arbitrator admonished him.

"You seen the bill of sale? That place is ours."

Daniel's grandson tried to calm him down, but Daniel fumed and shouted, his face turning redder by the minute.

"Please." Mary interrupted his diatribe, her voice a little shaky. "I believe, despite there being no record of a title change, that Mr. Hopkins' bill of sale is a legal contract."

Everyone in the room gaped at her.

Betty whirled toward Mary. "What on earth are you talking about? You just said you hadn't found any record of a title change."

"If you'll let me explain . . ." She pulled the diary from her tote and waited for a nod from the arbitrator.

"Eleanor Emerson Blakely, Betty Emerson's sister-in-law, discovered this diary

337

yesterday among some family memorabilia," Mary began.

"I did not expect that diary to be used against us, Mary. If I had, I certainly would not have passed it on to you."

"I understand, Eleanor. And I'm truly sorry." Mary briefly described the author of the diary and the young woman's relationship to William Emerson.

"He's the one what killed Caleb!" Daniel burst out, and his grandson grabbed his arm to hush him up.

"Actually, that's not true." Mary stared Daniel down for a moment until he stopped trying to yank away from Harry. "If I may, I'd like to read a few passages from Alice's diary."

She had marked the telling pages and opened the book. She read, "August 24, 1843: At dinner tonight, Mama asked Daddy why he wasn't charging Mrs. Hopkins for cornmeal. Mama usually has sympathy for the widow Hopkins, and they're really good friends, but she has been cranky all day. He told her that he was returning a favor owed to the Hopkinses, who once saved our family's skin. I didn't know what he was talking about and neither did Mama. Daddy explained a long time ago, when times were really hard, somebody named

James Hopkins helped Isaac Emerson —
that's Daddy's great-great-granddaddy —
by giving him some money to feed his
children. He had a lot of them."

Mary looked up from the diary. Everyone
was listening intently, gazing at her like
children used to when she'd been doing
story time at the library. Unlike the children,
however, they were not smiling or squirm-
ing in their seats.

"I can confirm from the census record
that Isaac had twelve children, which you'll
agree is a lot of mouths to feed," she
continued. "I believe the money referred to
is the five British pounds, which the lawsuit
contends James Hopkins gave Isaac Emerson to help him take care of his family. It
appears Isaac very likely signed over the bill
of sale as collateral."

With a shocked expression, Betty leaned
away, putting some distance between herself
and Mary. "What are you doing? The mill is
ours. It's the Emerson mill and always has
been." The deep hurt of betrayal rang
through the conference room.

"I'm sorry." Tears of regret burned the
backs of Mary's eyes as she retrieved the
mill's ledger from her tote.

"Like I said, the mill ain't yours!" Daniel
muttered.

The arbitrator held up his hand for silence. "Please continue, Mrs. Fisher."

Pressing her lips together, Mary took a moment to control her emotions. She cleared her throat. "From reading this diary, I've concluded the two families were such good friends and neighbors that James Hopkins refused to record the sale of the mill. He was, after all, a fisherman by trade. What would he have done with the mill? Chances were good he knew nothing about grinding corn."

Mary swallowed and continued. "That would explain why I was unable to find any record of a title or deed transfer. I do have a ledger written by William Emerson that confirms what Alice wrote in her diary. Her father was not charging Martha Hopkins for cornmeal. I believe that William Emerson made the effort to pay back that debt many times over by providing cornmeal to Martha Hopkins at no charge over the years."

Mary placed the ledger on the table and showed how she had reached that conclusion by identifying the sketch of the woman in black. "The lack of tally marks indicates that the widow made no payment for the cornmeal."

"Then if William paid off the debt," Eleanor said, "the Hopkinses have no claim on the mill or the land."

"This William fellow didn't pay back Isaac," Daniel insisted. "So it doesn't matter one whit what William did."

"Mr. Goodhue," Rob interrupted. "I think it is obvious from both the facts and the statement in the diary that Mr. Hopkins' intent was not to own the gristmill. County records clearly indicate the Emersons have paid property taxes each and every year since the earliest records, which is reason enough to establish their ownership. And, as we all know, possession is nine-tenths of the —"

"I disagree," Daniel's young attorney interrupted. "Mr. Hopkins has presented a valid bill of sale. That the transfer of title was not recorded does not change the facts. Isaac Emerson, in good faith and in exchange for value, sold the mill to James Hopkins. The mill should therefore rightfully belong to the descendants of James Hopkins."

Everyone on both sides of the table started talking at once, shouting to be heard over one another.

Feeling like a traitor, Mary returned the diary and ledger to her tote. She prayed Betty would forgive her, although she knew it might take time.

Meanwhile, Daniel was looking ever so proud of himself. Although the arbitrator hadn't ruled yet, Daniel looked confident he'd won.

But why does he want that run-down mill? she wondered yet again.

She leaned forward. "Daniel, what do you plan to do with the mill?"

He cut her a look. "What's it matter to you?"

"I'm curious. And I think the Emersons deserve an answer."

He wiped the back of his hand across his mouth. "I know a guy who wants that land. He's gonna build some fancy condos. He'll turn a pretty penny on the deal, but he's gonna pay me a bundle first."

Betty gasped, and Evan put his arm around his mother's shoulders.

Mary tilted her head in thought. "Have you spoken to the city planning department about the condo idea?"

"Nope. No need to. My buddy will take care of that."

"Maybe not, Daniel." She told him and the others about the zoning restrictions. "Your friend won't be able to build anything on that land, so he isn't going to buy the land. Instead, you'll probably have to pay to tear down the mill because it's a public hazard. That will cost you a lot of money."

"Thousands of dollars, according to the estimate I got," Evan added.

Daniel snarled at her. "That's another one of your lies."

"No, it isn't." Mary checked up and down the table. Harry Hopkins seemed like a reasonable man. Certainly his wife was.

She turned to the arbitrator. "If I may, I have a suggestion that may satisfy both parties in this matter without costing either of them a great deal of money."

"I'm all ears, Mrs. Fisher."

She acknowledged his permission with a slight dip of her head. "Assuming Mr. Goodhue will be ruling in Mr. Hopkins' favor, Daniel will find himself liable for the destruction of an unsafe building. Meanwhile, the Emersons will lose a beloved part of their heritage. I'm sure you've all heard the story of Solomon in the Bible when he was confronted by two women who both claimed to be the mother of a certain baby."

Everyone nodded, except Daniel, who continued to look at her with suspicion and distrust.

"Solomon, in his wisdom, decided that since the women could not reach an agreement, he would cut the baby in half. The baby's real mother immediately stepped forward and pleaded with Solomon to give the baby to the other woman so her child could live, even though she'd lose him to another. While our current situation isn't quite the same as the one Solomon faced, I think we can apply his wisdom to resolve this."

The Hopkinses glanced at one another. Goodhue seemed willing to listen.

"I have not revealed to Mr. Hopkins that I found something in the mill in addition to the ledger. Hidden behind a false wall, I discovered some valuable coins and a British uniform."

"If they were in the mill, they're mine," Daniel blustered, his determination twisting his features into an ugly mask. "You can turn them over to me right now."

"I think not, Daniel. The coins are dated 1775, well before Isaac needed money to feed his family and sold the mill to your ancestor. Therefore, the coins and British uniform from the Revolutionary War belong to my sister. Their combined value is such that it would provide a very good start for restoring the mill."

Evan confirmed that would be true.

"What if I just want to tear it down?" Daniel asked.

"Then you would be liable for the cost, wouldn't you?" Mary replied blandly. "But if you and the Emerson family could share in the ownership and operation of the mill, then the Emersons can restore it, and the mill might become known as the Emerson-Hopkins gristmill in Ivy Bay and would probably be listed as a registered historic landmark."

Shaking his head, Daniel muttered under his breath again.

Betty said, "Oh, I don't think that would work at all."

Mary looked to Goodhue for help.

"Ladies and gentlemen, Mrs. Fisher has proposed a very interesting compromise, which I feel has a great deal of merit. I think each side should take a minute to consider her suggestion."

Daniel, his grandson, and their attorney huddled on the opposite side of the table.

Betty, Evan, Eleanor, and Rob Dunlap did the same on the Emerson side. Mary sat staring off into the distance, worried about what she had done and the effect it would have on her sister and their relationship.

Lincoln touched her arm. "Well done, Mary. A smart solution, in my mind. A fine old building restored, and no harm done to either side. Your efforts would set an example for others in the antiquities business."

She thanked Lincoln, but her heart still ached.

The discussion between Daniel and his grandson grew heated. After a bit, Daniel stood and slammed his chair back against the wall. "Do any fool thing you want. I wash my hands of the whole thing. It's your worry now." He snatched the bill of sale, slapped it down in front of Harry, and stormed out the door.

After a quiet moment, Harry said, "I apologize for my grandfather. He shouldn't have made such a scene. He's been pretty emotional about the mill."

"No need to apologize," Goodhue said. "But since your grandfather has left matters in your hands, we'd be interested to know what your decision is."

Harry took his wife's hand. "Jill and I don't have any interest in tearing down the old mill. But it sounds like we have some responsibility toward the place since somehow we seem to own it now." He looked directly at Betty. "Seems to me our two families were close at one time, then things sort of got out of hand and a feud started up. I think if we could work together, our kids would be right proud to have the

Hopkins name on the mill beside the Emersons."

"I agree with my husband," Jill said, directing her words to Mary. "I think the Lord had a hand in you finding a solution we can all live with."

Jill's support meant a lot to Mary, and she smiled in gratitude. "I have some information about that feud, if you'd like to hear it," Mary said.

Harry glanced at Jill, who nodded.

"From what I understand, Caleb Hopkins went missing the night of the October gale in 1841. Over time, some members of the community, probably someone in the Hopkins family, began to blame William Emerson for Caleb's death. As I can best reconstruct what happened, Caleb — who had been drinking at the Horse Head Tavern, which was close to the mill — argued with William and probably followed him home.

"The rain was coming down very hard; visibility must have been poor. Caleb made a misstep and fell in the race by the mill. Few fishermen at that time could swim, so he was dragged out to sea. His official cause of death, according to the funeral home in Provincetown where his body washed up sometime later, was accidental drowning." She passed a copy of the report across the table. "For the sake of family harmony, it's worth considering."

"And that's what my grandfather's been raging on about all these years?" Harry asked.

"I'm afraid so."

The young man blew out a sigh and looked at Betty. "So what do you think, Mrs. Emerson? Can we work together on this?"

Her features were strained and her eyes puffy. "I think it's high time that the Emerson and Hopkins families put the past behind them, Harry." She produced a wavering smile for him and Jill. "And I think Elizabeth Emerson and Martha Hopkins would be the first to tell us so."

NINETEEN

The mid-September weather cooperated to provide a perfect day for the Ivy Bay Historic Walking Tour.

Tourists began to wander into the bookshop starting about two o'clock. Ashley faithfully stamped the walking tour tickets as the guests entered. Rebecca had made her daughter a colonial costume with a puffy white hat.

Mary, whose costuming effort was limited to a long cotton skirt and blouse, provided commentary for those who were interested in the building's history.

"This building was constructed over two hundred years ago using handmade bricks. For those of you who know something about bricks, these are slightly smaller than the current standard size."

At this point in her talk, one man actually got out a measuring tape and started measuring the bricks. Mary couldn't help but smile.

"Until recently, the building housed the town's archives, all the property records, titles and transfers, and tax records. That information is now stored in the county clerk's office down the street."

Mary intentionally skipped the history of her own uncle George having an auction house in this building. The details of that were too complicated to relate in a few short minutes. "Before that, this was an apothecary. We have several books on the history of Ivy Bay and Cape Cod."

Mary had made sure she had a full display on hand. "Plus we have replicas of early plot maps of the town and surrounding area."

As she finished her general talk, she chatted informally with visitors and invited them to help themselves to punch and cookies on the back patio.

By late afternoon, her voice was giving out and she was curious to see how the tour was going elsewhere. She left Rebecca to handle the tour-guide role and stepped outside.

The sidewalks were even more crowded with pedestrians than on a typical summer weekend, many of them checking the maps Jerry Avakian had printed for the tour.

She walked across the street to Gems and Antiques, only to find the store so crowded she couldn't get in the door.

After checking a few more shops, the owners happy with the number of visitors they'd had and accompanying sales they'd made, Mary decided to check on Dorothy Johnson.

Because of the line waiting to enter Dorothy's house, Mary slipped around to the rear of the house and entered via the back door. She followed the sound of Dorothy's voice to the great room. Dorothy was dressed in fine Victorian style; her gown had a voluminous skirt, snug bodice trimmed in lace and ribbon, and wide pagoda sleeves. Even her shoes were period style, white kid with side-laced boots. She was talking to a group of tourists.

"When guests arrive, they are greeted in the foyer and then escorted into what is called a great room, which you might call a living room." She gestured with a gloved hand at the paintings on the wall. "All these paintings are original oils, many by local artists. There are several fine galleries in Ivy Bay and elsewhere on the Cape that you might wish to visit."

Mary spotted Henry and eased across the room to stand next to him. "How is it going?"

He grinned and winked. "I've rarely seen Dorothy this happy. She's eating up all the attention."

Mary smiled back at him. "I'm glad. Looks like her house is a popular stop on the tour." She listened as Dorothy talked so proudly about her 1892 home for a few more minutes. Among the crowd, she spotted Lincoln in his dark raincoat. She smiled, and he nodded in return.

"Be sure Dorothy makes it to the special committee meeting tonight," she whispered to Henry. "Jerry Avakian will have a check for her."

"So soon?"

"He's already tallied the expenses, so once the ticket sales are added, we'll know what the profit will be."

Henry glanced toward Dorothy. "I'll be sure she gets there. She's going to be very surprised. Earlier today, she told me she was thinking about selling her house and moving into a condo."

"Now she won't have to." Mary let herself out the back, the same way she had come in. She wanted to visit the mill to see how Betty, Evan, and the Hopkinses were getting along. Betty had been cool toward her since the hearing. That worried Mary. Would their relationship ever return to the warmth they'd had before the deposition?

Evan had created a very nice display of the old gristmill photos, plus he'd mounted an artist's rendering of what the Emerson-Hopkins gristmill would look like after restoration.

Apparently, there hadn't been any need to worry about the two families getting along. Betty and Jill Sanderson were passing out pieces of cornmeal-mush bread made from an original colonial recipe. Meanwhile, Daniel, dressed in his fisherman's overalls, was strutting around explaining how people lived in the 1600s as if he'd been there himself.

Mary plucked a piece of bread from Betty's tray. "Are you doing all right here?"

"We are." She glanced around at a crowd of maybe twenty people who were examining the photos. "Do you know the best part of this?"

"The money we're raising for Dorothy?"

"That, too, but I was thinking about the feud between the Emersons and Hopkinses." She gestured toward Evan, who was talking to Harry Hopkins like they were old buddies. "Whatever misunderstandings and hurt feelings there were between the two families is now in the past. The feud is over."

That news warmed Mary's heart, but she

still wondered how Betty felt about her and the revelation about mill ownership at the deposition. They hadn't really talked about the meeting yet or its outcome.

"You're the one who ended the feud, Mary." Betty set her tray down on a table. "I owe you an apology for being so upset during the deposition. You found out the truth and you had to tell us. It was the right thing to do. The Christian thing to do."

Tears filled Mary's eyes. "I was so worried you'd resent me, Bets. I didn't know what to do."

The sisters fell into each other's arms, hugging and crying, without saying a word. Their family ties were too strong for a dispute over an ancient mill to break them apart.

The special meeting of the walking tour committee was called for eight o'clock at the bookshop. As the members squeezed inside, they were all jabbering about the success of the event and talking about repeating it next year.

Dorothy arrived, still in her costume, which now looked a little rumpled, as did her blonde hair. She and Betty took seats in the comfortable chairs at the back of the shop.

"All right, everyone." Mary waved her hand for attention. "I know you're excited about our success, but it's getting late. We have one big chore left to do. We have to vote on who should receive the proceeds from the tour in order to restore a historic building in Ivy Bay. Do I have a nomination?"

Betty's hand shot up as she and her sister had planned. "I nominate Dorothy Johnson and her exquisite 1892 Victorian."

Dorothy's eyes registered surprise, and she opened her mouth to say something, but she was cut off by Benjamin. "I second that."

"All in favor?"

A chorus of ayes carried the unanimous vote.

"But —" Dorothy protested, her cheeks flushing.

"Jerry, would you please present Dorothy with her check?"

"Happy to." He held up the check and announced the amount. Everyone except Dorothy, whose jaw seemed to have come loose, cheered. "Because of your outstanding contribution to the success of the walking tour, I'm proud to hand you the check for the proceeds, with the committee's deepest thanks."

With a trembling hand, Dorothy took the check with just two fingers as though it might burn her. "I didn't . . . I had no idea."

"You weren't supposed to know," Jerry said.

Blinking back tears, Dorothy looked up at Mary. "You did this, didn't you?"

"We all did it together, Dorothy. You're an important part of this community, and your home is part of Ivy Bay's history."

Tears began to spill down Dorothy's cheeks, and Mary realized that by sharing the Lord's grace with Dorothy, she had received the greater gift of His love.

By the time Betty and Mary got home, it was ten o'clock. Both of them slipped off their shoes the moment they stepped inside the house.

"I don't know about you," Mary said, "but I'm exhausted. I could sleep for a week."

"You'd deserve it. You pulled the tour together in record time."

"I had a lot of people helping, including you." She picked up her shoes. "Well, I'm off to bed."

"Me too." Betty turned toward her room and immediately halted. "Oh, I forgot to tell you the most interesting thing I learned about the mill tonight." Her eyes glittered with the hint of a secret to be shared.

"What's that?"

"Daniel and I were talking earlier this afternoon. He told me he'd wanted the mill land to sell to that developer, but he never intended to get rid of the buhrstone."

"Why on earth not? What was he planning to do with it?"

"If you can imagine, Daniel wanted to keep the buhrstone for sentimental reasons. He'd proposed to his wife one Sunday afternoon when they'd walked up to the mill. He'd been courting her for some time. After she said yes, he carved their initials in the stone."

Ironically, it was the same place where Edward had proposed to Betty. Although when Mary mentally tried to picture Daniel doing something so romantic, the image failed to appear. "Their initials?"

"He showed me. He'd carved 'DH + JC' inside a heart. Isn't that sweet?"

Mary's brain struggled to process what Betty had said. "Maybe that explains why he always seemed to be at the mill when I showed up. He was visiting the spot where he'd proposed to his wife. He wasn't looking for the treasure at all." She gasped when another thought occurred to her. "One time when he was leaving, he patted that old stone with his hand. A loving caress where he had carved their initials, perhaps."

"Entirely possible."

"Goodness! Who knew that cranky old man was a secret romantic?" She shook her head and laughed. "I misjudged him terribly, didn't I?"

"I'm afraid we all did." She hugged Mary. "But now we know he was doing all he could to cover up the fact that he's lonely. I think maybe I'll invite him to go to church with us one of these days. Maybe we can coax Henry into getting Daniel active in the men's group."

Mary chuckled. "Betty Emerson, you are one of a kind and so dear to me; I don't know what I'd do without you."

"You know," Betty said quietly, "I think Edward would be pleased how this has all worked out, both for the families and the mill."

"I do too, Bets."

They hugged again. Then it was time for them both to get a good night's sleep. Mary suspected it wouldn't be long before another mystery popped up.

A CONVERSATION WITH CHARLOTTE CARTER

Q: *What draws you to Mary's Bookshop as a writer?*

A: I live in Southern California, and I've never visited Cape Cod. It was wonderful to learn more about the beauty of that area. I see a trip to the "real" Ivy Bay in my future.

Q: *Which character in the series do you most relate to?*

A: I loved writing about Mary, a mature woman who is an amateur sleuth and good at it too. She'd make a good role model for our younger friends.

Q: *If you could open a bookshop anywhere, where would it be? And what kind of bookshop would it be?*

A: I'd open a bookshop on the beach in Redondo Beach, California. The only problem I'd have would be responsibly staying in the shop instead of taking a book out on the beach to read while watching the waves lapping against the shore. The book might be romance, adventure, suspense, or even a good biography.

On second thought, maybe I'd have my bookstore in the mountains. The scent of pine trees and the wind whispering through the treetops. . . .

Q: *What is your favorite mystery book/author? Why?*

A: I read most of James Patterson's books and particularly enjoy the Women's Murder Club series.

Q: *Have you ever had to solve a mystery? Tell us about it.*

A: The biggest mysteries my husband and I ever solve are finding an important paper that we've put down somewhere, where we've left our dark glasses, and discovering what happened this time to the little pocketknife he carries in his pants pocket. Guess we live a pretty quiet life!

Q: *Mary loves to make new ice-cream flavors and enjoys reading mystery novels. What are some of your hobbies?*

A: I've never been good at crafts; my feet

perspire when I knit. So I write and read, a lot, and sometimes I perform stand-up comedy. Having an audience laugh at my jokes is a wonderful experience.

Q: *Mary's two favorite confidants are her sister Betty and her old friend Henry. Who are your greatest confidants?*

A: I've fairly recently reconnected with a few of my high school friends, which has been great fun. I have another group of friends who I worked with in the late 1950s. We get together three or four times a year for lunch. And, not surprisingly, I have made exceptionally good friends through my writing group.

Q: *Please tell us about your family!*

A: I'm particularly proud of my grand-children. (No surprise there, huh?) Our oldest granddaughter is in college on a full-ride volleyball scholarship. Our oldest grandson, still in high school, performs in a group that provides youth programs at church camps all across California. The three youngest boys all have special talents that they're developing to match their older siblings.

CRANBERRY-BANANA JAM

Since there are cranberry bogs in Ivy Bay, I so wanted Mary to make some cranberry-banana jam, a recipe I picked up when my husband and I were living in Anchorage, Alaska. But the season was wrong in *Reading the Clues.* But I'll share the recipe with you anyway. The bananas take the tang out of the cranberries, making for a delicious addition to your toast or bagel.

3 cups cranberries
1 cup mashed banana
7 cups sugar
1 package of Certo or other fruit pectin

Clean and sterilize your canning equipment. In a large saucepan, combine the cranberries, banana, and sugar. Bring to a rolling boil on high heat, stirring constantly. Stir in the pectin. Remove from heat and run a metal spoon over the top to skim off any foam. Ladle the mixture into prepared jars, leaving 1/8 of an inch of room. Wipe jars and cover with lids; screw on tightly. Lower jars into your canner. Add boiling water — make sure water covers the jars by two inches. Cover and bring water to a gentle boil. Leave for ten minutes. Remove and cool jars.

ABOUT THE AUTHOR

An author of more than fifty romance, cozy mystery, and inspirational titles, **Charlotte Carter** lives in Southern California with her husband of fifty years and their cat, Mittens — an equal-opportunity lap cat. They have two married daughters and five grandchildren. When she's not writing, Charlotte does a little stand-up comedy — G-rated humor for grown-ups — and teaches workshops on the craft of writing.

Visit her Web site at www.CharlotteCarter.com.

The employees of Thorndike Press hope you have enjoyed this Large Print book. All our Thorndike, Wheeler, and Kennebec Large Print titles are designed for easy reading, and all our books are made to last. Other Thorndike Press Large Print books are available at your library, through selected bookstores, or directly from us.

For information about titles, please call:
(800) 223-1244

or visit our Web site at:
http://gale.cengage.com/thorndike

To share your comments, please write:
Publisher
Thorndike Press
10 Water St., Suite 310
Waterville, ME 04901

I

On an exceptionally hot evening early in July a young man came out of the garret in which he lodged in S—— Place and walked slowly, as though in hesitation, towards K—— bridge.

He had successfully avoided meeting his landlady on the staircase. His garret was under the roof of a high, five-storied house and was more like a cupboard than a room. The landlady who provided him with garret, dinners, and attendance, lived on the floor below, and every time he went out he was obliged to pass her kitchen, the door of which invariably stood open. And each time he passed, the young man had a sick, frightened feeling, which made him scowl and feel ashamed. He was hopelessly in debt to his landlady, and was afraid of meeting her.

This was not because he was cowardly and abject, quite the contrary; but for some time past he had been in an overstrained irritable condition, verging on hypochondria. He had become so completely absorbed in himself, and isolated from his fellows that he dreaded meeting, not only his landlady, but anyone at all. He was crushed by poverty, but the anxieties of his position had of late ceased to weigh upon him. He had given up attending to matters of practical importance; he had lost all desire to do so. Nothing that any landlady could do had a real terror for him. But to be stopped on the stairs, to be forced to listen to her trivial, irrelevant gossip, to pestering demands for payment, threats and complaints, and to rack his brains for excuses, to prevaricate, to lie—no, rather than that, he would creep down the stairs like a cat and slip out unseen.

This evening, however, on coming out into the street, he became acutely aware of his fears.

"I want to attempt a thing *like that* and am frightened by these trifles," he thought, with an odd smile. "Hm... yes, all is in a man's hands and he lets it all slip from cowardice, that's an axiom. It would be interesting to know what it is men are most afraid of. Taking a new step, uttering a new word is what they fear most.... But I am talking too much. It's because I chatter that I do nothing. Or perhaps it is that I chatter because I do nothing. I've learned to chatter this last month, lying for days together in my den thinking... of Jack the Giant-killer. Why am I going there now? Am I capable of *that*? Is *that* serious? It is not serious at all. It's simply a fantasy to amuse myself; a plaything! Yes, maybe it is a plaything."

The heat in the street was terrible: and the airlessness, the bustle and the plaster, scaffolding, bricks, and dust all about him, and that special Petersburg stench, so familiar to all who are unable to get out of town in summer—all worked painfully upon the young man's already overwrought nerves. The insufferable stench from the pothouses, which are particularly numerous in that part of the town, and the drunken men whom he met continually, although it was a working day, completed the revolting misery of the picture. An expression of the profoundest disgust gleamed for a moment in the young man's refined face. He was, by the way, exceptionally handsome, above the average in height, slim, well-built, with beautiful dark eyes and dark brown hair. Soon he sank into deep thought, or more accurately speaking into a complete blankness of mind; he walked along not observing what was about him and not caring to observe it. From time to time, he would mutter something, from the habit of talking to himself, to which he had just confessed. At these moments he would become conscious that his ideas were sometimes in a tangle and that he was very weak; for two days he had scarcely tasted food.

He was so badly dressed that even a man accustomed to shabbiness would have been ashamed to be seen in the street in such rags. In that quarter of the town, however, scarcely any shortcoming in dress would have created surprise. Owing to the proximity of the Hay Market, the number of establishments of bad character, the preponderance of the trading and working class population crowded in these streets and alleys in the heart of Petersburg, types so various were to be seen in the streets that no figure, however queer, would have caused surprise. But there was such accumulated bitterness and contempt in the young man's heart, that, in spite of all the fastidiousness of youth, he minded his rags least of all in the street. It was a different matter when he met with acquaintances or with former fellow students, whom, indeed, he disliked meeting at any time. And yet when a drunken man who, for some unknown reason, was being taken somewhere in a huge wagon dragged by a heavy dray horse, suddenly shouted at him as he drove past: "Hey there, German hatter" bawling at the top of his voice and pointing at him—the young man stopped suddenly and clutched tremulously at his hat. It was a tall round hat from Zimmerman's, but completely worn out, rusty with age, all torn and bespattered, brimless and bent on one side in a most unseemly fashion. Not shame, however, but quite another feeling akin to terror had overtaken him.

"I knew it," he muttered in confusion, "I thought so! That's the worst of all! Why, a stupid thing like this, the most trivial detail might spoil the whole plan. Yes, my hat is too noticeable.... It looks absurd and that makes it noticeable.... With my rags I ought to wear a cap, any sort of old pancake, but not this grotesque thing. Nobody wears such a hat, it would be noticed a mile off, it would be remembered.... What matters is that people would remember it, and that would give them a clue. For this business one should be as little conspicuous as possible.... Trifles, trifles are what matter! Why, it's just such trifles that always ruin everything...."

He had not far to go; he knew indeed how many steps it was from the gate of his lodging house: exactly seven hundred and thirty. He had counted them once when he had been lost in dreams. At the time he had put no faith in those dreams and was only tantalising himself by their hideous but daring recklessness. Now, a month later, he had begun to look upon them differently, and, in spite of the monologues in which he jeered at his own impotence and indecision, he had involuntarily come to regard this "hideous" dream as an exploit to be attempted, although he still did not realise this himself. He was positively going now for a "rehearsal" of his project, and at every step his excitement grew more and more violent.

With a sinking heart and a nervous tremor, he went up to a huge house which on one side looked on to the canal, and on the other into the street. This house was let out in tiny tenements and was inhabited by working people of all kinds—tailors, locksmiths, cooks, Germans of sorts, girls picking up a living as best they could, petty clerks, etc. There was a continual coming and going through the two gates and in the two courtyards of the house. Three or four doorkeepers were employed on the building. The young man was very glad to meet none of them, and at once slipped unnoticed through the door on the right, and up the staircase. It was a back staircase, dark and narrow, but he was familiar with it already, and knew his way, and he liked all these surroundings: in such darkness even the most inquisitive eyes were not to be dreaded.

"If I am so scared now, what would it be if it somehow came to pass that I were really going to do it?" he could not help asking himself as he reached the fourth storey. There his progress was barred by some porters who were engaged in moving furniture out of a flat. He knew that the flat had been occupied by a German clerk in the civil service, and his family. This German was moving out then, and so the fourth floor on this staircase would be untenanted except by the old woman. "That's a good thing anyway," he thought to himself, as he rang the bell of the old woman's flat. The bell gave a faint tinkle as though it were made of tin and not of copper. The little flats in such houses always have bells that ring like that. He had forgotten the note of that bell, and now its peculiar tinkle seemed to remind him of something and to bring it clearly before him.... He started, his nerves were terribly overstrained by now. In a little while, the door was opened a tiny crack: the old woman eyed her visitor with evident distrust through the crack, and nothing could be seen but her little eyes, glittering in the darkness. But, seeing a number of people on the landing, she grew bolder, and opened the door wide. The young man stepped into the dark entry, which was partitioned off from the tiny kitchen. The old woman stood facing him in silence and looking inquiringly at him. She was a diminutive, withered up old woman of sixty, with sharp malignant eyes and a sharp little nose. Her colourless, somewhat grizzled hair was thickly smeared with oil, and she wore no kerchief over it. Round her thin long neck, which looked like a

2

hen's leg, was knotted some sort of flannel rag, and, in spite of the heat, there hung flapping on her shoulders, a mangy fur cape, yellow with age. The old woman coughed and groaned at every instant. The young man must have looked at her with a rather peculiar expression, for a gleam of mistrust came into her eyes again.

"Raskolnikov, a student, I came here a month ago," the young man made haste to mutter, with a half bow, remembering that he ought to be more polite.

"I remember, my good sir, I remember quite well your coming here," the old woman said distinctly, still keeping her inquiring eyes on his face.

"And here… I am again on the same errand," Raskolnikov continued, a little disconcerted and surprised at the old woman's mistrust. "Perhaps she is always like that though, only I did not notice it the other time," he thought with an uneasy feeling.

The old woman paused, as though hesitating; then stepped on one side, and pointing to the door of the room, she said, letting her visitor pass in front of her:

"Step in, my good sir."

The little room into which the young man walked, with yellow paper on the walls, geraniums and muslin curtains in the windows, was brightly lighted up at that moment by the setting sun.

"So the sun will shine like this *then* too!" flashed as it were by chance through Raskolnikov's mind, and with a rapid glance he scanned everything in the room, trying as far as possible to notice and remember its arrangement. But there was nothing special in the room. The furniture, all very old and of yellow wood, consisted of a sofa with a huge bent wooden back, an oval table in front of the sofa, a dressing-table with a looking-glass fixed on it between the windows, chairs along the walls and two or three halfpenny prints in yellow frames, representing German damsels with birds in their hands—that was all. In the corner a light was burning before a small icon. Everything was very clean; the floor and the furniture were brightly polished; everything shone.

"Lizaveta's work," thought the young man. There was not a speck of dust to be seen in the whole flat.

"It's in the houses of spiteful old widows that one finds such cleanliness," Raskolnikov thought again, and he stole a curious glance at the cotton curtain over the door leading into another tiny room, in which stood the old woman's bed and chest of drawers and into which he had never looked before. These two rooms made up the whole flat.

"What do you want?" the old woman said severely, coming into the room and, as before, standing in front of him so as to look him straight in the face.

"I've brought something to pawn here," and he drew out of his pocket an old-fashioned flat silver watch, on the back of which was engraved a globe; the chain was of steel.

"But the time is up for your last pledge. The month was up the day before yesterday."

"I will bring you the interest for another month; wait a little."

"But that's for me to do as I please, my good sir, to wait or to sell your pledge at once."

"How much will you give me for the watch, Alyona Ivanovna?"

"You come with such trifles, my good sir, it's scarcely worth anything. I gave you two roubles last time for your ring and one could buy it quite new at a jeweler's for a rouble and a half."

"Give me four roubles for it, I shall redeem it, it was my father's. I shall be getting some money soon."

"A rouble and a half, and interest in advance, if you like!"

"A rouble and a half!" cried the young man.

"Please yourself"—and the old woman handed him back the watch. The young man took it, and was so angry that he was on the point of going away; but checked himself at once, remembering that there was nowhere else he could go, and that he had had another object also in coming.

"Hand it over," he said roughly.

The old woman fumbled in her pocket for her keys, and disappeared behind the curtain into the other room. The young man, left standing alone in the middle of the room, listened inquisitively, thinking. He could hear her unlocking the chest of drawers.

"It must be the top drawer," he reflected. "So she carries the keys in a pocket on the right. All in one bunch on a steel ring.… And there's one key there, three times as big as all the others, with

3

deep notches; that can't be the key of the chest of drawers... then there must be some other chest or strongbox... that's worth knowing. Strongboxes always have keys like that... but how degrading it all is."

The old woman came back.

"Here, sir: as we say ten kopecks the rouble a month, so I must take fifteen kopecks from a rouble and a half for the month in advance. But for the two roubles I lent you before, you owe me now twenty kopecks on the same reckoning in advance. That makes thirty-five kopecks altogether. So I must give you a rouble and fifteen kopecks for the watch. Here it is."

"What! only a rouble and fifteen kopecks now!"

"Just so."

The young man did not dispute it and took the money. He looked at the old woman, and was in no hurry to get away, as though there was still something he wanted to say or to do, but he did not himself quite know what.

"I may be bringing you something else in a day or two, Alyona Ivanovna—a valuable thing—silver—a cigarette-box, as soon as I get it back from a friend..." he broke off in confusion.

"Well, we will talk about it then, sir."

"Goodbye—are you always at home alone, your sister is not here with you?" He asked her as casually as possible as he went out into the passage.

"What business is she of yours, my good sir?"

"Oh, nothing particular, I simply asked. You are too quick.... Good day, Alyona Ivanovna."

Raskolnikov went out in complete confusion. This confusion became more and more intense. As he went down the stairs, he even stopped short, two or three times, as though suddenly struck by some thought. When he was in the street he cried out, "Oh, God, how loathsome it all is! and can I, can I possibly.... No, it's nonsense, it's rubbish!" he added resolutely. "And how could such an atrocious thing come into my head? What filthy things my heart is capable of. Yes, filthy above all, disgusting, loathsome, loathsome!—and for a whole month I've been...." But no words, no exclamations, could express his agitation. The feeling of intense repulsion, which had begun to oppress and torture his heart while he was on his way to the old woman, had by now reached such a pitch and had taken such a definite form that he did not know what to do with himself to escape from his wretchedness. He walked along the pavement like a drunken man, regardless of the passersby, and jostling against them, and only came to his senses when he was in the next street. Looking round, he noticed that he was standing close to a tavern which was entered by steps leading from the pavement to the basement. At that instant two drunken men came out at the door, and abusing and supporting one another, they mounted the steps. Without stopping to think, Raskolnikov went down the steps at once. Till that moment he had never been into a tavern, but now he felt giddy and was tormented by a burning thirst. He longed for a drink of cold beer, and attributed his sudden weakness to the want of food. He sat down at a sticky little table in a dark and dirty corner; ordered some beer, and eagerly drank off the first glassful. At once he felt easier; and his thoughts became clear.

"All that's nonsense," he said hopefully, "and there is nothing in it all to worry about! It's simply physical derangement. Just a glass of beer, a piece of dry bread—and in one moment the brain is stronger, the mind is clearer and the will is firm! Phew, how utterly petty it all is!"

But in spite of this scornful reflection, he was by now looking cheerful as though he were suddenly set free from a terrible burden: and he gazed round in a friendly way at the people in the room. But even at that moment he had a dim foreboding that this happier frame of mind was also not normal.

There were few people at the time in the tavern. Besides the two drunken men he had met on the steps, a group consisting of about five men and a girl with a concertina had gone out at the same time. Their departure left the room quiet and rather empty. The persons still in the tavern were a man who appeared to be an artisan, drunk, but not extremely so, sitting before a pot of beer, and his companion, a huge, stout man with a grey beard, in a short full-skirted coat. He was very drunk: and had dropped asleep on the bench; every now and then, he began as though in his sleep, cracking his fingers, with his arms wide apart and the upper part of his body bounding

4

about on the bench, while he hummed some meaningless refrain, trying to recall some such lines as these:
"His wife a year he fondly loved

His wife a—a year he—fondly loved."
Or suddenly waking up again:
"Walking along the crowded row

He met the one he used to know."
But no one shared his enjoyment: his silent companion looked with positive hostility and mistrust at all these manifestations. There was another man in the room who looked somewhat like a retired government clerk. He was sitting apart, now and then sipping from his pot and looking round at the company. He, too, appeared to be in some agitation.

Raskolnikov was not used to crowds, and, as we said before, he avoided society of every sort, more especially of late. But now all at once he felt a desire to be with other people. Something new seemed to be taking place within him, and with it he felt a sort of thirst for company. He was so weary after a whole month of concentrated wretchedness and gloomy excitement that he longed to rest, if only for a moment, in some other world, whatever it might be; and, in spite of the filthiness of the surroundings, he was glad now to stay in the tavern.

The master of the establishment was in another room, but he frequently came down some steps into the main room, his jaunty, tarred boots with red turnover tops coming into view each time before the rest of his person. He wore a full coat and a horribly greasy black satin waistcoat, with no cravat, and his whole face seemed smeared with oil like an iron lock. At the counter stood a boy of about fourteen, and there was another boy somewhat younger who handed whatever was wanted. On the counter lay some sliced cucumber, some pieces of dried black bread, and some fish, chopped up small, all smelling very bad. It was insufferably close, and so heavy with the fumes of spirits that five minutes in such an atmosphere might well make a man drunk.

There are chance meetings with strangers that interest us from the first moment, before a word is spoken. Such was the impression made on Raskolnikov by the person sitting a little distance from him, who looked like a retired clerk. The young man often recalled this impression afterwards, and even ascribed it to presentiment. He looked repeatedly at the clerk, partly no doubt because the latter was staring persistently at him, obviously anxious to enter into conversation. At the other persons in the room, including the tavern-keeper, the clerk looked as though he were used to their company, and weary of it, showing a shade of condescending contempt for them as persons of station and culture inferior to his own, with whom it would be useless for him to converse. He was a man over fifty, bald and grizzled, of medium height, and stoutly built. His face, bloated from continual drinking, was of a yellow, even greenish, tinge, with swollen eyelids out of which keen reddish eyes gleamed like little chinks. But there was something very strange in him; there was a light in his eyes as though of intense feeling—perhaps there were even thought and intelligence, but at the same time there was a gleam of something like madness. He was wearing an old and hopelessly ragged black dress coat, with all its buttons missing except one, and that one he had buttoned, evidently clinging to this last trace of respectability. A crumpled shirt front, covered with spots and stains, protruded from his canvas waistcoat. Like a clerk, he wore no beard, nor moustache, but had been so long unshaven that his chin looked like a stiff greyish brush. And there was something respectable and like an official about his manner too. But he was restless; he ruffled up his hair and from time to time let his head drop into his hands dejectedly resting his ragged elbows on the stained and sticky table. At last he looked straight at Raskolnikov, and said loudly and resolutely:

"May I venture, honoured sir, to engage you in polite conversation? Forasmuch as, though your exterior would not command respect, my experience admonishes me that you are a man of education and not accustomed to drinking. I have always respected education when in conjunction with genuine sentiments, and I am besides a titular counsellor in rank. Marmeladov—such is my name; titular counsellor. I make bold to inquire—have you been in the service?"

"No, I am studying," answered the young man, somewhat surprised at the grandiloquent style of the speaker and also at being so directly addressed. In spite of the momentary desire he had just been feeling for company of any sort, on being actually spoken to he felt immediately his habitual irritable and uneasy aversion for any stranger who approached or attempted to approach him.

"A student then, or formerly a student," cried the clerk. "Just what I thought! I'm a man of experience, immense experience, sir," and he tapped his forehead with his fingers in self-approval. "You've been a student or have attended some learned institution!... But allow me...." He got up, staggered, took up his jug and glass, and sat down beside the young man, facing him a little sideways. He was drunk, but spoke fluently and boldly, only occasionally losing the thread of his sentences and drawling his words. He pounced upon Raskolnikov as greedily as though he too had not spoken to a soul for a month.

"Honoured sir," he began almost with solemnity, "poverty is not a vice, that's a true saying. Yet I know too that drunkenness is not a virtue, and that that's even truer. But beggary, honoured sir, beggary is a vice. In poverty you may still retain your innate nobility of soul, but in beggary—never—no one. For beggary a man is not chased out of human society with a stick, he is swept out with a broom, so as to make it as humiliating as possible; and quite right, too, forasmuch as in beggary I am ready to be the first to humiliate myself. Hence the pothouse! Honoured sir, a month ago Mr. Lebeziatnikov gave my wife a beating, and my wife is a very different matter from me! Do you understand? Allow me to ask you another question out of simple curiosity: have you ever spent a night on a hay barge, on the Neva?"

"No, I have not happened to," answered Raskolnikov. "What do you mean?"

"Well, I've just come from one and it's the fifth night I've slept so...." He filled his glass, emptied it and paused. Bits of hay were in fact clinging to his clothes and sticking to his hair. It seemed quite probable that he had not undressed or washed for the last five days. His hands, particularly, were filthy. They were fat and red, with black nails.

His conversation seemed to excite a general though languid interest. The boys at the counter fell to sniggering. The innkeeper came down from the upper room, apparently on purpose to listen to the "funny fellow" and sat down at a little distance, yawning lazily, but with dignity. Evidently Marmeladov was a familiar figure here, and he had most likely acquired his weakness for high-flown speeches from the habit of frequently entering into conversation with strangers of all sorts in the tavern. This habit develops into a necessity in some drunkards, and especially in those who are looked after sharply and kept in order at home. Hence in the company of other drinkers they try to justify themselves and even if possible obtain consideration.

"Funny fellow!" pronounced the innkeeper. "And why don't you work, why aren't you at your duty, if you are in the service?"

"Why am I not at my duty, honoured sir," Marmeladov went on, addressing himself exclusively to Raskolnikov, as though it had been he who put that question to him. "Why am I not at my duty? Does not my heart ache to think what a useless worm I am? A month ago when Mr. Lebeziatnikov beat my wife with his own hands, and I lay drunk, didn't I suffer? Excuse me, young man, has it ever happened to you... hm... well, to petition hopelessly for a loan?"

"Yes, it has. But what do you mean by hopelessly?"

"Hopelessly in the fullest sense, when you know beforehand that you will get nothing by it. You know, for instance, beforehand with positive certainty that this man, this most reputable and exemplary citizen, will on no consideration give you money; and indeed I ask you why should he? For he knows of course that I shan't pay it back. From compassion? But Mr. Lebeziatnikov who keeps up with modern ideas explained the other day that compassion is forbidden nowadays by science itself, and that that's what is done now in England, where there is political economy. Why, I ask you, should he give it to me? And yet though I know beforehand that he won't, I set off to him and..."

"Why do you go?" put in Raskolnikov.

"Well, when one has no one, nowhere else one can go! For every man must have somewhere to go. Since there are times when one absolutely must go somewhere! When my own daughter first went out with a yellow ticket, then I had to go... (for my daughter has a yellow passport)," he added in parenthesis, looking with a certain uneasiness at the young man. "No matter, sir, no matter!" he went on hurriedly and with apparent composure when both the boys at the counter guffawed and even the innkeeper smiled—"No matter, I am not confounded by the wagging of their heads; for everyone knows everything about it already, and all that is secret is made open.

7

And I accept it all, not with contempt, but with humility. So be it! So be it! 'Behold the man!' Excuse me, young man, can you.... No, to put it more strongly and more distinctly; not *can* you but *dare* you, looking upon me, assert that I am not a pig?"

The young man did not answer a word.

"Well," the orator began again stolidly and with even increased dignity, after waiting for the laughter in the room to subside. "Well, so be it, I am a pig, but she is a lady! I have the semblance of a beast, but Katerina Ivanovna, my spouse, is a person of education and an officer's daughter. Granted, granted, I am a scoundrel, but she is a woman of a noble heart, full of sentiments, refined by education. And yet... oh, if only she felt for me! Honoured sir, honoured sir, you know every man ought to have at least one place where people feel for him! But Katerina Ivanovna, though she is magnanimous, she is unjust.... And yet, although I realise that when she pulls my hair she only does it out of pity—for I repeat without being ashamed, she pulls my hair, young man," he declared with redoubled dignity, hearing the sniggering again—"but, my God, if she would but once.... But no, no! It's all in vain and it's no use talking! No use talking! For more than once, my wish did come true and more than once she has felt for me but... such is my fate and I am a beast by nature!"

"Rather!" assented the innkeeper yawning. Marmeladov struck his fist resolutely on the table.

"Such is my fate! Do you know, sir, do you know, I have sold her very stockings for drink? Not her shoes—that would be more or less in the order of things, but her stockings, her stockings I have sold for drink! Her mohair shawl I sold for drink, a present to her long ago, her own property, not mine; and we live in a cold room and she caught cold this winter and has begun coughing and spitting blood too. We have three little children and Katerina Ivanovna is at work from morning till night; she is scrubbing and cleaning and washing the children, for she's been used to cleanliness from a child. But her chest is weak and she has a tendency to consumption and I feel it! Do you suppose I don't feel it? And the more I drink the more I feel it. That's why I drink too. I try to find sympathy and feeling in drink.... I drink so that I may suffer twice as much!" And as though in despair he laid his head down on the table.

"Young man," he went on, raising his head again, "in your face I seem to read some trouble of mind. When you came in I read it, and that was why I addressed you at once. For in unfolding to you the story of my life, I do not wish to make myself a laughingstock before these idle listeners, who indeed know all about it already, but I am looking for a man of feeling and education. Know then that my wife was educated in a high-class school for the daughters of noblemen, and on leaving she danced the shawl dance before the governor and other personages for which she was presented with a gold medal and a certificate of merit. The medal... well, the medal of course was sold—long ago, hm... but the certificate of merit is in her trunk still and not long ago she showed it to our landlady. And although she is most continually on bad terms with the landlady, yet she wanted to tell someone or other of her past honours and of the happy days that are gone. I don't condemn her for it, I don't blame her, for the one thing left her is recollection of the past, and all the rest is dust and ashes. Yes, yes, she is a lady of spirit, proud and determined. She scrubs the floors herself and has nothing but black bread to eat, but won't allow herself to be treated with disrespect. That's why she would not overlook Mr. Lebeziatnikov's rudeness to her, and so when he gave her a beating for it, she took to her bed more from the hurt to her feelings than from the blows. She was a widow when I married her, with three children, one smaller than the other. She married her first husband, an infantry officer, for love, and ran away with him from her father's house. She was exceedingly fond of her husband; but he gave way to cards, got into trouble and with that he died. He used to beat her at the end: and although she paid him back, of which I have authentic documentary evidence, to this day she speaks of him with tears and she throws him up to me; and I am glad, I am glad that, though only in imagination, she should think of herself as having once been happy.... And she was left at his death with three children in a wild and remote district where I happened to be at the time; and she was left in such hopeless poverty that, although I have seen many ups and downs of all sort, I don't feel equal to describing it even. Her relations had all thrown her off. And she was proud, too, excessively proud.... And then, honoured sir, and then, I, being at the time a widower, with a daughter of fourteen left me by my first wife, offered her my hand, for I could not bear the sight of such suffering. You can judge the extremity of her calamities, that she, a woman of education and culture and distinguished family, should have consented to be my wife. But she did! Weeping and sobbing and wringing her hands, she married me! For she had nowhere to turn! Do you understand, sir, do you understand what it means when you have absolutely nowhere to turn? No, that you don't understand yet.... And for a whole year, I performed my duties conscientiously and faithfully, and did not touch this" (he tapped the jug with his finger), "for I have feelings. But even so, I could not please her; and then I lost my place too, and that through no fault of mine but through changes in the office; and then I did touch it! ... It will be a year and a half ago soon since we found ourselves at last after many wanderings and numerous calamities in this magnificent capital, adorned with innumerable monuments. Here I obtained a situation.... I obtained it and I lost it again. Do you understand? This time it was through my own fault I lost it: for my weakness had come out.... We have now part of a room at Amalia Fyodorovna Lippevechsel's; and what we live upon and what we pay our rent with, I could not say. There are a lot of people living there besides ourselves. Dirt and disorder, a perfect Bedlam ... hm ... yes ... And meanwhile my daughter by my first wife has grown up; and what my daughter has had to put up with from her stepmother whilst she was growing up, I won't speak of. For, though Katerina Ivanovna is full of generous feelings, she is a spirited lady, irritable and short-tempered.... Yes. But it's no use going over that! Sonia, as you may well fancy, has had no education. I did make an effort four years ago to give her a course of geography and universal history, but as I was not very well up in those subjects myself and we had no suitable books, and what books we had ... hm, anyway we have not even those now, so all our instruction came to an end. We stopped at Cyrus of Persia. Since she has attained years of maturity, she has read other books of romantic tendency and of late she had read with great interest a book she got through Mr. Lebeziatnikov, Lewes' *Physiology*—do you know it?—and even recounted extracts from it to us: and that's the whole of her education. And now may I venture to address you, honoured sir, on my own account with a private question. Do you suppose that a respectable poor girl can earn much by honest work? Not fifteen farthings a day can she earn, if she is respectable and has no special talent and that without putting her work down for an instant! And what's more, Ivan Ivanitch Klopstock the civil counsellor—have you heard of him?—has not to this day paid her for the half-dozen linen shirts she made him and drove her roughly away, stamping and reviling her, on the pretext that the shirt collars were not made like the pattern and were put in askew. And there are the little ones hungry.... And Katerina Ivanovna walking up and down and wringing her hands, her cheeks flushed red, as they always are in that disease: 'Here you live with us,' says she, 'you eat and drink and are kept warm and you do nothing to help.' And much she gets to eat and drink when there is not a crust for the little ones for three days! I was lying at the time ... well, what of it! I was lying drunk and I heard my Sonia speaking (she is a gentle creature with a soft little voice ... fair hair and such a pale, thin little face). She said: 'Katerina Ivanovna, am I really to do a thing like that?' And Darya Frantsovna, a woman of evil character and very well known to the police, had two or three times tried to get at her through the landlady. 'And why not?' said Katerina Ivanovna with a jeer, 'you are something mighty precious to be so careful of!' But don't blame her, don't blame her, honoured sir, don't blame her! She was not herself when she spoke, but driven to distraction by her illness and the crying of the hungry children; and it was said more to wound her than anything else.... For that's Katerina Ivanovna's character, and when children cry, even from hunger, she falls to beating them at once. At six o'clock I saw Sonia get up, put on her kerchief and her cape, and go out of the room and about nine o'clock she came back. She walked straight up to Katerina Ivanovna and she laid thirty roubles on the table before her in silence. She did not utter a word, she did not even look at her, she simply picked up our big green *drap de dames* shawl (we have a shawl, made of *drap de dames*), put it over her head and face and lay down on the bed with her face to the wall; only her little shoulders and her body kept shuddering.... And I went on lying there, just as before.... And then I saw, young man, I saw Katerina Ivanovna, in the same silence go up to Sonia's little bed; she was on her knees all the evening kissing Sonia's feet, and would not get up,

9

and then they both fell asleep in each other's arms... together, together... yes... and I... lay drunk."

Marmeladov stopped short, as though his voice had failed him. Then he hurriedly filled his glass, drank, and cleared his throat.

"Since then, sir," he went on after a brief pause—"Since then, owing to an unfortunate occurrence and through information given by evil-intentioned persons—in all which Darya Frantsovna took a leading part on the pretext that she had been treated with want of respect— since then my daughter Sofya Semyonovna has been forced to take a yellow ticket, and owing to that she is unable to go on living with us. For our landlady, Amalia Fyodorovna would not hear of it (though she had backed up Darya Frantsovna before) and Mr. Lebeziatnikov too... hm.... All the trouble between him and Katerina Ivanovna was on Sonia's account. At first he was for making up to Sonia himself and then all of a sudden he stood on his dignity: 'how,' said he, 'can a highly educated man like me live in the same rooms with a girl like that?' And Katerina Ivanovna would not let it pass, she stood up for her... and so that's how it happened. And Sonia comes to us now, mostly after dark; she comforts Katerina Ivanovna and gives her all she can.... She has a room at the Kapernaumovs' the tailors, she lodges with them; Kapernaumov is a lame man with a cleft palate and all of his numerous family have cleft palates too. And his wife, too, has a cleft palate. They all live in one room, but Sonia has her own, partitioned off.... Hm... yes... very poor people and all with cleft palates... yes. Then I got up in the morning, and put on my rags, lifted up my hands to heaven and set off to his excellency Ivan Afanasyvitch. His excellency Ivan Afanasyvitch, do you know him? No? Well, then, it's a man of God you don't know. He is wax... wax before the face of the Lord; even as wax melteth!... His eyes were dim when he heard my story. 'Marmeladov, once already you have deceived my expectations... I'll take you once more on my own responsibility'—that's what he said, 'remember,' he said, 'and now you can go.' I kissed the dust at his feet—in thought only, for in reality he would not have allowed me to do it, being a statesman and a man of modern political and enlightened ideas. I returned home, and when I announced that I'd been taken back into the service and should receive a salary, heavens, what a to-do there was!..."

Marmeladov stopped again in violent excitement. At that moment a whole party of revellers already drunk came in from the street, and the sounds of a hired concertina and the cracked piping voice of a child of seven singing "The Hamlet" were heard in the entry. The room was filled with noise. The tavern-keeper and the boys were busy with the newcomers. Marmeladov paying no attention to the new arrivals continued his story. He appeared by now to be extremely weak, but as he became more and more drunk, he became more and more talkative. The recollection of his recent success in getting the situation seemed to revive him, and was positively reflected in a sort of radiance on his face. Raskolnikov listened attentively.

"That was five weeks ago, sir. Yes.... As soon as Katerina Ivanovna and Sonia heard of it, mercy on us, it was as though I stepped into the kingdom of Heaven. It used to be: you can lie like a beast, nothing but abuse. Now they were walking on tiptoe, hushing the children. 'Semyon Zaharovitch is tired with his work at the office, he is resting, shh!' They made me coffee before I went to work and boiled cream for me! They began to get real cream for me, do you hear that? And how they managed to get together the money for a decent outfit—eleven roubles, fifty kopecks, I can't guess. Boots, cotton shirtfronts—most magnificent, a uniform, they got up all in splendid style, for eleven roubles and a half. The first morning I came back from the office I found Katerina Ivanovna had cooked two courses for dinner—soup and salt meat with horseradish—which we had never dreamed of till then. She had not any dresses... none at all, but she got herself up as though she were going on a visit; and not that she'd anything to do it with, she smartened herself up with nothing at all, she'd done her hair nicely, put on a clean collar of some sort, cuffs, and there she was, quite a different person, she was younger and better looking. Sonia, my little darling, had only helped with money 'for the time,' she said, 'it won't do for me to come and see you too often. After dark maybe when no one can see.' Do you hear, do you hear? I lay down for a nap after dinner and what do you think: though Katerina Ivanovna had quarrelled to the last degree with our landlady Amalia Fyodorovna only a week before, she could

10

not resist then asking her in to coffee. For two hours they were sitting, whispering together. 'Semyon Zaharovitch is in the service again, now, and receiving a salary,' says she, 'and he went himself to his excellency and his excellency himself came out to him, made all the others wait and led Semyon Zaharovitch by the hand before everybody into his study.' Do you hear, do you hear? 'To be sure,' says he, 'Semyon Zaharovitch, remembering your past services,' says he, 'and in spite of your propensity to that foolish weakness, since you promise now and since moreover we've got on badly without you,' (do you hear, do you hear;) 'and so,' says he, 'I rely now on your word as a gentleman.' And all that, let me tell you, she has simply made up for herself, and not simply out of wantonness, for the sake of bragging; no, she believes it all herself, she amuses herself with her own fancies, upon my word she does! And I don't blame her for it, no, I don't blame her!... Six days ago when I brought her my first earnings in full—twenty-three roubles forty kopecks altogether—she called me her poppet: 'poppet,' said she, 'my little poppet.' And when we were by ourselves, you understand? You would not think me a beauty, you would not think much of me as a husband, would you?... Well, she pinched my cheek, 'my little poppet,' said she."

Marmeladov broke off, tried to smile, but suddenly his chin began to twitch. He controlled himself however. The tavern, the degraded appearance of the man, the five nights in the hay barge, and the pot of spirits, and yet this poignant love for his wife and children bewildered his listener. Raskolnikov listened intently but with a sick sensation. He felt vexed that he had come here.

"Honoured sir, honoured sir," cried Marmeladov recovering himself—"Oh, sir, perhaps all this seems a laughing matter to you, as it does to others, and perhaps I am only worrying you with the stupidity of all the trivial details of my home life, but it is not a laughing matter to me. For I can feel it all.... And the whole of that heavenly day of my life and the whole of that evening I passed in fleeting dreams of how I would arrange it all, and how I would dress all the children, and how I should give her rest, and how I should rescue my own daughter from dishonour and restore her to the bosom of her family.... And a great deal more.... Quite excusable, sir. Well, then, sir" (Marmeladov suddenly gave a sort of start, raised his head and gazed intently at his listener) "well, on the very next day after all those dreams, that is to say, exactly five days ago, in the evening, by a cunning trick, like a thief in the night, I stole from Katerina Ivanovna the key of her box, took out what was left of my earnings, how much it was I have forgotten, and now look at me, all of you! It's the fifth day since I left home, and they are looking for me there and it's the end of my employment, and my uniform is lying in a tavern on the Egyptian bridge. I exchanged it for the garments I have on... and it's the end of everything!"

Marmeladov struck his forehead with his fist, clenched his teeth, closed his eyes and leaned heavily with his elbow on the table. But a minute later his face suddenly changed and with a certain assumed slyness and affectation of bravado, he glanced at Raskolnikov, laughed and said:

"This morning I went to see Sonia, I went to ask her for a pick-me-up! He-he-he!"

"You don't say she gave it to you?" cried one of the newcomers; he shouted the words and went off into a guffaw.

"This very quart was bought with her money," Marmeladov declared, addressing himself exclusively to Raskolnikov. "Thirty kopecks she gave me with her own hands, her last, all she had, as I saw.... She said nothing, she only looked at me without a word.... Not on earth, but up yonder... they grieve over men, they weep, but they don't blame them, they don't blame them! But it hurts more, it hurts more when they don't blame! Thirty kopecks yes! And maybe she needs them now, eh? What do you think, my dear sir? For now she's got to keep up her appearance. It costs money, that smartness, that special smartness, you know? Do you understand? And there's pomatum, too, you see, she must have things; petticoats, starched ones, shoes, too, real jaunty ones to show off her foot when she has to step over a puddle. Do you understand, sir, do you understand what all that smartness means? And here I, her own father, here I took thirty kopecks of that money for a drink! And I am drinking it! And I have already drunk it! Come, who will have pity on a man like me, eh? Are you sorry for me, sir, or not? Tell me, sir, are you sorry or not? He-he-he!"

He would have filled his glass, but there was no drink left. The pot was empty.

"What are you to be pitied for?" shouted the tavern-keeper who was again near them.

Shouts of laughter and even oaths followed. The laughter and the oaths came from those who were listening and also from those who had heard nothing but were simply looking at the figure of the discharged government clerk.

"To be pitied! Why am I to be pitied?" Marmeladov suddenly declaimed, standing up with his arm outstretched, as though he had been only waiting for that question.

"Why am I to be pitied, you say? Yes! there's nothing to pity me for! I ought to be crucified, crucified on a cross, not pitied! Crucify me, oh judge, crucify me but pity me! And then I will go of myself to be crucified, for it's not merrymaking I seek but tears and tribulation!... Do you suppose, you that sell, that this pint of yours has been sweet to me? It was tribulation I sought at the bottom of it, tears and tribulation, and have found it, and I have tasted it; but He will pity us Who has had pity on all men, Who has understood all men and all things, He is the One, He too is the judge. He will come in that day and He will ask: 'Where is the daughter who gave herself for her cross, consumptive stepmother and for the little children of another? Where is the daughter who had pity upon the filthy drunkard, her earthly father, undismayed by his beastliness?' And He will say, 'Come to me! I have already forgiven thee once.... I have forgiven thee once.... Thy sins which are many are forgiven thee for thou hast loved much....' And he will forgive my Sonia, He will forgive, I know it... I felt it in my heart when I was with her just now! And He will judge and will forgive all, the good and the evil, the wise and the meek.... And when He has done with all of them, then He will summon us. 'You too come forth,' He will say, 'Come forth ye drunkards, come forth, ye weak ones, come forth, ye children of shame!' And we shall all come forth, without shame and shall stand before him. And He will say unto us, 'Ye are swine, made in the Image of the Beast and with his mark; but come ye also!' And the wise ones and those of understanding will say, 'Oh Lord, why dost Thou receive these men?' And He will say, 'This is why I receive them, oh ye wise, this is why I receive them, oh ye of understanding, that not one of them believed himself to be worthy of this.' And He will hold out His hands to us and we shall fall down before him... and we shall weep... and we shall understand all things! Then we shall understand all!... and all will understand, Katerina Ivanovna even... she will understand.... Lord, Thy kingdom come!" And he sank down on the bench exhausted, and helpless, looking at no one, apparently oblivious of his surroundings and plunged in deep thought. His words had created a certain impression; there was a moment of silence; but soon laughter and oaths were heard again.

"That's his notion!"

"Talked himself silly!"

"A fine clerk he is!"

And so on, and so on.

"Let us go, sir," said Marmeladov all at once, raising his head and addressing Raskolnikov— "come along with me... Kozel's house, looking into the yard. I'm going to Katerina Ivanovna— time I did."

Raskolnikov had for some time been wanting to go and he had meant to help him. Marmeladov was much unsteadier on his legs than in his speech and leaned heavily on the young man. They had two or three hundred paces to go. The drunken man was more and more overcome by dismay and confusion as they drew nearer the house.

"It's not Katerina Ivanovna I am afraid of now," he muttered in agitation—"and that she will begin pulling my hair. What does my hair matter! Bother my hair! That's what I say! Indeed it will be better if she does begin pulling it, that's not what I am afraid of... it's her eyes I am afraid of... yes, her eyes... the red on her cheeks, too, frightens me... and her breathing too.... Have you noticed how people in that disease breathe... when they are excited? I am frightened of the children's crying, too.... For if Sonia has not taken them food... I don't know what's happened! I don't know! But blows I am not afraid of.... Know, sir, that such blows are not a pain to me, but even an enjoyment. In fact I can't get on without it.... It's better so. Let her strike me, it relieves her heart... it's better so... There is the house. The house of Kozel, the cabinetmaker... a German, well-to-do. Lead the way!"

12

They went in from the yard and up to the fourth storey. The staircase got darker and darker as they went up. It was nearly eleven o'clock and although in summer in Petersburg there is no real night, yet it was quite dark at the top of the stairs.

A grimy little door at the very top of the stairs stood ajar. A very poor-looking room about ten paces long was lighted up by a candle-end; the whole of it was visible from the entrance. It was all in disorder, littered up with rags of all sorts, especially children's garments. Across the furthest corner was stretched a ragged sheet. Behind it probably was the bed. There was nothing in the room except two chairs and a sofa covered with American leather, full of holes, before which stood an old deal kitchen-table, unpainted and uncovered. At the edge of the table stood a smoldering tallow-candle in an iron candlestick. It appeared that the family had a room to themselves, not part of a room, but their room was practically a passage. The door leading to the other rooms, or rather cupboards, into which Amalia Lippevechsel's flat was divided stood half open, and there was shouting, uproar and laughter within. People seemed to be playing cards and drinking tea there. Words of the most unceremonious kind flew out from time to time.

Raskolnikov recognised Katerina Ivanovna at once. She was a rather tall, slim and graceful woman, terribly emaciated, with magnificent dark brown hair and with a hectic flush in her cheeks. She was pacing up and down in her little room, pressing her hands against her chest; her lips were parched and her breathing came in nervous broken gasps. Her eyes glittered as in fever and looked about with a harsh immovable stare. And that consumptive and excited face with the last flickering light of the candle-end playing upon it made a sickening impression. She seemed to Raskolnikov about thirty years old and was certainly a strange wife for Marmeladov.... She had not heard them and did not notice them coming in. She seemed to be lost in thought, hearing and seeing nothing. The room was close, but she had not opened the window; a stench rose from the staircase, but the door on to the stairs was not closed. From the inner rooms clouds of tobacco smoke floated in, she kept coughing, but did not close the door. The youngest child, a girl of six, was asleep, sitting curled up on the floor with her head on the sofa. A boy a year older stood crying and shaking in the corner, probably he had just had a beating. Beside him stood a girl of nine years old, tall and thin, wearing a thin and ragged chemise with an ancient cashmere pelisse flung over her bare shoulders, long outgrown and barely reaching her knees. Her arm, as thin as a stick, was round her brother's neck. She was trying to comfort him, whispering something to him, and doing all she could to keep him from whimpering again. At the same time her large dark eyes, which looked larger still from the thinness of her frightened face, were watching her mother with alarm. Marmeladov did not enter the door, but dropped on his knees in the very doorway, pushing Raskolnikov in front of him. The woman seeing a stranger stopped indifferently facing him, coming to herself for a moment and apparently wondering what he had come for. But evidently she decided that he was going into the next room, as he had to pass through hers to get there. Taking no further notice of him, she walked towards the outer door to close it and uttered a sudden scream on seeing her husband on his knees in the doorway.

"Ah!" she cried out in a frenzy, "he has come back! The criminal! the monster!... And where is the money? What's in your pocket, show me! And your clothes are all different! Where are your clothes? Where is the money! Speak!"

And she fell to searching him. Marmeladov submissively and obediently held up both arms to facilitate the search. Not a farthing was there.

"Where is the money?" she cried—"Mercy on us, can he have drunk it all? There were twelve silver roubles left in the chest!" and in a fury she seized him by the hair and dragged him into the room. Marmeladov seconded her efforts by meekly crawling along on his knees.

"And this is a consolation to me! This does not hurt me, but is a positive con-so-la-tion, ho-nou-red sir," he called out, shaken to and fro by his hair and even once striking the ground with his forehead. The child asleep on the floor woke up, and began to cry. The boy in the corner losing all control began trembling and screaming and rushed to his sister in violent terror, almost in a fit. The eldest girl was shaking like a leaf.

"He's drunk it! he's drunk it all," the poor woman screamed in despair—"and his clothes are gone! And they are hungry, hungry!"—and wringing her hands she pointed to the children. "Oh, accursed life! And you, are you not ashamed?"—she pounced all at once upon Raskolnikov—"from the tavern! Have you been drinking with him? You have been drinking with him, too! Go away!"

The young man was hastening away without uttering a word. The inner door was thrown wide open and inquisitive faces were peering in at it. Coarse laughing faces with pipes and cigarettes and heads wearing caps thrust themselves in at the doorway. Further in could be seen figures in dressing gowns flung open, in costumes of unseemly scantiness, some of them with cards in their hands. They were particularly diverted, when Marmeladov, dragged about by his hair, shouted that it was a consolation to him. They even began to come into the room; at last a sinister shrill outcry was heard: this came from Amalia Lippevechsel herself pushing her way amongst them and trying to restore order after her own fashion and for the hundredth time to frighten the poor woman by ordering her with coarse abuse to clear out of the room next day. As he went out, Raskolnikov had time to put his hand into his pocket, to snatch up the coppers he had received in exchange for his rouble in the tavern and to lay them unnoticed on the window. Afterwards on the stairs, he changed his mind and would have gone back.

"What a stupid thing I've done," he thought to himself, "they have Sonia and I want it myself." But reflecting that it would be impossible to take it back now and that in any case he would not have taken it, he dismissed it with a wave of his hand and went back to his lodging. "Sonia wants pomatum too," he said as he walked along the street, and he laughed malignantly—"such smartness costs money.... Hm! And maybe Sonia herself will be bankrupt today, for there is always a risk, hunting big game... digging for gold... then they would all be without a crust tomorrow except for my money. Hurrah for Sonia! What a mine they've dug there! And they're making the most of it! Yes, they are making the most of it! They've wept over it and grown used to it. Man grows used to everything, the scoundrel!"

He sank into thought.

"And what if I am wrong," he cried suddenly after a moment's thought. "What if man is not really a scoundrel, man in general, I mean, the whole race of mankind—then all the rest is prejudice, simply artificial terrors and there are no barriers and it's all as it should be."

14

He waked up late next day after a broken sleep. But his sleep had not refreshed him; he waked up bilious, irritable, ill-tempered, and looked with hatred at his room. It was a tiny cupboard of a room about six paces in length. It had a poverty-stricken appearance with its dusty yellow paper peeling off the walls, and it was so low-pitched that a man of more than average height was ill at ease in it and felt every moment that he would knock his head against the ceiling. The furniture was in keeping with the room: there were three old chairs, rather rickety; a painted table in the corner on which lay a few manuscripts and books; the dust that lay thick upon them showed that they had been long untouched. A big clumsy sofa occupied almost the whole of one wall and half the floor space of the room; it was once covered with chintz, but was now in rags and served Raskolnikov as a bed. Often he went to sleep on it, as he was, without undressing, without sheets, wrapped in his old student's overcoat, with his head on one little pillow, under which he heaped up all the linen he had, clean and dirty, by way of a bolster. A little table stood in front of the sofa.

It would have been difficult to sink to a lower ebb of disorder, but to Raskolnikov in his present state of mind this was positively agreeable. He had got completely away from everyone, like a tortoise in its shell, and even the sight of a servant girl who had to wait upon him and looked sometimes into his room made him writhe with nervous irritation. He was in the condition that overtakes some monomaniacs entirely concentrated upon one thing. His landlady had for the last fortnight given up sending him in meals, and he had not yet thought of expostulating with her, though he went without his dinner. Nastasya, the cook and only servant, was rather pleased at the lodger's mood and had entirely given up sweeping and doing his room, only once a week or so she would stray into his room with a broom. She waked him up that day.

"Get up, why are you asleep?" she called to him. "It's past nine, I have brought you some tea; will you have a cup? I should think you're fairly starving?"

Raskolnikov opened his eyes, started and recognised Nastasya.

"From the landlady, eh?" he asked, slowly and with a sickly face sitting up on the sofa.

"From the landlady, indeed!"

She set before him her own cracked teapot full of weak and stale tea and laid two yellow lumps of sugar by the side of it.

"Here, Nastasya, take it please," he said, fumbling in his pocket (for he had slept in his clothes) and taking out a handful of coppers—"run and buy me a loaf. And get me a little sausage, the cheapest, at the pork-butcher's."

"The loaf I'll fetch you this very minute, but wouldn't you rather have some cabbage soup instead of sausage? It's capital soup, yesterday's. I saved it for you yesterday, but you came in late. It's fine soup."

When the soup had been brought, and he had begun upon it, Nastasya sat down beside him on the sofa and began chatting. She was a country peasant-woman and a very talkative one.

"Praskovya Pavlovna means to complain to the police about you," she said.

He scowled.

"To the police? What does she want?"

"You don't pay her money and you won't turn out of the room. That's what she wants, to be sure."

"The devil, that's the last straw," he muttered, grinding his teeth, "no, that would not suit me... just now. She is a fool," he added aloud. "I'll go and talk to her today."

15

"Fool she is and no mistake, just as I am. But why, if you are so clever, do you lie here like a sack and have nothing to show for it? One time you used to go out, you say, to teach children. But why is it you do nothing now?"

"I am doing..." Raskolnikov began sullenly and reluctantly.

"What are you doing?"

"Work..."

"What sort of work?"

"I am thinking," he answered seriously after a pause.

Nastasya was overcome with a fit of laughter. She was given to laughter and when anything amused her, she laughed inaudibly, quivering and shaking all over till she felt ill.

"And have you made much money by your thinking?" she managed to articulate at last.

"One can't go out to give lessons without boots. And I'm sick of it."

"Don't quarrel with your bread and butter."

"They pay so little for lessons. What's the use of a few coppers?" he answered, reluctantly, as though replying to his own thought.

"And you want to get a fortune all at once?"

He looked at her strangely.

"Yes, I want a fortune," he answered firmly, after a brief pause.

"Don't be in such a hurry, you quite frighten me! Shall I get you the loaf or not?"

"As you please."

"Ah, I forgot! A letter came for you yesterday when you were out."

"A letter? for me! from whom?"

"I can't say. I gave three kopecks of my own to the postman for it. Will you pay me back?"

"Then bring it to me, for God's sake, bring it," cried Raskolnikov greatly excited—"good God!"

A minute later the letter was brought him. That was it: from his mother, from the province of R——. He turned pale when he took it. It was a long while since he had received a letter, but another feeling also suddenly stabbed his heart.

"Nastasya, leave me alone, for goodness' sake; here are your three kopecks, but for goodness' sake, make haste and go!"

The letter was quivering in his hand; he did not want to open it in her presence; he wanted to be left *alone* with this letter. When Nastasya had gone out, he lifted it quickly to his lips and kissed it; then he gazed intently at the address, the small, sloping handwriting, so dear and familiar, of the mother who had once taught him to read and write. He delayed; he seemed almost afraid of something. At last he opened it; it was a thick heavy letter, weighing over two ounces, two large sheets of note paper were covered with very small handwriting.

"MY DEAR RODYA," wrote his mother—"it's two months since I last had a talk with you by letter which has distressed me and even kept me awake at night, thinking. But I am sure you will not blame me for my inevitable silence. You know how I love you; you are all we have to look to, Dounia and I, you are our all, our one hope, our one stay. What a grief it was to me when I heard that you had given up the university some months ago, for want of means to keep yourself and that you had lost your lessons and your other work! How could I help you out of my hundred and twenty roubles a year pension? The fifteen roubles I sent you four months ago I borrowed, as you know, on security of my pension, from Vassily Ivanovitch Vahrushin a merchant of this town. He is a kindhearted man and was a friend of your father's too. But having given him the right to receive the pension, I had to wait till the debt was paid off and that is only just done, so that I've been unable to send you anything all this time. But now, thank God, I believe I shall be able to send you something more and in fact we may congratulate ourselves on our good fortune now, of which I hasten to inform you. In the first place, would you have guessed, dear Rodya, that your sister has been living with me for the last six weeks and we shall not be separated in the future. Thank God, her sufferings are over, but I will tell you everything in order, so that you may know just how everything has happened and all that we have hitherto concealed from you. When you wrote to me two months ago that you had heard that Dounia had a great deal to put up with in the

16

Svidrigraïlovs' house, when you wrote that and asked me to tell you all about it—what could I write in answer to you? If I had written the whole truth to you, I dare say you would have thrown up everything and have come to us, even if you had to walk all the way, for I know your character and your feelings, and you would not let your sister be insulted. I was in despair myself, but what could I do? And, besides, I did not know the whole truth myself then. What made it all so difficult was that Dounia received a hundred roubles in advance when she took the place as governess in their family, on condition of part of her salary being deducted every month, and so it was impossible to throw up the situation without repaying the debt. This sum (now I can explain it all to you, my precious Rodya) she took chiefly in order to send you sixty roubles, which you needed so terribly then and which you received from us last year. We deceived you then, writing that this money came from Dounia's savings, but that was not so, and now I tell you all about it, because, thank God, things have suddenly changed for the better, and that you may know how Dounia loves you and what a heart she has. At first indeed Mr. Svidrigaïlov treated her very rudely and used to make disrespectful and jeering remarks at table.... But I don't want to go into all those painful details, so as not to worry you for nothing when it is now all over. In short, in spite of the kind and generous behaviour of Marfa Petrovna, Mr. Svidrigaïlov's wife, and all the rest of the household, Dounia had a very hard time, especially when Mr. Svidrigaïlov, relapsing into his old regimental habits, was under the influence of Bacchus. And how do you think it was all explained later on? Would you believe that the crazy fellow had conceived a passion for Dounia from the beginning, but had concealed it under a show of rudeness and contempt. Possibly he was ashamed and horrified himself at his own flighty hopes, considering his years and his being the father of a family; and that made him angry with Dounia. And possibly, too, he hoped by his rude and sneering behaviour to hide the truth from others. But at last he lost all control and had the face to make Dounia an open and shameful proposal, promising her all sorts of inducements and offering, besides, to throw up everything and take her to another estate of his, or even abroad. You can imagine all she went through! To leave her situation at once was impossible not only on account of the money debt, but also to spare the feelings of Marfa Petrovna, whose suspicions would have been aroused: and then Dounia would have been the cause of a rupture in the family. And it would have meant a terrible scandal for Dounia too; that would have been inevitable. There were various other reasons owing to which Dounia could not hope to escape from that awful house for another six weeks. You know Dounia, of course; you know how clever she is and what a strong will she has. Dounia can endure a great deal and even in the most difficult cases she has the fortitude to maintain her firmness. She did not even write to me about everything for fear of upsetting me, although we were constantly in communication. It all ended very unexpectedly. Marfa Petrovna accidentally overheard her husband imploring Dounia in the garden, and, putting quite a wrong interpretation on the position, threw the blame upon her, believing her to be the cause of it all. An awful scene took place between them on the spot in the garden; Marfa Petrovna went so far as to strike Dounia, refused to hear anything and was shouting at her for a whole hour and then gave orders that Dounia should be packed off at once to me in a plain peasant's cart, into which they flung all her things, her linen and her clothes, all pell-mell, without folding it up and packing it. And a heavy shower of rain came on, too, and Dounia, insulted and put to shame, had to drive with a peasant in an open cart all the seventeen *versts* into town. Only think now what answer could I have sent to the letter I received from you two months ago and what could I have written? I was in despair; I dared not write to you the truth because you would have been very unhappy, mortified and indignant, and yet what could you do? You could only perhaps ruin yourself, and, besides, Dounia would not allow it; and fill up my letter with trifles when my heart was so full of sorrow, I could not. For a whole month the town was full of gossip about this scandal, and it came to such a pass that Dounia and I dared not even go to church on account of the contemptuous looks, whispers, and even remarks made aloud about us. All our acquaintances avoided us, nobody even bowed to us in the street, and I learnt that some shopmen and clerks were intending to insult us in a shameful way, smearing the gates of our house with pitch, so that the landlord began to tell us we must leave. All this was set going by Marfa Petrovna who managed to slander Dounia and throw dirt at her in every family. She knows everyone in the neighbourhood, and that

17

month she was continually coming into the town, and as she is rather talkative and fond of gossiping about her family affairs and particularly of complaining to all and each of her husband—which is not at all right—so in a short time she had spread her story not only in the town, but over the whole surrounding district. It made me ill, but Dounia bore it better than I did, and if only you could have seen how she endured it all and tried to comfort me and cheer me up! She is an angel! But by God's mercy, our sufferings were cut short: Mr. Svidrigaïlov returned to his senses and repented and, probably feeling sorry for Dounia, he laid before Marfa Petrovna a complete and unmistakable proof of Dounia's innocence, in the form of a letter Dounia had been forced to write and give to him, before Marfa Petrovna came upon them in the garden. This letter, which remained in Mr. Svidrigaïlov's hands after her departure, she had written to refuse personal explanations and secret interviews, for which he was entreating her. In that letter she reproached him with great heat and indignation for the baseness of his behaviour in regard to Marfa Petrovna, reminding him that he was the father and head of a family and telling him how infamous it was of him to torment and make unhappy a defenceless girl, unhappy enough already. Indeed, dear Rodya, the letter was so nobly and touchingly written that I sobbed when I read it and to this day I cannot read it without tears. Moreover, the evidence of the servants, too, cleared Dounia's reputation; they had seen and known a great deal more than Mr. Svidrigaïlov had himself supposed—as indeed is always the case with servants. Marfa Petrovna was completely taken aback, and 'again crushed' as she said herself to us, but she was completely convinced of Dounia's innocence. The very next day, being Sunday, she went straight to the Cathedral, knelt down and prayed with tears to Our Lady to give her strength to bear this new trial and to do her duty. Then she came straight from the Cathedral to us, told us the whole story, wept bitterly and, fully penitent, she embraced Dounia and besought her to forgive her. The same morning without any delay, she went round to all the houses in the town and everywhere, shedding tears, she asserted in the most flattering terms Dounia's innocence and the nobility of her feelings and her behavior. What was more, she showed and read to everyone the letter in Dounia's own handwriting to Mr. Svidrigaïlov and even allowed them to take copies of it—which I must say I think was superfluous. In this way she was busy for several days in driving about the whole town, because some people had taken offence through precedence having been given to others. And therefore they had to take turns, so that in every house she was expected before she arrived, and everyone knew that on such and such a day Marfa Petrovna would be reading the letter in such and such a place and people assembled for every reading of it, even many who had heard it several times already both in their own houses and in other people's. In my opinion a great deal, a very great deal of all this was unnecessary; but that's Marfa Petrovna's character. Anyway she succeeded in completely reestablishing Dounia's reputation and the whole ignominy of this affair rested as an indelible disgrace upon her husband, as the only person to blame, so that I really began to feel sorry for him; it was really treating the crazy fellow too harshly. Dounia was at once asked to give lessons in several families, but she refused. All of a sudden everyone began to treat her with marked respect and all this did much to bring about the event by which, one may say, our whole fortunes are now transformed. You must know, dear Rodya, that Dounia has a suitor and that she has already consented to marry him. I hasten to tell you all about the matter, and though it has been arranged without asking your consent, I think you will not be aggrieved with me or with your sister on that account, for you will see that we could not wait and put off our decision till we heard from you. And you could not have judged all the facts without being on the spot. This was how it happened. He is already of the rank of a counsellor, Pyotr Petrovitch Luzhin, and is distantly related to Marfa Petrovna, who has been very active in bringing the match about. It began with his expressing through her his desire to make our acquaintance. He was properly received, drank coffee with us and the very next day he sent us a letter in which he very courteously made an offer and begged for a speedy and decided answer. He is a very busy man and is in a great hurry to get to Petersburg, so that every moment is precious to him. At first, of course, we were greatly surprised, as it had all happened so quickly and unexpectedly. We thought and talked it over the whole day. He is a well-to-do man, to be depended upon, he has two posts in the government and has already made his fortune. It is true that he is forty-five years old, but he is of a fairly prepossessing appearance and might still be thought attractive by women, and he is altogether a very respectable and presentable man, only he seems a little morose and somewhat conceited. But possibly that may only be the impression he makes at first sight. And beware, dear Rodya, when he comes to Petersburg, as he shortly will do, beware of judging him too hastily and severely, as your way is, if there is anything you do not like in him at first sight. I give you this warning, although I feel sure that he will make a favourable impression upon you. Moreover, in order to understand any man one must be deliberate and careful to avoid forming prejudices and mistaken ideas, which are very difficult to correct and get over afterwards. And Pyotr Petrovitch, judging by many indications, is a thoroughly estimable man. At his first visit, indeed, he told us that he was a practical man, but still he shares, as he expressed it, many of the convictions 'of our most rising generation' and he is an opponent of all prejudices. He said a good deal more, for he seems a little conceited and likes to be listened to, but this is scarcely a vice. I, of course, understood very little of it, but Dounia explained to me that, though he is not a man of great education, he is clever and seems to be good-natured. You know your sister's character, Rodya. She is a resolute, sensible, patient and generous girl, but she has a passionate heart, as I know very well. Of course, there is no great love either on his side, or on hers, but Dounia is a clever girl and has the heart of an angel, and will make it her duty to make her husband happy who on his side will make her happiness his care. Of that we have no good reason to doubt, though it must be admitted the matter has been arranged in great haste. Besides he is a man of great prudence and he will see, to be sure, of himself, that his own happiness will be the more secure, the happier Dounia is with him. And as for some defects of character, for some habits and even certain differences of opinion—which indeed are inevitable even in the happiest marriages—Dounia has said that, as regards all that, she relies on herself, that there is nothing to be uneasy about, and that she is ready to put up with a great deal, if only their future relationship can be an honourable and straightforward one. He struck me, for instance, at first, as rather abrupt, but that may well come from his being an outspoken man, and that is no doubt how it is. For instance, at his second visit, after he had received Dounia's consent, in the course of conversation, he declared that before making Dounia's acquaintance, he had made up his mind to marry a girl of good reputation, without dowry and, above all, one who had experienced poverty, because, as he explained, a man ought not to be indebted to his wife, but that it is better for a wife to look upon her husband as her benefactor. I must add that he expressed it more nicely and politely than I have done, for I have forgotten his actual phrases and only remember the meaning. And, besides, it was obviously not said of design, but slipped out in the heat of conversation, so that he tried afterwards to correct himself and smooth it over, but all the same it did strike me as somewhat rude, and I said so afterwards to Dounia. But Dounia was vexed, and answered that 'words are not deeds,' and that, of course, is perfectly true. Dounia did not sleep all night before she made up her mind, and, thinking that I was asleep, she got out of bed and was walking up and down the room all night; at last she knelt down before the icon and prayed long and fervently and in the morning she told me that she had decided.

"I have mentioned already that Pyotr Petrovitch is just setting off for Petersburg, where he has a great deal of business, and he wants to open a legal bureau. He has been occupied for many years in conducting civil and commercial litigation, and only the other day he won an important case. He has to be in Petersburg because he has an important case before the Senate. So, Rodya dear, he may be of the greatest use to you, in every way indeed, and Dounia and I have agreed that from this very day you could definitely enter upon your career and might consider that your future is marked out and assured for you. Oh, if only this comes to pass! This would be such a benefit that we could only look upon it as a providential blessing. Dounia is dreaming of nothing else. We have even ventured already to drop a few words on the subject to Pyotr Petrovitch. He was cautious in his answer, and said that, of course, as he could not get on without a secretary, it would be better to be paying a salary to a relation than to a stranger, if only the former were fitted for the duties (as though there could be doubt of your being fitted!) but then he expressed doubts whether your studies at the university would leave you time for work at his office. The matter dropped for the time, but Dounia is thinking of nothing else now. She has been in a sort of fever for the last few days, and has already made a regular plan for your becoming in the end an associate and even a partner in Pyotr Petrovitch's business, which might well be, seeing that you are a student of law. I am in complete agreement with her, Rodya, and share all her plans and hopes, and think there is every probability of realising them. And in spite of Pyotr Petrovitch's evasiveness, very natural at present (since he does not know you), Dounia is firmly persuaded that she will gain everything by her good influence over her future husband; this she is reckoning upon. Of course we are careful not to talk of any of these more remote plans to Pyotr Petrovitch, especially of your becoming his partner. He is a practical man and might take this very coldly, it might all seem to him simply a daydream. Nor has either Dounia or I breathed a word to him of the great hopes we have of his helping us to pay for your university studies; we have not spoken of it in the first place, because it will come to pass of itself, later on, and he will no doubt without wasting words offer to do it of himself, (as though he could refuse Dounia that) the more readily since you may by your own efforts become his right hand in the office, and receive this assistance not as a charity, but as a salary earned by your own work. Dounia wants to arrange it all like this and I quite agree with her. And we have not spoken of our plans for another reason, that is, because I particularly wanted you to feel on an equal footing when you first meet him. When Dounia spoke to him with enthusiasm about you, he answered that one could never judge of a man without seeing him close, for oneself, and that he looked forward to forming his own opinion when he makes your acquaintance. Do you know, my precious Rodya, I think that perhaps for some reasons (nothing to do with Pyotr Petrovitch though, simply for my own personal, perhaps old-womanish, fancies) I should do better to go on living by myself, apart, than with them, after the wedding. I am convinced that he will be generous and delicate enough to invite me and to urge me to remain with my daughter for the future, and if he has said nothing about it hitherto, it is simply because it has been taken for granted; but I shall refuse. I have noticed more than once in my life that husbands don't quite get on with their mothers-in-law, and I don't want to be the least bit in anyone's way, and for my own sake, too, would rather be quite independent, so long as I have a crust of bread of my own, and such children as you and Dounia. If possible, I would settle somewhere near you, for the most joyful piece of news, dear Rodya, I have kept for the end of my letter: know then, my dear boy, that we may, perhaps, be all together in a very short time and may embrace one another again after a separation of almost three years! It is settled *for certain* that Dounia and I are to set off for Petersburg, exactly when I don't know, but very, very soon, possibly in a week. It all depends on Pyotr Petrovitch who will let us know when he has had time to look round him in Petersburg. To suit his own arrangements he is anxious to have the ceremony as soon as possible, even before the fast of Our Lady, if it could be managed, or if that is too soon to be ready, immediately after. Oh, with what happiness I shall press you to my heart! Dounia is all excitement at the joyful thought of seeing you, she said one day in joke that she would be ready to marry Pyotr Petrovitch for that alone. She is an angel! She is not writing anything to you now, and has only told me to write that she has so much, so much to tell you that she is not going to take up her pen now, for a few lines would tell you nothing, and it would only mean upsetting herself; she bids me send you her love and innumerable kisses. But although we shall be meeting so soon, perhaps I shall send you as much money as I can in a day or two. Now that everyone has heard that Dounia is to marry Pyotr Petrovitch, my credit has suddenly improved and I know that Afanasy Ivanovitch will trust me now even to seventy-five roubles on the security of my pension, so that perhaps I shall be able to send you twenty-five or even thirty roubles. I would send you more, but I am uneasy about our travelling expenses; for though Pyotr Petrovitch has been so kind as to undertake part of the expenses of the journey, that is to say, he has taken upon himself the conveyance of our bags and big trunk (which will be conveyed through some acquaintances of his), we must reckon upon some expense on our arrival in Petersburg, where we can't be left without a halfpenny, at least for the first few days. But we have calculated it all, Dounia and I, to the last penny, and we see that the journey will not cost very much. It is only ninety *versts* from us to the railway and we have come to an agreement with a driver we know, so as to be in readiness; and from there Dounia and I can travel quite comfortably third class. So that I may very likely be able to send to you not twenty-five, but thirty roubles. But enough; I have covered two sheets already and there is no space left for more; our whole history, but so many events have happened! And now, my precious Rodya, I embrace you and send you a mother's blessing till we meet. Love Dounia your sister, Rodya; love her as she loves you and understand that she loves you beyond everything, more than herself. She is an angel and you, Rodya, you are everything to us—our one hope, our one consolation. If only you are happy, we shall be happy. Do you still say your prayers, Rodya, and believe in the mercy of our Creator and our Redeemer? I am afraid in my heart that you may have been visited by the new spirit of infidelity that is abroad today; If it is so, I pray for you. Remember, dear boy, how in your childhood, when your father was living, you used to lisp your prayers at my knee, and how happy we all were in those days. Goodbye, till we meet then—I embrace you warmly, warmly, with many kisses.

"Yours till death,
PULCHERIA RASKOLNIKOV."

Almost from the first, while he read the letter, Raskolnikov's face was wet with tears; but when he finished it, his face was pale and distorted and a bitter, wrathful and malignant smile was on his lips. He laid his head down on his threadbare dirty pillow and pondered, pondered a long time. His heart was beating violently, and his brain was in a turmoil. At last he felt cramped and stifled in the little yellow room that was like a cupboard or a box. His eyes and his mind craved for space. He took up his hat and went out, this time without dread of meeting anyone; he had forgotten his dread. He turned in the direction of the Vassilyevsky Ostrov, walking along Vassilyevsky Prospect, as though hastening on some business, but he walked, as his habit was, without noticing his way, muttering and even speaking aloud to himself, to the astonishment of the passersby. Many of them took him to be drunk.

21

His mother's letter had been a torture to him, but as regards the chief fact in it, he had felt not one moment's hesitation, even whilst he was reading the letter. The essential question was settled, and irrevocably settled, in his mind: "Never such a marriage while I am alive and Mr. Luzhin be damned!" "The thing is perfectly clear," he muttered to himself, with a malignant smile anticipating the triumph of his decision. "No, mother, no, Dounia, you won't deceive me! and then they apologise for not asking my advice and for taking the decision without me! I dare say! They imagine it is arranged now and can't be broken off; but we will see whether it can or not! A magnificent excuse: 'Pyotr Petrovitch is such a busy man that even his wedding has to be in post-haste, almost by express.' No, Dounia, I see it all and I know what you want to say to me; and I know too what you were thinking about, when you walked up and down all night, and what your prayers were like before the Holy Mother of Kazan who stands in mother's bedroom. Bitter is the ascent to Golgotha.... Hm... so it is finally settled; you have determined to marry a sensible business man, Avdotya Romanovna, one who has a fortune (has *already* made his fortune, that is so much more solid and impressive), a man who holds two government posts and who shares the ideas of our most rising generation, as mother writes, and who *seems* to be kind, as Dounia herself observes. That *seems* beats everything! And that very Dounia for that very '*seems*' is marrying him! Splendid! splendid!

"... But I should like to know why mother has written to me about 'our most rising generation'? Simply as a descriptive touch, or with the idea of prepossessing me in favour of Mr. Luzhin? Oh, the cunning of them! I should like to know one thing more: how far they were open with one another that day and night and all this time since? Was it all put into *words*, or did both understand that they had the same thing at heart and in their minds, so that there was no need to speak of it aloud, and better not to speak of it. Most likely it was partly like that, from mother's letter it's evident: he struck her as rude *a little*, and mother in her simplicity took her observations to Dounia. And she was sure to be vexed and 'answered her angrily.' I should think so! Who would not be angered when it was quite clear without any naive questions and when it was understood that it was useless to discuss it. And why does she write to me, 'love Dounia, Rodya, and she loves you more than herself'? Has she a secret conscience-prick at sacrificing her daughter to her son? 'You are our one comfort, you are everything to us.' Oh, mother!"

His bitterness grew more and more intense, and if he had happened to meet Mr. Luzhin at the moment, he might have murdered him.

"Hm... yes, that's true," he continued, pursuing the whirling ideas that chased each other in his brain, "it is true that 'it needs time and care to get to know a man,' but there is no mistake about Mr. Luzhin. The chief thing is he is 'a man of business and *seems* kind,' that was something, wasn't it, to send the bags and big box for them! A kind man, no doubt after that! But his *bride* and her mother are to drive in a peasant's cart covered with sacking (I know, I have been driven in it). No matter! It is only ninety *versts* and then they can 'travel very comfortably, third class,' for a thousand *versts*! Quite right, too. One must cut one's coat according to one's cloth, but what about you, Mr. Luzhin? She is your bride.... And you must be aware that her mother has to raise money on her pension for the journey. To be sure it's a matter of business, a partnership for mutual benefit, with equal shares and expenses;—food and drink provided, but pay for your tobacco. The business man has got the better of them, too. The luggage will cost less than their fares and very likely go for nothing. How is it that they don't both see all that, or is it that they don't want to see? And they are pleased, pleased! And to think that this is only the first blossoming, and that the real fruits are to come! But what really matters is not the stinginess, is not the meanness, but the *tone* of the whole thing. For that will be the tone after marriage, it's a foretaste of it. And mother too, why should she be so lavish? What will she have by the time she gets to Petersburg? Three silver roubles or two 'paper ones' as *she* says... that old woman... hm. What does she expect to live upon in Petersburg afterwards? She has her reasons already for guessing that she *could not* live with Dounia after the marriage, even for the first few months. The good man has no doubt let slip something on that subject also, though mother would deny it: 'I shall refuse,' says she. On whom is she reckoning then? Is she counting on what is left of her hundred and twenty roubles of pension when Afanasy Ivanovitch's debt is paid? She knits woollen shawls and embroiders cuffs, ruining her old eyes. And all her shawls don't add more than twenty roubles a year to her hundred and twenty, I know that. So she is building all her hopes all the time on Mr. Luzhin's generosity; 'he will offer it of himself, he will press it on me.' You may wait a long time for that! That's how it always is with these Schilleresque noble hearts; till the last moment every goose is a swan with them, till the last moment, they hope for the best and will see nothing wrong, and although they have an inkling of the other side of the picture, yet they won't face the truth till they are forced to; the very thought of it makes them shiver; they thrust the truth away with both hands, until the man they deck out in false colours puts a fool's cap on them with his own hands. I should like to know whether Mr. Luzhin has any orders of merit; I bet he has the Anna in his buttonhole and that he puts it on when he goes to dine with contractors or merchants. He will be sure to have it for his wedding, too! Enough of him, confound him!

"Well,... mother I don't wonder at, it's like her, God bless her, but how could Dounia? Dounia darling, as though I did not know you! You were nearly twenty when I saw you last: I understood you then. Mother writes that 'Dounia can put up with a great deal.' I know that very well. I knew that two years and a half ago, and for the last two and a half years I have been thinking about it, thinking of just that, that 'Dounia can put up with a great deal.' If she could put up with Mr. Svidrigaïlov and all the rest of it, she certainly can put up with a great deal. And now mother and she have taken it into their heads that she can put up with Mr. Luzhin, who propounds the theory of the superiority of wives raised from destitution and owing everything to their husband's bounty—who propounds it, too, almost at the first interview. Granted that he 'let it slip,' though he is a sensible man, (yet maybe it was not a slip at all, but he meant to make himself clear as soon as possible) but Dounia, Dounia? She understands the man, of course, but she will have to live with the man. Why! she'd live on black bread and water, she would not sell her soul, she would not barter her moral freedom for comfort; she would not barter it for all Schleswig-Holstein, much less Mr. Luzhin's money. No, Dounia was not that sort when I knew her and... she is still the same, of course! Yes, there's no denying, the Svidrigaïlovs are a bitter pill! It's a bitter thing to spend one's life a governess in the provinces for two hundred roubles, but I know she would rather be a nigger on a plantation or a Lett with a German master than degrade her soul, and her moral dignity, by binding herself forever to a man whom she does not respect and with whom she has nothing in common—for her own advantage. And if Mr. Luzhin had been of unalloyed gold, or one huge diamond, she would never have consented to become his legal concubine. Why is she consenting then? What's the point of it? What's the answer? It's clear enough: for herself, for her comfort, to save her life she would not sell herself, but for someone else she is doing it! For one she loves, for one she adores, she will sell herself! That's what it all amounts to; for her brother, for her mother, she will sell herself! She will sell everything! In such cases, 'we overcome our moral feeling if necessary,' freedom, peace, conscience even, all, all are brought into the market. Let my life go, if only my dear ones may be happy! More than that, we become casuists, we learn to be Jesuitical and for a time maybe we can soothe ourselves, we can persuade ourselves that it is one's duty for a good object. That's just like us, it's as clear as daylight. It's clear that Rodion Romanovitch Raskolnikov is the central figure in the business, and no one else. Oh, yes, she can ensure his happiness, keep him in the university, make him a partner in the office, make his whole future secure; perhaps he may even be a rich man later on, prosperous, respected, and may even end his life a famous man! But my mother? It's all Rodya, precious Rodya, her first born! For such a son who would not sacrifice such a daughter! Oh, loving, over-partial hearts! Why, for his sake we would not shrink even from Sonia's fate. Sonia, Sonia Marmeladov, the eternal victim so long as the world lasts. Have you taken the measure of your sacrifice, both of you? Is it right? Can you bear it? Is it any use? Is there sense in it? And let me tell you, Dounia, Sonia's life is no worse than life with Mr. Luzhin. 'There can be no question of love,' mother writes. And what if there can be no respect either, if on the contrary there is aversion, contempt, repulsion, what then? So you will have to 'keep up your appearance,' too. Is not that so? Do you understand what that smartness means? Do you understand that the Luzhin smartness is just the same thing as Sonia's and may be worse, viler, baser, because in your case, Dounia, it's a bargain for luxuries, after all, but with Sonia it's simply a question of starvation. It has to be paid for, it has to be paid for, Dounia, this smartness. And what if it's more than you can bear afterwards, if you regret it? The bitterness, the misery, the curses, the tears hidden from all the world, for you are not a Marfa Petrovna. And how will your mother feel then? Even now she is uneasy, she is worried, but then, when she sees it all clearly? And I? Yes, indeed, what have you taken me for? I won't have your sacrifice, Dounia, I won't have it, mother! It shall not be, so long as I am alive, it shall not, it shall not! I won't accept it!"

He suddenly paused in his reflection and stood still.

"It shall not be? But what are you going to do to prevent it? You'll forbid it? And what right have you? What can you promise them on your side to give you such a right? Your whole life, your whole future, you will devote to them *when you have finished your studies and obtained a post?* Yes, we have heard all that before, and that's all *words*, but now? Now something must be done, now, do you understand that? And what are you doing now? You are living upon them. They borrow on their hundred roubles pension. They borrow from the Svidrigaïlovs. How are you going to save them from Svidrigaïlovs, from Afanasy Ivanovitch Vahrushin, oh, future millionaire Zeus who would arrange their lives for them? In another ten years? In another ten years, mother will be blind with knitting shawls, maybe with weeping too. She will be worn to a shadow with fasting; and my sister? Imagine for a moment what may have become of your sister in ten years? What may happen to her during those ten years? Can you fancy?"

So he tortured himself, fretting himself with such questions, and finding a kind of enjoyment in it. And yet all these questions were not new ones suddenly confronting him, they were old familiar aches. It was long since they had first begun to grip and rend his heart. Long, long ago his present anguish had its first beginnings; it had waxed and gathered strength, it had matured and concentrated, until it had taken the form of a fearful, frenzied and fantastic question, which tortured his heart and mind, clamouring insistently for an answer. Now his mother's letter had burst on him like a thunderclap. It was clear that he must not now suffer passively, worrying himself over unsolved questions, but that he must do something, do it at once, and do it quickly. Anyway he must decide on something, or else…

"Or throw up life altogether!" he cried suddenly, in a frenzy—"accept one's lot humbly as it is, once for all and stifle everything in oneself, giving up all claim to activity, life and love!"

"Do you understand, sir, do you understand what it means when you have absolutely nowhere to turn?" Marmeladov's question came suddenly into his mind, "for every man must have somewhere to turn…."

He gave a sudden start; another thought, that he had had yesterday, slipped back into his mind. But he did not start at the thought recurring to him, for he knew, he had *felt beforehand*, that it must come back, he was expecting it; besides it was not only yesterday's thought. The difference was that a month ago, yesterday even, the thought was a mere dream: but now… now it appeared not a dream at all, it had taken a new menacing and quite unfamiliar shape, and he suddenly became aware of this himself…. He felt a hammering in his head, and there was a darkness before his eyes.

He looked round hurriedly, he was searching for something. He wanted to sit down and was looking for a seat; he was walking along the K—— Boulevard. There was a seat about a hundred paces in front of him. He walked towards it as fast he could; but on the way he met with a little adventure which absorbed all his attention. Looking for the seat, he had noticed a woman walking some twenty paces in front of him, but at first he took no more notice of her than of other objects that crossed his path. It had happened to him many times going home not to notice the road by which he was going, and he was accustomed to walk like that. But there was at first sight something so strange about the woman in front of him, that gradually his attention was riveted upon her, at first reluctantly and, as it were, resentfully, and then more and more intently. He felt a sudden desire to find out what it was that was so strange about the woman. In the first place, she appeared to be a girl quite young, and she was walking in the great heat bareheaded and with no parasol or gloves, waving her arms about in an absurd way. She had on a dress of some light silky material, but put on strangely awry, not properly hooked up, and torn open at the top of the skirt, close to the waist: a great piece was rent and hanging loose. A little kerchief was flung about her bare throat, but lay slanting on one side. The girl was walking unsteadily, too, stumbling and staggering from side to side. She drew Raskolnikov's whole attention at last. He overtook the girl at the seat, but, on reaching it, she dropped down on it, in the corner; she let her head sink on the back of the seat and closed her eyes, apparently in extreme exhaustion. Looking at her closely, he saw at once that she was completely drunk. It was a strange and shocking sight. He could hardly believe that he was not mistaken. He saw before him the face of a quite young, fair-haired girl— sixteen, perhaps not more than fifteen, years old, pretty little face, but flushed and heavy looking and, as it were, swollen. The girl seemed hardly to know what she was doing; she crossed one leg over the other, lifting it indecorously, and showed every sign of being unconscious that she was in the street.

Raskolnikov did not sit down, but he felt unwilling to leave her, and stood facing her in perplexity. This boulevard was never much frequented; and now, at two o'clock, in the stifling heat, it was quite deserted. And yet on the further side of the boulevard, about fifteen paces away, a gentleman was standing on the edge of the pavement. He, too, would apparently have liked to approach the girl with some object of his own. He, too, had probably seen her in the distance and had followed her, but found Raskolnikov in his way. He looked angrily at him, though he tried to escape his notice, and stood impatiently biding his time, till the unwelcome man in rags should have moved away. His intentions were unmistakable. The gentleman was a plump, thickly-set man, about thirty, fashionably dressed, with a high colour, red lips and moustaches. Raskolnikov felt furious; he had a sudden longing to insult this fat dandy in some way. He left the girl for a moment and walked towards the gentleman.

"Hey! You Svidrigaïlov! What do you want here?" he shouted, clenching his fists and laughing, spluttering with rage.

"What do you mean?" the gentleman asked sternly, scowling in haughty astonishment.

"Get away, that's what I mean."

"How dare you, you low fellow!"

He raised his cane. Raskolnikov rushed at him with his fists, without reflecting that the stout gentleman was a match for two men like himself. But at that instant someone seized him from behind, and a police constable stood between them.

"That's enough, gentlemen, no fighting, please, in a public place. What do you want? Who are you?" he asked Raskolnikov sternly, noticing his rags.

Raskolnikov looked at him intently. He had a straightforward, sensible, soldierly face, with grey moustaches and whiskers.

"You are just the man I want," Raskolnikov cried, catching at his arm. "I am a student, Raskolnikov.... You may as well know that too," he added, addressing the gentleman, "come along, I have something to show you."

And taking the policeman by the hand he drew him towards the seat.

"Look here, hopelessly drunk, and she has just come down the boulevard. There is no telling who and what she is, she does not look like a professional. It's more likely she has been given drink and deceived somewhere... for the first time... you understand? and they've put her out into the street like that. Look at the way her dress is torn, and the way it has been put on: she has been dressed by somebody, she has not dressed herself, and dressed by unpractised hands, by a man's hands; that's evident. And now look there: I don't know that dandy with whom I was going to fight, I see him for the first time, but he, too, has seen her on the road, just now, drunk, not knowing what she is doing, and now he is very eager to get hold of her, to get her away somewhere while she is in this state... that's certain, believe me, I am not wrong. I saw him myself watching her and following her, but I prevented him, and he is just waiting for me to go away. Now he has walked away a little, and is standing still, pretending to make a cigarette.... Think how can we keep her out of his hands, and how are we to get her home?"

The policeman saw it all in a flash. The stout gentleman was easy to understand, he turned to consider the girl. The policeman bent over to examine her more closely, and his face worked with genuine compassion.

"Ah, what a pity!" he said, shaking his head—"why, she is quite a child! She has been deceived, you can see that at once. Listen, lady," he began addressing her, "where do you live?" The girl opened her weary and sleepy-looking eyes, gazed blankly at the speaker and waved her hand.

"Here," said Raskolnikov feeling in his pocket and finding twenty kopecks, "here, call a cab and tell him to drive her to her address. The only thing is to find out her address!"

"Missy, missy!" the policeman began again, taking the money. "I'll fetch you a cab and take you home myself. Where shall I take you, eh? Where do you live?"

"Go away! They won't let me alone," the girl muttered, and once more waved her hand.

"Ach, ach, how shocking! It's shameful, missy, it's a shame!" He shook his head again, shocked, sympathetic and indignant.

"It's a difficult job," the policeman said to Raskolnikov, and as he did so, he looked him up and down in a rapid glance. He, too, must have seemed a strange figure to him: dressed in rags and handing him money!

"Did you meet her far from here?" he asked him.

"I tell you she was walking in front of me, staggering, just here, in the boulevard. She only just reached the seat and sank down on it."

"Ah, the shameful things that are done in the world nowadays, God have mercy on us! An innocent creature like that, drunk already! She has been deceived, that's a sure thing. See how her dress has been torn too.... Ah, the vice one sees nowadays! And as likely as not she belongs to gentlefolk too, poor ones maybe.... There are many like that nowadays. She looks refined, too, as though she were a lady," and he bent over her once more.

Perhaps he had daughters growing up like that, "looking like ladies and refined" with pretensions to gentility and smartness....

"The chief thing is," Raskolnikov persisted, "to keep her out of this scoundrel's hands! Why should he outrage her! It's as clear as day what he is after; ah, the brute, he is not moving off!"

Raskolnikov spoke aloud and pointed to him. The gentleman heard him, and seemed about to fly into a rage again, but thought better of it, and confined himself to a contemptuous look. He then walked slowly another ten paces away and again halted.

"Keep her out of his hands we can," said the constable thoughtfully, "if only she'd tell us where to take her, but as it is.... Missy, hey, missy!" he bent over her once more.

She opened her eyes fully all of a sudden, looked at him intently, as though realising something, got up from the seat and walked away in the direction from which she had come. "Oh shameful wretches, they won't let me alone!" she said, waving her hand again. She walked quickly, though staggering as before. The dandy followed her, but along another avenue, keeping his eye on her.

"Don't be anxious, I won't let him have her," the policeman said resolutely, and he set off after them.

"Ah, the vice one sees nowadays!" he repeated aloud, sighing.

At that moment something seemed to sting Raskolnikov; in an instant a complete revulsion of feeling came over him.

"Hey, here!" he shouted after the policeman.

The latter turned round.

"Let them be! What is it to do with you? Let her go! Let him amuse himself." He pointed at the dandy, "What is it to do with you?"

The policeman was bewildered, and stared at him open-eyed. Raskolnikov laughed.

26

"Well!" ejaculated the policeman, with a gesture of contempt, and he walked after the dandy and the girl, probably taking Raskolnikov for a madman or something even worse.

"He has carried off my twenty kopecks," Raskolnikov murmured angrily when he was left alone. "Well, let him take as much from the other fellow to allow him to have the girl and so let it end. And why did I want to interfere? Is it for me to help? Have I any right to help? Let them devour each other alive—what is to me? How did I dare to give him twenty kopecks? Were they mine?"

In spite of those strange words he felt very wretched. He sat down on the deserted seat. His thoughts strayed aimlessly.... He found it hard to fix his mind on anything at that moment. He longed to forget himself altogether, to forget everything, and then to wake up and begin life anew....

"Poor girl!" he said, looking at the empty corner where she had sat—"She will come to herself and weep, and then her mother will find out.... She will give her a beating, a horrible, shameful beating and then maybe, turn her out of doors.... And even if she does not, the Darya Frantsovnas will get wind of it, and the girl will soon be slipping out on the sly here and there. Then there will be the hospital directly (that's always the luck of those girls with respectable mothers, who go wrong on the sly) and then... again the hospital... drink... the taverns... and more hospital, in two or three years—a wreck, and her life over at eighteen or nineteen.... Have not I seen cases like that? And how have they been brought to it? Why, they've all come to it like that. Ugh! But what does it matter? That's as it should be, they tell us. A certain percentage, they tell us, must every year go... that way... to the devil, I suppose, so that the rest may remain chaste, and not interfered with. A percentage! What splendid words they have; they are so scientific, so consolatory.... Once you've said 'percentage' there's nothing more to worry about. If we had any other word... maybe we might feel more uneasy.... But what if Dounia were one of the percentage! Of another one if not that one?

"But where am I going?" he thought suddenly. "Strange, I came out for something. As soon as I had read the letter I came out.... I was going to Vassilyevsky Ostrov, to Razumihin. That's what it was... now I remember. What for, though? And what put the idea of going to Razumihin into my head just now? That's curious."

He wondered at himself. Razumihin was one of his old comrades at the university. It was remarkable that Raskolnikov had hardly any friends at the university; he kept aloof from everyone, went to see no one, and did not welcome anyone who came to see him, and indeed everyone soon gave him up. He took no part in the students' gatherings, amusements or conversations. He worked with great intensity without sparing himself, and he was respected for this, but no one liked him. He was very poor, and there was a sort of haughty pride and reserve about him, as though he were keeping something to himself. He seemed to some of his comrades to look down upon them all as children, as though he were superior in development, knowledge and convictions, as though their beliefs and interests were beneath him.

With Razumihin he had got on, or, at least, he was more unreserved and communicative with him. Indeed it was impossible to be on any other terms with Razumihin. He was an exceptionally good-humoured and candid youth, good-natured to the point of simplicity, though both depth and dignity lay concealed under that simplicity. The better of his comrades understood this, and all were fond of him. He was extremely intelligent, though he was certainly rather a simpleton at times. He was of striking appearance—tall, thin, black-haired and always badly shaved. He was sometimes uproarious and was reputed to be of great physical strength. One night, when out in a festive company, he had with one blow laid a gigantic policeman on his back. There was no limit to his drinking powers, but he could abstain from drink altogether; he sometimes went too far in his pranks; but he could do without pranks altogether. Another thing striking about Razumihin, no failure distressed him, and it seemed as though no unfavourable circumstances could crush him. He could lodge anywhere, and bear the extremes of cold and hunger. He was very poor, and kept himself entirely on what he could earn by work of one sort or another. He knew of no end of resources by which to earn money. He spent one whole winter without lighting his stove, and used to declare that he liked it better, because one slept more soundly in the cold. For the present he, too, had been obliged to give up the university, but it was only for a time, and he was working with all his might to save enough to return to his studies again. Raskolnikov had not been to see him for the last four months, and Razumihin did not even know his address. About two months before, they had met in the street, but Raskolnikov had turned away and even crossed to the other side that he might not be observed. And though Razumihin noticed him, he passed him by, as he did not want to annoy him.

V

"Of course, I've been meaning lately to go to Razumihin's to ask for work, to ask him to get me lessons or something…" Raskolnikov thought, "but what help can he be to me now? Suppose he gets me lessons, suppose he shares his last farthing with me, if he has any farthings, so that I could get some boots and make myself tidy enough to give lessons… hm… Well and what then? What shall I do with the few coppers I earn? That's not what I want now. It's really absurd for me to go to Razumihin.…"

The question why he was now going to Razumihin agitated him even more than he was himself aware; he kept uneasily seeking for some sinister significance in this apparently ordinary action.

"Could I have expected to set it all straight and to find a way out by means of Razumihin alone?" he asked himself in perplexity.

He pondered and rubbed his forehead, and, strange to say, after long musing, suddenly, as if it were spontaneously and by chance, a fantastic thought came into his head.

"Hm… to Razumihin's," he said all at once, calmly, as though he had reached a final determination. "I shall go to Razumihin's of course, but… not now. I shall go to him… on the next day after It, when It will be over and everything will begin afresh.…"

And suddenly he realised what he was thinking.

"After It," he shouted, jumping up from the seat, "but is It really going to happen? Is it possible it really will happen?" He left the seat, and went off almost at a run; he meant to turn back, homewards, but the thought of going home suddenly filled him with intense loathing; in that hole, in that awful little cupboard of his, all *this* had for a month past been growing up in him; and he walked on at random.

His nervous shudder had passed into a fever that made him feel shivering; in spite of the heat he felt cold. With a kind of effort he began almost unconsciously, from some inner craving, to stare at all the objects before him, as though looking for something to distract his attention; but he did not succeed, and kept dropping every moment into brooding. When with a start he lifted his head again and looked round, he forgot at once what he had just been thinking about and even where he was going. In this way he walked right across Vassilyevsky Ostrov, came out on to the Lesser Neva, crossed the bridge and turned towards the islands. The greenness and freshness were at first restful to his weary eyes after the dust of the town and the huge houses that hemmed him in and weighed upon him. Here there were no taverns, no stifling closeness, no stench. But soon these new pleasant sensations passed into morbid irritability. Sometimes he stood still before a brightly painted summer villa standing among green foliage, he gazed through the fence, he saw in the distance smartly dressed women on the verandahs and balconies, and children running in the gardens. The flowers especially caught his attention; he gazed at them longer than at anything. He was met, too, by luxurious carriages and by men and women on horseback; he watched them with curious eyes and forgot about them before they had vanished from his sight. Once he stood still and counted his money; he found he had thirty kopecks. "Twenty to the policeman, three to Nastasya for the letter, so I must have given forty-seven or fifty to the Marmeladovs yesterday," he thought, reckoning it up for some unknown reason, but he soon forgot with what object he had taken the money out of his pocket. He recalled it on passing an eating-house or tavern, and felt that he was hungry.… Going into the tavern he drank a glass of vodka and ate a pie of some sort. He finished eating it as he walked away. It was a long while since he had taken vodka and it had an effect upon him at once, though he only drank a wineglassful. His legs felt suddenly heavy and a great drowsiness came upon him. He turned homewards, but reaching Petrovsky Ostrov he stopped completely exhausted, turned off the road into the bushes, sank down upon the grass and instantly fell asleep.

In a morbid condition of the brain, dreams often have a singular actuality, vividness, and extraordinary semblance of reality. At times monstrous images are created, but the setting and the whole picture are so truth-like and filled with details so delicate, so unexpectedly, but so artistically consistent, that the dreamer, were he an artist like Pushkin or Turgenev even, could never have invented them in the waking state. Such sick dreams always remain long in the memory and make a powerful impression on the overwrought and deranged nervous system.

Raskolnikov had a fearful dream. He dreamt he was back in his childhood in the little town of his birth. He was a child about seven years old, walking into the country with his father on the evening of a holiday. It was a grey and heavy day, the country was exactly as he remembered it; indeed he recalled it far more vividly in his dream than he had done in memory. The little town stood on a level flat as bare as the hand, not even a willow near it; only in the far distance, a copse lay, a dark blur on the very edge of the horizon. A few paces beyond the last market garden stood a tavern, a big tavern, which had always aroused in him a feeling of aversion, even of fear, when he walked by it with his father. There was always a crowd there, always shouting, laughter and abuse, hideous hoarse singing and often fighting. Drunken and horrible-looking figures were hanging about the tavern. He used to cling close to his father, trembling all over when he met them. Near the tavern the road became a dusty track, the dust of which was always black. It was a winding road, and about a hundred paces further on, it turned to the right to the graveyard. In the middle of the graveyard stood a stone church with a green cupola where he used to go to mass two or three times a year with his father and mother, when a service was held in memory of his grandmother, who had long been dead, and whom he had never seen. On these occasions they used to take on a white dish tied up in a table napkin a special sort of rice pudding with raisins stuck in it in the shape of a cross. He loved that church, the old-fashioned, unadorned icons and the old priest with the shaking head. Near his grandmother's grave, which was marked by a stone, was the little grave of his younger brother who had died at six months old. He did not remember him at all, but he had been told about his little brother, and whenever he visited the graveyard he used religiously and reverently to cross himself and to bow down and kiss the little grave. And now he dreamt that he was walking with his father past the tavern on the way to the graveyard; he was holding his father's hand and looking with dread at the tavern. A peculiar circumstance attracted his attention: there seemed to be some kind of festivity going on, there were crowds of gaily dressed townspeople, peasant women, their husbands, and riffraff of all sorts, all singing and all more or less drunk. Near the entrance of the tavern stood a cart, but a strange cart. It was one of those big carts usually drawn by heavy carthorses and laden with casks of wine or other heavy goods. He always liked looking at those great carthorses, with their long manes, thick legs, and slow even pace, drawing along a perfect mountain with no appearance of effort, as though it were easier going with a load than without it. But now, strange to say, in the shafts of such a cart he saw a thin little sorrel beast, one of those peasants' nags which he had often seen straining their utmost under a heavy load of wood or hay, especially when the wheels were stuck in the mud or in a rut. And the peasants would beat them so cruelly, sometimes even about the nose and eyes, and he felt so sorry, so sorry for them that he almost cried, and his mother always used to take him away from the window. All of a sudden there was a great uproar of shouting, singing and the balalaika, and from the tavern a number of big and very drunken peasants came out, wearing red and blue shirts and coats thrown over their shoulders.

"Get in, get in!" shouted one of them, a young thick-necked peasant with a fleshy face red as a carrot. "I'll take you all, get in!"

But at once there was an outbreak of laughter and exclamations in the crowd.

"Take us all with a beast like that!"

"Why, Mikolka, are you crazy to put a nag like that in such a cart?"

"And this mare is twenty if she is a day, mates!"

"Get in, I'll take you all," Mikolka shouted again, leaping first into the cart, seizing the reins and standing straight up in front. "The bay has gone with Matvey," he shouted from the cart—

"and this brute, mates, is just breaking my heart, I feel as if I could kill her. She's just eating her head off. Get in, I tell you! I'll make her gallop! She'll gallop!" and he picked up the whip, preparing himself with relish to flog the little mare.

"Get in! Come along!" The crowd laughed. "D'you hear, she'll gallop!"

"Gallop indeed! She has not had a gallop in her for the last ten years!"

"She'll jog along!"

"Don't you mind her, mates, bring a whip each of you, get ready!"

"All right! Give it to her!"

They all clambered into Mikolka's cart, laughing and making jokes. Six men got in and there was still room for more. They hauled in a fat, rosy-cheeked woman. She was dressed in red cotton, in a pointed, beaded headdress and thick leather shoes; she was cracking nuts and laughing. The crowd round them was laughing too and indeed, how could they help laughing? That wretched nag was to drag all the cartload of them at a gallop! Two young fellows in the cart were just getting whips ready to help Mikolka. With the cry of "now," the mare tugged with all her might, but far from galloping, could scarcely move forward; she struggled with her legs, gasping and shrinking from the blows of the three whips which were showered upon her like hail. The laughter in the cart and in the crowd was redoubled, but Mikolka flew into a rage and furiously thrashed the mare, as though he supposed she really could gallop.

"Let me get in, too, mates," shouted a young man in the crowd whose appetite was aroused.

"Get in, all get in," cried Mikolka, "she will draw you all. I'll beat her to death!" And he thrashed and thrashed at the mare, beside himself with fury.

"Father, father," he cried, "father, what are they doing? Father, they are beating the poor horse!"

"Come along, come along!" said his father. "They are drunken and foolish, they are in fun; come away, don't look!" and he tried to draw him away, but he tore himself away from his hand, and, beside himself with horror, ran to the horse. The poor beast was in a bad way. She was gasping, standing still, then tugging again and almost falling.

"Beat her to death," cried Mikolka, "it's come to that. I'll do for her!"

"What are you about, are you a Christian, you devil?" shouted an old man in the crowd.

"Did anyone ever see the like? A wretched nag like that pulling such a cartload," said another.

"You'll kill her," shouted the third.

"Don't meddle! It's my property, I'll do what I choose. Get in, more of you! Get in, all of you! I will have her go at a gallop!..."

All at once laughter broke into a roar and covered everything: the mare, roused by the shower of blows, began feebly kicking. Even the old man could not help smiling. To think of a wretched little beast like that trying to kick!

Two lads in the crowd snatched up whips and ran to the mare to beat her about the ribs. One ran each side.

"Hit her in the face, in the eyes, in the eyes," cried Mikolka.

"Give us a song, mates," shouted someone in the cart and everyone in the cart joined in a riotous song, jingling a tambourine and whistling. The woman went on cracking nuts and laughing.

... He ran beside the mare, ran in front of her, saw her being whipped across the eyes, right in the eyes! He was crying, he felt choking, his tears were streaming. One of the men gave him a cut with the whip across the face, he did not feel it. Wringing his hands and screaming, he rushed up to the grey-headed old man with the grey beard, who was shaking his head in disapproval. One woman seized him by the hand and would have taken him away, but he tore himself from her and ran back to the mare. She was almost at the last gasp, but began kicking once more.

"I'll teach you to kick," Mikolka shouted ferociously. He threw down the whip, bent forward and picked up from the bottom of the cart a long, thick shaft, he took hold of one end with both hands and with an effort brandished it over the mare.

"He'll crush her," was shouted round him. "He'll kill her!"

31

"It's my property," shouted Mikolka and brought the shaft down with a swinging blow. There was a sound of a heavy thud.

"Thrash her, thrash her! Why have you stopped?" shouted voices in the crowd.

And Mikolka swung the shaft a second time and it fell a second time on the spine of the luckless mare. She sank back on her haunches, but lurched forward and tugged forward with all her force, tugged first on one side and then on the other, trying to move the cart. But the six whips were attacking her in all directions, and the shaft was raised again and fell upon her a third time, then a fourth, with heavy measured blows. Mikolka was in a fury that he could not kill her at one blow.

"She's a tough one," was shouted in the crowd.

"She'll fall in a minute, mates, there will soon be an end of her," said an admiring spectator in the crowd.

"Fetch an axe to her! Finish her off," shouted a third.

"I'll show you! Stand off," Mikolka screamed frantically; he threw down the shaft, stooped down in the cart and picked up an iron crowbar. "Look out," he shouted, and with all his might he dealt a stunning blow at the poor mare. The blow fell; the mare staggered, sank back, tried to pull, but the bar fell again with a swinging blow on her back and she fell on the ground like a log.

"Finish her off," shouted Mikolka and he leapt beside himself, out of the cart. Several young men, also flushed with drink, seized anything they could come across—whips, sticks, poles, and ran to the dying mare. Mikolka stood on one side and began dealing random blows with the crowbar. The mare stretched out her head, drew a long breath and died.

"You butchered her," someone shouted in the crowd.

"Why wouldn't she gallop then?"

"My property!" shouted Mikolka, with bloodshot eyes, brandishing the bar in his hands. He stood as though regretting that he had nothing more to beat.

"No mistake about it, you are not a Christian," many voices were shouting in the crowd.

But the poor boy, beside himself, made his way, screaming, through the crowd to the sorrel nag, put his arms round her bleeding dead head and kissed it, kissed the eyes and kissed the lips.... Then he jumped up and flew in a frenzy with his little fists out at Mikolka. At that instant his father, who had been running after him, snatched him up and carried him out of the crowd.

"Come along, come! Let us go home," he said to him.

"Father! Why did they ... kill ... the poor horse!" he sobbed, but his voice broke and the words came in shrieks from his panting chest.

"They are drunk.... They are brutal... it's not our business!" said his father. He put his arms round his father but he felt choked, choked. He tried to draw a breath, to cry out—and woke up.

He waked up, gasping for breath, his hair soaked with perspiration, and stood up in terror.

"Thank God, that was only a dream," he said, sitting down under a tree and drawing deep breaths. "But what is it? Is it some fever coming on? Such a hideous dream!"

He felt utterly broken: darkness and confusion were in his soul. He rested his elbows on his knees and leaned his head on his hands.

"Good God!" he cried, "can it be, can it be, that I shall really take an axe, that I shall strike her on the head, split her skull open... that I shall tread in the sticky warm blood, break the lock, steal and tremble; hide, all spattered in the blood... with the axe.... Good God, can it be?"

He was shaking like a leaf as he said this.

"But why am I going on like this?" he continued, sitting up again, as it were in profound amazement. "I knew that I could never bring myself to it, so what have I been torturing myself for till now? Yesterday, yesterday, when I went to make that... *experiment*, yesterday I realised completely that I could never bear to do it.... Why am I going over it again, then? Why am I hesitating? As I came down the stairs yesterday, I said myself that it was base, loathsome, vile, vile... the very thought of it made me feel sick and filled me with horror.

"No, I couldn't do it, I couldn't do it! Granted, granted that there is no flaw in all that reasoning, that all that I have concluded this last month is clear as day, true as arithmetic.... My

God! Anyway I couldn't bring myself to it! I couldn't do it, I couldn't do it! Why, why then am I still…?"

He rose to his feet, looked round in wonder as though surprised at finding himself in this place, and went towards the bridge. He was pale, his eyes glowed, he was exhausted in every limb, but he seemed suddenly to breathe more easily. He felt he had cast off that fearful burden that had so long been weighing upon him, and all at once there was a sense of relief and peace in his soul. "Lord," he prayed, "show me my path—I renounce that accursed… dream of mine."

Crossing the bridge, he gazed quietly and calmly at the Neva, at the glowing red sun setting in the glowing sky. In spite of his weakness he was not conscious of fatigue. It was as though an abscess that had been forming for a month past in his heart had suddenly broken. Freedom, freedom! He was free from that spell, that sorcery, that obsession!

Later on, when he recalled that time and all that happened to him during those days, minute by minute, point by point, he was superstitiously impressed by one circumstance, which, though in itself not very exceptional, always seemed to him afterwards the predestined turning-point of his fate. He could never understand and explain to himself why, when he was tired and worn out, when it would have been more convenient for him to go home by the shortest and most direct way, he had returned by the Hay Market where he had no need to go. It was obviously and quite unnecessarily out of his way, though not much so. It is true that it happened to him dozens of times to return home without noticing what streets he passed through. But why, he was always asking himself, why had such an important, such a decisive and at the same time such an absolutely chance meeting happened in the Hay Market (where he had moreover no reason to go) at the very hour, the very minute of his life when he was just in the very mood and in the very circumstances in which that meeting was able to exert the gravest and most decisive influence on his whole destiny? As though it had been lying in wait for him on purpose!

It was about nine o'clock when he crossed the Hay Market. At the tables and the barrows, at the booths and the shops, all the market people were closing their establishments or clearing away and packing up their wares and, like their customers, were going home. Rag pickers and costermongers of all kinds were crowding round the taverns in the dirty and stinking courtyards of the Hay Market. Raskolnikov particularly liked this place and the neighbouring alleys, when he wandered aimlessly in the streets. Here his rags did not attract contemptuous attention, and one could walk about in any attire without scandalising people. At the corner of an alley a huckster and his wife had two tables set out with tapes, thread, cotton handkerchiefs, etc. They, too, had got up to go home, but were lingering in conversation with a friend, who had just come up to them. This friend was Lizaveta Ivanovna, or, as everyone called her, Lizaveta, the younger sister of the old pawnbroker, Alyona Ivanovna, whom Raskolnikov had visited the previous day to pawn his watch and make his *experiment*.… He already knew all about Lizaveta and she knew him a little too. She was a single woman of about thirty-five, tall, clumsy, timid, submissive and almost idiotic. She was a complete slave and went in fear and trembling of her sister, who made her work day and night, and even beat her. She was standing with a bundle before the huckster and his wife, listening earnestly and doubtfully. They were talking of something with special warmth. The moment Raskolnikov caught sight of her, he was overcome by a strange sensation as it were of intense astonishment, though there was nothing astonishing about this meeting.

"You could make up your mind for yourself, Lizaveta Ivanovna," the huckster was saying aloud. "Come round tomorrow about seven. They will be here too."

"Tomorrow?" said Lizaveta slowly and thoughtfully, as though unable to make up her mind.

"Upon my word, what a fright you are in of Alyona Ivanovna," gabbled the huckster's wife, a lively little woman. "I look at you, you are like some little babe. And she is not your own sister either—nothing but a stepsister and what a hand she keeps over you!"

"But this time don't say a word to Alyona Ivanovna," her husband interrupted; "that's my advice, but come round to us without asking. It will be worth your while. Later on your sister herself may have a notion."

"Am I to come?"

"About seven o'clock tomorrow. And they will be here. You will be able to decide for yourself."

"And we'll have a cup of tea," added his wife.

"All right, I'll come," said Lizaveta, still pondering, and she began slowly moving away.

Raskolnikov had just passed and heard no more. He passed softly, unnoticed, trying not to miss a word. His first amazement was followed by a thrill of horror, like a shiver running down his spine. He had learnt, he had suddenly quite unexpectedly learnt, that the next day at seven o'clock Lizaveta, the old woman's sister and only companion, would be away from home and that therefore at seven o'clock precisely the old woman *would be left alone*.

He was only a few steps from his lodging. He went in like a man condemned to death. He thought of nothing and was incapable of thinking; but he felt suddenly in his whole being that he had no more freedom of thought, no will, and that everything was suddenly and irrevocably decided.

Certainly, if he had to wait whole years for a suitable opportunity, he could not reckon on a more certain step towards the success of the plan than that which had just presented itself. In any case, it would have been difficult to find out beforehand and with certainty, with greater exactness and less risk, and without dangerous inquiries and investigations, that next day at a certain time an old woman, on whose life an attempt was contemplated, would be at home and entirely alone.

Later on Raskolnikov happened to find out why the huckster and his wife had invited Lizaveta. It was a very ordinary matter and there was nothing exceptional about it. A family who had come to the town and been reduced to poverty were selling their household goods and clothes, all women's things. As the things would have fetched little in the market, they were looking for a dealer. This was Lizaveta's business. She undertook such jobs and was frequently employed, as she was very honest and always fixed a fair price and stuck to it. She spoke as a rule little and, as we have said already, she was very submissive and timid.

But Raskolnikov had become superstitious of late. The traces of superstition remained in him long after, and were almost ineradicable. And in all this he was always afterwards disposed to see something strange and mysterious, as it were, the presence of some peculiar influences and coincidences. In the previous winter a student he knew called Pokorev, who had left for Harkov, had chanced in conversation to give him the address of Alyona Ivanovna, the old pawnbroker, in case he might want to pawn anything. For a long while he did not go to her, for he had lessons and managed to get along somehow. Six weeks ago he had remembered the address; he had two articles that could be pawned: his father's old silver watch and a little gold ring with three red stones, a present from his sister at parting. He decided to take the ring. When he found the old woman he had felt an insurmountable repulsion for her at the first glance, though he knew nothing special about her. He got two roubles from her and went into a miserable little tavern on his way home. He asked for tea, sat down and sank into deep thought. A strange idea was pecking at his brain like a chicken in the egg, and very, very much absorbed him.

Almost beside him at the next table there was sitting a student, whom he did not know and had never seen, and with him a young officer. They had played a game of billiards and began drinking tea. All at once he heard the student mention to the officer the pawnbroker Alyona Ivanovna and give him her address. This of itself seemed strange to Raskolnikov; he had just come from her and here at once he heard her name. Of course it was a chance, but he could not shake off a very extraordinary impression, and here someone seemed to be speaking expressly for him; the student began telling his friend various details about Alyona Ivanovna.

"She is first-rate," he said. "You can always get money from her. She is as rich as a Jew, she can give you five thousand roubles at a time and she is not above taking a pledge for a rouble. Lots of our fellows have had dealings with her. But she is an awful old harpy...."

And he began describing how spiteful and uncertain she was, how if you were only a day late with your interest the pledge was lost; how she gave a quarter of the value of an article and took five and even seven percent a month on it and so on. The student chattered on, saying that she had a sister Lizaveta, whom the wretched little creature was continually beating, and kept in complete bondage like a small child, though Lizaveta was at least six feet high.

"There's a phenomenon for you," cried the student and he laughed.

They began talking about Lizaveta. The student spoke about her with a peculiar relish and was continually laughing and the officer listened with great interest and asked him to send Lizaveta to do some mending for him. Raskolnikov did not miss a word and learned everything about her. Lizaveta was younger than the old woman and was her half-sister, being the child of a different mother. She was thirty-five. She worked day and night for her sister, and besides doing the cooking and the washing, she did sewing and worked as a charwoman and gave her sister all she earned. She did not dare to accept an order or job of any kind without her sister's permission. The old woman had already made her will, and Lizaveta knew of it, and by this will she would not get a farthing; nothing but the movables, chairs and so on; all the money was left to a monastery in the province of N——, that prayers might be said for her in perpetuity. Lizaveta was of lower rank than her sister, unmarried and awfully uncouth in appearance, remarkably tall with long feet that looked as if they were bent outwards. She always wore battered goatskin shoes, and was clean in her person. What the student expressed most surprise and amusement about was the fact that Lizaveta was continually with child.

"But you say she is hideous?" observed the officer.

"Yes, she is so dark-skinned and looks like a soldier dressed up, but you know she is not at all hideous. She has such a good-natured face and eyes. Strikingly so. And the proof of it is that lots of people are attracted by her. She is such a soft, gentle creature, ready to put up with anything, always willing, willing to do anything. And her smile is really very sweet."

"You seem to find her attractive yourself," laughed the officer.

"From her queerness. No, I'll tell you what. I could kill that damned old woman and make off with her money, I assure you, without the faintest conscience-prick," the student added with warmth. The officer laughed again while Raskolnikov shuddered. How strange it was!

"Listen, I want to ask you a serious question," the student said hotly. "I was joking of course, but look here; on one side we have a stupid, senseless, worthless, spiteful, ailing, horrid old woman, not simply useless but doing actual mischief, who has not an idea what she is living for herself, and who will die in a day or two in any case. You understand? You understand?"

"Yes, yes, I understand," answered the officer, watching his excited companion attentively.

"Well, listen then. On the other side, fresh young lives thrown away for want of help and by thousands, on every side! A hundred thousand good deeds could be done and helped, on that old woman's money which will be buried in a monastery! Hundreds, thousands perhaps, might be set on the right path; dozens of families saved from destitution, from ruin, from vice, from the Lock hospitals—and all with her money. Kill her, take her money and with the help of it devote oneself to the service of humanity and the good of all. What do you think, would not one tiny crime be wiped out by thousands of good deeds? For one life thousands would be saved from corruption and decay. One death, and a hundred lives in exchange—it's simple arithmetic! Besides, what value has the life of that sickly, stupid, ill-natured old woman in the balance of existence! No more than the life of a louse, of a black-beetle, less in fact because the old woman is doing harm. She is wearing out the lives of others; the other day she bit Lizaveta's finger out of spite; it almost had to be amputated."

"Of course she does not deserve to live," remarked the officer, "but there it is, it's nature."

"Oh, well, brother, but we have to correct and direct nature, and, but for that, we should drown in an ocean of prejudice. But for that, there would never have been a single great man. They talk of duty, conscience—I don't want to say anything against duty and conscience;—but the point is, what do we mean by them? Stay, I have another question to ask you. Listen!"

"No, you stay, I'll ask you a question. Listen!"

"Well?"

"You are talking and speechifying away, but tell me, would you kill the old woman *yourself*?"

"Of course not! I was only arguing the justice of it.... It's nothing to do with me...."

"But I think, if you would not do it yourself, there's no justice about it.... Let us have another game."

Raskolnikov was violently agitated. Of course, it was all ordinary youthful talk and thought, such as he had often heard before in different forms and on different themes. But why had he happened to hear such a discussion and such ideas at the very moment when his own brain was just conceiving... *the very same ideas*? And why, just at the moment when he had brought away the embryo of his idea from the old woman had he dropped at once upon a conversation about her? This coincidence always seemed strange to him. This trivial talk in a tavern had an immense influence on him in his later action; as though there had really been in it something preordained, some guiding hint....

On returning from the Hay Market he flung himself on the sofa and sat for a whole hour without stirring. Meanwhile it got dark; he had no candle and, indeed, it did not occur to him to light up. He could never recollect whether he had been thinking about anything at that time. At last he was conscious of his former fever and shivering, and he realised with relief that he could lie down on the sofa. Soon heavy, leaden sleep came over him, as it were crushing him.

He slept an extraordinarily long time and without dreaming. Nastasya, coming into his room at ten o'clock the next morning, had difficulty in rousing him. She brought him in tea and bread. The tea was again the second brew and again in her own teapot.

"My goodness, how he sleeps!" she cried indignantly. "And he is always asleep."

He got up with an effort. His head ached, he stood up, took a turn in his garret and sank back on the sofa again.

"Going to sleep again," cried Nastasya. "Are you ill, eh?"

He made no reply.

"Do you want some tea?"

"Afterwards," he said with an effort, closing his eyes again and turning to the wall.

Nastasya stood over him.

"Perhaps he really is ill," she said, turned and went out. She came in again at two o'clock with soup. He was lying as before. The tea stood untouched. Nastasya felt positively offended and began wrathfully rousing him.

"Why are you lying like a log?" she shouted, looking at him with repulsion.

He got up, and sat down again, but said nothing and stared at the floor.

"Are you ill or not?" asked Nastasya and again received no answer. "You'd better go out and get a breath of air," she said after a pause. "Will you eat it or not?"

"Afterwards," he said weakly. "You can go."

And he motioned her out.

She remained a little longer, looked at him with compassion and went out.

A few minutes afterwards, he raised his eyes and looked for a long while at the tea and the soup. Then he took the bread, took up a spoon and began to eat.

He ate a little, three or four spoonfuls, without appetite, as it were mechanically. His head ached less. After his meal he stretched himself on the sofa again, but now he could not sleep; he lay without stirring, with his face in the pillow. He was haunted by daydreams and such strange daydreams; in one, that kept recurring, he fancied that he was in Africa, in Egypt, in some sort of oasis. The caravan was resting, the camels were peacefully lying down; the palms stood all around in a complete circle; all the party were at dinner. But he was drinking water from a spring which flowed gurgling close by. And it was so cool, it was wonderful, wonderful, blue, cold water running among the particoloured stones and over the clean sand which glistened here and there like gold.... Suddenly he heard a clock strike. He started, roused himself, raised his head, looked out of the window, and seeing how late it was, suddenly jumped up wide awake as though someone had pulled him off the sofa. He crept on tiptoe to the door, stealthily opened it and began listening on the staircase. His heart beat terribly. But all was quiet on the stairs as if everyone was asleep.... It seemed to him strange and monstrous that he could have slept in such forgetfulness from the previous day and had done nothing, had prepared nothing yet.... And meanwhile perhaps it had struck six. And his drowsiness and stupefaction were followed by an extraordinary, feverish, as it were distracted haste. But the preparations to be made were few. He concentrated all his energies on thinking of everything and forgetting nothing; and his heart kept beating and thumping so that he could hardly breathe. First he had to make a noose and sew it into his overcoat—a work of a moment. He rummaged under his pillow and picked out amongst the linen stuffed away under it, a worn out, old unwashed shirt. From its rags he tore a long strip, a couple of inches wide and about sixteen inches long. He folded this strip in two, took off his wide, strong summer overcoat of some stout cotton material (his only outer garment) and began sewing the two ends of the rag on the inside, under the left armhole. His hands shook as he sewed, but he did it successfully so that nothing showed outside when he put the coat on again. The needle and thread he had got ready long before and they lay on his table in a piece of paper. As for the noose, it was a very ingenious device of his own; the noose was intended for the axe. It was impossible for him to carry the axe through the street in his hands. And if hidden under his coat he would still have had to support it with his hand, which would have been noticeable. Now he had only to put the head of the axe in the noose, and it would hang quietly under his arm on the inside. Putting his hand in his coat pocket, he could hold the end of the handle all the way, so that it did not swing; and as the coat was very full, a regular sack in fact, it could not be seen from outside that he was holding something with the hand that was in the pocket. This noose, too, he had designed a fortnight before.

When he had finished with this, he thrust his hand into a little opening between his sofa and the floor, fumbled in the left corner and drew out the *pledge*, which he had got ready long before and hidden there. This pledge was, however, only a smoothly planed piece of wood the size and thickness of a silver cigarette case. He picked up this piece of wood in one of his wanderings in a courtyard where there was some sort of a workshop. Afterwards he had added to the wood a thin smooth piece of iron, which he had also picked up at the same time in the street. Putting the iron which was a little the smaller on the piece of wood, he fastened them very firmly, crossing and re-crossing the thread round them; then wrapped them carefully and daintily in clean white paper and tied up the parcel so that it would be very difficult to untie it. This was in order to divert the attention of the old woman for a time, while she was trying to undo the knot, and so to gain a moment. The iron strip was added to give weight, so that the woman might not guess the first minute that the "thing" was made of wood. All this had been stored by him beforehand under the sofa. He had only just got the pledge out when he heard someone suddenly about in the yard.

"It struck six long ago."

"Long ago! My God!"

He rushed to the door, listened, caught up his hat and began to descend his thirteen steps cautiously, noiselessly, like a cat. He had still the most important thing to do—to steal the axe from the kitchen. That the deed must be done with an axe he had decided long ago. He had also a pocket pruning-knife, but he could not rely on the knife and still less on his own strength, and so resolved finally on the axe. We may note in passing, one peculiarity in regard to all the final resolutions taken by him in the matter; they had one strange characteristic: the more final they were, the more hideous and the more absurd they at once became in his eyes. In spite of all his agonising inward struggle, he never for a single instant all that time could believe in the carrying out of his plans.

And, indeed, if it had ever happened that everything to the least point could have been considered and finally settled, and no uncertainty of any kind had remained, he would, it seems, have renounced it all as something absurd, monstrous and impossible. But a whole mass of unsettled points and uncertainties remained. As for getting the axe, that trifling business cost him no anxiety, for nothing could be easier. Nastasya was continually out of the house, especially in the evenings; she would run in to the neighbours or to a shop, and always left the door ajar. It was the one thing the landlady was always scolding her about. And so, when the time came, he would only have to go quietly into the kitchen and to take the axe, and an hour later (when everything was over) go in and put it back again. But these were doubtful points. Supposing he returned an hour later to put it back, and Nastasya had come back and was on the spot. He would of course have to go by and wait till she went out again. But supposing she were in the meantime to miss the axe, look for it, make an outcry—that would mean suspicion or at least grounds for suspicion.

But those were all trifles which he had not even begun to consider, and indeed he had no time. He was thinking of the chief point, and put off trifling details, until *he could believe in it all*. But that seemed utterly unattainable. So it seemed to himself at least. He could not imagine, for instance, that he would sometime leave off thinking, get up and simply go there.... Even his late experiment (i.e. his visit with the object of a final survey of the place) was simply an attempt at an experiment, far from being the real thing, as though one should say "come, let us go and try it—

why dream about it!"—and at once he had broken down and had run away cursing, in a frenzy with himself. Meanwhile it would seem, as regards the moral question, that his analysis was complete; his casuistry had become keen as a razor, and he could not find rational objections in himself. But in the last resort he simply ceased to believe in himself, and doggedly, slavishly sought arguments in all directions, fumbling for them, as though someone were forcing and drawing him to it.

At first—long before indeed—he had been much occupied with one question; why almost all crimes are so badly concealed and so easily detected, and why almost all criminals leave such obvious traces? He had come gradually to many different and curious conclusions, and in his opinion the chief reason lay not so much in the material impossibility of concealing the crime, as in the criminal himself. Almost every criminal is subject to a failure of will and reasoning power by a childish and phenomenal heedlessness, at the very instant when prudence and caution are most essential. It was his conviction that this eclipse of reason and failure of will power attacked a man like a disease, developed gradually and reached its highest point just before the perpetration of the crime, continued with equal violence at the moment of the crime and for longer or shorter time after, according to the individual case, and then passed off like any other disease. The question whether the disease gives rise to the crime, or whether the crime from its own peculiar nature is always accompanied by something of the nature of disease, he did not yet feel able to decide.

When he reached these conclusions, he decided that in his own case there could not be such a morbid reaction, that his reason and will would remain unimpaired at the time of carrying out his design, for the simple reason that his design was "not a crime...." We will omit all the process by means of which he arrived at this last conclusion; we have run too far ahead already.... We may add only that the practical, purely material difficulties of the affair occupied a secondary position in his mind. "One has but to keep all one's willpower and reason to deal with them, and they will all be overcome at the time when once one has familiarised oneself with the minutest details of the business...." But this preparation had never been begun. His final decisions were what he came to trust least, and when the hour struck, it all came to pass quite differently, as it were accidentally and unexpectedly.

One trifling circumstance upset his calculations, before he had even left the staircase. When he reached the landlady's kitchen, the door of which was open as usual, he glanced cautiously in to see whether, in Nastasya's absence, the landlady herself was there, or if not, whether the door to her own room was closed, so that she might not peep out when he went in for the axe. But what was his amazement when he suddenly saw that Nastasya was not only at home in the kitchen, but was occupied there, taking linen out of a basket and hanging it on a line. Seeing him, she left off hanging the clothes, turned to him and stared at him all the time he was passing. He turned away his eyes, and walked past as though he noticed nothing. But it was the end of everything; he had not the axe! He was overwhelmed.

"What made me think," he reflected, as he went under the gateway, "what made me think that she would be sure not to be at home at that moment! Why, why, why did I assume this so certainly?"

He was crushed and even humiliated. He could have laughed at himself in his anger.... A dull animal rage boiled within him.

He stood hesitating in the gateway. To go into the street, to go a walk for appearance' sake was revolting; to go back to his room, even more revolting. "And what a chance I have lost for ever!" he muttered, standing aimlessly in the gateway, just opposite the porter's little dark room, which was also open. Suddenly he started. From the porter's room, two paces away from him, something shining under the bench to the right caught his eye.... He looked about him—nobody. He approached the room on tiptoe, went down two steps into it and in a faint voice called the porter. "Yes, not at home! Somewhere near though, in the yard, for the door is wide open." He dashed to the axe (it was an axe) and pulled it out from under the bench, where it lay between two chunks of wood; at once, before going out, he made it fast in the noose, he thrust both hands into his pockets and went out of the room; no one had noticed him! "When reason fails, the devil helps!" he thought with a strange grin. This chance raised his spirits extraordinarily.

He walked along quietly and sedately, without hurry, to avoid awakening suspicion. He scarcely looked at the passersby, tried to escape looking at their faces at all, and to be as little noticeable as possible. Suddenly he thought of his hat. "Good heavens! I had the money the day before yesterday and did not get a cap to wear instead!" A curse rose from the bottom of his soul.

Glancing out of the corner of his eye into a shop, he saw by a clock on the wall that it was ten minutes past seven. He had to make haste and at the same time to go someway round, so as to approach the house from the other side....

When he had happened to imagine all this beforehand, he had sometimes thought that he would be very much afraid. But he was not very much afraid now, was not afraid at all, indeed. His mind was even occupied by irrelevant matters, but by nothing for long. As he passed the Yusupov garden, he was deeply absorbed in considering the building of great fountains, and of their refreshing effect on the atmosphere in all the squares. By degrees he passed to the conviction that if the summer garden were extended to the field of Mars, and perhaps joined to the garden of the Mihailovsky Palace, it would be a splendid thing and a great benefit to the town. Then he was interested by the question why in all great towns men are not simply driven by necessity, but in some peculiar way inclined to live in those parts of the town where there are no gardens nor fountains; where there is most dirt and smell and all sorts of nastiness. Then his own walks through the Hay Market came back to his mind, and for a moment he waked up to reality. "What nonsense!" he thought, "better think of nothing at all!"

"So probably men led to execution clutch mentally at every object that meets them on the way," flashed through his mind, but simply flashed, like lightning; he made haste to dismiss this thought.... And by now he was near; here was the house, here was the gate. Suddenly a clock somewhere struck once. "What! can it be half-past seven? Impossible, it must be fast!"

Luckily for him, everything went well again at the gates. At that very moment, as though expressly for his benefit, a huge wagon of hay had just driven in at the gate, completely screening him as he passed under the gateway, and the wagon had scarcely had time to drive through into the yard, before he had slipped in a flash to the right. On the other side of the wagon he could hear shouting and quarrelling; but no one noticed him and no one met him. Many windows looking into that huge quadrangular yard were open at that moment, but he did not raise his head—he had not the strength to. The staircase leading to the old woman's room was close by, just on the right of the gateway. He was already on the stairs....

Drawing a breath, pressing his hand against his throbbing heart, and once more feeling for the axe and setting it straight, he began softly and cautiously ascending the stairs, listening every minute. But the stairs, too, were quite deserted; all the doors were shut; he met no one. One flat indeed on the first floor was wide open and painters were at work in it, but they did not glance at him. He stood still, thought a minute and went on. "Of course it would be better if they had not been here, but... it's two storeys above them."

And there was the fourth storey, here was the door, here was the flat opposite, the empty one. The flat underneath the old woman's was apparently empty also; the visiting card nailed on the door had been torn off—they had gone away!... He was out of breath. For one instant the thought floated through his mind, "Shall I go back?" But he made no answer and began listening at the old woman's door, a dead silence. Then he listened again on the staircase, listened long and intently... then looked about him for the last time, pulled himself together, drew himself up, and once more tried the axe in the noose. "Am I very pale?" he wondered. "Am I not evidently agitated? She is mistrustful.... Had I better wait a little longer... till my heart leaves off thumping?"

But his heart did not leave off. On the contrary, as though to spite him, it throbbed more and more violently. He could stand it no longer, he slowly put out his hand to the bell and rang. Half a minute later he rang again, more loudly.

No answer. To go on ringing was useless and out of place. The old woman was, of course, at home, but she was suspicious and alone. He had some knowledge of her habits... and once more

40

he put his ear to the door. Either his senses were peculiarly keen (which it is difficult to suppose), or the sound was really very distinct. Anyway, he suddenly heard something like the cautious touch of a hand on the lock and the rustle of a skirt at the very door. Someone was standing stealthily close to the lock and just as he was doing on the outside was secretly listening within, and seemed to have her ear to the door.... He moved a little on purpose and muttered something aloud that he might not have the appearance of hiding, then rang a third time, but quietly, soberly, and without impatience, Recalling it afterwards, that moment stood out in his mind vividly, distinctly, forever; he could not make out how he had had such cunning, for his mind was as it were clouded at moments and he was almost unconscious of his body.... An instant later he heard the latch unfastened.

The door was as before opened a tiny crack, and again two sharp and suspicious eyes stared at him out of the darkness. Then Raskolnikov lost his head and nearly made a great mistake.

Fearing the old woman would be frightened by their being alone, and not hoping that the sight of him would disarm her suspicions, he took hold of the door and drew it towards him to prevent the old woman from attempting to shut it again. Seeing this she did not pull the door back, but she did not let go the handle so that he almost dragged her out with it on to the stairs. Seeing that she was standing in the doorway not allowing him to pass, he advanced straight upon her. She stepped back in alarm, tried to say something, but seemed unable to speak and stared with open eyes at him.

"Good evening, Alyona Ivanovna," he began, trying to speak easily, but his voice would not obey him, it broke and shook. "I have come… I have brought something… but we'd better come in… to the light.…"

And leaving her, he passed straight into the room uninvited. The old woman ran after him; her tongue was unloosed.

"Good heavens! What it is? Who is it? What do you want?"

"Why, Alyona Ivanovna, you know me… Raskolnikov… here, I brought you the pledge I promised the other day…" And he held out the pledge.

The old woman glanced for a moment at the pledge, but at once stared in the eyes of her uninvited visitor. She looked intently, maliciously and mistrustfully. A minute passed; he even fancied something like a sneer in her eyes, as though she had already guessed everything. He felt that he was losing his head, that he was almost frightened, so frightened that if she were to look like that and not say a word for another half minute, he thought he would have run away from her.

"Why do you look at me as though you did not know me?" he said suddenly, also with malice. "Take it if you like, if not I'll go elsewhere, I am in a hurry."

He had not even thought of saying this, but it was suddenly said of itself. The old woman recovered herself, and her visitor's resolute tone evidently restored her confidence.

"But why, my good sir, all of a minute.… What is it?" she asked, looking at the pledge.

"The silver cigarette case; I spoke of it last time, you know."

She held out her hand.

"But how pale you are, to be sure… and your hands are trembling too? Have you been bathing, or what?"

"Fever," he answered abruptly. "You can't help getting pale… if you've nothing to eat," he added, with difficulty articulating the words.

His strength was failing him again. But his answer sounded like the truth; the old woman took the pledge.

"What is it?" she asked once more, scanning Raskolnikov intently, and weighing the pledge in her hand.

"A thing… cigarette case.… Silver.… Look at it."

"It does not seem somehow like silver.… How he has wrapped it up!"

Trying to untie the string and turning to the window, to the light (all her windows were shut, in spite of the stifling heat), she left him altogether for some seconds and stood with her back to him. He unbuttoned his coat and freed the axe from the noose, but did not yet take it out altogether, simply holding it in his right hand under the coat. His hands were fearfully weak, he felt them every moment growing more numb and more wooden. He was afraid he would let the axe slip and fall.... A sudden giddiness came over him.

"But what has he tied it up like this for?" the old woman cried with vexation and moved towards him.

He had not a minute more to lose. He pulled the axe quite out, swung it with both arms, scarcely conscious of himself, and almost without effort, almost mechanically, brought the blunt side down on her head. He seemed not to use his own strength in this. But as soon as he had once brought the axe down, his strength returned to him.

The old woman was as always bareheaded. Her thin, light hair, streaked with grey, thickly smeared with grease, was plaited in a rat's tail and fastened by a broken horn comb which stood out on the nape of her neck. As she was so short, the blow fell on the very top of her skull. She cried out, but very faintly, and suddenly sank all of a heap on the floor, raising her hands to her head. In one hand she still held "the pledge." Then he dealt her another and another blow with the blunt side and on the same spot. The blood gushed as from an overturned glass, the body fell back. He stepped back, let it fall, and at once bent over her face; she was dead. Her eyes seemed to be starting out of their sockets, the brow and the whole face were drawn and contorted convulsively.

He laid the axe on the ground near the dead body and felt at once in her pocket (trying to avoid the streaming body)—the same right-hand pocket from which she had taken the key on his last visit. He was in full possession of his faculties, free from confusion or giddiness, but his hands were still trembling. He remembered afterwards that he had been particularly collected and careful, trying all the time not to get smeared with blood.... He pulled out the keys at once, they were all, as before, in one bunch on a steel ring. He ran at once into the bedroom with them. It was a very small room with a whole shrine of holy images. Against the other wall stood a big bed, very clean and covered with a silk patchwork wadded quilt. Against a third wall was a chest of drawers. Strange to say, so soon as he began to fit the keys into the chest, so soon as he heard their jingling, a convulsive shudder passed over him. He suddenly felt tempted again to give it all up and go away. But that was only for an instant; it was too late to go back. He positively smiled at himself, when suddenly another terrifying idea occurred to his mind. He suddenly fancied that the old woman might be still alive and might recover her senses. Leaving the keys in the chest, he ran back to the body, snatched up the axe and lifted it once more over the old woman, but did not bring it down. There was no doubt that she was dead. Bending down and examining her again more closely, he saw clearly that the skull was broken and even battered in on one side. He was about to feel it with his finger, but drew back his hand and indeed it was evident without that. Meanwhile there was a perfect pool of blood. All at once he noticed a string on her neck; he tugged at it, but the string was strong and did not snap and besides, it was soaked with blood. He tried to pull it out from the front of the dress, but something held it and prevented its coming. In his impatience he raised the axe again to cut the string from above on the body, but did not dare, and with difficulty, smearing his hand and the axe in the blood, after two minutes' hurried effort, he cut the string and took it off without touching the body with the axe; he was not mistaken—it was a purse. On the string were two crosses, one of Cyprus wood and one of copper, and an image in silver filigree, and with them a small greasy chamois leather purse with a steel rim and ring. The purse was stuffed very full; Raskolnikov thrust it in his pocket without looking at it, flung the crosses on the old woman's body and rushed back into the bedroom, this time taking the axe with him.

He was in terrible haste, he snatched the keys, and began trying them again. But he was unsuccessful. They would not fit in the locks. It was not so much that his hands were shaking, but that he kept making mistakes; though he saw for instance that a key was not the right one and would not fit, still he tried to put it in. Suddenly he remembered and realised that the big key with the deep notches, which was hanging there with the small keys could not possibly belong to the chest of drawers (on his last visit this had struck him), but to some strong box, and that everything perhaps was hidden in that box. He left the chest of drawers, and at once felt under the bedstead, knowing that old women usually keep boxes under their beds. And so it was; there was a good-sized box under the bed, at least a yard in length, with an arched lid covered with red leather and studded with steel nails. The notched key fitted at once and unlocked it. At the top, under a white sheet, was a coat of red brocade lined with hareskin; under it was a silk dress, then a shawl and it seemed as though there was nothing below but clothes. The first thing he did was to wipe his bloodstained hands on the red brocade. "It's red, and on red blood will be less noticeable," the thought passed through his mind; then he suddenly came to himself. "Good God, am I going out of my senses?" he thought with terror.

But no sooner did he touch the clothes than a gold watch slipped from under the fur coat. He made haste to turn them all over. There turned out to be various articles made of gold among the clothes—probably all pledges, unredeemed or waiting to be redeemed—bracelets, chains, earrings, pins and such things. Some were in cases, others simply wrapped in newspaper, carefully and exactly folded, and tied round with tape. Without any delay, he began filling up the pockets of his trousers and overcoat without examining or undoing the parcels and cases; but he had not time to take many....

He suddenly heard steps in the room where the old woman lay. He stopped short and was still as death. But all was quiet, so it must have been his fancy. All at once he heard distinctly a faint cry, as though someone had uttered a low broken moan. Then again dead silence for a minute or two. He sat squatting on his heels by the box and waited holding his breath. Suddenly he jumped up, seized the axe and ran out of the bedroom.

In the middle of the room stood Lizaveta with a big bundle in her arms. She was gazing in stupefaction at her murdered sister, white as a sheet and seeming not to have the strength to cry out. Seeing him run out of the bedroom, she began faintly quivering all over, like a leaf, a shudder ran down her face; she lifted her hand, opened her mouth, but still did not scream. She began slowly backing away from him into the corner, staring intently, persistently at him, but still uttered no sound, as though she could not get breath to scream. He rushed at her with the axe; her mouth twitched piteously, as one sees babies' mouths, when they begin to be frightened, stare intently at what frightens them and are on the point of screaming. And this hapless Lizaveta was so simple and had been so thoroughly crushed and scared that she did not even raise a hand to guard her face, though that was the most necessary and natural action at the moment, for the axe was raised over her face. She only put up her empty left hand, but not to her face, slowly holding it out before her as though motioning him away. The axe fell with the sharp edge just on the skull and split at one blow all the top of the head. She fell heavily at once. Raskolnikov completely lost his head, snatching up her bundle, dropped it again and ran into the entry.

Fear gained more and more mastery over him, especially after this second, quite unexpected murder. He longed to run away from the place as fast as possible. And if at that moment he had been capable of seeing and reasoning more correctly, if he had been able to realise all the difficulties of his position, the hopelessness, the hideousness and the absurdity of it, if he could have understood how many obstacles and, perhaps, crimes he had still to overcome or to commit, to get out of that place and to make his way home, it is very possible that he would have flung up everything, and would have gone to give himself up, and not from fear, but from simple horror and loathing of what he had done. The feeling of loathing especially surged up within him and grew stronger every minute. He would not now have gone to the box or even into the room for anything in the world.

But a sort of blankness, even dreaminess, had begun by degrees to take possession of him; at moments he forgot himself, or rather, forgot what was of importance, and caught at trifles. Glancing, however, into the kitchen and seeing a bucket half full of water on a bench, he bethought him of washing his hands and the axe. His hands were sticky with blood. He dropped the axe with the blade in the water, snatched a piece of soap that lay in a broken saucer on the window, and began washing his hands in the bucket. When they were clean, he took out the axe, washed the blade and spent a long time, about three minutes, washing the wood where there were spots of blood rubbing them with soap. Then he wiped it all with some linen that was hanging to dry on a line in the kitchen and then he was a long while attentively examining the axe at the window. There was no trace left on it, only the wood was still damp. He carefully hung the axe in the noose under his coat. Then as far as was possible, in the dim light in the kitchen, he looked over his overcoat, his trousers and his boots. At the first glance there seemed to be nothing but stains on the boots. He wetted the rag and rubbed the boots. But he knew he was not looking thoroughly, that there might be something quite noticeable that he was overlooking. He stood in the middle of the room, lost in thought. Dark agonising ideas rose in his mind—the idea that he was mad and that at that moment he was incapable of reasoning, of protecting himself, that he ought perhaps to be doing something utterly different from what he was now doing. "Good God!" he muttered "I must fly, fly," and he rushed into the entry. But here a shock of terror awaited him such as he had never known before.

He stood and gazed and could not believe his eyes: the door, the outer door from the stairs, at which he had not long before waited and rung, was standing unfastened and at least six inches open. No lock, no bolt, all the time, all that time! The old woman had not shut it after him perhaps as a precaution. But, good God! Why, he had seen Lizaveta afterwards! And how could he, how could he have failed to reflect that she must have come in somehow! She could not have come through the wall!

He dashed to the door and fastened the latch.

"But no, the wrong thing again! I must get away, get away...."

He unfastened the latch, opened the door and began listening on the staircase.

He listened a long time. Somewhere far away, it might be in the gateway, two voices were loudly and shrilly shouting, quarrelling and scolding. "What are they about?" He waited patiently. At last all was still, as though suddenly cut off; they had separated. He was meaning to go out, but suddenly, on the floor below, a door was noisily opened and someone began going downstairs humming a tune. "How is it they all make such a noise?" flashed through his mind. Once more he closed the door and waited. At last all was still, not a soul stirring. He was just taking a step towards the stairs when he heard fresh footsteps.

The steps sounded very far off, at the very bottom of the stairs, but he remembered quite clearly and distinctly that from the first sound he began for some reason to suspect that this was someone coming *there*, to the fourth floor, to the old woman. Why? Were the sounds somehow peculiar, significant? The steps were heavy, even and unhurried. Now *he* had passed the first floor, now he was mounting higher, it was growing more and more distinct! He could hear his heavy breathing. And now the third storey had been reached. Coming here! And it seemed to him all at once that he was turned to stone, that it was like a dream in which one is being pursued, nearly caught and will be killed, and is rooted to the spot and cannot even move one's arms.

At last when the unknown was mounting to the fourth floor, he suddenly started, and succeeded in slipping neatly and quickly back into the flat and closing the door behind him. Then he took the hook and softly, noiselessly, fixed it in the catch. Instinct helped him. When he had done this, he crouched holding his breath, by the door. The unknown visitor was by now also at the door. They were now standing opposite one another, as he had just before been standing with the old woman, when the door divided them and he was listening.

The visitor panted several times. "He must be a big, fat man," thought Raskolnikov, squeezing the axe in his hand. It seemed like a dream indeed. The visitor took hold of the bell and rang it loudly.

As soon as the tin bell tinkled, Raskolnikov seemed to be aware of something moving in the room. For some seconds he listened quite seriously. The unknown rang again, waited and suddenly tugged violently and impatiently at the handle of the door. Raskolnikov gazed in horror at the hook shaking in its fastening, and in blank terror expected every minute that the fastening would be pulled out. It certainly did seem possible, so violently was he shaking it. He was tempted to hold the fastening, but *he* might be aware of it. A giddiness came over him again. "I shall fall down!" flashed through his mind, but the unknown began to speak and he recovered himself at once.

"What's up? Are they asleep or murdered? D-damn them!" he bawled in a thick voice, "Hey, Alyona Ivanovna, old witch! Lizaveta Ivanovna, hey, my beauty! open the door! Oh, damn them! Are they asleep or what?"

And again, enraged, he tugged with all his might a dozen times at the bell. He must certainly be a man of authority and an intimate acquaintance.

At this moment light hurried steps were heard not far off, on the stairs. Someone else was approaching. Raskolnikov had not heard them at first.

"You don't say there's no one at home," the newcomer cried in a cheerful, ringing voice, addressing the first visitor, who still went on pulling the bell. "Good evening, Koch."

"From his voice he must be quite young," thought Raskolnikov.

"Who the devil can tell? I've almost broken the lock," answered Koch. "But how do you come to know me?"

"Why! The day before yesterday I beat you three times running at billiards at Gambrinus'."

"Oh!"

"So they are not at home? That's queer. It's awfully stupid though. Where could the old woman have gone? I've come on business."

"Yes; and I have business with her, too."

"Well, what can we do? Go back, I suppose, Aie—aie! And I was hoping to get some money!" cried the young man.

"We must give it up, of course, but what did she fix this time for? The old witch fixed the time for me to come herself. It's out of my way. And where the devil she can have got to, I can't make out. She sits here from year's end to year's end, the old hag; her legs are bad and yet here all of a sudden she is out for a walk!"

"Hadn't we better ask the porter?"

"What?"

"Where she's gone and when she'll be back."

"Hm.... Damn it all!... We might ask.... But you know she never does go anywhere."

And he once more tugged at the door-handle.

"Damn it all. There's nothing to be done, we must go!"

"Stay!" cried the young man suddenly. "Do you see how the door shakes if you pull it?"

"Well?"

"That shows it's not locked, but fastened with the hook! Do you hear how the hook clanks?"

"Well?"

"Why, don't you see? That proves that one of them is at home. If they were all out, they would have locked the door from the outside with the key and not with the hook from inside. There, do you hear how the hook is clanking? To fasten the hook on the inside they must be at home, don't you see. So there they are sitting inside and don't open the door!"

"Well! And so they must be!" cried Koch, astonished. "What are they about in there?" And he began furiously shaking the door.

"Stay!" cried the young man again. "Don't pull at it! There must be something wrong.... Here, you've been ringing and pulling at the door and still they don't open! So either they've both fainted or..."

"What?"

"I tell you what. Let's go fetch the porter, let him wake them up."

"All right."

Both were going down.

"Stay. You stop here while I run down for the porter."

"What for?"

"Well, you'd better."

"All right."

"I'm studying the law you see! It's evident, e-vi-dent there's something wrong here!" the young man cried hotly, and he ran downstairs.

Koch remained. Once more he softly touched the bell which gave one tinkle, then gently, as though reflecting and looking about him, began touching the door-handle pulling it and letting it go to make sure once more that it was only fastened by the hook. Then puffing and panting he bent down and began looking at the keyhole: but the key was in the lock on the inside and so nothing could be seen.

Raskolnikov stood keeping tight hold of the axe. He was in a sort of delirium. He was even making ready to fight when they should come in. While they were knocking and talking together, the idea several times occurred to him to end it all at once and shout to them through the door. Now and then he was tempted to swear at them, to jeer at them, while they could not open the door! "Only make haste!" was the thought that flashed through his mind.

"But what the devil is he about?..." Time was passing, one minute, and another—no one came. Koch began to be restless.

"What the devil?" he cried suddenly and in impatience deserting his sentry duty, he, too, went down, hurrying and thumping with his heavy boots on the stairs. The steps died away.

"Good heavens! What am I to do?"

Raskolnikov unfastened the hook, opened the door—there was no sound. Abruptly, without any thought at all, he went out, closing the door as thoroughly as he could, and went downstairs.

He had gone down three flights when he suddenly heard a loud voice below—where could he go! There was nowhere to hide. He was just going back to the flat.

"Hey there! Catch the brute!"

Somebody dashed out of a flat below, shouting, and rather fell than ran down the stairs, bawling at the top of his voice.

"Mitka! Mitka! Mitka! Mitka! Mitka! Blast him!"

The shout ended in a shriek; the last sounds came from the yard; all was still. But at the same instant several men talking loud and fast began noisily mounting the stairs. There were three or four of them. He distinguished the ringing voice of the young man. "Hey!"

Filled with despair he went straight to meet them, feeling "come what must!" If they stopped him—all was lost; if they let him pass—all was lost too; they would remember him. They were approaching; they were only a flight from him—and suddenly deliverance! A few steps from him on the right, there was an empty flat with the door wide open, the flat on the second floor where the painters had been at work, and which, as though for his benefit, they had just left. It was they, no doubt, who had just run down, shouting. The floor had only just been painted, in the middle of the room stood a pail and a broken pot with paint and brushes. In one instant he had whisked in at the open door and hidden behind the wall and only in the nick of time; they had already reached the landing. Then they turned and went on up to the fourth floor, talking loudly. He waited, went out on tiptoe and ran down the stairs.

No one was on the stairs, nor in the gateway. He passed quickly through the gateway and turned to the left in the street.

He knew, he knew perfectly well that at that moment they were at the flat, that they were greatly astonished at finding it unlocked, as the door had just been fastened, that by now they were looking at the bodies, that before another minute had passed they would guess and completely realise that the murderer had just been there, and had succeeded in hiding somewhere, slipping by them and escaping. They would guess most likely that he had been in the empty flat, while they were going upstairs. And meanwhile he dared not quicken his pace much, though the next turning was still nearly a hundred yards away. "Should he slip through some gateway and wait somewhere in an unknown street? No, hopeless! Should he fling away the axe? Should he take a cab? Hopeless, hopeless!"

At last he reached the turning. He turned down it more dead than alive. Here he was half way to safety, and he understood it; it was less risky because there was a great crowd of people, and he was lost in it like a grain of sand. But all he had suffered had so weakened him that he could scarcely move. Perspiration ran down him in drops, his neck was all wet. "My word, he has been going it!" someone shouted at him when he came out on the canal bank.

He was only dimly conscious of himself now, and the farther he went the worse it was. He remembered however, that on coming out on to the canal bank, he was alarmed at finding few people there and so being more conspicuous, and he had thought of turning back. Though he was almost falling from fatigue, he went a long way round so as to get home from quite a different direction.

He was not fully conscious when he passed through the gateway of his house! He was already on the staircase before he recollected the axe. And yet he had a very grave problem before him, to put it back and to escape observation as far as possible in doing so. He was of course incapable of reflecting that it might perhaps be far better not to restore the axe at all, but to drop it later on in somebody's yard. But it all happened fortunately, the door of the porter's room was closed but not locked, so that it seemed most likely that the porter was at home. But he had so completely lost all power of reflection that he walked straight to the door and opened it. If the porter had asked him, "What do you want?" he would perhaps have simply handed him the axe. But again the porter was not at home, and he succeeded in putting the axe back under the bench, and even covering it with the chunk of wood as before. He met no one, not a soul, afterwards on the way to his room; the landlady's door was shut. When he was in his room, he flung himself on the sofa just as he was— he did not sleep, but sank into blank forgetfulness. If anyone had come into his room then, he would have jumped up at once and screamed. Scraps and shreds of thoughts were simply swarming in his brain, but he could not catch at one, he could not rest on one, in spite of all his efforts....

PART II

49

So he lay a very long while. Now and then he seemed to wake up, and at such moments he noticed that it was far into the night, but it did not occur to him to get up. At last he noticed that it was beginning to get light. He was lying on his back, still dazed from his recent oblivion. Fearful, despairing cries rose shrilly from the street, sounds which he heard every night, indeed, under his window after two o'clock. They woke him up now.

"Ah! the drunken men are coming out of the taverns," he thought, "it's past two o'clock," and at once he leaped up, as though someone had pulled him from the sofa.

"What! Past two o'clock!"

He sat down on the sofa—and instantly recollected everything! All at once, in one flash, he recollected everything.

For the first moment he thought he was going mad. A dreadful chill came over him; but the chill was from the fever that had begun long before in his sleep. Now he was suddenly taken with violent shivering, so that his teeth chattered and all his limbs were shaking. He opened the door and began listening—everything in the house was asleep. With amazement he gazed at himself and everything in the room around him, wondering how he could have come in the night before without fastening the door, and have flung himself on the sofa without undressing, without even taking his hat off. It had fallen off and was lying on the floor near his pillow.

"If anyone had come in, what would he have thought? That I'm drunk but…"

He rushed to the window. There was light enough, and he began hurriedly looking himself all over from head to foot, all his clothes; were there no traces? But there was no doing it like that; shivering with cold, he began taking off everything and looking over again. He turned everything over to the last threads and rags, and mistrusting himself, went through his search three times.

But there seemed to be nothing, no trace, except in one place, where some thick drops of congealed blood were clinging to the frayed edge of his trousers. He picked up a big claspknife and cut off the frayed threads. There seemed to be nothing more.

Suddenly he remembered that the purse and the things he had taken out of the old woman's box were still in his pockets! He had not thought till then of taking them out and hiding them! He had not even thought of them while he was examining his clothes! What next? Instantly he rushed to take them out and fling them on the table. When he had pulled out everything, and turned the pocket inside out to be sure there was nothing left, he carried the whole heap to the corner. The paper had come off the bottom of the wall and hung there in tatters. He began stuffing all the things into the hole under the paper: "They're in! All out of sight, and the purse too!" he thought gleefully, getting up and gazing blankly at the hole which bulged out more than ever. Suddenly he shuddered all over with horror; "My God!" he whispered in despair: "what's the matter with me? Is that hidden? Is that the way to hide things?"

He had not reckoned on having trinkets to hide. He had only thought of money, and so had not prepared a hiding-place.

"But now, now, what am I glad of?" he thought, "Is that hiding things? My reason's deserting me—simply!"

He sat down on the sofa in exhaustion and was at once shaken by another unbearable fit of shivering. Mechanically he drew from a chair beside him his old student's winter coat, which was still warm though almost in rags, covered himself up with it and once more sank into drowsiness and delirium. He lost consciousness.

Not more than five minutes had passed when he jumped up a second time, and at once pounced in a frenzy on his clothes again.

"How could I go to sleep again with nothing done? Yes, yes; I have not taken the loop off the armhole! I forgot it, forgot a thing like that! Such a piece of evidence!"

He pulled off the noose, hurriedly cut it to pieces and threw the bits among his linen under the pillow.

"Pieces of torn linen couldn't rouse suspicion, whatever happened; I think not, I think not, anyway!" he repeated, standing in the middle of the room, and with painful concentration he fell to gazing about him again, at the floor and everywhere, trying to make sure he had not forgotten anything. The conviction that all his faculties, even memory, and the simplest power of reflection were failing him, began to be an insufferable torture.

"Surely it isn't beginning already! Surely it isn't my punishment coming upon me? It is!"

The frayed rags he had cut off his trousers were actually lying on the floor in the middle of the room, where anyone coming in would see them!

"What is the matter with me!" he cried again, like one distraught.

Then a strange idea entered his head; that, perhaps, all his clothes were covered with blood, that, perhaps, there were a great many stains, but that he did not see them, did not notice them because his perceptions were failing, were going to pieces… his reason was clouded.... Suddenly he remembered that there had been blood on the purse too. "Ah! Then there must be blood on the pocket too, for I put the wet purse in my pocket!"

In a flash he had turned the pocket inside out and, yes!—there were traces, stains on the lining of the pocket!

"So my reason has not quite deserted me, so I still have some sense and memory, since I guessed it of myself," he thought triumphantly, with a deep sigh of relief; "it's simply the weakness of fever, a moment's delirium," and he tore the whole lining out of the left pocket of his trousers. At that instant the sunlight fell on his left boot; on the sock which poked out from the boot, he fancied there were traces! He flung off his boots; "traces indeed! The tip of the sock was soaked with blood;" he must have unwarily stepped into that pool.... "But what am I to do with this now? Where am I to put the sock and rags and pocket?"

He gathered them all up in his hands and stood in the middle of the room.

"In the stove? But they would ransack the stove first of all. Burn them? But what can I burn them with? There are no matches even. No, better go out and throw it all away somewhere. Yes, better throw it away," he repeated, sitting down on the sofa again, "and at once, this minute, without lingering…"

But his head sank on the pillow instead. Again the unbearable icy shivering came over him; again he drew his coat over him.

And for a long while, for some hours, he was haunted by the impulse to "go off somewhere at once, this moment, and fling it all away, so that it may be out of sight and done with, at once, at once!" Several times he tried to rise from the sofa, but could not.

He was thoroughly waked up at last by a violent knocking at his door.

"Open, do, are you dead or alive? He keeps sleeping here!" shouted Nastasya, banging with her fist on the door. "For whole days together he's snoring here like a dog! A dog he is too. Open, I tell you. It's past ten."

"Maybe he's not at home," said a man's voice.

"Ha! that's the porter's voice.... What does he want?"

He jumped up and sat on the sofa. The beating of his heart was a positive pain.

"Then who can have latched the door?" retorted Nastasya. "He's taken to bolting himself in! As if he were worth stealing! Open, you stupid, wake up!"

"What do they want? Why the porter? All's discovered. Resist or open? Come what may!…"

He half rose, stooped forward and unlatched the door.

His room was so small that he could undo the latch without leaving the bed. Yes; the porter and Nastasya were standing there.

Nastasya stared at him in a strange way. He glanced with a defiant and desperate air at the porter, who without a word held out a grey folded paper sealed with bottle-wax.

"A notice from the office," he announced, as he gave him the paper.

"From what office?"

"A summons to the police office, of course. You know which office."

51

"To the police?... What for?..."

"How can I tell? You're sent for, so you go."

The man looked at him attentively, looked round the room and turned to go away.

"He's downright ill!" observed Nastasya, not taking her eyes off him. The porter turned his head for a moment. "He's been in a fever since yesterday," she added.

Raskolnikov made no response and held the paper in his hands, without opening it. "Don't you get up then," Nastasya went on compassionately, seeing that he was letting his feet down from the sofa. "You're ill, and so don't go; there's no such hurry. What have you got there?"

He looked; in his right hand he held the shreds he had cut from his trousers, the sock, and the rags of the pocket. So he had been asleep with them in his hand. Afterwards reflecting upon it, he remembered that half waking up in his fever, he had grasped all this tightly in his hand and so fallen asleep again.

"Look at the rags he's collected and sleeps with them, as though he has got hold of a treasure..."

And Nastasya went off into her hysterical giggle.

Instantly he thrust them all under his great coat and fixed his eyes intently upon her. Far as he was from being capable of rational reflection at that moment, he felt that no one would behave like that with a person who was going to be arrested. "But... the police?"

"You'd better have some tea! Yes? I'll bring it, there's some left."

"No... I'm going; I'll go at once," he muttered, getting on to his feet.

"Why, you'll never get downstairs!"

"Yes, I'll go."

"As you please."

She followed the porter out.

At once he rushed to the light to examine the sock and the rags.

"There are stains, but not very noticeable; all covered with dirt, and rubbed and already discoloured. No one who had no suspicion could distinguish anything. Nastasya from a distance could not have noticed, thank God!" Then with a tremor he broke the seal of the notice and began reading; he was a long while reading, before he understood. It was an ordinary summons from the district police-station to appear that day at half-past nine at the office of the district superintendent.

"But when has such a thing happened? I never have anything to do with the police! And why just today?" he thought in agonising bewilderment. "Good God, only get it over soon!"

He was flinging himself on his knees to pray, but broke into laughter—not at the idea of prayer, but at himself.

He began, hurriedly dressing. "If I'm lost, I am lost, I don't care! Shall I put the sock on?" he suddenly wondered, "it will get dustier still and the traces will be gone."

But no sooner had he put it on than he pulled it off again in loathing and horror. He pulled it off, but reflecting that he had no other socks, he picked it up and put it on again—and again he laughed.

"That's all conventional, that's all relative, merely a way of looking at it," he thought in a flash, but only on the top surface of his mind, while he was shuddering all over, "there, I've got it on! I have finished by getting it on!"

But his laughter was quickly followed by despair.

"No, it's too much for me..." he thought. His legs shook. "From fear," he muttered. His head swam and ached with fever. "It's a trick! They want to decoy me there and confound me over everything," he mused, as he went out on to the stairs—"the worst of it is I'm almost lightheaded... I may blurt out something stupid..."

On the stairs he remembered that he was leaving all the things just as they were in the hole in the wall, "and very likely, it's on purpose to search when I'm out," he thought, and stopped short. But he was possessed by such despair, such cynicism of misery, if one may so call it, that with a wave of his hand he went on. "Only to get it over!"

In the street the heat was insufferable again; not a drop of rain had fallen all those days. Again dust, bricks and mortar, again the stench from the shops and pothouses, again the drunken men, the Finnish pedlars and half-broken-down cabs. The sun shone straight in his eyes, so that it hurt him to look out of them, and he felt his head going round—as a man in a fever is apt to feel when he comes out into the street on a bright sunny day.

When he reached the turning into *the* street, in an agony of trepidation he looked down it... at *the* house... and at once averted his eyes.

"If they question me, perhaps I'll simply tell," he thought, as he drew near the police-station.

The police-station was about a quarter of a mile off. It had lately been moved to new rooms on the fourth floor of a new house. He had been once for a moment in the old office but long ago. Turning in at the gateway, he saw on the right a flight of stairs which a peasant was mounting with a book in his hand. "A house-porter, no doubt; so then, the office is here," and he began ascending the stairs on the chance. He did not want to ask questions of anyone.

"I'll go in, fall on my knees, and confess everything..." he thought, as he reached the fourth floor.

The staircase was steep, narrow and all sloppy with dirty water. The kitchens of the flats opened on to the stairs and stood open almost the whole day. So there was a fearful smell and heat. The staircase was crowded with porters going up and down with their books under their arms, policemen, and persons of all sorts and both sexes. The door of the office, too, stood wide open. Peasants stood waiting within. There, too, the heat was stifling and there was a sickening smell of fresh paint and stale oil from the newly decorated rooms.

After waiting a little, he decided to move forward into the next room. All the rooms were small and low-pitched. A fearful impatience drew him on and on. No one paid attention to him. In the second room some clerks sat writing, dressed hardly better than he was, and rather a queer-looking set. He went up to one of them.

"What is it?"

He showed the notice he had received.

"You are a student?" the man asked, glancing at the notice.

"Yes, formerly a student."

The clerk looked at him, but without the slightest interest. He was a particularly unkempt person with the look of a fixed idea in his eye.

"There would be no getting anything out of him, because he has no interest in anything," thought Raskolnikov.

"Go in there to the head clerk," said the clerk, pointing towards the furthest room.

He went into that room—the fourth in order; it was a small room and packed full of people, rather better dressed than in the outer rooms. Among them were two ladies. One, poorly dressed in mourning, sat at the table opposite the chief clerk, writing something at his dictation. The other, a very stout, buxom woman with a purplish-red, blotchy face, excessively smartly dressed with a brooch on her bosom as big as a saucer, was standing on one side, apparently waiting for something. Raskolnikov thrust his notice upon the head clerk. The latter glanced at it, said: "Wait a minute," and went on attending to the lady in mourning.

He breathed more freely. "It can't be that!"

By degrees he began to regain confidence, he kept urging himself to have courage and be calm.

"Some foolishness, some trifling carelessness, and I may betray myself! Hm... it's a pity there's no air here," he added, "it's stifling.... It makes one's head dizzier than ever... and one's mind too..."

He was conscious of a terrible inner turmoil. He was afraid of losing his self-control; he tried to catch at something and fix his mind on it, something quite irrelevant, but he could not succeed in this at all. Yet the head clerk greatly interested him, he kept hoping to see through him and guess something from his face.

He was a very young man, about two and twenty, with a dark mobile face that looked older than his years. He was fashionably dressed and foppish, with his hair parted in the middle, well combed and pomaded, and wore a number of rings on his well-scrubbed fingers and a gold chain on his waistcoat. He said a couple of words in French to a foreigner who was in the room, and said them fairly correctly.

"Luise Ivanovna, you can sit down," he said casually to the gaily-dressed, purple-faced lady, who was still standing as though not venturing to sit down, though there was a chair beside her.

"*Ich danke*," said the latter, and softly, with a rustle of silk she sank into the chair. Her light blue dress trimmed with white lace floated about the table like an air-balloon and filled almost half the room. She smelt of scent. But she was obviously embarrassed at filling half the room and smelling so strongly of scent; and though her smile was impudent as well as cringing, it betrayed evident uneasiness.

The lady in mourning had done at last, and got up. All at once, with some noise, an officer walked in very jauntily, with a peculiar swing of his shoulders at each step. He tossed his cockaded cap on the table and sat down in an easy-chair. The small lady positively skipped from her seat on seeing him, and fell to curtsying in a sort of ecstasy; but the officer took not the smallest notice of her, and she did not venture to sit down again in his presence. He was the assistant superintendent. He had a reddish moustache that stood out horizontally on each side of his face, and extremely small features, expressive of nothing much except a certain insolence. He looked askance and rather indignantly at Raskolnikov; he was so very badly dressed, and in spite of his humiliating position, his bearing was by no means in keeping with his clothes. Raskolnikov had unwarily fixed a very long and direct look on him, so that he felt positively affronted.

"What do you want?" he shouted, apparently astonished that such a ragged fellow was not annihilated by the majesty of his glance.

"I was summoned... by a notice..." Raskolnikov faltered.

"For the recovery of money due, from *the student*," the head clerk interfered hurriedly, tearing himself from his papers. "Here!" and he flung Raskolnikov a document and pointed out the place. "Read that!"

"Money? What money?" thought Raskolnikov, "but... then... it's certainly not *that*."

And he trembled with joy. He felt sudden intense indescribable relief. A load was lifted from his back.

"And pray, what time were you directed to appear, sir?" shouted the assistant superintendent, seeming for some unknown reason more and more aggrieved. "You are told to come at nine, and now it's twelve!"

"The notice was only brought me a quarter of an hour ago," Raskolnikov answered loudly over his shoulder. To his own surprise, he, too, grew suddenly angry and found a certain pleasure in it. "And it's enough that I have come here ill with fever."

"Kindly refrain from shouting!"

"I'm not shouting, I'm speaking very quietly, it's you who are shouting at me. I'm a student, and allow no one to shout at me."

The assistant superintendent was so furious that for the first minute he could only splutter inarticulately. He leaped up from his seat.

"Be silent! You are in a government office. Don't be impudent, sir!"

"You're in a government office, too," cried Raskolnikov, "and you're smoking a cigarette as well as shouting, so you are showing disrespect to all of us."

He felt an indescribable satisfaction at having said this.

The head clerk looked at him with a smile. The angry assistant superintendent was obviously disconcerted.

"That's not your business!" he shouted at last with unnatural loudness. "Kindly make the declaration demanded of you. Show him. Alexandr Grigorievitch. There is a complaint against you! You don't pay your debts! You're a fine bird!"

But Raskolnikov was not listening now; he had eagerly clutched at the paper, in haste to find an explanation. He read it once, and a second time, and still did not understand.

"What is this?" he asked the head clerk.

"It is for the recovery of money on an IOU, a writ. You must either pay it, with all expenses, costs and so on, or give a written declaration when you can pay it, and at the same time an undertaking not to leave the capital without payment, and nor to sell or conceal your property. The creditor is at liberty to sell your property, and proceed against you according to the law."

"But I… am not in debt to anyone!"

"That's not our business. Here, an IOU for a hundred and fifteen roubles, legally attested, and due for payment, has been brought us for recovery, given by you to the widow of the assessor Zarnitsyn, nine months ago, and paid over by the widow Zarnitsyn to one Mr. Tchebarov. We therefore summon you, hereupon."

"But she is my landlady!"

"And what if she is your landlady?"

The head clerk looked at him with a condescending smile of compassion, and at the same time with a certain triumph, as at a novice under fire for the first time—as though he would say: "Well, how do you feel now?" But what did he care now for an IOU, for a writ of recovery! Was that worth worrying about now, was it worth attention even! He stood, he read, he listened, he answered, he even asked questions himself, but all mechanically. The triumphant sense of security, of deliverance from overwhelming danger, that was what filled his whole soul that moment without thought for the future, without analysis, without suppositions or surmises, without doubts and without questioning. It was an instant of full, direct, purely instinctive joy. But at that very moment something like a thunderstorm took place in the office. The assistant superintendent, still shaken by Raskolnikov's disrespect, still fuming and obviously anxious to keep up his wounded dignity, pounced on the unfortunate smart lady, who had been gazing at him ever since he came in with an exceedingly silly smile.

"You shameful hussy!" he shouted suddenly at the top of his voice. (The lady in mourning had left the office.) "What was going on at your house last night? Eh! A disgrace again, you're a scandal to the whole street. Fighting and drinking again. Do you want the house of correction? Why, I have warned you ten times over that I would not let you off the eleventh! And here you are again, again, you… you…!"

The paper fell out of Raskolnikov's hands, and he looked wildly at the smart lady who was so unceremoniously treated. But he soon saw what it meant, and at once began to find positive amusement in the scandal. He listened with pleasure, so that he longed to laugh and laugh… all his nerves were on edge.

"Ilya Petrovitch!" the head clerk was beginning anxiously, but stopped short, for he knew from experience that the enraged assistant could not be stopped except by force.

As for the smart lady, at first she positively trembled before the storm. But, strange to say, the more numerous and violent the terms of abuse became, the more amiable she looked, and the more seductive the smiles she lavished on the terrible assistant. She moved uneasily, and curtsied incessantly, waiting impatiently for a chance of putting in her word: and at last she found it.

"There was no sort of noise or fighting in my house, Mr. Captain," she pattered all at once, like peas dropping, speaking Russian confidently, though with a strong German accent, "and no sort of scandal, and his honour came drunk, and it's the whole truth I am telling, Mr. Captain, and I am not to blame.… Mine is an honourable house, Mr. Captain, and honourable behaviour, Mr. Captain, and I always, always dislike any scandal myself. But he came quite tipsy, and asked for three bottles again, and then he lifted up one leg, and began playing the pianoforte with one foot, and that is not at all right in an honourable house, and he *ganz* broke the piano, and it was very bad manners indeed and I said so. And he took up a bottle and began hitting everyone with it. And then I called the porter, and Karl came, and he took Karl and hit him in the eye; and he hit Henriette in the eye, too, and gave me five slaps on the cheek. And it was so ungentlemanly in an honourable house, Mr. Captain, and I screamed. And he opened the window over the canal, and stood in the window, squealing like a little pig; it was a disgrace. The idea of squealing like a little pig at the window into the street! Fie upon him! And Karl pulled him away from the window by his coat, and it is true, Mr. Captain, he tore *sein rock*. And then he shouted that *man muss* pay him fifteen roubles damages. And I did pay him, Mr. Captain, five roubles for *sein rock*. And he is an ungentlemanly visitor and caused all the scandal. 'I will show you up,' he said, 'for I can write to all the papers about you.'"

"Then he was an author?"

"Yes, Mr. Captain, and what an ungentlemanly visitor in an honourable house...."

"Now then! Enough! I have told you already..."

"Ilya Petrovitch!" the head clerk repeated significantly.

The assistant glanced rapidly at him; the head clerk slightly shook his head.

"... So I tell you this, most respectable Luise Ivanovna, and I tell it you for the last time," the assistant went on. "If there is a scandal in your honourable house once again, I will put you yourself in the lockup, as it is called in polite society. Do you hear? So a literary man, an author took five roubles for his coattail in an 'honourable house'? A nice set, these authors!"

And he cast a contemptuous glance at Raskolnikov. "There was a scandal the other day in a restaurant, too. An author had eaten his dinner and would not pay; 'I'll write a satire on you,' says he. And there was another of them on a steamer last week used the most disgraceful language to the respectable family of a civil councillor, his wife and daughter. And there was one of them turned out of a confectioner's shop the other day. They are like that, authors, literary men, students, town-criers.... Pfoo! You get along! I shall look in upon you myself one day. Then you had better be careful! Do you hear?"

With hurried deference, Luise Ivanovna fell to curtsying in all directions, and so curtsied herself to the door. But at the door, she stumbled backwards against a good-looking officer with a fresh, open face and splendid thick fair whiskers. This was the superintendent of the district himself, Nikodim Fomitch. Luise Ivanovna made haste to curtsy almost to the ground, and with mincing little steps, she fluttered out of the office.

"Again thunder and lightning—a hurricane!" said Nikodim Fomitch to Ilya Petrovitch in a civil and friendly tone. "You are aroused again, you are fuming again! I heard it on the stairs!"

"Well, what then!" Ilya Petrovitch drawled with gentlemanly nonchalance; and he walked with some papers to another table, with a jaunty swing of his shoulders at each step. "Here, if you will kindly look: an author, or a student, has been one at least, does not pay his debts, has given an IOU, won't clear out of his room, and complaints are constantly being lodged against him, and here he has been pleased to make a protest against my smoking in his presence! He behaves like a cad himself, and just look at him, please. Here's the gentleman, and very attractive he is!"

"Poverty is not a vice, my friend, but we know you go off like powder, you can't bear a slight, I daresay you took offence at something and went too far yourself," continued Nikodim Fomitch, turning affably to Raskolnikov. "But you were wrong there; he is a capital fellow, I assure you, but explosive, explosive! He gets hot, fires up, boils over, and no stopping him! And then it's all over! And at the bottom he's a heart of gold! His nickname in the regiment was the 'Explosive Lieutenant.'..."

"And what a regiment it was, too," cried Ilya Petrovitch, much gratified at this agreeable banter, though still sulky.

Raskolnikov had a sudden desire to say something exceptionally pleasant to them all. "Excuse me, Captain," he began easily, suddenly addressing Nikodim Fomitch, "will you enter into my position?... I am ready to ask pardon, if I have been ill-mannered. I am a poor student, sick and shattered" ("shattered" was the word he used) "by poverty. I am not studying, because I cannot keep myself now, but I shall get money.... I have a mother and sister in the province of X——. They will send it to me, and I will pay. My landlady is a good-hearted woman, but she is so exasperated at my having lost my lessons, and not paying her for the last four months, that she does not even send up my dinner... and I don't understand this IOU at all. She is asking me to pay her on this IOU. How am I to pay her? Judge for yourselves!..."

"But that is not our business, you know," the head clerk was observing.

"Yes, yes. I perfectly agree with you. But allow me to explain..." Raskolnikov put in again, still addressing Nikodim Fomitch, but trying his best to address Ilya Petrovitch also, though the latter persistently appeared to be rummaging among his papers and to be contemptuously oblivious of him. "Allow me to explain that I have been living with her for nearly three years and at first... at first... for why should I not confess it, at the very beginning I promised to marry her daughter, it was a verbal promise, freely given... she was a girl... indeed, I liked her, though I was not in love with her... a youthful affair in fact... that is, I mean to say, that my landlady gave me credit freely in those days, and I led a life of... I was very heedless..."

"Nobody asks you for these personal details, sir, we've no time to waste," Ilya Petrovitch interposed roughly and with a note of triumph; but Raskolnikov stopped him hotly, though he suddenly found it exceedingly difficult to speak.

"But excuse me, excuse me. It is for me to explain... how it all happened... In my turn... though I agree with you... it is unnecessary. But a year ago, the girl died of typhus. I remained lodging there as before, and when my landlady moved into her present quarters, she said to me... and in a friendly way... that she had complete trust in me, but still, would I not give her an IOU for one hundred and fifteen roubles, all the debt I owed her. She said if only I gave her that, she would trust me again, as much as I liked, and that she would never, never—those were her own words—make use of that IOU till I could pay of myself... and now, when I have lost my lessons and have nothing to eat, she takes action against me. What am I to say to that?"

"All these affecting details are no business of ours." Ilya Petrovitch interrupted rudely. "You must give a written undertaking but as for your love affairs and all these tragic events, we have nothing to do with that."

"Come now... you are harsh," muttered Nikodim Fomitch, sitting down at the table and also beginning to write. He looked a little ashamed.

"Write!" said the head clerk to Raskolnikov.

"Write what?" the latter asked, gruffly.

"I will dictate to you."

Raskolnikov fancied that the head clerk treated him more casually and contemptuously after his speech, but strange to say he suddenly felt completely indifferent to anyone's opinion, and this revulsion took place in a flash, in one instant. If he had cared to think a little, he would have been amazed indeed that he could have talked to them like that a minute before, forcing his feelings upon them. And where had those feelings come from? Now if the whole room had been filled, not with police officers, but with those nearest and dearest to him, he would not have found one human word for them, so empty was his heart. A gloomy sensation of agonising, everlasting solitude and remoteness, took conscious form in his soul. It was not the meanness of his sentimental effusions before Ilya Petrovitch, nor the meanness of the latter's triumph over him that had caused this sudden revulsion in his heart. Oh, what had he to do now with his own baseness, with all these petty vanities, officers, German women, debts, police-offices? If he had been sentenced to be burnt at that moment, he would not have stirred, would hardly have heard the sentence to the end. Something was happening to him entirely new, sudden and unknown. It was not that he understood, but he felt clearly with all the intensity of sensation that he could never more appeal to these people in the police-office with sentimental effusions like his recent outburst, or with anything whatever; and that if they had been his own brothers and sisters and not police-officers, it would have been utterly out of the question to appeal to them in any circumstance of life. He had never experienced such a strange and awful sensation. And what was most agonising—it was more a sensation than a conception or idea, a direct sensation, the most agonising of all the sensations he had known in his life.

The head clerk began dictating to him the usual form of declaration, that he could not pay, that he undertook to do so at a future date, that he would not leave the town, nor sell his property, and so on.

"But you can't write, you can hardly hold the pen," observed the head clerk, looking with curiosity at Raskolnikov. "Are you ill?"

"Yes, I am giddy. Go on!"

"That's all. Sign it."

The head clerk took the paper, and turned to attend to others.

Raskolnikov gave back the pen; but instead of getting up and going away, he put his elbows on the table and pressed his head in his hands. He felt as if a nail were being driven into his skull. A strange idea suddenly occurred to him, to get up at once, to go up to Nikodim Fomitch, and tell him everything that had happened yesterday, and then to go with him to his lodgings and to show him the things in the hole in the corner. The impulse was so strong that he got up from his seat to carry it out. "Hadn't I better think a minute?" flashed through his mind. "No, better cast off the burden without thinking." But all at once he stood still, rooted to the spot. Nikodim Fomitch was talking eagerly with Ilya Petrovitch, and the words reached him:

"It's impossible, they'll both be released. To begin with, the whole story contradicts itself. Why should they have called the porter, if it had been their doing? To inform against themselves? Or as a blind? No, that would be too cunning! Besides, Pestryakov, the student, was seen at the gate by both the porters and a woman as he went in. He was walking with three friends, who left him only at the gate, and he asked the porters to direct him, in the presence of the friends. Now, would he have asked his way if he had been going with such an object? As for Koch, he spent half an hour at the silversmith's below, before he went up to the old woman and he left him at exactly a quarter to eight. Now just consider…"

"But excuse me, how do you explain this contradiction? They state themselves that they knocked and the door was locked; yet three minutes later when they went up with the porter, it turned out the door was unfastened."

"That's just it; the murderer must have been there and bolted himself in; and they'd have caught him for a certainty if Koch had not been an ass and gone to look for the porter too. *He* must have seized the interval to get downstairs and slip by them somehow. Koch keeps crossing himself and saying: 'If I had been there, he would have jumped out and killed me with his axe.' He is going to have a thanksgiving service—ha, ha!"

"And no one saw the murderer?"

"They might well not see him; the house is a regular Noah's Ark," said the head clerk, who was listening.

"It's clear, quite clear," Nikodim Fomitch repeated warmly.

"No, it is anything but clear," Ilya Petrovitch maintained.

Raskolnikov picked up his hat and walked towards the door, but he did not reach it.…

When he recovered consciousness, he found himself sitting in a chair, supported by someone on the right side, while someone else was standing on the left, holding a yellowish glass filled with yellow water, and Nikodim Fomitch standing before him, looking intently at him. He got up from the chair.

"What's this? Are you ill?" Nikodim Fomitch asked, rather sharply.

"He could hardly hold his pen when he was signing," said the head clerk, settling back in his place, and taking up his work again.

"Have you been ill long?" cried Ilya Petrovitch from his place, where he, too, was looking through papers. He had, of course, come to look at the sick man when he fainted, but retired at once when he recovered.

"Since yesterday," muttered Raskolnikov in reply.

"Did you go out yesterday?"

"Yes."

"Though you were ill?"

"Yes."

"At what time?"

"About seven."

"And where did you go, may I ask?"

"Along the street."

"Short and clear."

Raskolnikov, white as a handkerchief, had answered sharply, jerkily, without dropping his black feverish eyes before Ilya Petrovitch's stare.

"He can scarcely stand upright. And you…" Nikodim Fomitch was beginning.

"No matter," Ilya Petrovitch pronounced rather peculiarly.

Nikodim Fomitch would have made some further protest, but glancing at the head clerk who was looking very hard at him, he did not speak. There was a sudden silence. It was strange.

"Very well, then," concluded Ilya Petrovitch, "we will not detain you."

Raskolnikov went out. He caught the sound of eager conversation on his departure, and above the rest rose the questioning voice of Nikodim Fomitch. In the street, his faintness passed off completely.

"A search—there will be a search at once," he repeated to himself, hurrying home. "The brutes! they suspect."

His former terror mastered him completely again.

"And what if there has been a search already? What if I find them in my room?"

But here was his room. Nothing and no one in it. No one had peeped in. Even Nastasya had not touched it. But heavens! how could he have left all those things in the hole?

He rushed to the corner, slipped his hand under the paper, pulled the things out and lined his pockets with them. There were eight articles in all: two little boxes with earrings or something of the sort, he hardly looked to see; then four small leather cases. There was a chain, too, merely wrapped in newspaper and something else in newspaper, that looked like a decoration.... He put them all in the different pockets of his overcoat, and the remaining pocket of his trousers, trying to conceal them as much as possible. He took the purse, too. Then he went out of his room, leaving the door open. He walked quickly and resolutely, and though he felt shattered, he had his senses about him. He was afraid of pursuit, he was afraid that in another half-hour, another quarter of an hour perhaps, instructions would be issued for his pursuit, and so at all costs, he must hide all traces before then. He must clear everything up while he still had some strength, some reasoning power left him.... Where was he to go?

That had long been settled: "Fling them into the canal, and all traces hidden in the water, the thing would be at an end." So he had decided in the night of his delirium when several times he had had the impulse to get up and go away, to make haste, and get rid of it all. But to get rid of it, turned out to be a very difficult task. He wandered along the bank of the Ekaterininsky Canal for half an hour or more and looked several times at the steps running down to the water, but he could not think of carrying out his plan; either rafts stood at the steps' edge, and women were washing clothes on them, or boats were moored there, and people were swarming everywhere. Moreover he could be seen and noticed from the banks on all sides; it would look suspicious for a man to go down on purpose, stop, and throw something into the water. And what if the boxes were to float instead of sinking? And of course they would. Even as it was, everyone he met seemed to stare and look round, as if they had nothing to do but to watch him. "Why is it, or can it be my fancy?" he thought.

At last the thought struck him that it might be better to go to the Neva. There were not so many people there, he would be less observed, and it would be more convenient in every way, above all it was further off. He wondered how he could have been wandering for a good half-hour, worried and anxious in this dangerous past without thinking of it before. And that half-hour he had lost over an irrational plan, simply because he had thought of it in delirium! He had become extremely absent and forgetful and he was aware of it. He certainly must make haste.

He walked towards the Neva along V—— Prospect, but on the way another idea struck him. "Why to the Neva? Would it not be better to go somewhere far off, to the Islands again, and there hide the things in some solitary place, in a wood or under a bush, and mark the spot perhaps?" And though he felt incapable of clear judgment, the idea seemed to him a sound one. But he was not destined to go there. For coming out of V—— Prospect towards the square, he saw on the left a passage leading between two blank walls to a courtyard. On the right hand, the blank unwhitewashed wall of a four-storied house stretched far into the court; on the left, a wooden hoarding ran parallel with it for twenty paces into the court, and then turned sharply to the left. Here was a deserted fenced-off place where rubbish of different sorts was lying. At the end of the court, the corner of a low, smutty, stone shed, apparently part of some workshop, peeped from behind the hoarding. It was probably a carriage builder's or carpenter's shed; the whole place from the entrance was black with coal dust. Here would be the place to throw it, he thought. Not seeing anyone in the yard, he slipped in, and at once saw near the gate a sink, such as is often put in yards where there are many workmen or cabdrivers; and on the hoarding above had been scribbled in chalk the time-honoured witticism, "Standing here strictly forbidden." This was all the better, for there would be nothing suspicious about his going in. "Here I could throw it all in a heap and get away!"

Looking round once more, with his hand already in his pocket, he noticed against the outer wall, between the entrance and the sink, a big unhewn stone, weighing perhaps sixty pounds. The other side of the wall was a street. He could hear passersby, always numerous in that part, but he could not be seen from the entrance, unless someone came in from the street, which might well happen indeed, so there was need of haste.

He bent down over the stone, seized the top of it firmly in both hands, and using all his strength turned it over. Under the stone was a small hollow in the ground, and he immediately emptied his pocket into it. The purse lay at the top, and yet the hollow was not filled up. Then he seized the stone again and with one twist turned it back, so that it was in the same position again, though it stood a very little higher. But he scraped the earth about it and pressed it at the edges with his foot. Nothing could be noticed.

Then he went out, and turned into the square. Again an intense, almost unbearable joy overwhelmed him for an instant, as it had in the police-office. "I have buried my tracks! And who, who can think of looking under that stone? It has been lying there most likely ever since the house was built, and will lie as many years more. And if it were found, who would think of me? It is all over! No clue!" And he laughed. Yes, he remembered that he began laughing a thin, nervous noiseless laugh, and went on laughing all the time he was crossing the square. But when he reached the K—— Boulevard where two days before he had come upon that girl, his laughter suddenly ceased. Other ideas crept into his mind. He felt all at once that it would be loathsome to pass that seat on which after the girl was gone, he had sat and pondered, and that it would be hateful, too, to meet that whiskered policeman to whom he had given the twenty kopecks: "Damn him!"

He walked, looking about him angrily and distractedly. All his ideas now seemed to be circling round some single point, and he felt that there really was such a point, and that now, now, he was left facing that point—and for the first time, indeed, during the last two months.

"Damn it all!" he thought suddenly, in a fit of ungovernable fury. "If it has begun, then it has begun. Hang the new life! Good Lord, how stupid it is!… And what lies I told today! How despicably I fawned upon that wretched Ilya Petrovitch! But that is all folly! What do I care for them all, and my fawning upon them! It is not that at all! It is not that at all!"

Suddenly he stopped; a new utterly unexpected and exceedingly simple question perplexed and bitterly confounded him.

"If it all has really been done deliberately and not idiotically, if I really had a certain and definite object, how is it I did not even glance into the purse and don't know what I had there, for which I have undergone these agonies, and have deliberately undertaken this base, filthy degrading business? And here I wanted at once to throw into the water the purse together with all the things which I had not seen either… how's that?"

Yes, that was so, that was all so. Yet he had known it all before, and it was not a new question for him, even when it was decided in the night without hesitation and consideration, as though so it must be, as though it could not possibly be otherwise…. Yes, he had known it all, and understood it all; it surely had all been settled even yesterday at the moment when he was bending over the box and pulling the jewel-cases out of it…. Yes, so it was.

"It is because I am very ill," he decided grimly at last, "I have been worrying and fretting myself, and I don't know what I am doing…. Yesterday and the day before yesterday and all this time I have been worrying myself…. I shall get well and I shall not worry…. But what if I don't get well at all? Good God, how sick I am of it all!"

He walked on without resting. He had a terrible longing for some distraction, but he did not know what to do, what to attempt. A new overwhelming sensation was gaining more and more mastery over him every moment; this was an immeasurable, almost physical, repulsion for everything surrounding him, an obstinate, malignant feeling of hatred. All who met him were loathsome to him—he loathed their faces, their movements, their gestures. If anyone had addressed him, he felt that he might have spat at him or bitten him. . . .

He stopped suddenly, on coming out on the bank of the Little Neva, near the bridge to Vassilyevsky Ostrov. "Why, he lives here, in that house," he thought, "why, I have not come to Razumihin of my own accord! Here it's the same thing over again. . . . Very interesting to know, though; have I come on purpose or have I simply walked here by chance? Never mind, I said the day before yesterday that I would go and see him the day *after*; well, and so I will! Besides I really cannot go further now."

He went up to Razumihin's room on the fifth floor.

The latter was at home in his garret, busily writing at the moment, and he opened the door himself. It was four months since they had seen each other. Razumihin was sitting in a ragged dressing-gown, with slippers on his bare feet, unkempt, unshaven and unwashed. His face showed surprise.

"Is it you?" he cried. He looked his comrade up and down; then after a brief pause, he whistled. "As hard up as all that! Why, brother, you've cut me out!" he added, looking at Raskolnikov's rags. "Come sit down, you are tired, I'll be bound."

And when he had sunk down on the American leather sofa, which was in even worse condition than his own, Razumihin saw at once that his visitor was ill.

"Why, you are seriously ill, do you know that?" He began feeling his pulse. Raskolnikov pulled away his hand.

"Never mind," he said, "I have come for this: I have no lessons. . . . I wanted, . . . but I don't really want lessons. . . ."

"But I say! You are delirious, you know!" Razumihin observed, watching him carefully.

"No, I am not."

Raskolnikov got up from the sofa. As he had mounted the stairs to Razumihin's, he had not realised that he would be meeting his friend face to face. Now, in a flash, he knew, that what he was least of all disposed for at that moment was to be face to face with anyone in the wide world. His spleen rose within him. He almost choked with rage at himself as soon as he crossed Razumihin's threshold.

"Goodbye," he said abruptly, and walked to the door.

"Stop, stop! You queer fish."

"I don't want to," said the other, again pulling away his hand.

"Then why the devil have you come? Are you mad, or what? Why, this is . . . almost insulting! I won't let you go like that."

"Well, then, I came to you because I know no one but you who could help . . . to begin . . . because you are kinder than anyone—cleverer, I mean, and can judge . . . and now I see that I want nothing. Do you hear? Nothing at all . . . no one's services . . . no one's sympathy. I am by myself . . . alone. Come, that's enough. Leave me alone."

"Stay a minute, you sweep! You are a perfect madman. As you like for all I care. I have no lessons, do you see, and I don't care about that, but there's a bookseller, Heruvimov—and he takes the place of a lesson. I would not exchange him for five lessons. He's doing publishing of a kind, and issuing natural science manuals and what a circulation they have! The very titles are worth the money! You always maintained that I was a fool, but by Jove, my boy, there are greater fools than I am! Now he is setting up for being advanced, not that he has an inkling of anything, but, of course, I encourage him. Here are two signatures of the German text—in my opinion, the crudest charlatanism; it discusses the question, 'Is woman a human being?' And, of course, triumphantly proves that she is. Heruvimov is going to bring out this work as a contribution to the woman question; I am translating it; he will expand these two and a half signatures into six, we shall make up a gorgeous title half a page long and bring it out at half a rouble. It will do! He pays me six roubles the signature, it works out to about fifteen roubles for the job, and I've had six already in advance. When we have finished this, we are going to begin a translation about whales, and then some of the dullest scandals out of the second part of *Les Confessions* we have marked for translation; somebody has told Heruvimov, that Rousseau was a kind of Radishchev. You may be sure I don't contradict him, hang him! Well, would you like to do the second signature of 'Is woman a human being?' If you would, take the German and pens and paper—all those are provided, and take three roubles; for as I have had six roubles in advance on the whole thing, three roubles come to you for your share. And when you have finished the signature there will be another three roubles for you. And please don't think I am doing you a service; quite the contrary, as soon as you came in, I saw how you could help me; to begin with, I am weak in spelling, and secondly, I am sometimes utterly adrift in German, so that I make it up as I go along for the most part. The only comfort is, that it's bound to be a change for the better. Though who can tell, maybe it's sometimes for the worse. Will you take it?"

Raskolnikov took the German sheets in silence, took the three roubles and without a word went out. Razumihin gazed after him in astonishment. But when Raskolnikov was in the next street, he turned back, mounted the stairs to Razumihin's again and laying on the table the German article and the three roubles, went out again, still without uttering a word.

"Are you raving, or what?" Razumihin shouted, roused to fury at last. "What farce is this? You'll drive me crazy too... what did you come to see me for, damn you?"

"I don't want... translation," muttered Raskolnikov from the stairs.

"Then what the devil do you want?" shouted Razumihin from above. Raskolnikov continued descending the staircase in silence.

"Hey, there! Where are you living?"

No answer.

"Well, confound you then!"

But Raskolnikov was already stepping into the street. On the Nikolaevsky Bridge he was roused to full consciousness again by an unpleasant incident. A coachman, after shouting at him two or three times, gave him a violent lash on the back with his whip, for having almost fallen under his horses' hoofs. The lash so infuriated him that he dashed away to the railing (for some unknown reason he had been walking in the very middle of the bridge in the traffic). He angrily clenched and ground his teeth. He heard laughter, of course.

"Serves him right!"

"A pickpocket I dare say."

"Pretending to be drunk, for sure, and getting under the wheels on purpose; and you have to answer for him."

"It's a regular profession, that's what it is."

But while he stood at the railing, still looking angry and bewildered after the retreating carriage, and rubbing his back, he suddenly felt someone thrust money into his hand. He looked. It was an elderly woman in a kerchief and goatskin shoes, with a girl, probably her daughter, wearing a hat, and carrying a green parasol.

"Take it, my good man, in Christ's name."

He took it and they passed on. It was a piece of twenty kopecks. From his dress and appearance they might well have taken him for a beggar asking alms in the streets, and the gift of the twenty kopecks he doubtless owed to the blow, which made them feel sorry for him.

He closed his hand on the twenty kopecks, walked on for ten paces, and turned facing the Neva, looking towards the palace. The sky was without a cloud and the water was almost bright blue, which is so rare in the Neva. The cupola of the cathedral, which is seen at its best from the bridge about twenty paces from the chapel, glittered in the sunlight, and in the pure air every ornament on it could be clearly distinguished. The pain from the lash went off, and Raskolnikov forgot about it; one uneasy and not quite definite idea occupied him now completely. He stood still, and gazed long and intently into the distance; this spot was especially familiar to him. When he was attending the university, he had hundreds of times—generally on his way home—stood still on this spot, gazed at this truly magnificent spectacle and almost always marvelled at a vague and mysterious emotion it roused in him. It left him strangely cold; this gorgeous picture was for him blank and lifeless. He wondered every time at his sombre and enigmatic impression and, mistrusting himself, put off finding the explanation of it. He vividly recalled those old doubts and perplexities, and it seemed to him that it was no mere chance that he recalled them now. It struck him as strange and grotesque, that he should have stopped at the same spot as before, as though he actually imagined he could think the same thoughts, be interested in the same theories and pictures that had interested him... so short a time ago. He felt it almost amusing, and yet it wrung his heart. Deep down, hidden far away out of sight all that seemed to him now—all his old past, his old thoughts, his old problems and theories, his old impressions and that picture and himself and all, all.... He felt as though he were flying upwards, and everything were vanishing from his sight. Making an unconscious movement with his hand, he suddenly became aware of the piece of money in his fist. He opened his hand, stared at the coin, and with a sweep of his arm flung it into the water; then he turned and went home. It seemed to him, he had cut himself off from everyone and from everything at that moment.

Evening was coming on when he reached home, so that he must have been walking about six hours. How and where he came back he did not remember. Undressing, and quivering like an overdriven horse, he lay down on the sofa, drew his greatcoat over him, and at once sank into oblivion....

It was dusk when he was waked up by a fearful scream. Good God, what a scream! Such unnatural sounds, such howling, wailing, grinding, tears, blows and curses he had never heard.

He could never have imagined such brutality, such frenzy. In terror he sat up in bed, almost swooning with agony. But the fighting, wailing and cursing grew louder and louder. And then to his intense amazement he caught the voice of his landlady. She was howling, shrieking and wailing, rapidly, hurriedly, incoherently, so that he could not make out what she was talking about; she was beseeching, no doubt, not to be beaten, for she was being mercilessly beaten on the stairs. The voice of her assailant was so horrible from spite and rage that it was almost a croak; but he, too, was saying something, and just as quickly and indistinctly, hurrying and spluttering. All at once Raskolnikov trembled; he recognised the voice—it was the voice of Ilya Petrovitch. Ilya Petrovitch here and beating the landlady! He is kicking her, banging her head against the steps—that's clear, that can be told from the sounds, from the cries and the thuds. How is it, is the world topsy-turvy? He could hear people running in crowds from all the storeys and all the staircases; he heard voices, exclamations, knocking, doors banging. "But why, why, and how could it be?" he repeated, thinking seriously that he had gone mad. But no, he heard too distinctly! And they would come to him next, "for no doubt... it's all about that... about yesterday.... Good God!" He would have fastened his door with the latch, but he could not lift his hand... besides, it would be useless. Terror gripped his heart like ice, tortured him and numbed him.... But at last all this uproar, after continuing about ten minutes, began gradually to subside. The landlady was moaning and groaning; Ilya Petrovitch was still uttering threats and curses.... But at last he, too, seemed to be silent, and now he could not be heard. "Can he have gone away? Good Lord!" Yes, and now the landlady is going too, still weeping and moaning... and then her door slammed.... Now the crowd was going from the stairs to their rooms, exclaiming, disputing, calling to one another, raising their voices to a shout, dropping them to a whisper. There must have been numbers of them—almost all the inmates of the block. "But, good God, how could it be! And why, why had he come here!"

Raskolnikov sank worn out on the sofa, but could not close his eyes. He lay for half an hour in such anguish, such an intolerable sensation of infinite terror as he had never experienced before. Suddenly a bright light flashed into his room. Nastasya came in with a candle and a plate of soup. Looking at him carefully and ascertaining that he was not asleep, she set the candle on the table and began to lay out what she had brought—bread, salt, a plate, a spoon.

"You've eaten nothing since yesterday, I warrant. You've been trudging about all day, and you're shaking with fever."

"Nastasya... what were they beating the landlady for?"

She looked intently at him.

"Who beat the landlady?"

"Just now... half an hour ago, Ilya Petrovitch, the assistant superintendent, on the stairs.... Why was he ill-treating her like that, and... why was he here?"

Nastasya scrutinised him, silent and frowning, and her scrutiny lasted a long time. He felt uneasy, even frightened at her searching eyes.

"Nastasya, why don't you speak?" he said timidly at last in a weak voice.

"It's the blood," she answered at last softly, as though speaking to herself.

"Blood? What blood?" he muttered, growing white and turning towards the wall.

Nastasya still looked at him without speaking.

"Nobody has been beating the landlady," she declared at last in a firm, resolute voice.

He gazed at her, hardly able to breathe.

"I heard it myself.... I was not asleep... I was sitting up," he said still more timidly. "I listened a long while. The assistant superintendent came.... Everyone ran out on to the stairs from all the flats."

"No one has been here. That's the blood crying in your ears. When there's no outlet for it and it gets clotted, you begin fancying things.... Will you eat something?"

He made no answer. Nastasya still stood over him, watching him.

"Give me something to drink... Nastasya."

She went downstairs and returned with a white earthenware jug of water. He remembered only swallowing one sip of the cold water and spilling some on his neck. Then followed forgetfulness.

65

He was not completely unconscious, however, all the time he was ill; he was in a feverish state, sometimes delirious, sometimes half conscious. He remembered a great deal afterwards. Sometimes it seemed as though there were a number of people round him; they wanted to take him away somewhere, there was a great deal of squabbling and discussing about him. Then he would be alone in the room; they had all gone away afraid of him, and only now and then opened the door a crack to look at him; they threatened him, plotted something together, laughed, and mocked at him. He remembered Nastasya often at his bedside; he distinguished another person, too, whom he seemed to know very well, though he could not remember who he was, and this fretted him, even made him cry. Sometimes he fancied he had been lying there a month; at other times it all seemed part of the same day. But of *that*—of *that* he had no recollection, and yet every minute he felt that he had forgotten something he ought to remember. He worried and tormented himself trying to remember, moaned, flew into a rage, or sank into awful, intolerable terror. Then he struggled to get up, would have run away, but someone always prevented him by force, and he sank back into impotence and forgetfulness. At last he returned to complete consciousness.

It happened at ten o'clock in the morning. On fine days the sun shone into the room at that hour, throwing a streak of light on the right wall and the corner near the door. Nastasya was standing beside him with another person, a complete stranger, who was looking at him very inquisitively. He was a young man with a beard, wearing a full, short-waisted coat, and looked like a messenger. The landlady was peeping in at the half-opened door. Raskolnikov sat up.

"Who is this, Nastasya?" he asked, pointing to the young man.

"I say, he's himself again!" she said.

"He is himself," echoed the man.

Concluding that he had returned to his senses, the landlady closed the door and disappeared. She was always shy and dreaded conversations or discussions. She was a woman of forty, not at all bad-looking, fat and buxom, with black eyes and eyebrows, good-natured from fatness and laziness, and absurdly bashful.

"Who... are you?" he went on, addressing the man. But at that moment the door was flung open, and, stooping a little, as he was so tall, Razumihin came in.

"What a cabin it is!" he cried. "I am always knocking my head. You call this a lodging! So you are conscious, brother? I've just heard the news from Pashenka."

"He has just come to," said Nastasya.

"Just come to," echoed the man again, with a smile.

"And who are you?" Razumihin asked, suddenly addressing him. "My name is Vrazumihin, at your service; not Razumihin, as I am always called, but Vrazumihin, a student and gentleman; and he is my friend. And who are you?"

"I am the messenger from our office, from the merchant Shelopaev, and I've come on business."

"Please sit down." Razumihin seated himself on the other side of the table. "It's a good thing you've come to, brother," he went on to Raskolnikov. "For the last four days you have scarcely eaten or drunk anything. We had to give you tea in spoonfuls. I brought Zossimov to see you twice. You remember Zossimov? He examined you carefully and said at once it was nothing serious—something seemed to have gone to your head. Some nervous nonsense, the result of bad feeding, he says you have not had enough beer and radish, but it's nothing much, it will pass and you will be all right. Zossimov is a first-rate fellow! He is making quite a name. Come, I won't keep you," he said, addressing the man again. "Will you explain what you want? You must know, Rodya, this is the second time they have sent from the office; but it was another man last time, and I talked to him. Who was it came before?"

"That was the day before yesterday, I venture to say, if you please, sir. That was Alexey Semyonovitch; he is in our office, too."

"He was more intelligent than you, don't you think so?"

"Yes, indeed, sir, he is of more weight than I am."

"Quite so; go on."

"At your mamma's request, through Afanasy Ivanovitch Vahrushin, of whom I presume you have heard more than once, a remittance is sent to you from our office," the man began, addressing Raskolnikov. "If you are in an intelligible condition, I've thirty-five roubles to remit to you, as Semyon Semyonovitch has received from Afanasy Ivanovitch at your mamma's request instructions to that effect, as on previous occasions. Do you know him, sir?"

"Yes, I remember... Vahrushin," Raskolnikov said dreamily.

"You hear, he knows Vahrushin," cried Razumihin. "He is in 'an intelligible condition'! And I see you are an intelligent man too. Well, it's always pleasant to hear words of wisdom."

"That's the gentleman, Vahrushin, Afanasy Ivanovitch. And at the request of your mamma, who has sent you a remittance once before in the same manner through him, he did not refuse this time also, and sent instructions to Semyon Semyonovitch some days since to hand you thirty-five roubles in the hope of better to come."

"That 'hoping for better to come' is the best thing you've said, though 'your mamma' is not bad either. Come then, what do you say? Is he fully conscious, eh?"

"That's all right. If only he can sign this little paper."

"He can scrawl his name. Have you got the book?"

"Yes, here's the book."

"Give it to me. Here, Rodya, sit up. I'll hold you. Take the pen and scribble 'Raskolnikov' for him. For just now, brother, money is sweeter to us than treacle."

"I don't want it," said Raskolnikov, pushing away the pen.

"Not want it?"

"I won't sign it."

"How the devil can you do without signing it?"

"I don't want... the money."

"Don't want the money! Come, brother, that's nonsense, I bear witness. Don't trouble, please, it's only that he is on his travels again. But that's pretty common with him at all times though.... You are a man of judgment and we will take him in hand, that is, more simply, take his hand and he will sign it. Here."

"But I can come another time."

"No, no. Why should we trouble you? You are a man of judgment.... Now, Rodya, don't keep your visitor, you see he is waiting," and he made ready to hold Raskolnikov's hand in earnest.

"Stop, I'll do it alone," said the latter, taking the pen and signing his name.

The messenger took out the money and went away.

"Bravo! And now, brother, are you hungry?"

"Yes," answered Raskolnikov.

"Is there any soup?"

"Some of yesterday's," answered Nastasya, who was still standing there.

"With potatoes and rice in it?"

"Yes."

"I know it by heart. Bring soup and give us some tea."

"Very well."

Raskolnikov looked at all this with profound astonishment and a dull, unreasoning terror. He made up his mind to keep quiet and see what would happen. "I believe I am not wandering. I believe it's reality," he thought.

67

In a couple of minutes Nastasya returned with the soup, and announced that the tea would be ready directly. With the soup she brought two spoons, two plates, salt, pepper, mustard for the beef, and so on. The table was set as it had not been for a long time. The cloth was clean.

"It would not be amiss, Nastasya, if Praskovya Pavlovna were to send us up a couple of bottles of beer. We could empty them."

"Well, you are a cool hand," muttered Nastasya, and she departed to carry out his orders.

Raskolnikov still gazed wildly with strained attention. Meanwhile Razumihin sat down on the sofa beside him, as clumsily as a bear put his left arm round Raskolnikov's head, although he was able to sit up, and with his right hand gave him a spoonful of soup, blowing on it that it might not burn him. But the soup was only just warm. Raskolnikov swallowed one spoonful greedily, then a second, then a third. But after giving him a few more spoonfuls of soup, Razumihin suddenly stopped, and said that he must ask Zossimov whether he ought to have more.

Nastasya came in with two bottles of beer.

"And will you have tea?"

"Yes."

"Cut along, Nastasya, and bring some tea, for tea we may venture on without the faculty. But here is the beer!" He moved back to his chair, pulled the soup and meat in front of him, and began eating as though he had not touched food for three days.

"I must tell you, Rodya, I dine like this here every day now," he mumbled with his mouth full of beef, "and it's all Pashenka, your dear little landlady, who sees to that; she loves to do anything for me. I don't ask for it, but, of course, I don't object. And here's Nastasya with the tea. She is a quick girl. Nastasya, my dear, won't you have some beer?"

"Get along with your nonsense!"

"A cup of tea, then?"

"A cup of tea, maybe."

"Pour it out. Stay, I'll pour it out myself. Sit down."

He poured out two cups, left his dinner, and sat on the sofa again. As before, he put his left arm round the sick man's head, raised him up and gave him tea in spoonfuls, again blowing each spoonful steadily and earnestly, as though this process was the principal and most effective means towards his friend's recovery. Raskolnikov said nothing and made no resistance, though he felt quite strong enough to sit up on the sofa without support and could not merely have held a cup or a spoon, but even perhaps could have walked about. But from some queer, almost animal, cunning he conceived the idea of hiding his strength and lying low for a time, pretending if necessary not to be yet in full possession of his faculties, and meanwhile listening to find out what was going on. Yet he could not overcome his sense of repugnance. After sipping a dozen spoonfuls of tea, he suddenly released his head, pushed the spoon away capriciously, and sank back on the pillow. There were actually real pillows under his head now, down pillows in clean cases, he observed that, too, and took note of it.

"Pashenka must give us some raspberry jam today to make him some raspberry tea," said Razumihin, going back to his chair and attacking his soup and beer again.

"And where is she to get raspberries for you?" asked Nastasya, balancing a saucer on her five outspread fingers and sipping tea through a lump of sugar.

"She'll get it at the shop, my dear. You see, Rodya, all sorts of things have been happening while you have been laid up. When you decamped in that rascally way without leaving your address, I felt so angry that I resolved to find you out and punish you. I set to work that very day. How I ran about making inquiries for you! This lodging of yours I had forgotten, though I never remembered it, indeed, because I did not know it; and as for your old lodgings, I could only remember it was at the Five Corners, Harlamov's house. I kept trying to find that Harlamov's house, and afterwards it turned out that it was not Harlamov's, but Buch's. How one muddles up sound sometimes! So I lost my temper, and I went on the chance to the address bureau next day, and only fancy, in two minutes they looked you up! Your name is down there."

"My name!"

"I should think so; and yet a General Kobelev they could not find while I was there. Well, it's a long story. But as soon as I did land on this place, I soon got to know all your affairs—all, all, brother, I know everything; Nastasya here will tell you. I made the acquaintance of Nikodim Fomitch and Ilya Petrovitch, and the house-porter and Mr. Zametov, Alexandr Grigorievitch, the head clerk in the police office, and, last, but not least, of Pashenka; Nastasya here knows...."

"He's got round her," Nastasya murmured, smiling slyly.

"Why don't you put the sugar in your tea, Nastasya Nikiforovna?"

"You are a one!" Nastasya cried suddenly, going off into a giggle. "I am not Nikiforovna, but Petrovna," she added suddenly, recovering from her mirth.

"I'll make a note of it. Well, brother, to make a long story short, I was going in for a regular explosion here to uproot all malignant influences in the locality, but Pashenka won the day. I had not expected, brother, to find her so... prepossessing. Eh, what do you think?"

Raskolnikov did not speak, but he still kept his eyes fixed upon him, full of alarm.

"And all that could be wished, indeed, in every respect," Razumihin went on, not at all embarrassed by his silence.

"Ah, the sly dog!" Nastasya shrieked again. This conversation afforded her unspeakable delight.

"It's a pity, brother, that you did not set to work in the right way at first. You ought to have approached her differently. She is, so to speak, a most unaccountable character. But we will talk about her character later.... How could you let things come to such a pass that she gave up sending you your dinner? And that IOU? You must have been mad to sign an IOU. And that promise of marriage when her daughter, Natalya Yegorovna, was alive?... I know all about it! But I see that's a delicate matter and I am an ass; forgive me. But, talking of foolishness, do you know Praskovya Pavlovna is not nearly so foolish as you would think at first sight?"

"No," mumbled Raskolnikov, looking away, but feeling that it was better to keep up the conversation.

"She isn't, is she?" cried Razumihin, delighted to get an answer out of him. "But she is not very clever either, eh? She is essentially, essentially an unaccountable character! I am sometimes quite at a loss, I assure you.... She must be forty; she says she is thirty-six, and of course she has every right to say so. But I swear I judge her intellectually, simply from the metaphysical point of view; there is a sort of symbolism sprung up between us, a sort of algebra or whatnot! I don't understand it! Well, that's all nonsense. Only, seeing that you are not a student now and have lost your lessons and your clothes, and that through the young lady's death she has no need to treat you as a relation, she suddenly took fright; and as you hid in your den and dropped all your old relations with her, she planned to get rid of you. And she's been cherishing that design a long time, but was sorry to lose the IOU, for you assured her yourself that your mother would pay."

"It was base of me to say that.... My mother herself is almost a beggar... and I told a lie to keep my lodging... and be fed," Raskolnikov said loudly and distinctly.

"Yes, you did very sensibly. But the worst of it is that at that point Mr. Tchebarov turns up, a business man. Pashenka would never have thought of doing anything on her own account, she is too retiring; but the business man is by no means retiring, and first thing he puts the question, 'Is there any hope of realising the IOU?' Answer: there is, because he has a mother who would save her Rodya with her hundred and twenty-five roubles pension, if she has to starve herself; and a sister, too, who would go into bondage for his sake. That's what he was building upon.... Why do you start? I know all the ins and outs of your affairs now, my dear boy—it's not for nothing that you were so open with Pashenka when you were her prospective son-in-law, and I say all this as a friend.... But I tell you what it is; an honest and sensitive man is open; and a business man 'listens and goes on eating' you up. Well, then she gave the IOU by way of payment to this Tchebarov, and without hesitation he made a formal demand for payment. When I heard of all this I wanted to blow him up, too, to clear my conscience, but by that time harmony reigned between me and Pashenka, and I insisted on stopping the whole affair, engaging that you would pay. I went security for you, brother. Do you understand? We called Tchebarov, flung him ten roubles and got the IOU back from him, and here I have the honour of presenting it to you. She trusts your word now. Here, take it, you see I have torn it."

Razumihin put the note on the table. Raskolnikov looked at him and turned to the wall without uttering a word. Even Razumihin felt a twinge.

"I see, brother," he said a moment later, "that I have been playing the fool again. I thought I should amuse you with my chatter, and I believe I have only made you cross."

"Was it you I did not recognise when I was delirious?" Raskolnikov asked, after a moment's pause without turning his head.

"Yes, and you flew into a rage about it, especially when I brought Zametov one day."

"Zametov? The head clerk? What for?" Raskolnikov turned round quickly and fixed his eyes on Razumihin.

"What's the matter with you?... What are you upset about? He wanted to make your acquaintance because I talked to him a lot about you.... How could I have found out so much except from him? He is a capital fellow, brother, first-rate... in his own way, of course. Now we are friends—see each other almost every day. I have moved into this part, you know. I have only just moved. I've been with him to Luise Ivanovna once or twice.... Do you remember Luise, Luise Ivanovna?

"Did I say anything in delirium?"

"I should think so! You were beside yourself."

"What did I rave about?"

"What next? What did you rave about? What people do rave about.... Well, brother, now I must not lose time. To work." He got up from the table and took up his cap.

"What did I rave about?"

"How he keeps on! Are you afraid of having let out some secret? Don't worry yourself; you said nothing about a countess. But you said a lot about a bulldog, and about earrings and chains, and about Krestovsky Island, and some porter, and Nikodim Fomitch and Ilya Petrovitch, the assistant superintendent. And another thing that was of special interest to you was your own sock. You whined, 'Give me my sock.' Zametov hunted all about your room for your socks, and with his own scented, ring-bedecked fingers he gave you the rag. And only then were you comforted, and for the next twenty-four hours you held the wretched thing in your hand; we could not get it from you. It is most likely somewhere under your quilt at this moment. And then you asked so piteously for fringe for your trousers. We tried to find out what sort of fringe, but we could not make it out. Now to business! Here are thirty-five roubles; I take ten of them, and shall give you an account of them in an hour or two. I will let Zossimov know at the same time, though he ought to have been here long ago, for it is nearly twelve. And you, Nastasya, look in pretty often while I am away, to see whether he wants a drink or anything else. And I will tell Pashenka what is wanted myself. Goodbye!"

"He calls her Pashenka! Ah, he's a deep one!" said Nastasya as he went out; then she opened the door and stood listening, but could not resist running downstairs after him. She was very eager to hear what he would say to the landlady. She was evidently quite fascinated by Razumihin.

No sooner had she left the room than the sick man flung off the bedclothes and leapt out of bed like a madman. With burning, twitching impatience he had waited for them to be gone so that he might set to work. But to what work? Now, as though to spite him, it eluded him.

"Good God, only tell me one thing: do they know of it yet or not? What if they know it and are only pretending, mocking me while I am laid up, and then they will come in and tell me that it's been discovered long ago and that they have only... What am I to do now? That's what I've forgotten, as though on purpose; forgotten it all at once, I remembered a minute ago."

He stood in the middle of the room and gazed in miserable bewilderment about him; he walked to the door, opened it, listened; but that was not what he wanted. Suddenly, as though recalling something, he rushed to the corner where there was a hole under the paper, began examining it, put his hand into the hole, fumbled—but that was not it. He went to the stove, opened it and began rummaging in the ashes; the frayed edges of his trousers and the rags cut off his pocket were lying there just as he had thrown them. No one had looked, then! Then he remembered the sock about which Razumihin had just been telling him. Yes, there it lay on the sofa under the quilt, but it was so covered with dust and grime that Zametov could not have seen anything on it.

"Bah, Zametov! The police office! And why am I sent for to the police office? Where's the notice? Bah! I am mixing it up; that was then. I looked at my sock then, too, but now ... now I have been ill. But what did Zametov come for? Why did Razumihin bring him?" he muttered, helplessly sitting on the sofa again. "What does it mean? Am I still in delirium, or is it real? I believe it is real.... Ah, I remember; I must escape! Make haste to escape. Yes, I must, I must escape! Yes ... but where? And where are my clothes? I've no boots. They've taken them away! They've hidden them! I understand! Ah, here is my coat—they passed that over! And here is money on the table, thank God! And here's the IOU ... I'll take the money and go and take another lodging. They won't find me! ... Yes, but the address bureau? They'll find me, Razumihin will find me. Better escape altogether... far away... to America, and let them do their worst! And take the IOU... it would be of use there.... What else shall I take? They think I am ill! They don't know that I can walk, ha-ha-ha! I could see by their eyes that they know all about it! If only I could get downstairs! And what if they have set a watch there—policemen! What's this tea? Ah, and here is beer left, half a bottle, cold!"

He snatched up the bottle, which still contained a glassful of beer, and gulped it down with relish, as though quenching a flame in his breast. But in another minute the beer had gone to his head, and a faint and even pleasant shiver ran down his spine. He lay down and pulled the quilt over him. His sick and incoherent thoughts grew more and more disconnected, and soon a light, pleasant drowsiness came upon him. With a sense of comfort he nestled his head into the pillow, wrapped more closely about him the soft, wadded quilt which had replaced the old, ragged greatcoat, sighed softly and sank into a deep, sound, refreshing sleep.

He woke up, hearing someone come in. He opened his eyes and saw Razumihin standing in the doorway, uncertain whether to come in or not. Raskolnikov sat up quickly on the sofa and gazed at him, as though trying to recall something.

"Ah, you are not asleep! Here I am! Nastasya, bring in the parcel!" Razumihin shouted down the stairs. "You shall have the account directly."

"What time is it?" asked Raskolnikov, looking round uneasily.

"Yes, you had a fine sleep, brother, it's almost evening, it will be six o'clock directly. You have slept more than six hours."

"Good heavens! Have I?"

"And why not? It will do you good. What's the hurry? A tryst, is it? We've all time before us. I've been waiting for the last three hours for you; I've been up twice and found you asleep. I've called on Zossimov twice; not at home, only fancy! But no matter, he will turn up. And I've been out on my own business, too. You know I've been moving today, moving with my uncle. I have an uncle living with me now. But that's no matter, to business. Give me the parcel, Nastasya. We will open it directly. And how do you feel now, brother?"

"I am quite well, I am not ill. Razumihin, have you been here long?"

"I tell you I've been waiting for the last three hours."

"No, before."

"How do you mean?"

"How long have you been coming here?"

"Why I told you all about it this morning. Don't you remember?"

Raskolnikov pondered. The morning seemed like a dream to him. He could not remember alone, and looked inquiringly at Razumihin.

"Hm!" said the latter, "he has forgotten. I fancied then that you were not quite yourself. Now you are better for your sleep.... You really look much better. First-rate! Well, to business. Look here, my dear boy."

He began untying the bundle, which evidently interested him.

"Believe me, brother, this is something specially near my heart. For we must make a man of you. Let's begin from the top. Do you see this cap?" he said, taking out of the bundle a fairly good though cheap and ordinary cap. "Let me try it on."

"Presently, afterwards," said Raskolnikov, waving it off pettishly.

"Come, Rodya, my boy, don't oppose it, afterwards will be too late; and I shan't sleep all night, for I bought it by guess, without measure. Just right!" he cried triumphantly, fitting it on, "just your size! A proper head-covering is the first thing in dress and a recommendation in its own way. Tolstyakov, a friend of mine, is always obliged to take off his pudding basin when he goes into any public place where other people wear their hats or caps. People think he does it from slavish politeness, but it's simply because he is ashamed of his bird's nest; he is such a boastful fellow! Look, Nastasya, here are two specimens of headgear: this Palmerston"—he took from the corner Raskolnikov's old, battered hat, which for some unknown reason, he called a Palmerston—"or this jewel! Guess the price, Rodya, what do you suppose I paid for it, Nastasya!" he said, turning to her, seeing that Raskolnikov did not speak.

"Twenty kopecks, no more, I dare say," answered Nastasya.

"Twenty kopecks, silly!" he cried, offended. "Why, nowadays you would cost more than that— eighty kopecks! And that only because it has been worn. And it's bought on condition that when's it's worn out, they will give you another next year. Yes, on my word! Well, now let us pass to the United States of America, as they called them at school. I assure you I am proud of these breeches," and he exhibited to Raskolnikov a pair of light, summer trousers of grey woollen material. "No holes, no spots, and quite respectable, although a little worn; and a waistcoat to match, quite in the fashion. And its being worn really is an improvement, it's softer, smoother.... You see, Rodya, to my thinking, the great thing for getting on in the world is always to keep to the seasons; if you don't insist on having asparagus in January, you keep your money in your purse; and it's the same with this purchase. It's summer now, so I've been buying summer things— warmer materials will be wanted for autumn, so you will have to throw these away in any case... especially as they will be done for by then from their own lack of coherence if not your higher standard of luxury. Come, price them! What do you say? Two roubles twenty-five kopecks! And remember the condition: if you wear these out, you will have another suit for nothing! They only do business on that system at Fedyaev's; if you've bought a thing once, you are satisfied for life, for you will never go there again of your own free will. Now for the boots. What do you say? You see that they are a bit worn, but they'll last a couple of months, for it's foreign work and foreign leather; the secretary of the English Embassy sold them last week—he had only worn them six days, but he was very short of cash. Price—a rouble and a half. A bargain?"

"But perhaps they won't fit," observed Nastasya.

"Not fit? Just look!" and he pulled out of his pocket Raskolnikov's old, broken boot, stiffly coated with dry mud. "I did not go empty-handed—they took the size from this monster. We all did our best. And as to your linen, your landlady has seen to that. Here, to begin with are three shirts, hempen but with a fashionable front.... Well now then, eighty kopecks the cap, two roubles twenty-five kopecks the suit—together three roubles five kopecks—a rouble and a half for the boots—for, you see, they are very good—and that makes four roubles fifty-five kopecks; five roubles for the underclothes—they were bought in the lot—which makes exactly nine roubles fifty-five kopecks. Forty-five kopecks change in coppers. Will you take it? And so, Rodya, you are set up with a complete new rig-out, for your overcoat will serve, and even has a style of its own. That comes from getting one's clothes from Sharmer's! As for your socks and other things, I leave them to you; we've twenty-five roubles left. And as for Pashenka and paying for your lodging, don't you worry. I tell you she'll trust you for anything. And now, brother, let me change your linen, for I daresay you will throw off your illness with your shirt."

"Let me be! I don't want to!" Raskolnikov waved him off. He had listened with disgust to Razumihin's efforts to be playful about his purchases.

"Come, brother, don't tell me I've been trudging around for nothing," Razumihin insisted. "Nastasya, don't be bashful, but help me—that's it," and in spite of Raskolnikov's resistance he changed his linen. The latter sank back on the pillows and for a minute or two said nothing.

"It will be long before I get rid of them," he thought. "What money was all that bought with?" he asked at last, gazing at the wall.

"Money? Why, your own, what the messenger brought from Vahrushin, your mother sent it. Have you forgotten that, too?"

"I remember now," said Raskolnikov after a long, sullen silence. Razumihin looked at him, frowning and uneasy.

The door opened and a tall, stout man whose appearance seemed familiar to Raskolnikov came in.

Zossimov was a tall, fat man with a puffy, colourless, clean-shaven face and straight flaxen hair. He wore spectacles, and a big gold ring on his fat finger. He was twenty-seven. He had on a light grey fashionable loose coat, light summer trousers, and everything about him loose, fashionable and spick and span; his linen was irreproachable, his watch-chain was massive. In manner he was slow and, as it were, nonchalant, and at the same time studiously free and easy; he made efforts to conceal his self-importance, but it was apparent at every instant. All his acquaintances found him tedious, but said he was clever at his work.

"I've been to you twice today, brother. You see, he's come to himself," cried Razumihin.

"I see, I see; and how do we feel now, eh?" said Zossimov to Raskolnikov, watching him carefully and, sitting down at the foot of the sofa, he settled himself as comfortably as he could.

"He is still depressed," Razumihin went on. "We've just changed his linen and he almost cried."

"That's very natural; you might have put it off if he did not wish it.... His pulse is first-rate. Is your head still aching, eh?"

"I am well, I am perfectly well!" Raskolnikov declared positively and irritably. He raised himself on the sofa and looked at them with glittering eyes, but sank back on to the pillow at once and turned to the wall. Zossimov watched him intently.

"Very good.... Going on all right," he said lazily. "Has he eaten anything?"

They told him, and asked what he might have.

"He may have anything... soup, tea... mushrooms and cucumbers, of course, you must not give him; he'd better not have meat either, and... but no need to tell you that!" Razumihin and he looked at each other. "No more medicine or anything. I'll look at him again tomorrow. Perhaps, today even... but never mind..."

"Tomorrow evening I shall take him for a walk," said Razumihin. "We are going to the Yusupov garden and then to the Palais de Cristal."

"I would not disturb him tomorrow at all, but I don't know... a little, maybe... but we'll see."

"Ach, what a nuisance! I've got a housewarming party tonight; it's only a step from here. Couldn't he come? He could lie on the sofa. You are coming?" Razumihin said to Zossimov. "Don't forget, you promised."

"All right, only rather later. What are you going to do?"

"Oh, nothing—tea, vodka, herrings. There will be a pie... just our friends."

"And who?"

"All neighbours here, almost all new friends, except my old uncle, and he is new too—he only arrived in Petersburg yesterday to see to some business of his. We meet once in five years."

"What is he?"

"He's been stagnating all his life as a district postmaster; gets a little pension. He is sixty-five—not worth talking about.... But I am fond of him. Porfiry Petrovitch, the head of the Investigation Department here... But you know him."

"Is he a relation of yours, too?"

"A very distant one. But why are you scowling? Because you quarrelled once, won't you come then?"

"I don't care a damn for him."

"So much the better. Well, there will be some students, a teacher, a government clerk, a musician, an officer and Zametov."

"Do tell me, please, what you or he"—Zossimov nodded at Raskolnikov—"can have in common with this Zametov?"

"Oh, you particular gentleman! Principles! You are worked by principles, as it were by springs; you won't venture to turn round on your own account. If a man is a nice fellow, that's the only principle I go upon. Zametov is a delightful person."

"Though he does take bribes."

"Well, he does! and what of it? I don't care if he does take bribes," Razumihin cried with unnatural irritability. "I don't praise him for taking bribes. I only say he is a nice man in his own way! But if one looks at men in all ways—are there many good ones left? Why, I am sure I shouldn't be worth a baked onion myself... perhaps with you thrown in."

"That's too little; I'd give two for you."

"And I wouldn't give more than one for you. No more of your jokes! Zametov is no more than a boy. I can pull his hair and one must draw him not repel him. You'll never improve a man by repelling him, especially a boy. One has to be twice as careful with a boy. Oh, you progressive dullards! You don't understand. You harm yourselves running another man down.... But if you want to know, we really have something in common."

"I should like to know what."

"Why, it's all about a house-painter.... We are getting him out of a mess! Though indeed there's nothing to fear now. The matter is absolutely self-evident. We only put on steam."

"A painter?"

"Why, haven't I told you about it? I only told you the beginning then about the murder of the old pawnbroker-woman. Well, the painter is mixed up in it..."

"Oh, I heard about that murder before and was rather interested in it... partly... for one reason.... I read about it in the papers, too...."

"Lizaveta was murdered, too," Nastasya blurted out, suddenly addressing Raskolnikov. She remained in the room all the time, standing by the door listening.

"Lizaveta," murmured Raskolnikov hardly audibly.

"Lizaveta, who sold old clothes. Didn't you know her? She used to come here. She mended a shirt for you, too."

Raskolnikov turned to the wall where in the dirty, yellow paper he picked out one clumsy, white flower with brown lines on it and began examining how many petals there were in it, how many scallops in the petals and how many lines on them. He felt his arms and legs as lifeless as though they had been cut off. He did not attempt to move, but stared obstinately at the flower.

"But what about the painter?" Zossimov interrupted Nastasya's chatter with marked displeasure. She sighed and was silent.

"Why, he was accused of the murder," Razumihin went on hotly.

"Was there evidence against him then?"

"Evidence, indeed! Evidence that was no evidence, and that's what we have to prove. It was just as they pitched on those fellows, Koch and Pestryakov, at first. Foo! how stupidly it's all done, it makes one sick, though it's not one's business! Pestryakov may be coming tonight.... By the way, Rodya, you've heard about the business already; it happened before you were ill, the day before you fainted at the police office while they were talking about it."

Zossimov looked curiously at Raskolnikov. He did not stir.

"But I say, Razumihin, I wonder at you. What a busybody you are!" Zossimov observed.

"Maybe I am, but we will get him off anyway," shouted Razumihin, bringing his fist down on the table. "What's the most offensive is not their lying—one can always forgive lying—lying is a delightful thing, for it leads to truth—what is offensive is that they lie and worship their own lying.... I respect Porfiry, but... What threw them out at first? The door was locked, and when they came back with the porter it was open. So it followed that Koch and Pestryakov were the murderers—that was their logic!"

"But don't excite yourself; they simply detained them, they could not help that.... And, by the way, I've met that man Koch. He used to buy unredeemed pledges from the old woman? Eh?"

"Yes, he is a swindler. He buys up bad debts, too. He makes a profession of it. But enough of him! Do you know what makes me angry? It's their sickening rotten, petrified routine.... And this case might be the means of introducing a new method. One can show from the psychological data alone how to get on the track of the real man. 'We have facts,' they say. But facts are not everything—at least half the business lies in how you interpret them!"

"Can you interpret them, then?"

"Anyway, one can't hold one's tongue when one has a feeling, a tangible feeling, that one might be a help if only.... Eh! Do you know the details of the case?"

"I am waiting to hear about the painter."

"Oh, yes! Well, here's the story. Early on the third day after the murder, when they were still dandling Koch and Pestryakov—though they accounted for every step they took and it was as plain as a pikestaff—an unexpected fact turned up. A peasant called Dushkin, who keeps a dram-shop facing the house, brought to the police office a jeweller's case containing some gold earrings, and told a long rigamarole. 'The day before yesterday, just after eight o'clock'—mark the day and the hour!—'a journeyman house-painter, Nikolay, who had been in to see me already that day, brought me this box of gold earrings and stones, and asked me to give him two roubles for them. When I asked him where he got them, he said that he picked them up in the street. I did not ask him anything more.' I am telling you Dushkin's story. 'I gave him a note'—a rouble that is—'for I thought if he did not pawn it with me he would with another. It would all come to the same thing—he'd spend it on drink, so the thing had better be with me. The further you hide it the quicker you will find it, and if anything turns up, if I hear any rumours, I'll take it to the police.' Of course, that's all taradiddle; he lies like a horse, for I know this Dushkin, he is a pawnbroker and a receiver of stolen goods, and he did not cheat Nikolay out of a thirty-rouble trinket in order to give it to the police. He was simply afraid. But no matter, to return to Dushkin's story. 'I've known this peasant, Nikolay Dementyev, from a child; he comes from the same province and district of Zaraïsk, we are both Ryazan men. And though Nikolay is not a drunkard, he drinks, and I knew he had a job in that house, painting work with Dmitri, who comes from the same village, too. As soon as he got the rouble he changed it, had a couple of glasses, took his change and went out. But I did not see Dmitri with him then. And the next day I heard that someone had murdered Alyona Ivanovna and her sister, Lizaveta Ivanovna, with an axe. I knew them, and I felt suspicious about the earrings at once, for I knew the murdered woman lent money on pledges. I went to the house, and began to make careful inquiries without saying a word to anyone. First of all I asked, "Is Nikolay here?" Dmitri told me that Nikolay had gone off on the spree; he had come home at daybreak drunk, stayed in the house about ten minutes, and went out again. Dmitri didn't see him again and is finishing the job alone. And their job is on the same staircase as the murder, on the second floor. When I heard all that I did not say a word to anyone'—that's Dushkin's tale—'but I found out what I could about the murder, and went home feeling as suspicious as ever. And at eight o'clock this morning'—that was the third day, you understand—'I saw Nikolay coming in, not sober, though not to say very drunk—he could understand what was said to him. He sat down on the bench and did not speak. There was only one stranger in the bar and a man I knew asleep on a bench and our two boys. "Have you seen Dmitri?" said I. "No, I haven't," said he. "And you've not been here either?" "Not since the day before yesterday," said he. "And where did you sleep last night?" "In Peski, with the Kolomensky men." "And where did you get those earrings?" I asked. "I found them in the street," and the way he said it was a bit queer; he did not look at me. "Did you hear what happened that very evening, at that very hour, on that same staircase?" said I. "No," said he, "I had not heard," and all the while he was listening, his eyes were staring out of his head and he turned as white as chalk. I told him all about it and he took his hat and began getting up. I wanted to keep him. "Wait a bit, Nikolay," said I, "won't you have a drink?" And I signed to the boy to hold the door, and I came out from behind the bar; but he darted out and down the street to the turning at a run. I have not seen him since. Then my doubts were at an end—it was his doing, as clear as could be....'"

"I should think so," said Zossimov.

"Wait! Hear the end. Of course they sought high and low for Nikolay; they detained Dushkin and searched his house; Dmitri, too, was arrested; the Kolomensky men also were turned inside out. And the day before yesterday they arrested Nikolay in a tavern at the end of the town. He had gone there, taken the silver cross off his neck and asked for a dram for it. They gave it to him. A few minutes afterwards the woman went to the cowshed, and through a crack in the wall she saw in the stable adjoining he had made a noose of his sash from the beam, stood on a block of wood, and was trying to put his neck in the noose. The woman screeched her hardest; people ran in. 'So that's what you are up to!' 'Take me,' he says, 'to such-and-such a police officer; I'll confess everything.' Well, they took him to that police station—that is here—with a suitable escort. So they asked him this and that, how old he is, 'twenty-two,' and so on. At the question, 'When you were working with Dmitri, didn't you see anyone on the staircase at such-and-such a time?'— answer: 'To be sure folks may have gone up and down, but I did not notice them.' 'And didn't you hear anything, any noise, and so on?' 'We heard nothing special.' 'And did you hear, Nikolay, that on the same day Widow So-and-so and her sister were murdered and robbed?' 'I never knew a thing about it. The first I heard of it was from Afanasy Pavlovitch the day before yesterday.' 'And where did you find the earrings?' 'I found them on the pavement.' 'Why didn't you go to work with Dmitri the other day?' 'Because I was drinking.' 'And where were you drinking?' 'Oh, in such-and-such a place.' 'Why did you run away from Dushkin's?' 'Because I was awfully frightened.' 'What were you frightened of?' 'That I should be accused.' 'How could you be frightened, if you felt free from guilt?' Now, Zossimov, you may not believe me, that question was put literally in those words. I know it for a fact, it was repeated to me exactly! What do you say to that?"

"Well, anyway, there's the evidence."

"I am not talking of the evidence now, I am talking about that question, of their own idea of themselves. Well, so they squeezed and squeezed him and he confessed: 'I did not find it in the street, but in the flat where I was painting with Dmitri.' 'And how was that?' 'Why, Dmitri and I were painting there all day, and we were just getting ready to go, and Dmitri took a brush and painted my face, and he ran off and I after him. I ran after him, shouting my hardest, and at the bottom of the stairs I ran right against the porter and some gentlemen—and how many gentlemen were there I don't remember. And the porter swore at me, and the other porter swore, too, and the porter's wife came out, and swore at us, too; and a gentleman came into the entry with a lady, and he swore at us, too, for Dmitri and I lay right across the way. I got hold of Dmitri's hair and knocked him down and began beating him. And Dmitri, too, caught me by the hair and began beating me. But we did it all not for temper but in a friendly way, for sport. And then Dmitri escaped and ran into the street, and I ran after him; but I did not catch him, and went back to the flat alone; I had to clear up my things. I began putting them together, expecting Dmitri to come, and there in the passage, in the corner by the door, I stepped on the box. I saw it lying there wrapped up in paper. I took off the paper, saw some little hooks, undid them, and in the box were the earrings....'"

"Behind the door? Lying behind the door? Behind the door?" Raskolnikov cried suddenly, staring with a blank look of terror at Razumihin, and he slowly sat up on the sofa, leaning on his hand.

"Yes... why? What's the matter? What's wrong?" Razumihin, too, got up from his seat.

"Nothing," Raskolnikov answered faintly, turning to the wall. All were silent for a while.

"He must have waked from a dream," Razumihin said at last, looking inquiringly at Zossimov. The latter slightly shook his head.

"Well, go on," said Zossimov. "What next?"

"What next? As soon as he saw the earrings, forgetting Dmitri and everything, he took up his cap and ran to Dushkin and, as we know, got a rouble from him. He told a lie saying he found them in the street, and went off drinking. He keeps repeating his old story about the murder: 'I know nothing of it, never heard of it till the day before yesterday.' 'And why didn't you come to the police till now?' 'I was frightened.' 'And why did you try to hang yourself?' 'From anxiety.'

'What anxiety?' 'That I should be accused of it.' Well, that's the whole story. And now what do you suppose they deduced from that?"

"Why, there's no supposing. There's a clue, such as it is, a fact. You wouldn't have your painter set free?"

"Now they've simply taken him for the murderer. They haven't a shadow of doubt."

"That's nonsense. You are excited. But what about the earrings? You must admit that, if on the very same day and hour earrings from the old woman's box have come into Nikolay's hands, they must have come there somehow. That's a good deal in such a case."

"How did they get there? How did they get there?" cried Razumihin. "How can you, a doctor, whose duty it is to study man and who has more opportunity than anyone else for studying human nature—how can you fail to see the character of the man in the whole story? Don't you see at once that the answers he has given in the examination are the holy truth? They came into his hand precisely as he has told us—he stepped on the box and picked it up."

"The holy truth! But didn't he own himself that he told a lie at first?"

"Listen to me, listen attentively. The porter and Koch and Pestryakov and the other porter and the wife of the first porter and the woman who was sitting in the porter's lodge and the man Kryukov, who had just got out of a cab at that minute and went in at the entry with a lady on his arm, that is eight or ten witnesses, agree that Nikolay had Dmitri on the ground, was lying on him beating him, while Dmitri hung on to his hair, beating him, too. They lay right across the way, blocking the thoroughfare. They were sworn at on all sides while they 'like children' (the very words of the witnesses) were falling over one another, squealing, fighting and laughing with the funniest faces, and, chasing one another like children, they ran into the street. Now take careful note. The bodies upstairs were warm, you understand, warm when they found them! If they, or Nikolay alone, had murdered them and broken open the boxes, or simply taken part in the robbery, allow me to ask you one question: do their state of mind, their squeals and giggles and childish scuffling at the gate fit in with axes, bloodshed, fiendish cunning, robbery? They'd just killed them, not five or ten minutes before, for the bodies were still warm, and at once, leaving the flat open, knowing that people would go there at once, flinging away their booty, they rolled about like children, laughing and attracting general attention. And there are a dozen witnesses to swear to that!"

"Of course it is strange! It's impossible, indeed, but..."

"No, brother, no *buts*. And if the earrings being found in Nikolay's hands at the very day and hour of the murder constitutes an important piece of circumstantial evidence against him—although the explanation given by him accounts for it, and therefore it does not tell seriously against him—one must take into consideration the facts which prove him innocent, especially as they are facts that *cannot be denied*. And do you suppose, from the character of our legal system, that they will accept, or that they are in a position to accept, this fact—resting simply on a psychological impossibility—as irrefutable and conclusively breaking down the circumstantial evidence for the prosecution? No, they won't accept it, they certainly won't, because they found the jewel-case and the man tried to hang himself, 'which he could not have done if he hadn't felt guilty.' That's the point, that's what excites me, you must understand!"

"Oh, I see you are excited! Wait a bit. I forgot to ask you; what proof is there that the box came from the old woman?"

"That's been proved," said Razumihin with apparent reluctance, frowning. "Koch recognised the jewel-case and gave the name of the owner, who proved conclusively that it was his."

"That's bad. Now another point. Did anyone see Nikolay at the time that Koch and Pestryakov were going upstairs at first, and is there no evidence about that?"

"Nobody did see him," Razumihin answered with vexation. "That's the worst of it. Even Koch and Pestryakov did not notice them on their way upstairs, though, indeed, their evidence could not have been worth much. They said they saw the flat was open, and that there must be work going on in it, but they took no special notice and could not remember whether there actually were men at work in it."

"Hm!... So the only evidence for the defence is that they were beating one another and laughing. That constitutes a strong presumption, but... How do you explain the facts yourself?"

"How do I explain them? What is there to explain? It's clear. At any rate, the direction in which explanation is to be sought is clear, and the jewel-case points to it. The real murderer dropped those earrings. The murderer was upstairs, locked in, when Koch and Pestryakov knocked at the door. Koch, like an ass, did not stay at the door; so the murderer popped out and ran down, too; for he had no other way of escape. He hid from Koch, Pestryakov and the porter in the flat when Nikolay and Dmitri had just run out of it. He stopped there while the porter and others were going upstairs, waited till they were out of hearing, and then went calmly downstairs at the very minute when Dmitri and Nikolay ran out into the street and there was no one in the entry; possibly he was seen, but not noticed. There are lots of people going in and out. He must have dropped the earrings out of his pocket when he stood behind the door, and did not notice he dropped them, because he had other things to think of. The jewel-case is a conclusive proof that he did stand there.... That's how I explain it."

"Too clever! No, my boy, you're too clever. That beats everything."

"But, why, why?"

"Why, because everything fits too well... it's too melodramatic."

"A-ach!" Razumihin was exclaiming, but at that moment the door opened and a personage came in who was a stranger to all present.

This was a gentleman no longer young, of a stiff and portly appearance, and a cautious and sour countenance. He began by stopping short in the doorway, staring about him with offensive and undisguised astonishment, as though asking himself what sort of place he had come to. Mistrustfully and with an affectation of being alarmed and almost affronted, he scanned Raskolnikov's low and narrow "cabin." With the same amazement he stared at Raskolnikov, who lay undressed, dishevelled, unwashed, on his miserable dirty sofa, looking fixedly at him. Then with the same deliberation he scrutinised the uncouth, unkempt figure and unshaven face of Razumihin, who looked him boldly and inquiringly in the face without rising from his seat. A constrained silence lasted for a couple of minutes, and then, as might be expected, some scene-shifting took place. Reflecting, probably from certain fairly unmistakable signs, that he would get nothing in this "cabin" by attempting to overawe them, the gentleman softened somewhat, and civilly, though with some severity, emphasising every syllable of his question, addressed Zossimov:

"Rodion Romanovitch Raskolnikov, a student, or formerly a student?"

Zossimov made a slight movement, and would have answered, had not Razumihin anticipated him.

"Here he is lying on the sofa! What do you want?"

This familiar "what do you want" seemed to cut the ground from the feet of the pompous gentleman. He was turning to Razumihin, but checked himself in time and turned to Zossimov again.

"This is Raskolnikov," mumbled Zossimov, nodding towards him. Then he gave a prolonged yawn, opening his mouth as wide as possible. Then he lazily put his hand into his waistcoat-pocket, pulled out a huge gold watch in a round hunter's case, opened it, looked at it and as slowly and lazily proceeded to put it back.

Raskolnikov himself lay without speaking, on his back, gazing persistently, though without understanding, at the stranger. Now that his face was turned away from the strange flower on the paper, it was extremely pale and wore a look of anguish, as though he had just undergone an agonising operation or just been taken from the rack. But the newcomer gradually began to arouse his attention, then his wonder, then suspicion and even alarm. When Zossimov said "This is Raskolnikov" he jumped up quickly, sat on the sofa and with an almost defiant, but weak and breaking, voice articulated:

"Yes, I am Raskolnikov! What do you want?"

The visitor scrutinised him and pronounced impressively:

"Pyotr Petrovitch Luzhin. I believe I have reason to hope that my name is not wholly unknown to you?"

But Raskolnikov, who had expected something quite different, gazed blankly and dreamily at him, making no reply, as though he heard the name of Pyotr Petrovitch for the first time.

"Is it possible that you can up to the present have received no information?" asked Pyotr Petrovitch, somewhat disconcerted.

In reply Raskolnikov sank languidly back on the pillow, put his hands behind his head and gazed at the ceiling. A look of dismay came into Luzhin's face. Zossimov and Razumihin stared at him more inquisitively than ever, and at last he showed unmistakable signs of embarrassment.

"I had presumed and calculated," he faltered, "that a letter posted more than ten days, if not a fortnight ago..."

"I say, why are you standing in the doorway?" Razumihin interrupted suddenly. "If you've something to say, sit down. Nastasya and you are so crowded. Nastasya, make room. Here's a chair, thread your way in!"

He moved his chair back from the table, made a little space between the table and his knees, and waited in a rather cramped position for the visitor to "thread his way in." The minute was so chosen that it was impossible to refuse, and the visitor squeezed his way through, hurrying and stumbling. Reaching the chair, he sat down, looking suspiciously at Razumihin.

"No need to be nervous," the latter blurted out. "Rodya has been ill for the last five days and delirious for three, but now he is recovering and has got an appetite. This is his doctor, who has just had a look at him. I am a comrade of Rodya's, like him, formerly a student, and now I am nursing him; so don't you take any notice of us, but go on with your business."

"Thank you. But shall I not disturb the invalid by my presence and conversation?" Pyotr Petrovitch asked of Zossimov.

"N-no," mumbled Zossimov; "you may amuse him." He yawned again.

"He has been conscious a long time, since the morning," went on Razumihin, whose familiarity seemed so much like unaffected good-nature that Pyotr Petrovitch began to be more cheerful, partly, perhaps, because this shabby and impudent person had introduced himself as a student.

"Your mamma," began Luzhin.

"Hm!" Razumihin cleared his throat loudly. Luzhin looked at him inquiringly.

"That's all right, go on."

Luzhin shrugged his shoulders.

"Your mamma had commenced a letter to you while I was sojourning in her neighbourhood. On my arrival here I purposely allowed a few days to elapse before coming to see you, in order that I might be fully assured that you were in full possession of the tidings; but now, to my astonishment…"

"I know, I know!" Raskolnikov cried suddenly with impatient vexation. "So you are the fiancé? I know, and that's enough!"

There was no doubt about Pyotr Petrovitch's being offended this time, but he said nothing. He made a violent effort to understand what it all meant. There was a moment's silence.

Meanwhile Raskolnikov, who had turned a little towards him when he answered, began suddenly staring at him again with marked curiosity, as though he had not had a good look at him yet, or as though something new had struck him; he rose from his pillow on purpose to stare at him. There certainly was something peculiar in Pyotr Petrovitch's whole appearance, something which seemed to justify the title of "fiancé" so unceremoniously applied to him. In the first place, it was evident, far too much so indeed, that Pyotr Petrovitch had made eager use of his few days in the capital to get himself up and rig himself out in expectation of his betrothed—a perfectly innocent and permissible proceeding, indeed. Even his own, perhaps too complacent, consciousness of the agreeable improvement in his appearance might have been forgiven in such circumstances, seeing that Pyotr Petrovitch had taken up the role of fiancé. All his clothes were fresh from the tailor's and were all right, except for being too new and too distinctly appropriate. Even the stylish new round hat had the same significance. Pyotr Petrovitch treated it too respectfully and held it too carefully in his hands. The exquisite pair of lavender gloves, real Louvain, told the same tale, if only from the fact of his not wearing them, but carrying them in his hand for show. Light and youthful colours predominated in Pyotr Petrovitch's attire. He wore a charming summer jacket of a fawn shade, light thin trousers, a waistcoat of the same, new and fine linen, a cravat of the lightest cambric with pink stripes on it, and the best of it was, this all suited Pyotr Petrovitch. His very fresh and even handsome face looked younger than his forty-five years at all times. His dark, mutton-chop whiskers made an agreeable setting on both sides, growing thickly upon his shining, clean-shaven chin. Even his hair, touched here and there with grey, though it had been combed and curled at a hairdresser's, did not give him a stupid appearance, as curled hair usually does, by inevitably suggesting a German on his wedding-day. If there really was something unpleasing and repulsive in his rather good-looking and imposing countenance, it was due to quite other causes. After scanning Mr. Luzhin unceremoniously, Raskolnikov smiled malignantly, sank back on the pillow and stared at the ceiling as before.

But Mr. Luzhin hardened his heart and seemed to determine to take no notice of their oddities.

"I feel the greatest regret at finding you in this situation," he began, again breaking the silence with an effort. "If I had been aware of your illness I should have come earlier. But you know what business is. I have, too, a very important legal affair in the Senate, not to mention other preoccupations which you may well conjecture. I am expecting your mamma and sister any minute."

Raskolnikov made a movement and seemed about to speak; his face showed some excitement. Pyotr Petrovitch paused, waited, but as nothing followed, he went on:

"... Any minute. I have found a lodging for them on their arrival."

"Where?" asked Raskolnikov weakly.

"Very near here, in Bakaleyev's house."

"That's in Voskresensky," put in Razumihin. "There are two storeys of rooms, let by a merchant called Yushin; I've been there."

"Yes, rooms..."

"A disgusting place—filthy, stinking and, what's more, of doubtful character. Things have happened there, and there are all sorts of queer people living there. And I went there about a scandalous business. It's cheap, though..."

"I could not, of course, find out so much about it, for I am a stranger in Petersburg myself," Pyotr Petrovitch replied huffily. "However, the two rooms are exceedingly clean, and as it is for so short a time... I have already taken a permanent, that is, our future flat," he said, addressing Raskolnikov, "and I am having it done up. And meanwhile I am myself cramped for room in a lodging with my friend Andrey Semyonovitch Lebeziatnikov, in the flat of Madame Lippevechsel; it was he who told me of Bakaleyev's house, too..."

"Lebeziatnikov?" said Raskolnikov slowly, as if recalling something.

"Yes, Andrey Semyonovitch Lebeziatnikov, a clerk in the Ministry. Do you know him?"

"Yes... no," Raskolnikov answered.

"Excuse me, I fancied so from your inquiry. I was once his guardian.... A very nice young man and advanced. I like to meet young people: one learns new things from them." Luzhin looked round hopefully at them all.

"How do you mean?" asked Razumihin.

"In the most serious and essential matters," Pyotr Petrovitch replied, as though delighted at the question. "You see, it's ten years since I visited Petersburg. All the novelties, reforms, ideas have reached us in the provinces, but to see it all more clearly one must be in Petersburg. And it's my notion that you observe and learn most by watching the younger generation. And I confess I am delighted..."

"At what?"

"Your question is a wide one. I may be mistaken, but I fancy I find clearer views, more, so to say, criticism, more practicality..."

"That's true," Zossimov let drop.

"Nonsense! There's no practicality." Razumihin flew at him. "Practicality is a difficult thing to find; it does not drop down from heaven. And for the last two hundred years we have been divorced from all practical life. Ideas, if you like, are fermenting," he said to Pyotr Petrovitch, "and desire for good exists, though it's in a childish form, and honesty you may find, although there are crowds of brigands. Anyway, there's no practicality. Practicality goes well shod."

"I don't agree with you," Pyotr Petrovitch replied, with evident enjoyment. "Of course, people do get carried away and make mistakes, but one must have indulgence; those mistakes are merely evidence of enthusiasm for the cause and of abnormal external environment. If little has been done, the time has been but short; of means I will not speak. It's my personal view, if you care to know, that something has been accomplished already. New valuable ideas, new valuable works are circulating in the place of our old dreamy and romantic authors. Literature is taking a maturer form, many injurious prejudices have been rooted up and turned into ridicule.... In a word, we have cut ourselves off irrevocably from the past, and that, to my thinking, is a great thing..."

"He's learnt it by heart to show off!" Raskolnikov pronounced suddenly.

"What?" asked Pyotr Petrovitch, not catching his words; but he received no reply.

"That's all true," Zossimov hastened to interpose.

"Isn't it so?" Pyotr Petrovitch went on, glancing affably at Zossimov. "You must admit," he went on, addressing Razumihin with a shade of triumph and superciliousness—he almost added "young man"—"that there is an advance, or, as they say now, progress in the name of science and economic truth..."

"A commonplace."

"No, not a commonplace! Hitherto, for instance, if I were told, 'love thy neighbour,' what came of it?" Pyotr Petrovitch went on, perhaps with excessive haste. "It came to my tearing my coat in half to share with my neighbour and we both were left half naked. As a Russian proverb has it, 'Catch several hares and you won't catch one.' Science now tells us, love yourself before all men, for everything in the world rests on self-interest. You love yourself and manage your own affairs properly and your coat remains whole. Economic truth adds that the better private affairs are organised in society—the more whole coats, so to say—the firmer are its foundations and the better is the common welfare organised too. Therefore, in acquiring wealth solely and exclusively for myself, I am acquiring, so to speak, for all, and helping to bring to pass my neighbour's getting a little more than a torn coat; and that not from private, personal liberality, but as a consequence of the general advance. The idea is simple, but unhappily it has been a long time reaching us, being hindered by idealism and sentimentality. And yet it would seem to want very little wit to perceive it..."

"Excuse me, I've very little wit myself," Razumihin cut in sharply, "and so let us drop it. I began this discussion with an object, but I've grown so sick during the last three years of this chattering to amuse oneself, of this incessant flow of commonplaces, always the same, that, by Jove, I blush even when other people talk like that. You are in a hurry, no doubt, to exhibit your acquirements; and I don't blame you, that's quite pardonable. I only wanted to find out what sort of man you are, for so many unscrupulous people have got hold of the progressive cause of late and have so distorted in their own interests everything they touched, that the whole cause has been dragged in the mire. That's enough!"

"Excuse me, sir," said Luzhin, affronted, and speaking with excessive dignity. "Do you mean to suggest so unceremoniously that I too..."

"Oh, my dear sir... how could I?... Come, that's enough," Razumihin concluded, and he turned abruptly to Zossimov to continue their previous conversation.

Pyotr Petrovitch had the good sense to accept the disavowal. He made up his mind to take leave in another minute or two.

"I trust our acquaintance," he said, addressing Raskolnikov, "may, upon your recovery and in view of the circumstances of which you are aware, become closer... Above all, I hope for your return to health..."

Raskolnikov did not even turn his head. Pyotr Petrovitch began getting up from his chair.

"One of her customers must have killed her," Zossimov declared positively.

"Not a doubt of it," replied Razumihin. "Porfiry doesn't give his opinion, but is examining all who have left pledges with her there."

"Examining them?" Raskolnikov asked aloud.

"Yes. What then?"

"Nothing."

"How does he get hold of them?" asked Zossimov.

"Koch has given the names of some of them, other names are on the wrappers of the pledges and some have come forward of themselves."

"It must have been a cunning and practised ruffian! The boldness of it! The coolness!"

"That's just what it wasn't!" interposed Razumihin. "That's what throws you all off the scent. But I maintain that he is not cunning, not practised, and probably this was his first crime! The supposition that it was a calculated crime and a cunning criminal doesn't work. Suppose him to have been inexperienced, and it's clear that it was only a chance that saved him—and chance may do anything. Why, he did not foresee obstacles, perhaps! And how did he set to work? He took jewels worth ten or twenty roubles, stuffing his pockets with them, ransacked the old woman's trunks, her rags—and they found fifteen hundred roubles, besides notes, in a box in the top drawer of the chest! He did not know how to rob; he could only murder. It was his first crime, I assure you, his first crime; he lost his head. And he got off more by luck than good counsel!"

"You are talking of the murder of the old pawnbroker, I believe?" Pyotr Petrovitch put in, addressing Zossimov. He was standing, hat and gloves in hand, but before departing he felt disposed to throw off a few more intellectual phrases. He was evidently anxious to make a favourable impression and his vanity overcame his prudence.

"Yes. You've heard of it?"

"Oh, yes, being in the neighbourhood."

"Do you know the details?"

"I can't say that; but another circumstance interests me in the case—the whole question, so to say. Not to speak of the fact that crime has been greatly on the increase among the lower classes during the last five years, not to speak of the cases of robbery and arson everywhere, what strikes me as the strangest thing is that in the higher classes, too, crime is increasing proportionately. In one place one hears of a student's robbing the mail on the high road; in another place people of good social position forge false banknotes; in Moscow of late a whole gang has been captured who used to forge lottery tickets, and one of the ringleaders was a lecturer in universal history; then our secretary abroad was murdered from some obscure motive of gain.... And if this old woman, the pawnbroker, has been murdered by someone of a higher class in society—for peasants don't pawn gold trinkets—how are we to explain this demoralisation of the civilised part of our society?"

"There are many economic changes," put in Zossimov.

"How are we to explain it?" Razumihin caught him up. "It might be explained by our inveterate impracticality."

"How do you mean?"

"What answer had your lecturer in Moscow to make to the question why he was forging notes? 'Everybody is getting rich one way or another, so I want to make haste to get rich too.' I don't remember the exact words, but the upshot was that he wants money for nothing, without waiting or working! We've grown used to having everything ready-made, to walking on crutches, to having our food chewed for us. Then the great hour struck,[1] and every man showed himself in his true colours."

"But morality? And so to speak, principles..."

"But why do you worry about it?" Raskolnikov interposed suddenly. "It's in accordance with your theory!"

"In accordance with my theory?"

"Why, carry out logically the theory you were advocating just now, and it follows that people may be killed..."

"Upon my word!" cried Luzhin.

"No, that's not so," put in Zossimov.

Raskolnikov lay with a white face and twitching upper lip, breathing painfully.

"There's a measure in all things," Luzhin went on superciliously. "Economic ideas are not an incitement to murder, and one has but to suppose..."

"And is it true," Raskolnikov interposed once more suddenly, again in a voice quivering with fury and delight in insulting him, "is it true that you told your fiancée... within an hour of her acceptance, that what pleased you most... was that she was a beggar... because it was better to raise a wife from poverty, so that you may have complete control over her, and reproach her with your being her benefactor?"

"Upon my word," Luzhin cried wrathfully and irritably, crimson with confusion, "to distort my words in this way! Excuse me, allow me to assure you that the report which has reached you, or rather, let me say, has been conveyed to you, has no foundation in truth, and I… suspect who… in a word… this arrow… in a word, your mamma… She seemed to me in other things, with all her excellent qualities, of a somewhat high-flown and romantic way of thinking…. But I was a thousand miles from supposing that she would misunderstand and misrepresent things in so fanciful a way…. And indeed… indeed…"

"I tell you what," cried Raskolnikov, raising himself on his pillow and fixing his piercing, glittering eyes upon him, "I tell you what."

"What?" Luzhin stood still, waiting with a defiant and offended face. Silence lasted for some seconds.

"Why, if ever again… you dare to mention a single word… about my mother… I shall send you flying downstairs!"

"What's the matter with you?" cried Razumihin.

"So that's how it is?" Luzhin turned pale and bit his lip. "Let me tell you, sir," he began deliberately, doing his utmost to restrain himself but breathing hard, "at the first moment I saw you you were ill-disposed to me, but I remained here on purpose to find out more. I could forgive a great deal in a sick man and a connection, but you… never after this…"

"I am not ill," cried Raskolnikov.

"So much the worse…"

"Go to hell!"

But Luzhin was already leaving without finishing his speech, squeezing between the table and the chair; Razumihin got up this time to let him pass. Without glancing at anyone, and not even nodding to Zossimov, who had for some time been making signs to him to let the sick man alone, he went out, lifting his hat to the level of his shoulders to avoid crushing it as he stooped to go out of the door. And even the curve of his spine was expressive of the horrible insult he had received.

"How could you—how could you!" Razumihin said, shaking his head in perplexity.

"Let me alone—let me alone all of you!" Raskolnikov cried in a frenzy. "Will you ever leave off tormenting me? I am not afraid of you! I am not afraid of anyone, anyone now! Get away from me! I want to be alone, alone, alone!"

"Come along," said Zossimov, nodding to Razumihin.

"But we can't leave him like this!"

"Come along," Zossimov repeated insistently, and he went out. Razumihin thought a minute and ran to overtake him.

"It might be worse not to obey him," said Zossimov on the stairs. "He mustn't be irritated."

"What's the matter with him?"

"If only he could get some favourable shock, that's what would do it! At first he was better…. You know he has got something on his mind! Some fixed idea weighing on him…. I am very much afraid so; he must have!"

"Perhaps it's that gentleman, Pyotr Petrovitch. From his conversation I gather he is going to marry his sister, and that he had received a letter about it just before his illness…."

"Yes, confound the man! he may have upset the case altogether. But have you noticed, he takes no interest in anything, he does not respond to anything except one point on which he seems excited—that's the murder?"

"Yes, yes," Razumihin agreed, "I noticed that, too. He is interested, frightened. It gave him a shock on the day he was ill in the police office; he fainted."

"Tell me more about that this evening and I'll tell you something afterwards. He interests me very much! In half an hour I'll go and see him again…. There'll be no inflammation though."

"Thanks! And I'll wait with Pashenka meantime and will keep watch on him through Nastasya…."

Raskolnikov, left alone, looked with impatience and misery at Nastasya, but she still lingered.

"Won't you have some tea now?" she asked.

"Later! I am sleepy! Leave me."

He turned abruptly to the wall; Nastasya went out.

But as soon as she went out, he got up, latched the door, undid the parcel which Razumihin had brought in that evening and had tied up again and began dressing. Strange to say, he seemed immediately to have become perfectly calm; not a trace of his recent delirium nor of the panic fear that had haunted him of late. It was the first moment of a strange sudden calm. His movements were precise and definite; a firm purpose was evident in them. "Today, today," he muttered to himself. He understood that he was still weak, but his intense spiritual concentration gave him strength and self-confidence. He hoped, moreover, that he would not fall down in the street. When he had dressed in entirely new clothes, he looked at the money lying on the table, and after a moment's thought put it in his pocket. It was twenty-five roubles. He took also all the copper change from the ten roubles spent by Razumihin on the clothes. Then he softly unlatched the door, went out, slipped downstairs and glanced in at the open kitchen door. Nastasya was standing with her back to him, blowing up the landlady's samovar. She heard nothing. Who would have dreamed of his going out, indeed? A minute later he was in the street.

It was nearly eight o'clock, the sun was setting. It was as stifling as before, but he eagerly drank in the stinking, dusty town air. His head felt rather dizzy; a sort of savage energy gleamed suddenly in his feverish eyes and his wasted, pale and yellow face. He did not know and did not think where he was going, he had one thought only: "that all *this* must be ended today, once for all, immediately; that he would not return home without it, because he *would not go on living like that*." How, with what to make an end? He had not an idea about it, he did not even want to think of it. He drove away thought; thought tortured him. All he knew, all he felt was that everything must be changed "one way or another," he repeated with desperate and immovable self-confidence and determination.

From old habit he took his usual walk in the direction of the Hay Market. A dark-haired young man with a barrel organ was standing in the road in front of a little general shop and was grinding out a very sentimental song. He was accompanying a girl of fifteen, who stood on the pavement in front of him. She was dressed up in a crinoline, a mantle and a straw hat with a flame-coloured feather in it, all very old and shabby. In a strong and rather agreeable voice, cracked and coarsened by street singing, she sang in hope of getting a copper from the shop. Raskolnikov joined two or three listeners, took out a five kopeck piece and put it in the girl's hand. She broke off abruptly on a sentimental high note, shouted sharply to the organ grinder "Come on," and both moved on to the next shop.

"Do you like street music?" said Raskolnikov, addressing a middle-aged man standing idly by him. The man looked at him, startled and wondering.

"I love to hear singing to a street organ," said Raskolnikov, and his manner seemed strangely out of keeping with the subject—"I like it on cold, dark, damp autumn evenings—they must be damp—when all the passersby have pale green, sickly faces, or better still when wet snow is falling straight down, when there's no wind—you know what I mean?—and the street lamps shine through it…"

"I don't know…. Excuse me…" muttered the stranger, frightened by the question and Raskolnikov's strange manner, and he crossed over to the other side of the street.

Raskolnikov walked straight on and came out at the corner of the Hay Market, where the huckster and his wife had talked with Lizaveta; but they were not there now. Recognising the place, he stopped, looked round and addressed a young fellow in a red shirt who stood gaping before a corn chandler's shop.

"Isn't there a man who keeps a booth with his wife at this corner?"

"All sorts of people keep booths here," answered the young man, glancing superciliously at Raskolnikov.

"What's his name?"

"What he was christened."

"Aren't you a Zaraïsky man, too? Which province?"

The young man looked at Raskolnikov again.

"It's not a province, your excellency, but a district. Graciously forgive me, your excellency!"

"Is that a tavern at the top there?"

"Yes, it's an eating-house and there's a billiard-room and you'll find princesses there too.... La-la!"

Raskolnikov crossed the square. In that corner there was a dense crowd of peasants. He pushed his way into the thickest part of it, looking at the faces. He felt an unaccountable inclination to enter into conversation with people. But the peasants took no notice of him; they were all shouting in groups together. He stood and thought a little and took a turning to the right in the direction of V——.

He had often crossed that little street which turns at an angle, leading from the marketplace to Sadovy Street. Of late he had often felt drawn to wander about this district, when he felt depressed, that he might feel more so.

Now he walked along, thinking of nothing. At that point there is a great block of buildings, entirely let out in dram shops and eating-houses; women were continually running in and out, bareheaded and in their indoor clothes. Here and there they gathered in groups, on the pavement, especially about the entrances to various festive establishments in the lower storeys. From one of these a loud din, sounds of singing, the tinkling of a guitar and shouts of merriment, floated into the street. A crowd of women were thronging round the door; some were sitting on the steps, others on the pavement, others were standing talking. A drunken soldier, smoking a cigarette, was walking near them in the road, swearing; he seemed to be trying to find his way somewhere, but had forgotten where. One beggar was quarrelling with another, and a man dead drunk was lying right across the road. Raskolnikov joined the throng of women, who were talking in husky voices. They were bareheaded and wore cotton dresses and goatskin shoes. There were women of forty and some not more than seventeen; almost all had blackened eyes.

He felt strangely attracted by the singing and all the noise and uproar in the saloon below... someone could be heard within dancing frantically, marking time with his heels to the sounds of the guitar and of a thin falsetto voice singing a jaunty air. He listened intently, gloomily and dreamily, bending down at the entrance and peeping inquisitively in from the pavement.

"Oh, my handsome soldier

Don't beat me for nothing,"

trilled the thin voice of the singer. Raskolnikov felt a great desire to make out what he was singing, as though everything depended on that.

"Shall I go in?" he thought. "They are laughing. From drink. Shall I get drunk?"

"Won't you come in?" one of the women asked him. Her voice was still musical and less thick than the others, she was young and not repulsive—the only one of the group.

"Why, she's pretty," he said, drawing himself up and looking at her.

She smiled, much pleased at the compliment.

"You're very nice looking yourself," she said.

"Isn't he thin though!" observed another woman in a deep bass. "Have you just come out of a hospital?"

"They're all generals' daughters, it seems, but they have all snub noses," interposed a tipsy peasant with a sly smile on his face, wearing a loose coat. "See how jolly they are."

"Go along with you!"

"I'll go, sweetie!"

And he darted down into the saloon below. Raskolnikov moved on.

"I say, sir," the girl shouted after him.

"What is it?"

She hesitated.

"I'll always be pleased to spend an hour with you, kind gentleman, but now I feel shy. Give me six kopecks for a drink, there's a nice young man!"

Raskolnikov gave her what came first—fifteen kopecks.

"Ah, what a good-natured gentleman!"

"What's your name?"

"Ask for Duclida."

"Well, that's too much," one of the women observed, shaking her head at Duclida. "I don't know how you can ask like that. I believe I should drop with shame...."

Raskolnikov looked curiously at the speaker. She was a pockmarked wench of thirty, covered with bruises, with her upper lip swollen. She made her criticism quietly and earnestly. "Where is it," thought Raskolnikov. "Where is it I've read that someone condemned to death says or thinks, an hour before his death, that if he had to live on some high rock, on such a narrow ledge that he'd only room to stand, and the ocean, everlasting darkness, everlasting solitude, everlasting tempest around him, if he had to remain standing on a square yard of space all his life, a thousand years, eternity, it were better to live so than to die at once! Only to live, to live and live! Life, whatever it may be!... How true it is! Good God, how true! Man is a vile creature!... And vile is he who calls him vile for that," he added a moment later.

He went into another street. "Bah, the Palais de Cristal! Razumihin was just talking of the Palais de Cristal. But what on earth was it I wanted? Yes, the newspapers.... Zossimov said he'd read it in the papers. Have you the papers?" he asked, going into a very spacious and positively clean restaurant, consisting of several rooms, which were, however, rather empty. Two or three people were drinking tea, and in a room further away were sitting four men drinking champagne. Raskolnikov fancied that Zametov was one of them, but he could not be sure at that distance. "What if it is?" he thought.

"Will you have vodka?" asked the waiter.

"Give me some tea and bring me the papers, the old ones for the last five days, and I'll give you something."

"Yes, sir, here's today's. No vodka?"

The old newspapers and the tea were brought. Raskolnikov sat down and began to look through them.

"Oh, damn... these are the items of intelligence. An accident on a staircase, spontaneous combustion of a shopkeeper from alcohol, a fire in Peski... a fire in the Petersburg quarter... another fire in the Petersburg quarter... and another fire in the Petersburg quarter.... Ah, here it is!" He found at last what he was seeking and began to read it. The lines danced before his eyes, but he read it all and began eagerly seeking later additions in the following numbers. His hands shook with nervous impatience as he turned the sheets. Suddenly someone sat down beside him at his table. He looked up, it was the head clerk Zametov, looking just the same, with the rings on his fingers and the watch-chain, with the curly, black hair, parted and pomaded, with the smart waistcoat, rather shabby coat and doubtful linen. He was in a good humour, at least he was smiling very gaily and good-humouredly. His dark face was rather flushed from the champagne he had drunk.

"What, you here?" he began in surprise, speaking as though he'd known him all his life. "Why, Razumihin told me only yesterday you were unconscious. How strange! And do you know I've been to see you?"

Raskolnikov knew he would come up to him. He laid aside the papers and turned to Zametov. There was a smile on his lips, and a new shade of irritable impatience was apparent in that smile.

"I know you have," he answered. "I've heard it. You looked for my sock.... And you know Razumihin has lost his heart to you? He says you've been with him to Luise Ivanovna's—you know, the woman you tried to befriend, for whom you winked to the Explosive Lieutenant and he would not understand. Do you remember? How could he fail to understand—it was quite clear, wasn't it?"

"What a hot head he is!"

"The explosive one?"

"No, your friend Razumihin."

"You must have a jolly life, Mr. Zametov; entrance free to the most agreeable places. Who's been pouring champagne into you just now?"

"We've just been... having a drink together.... You talk about pouring it into me!"

"By way of a fee! You profit by everything!" Raskolnikov laughed, "it's all right, my dear boy," he added, slapping Zametov on the shoulder. "I am not speaking from temper, but in a friendly way, for sport, as that workman of yours said when he was scuffling with Dmitri, in the case of the old woman...."

"How do you know about it?"

"Perhaps I know more about it than you do."

"How strange you are.... I am sure you are still very unwell. You oughtn't to have come out."

"Oh, do I seem strange to you?"

"Yes. What are you doing, reading the papers?"

"Yes."

"There's a lot about the fires."

"No, I am not reading about the fires." Here he looked mysteriously at Zametov; his lips were twisted again in a mocking smile. "No, I am not reading about the fires," he went on, winking at Zametov. "But confess now, my dear fellow, you're awfully anxious to know what I am reading about?"

"I am not in the least. Mayn't I ask a question? Why do you keep on...?"

"Listen, you are a man of culture and education?"

"I was in the sixth class at the gymnasium," said Zametov with some dignity.

"Sixth class! Ah, my cock-sparrow! With your parting and your rings—you are a gentleman of fortune. Foo! what a charming boy!" Here Raskolnikov broke into a nervous laugh right in Zametov's face. The latter drew back, more amazed than offended.

"Foo! how strange you are!" Zametov repeated very seriously. "I can't help thinking you are still delirious."

"I am delirious? You are fibbing, my cock-sparrow! So I am strange? You find me curious, do you?"

"Yes, curious."

"Shall I tell you what I was reading about, what I was looking for? See what a lot of papers I've made them bring me. Suspicious, eh?"

"Well, what is it?"

"You prick up your ears?"

"How do you mean—'prick up my ears'?"

"I'll explain that afterwards, but now, my boy, I declare to you... no, better 'I confess'... No, that's not right either; 'I make a deposition and you take it.' I depose that I was reading, that I was looking and searching...." he screwed up his eyes and paused. "I was searching—and came here on purpose to do it—for news of the murder of the old pawnbroker woman," he articulated at last, almost in a whisper, bringing his face exceedingly close to the face of Zametov. Zametov looked at him steadily, without moving or drawing his face away. What struck Zametov afterwards as the strangest part of it all was that silence followed for exactly a minute, and that they gazed at one another all the while.

"What if you have been reading about it?" he cried at last, perplexed and impatient. "That's no business of mine! What of it?"

"The same old woman," Raskolnikov went on in the same whisper, not heeding Zametov's explanation, "about whom you were talking in the police-office, you remember, when I fainted. Well, do you understand now?"

"What do you mean? Understand... what?" Zametov brought out, almost alarmed.

Raskolnikov's set and earnest face was suddenly transformed, and he suddenly went off into the same nervous laugh as before, as though utterly unable to restrain himself. And in one flash he recalled with extraordinary vividness of sensation a moment in the recent past, that moment when he stood with the axe behind the door, while the latch trembled and the men outside swore and shook it, and he had a sudden desire to shout at them, to swear at them, to put out his tongue at them, to mock them, to laugh, and laugh, and laugh!

"You are either mad, or…" began Zametov, and he broke off, as though stunned by the idea that had suddenly flashed into his mind.

"Or? Or what? What? Come, tell me!"

"Nothing," said Zametov, getting angry, "it's all nonsense!"

Both were silent. After his sudden fit of laughter Raskolnikov became suddenly thoughtful and melancholy. He put his elbow on the table and leaned his head on his hand. He seemed to have completely forgotten Zametov. The silence lasted for some time.

"Why don't you drink your tea? It's getting cold," said Zametov.

"What! Tea? Oh, yes.…" Raskolnikov sipped the glass, put a morsel of bread in his mouth and, suddenly looking at Zametov, seemed to remember everything and pulled himself together. At the same moment his face resumed its original mocking expression. He went on drinking tea.

"There have been a great many of these crimes lately," said Zametov. "Only the other day I read in the *Moscow News* that a whole gang of false coiners had been caught in Moscow. It was a regular society. They used to forge tickets!"

"Oh, but it was a long time ago! I read about it a month ago," Raskolnikov answered calmly. "So you consider them criminals?" he added, smiling.

"Of course they are criminals."

"They? They are children, simpletons, not criminals! Why, half a hundred people meeting for such an object—what an idea! Three would be too many, and then they want to have more faith in one another than in themselves! One has only to blab in his cups and it all collapses. Simpletons! They engaged untrustworthy people to change the notes—what a thing to trust to a casual stranger! Well, let us suppose that these simpletons succeed and each makes a million, and what follows for the rest of their lives? Each is dependent on the others for the rest of his life! Better hang oneself at once! And they did not know how to change the notes either; the man who changed the notes took five thousand roubles, and his hands trembled. He counted the first four thousand, but did not count the fifth thousand—he was in such a hurry to get the money into his pocket and run away. Of course he roused suspicion. And the whole thing came to a crash through one fool! Is it possible?"

"That his hands trembled?" observed Zametov, "yes, that's quite possible. That, I feel quite sure, is possible. Sometimes one can't stand things."

"Can't stand that?"

"Why, could you stand it then? No, I couldn't. For the sake of a hundred roubles to face such a terrible experience? To go with false notes into a bank where it's their business to spot that sort of thing! No, I should not have the face to do it. Would you?"

Raskolnikov had an intense desire again "to put his tongue out." Shivers kept running down his spine.

"I should do it quite differently," Raskolnikov began. "This is how I would change the notes: I'd count the first thousand three or four times backwards and forwards, looking at every note and then I'd set to the second thousand; I'd count that halfway through and then hold some fifty-rouble note to the light, then turn it, then hold it to the light again—to see whether it was a good one. 'I am afraid,' I would say, 'a relation of mine lost twenty-five roubles the other day through a false note,' and then I'd tell them the whole story. And after I began counting the third, 'No, excuse me,' I would say, 'I fancy I made a mistake in the seventh hundred in that second thousand, I am not sure.' And so I would give up the third thousand and go back to the second and so on to the end. And when I had finished, I'd pick out one from the fifth and one from the second thousand and take them again to the light and ask again, 'Change them, please,' and put the clerk into such a stew that he would not know how to get rid of me. When I'd finished and had gone out, I'd come back, 'No, excuse me,' and ask for some explanation. That's how I'd do it."

"Foo! what terrible things you say!" said Zametov, laughing. "But all that is only talk. I dare say when it came to deeds you'd make a slip. I believe that even a practised, desperate man cannot always reckon on himself, much less you and I. To take an example near home—that old woman murdered in our district. The murderer seems to have been a desperate fellow, he risked everything in open daylight, was saved by a miracle—but his hands shook, too. He did not succeed in robbing the place, he couldn't stand it. That was clear from the…"

Raskolnikov seemed offended.

"Clear? Why don't you catch him then?" he cried, maliciously gibing at Zametov.

"Well, they will catch him."

"Who? You? Do you suppose you could catch him? You've a tough job! A great point for you is whether a man is spending money or not. If he had no money and suddenly begins spending, he must be the man. So that any child can mislead you."

"The fact is they always do that, though," answered Zametov. "A man will commit a clever murder at the risk of his life and then at once he goes drinking in a tavern. They are caught spending money, they are not all as cunning as you are. You wouldn't go to a tavern, of course?"

Raskolnikov frowned and looked steadily at Zametov.

"You seem to enjoy the subject and would like to know how I should behave in that case, too?" he asked with displeasure.

"I should like to," Zametov answered firmly and seriously. Somewhat too much earnestness began to appear in his words and looks.

"Very much?"

"Very much!"

"All right then. This is how I should behave," Raskolnikov began, again bringing his face close to Zametov's, again staring at him and speaking in a whisper, so that the latter positively shuddered. "This is what I should have done. I should have taken the money and jewels, I should have walked out of there and have gone straight to some deserted place with fences round it and scarcely anyone to be seen, some kitchen garden or place of that sort. I should have looked out beforehand some stone weighing a hundredweight or more which had been lying in the corner from the time the house was built. I would lift that stone—there would sure to be a hollow under it, and I would put the jewels and money in that hole. Then I'd roll the stone back so that it would look as before, would press it down with my foot and walk away. And for a year or two, three maybe, I would not touch it. And, well, they could search! There'd be no trace."

"You are a madman," said Zametov, and for some reason he too spoke in a whisper, and moved away from Raskolnikov, whose eyes were glittering. He had turned fearfully pale and his upper lip was twitching and quivering. He bent down as close as possible to Zametov, and his lips began to move without uttering a word. This lasted for half a minute; he knew what he was doing, but could not restrain himself. The terrible word trembled on his lips, like the latch on that door; in another moment it will break out, in another moment he will let it go, he will speak out.

"And what if it was I who murdered the old woman and Lizaveta?" he said suddenly and—realised what he had done.

Zametov looked wildly at him and turned white as the tablecloth. His face wore a contorted smile.

"But is it possible?" he brought out faintly. Raskolnikov looked wrathfully at him.

"Own up that you believed it, yes, you did?"

"Not a bit of it, I believe it less than ever now," Zametov cried hastily.

"I've caught my cock-sparrow! So you did believe it before, if now you believe less than ever?"

"Not at all," cried Zametov, obviously embarrassed. "Have you been frightening me so as to lead up to this?"

"You don't believe it then? What were you talking about behind my back when I went out of the police-office? And why did the explosive lieutenant question me after I fainted? Hey, there," he shouted to the waiter, getting up and taking his cap, "how much?"

"Thirty kopecks," the latter replied, running up.

"And there is twenty kopecks for vodka. See what a lot of money!" he held out his shaking hand to Zametov with notes in it. "Red notes and blue, twenty-five roubles. Where did I get them? And where did my new clothes come from? You know I had not a kopeck. You've cross-examined my landlady, I'll be bound.... Well, that's enough! *Assez causé!* Till we meet again!"

He went out, trembling all over from a sort of wild hysterical sensation, in which there was an element of insufferable rapture. Yet he was gloomy and terribly tired. His face was twisted as after a fit. His fatigue increased rapidly. Any shock, any irritating sensation stimulated and revived his energies at once, but his strength failed as quickly when the stimulus was removed.

Zametov, left alone, sat for a long time in the same place, plunged in thought. Raskolnikov had unwittingly worked a revolution in his brain on a certain point and had made up his mind for him conclusively.

"Ilya Petrovitch is a blockhead," he decided.

Raskolnikov had hardly opened the door of the restaurant when he stumbled against Razumihin on the steps. They did not see each other till they almost knocked against each other. For a moment they stood looking each other up and down. Razumihin was greatly astounded, then anger, real anger gleamed fiercely in his eyes.

"So here you are!" he shouted at the top of his voice—"you ran away from your bed! And here I've been looking for you under the sofa! We went up to the garret. I almost beat Nastasya on your account. And here he is after all. Rodya! What is the meaning of it? Tell me the whole truth! Confess! Do you hear?"

"It means that I'm sick to death of you all and I want to be alone," Raskolnikov answered calmly.

"Alone? When you are not able to walk, when your face is as white as a sheet and you are gasping for breath! Idiot!... What have you been doing in the Palais de Cristal? Own up at once!"

"Let me go!" said Raskolnikov and tried to pass him. This was too much for Razumihin; he gripped him firmly by the shoulder.

"Let you go? You dare tell me to let you go? Do you know what I'll do with you directly? I'll pick you up, tie you up in a bundle, carry you home under my arm and lock you up!"

"Listen, Razumihin," Raskolnikov began quietly, apparently calm—"can't you see that I don't want your benevolence? A strange desire you have to shower benefits on a man who... curses them, who feels them a burden in fact! Why did you seek me out at the beginning of my illness? Maybe I was very glad to die. Didn't I tell you plainly enough today that you were torturing me, that I was... sick of you! You seem to want to torture people! I assure you that all that is seriously hindering my recovery, because it's continually irritating me. You saw Zossimov went away just now to avoid irritating me. You leave me alone too, for goodness' sake! What right have you, indeed, to keep me by force? Don't you see that I am in possession of all my faculties now? How, how can I persuade you not to persecute me with your kindness? I may be ungrateful, I may be mean, only let me be, for God's sake, let me be! Let me be, let me be!"

He began calmly, gloating beforehand over the venomous phrases he was about to utter, but finished, panting for breath, in a frenzy, as he had been with Luzhin.

Razumihin stood a moment, thought and let his hand drop.

"Well, go to hell then," he said gently and thoughtfully. "Stay," he roared, as Raskolnikov was about to move. "Listen to me. Let me tell you, that you are all a set of babbling, posing idiots! If you've any little trouble you brood over it like a hen over an egg. And you are plagiarists even in that! There isn't a sign of independent life in you! You are made of spermaceti ointment and you've lymph in your veins instead of blood. I don't believe in anyone of you! In any circumstances the first thing for all of you is to be unlike a human being! Stop!" he cried with redoubled fury, noticing that Raskolnikov was again making a movement—"hear me out! You know I'm having a housewarming this evening, I dare say they've arrived by now, but I left my uncle there—I just ran in—to receive the guests. And if you weren't a fool, a common fool, a perfect fool, if you were an original instead of a translation... you see, Rodya, I recognise you're a clever fellow, but you're a fool!—and if you weren't a fool you'd come round to me this evening instead of wearing out your boots in the street! Since you have gone out, there's no help for it! I'd give you a snug easy chair, my landlady has one... a cup of tea, company.... Or you could lie on the sofa—anyway you would be with us.... Zossimov will be there too. Will you come?"

"No."

"R-rubbish!" Razumihin shouted, out of patience. "How do you know? You can't answer for yourself! You don't know anything about it.... Thousands of times I've fought tooth and nail with people and run back to them afterwards.... One feels ashamed and goes back to a man! So remember, Potchinkov's house on the third storey...."

"Why, Mr. Razumihin, I do believe you'd let anybody beat you from sheer benevolence."

"Beat? Whom? Me? I'd twist his nose off at the mere idea! Potchinkov's house, 47, Babushkin's flat...."

"I shall not come, Razumihin." Raskolnikov turned and walked away.

"I bet you will," Razumihin shouted after him. "I refuse to know you if you don't! Stay, hey, is Zametov in there?"

"Yes."

"Did you see him?"

"Yes."

"Talked to him?"

"Yes."

"What about? Confound you, don't tell me then. Potchinkov's house, 47, Babushkin's flat, remember!"

Raskolnikov walked on and turned the corner into Sadovy Street. Razumihin looked after him thoughtfully. Then with a wave of his hand he went into the house but stopped short of the stairs.

"Confound it," he went on almost aloud. "He talked sensibly but yet... I am a fool! As if madmen didn't talk sensibly! And this was just what Zossimov seemed afraid of." He struck his finger on his forehead. "What if... how could I let him go off alone? He may drown himself.... Ach, what a blunder! I can't." And he ran back to overtake Raskolnikov, but there was no trace of him. With a curse he returned with rapid steps to the Palais de Cristal to question Zametov.

Raskolnikov walked straight to X—— Bridge, stood in the middle, and leaning both elbows on the rail stared into the distance. On parting with Razumihin, he felt so much weaker that he could scarcely reach this place. He longed to sit or lie down somewhere in the street. Bending over the water, he gazed mechanically at the last pink flush of the sunset, at the row of houses growing dark in the gathering twilight, at one distant attic window on the left bank, flashing as though on fire in the last rays of the setting sun, at the darkening water of the canal, and the water seemed to catch his attention. At last red circles flashed before his eyes, the houses seemed moving, the passersby, the canal banks, the carriages, all danced before his eyes. Suddenly he started, saved again perhaps from swooning by an uncanny and hideous sight. He became aware of someone standing on the right side of him; he looked and saw a tall woman with a kerchief on her head, with a long, yellow, wasted face and red sunken eyes. She was looking straight at him, but obviously she saw nothing and recognised no one. Suddenly she leaned her right hand on the parapet, lifted her right leg over the railing, then her left and threw herself into the canal. The filthy water parted and swallowed up its victim for a moment, but an instant later the drowning woman floated to the surface, moving slowly with the current, her head and legs in the water, her skirt inflated like a balloon over her back.

"A woman drowning! A woman drowning!" shouted dozens of voices; people ran up, both banks were thronged with spectators, on the bridge people crowded about Raskolnikov, pressing up behind him.

"Mercy on it! it's our Afrosinya!" a woman cried tearfully close by. "Mercy! save her! kind people, pull her out!"

"A boat, a boat!" was shouted in the crowd. But there was no need of a boat; a policeman ran down the steps to the canal, threw off his great coat and his boots and rushed into the water. It was easy to reach her: she floated within a couple of yards from the steps, he caught hold of her clothes with his right hand and with his left seized a pole which a comrade held out to him; the drowning woman was pulled out at once. They laid her on the granite pavement of the embankment. She soon recovered consciousness, raised her head, sat up and began sneezing and coughing, stupidly wiping her wet dress with her hands. She said nothing.

"She's drunk herself out of her senses," the same woman's voice wailed at her side. "Out of her senses. The other day she tried to hang herself, we cut her down. I ran out to the shop just now, left my little girl to look after her—and here she's in trouble again! A neighbour, gentleman, a neighbour, we live close by, the second house from the end, see yonder...."

The crowd broke up. The police still remained round the woman, someone mentioned the police station.... Raskolnikov looked on with a strange sensation of indifference and apathy. He felt disgusted. "No, that's loathsome... water... it's not good enough," he muttered to himself. "Nothing will come of it," he added, "no use to wait. What about the police office...? And why isn't Zametov at the police office? The police office is open till ten o'clock...." He turned his back to the railing and looked about him.

"Very well then!" he said resolutely; he moved from the bridge and walked in the direction of the police office. His heart felt hollow and empty. He did not want to think. Even his depression had passed, there was not a trace now of the energy with which he had set out "to make an end of it all." Complete apathy had succeeded to it.

"Well, it's a way out of it," he thought, walking slowly and listlessly along the canal bank. "Anyway I'll make an end, for I want to.... But is it a way out? What does it matter! There'll be the square yard of space—ha! But what an end! Is it really the end? Shall I tell them or not? Ah... damn! How tired I am! If I could find somewhere to sit or lie down soon! What I am most ashamed of is its being so stupid. But I don't care about that either! What idiotic ideas come into one's head."

To reach the police office he had to go straight forward and take the second turning to the left. It was only a few paces away. But at the first turning he stopped and, after a minute's thought, turned into a side street and went two streets out of his way, possibly without any object, or possibly to delay a minute and gain time. He walked, looking at the ground; suddenly someone seemed to whisper in his ear; he lifted his head and saw that he was standing at the very gate of *the* house. He had not passed it, he had not been near it since *that* evening. An overwhelming, unaccountable prompting drew him on. He went into the house, passed through the gateway, then into the first entrance on the right, and began mounting the familiar staircase to the fourth storey. The narrow, steep staircase was very dark. He stopped at each landing and looked round him with curiosity; on the first landing the framework of the window had been taken out. "That wasn't so then," he thought. Here was the flat on the second storey where Nikolay and Dmitri had been working. "It's shut up and the door newly painted. So it's to let." Then the third storey and the fourth. "Here!" He was perplexed to find the door of the flat wide open. There were men there, he could hear voices; he had not expected that. After brief hesitation he mounted the last stairs and went into the flat. It, too, was being done up; there were workmen in it. This seemed to amaze him; he somehow fancied that he would find everything as he left it, even perhaps the corpses in the same places on the floor. And now, bare walls, no furniture; it seemed strange. He walked to the window and sat down on the windowsill. There were two workmen, both young fellows, but one much younger than the other. They were papering the walls with a new white paper covered with lilac flowers, instead of the old, dirty, yellow one. Raskolnikov for some reason felt horribly annoyed by this. He looked at the new paper with dislike, as though he felt sorry to have it all so changed. The workmen had obviously stayed beyond their time and now they were hurriedly rolling up their paper and getting ready to go home. They took no notice of Raskolnikov's coming in; they were talking. Raskolnikov folded his arms and listened.

"She comes to me in the morning," said the elder to the younger, "very early, all dressed up. 'Why are you preening and prinking?' says I. 'I am ready to do anything to please you, Tit Vassilitch!' That's a way of going on! And she dressed up like a regular fashion book!"

"And what is a fashion book?" the younger one asked. He obviously regarded the other as an authority.

"A fashion book is a lot of pictures, coloured, and they come to the tailors here every Saturday, by post from abroad, to show folks how to dress, the male sex as well as the female. They're pictures. The gentlemen are generally wearing fur coats and for the ladies' fluffles, they're beyond anything you can fancy."

"There's nothing you can't find in Petersburg," the younger cried enthusiastically, "except father and mother, there's everything!"

"Except them, there's everything to be found, my boy," the elder declared sententiously.

Raskolnikov got up and walked into the other room where the strong box, the bed, and the chest of drawers had been; the room seemed to him very tiny without furniture in it. The paper was the same; the paper in the corner showed where the case of icons had stood. He looked at it and went to the window. The elder workman looked at him askance.

"What do you want?" he asked suddenly.

Instead of answering Raskolnikov went into the passage and pulled the bell. The same bell, the same cracked note. He rang it a second and a third time; he listened and remembered. The hideous and agonisingly fearful sensation he had felt then began to come back more and more vividly. He shuddered at every ring and it gave him more and more satisfaction.

"Well, what do you want? Who are you?" the workman shouted, going out to him. Raskolnikov went inside again.

"I want to take a flat," he said. "I am looking round."

"It's not the time to look at rooms at night! and you ought to come up with the porter."

"The floors have been washed, will they be painted?" Raskolnikov went on. "Is there no blood?"

"What blood?"

"Why, the old woman and her sister were murdered here. There was a perfect pool there."

"But who are you?" the workman cried, uneasy.

"Who am I?"

"Yes."

"You want to know? Come to the police station, I'll tell you."

The workmen looked at him in amazement.

"It's time for us to go, we are late. Come along, Alyoshka. We must lock up," said the elder workman.

"Very well, come along," said Raskolnikov indifferently, and going out first, he went slowly downstairs. "Hey, porter," he cried in the gateway.

At the entrance several people were standing, staring at the passersby; the two porters, a peasant woman, a man in a long coat and a few others. Raskolnikov went straight up to them.

"What do you want?" asked one of the porters.

"Have you been to the police office?"

"I've just been there. What do you want?"

"Is it open?"

"Of course."

"Is the assistant there?"

"He was there for a time. What do you want?"

Raskolnikov made no reply, but stood beside them lost in thought.

"He's been to look at the flat," said the elder workman, coming forward.

"Which flat?"

"Where we are at work. 'Why have you washed away the blood?' says he. 'There has been a murder here,' says he, 'and I've come to take it.' And he began ringing at the bell, all but broke it. 'Come to the police station,' says he. 'I'll tell you everything there.' He wouldn't leave us."

The porter looked at Raskolnikov, frowning and perplexed.

"Who are you?" he shouted as impressively as he could.

"I am Rodion Romanovitch Raskolnikov, formerly a student, I live in Shil's house, not far from here, flat Number 14, ask the porter, he knows me." Raskolnikov said all this in a lazy, dreamy voice, not turning round, but looking intently into the darkening street.

"Why have you been to the flat?"

"To look at it."

"What is there to look at?"

"Take him straight to the police station," the man in the long coat jerked in abruptly.

Raskolnikov looked intently at him over his shoulder and said in the same slow, lazy tones:

"Come along."

"Yes, take him," the man went on more confidently. "Why was he going into *that*, what's in his mind, eh?"

"He's not drunk, but God knows what's the matter with him," muttered the workman.

"But what do you want?" the porter shouted again, beginning to get angry in earnest—"Why are you hanging about?"

"You funk the police station then?" said Raskolnikov jeeringly.

"How funk it? Why are you hanging about?"

"He's a rogue!" shouted the peasant woman.

"Why waste time talking to him?" cried the other porter, a huge peasant in a full open coat and with keys on his belt. "Get along! He is a rogue and no mistake. Get along!"

And seizing Raskolnikov by the shoulder he flung him into the street. He lurched forward, but recovered his footing, looked at the spectators in silence and walked away.

"Strange man!" observed the workman.

"There are strange folks about nowadays," said the woman.

"You should have taken him to the police station all the same," said the man in the long coat.

"Better have nothing to do with him," decided the big porter. "A regular rogue! Just what he wants, you may be sure, but once take him up, you won't get rid of him.... We know the sort!"

"Shall I go there or not?" thought Raskolnikov, standing in the middle of the thoroughfare at the crossroads, and he looked about him, as though expecting from someone a decisive word. But no sound came, all was dead and silent like the stones on which he walked, dead to him, to him alone.... All at once at the end of the street, two hundred yards away, in the gathering dusk he saw a crowd and heard talk and shouts. In the middle of the crowd stood a carriage.... A light gleamed in the middle of the street. "What is it?" Raskolnikov turned to the right and went up to the crowd. He seemed to clutch at everything and smiled coldly when he recognised it, for he had fully made up his mind to go to the police station and knew that it would all soon be over.

VII

An elegant carriage stood in the middle of the road with a pair of spirited grey horses; there was no one in it, and the coachman had got off his box and stood by; the horses were being held by the bridle.... A mass of people had gathered round, the police standing in front. One of them held a lighted lantern which he was turning on something lying close to the wheels. Everyone was talking, shouting, exclaiming; the coachman seemed at a loss and kept repeating:

"What a misfortune! Good Lord, what a misfortune!"

Raskolnikov pushed his way in as far as he could, and succeeded at last in seeing the object of the commotion and interest. On the ground a man who had been run over lay apparently unconscious, and covered with blood; he was very badly dressed, but not like a workman. Blood was flowing from his head and face; his face was crushed, mutilated and disfigured. He was evidently badly injured.

"Merciful heaven!" wailed the coachman, "what more could I do? If I'd been driving fast or had not shouted to him, but I was going quietly, not in a hurry. Everyone could see I was going along just like everybody else. A drunken man can't walk straight, we all know.... I saw him crossing the street, staggering and almost falling. I shouted again and a second and a third time, then I held the horses in, but he fell straight under their feet! Either he did it on purpose or he was very tipsy.... The horses are young and ready to take fright... they started, he screamed... that made them worse. That's how it happened!"

"That's just how it was," a voice in the crowd confirmed.

"He shouted, that's true, he shouted three times," another voice declared.

"Three times it was, we all heard it," shouted a third.

But the coachman was not very much distressed and frightened. It was evident that the carriage belonged to a rich and important person who was awaiting it somewhere; the police, of course, were in no little anxiety to avoid upsetting his arrangements. All they had to do was to take the injured man to the police station and the hospital. No one knew his name.

Meanwhile Raskolnikov had squeezed in and stooped closer over him. The lantern suddenly lighted up the unfortunate man's face. He recognised him.

"I know him! I know him!" he shouted, pushing to the front. "It's a government clerk retired from the service, Marmeladov. He lives close by in Kozel's house.... Make haste for a doctor! I will pay, see?" He pulled money out of his pocket and showed it to the policeman. He was in violent agitation.

The police were glad that they had found out who the man was. Raskolnikov gave his own name and address, and, as earnestly as if it had been his father, he besought the police to carry the unconscious Marmeladov to his lodging at once.

"Just here, three houses away," he said eagerly, "the house belongs to Kozel, a rich German. He was going home, no doubt drunk. I know him, he is a drunkard. He has a family there, a wife, children, he has one daughter.... It will take time to take him to the hospital, and there is sure to be a doctor in the house. I'll pay, I'll pay! At least he will be looked after at home... they will help him at once. But he'll die before you get him to the hospital." He managed to slip something unseen into the policeman's hand. But the thing was straightforward and legitimate, and in any case help was closer here. They raised the injured man; people volunteered to help.

Kozel's house was thirty yards away. Raskolnikov walked behind, carefully holding Marmeladov's head and showing the way.

"This way, this way! We must take him upstairs head foremost. Turn round! I'll pay, I'll make it worth your while," he muttered.

Katerina Ivanovna had just begun, as she always did at every free moment, walking to and fro in her little room from window to stove and back again, with her arms folded across her chest, talking to herself and coughing. Of late she had begun to talk more than ever to her eldest girl, Polenka, a child of ten, who, though there was much she did not understand, understood very well that her mother needed her, and so always watched her with her big clever eyes and strove her utmost to appear to understand. This time Polenka was undressing her little brother, who had been unwell all day and was going to bed. The boy was waiting for her to take off his shirt, which had to be washed at night. He was sitting straight and motionless on a chair, with a silent, serious face, with his legs stretched out straight before him—heels together and toes turned out.

He was listening to what his mother was saying to his sister, sitting perfectly still with pouting lips and wide-open eyes, just as all good little boys have to sit when they are undressed to go to bed. A little girl, still younger, dressed literally in rags, stood at the screen, waiting for her turn. The door on to the stairs was open to relieve them a little from the clouds of tobacco smoke which floated in from the other rooms and brought on long terrible fits of coughing in the poor, consumptive woman. Katerina Ivanovna seemed to have grown even thinner during that week and the hectic flush on her face was brighter than ever.

"You wouldn't believe, you can't imagine, Polenka," she said, walking about the room, "what a happy luxurious life we had in my papa's house and how this drunkard has brought me, and will bring you all, to ruin! Papa was a civil colonel and only a step from being a governor; so that everyone who came to see him said, 'We look upon you, Ivan Mihailovitch, as our governor!' When I... when..." she coughed violently, "oh, cursed life," she cried, clearing her throat and pressing her hands to her breast, "when I... when at the last ball... at the marshal's... Princess Bezzemelny saw me—who gave me the blessing when your father and I were married, Polenka— she asked at once 'Isn't that the pretty girl who danced the shawl dance at the breaking-up?' (You must mend that tear, you must take your needle and darn it as I showed you, or tomorrow—cough, cough, cough—he will make the hole bigger," she articulated with effort.) "Prince Schegolskoy, a *kammerjunker*, had just come from Petersburg then... he danced the mazurka with me and wanted to make me an offer next day; but I thanked him in flattering expressions and told him that my heart had long been another's. That other was your father, Polya; papa was fearfully angry.... Is the water ready? Give me the shirt, and the stockings! Lida," said she to the youngest one, "you must manage without your chemise tonight... and lay your stockings out with it... I'll wash them together.... How is it that drunken vagabond doesn't come in? He has worn his shirt till it looks like a dish-clout, he has torn it to rags! I'd do it all together, so as not to have to work two nights running! Oh, dear! (Cough, cough, cough, cough!) Again! What's this?" she cried, noticing a crowd in the passage and the men, who were pushing into her room, carrying a burden. "What is it? What are they bringing? Mercy on us!"

"Where are we to put him?" asked the policeman, looking round when Marmeladov, unconscious and covered with blood, had been carried in.

"On the sofa! Put him straight on the sofa, with his head this way," Raskolnikov showed him.

"Run over in the road! Drunk!" someone shouted in the passage.

Katerina Ivanovna stood, turning white and gasping for breath. The children were terrified. Little Lida screamed, rushed to Polenka and clutched at her, trembling all over.

Having laid Marmeladov down, Raskolnikov flew to Katerina Ivanovna.

"For God's sake be calm, don't be frightened!" he said, speaking quickly, "he was crossing the road and was run over by a carriage, don't be frightened, he will come to, I told them bring him here... I've been here already, you remember? He will come to; I'll pay!"

"He's done it this time!" Katerina Ivanovna cried despairingly and she rushed to her husband.

Raskolnikov noticed at once that she was not one of those women who swoon easily. She instantly placed under the luckless man's head a pillow, which no one had thought of and began undressing and examining him. She kept her head, forgetting herself, biting her trembling lips and stifling the screams which were ready to break from her.

Raskolnikov meanwhile induced someone to run for a doctor. There was a doctor, it appeared, next door but one.

"I've sent for a doctor," he kept assuring Katerina Ivanovna, "don't be uneasy, I'll pay. Haven't you water?... and give me a napkin or a towel, anything, as quick as you can.... He is injured, but not killed, believe me.... We shall see what the doctor says!"

Katerina Ivanovna ran to the window; there, on a broken chair in the corner, a large earthenware basin full of water had been stood, in readiness for washing her children's and husband's linen that night. This washing was done by Katerina Ivanovna at night at least twice a week, if not oftener. For the family had come to such a pass that they were practically without change of linen, and Katerina Ivanovna could not endure uncleanliness and, rather than see dirt in the house, she preferred to wear herself out at night, working beyond her strength when the rest were asleep, so as to get the wet linen hung on a line and dry by the morning. She took up the basin of water at Raskolnikov's request, but almost fell down with her burden. But the latter had already succeeded in finding a towel, wetted it and began washing the blood off Marmeladov's face.

Katerina Ivanovna stood by, breathing painfully and pressing her hands to her breast. She was in need of attention herself. Raskolnikov began to realise that he might have made a mistake in having the injured man brought here. The policeman, too, stood in hesitation.

"Polenka," cried Katerina Ivanovna, "run to Sonia, make haste. If you don't find her at home, leave word that her father has been run over and that she is to come here at once... when she comes in. Run, Polenka! there, put on the shawl."

"Run your fastest!" cried the little boy on the chair suddenly, after which he relapsed into the same dumb rigidity, with round eyes, his heels thrust forward and his toes spread out.

Meanwhile the room had become so full of people that you couldn't have dropped a pin. The policemen left, all except one, who remained for a time, trying to drive out the people who came in from the stairs. Almost all Madame Lippevechsel's lodgers had streamed in from the inner rooms of the flat; at first they were squeezed together in the doorway, but afterwards they overflowed into the room. Katerina Ivanovna flew into a fury.

"You might let him die in peace, at least," she shouted at the crowd, "is it a spectacle for you to gape at? With cigarettes! (Cough, cough, cough!) You might as well keep your hats on.... And there is one in his hat!... Get away! You should respect the dead, at least!"

Her cough choked her—but her reproaches were not without result. They evidently stood in some awe of Katerina Ivanovna. The lodgers, one after another, squeezed back into the doorway with that strange inner feeling of satisfaction which may be observed in the presence of a sudden accident, even in those nearest and dearest to the victim, from which no living man is exempt, even in spite of the sincerest sympathy and compassion.

Voices outside were heard, however, speaking of the hospital and saying that they'd no business to make a disturbance here.

"No business to die!" cried Katerina Ivanovna, and she was rushing to the door to vent her wrath upon them, but in the doorway came face to face with Madame Lippevechsel who had only just heard of the accident and ran in to restore order. She was a particularly quarrelsome and irresponsible German.

"Ah, my God!" she cried, clasping her hands, "your husband drunken horses have trampled! To the hospital with him! I am the landlady!"

"Amalia Ludwigovna, I beg you to recollect what you are saying," Katerina Ivanovna began haughtily (she always took a haughty tone with the landlady that she might "remember her place" and even now could not deny herself this satisfaction). "Amalia Ludwigovna..."

"I have you once before told that you to call me Amalia Ludwigovna may not dare; I am Amalia Ivanovna."

"You are not Amalia Ivanovna, but Amalia Ludwigovna, and as I am not one of your despicable flatterers like Mr. Lebeziatnikov, who's laughing behind the door at this moment" (a laugh and a cry of "they are at it again" was in fact audible at the door) "so I shall always call you Amalia Ludwigovna, though I fail to understand why you dislike that name. You can see for yourself what has happened to Semyon Zaharovitch; he is dying. I beg you to close that door at once and to admit no one. Let him at least die in peace! Or I warn you the Governor-General, himself, shall be informed of your conduct tomorrow. The prince knew me as a girl; he remembers Semyon Zaharovitch well and has often been a benefactor to him. Everyone knows that Semyon Zaharovitch had many friends and protectors, whom he abandoned himself from an honourable pride, knowing his unhappy weakness, but now (she pointed to Raskolnikov) a generous young man has come to our assistance, who has wealth and connections and whom Semyon Zaharovitch has known from a child. You may rest assured, Amalia Ludwigovna…"

All this was uttered with extreme rapidity, getting quicker and quicker, but a cough suddenly cut short Katerina Ivanovna's eloquence. At that instant the dying man recovered consciousness and uttered a groan; she ran to him. The injured man opened his eyes and without recognition or understanding gazed at Raskolnikov who was bending over him. He drew deep, slow, painful breaths; blood oozed at the corners of his mouth and drops of perspiration came out on his forehead. Not recognising Raskolnikov, he began looking round uneasily. Katerina Ivanovna looked at him with a sad but stern face, and tears trickled from her eyes.

"My God! His whole chest is crushed! How he is bleeding," she said in despair. "We must take off his clothes. Turn a little, Semyon Zaharovitch, if you can," she cried to him.

Marmeladov recognised her.

"A priest," he articulated huskily.

Katerina Ivanovna walked to the window, laid her head against the window frame and exclaimed in despair:

"Oh, cursed life!"

"A priest," the dying man said again after a moment's silence.

"They've gone for him," Katerina Ivanovna shouted to him, he obeyed her shout and was silent. With sad and timid eyes he looked for her; she returned and stood by his pillow. He seemed a little easier but not for long.

Soon his eyes rested on little Lida, his favourite, who was shaking in the corner, as though she were in a fit, and staring at him with her wondering childish eyes.

"A-ah," he signed towards her uneasily. He wanted to say something.

"What now?" cried Katerina Ivanovna.

"Barefoot, barefoot!" he muttered, indicating with frenzied eyes the child's bare feet.

"Be silent," Katerina Ivanovna cried irritably, "you know why she is barefooted."

"Thank God, the doctor," exclaimed Raskolnikov, relieved.

The doctor came in, a precise little old man, a German, looking about him mistrustfully; he went up to the sick man, took his pulse, carefully felt his head and with the help of Katerina Ivanovna he unbuttoned the bloodstained shirt, and bared the injured man's chest. It was gashed, crushed and fractured, several ribs on the right side were broken. On the left side, just over the heart, was a large, sinister-looking yellowish-black bruise—a cruel kick from the horse's hoof. The doctor frowned. The policeman told him that he was caught in the wheel and turned round with it for thirty yards on the road.

"It's wonderful that he has recovered consciousness," the doctor whispered softly to Raskolnikov.

"What do you think of him?" he asked.

"He will die immediately."

"Is there really no hope?"

"Not the faintest! He is at the last gasp…. His head is badly injured, too… Hm… I could bleed him if you like, but… it would be useless. He is bound to die within the next five or ten minutes."

"Better bleed him then."

"If you like…. But I warn you it will be perfectly useless."

At that moment other steps were heard; the crowd in the passage parted, and the priest, a little, grey old man, appeared in the doorway bearing the sacrament. A policeman had gone for him at the time of the accident. The doctor changed places with him, exchanging glances with him. Raskolnikov begged the doctor to remain a little while. He shrugged his shoulders and remained.

All stepped back. The confession was soon over. The dying man probably understood little; he could only utter indistinct broken sounds. Katerina Ivanovna took little Lida, lifted the boy from the chair, knelt down in the corner by the stove and made the children kneel in front of her. The little girl was still trembling; but the boy, kneeling on his little bare knees, lifted his hand rhythmically, crossing himself with precision and bowed down, touching the floor with his forehead, which seemed to afford him especial satisfaction. Katerina Ivanovna bit her lips and held back her tears; she prayed, too, now and then pulling straight the boy's shirt, and managed to cover the girl's bare shoulders with a kerchief, which she took from the chest without rising from her knees or ceasing to pray. Meanwhile the door from the inner rooms was opened inquisitively again. In the passage the crowd of spectators from all the flats on the staircase grew denser and denser, but they did not venture beyond the threshold. A single candle-end lighted up the scene.

At that moment Polenka forced her way through the crowd at the door. She came in panting from running so fast, took off her kerchief, looked for her mother, went up to her and said, "She's coming, I met her in the street." Her mother made her kneel beside her.

Timidly and noiselessly a young girl made her way through the crowd, and strange was her appearance in that room, in the midst of want, rags, death and despair. She, too, was in rags, her attire was all of the cheapest, but decked out in gutter finery of a special stamp, unmistakably betraying its shameful purpose. Sonia stopped short in the doorway and looked about her bewildered, unconscious of everything. She forgot her fourth-hand, gaudy silk dress, so unseemly here with its ridiculous long train, and her immense crinoline that filled up the whole doorway, and her light-coloured shoes, and the parasol she brought with her, though it was no use at night, and the absurd round straw hat with its flaring flame-coloured feather. Under this rakishly-tilted hat was a pale, frightened little face with lips parted and eyes staring in terror. Sonia was a small thin girl of eighteen with fair hair, rather pretty, with wonderful blue eyes. She looked intently at the bed and the priest; she too was out of breath with running. At last whispers, some words in the crowd probably, reached her. She looked down and took a step forward into the room, still keeping close to the door.

The service was over. Katerina Ivanovna went up to her husband again. The priest stepped back and turned to say a few words of admonition and consolation to Katerina Ivanovna on leaving.

"What am I to do with these?" she interrupted sharply and irritably, pointing to the little ones.

"God is merciful; look to the Most High for succour," the priest began.

"Ach! He is merciful, but not to us."

"That's a sin, a sin, madam," observed the priest, shaking his head.

"And isn't that a sin?" cried Katerina Ivanovna, pointing to the dying man.

"Perhaps those who have involuntarily caused the accident will agree to compensate you, at least for the loss of his earnings."

"You don't understand!" cried Katerina Ivanovna angrily waving her hand. "And why should they compensate me? Why, he was drunk and threw himself under the horses! What earnings? He brought us in nothing but misery. He drank everything away, the drunkard! He robbed us to get drink, he wasted their lives and mine for drink! And thank God he's dying! One less to keep!"

"You must forgive in the hour of death, that's a sin, madam, such feelings are a great sin."

Katerina Ivanovna was busy with the dying man; she was giving him water, wiping the blood and sweat from his head, setting his pillow straight, and had only turned now and then for a moment to address the priest. Now she flew at him almost in a frenzy.

"Ah, father! That's words and only words! Forgive! If he'd not been run over, he'd have come home today drunk and his only shirt dirty and in rags and he'd have fallen asleep like a log, and I should have been sousing and rinsing till daybreak, washing his rags and the children's and then drying them by the window and as soon as it was daylight I should have been darning them. That's how I spend my nights!... What's the use of talking of forgiveness! I have forgiven as it is!"

A terrible hollow cough interrupted her words. She put her handkerchief to her lips and showed it to the priest, pressing her other hand to her aching chest. The handkerchief was covered with blood. The priest bowed his head and said nothing.

101

Marmeladov was in the last agony; he did not take his eyes off the face of Katerina Ivanovna, who was bending over him again. He kept trying to say something to her; he began moving his tongue with difficulty and articulating indistinctly, but Katerina Ivanovna, understanding that he wanted to ask her forgiveness, called peremptorily to him:

"Be silent! No need! I know what you want to say!" And the sick man was silent, but at the same instant his wandering eyes strayed to the doorway and he saw Sonia.

Till then he had not noticed her: she was standing in the shadow in a corner.

"Who's that? Who's that?" he said suddenly in a thick gasping voice, in agitation, turning his eyes in horror towards the door where his daughter was standing, and trying to sit up.

"Lie down! Lie do-own!" cried Katerina Ivanovna.

With unnatural strength he had succeeded in propping himself on his elbow. He looked wildly and fixedly for some time on his daughter, as though not recognising her. He had never seen her before in such attire. Suddenly he recognised her, crushed and ashamed in her humiliation and gaudy finery, meekly awaiting her turn to say goodbye to her dying father. His face showed intense suffering.

"Sonia! Daughter! Forgive!" he cried, and he tried to hold out his hand to her, but losing his balance, he fell off the sofa, face downwards on the floor. They rushed to pick him up, they put him on the sofa; but he was dying. Sonia with a faint cry ran up, embraced him and remained so without moving. He died in her arms.

"He's got what he wanted," Katerina Ivanovna cried, seeing her husband's dead body. "Well, what's to be done now? How am I to bury him! What can I give them tomorrow to eat?"

Raskolnikov went up to Katerina Ivanovna.

"Katerina Ivanovna," he began, "last week your husband told me all his life and circumstances.... Believe me, he spoke of you with passionate reverence. From that evening, when I learnt how devoted he was to you all and how he loved and respected you especially, Katerina Ivanovna, in spite of his unfortunate weakness, from that evening we became friends.... Allow me now... to do something... to repay my debt to my dead friend. Here are twenty roubles, I think—and if that can be of any assistance to you, then... I... in short, I will come again, I will be sure to come again... I shall, perhaps, come again tomorrow.... Goodbye!"

And he went quickly out of the room, squeezing his way through the crowd to the stairs. But in the crowd he suddenly jostled against Nikodim Fomitch, who had heard of the accident and had come to give instructions in person. They had not met since the scene at the police station, but Nikodim Fomitch knew him instantly.

"Ah, is that you?" he asked him.

"He's dead," answered Raskolnikov. "The doctor and the priest have been, all as it should have been. Don't worry the poor woman too much, she is in consumption as it is. Try and cheer her up, if possible... you are a kindhearted man, I know..." he added with a smile, looking straight in his face.

"But you are spattered with blood," observed Nikodim Fomitch, noticing in the lamplight some fresh stains on Raskolnikov's waistcoat.

"Yes... I'm covered with blood," Raskolnikov said with a peculiar air; then he smiled, nodded and went downstairs.

He walked down slowly and deliberately, feverish but not conscious of it, entirely absorbed in a new overwhelming sensation of life and strength that surged up suddenly within him. This sensation might be compared to that of a man condemned to death who has suddenly been pardoned. Halfway down the staircase he was overtaken by the priest on his way home; Raskolnikov let him pass, exchanging a silent greeting with him. He was just descending the last steps when he heard rapid footsteps behind him. Someone overtook him; it was Polenka. She was running after him, calling "Wait! wait!"

He turned round. She was at the bottom of the staircase and stopped short a step above him. A dim light came in from the yard. Raskolnikov could distinguish the child's thin but pretty little face, looking at him with a bright childish smile. She had run after him with a message which she was evidently glad to give.

102

"Tell me, what is your name?… and where do you live?" she said hurriedly in a breathless voice.

He laid both hands on her shoulders and looked at her with a sort of rapture. It was such a joy to him to look at her, he could not have said why.

"Who sent you?"

"Sister Sonia sent me," answered the girl, smiling still more brightly.

"I knew it was sister Sonia sent you."

"Mamma sent me, too… when sister Sonia was sending me, mamma came up, too, and said 'Run fast, Polenka.'"

"Do you love sister Sonia?"

"I love her more than anyone," Polenka answered with a peculiar earnestness, and her smile became graver.

"And will you love me?"

By way of answer he saw the little girl's face approaching him, her full lips naively held out to kiss him. Suddenly her arms as thin as sticks held him tightly, her head rested on his shoulder and the little girl wept softly, pressing her face against him.

"I am sorry for father," she said a moment later, raising her tear-stained face and brushing away the tears with her hands. "It's nothing but misfortunes now," she added suddenly with that peculiarly sedate air which children try hard to assume when they want to speak like grownup people.

"Did your father love you?"

"He loved Lida most," she went on very seriously without a smile, exactly like grownup people, "he loved her because she is little and because she is ill, too. And he always used to bring her presents. But he taught us to read and me grammar and scripture, too," she added with dignity. "And mother never used to say anything, but we knew that she liked it and father knew it, too. And mother wants to teach me French, for it's time my education began."

"And do you know your prayers?"

"Of course, we do! We knew them long ago. I say my prayers to myself as I am a big girl now, but Kolya and Lida say them aloud with mother. First they repeat the 'Ave Maria' and then another prayer: 'Lord, forgive and bless sister Sonia,' and then another, 'Lord, forgive and bless our second father.' For our elder father is dead and this is another one, but we do pray for the other as well."

"Polenka, my name is Rodion. Pray sometimes for me, too. 'And Thy servant Rodion,' nothing more."

"I'll pray for you all the rest of my life," the little girl declared hotly, and suddenly smiling again she rushed at him and hugged him warmly once more.

Raskolnikov told her his name and address and promised to be sure to come next day. The child went away quite enchanted with him. It was past ten when he came out into the street. In five minutes he was standing on the bridge at the spot where the woman had jumped in.

"Enough," he pronounced resolutely and triumphantly. "I've done with fancies, imaginary terrors and phantoms! Life is real! haven't I lived just now? My life has not yet died with that old woman! The Kingdom of Heaven to her—and now enough, madam, leave me in peace! Now for the reign of reason and light… and of will, and of strength… and now we will see! We will try our strength!" he added defiantly, as though challenging some power of darkness. "And I was ready to consent to live in a square of space!

"I am very weak at this moment, but… I believe my illness is all over. I knew it would be over when I went out. By the way, Potchinkov's house is only a few steps away. I certainly must go to Razumihin even if it were not close by… let him win his bet! Let us give him some satisfaction, too—no matter! Strength, strength is what one wants, you can get nothing without it, and strength must be won by strength—that's what they don't know," he added proudly and self-confidently and he walked with flagging footsteps from the bridge. Pride and self-confidence grew continually stronger in him; he was becoming a different man every moment. What was it had happened to work this revolution in him? He did not know himself; like a man catching at a straw, he suddenly

103

felt that he, too, "could live, that there was still life for him, that his life had not died with the old woman." Perhaps he was in too great a hurry with his conclusions, but he did not think of that.

"But I did ask her to remember 'Thy servant Rodion' in her prayers," the idea struck him. "Well, that was... in case of emergency," he added and laughed himself at his boyish sally. He was in the best of spirits.

He easily found Razumihin; the new lodger was already known at Potchinkov's and the porter at once showed him the way. Halfway upstairs he could hear the noise and animated conversation of a big gathering of people. The door was wide open on the stairs; he could hear exclamations and discussion. Razumihin's room was fairly large; the company consisted of fifteen people. Raskolnikov stopped in the entry, where two of the landlady's servants were busy behind a screen with two samovars, bottles, plates and dishes of pie and savouries, brought up from the landlady's kitchen. Raskolnikov sent in for Razumihin. He ran out delighted. At the first glance it was apparent that he had had a great deal to drink and, though no amount of liquor made Razumihin quite drunk, this time he was perceptibly affected by it.

"Listen," Raskolnikov hastened to say, "I've only just come to tell you you've won your bet and that no one really knows what may not happen to him. I can't come in; I am so weak that I shall fall down directly. And so good evening and goodbye! Come and see me tomorrow."

"Do you know what? I'll see you home. If you say you're weak yourself, you must..."

"And your visitors? Who is the curly-headed one who has just peeped out?"

"He? Goodness only knows! Some friend of uncle's, I expect, or perhaps he has come without being invited... I'll leave uncle with them, he is an invaluable person, pity I can't introduce you to him now. But confound them all now! They won't notice me, and I need a little fresh air, for you've come just in the nick of time—another two minutes and I should have come to blows! They are talking such a lot of wild stuff... you simply can't imagine what men will say! Though why shouldn't you imagine? Don't we talk nonsense ourselves? And let them... that's the way to learn not to!... Wait a minute, I'll fetch Zossimov."

Zossimov pounced upon Raskolnikov almost greedily; he showed a special interest in him; soon his face brightened.

"You must go to bed at once," he pronounced, examining the patient as far as he could, "and take something for the night. Will you take it? I got it ready some time ago... a powder."

"Two, if you like," answered Raskolnikov. The powder was taken at once.

"It's a good thing you are taking him home," observed Zossimov to Razumihin—"we shall see how he is tomorrow, today he's not at all amiss—a considerable change since the afternoon. Live and learn..."

"Do you know what Zossimov whispered to me when we were coming out?" Razumihin blurted out, as soon as they were in the street. "I won't tell you everything, brother, because they are such fools. Zossimov told me to talk freely to you on the way and get you to talk freely to me, and afterwards I am to tell him about it, for he's got a notion in his head that you are... mad or close on it. Only fancy! In the first place, you've three times the brains he has; in the second, if you are not mad, you needn't care a hang that he has got such a wild idea; and thirdly, that piece of beef whose specialty is surgery has gone mad on mental diseases, and what's brought him to this conclusion about you was your conversation today with Zametov."

"Zametov told you all about it?"

"Yes, and he did well. Now I understand what it all means and so does Zametov.... Well, the fact is, Rodya... the point is... I am a little drunk now.... But that's... no matter... the point is that this idea... you understand? was just being hatched in their brains... you understand? That is, no one ventured to say it aloud, because the idea is too absurd and especially since the arrest of that painter, that bubble's burst and gone for ever. But why are they such fools? I gave Zametov a bit of a thrashing at the time—that's between ourselves, brother; please don't let out a hint that you know of it; I've noticed he is a ticklish subject; it was at Luise Ivanovna's. But today, today it's all cleared up. That Ilya Petrovitch is at the bottom of it! He took advantage of your fainting at the police station, but he is ashamed of it himself now; I know that..."

Raskolnikov listened greedily. Razumihin was drunk enough to talk too freely.

"I fainted then because it was so close and the smell of paint," said Raskolnikov.

"No need to explain that! And it wasn't the paint only: the fever had been coming on for a month; Zossimov testifies to that! But how crushed that boy is now, you wouldn't believe! 'I am not worth his little finger,' he says. Yours, he means. He has good feelings at times, brother. But the lesson, the lesson you gave him today in the Palais de Cristal, that was too good for anything! You frightened him at first, you know, he nearly went into convulsions! You almost convinced him again of the truth of all that hideous nonsense, and then you suddenly—put out your tongue at him: 'There now, what do you make of it?' It was perfect! He is crushed, annihilated now! It was masterly, by Jove, it's what they deserve! Ah, that I wasn't there! He was hoping to see you awfully. Porfiry, too, wants to make your acquaintance…"

"Ah!… he too… but why did they put me down as mad?"

"Oh, not mad. I must have said too much, brother…. What struck him, you see, was that only that subject seemed to interest you; now it's clear why it did interest you; knowing all the circumstances… and how that irritated you and worked in with your illness… I am a little drunk, brother, only, confound him, he has some idea of his own… I tell you, he's mad on mental diseases. But don't you mind him…"

For half a minute both were silent.

"Listen, Razumihin," began Raskolnikov, "I want to tell you plainly: I've just been at a deathbed, a clerk who died… I gave them all my money… and besides I've just been kissed by someone who, if I had killed anyone, would just the same… in fact I saw someone else there… with a flame-coloured feather… but I am talking nonsense; I am very weak, support me… we shall be at the stairs directly…"

"What's the matter? What's the matter with you?" Razumihin asked anxiously.

"I am a little giddy, but that's not the point, I am so sad, so sad… like a woman. Look, what's that? Look, look!"

"What is it?"

"Don't you see? A light in my room, you see? Through the crack…"

They were already at the foot of the last flight of stairs, at the level of the landlady's door, and they could, as a fact, see from below that there was a light in Raskolnikov's garret.

"Queer! Nastasya, perhaps," observed Razumihin.

"She is never in my room at this time and she must be in bed long ago, but… I don't care! Goodbye!"

"What do you mean? I am coming with you, we'll come in together!"

"I know we are going in together, but I want to shake hands here and say goodbye to you here. So give me your hand, goodbye!"

"What's the matter with you, Rodya?"

"Nothing… come along… you shall be witness."

They began mounting the stairs, and the idea struck Razumihin that perhaps Zossimov might be right after all. "Ah, I've upset him with my chatter!" he muttered to himself.

When they reached the door they heard voices in the room.

"What is it?" cried Razumihin. Raskolnikov was the first to open the door; he flung it wide and stood still in the doorway, dumbfounded.

His mother and sister were sitting on his sofa and had been waiting an hour and a half for him. Why had he never expected, never thought of them, though the news that they had started, were on their way and would arrive immediately, had been repeated to him only that day? They had spent that hour and a half plying Nastasya with questions. She was standing before them and had told them everything by now. They were beside themselves with alarm when they heard of his "running away" today, ill and, as they understood from her story, delirious! "Good Heavens, what had become of him?" Both had been weeping, both had been in anguish for that hour and a half.

A cry of joy, of ecstasy, greeted Raskolnikov's entrance. Both rushed to him. But he stood like one dead; a sudden intolerable sensation struck him like a thunderbolt. He did not lift his arms to embrace them, he could not. His mother and sister clasped him in their arms, kissed him, laughed and cried. He took a step, tottered and fell to the ground, fainting.

Anxiety, cries of horror, moans… Razumihin who was standing in the doorway flew into the room, seized the sick man in his strong arms and in a moment had him on the sofa.

"It's nothing, nothing!" he cried to the mother and sister—"it's only a faint, a mere trifle! Only just now the doctor said he was much better, that he is perfectly well! Water! See, he is coming to himself, he is all right again!"

And seizing Dounia by the arm so that he almost dislocated it, he made her bend down to see that "he is all right again." The mother and sister looked on him with emotion and gratitude, as their Providence. They had heard already from Nastasya all that had been done for their Rodya during his illness, by this "very competent young man," as Pulcheria Alexandrovna Raskolnikov called him that evening in conversation with Dounia.

Raskolnikov got up, and sat down on the sofa. He waved his hand weakly to Razumihin to cut short the flow of warm and incoherent consolations he was addressing to his mother and sister, took them both by the hand and for a minute or two gazed from one to the other without speaking. His mother was alarmed by his expression. It revealed an emotion agonisingly poignant, and at the same time something immovable, almost insane. Pulcheria Alexandrovna began to cry.

Avdotya Romanovna was pale; her hand trembled in her brother's.

"Go home... with him," he said in a broken voice, pointing to Razumihin, "goodbye till tomorrow; tomorrow everything... Is it long since you arrived?"

"This evening, Rodya," answered Pulcheria Alexandrovna, "the train was awfully late. But, Rodya, nothing would induce me to leave you now! I will spend the night here, near you..."

"Don't torture me!" he said with a gesture of irritation.

"I will stay with him," cried Razumihin, "I won't leave him for a moment. Bother all my visitors! Let them rage to their hearts' content! My uncle is presiding there."

"How, how can I thank you!" Pulcheria Alexandrovna was beginning, once more pressing Razumihin's hands, but Raskolnikov interrupted her again.

"I can't have it! I can't have it!" he repeated irritably, "don't worry me! Enough, go away... I can't stand it!"

"Come, mamma, come out of the room at least for a minute," Dounia whispered in dismay; "we are distressing him, that's evident."

"Mayn't I look at him after three years?" wept Pulcheria Alexandrovna.

"Stay," he stopped them again, "you keep interrupting me, and my ideas get muddled.... Have you seen Luzhin?"

"No, Rodya, but he knows already of our arrival. We have heard, Rodya, that Pyotr Petrovitch was so kind as to visit you today," Pulcheria Alexandrovna added somewhat timidly.

"Yes... he was so kind... Dounia, I promised Luzhin I'd throw him downstairs and told him to go to hell...."

"Rodya, what are you saying! Surely, you don't mean to tell us..." Pulcheria Alexandrovna began in alarm, but she stopped, looking at Dounia.

Avdotya Romanovna was looking attentively at her brother, waiting for what would come next. Both of them had heard of the quarrel from Nastasya, so far as she had succeeded in understanding and reporting it, and were in painful perplexity and suspense.

"Dounia," Raskolnikov continued with an effort, "I don't want that marriage, so at the first opportunity tomorrow you must refuse Luzhin, so that we may never hear his name again."

"Good Heavens!" cried Pulcheria Alexandrovna.

"Brother, think what you are saying!" Avdotya Romanovna began impetuously, but immediately checked herself. "You are not fit to talk now, perhaps; you are tired," she added gently.

"You think I am delirious? No... You are marrying Luzhin for *my* sake. But I won't accept the sacrifice. And so write a letter before tomorrow, to refuse him... Let me read it in the morning and that will be the end of it!"

"That I can't do!" the girl cried, offended, "what right have you..."

"Dounia, you are hasty, too, be quiet, tomorrow... Don't you see..." the mother interposed in dismay. "Better come away!"

"He is raving," Razumihin cried tipsily, "or how would he dare! Tomorrow all this nonsense will be over... today he certainly did drive him away. That was so. And Luzhin got angry, too.... He made speeches here, wanted to show off his learning and he went out crestfallen...."

"Then it's true?" cried Pulcheria Alexandrovna.

"Goodbye till tomorrow, brother," said Dounia compassionately—"let us go, mother… Goodbye, Rodya."

"Do you hear, sister," he repeated after them, making a last effort, "I am not delirious; this marriage is—an infamy. Let me act like a scoundrel, but you mustn't… one is enough… and though I am a scoundrel, I wouldn't own such a sister. It's me or Luzhin! Go now…."

"But you're out of your mind! Despot!" roared Razumihin; but Raskolnikov did not and perhaps could not answer. He lay down on the sofa, and turned to the wall, utterly exhausted. Avdotya Romanovna looked with interest at Razumihin; her black eyes flashed; Razumihin positively started at her glance.

Pulcheria Alexandrovna stood overwhelmed.

"Nothing would induce me to go," she whispered in despair to Razumihin. "I will stay somewhere here… escort Dounia home."

"You'll spoil everything," Razumihin answered in the same whisper, losing patience—"come out on to the stairs, anyway. Nastasya, show a light! I assure you," he went on in a half whisper on the stairs—"that he was almost beating the doctor and me this afternoon! Do you understand? The doctor himself! Even he gave way and left him, so as not to irritate him. I remained downstairs on guard, but he dressed at once and slipped off. And he will slip off again if you irritate him, at this time of night, and will do himself some mischief…."

"What are you saying?"

"And Avdotya Romanovna can't possibly be left in those lodgings without you. Just think where you are staying! That blackguard Pyotr Petrovitch couldn't find you better lodgings… But you know I've had a little to drink, and that's what makes me… swear; don't mind it…."

"But I'll go to the landlady here," Pulcheria Alexandrovna insisted, "I'll beseech her to find some corner for Dounia and me for the night. I can't leave him like that, I cannot!"

This conversation took place on the landing just before the landlady's door. Nastasya lighted them from a step below. Razumihin was in extraordinary excitement. Half an hour earlier, while he was bringing Raskolnikov home, he had indeed talked too freely, but he was aware of it himself, and his head was clear in spite of the vast quantities he had imbibed. Now he was in a state bordering on ecstasy, and all that he had drunk seemed to fly to his head with redoubled effect. He stood with the two ladies, seizing both by their hands, persuading them, and giving them reasons with astonishing plainness of speech, and at almost every word he uttered, probably to emphasise his arguments, he squeezed their hands painfully as in a vise. He stared at Avdotya Romanovna without the least regard for good manners. They sometimes pulled their hands out of his huge bony paws, but far from noticing what was the matter, he drew them all the closer to him. If they'd told him to jump head foremost from the staircase, he would have done it without thought or hesitation in their service. Though Pulcheria Alexandrovna felt that the young man was really too eccentric and pinched her hand too much, in her anxiety over her Rodya she looked on his presence as providential, and was unwilling to notice all his peculiarities. But though Avdotya Romanovna shared her anxiety, and was not of timorous disposition, she could not see the glowing light in his eyes without wonder and almost alarm. It was only the unbounded confidence inspired by Nastasya's account of her brother's queer friend, which prevented her from trying to run away from him, and to persuade her mother to do the same. She realised, too, that even running away was perhaps impossible now. Ten minutes later, however, she was considerably reassured; it was characteristic of Razumihin that he showed his true nature at once, whatever mood he might be in, so that people quickly saw the sort of man they had to deal with.

"You can't go to the landlady, that's perfect nonsense!" he cried. "If you stay, though you are his mother, you'll drive him to a frenzy, and then goodness knows what will happen! Listen, I'll tell you what I'll do: Nastasya will stay with him now, and I'll conduct you both home, you can't be in the streets alone; Petersburg is an awful place in that way…. But no matter! Then I'll run straight back here and a quarter of an hour later, on my word of honour, I'll bring you news how he is, whether he is asleep, and all that. Then, listen! Then I'll run home in a twinkling—I've a lot of friends there, all drunk—I'll fetch Zossimov—that's the doctor who is looking after him, he is there, too, but he is not drunk; he is not drunk, he is never drunk! I'll drag him to Rodya, and then

109

to you, so that you'll get two reports in the hour—from the doctor, you understand, from the doctor himself, that's a very different thing from my account of him! If there's anything wrong, I swear I'll bring you here myself, but, if it's all right, you go to bed. And I'll spend the night here, in the passage, he won't hear me, and I'll tell Zossimov to sleep at the landlady's, to be at hand. Which is better for him: you or the doctor? So come home then! But the landlady is out of the question; it's all right for me, but it's out of the question for you: she wouldn't take you, for she's... for she's a fool... She'd be jealous on my account of Avdotya Romanovna and of you, too, if you want to know... of Avdotya Romanovna certainly. She is an absolutely, absolutely unaccountable character! But I am a fool, too!... No matter! Come along! Do you trust me? Come, do you trust me or not?"

"Let us go, mother," said Avdotya Romanovna, "he will certainly do what he has promised. He has saved Rodya already, and if the doctor really will consent to spend the night here, what could be better?"

"You see, you... you... understand me, because you are an angel!" Razumihin cried in ecstasy, "let us go! Nastasya! Fly upstairs and sit with him with a light; I'll come in a quarter of an hour."

Though Pulcheria Alexandrovna was not perfectly convinced, she made no further resistance. Razumihin gave an arm to each and drew them down the stairs. He still made her uneasy, as though he was competent and good-natured, was he capable of carrying out his promise? He seemed in such a condition....

"Ah, I see you think I am in such a condition!" Razumihin broke in upon her thoughts, guessing them, as he strolled along the pavement with huge steps, so that the two ladies could hardly keep up with him, a fact he did not observe, however. "Nonsense! That is... I am drunk like a fool, but that's not it; I am not drunk from wine. It's seeing you has turned my head... But don't mind me! Don't take any notice: I am talking nonsense, I am not worthy of you.... I am utterly unworthy of you! The minute I've taken you home, I'll pour a couple of pailfuls of water over my head in the gutter here, and then I shall be all right.... If only you knew how I love you both! Don't laugh, and don't be angry! You may be angry with anyone, but not with me! I am his friend, and therefore I am your friend, too, I want to be... I had a presentiment... Last year there was a moment... though it wasn't a presentiment really, for you seem to have fallen from heaven. And I expect I shan't sleep all night... Zossimov was afraid a little time ago that he would go mad... that's why he mustn't be irritated."

"What do you say?" cried the mother.

"Did the doctor really say that?" asked Avdotya Romanovna, alarmed.

"Yes, but it's not so, not a bit of it. He gave him some medicine, a powder, I saw it, and then your coming here.... Ah! It would have been better if you had come tomorrow. It's a good thing we went away. And in an hour Zossimov himself will report to you about everything. He is not drunk! And I shan't be drunk.... And what made me get so tight? Because they got me into an argument, damn them! I've sworn never to argue! They talk such trash! I almost came to blows! I've left my uncle to preside. Would you believe, they insist on complete absence of individualism and that's just what they relish! Not to be themselves, to be as unlike themselves as they can. That's what they regard as the highest point of progress. If only their nonsense were their own, but as it is..."

"Listen!" Pulcheria Alexandrovna interrupted timidly, but it only added fuel to the flames.

"What do you think?" shouted Razumihin, louder than ever, "you think I am attacking them for talking nonsense? Not a bit! I like them to talk nonsense. That's man's one privilege over all creation. Through error you come to the truth! I am a man because I err! You never reach any truth without making fourteen mistakes and very likely a hundred and fourteen. And a fine thing, too, in its way; but we can't even make mistakes on our own account! Talk nonsense, but talk your own nonsense, and I'll kiss you for it. To go wrong in one's own way is better than to go right in someone else's. In the first case you are a man, in the second you're no better than a bird. Truth won't escape you, but life can be cramped. There have been examples. And what are we doing now? In science, development, thought, invention, ideals, aims, liberalism, judgment, experience and everything, everything, everything, we are still in the preparatory class at school.

110

We prefer to live on other people's ideas, it's what we are used to! Am I right, am I right?" cried Razumihin, pressing and shaking the two ladies' hands.

"Oh, mercy, I do not know," cried poor Pulcheria Alexandrovna.

"Yes, yes... though I don't agree with you in everything," added Avdotya Romanovna earnestly and at once uttered a cry, for he squeezed her hand so painfully.

"Yes, you say yes... well after that you... you..." he cried in a transport, "you are a fount of goodness, purity, sense... and perfection. Give me your hand... you give me yours, too! I want to kiss your hands here at once, on my knees..." and he fell on his knees on the pavement, fortunately at that time deserted.

"Leave off, I entreat you, what are you doing?" Pulcheria Alexandrovna cried, greatly distressed.

"Get up, get up!" said Dounia laughing, though she, too, was upset.

"Not for anything till you let me kiss your hands! That's it! Enough! I get up and we'll go on! I am a luckless fool, I am unworthy of you and drunk... and I am ashamed.... I am not worthy to love you, but to do homage to you is the duty of every man who is not a perfect beast! And I've done homage.... Here are your lodgings, and for that alone Rodya was right in driving your Pyotr Petrovitch away.... How dare he! how dare he put you in such lodgings! It's a scandal! Do you know the sort of people they take in here? And you his betrothed! You are his betrothed? Yes? Well, then, I'll tell you, your fiancé is a scoundrel."

"Excuse me, Mr. Razumihin, you are forgetting..." Pulcheria Alexandrovna was beginning.

"Yes, yes, you are right, I did forget myself, I am ashamed of it," Razumihin made haste to apologise. "But... but you can't be angry with me for speaking so! For I speak sincerely and not because... hm, hm! That would be disgraceful; in fact not because I'm in... hm! Well, anyway, I won't say why, I daren't.... But we all saw today when he came in that that man is not of our sort. Not because he had his hair curled at the barber's, not because he was in such a hurry to show his wit, but because he is a spy, a speculator, because he is a skinflint and a buffoon. That's evident. Do you think him clever? No, he is a fool, a fool. And is he a match for you? Good heavens! Do you see, ladies?" he stopped suddenly on the way upstairs to their rooms, "though all my friends there are drunk, yet they are all honest, and though we do talk a lot of trash, and I do, too, yet we shall talk our way to the truth at last, for we are on the right path, while Pyotr Petrovitch... is not on the right path. Though I've been calling them all sorts of names just now, I do respect them all... though I don't respect Zametov, I like him, for he is a puppy, and that bullock Zossimov, because he is an honest man and knows his work. But enough, it's all said and forgiven. Is it forgiven? Well, then, let's go on. I know this corridor, I've been here, there was a scandal here at Number 3.... Where are you here? Which number? eight? Well, lock yourselves in for the night, then. Don't let anybody in. In a quarter of an hour I'll come back with news, and half an hour later I'll bring Zossimov, you'll see! Goodbye, I'll run."

"Good heavens, Dounia, what is going to happen?" said Pulcheria Alexandrovna, addressing her daughter with anxiety and dismay.

"Don't worry yourself, mother," said Dounia, taking off her hat and cape. "God has sent this gentleman to our aid, though he has come from a drinking party. We can depend on him, I assure you. And all that he has done for Rodya...."

"Ah. Dounia, goodness knows whether he will come! How could I bring myself to leave Rodya?... And how different, how different I had fancied our meeting! How sullen he was, as though not pleased to see us...."

Tears came into her eyes.

"No, it's not that, mother. You didn't see, you were crying all the time. He is quite unhinged by serious illness—that's the reason."

"Ah, that illness! What will happen, what will happen? And how he talked to you, Dounia!" said the mother, looking timidly at her daughter, trying to read her thoughts and, already half consoled by Dounia's standing up for her brother, which meant that she had already forgiven him. "I am sure he will think better of it tomorrow," she added, probing her further.

"And I am sure that he will say the same tomorrow… about that," Avdotya Romanovna said finally. And, of course, there was no going beyond that, for this was a point which Pulcheria Alexandrovna was afraid to discuss. Dounia went up and kissed her mother. The latter warmly embraced her without speaking. Then she sat down to wait anxiously for Razumihin's return, timidly watching her daughter who walked up and down the room with her arms folded, lost in thought. This walking up and down when she was thinking was a habit of Avdotya Romanovna's and the mother was always afraid to break in on her daughter's mood at such moments.

Razumihin, of course, was ridiculous in his sudden drunken infatuation for Avdotya Romanovna. Yet apart from his eccentric condition, many people would have thought it justified if they had seen Avdotya Romanovna, especially at that moment when she was walking to and fro with folded arms, pensive and melancholy. Avdotya Romanovna was remarkably good-looking; she was tall, strikingly well-proportioned, strong and self-reliant—the latter quality was apparent in every gesture, though it did not in the least detract from the grace and softness of her movements. In face she resembled her brother, but she might be described as really beautiful. Her hair was dark brown, a little lighter than her brother's; there was a proud light in her almost black eyes and yet at times a look of extraordinary kindness. She was pale, but it was a healthy pallor; her face was radiant with freshness and vigour. Her mouth was rather small; the full red lower lip projected a little as did her chin; it was the only irregularity in her beautiful face, but it gave it a peculiarly individual and almost haughty expression. Her face was always more serious and thoughtful than gay; but how well smiles, how well youthful, lighthearted, irresponsible, laughter suited her face! It was natural enough that a warm, open, simple-hearted, honest giant like Razumihin, who had never seen anyone like her and was not quite sober at the time, should lose his head immediately. Besides, as chance would have it, he saw Dounia for the first time transfigured by her love for her brother and her joy at meeting him. Afterwards he saw her lower lip quiver with indignation at her brother's insolent, cruel and ungrateful words—and his fate was sealed.

He had spoken the truth, moreover, when he blurted out in his drunken talk on the stairs that Praskovya Pavlovna, Raskolnikov's eccentric landlady, would be jealous of Pulcheria Alexandrovna as well as of Avdotya Romanovna on his account. Although Pulcheria Alexandrovna was forty-three, her face still retained traces of her former beauty; she looked much younger than her age, indeed, which is almost always the case with women who retain serenity of spirit, sensitiveness and pure sincere warmth of heart to old age. We may add in parenthesis that to preserve all this is the only means of retaining beauty to old age. Her hair had begun to grow grey and thin, there had long been little crow's foot wrinkles round her eyes, her cheeks were hollow and sunken from anxiety and grief, and yet it was a handsome face. She was Dounia over again, twenty years older, but without the projecting underlip. Pulcheria Alexandrovna was emotional, but not sentimental, timid and yielding, but only to a certain point. She could give way and accept a great deal even of what was contrary to her convictions, but there was a certain barrier fixed by honesty, principle and the deepest convictions which nothing would induce her to cross.

Exactly twenty minutes after Razumihin's departure, there came two subdued but hurried knocks at the door: he had come back.

"I won't come in, I haven't time," he hastened to say when the door was opened. "He sleeps like a top, soundly, quietly, and God grant he may sleep ten hours. Nastasya's with him; I told her not to leave till I came. Now I am fetching Zossimov, he will report to you and then you'd better turn in; I can see you are too tired to do anything…."

And he ran off down the corridor.

"What a very competent and… devoted young man!" cried Pulcheria Alexandrovna exceedingly delighted.

"He seems a splendid person!" Avdotya Romanovna replied with some warmth, resuming her walk up and down the room.

It was nearly an hour later when they heard footsteps in the corridor and another knock at the door. Both women waited this time completely relying on Razumihin's promise; he actually had succeeded in bringing Zossimov. Zossimov had agreed at once to desert the drinking party to go to Raskolnikov's, but he came reluctantly and with the greatest suspicion to see the ladies, mistrusting Razumihin in his exhilarated condition. But his vanity was at once reassured and flattered; he saw that they were really expecting him as an oracle. He stayed just ten minutes and succeeded in completely convincing and comforting Pulcheria Alexandrovna. He spoke with marked sympathy, but with the reserve and extreme seriousness of a young doctor at an important consultation. He did not utter a word on any other subject and did not display the slightest desire to enter into more personal relations with the two ladies. Remarking at his first entrance the dazzling beauty of Avdotya Romanovna, he endeavoured not to notice her at all during his visit and addressed himself solely to Pulcheria Alexandrovna. All this gave him extraordinary inward satisfaction. He declared that he thought the invalid at this moment going on very satisfactorily. According to his observations the patient's illness was due partly to his unfortunate material surroundings during the last few months, but it had partly also a moral origin, "was, so to speak, the product of several material and moral influences, anxieties, apprehensions, troubles, certain ideas... and so on." Noticing stealthily that Avdotya Romanovna was following his words with close attention, Zossimov allowed himself to enlarge on this theme. On Pulcheria Alexandrovna's anxiously and timidly inquiring as to "some suspicion of insanity," he replied with a composed and candid smile that his words had been exaggerated; that certainly the patient had some fixed idea, something approaching a monomania—he, Zossimov, was now particularly studying this interesting branch of medicine—but that it must be recollected that until today the patient had been in delirium and... and that no doubt the presence of his family would have a favourable effect on his recovery and distract his mind, "if only all fresh shocks can be avoided," he added significantly. Then he got up, took leave with an impressive and affable bow, while blessings, warm gratitude, and entreaties were showered upon him, and Avdotya Romanovna spontaneously offered her hand to him. He went out exceedingly pleased with his visit and still more so with himself.

"We'll talk tomorrow; go to bed at once!" Razumihin said in conclusion, following Zossimov out. "I'll be with you tomorrow morning as early as possible with my report."

"That's a fetching little girl, Avdotya Romanovna," remarked Zossimov, almost licking his lips as they both came out into the street.

"Fetching? You said fetching?" roared Razumihin and he flew at Zossimov and seized him by the throat. "If you ever dare.... Do you understand? Do you understand?" he shouted, shaking him by the collar and squeezing him against the wall. "Do you hear?"

"Let me go, you drunken devil," said Zossimov, struggling and when he had let him go, he stared at him and went off into a sudden guffaw. Razumihin stood facing him in gloomy and earnest reflection.

"Of course, I am an ass," he observed, sombre as a storm cloud, "but still... you are another."

"No, brother, not at all such another. I am not dreaming of any folly."

They walked along in silence and only when they were close to Raskolnikov's lodgings, Razumihin broke the silence in considerable anxiety.

"Listen," he said, "you're a first-rate fellow, but among your other failings, you're a loose fish, that I know, and a dirty one, too. You are a feeble, nervous wretch, and a mass of whims, you're getting fat and lazy and can't deny yourself anything—and I call that dirty because it leads one straight into the dirt. You've let yourself get so slack that I don't know how it is you are still a good, even a devoted doctor. You—a doctor—sleep on a feather bed and get up at night to your patients! In another three or four years you won't get up for your patients... But hang it all, that's not the point!... You are going to spend tonight in the landlady's flat here. (Hard work I've had to persuade her!) And I'll be in the kitchen. So here's a chance for you to get to know her better.... It's not as you think! There's not a trace of anything of the sort, brother...!"

"But I don't think!"

"Here you have modesty, brother, silence, bashfulness, a savage virtue... and yet she's sighing and melting like wax, simply melting! Save me from her, by all that's unholy! She's most prepossessing... I'll repay you, I'll do anything...."

Zossimov laughed more violently than ever.

"Well, you are smitten! But what am I to do with her?"

"It won't be much trouble, I assure you. Talk any rot you like to her, as long as you sit by her and talk. You're a doctor, too; try curing her of something. I swear you won't regret it. She has a piano, and you know, I strum a little. I have a song there, a genuine Russian one: 'I shed hot tears.' She likes the genuine article—and well, it all began with that song; Now you're a regular performer, a *maître*, a Rubinstein.... I assure you, you won't regret it!"

"But have you made her some promise? Something signed? A promise of marriage, perhaps?"

"Nothing, nothing, absolutely nothing of the kind! Besides she is not that sort at all.... Tchebarov tried that...."

"Well then, drop her!"

"But I can't drop her like that!"

"Why can't you?"

"Well, I can't, that's all about it! There's an element of attraction here, brother."

"Then why have you fascinated her?"

"I haven't fascinated her; perhaps I was fascinated myself in my folly. But she won't care a straw whether it's you or I, so long as somebody sits beside her, sighing.... I can't explain the position, brother... look here, you are good at mathematics, and working at it now... begin teaching her the integral calculus; upon my soul, I'm not joking, I'm in earnest, it'll be just the same to her. She will gaze at you and sigh for a whole year together. I talked to her once for two days at a time about the Prussian House of Lords (for one must talk of something)—she just sighed and perspired! And you mustn't talk of love—she's bashful to hysterics—but just let her see you can't tear yourself away—that's enough. It's fearfully comfortable; you're quite at home, you can read, sit, lie about, write. You may even venture on a kiss, if you're careful."

"But what do I want with her?"

"Ach, I can't make you understand! You see, you are made for each other! I have often been reminded of you!... You'll come to it in the end! So does it matter whether it's sooner or later? There's the featherbed element here, brother—ach! and not only that! There's an attraction here— here you have the end of the world, an anchorage, a quiet haven, the navel of the earth, the three fishes that are the foundation of the world, the essence of pancakes, of savoury fish-pies, of the evening samovar, of soft sighs and warm shawls, and hot stoves to sleep on—as snug as though you were dead, and yet you're alive—the advantages of both at once! Well, hang it, brother, what stuff I'm talking, it's bedtime! Listen. I sometimes wake up at night; so I'll go in and look at him. But there's no need, it's all right. Don't you worry yourself, yet if you like, you might just look in once, too. But if you notice anything—delirium or fever—wake me at once. But there can't be...."

II

Razumihin waked up next morning at eight o'clock, troubled and serious. He found himself confronted with many new and unlooked-for perplexities. He had never expected that he would ever wake up feeling like that. He remembered every detail of the previous day and he knew that a perfectly novel experience had befallen him, that he had received an impression unlike anything he had known before. At the same time he recognised clearly that the dream which had fired his imagination was hopelessly unattainable—so unattainable that he felt positively ashamed of it, and he hastened to pass to the other more practical cares and difficulties bequeathed him by that "thrice accursed yesterday."

The most awful recollection of the previous day was the way he had shown himself "base and mean," not only because he had been drunk, but because he had taken advantage of the young girl's position to abuse her fiancé in his stupid jealousy, knowing nothing of their mutual relations and obligations and next to nothing of the man himself. And what right had he to criticise him in that hasty and unguarded manner? Who had asked for his opinion? Was it thinkable that such a creature as Avdotya Romanovna would be marrying an unworthy man for money? So there must be something in him. The lodgings? But after all how could he know the character of the lodgings? He was furnishing a flat... Foo! how despicable it all was! And what justification was it that he was drunk? Such a stupid excuse was even more degrading! In wine is truth, and the truth had all come out, "that is, all the uncleanness of his coarse and envious heart"! And would such a dream ever be permissible to him, Razumihin? What was he beside such a girl—he, the drunken noisy braggart of last night? Was it possible to imagine so absurd and cynical a juxtaposition? Razumihin blushed desperately at the very idea and suddenly the recollection forced itself vividly upon him of how he had said last night on the stairs that the landlady would be jealous of Avdotya Romanovna... that was simply intolerable. He brought his fist down heavily on the kitchen stove, hurt his hand and sent one of the bricks flying.

"Of course," he muttered to himself a minute later with a feeling of self-abasement, "of course, all these infamies can never be wiped out or smoothed over... and so it's useless even to think of it, and I must go to them in silence and do my duty... in silence, too... and not ask forgiveness, and say nothing... for all is lost now!"

And yet as he dressed he examined his attire more carefully than usual. He hadn't another suit—if he had had, perhaps he wouldn't have put it on. "I would have made a point of not putting it on." But in any case he could not remain a cynic and a dirty sloven; he had no right to offend the feelings of others, especially when they were in need of his assistance and asking him to see them. He brushed his clothes carefully. His linen was always decent; in that respect he was especially clean.

He washed that morning scrupulously—he got some soap from Nastasya—he washed his hair, his neck and especially his hands. When it came to the question whether to shave his stubbly chin or not (Praskovya Pavlovna had capital razors that had been left by her late husband), the question was angrily answered in the negative. "Let it stay as it is! What if they think that I shaved on purpose to...? They certainly would think so! Not on any account!"

"And... the worst of it was he was so coarse, so dirty, he had the manners of a pothouse; and... and even admitting that he knew he had some of the essentials of a gentleman... what was there in that to be proud of? Everyone ought to be a gentleman and more than that... and all the same (he remembered) he, too, had done little things... not exactly dishonest, and yet.... And what thoughts he sometimes had; hm... and to set all that beside Avdotya Romanovna! Confound it! So

115

be it! Well, he'd make a point then of being dirty, greasy, pothouse in his manners and he wouldn't care! He'd be worse!"

He was engaged in such monologues when Zossimov, who had spent the night in Praskovya Pavlovna's parlour, came in.

He was going home and was in a hurry to look at the invalid first. Razumihin informed him that Raskolnikov was sleeping like a dormouse. Zossimov gave orders that they shouldn't wake him and promised to see him again about eleven.

"If he is still at home," he added. "Damn it all! If one can't control one's patients, how is one to cure them? Do you know whether *he* will go to them, or whether *they* are coming here?"

"They are coming, I think," said Razumihin, understanding the object of the question, "and they will discuss their family affairs, no doubt. I'll be off. You, as the doctor, have more right to be here than I."

"But I am not a father confessor; I shall come and go away; I've plenty to do besides looking after them."

"One thing worries me," interposed Razumihin, frowning. "On the way home I talked a lot of drunken nonsense to him... all sorts of things... and amongst them that you were afraid that he... might become insane."

"You told the ladies so, too."

"I know it was stupid! You may beat me if you like! Did you think so seriously?"

"That's nonsense, I tell you, how could I think it seriously? You, yourself, described him as a monomaniac when you fetched me to him... and we added fuel to the fire yesterday, you did, that is, with your story about the painter; it was a nice conversation, when he was, perhaps, mad on that very point! If only I'd known what happened then at the police station and that some wretch... had insulted him with this suspicion! Hm... I would not have allowed that conversation yesterday. These monomaniacs will make a mountain out of a molehill... and see their fancies as solid realities.... As far as I remember, it was Zametov's story that cleared up half the mystery, to my mind. Why, I know one case in which a hypochondriac, a man of forty, cut the throat of a little boy of eight, because he couldn't endure the jokes he made every day at table! And in this case his rags, the insolent police officer, the fever and this suspicion! All that working upon a man half frantic with hypochondria, and with his morbid exceptional vanity! That may well have been the starting-point of illness. Well, bother it all!... And, by the way, that Zametov certainly is a nice fellow, but hm... he shouldn't have told all that last night. He is an awful chatterbox!"

"But whom did he tell it to? You and me?"

"And Porfiry."

"What does that matter?"

"And, by the way, have you any influence on them, his mother and sister? Tell them to be more careful with him today...."

"They'll get on all right!" Razumihin answered reluctantly.

"Why is he so set against this Luzhin? A man with money and she doesn't seem to dislike him... and they haven't a farthing, I suppose? eh?"

"But what business is it of yours?" Razumihin cried with annoyance. "How can I tell whether they've a farthing? Ask them yourself and perhaps you'll find out...."

"Foo! what an ass you are sometimes! Last night's wine has not gone off yet.... Goodbye; thank your Praskovya Pavlovna from me for my night's lodging. She locked herself in, made no reply to my bonjour through the door; she was up at seven o'clock, the samovar was taken into her from the kitchen. I was not vouchsafed a personal interview...."

At nine o'clock precisely Razumihin reached the lodgings at Bakaleyev's house. Both ladies were waiting for him with nervous impatience. They had risen at seven o'clock or earlier. He entered looking as black as night, bowed awkwardly and was at once furious with himself for it. He had reckoned without his host: Pulcheria Alexandrovna fairly rushed at him, seized him by both hands and was almost kissing them. He glanced timidly at Avdotya Romanovna, but her proud countenance wore at that moment an expression of such gratitude and friendliness, such complete and unlooked-for respect (in place of the sneering looks and ill-disguised contempt he had expected), that it threw him into greater confusion than if he had been met with abuse. Fortunately there was a subject for conversation, and he made haste to snatch at it.

Hearing that everything was going well and that Rodya had not yet waked, Pulcheria Alexandrovna declared that she was glad to hear it, because "she had something which it was very, very necessary to talk over beforehand." Then followed an inquiry about breakfast and an invitation to have it with them; they had waited to have it with him. Avdotya Romanovna rang the bell: it was answered by a ragged dirty waiter, and they asked him to bring tea which was served at last, but in such a dirty and disorderly way that the ladies were ashamed. Razumihin vigorously attacked the lodgings, but, remembering Luzhin, stopped in embarrassment and was greatly relieved by Pulcheria Alexandrovna's questions, which showered in a continual stream upon him.

He talked for three quarters of an hour, being constantly interrupted by their questions, and succeeded in describing to them all the most important facts he knew of the last year of Raskolnikov's life, concluding with a circumstantial account of his illness. He omitted, however, many things, which were better omitted, including the scene at the police station with all its consequences. They listened eagerly to his story, and, when he thought he had finished and satisfied his listeners, he found that they considered he had hardly begun.

"Tell me, tell me! What do you think…? Excuse me, I still don't know your name!" Pulcheria Alexandrovna put in hastily.

"Dmitri Prokofitch."

"I should like very, very much to know, Dmitri Prokofitch… how he looks… on things in general now, that is, how can I explain, what are his likes and dislikes? Is he always so irritable? Tell me, if you can, what are his hopes and, so to say, his dreams? Under what influences is he now? In a word, I should like…"

"Ah, mother, how can he answer all that at once?" observed Dounia.

"Good heavens, I had not expected to find him in the least like this, Dmitri Prokofitch!"

"Naturally," answered Razumihin. "I have no mother, but my uncle comes every year and almost every time he can scarcely recognise me, even in appearance, though he is a clever man; and your three years' separation means a great deal. What am I to tell you? I have known Rodion for a year and a half; he is morose, gloomy, proud and haughty, and of late—and perhaps for a long time before—he has been suspicious and fanciful. He has a noble nature and a kind heart. He does not like showing his feelings and would rather do a cruel thing than open his heart freely. Sometimes, though, he is not at all morbid, but simply cold and inhumanly callous; it's as though he were alternating between two characters. Sometimes he is fearfully reserved! He says he is so busy that everything is a hindrance, and yet he lies in bed doing nothing. He doesn't jeer at things, not because he hasn't the wit, but as though he hadn't time to waste on such trifles. He never listens to what is said to him. He is never interested in what interests other people at any given moment. He thinks very highly of himself and perhaps he is right. Well, what more? I think your arrival will have a most beneficial influence upon him."

"God grant it may," cried Pulcheria Alexandrovna, distressed by Razumihin's account of her Rodya.

And Razumihin ventured to look more boldly at Avdotya Romanovna at last. He glanced at her often while he was talking, but only for a moment and looked away again at once. Avdotya Romanovna sat at the table, listening attentively, then got up again and began walking to and fro with her arms folded and her lips compressed, occasionally putting in a question, without stopping her walk. She had the same habit of not listening to what was said. She was wearing a dress of thin dark stuff and she had a white transparent scarf round her neck. Razumihin soon detected signs of extreme poverty in their belongings. Had Avdotya Romanovna been dressed like a queen, he felt that he would not be afraid of her, but perhaps just because she was poorly dressed and that he noticed all the misery of her surroundings, his heart was filled with dread and he began to be afraid of every word he uttered, every gesture he made, which was very trying for a man who already felt diffident.

"You've told us a great deal that is interesting about my brother's character… and have told it impartially. I am glad. I thought that you were too uncritically devoted to him," observed Avdotya

Romanovna with a smile. "I think you are right that he needs a woman's care," she added thoughtfully.

"I didn't say so; but I daresay you are right, only…"

"What?"

"He loves no one and perhaps he never will," Razumihin declared decisively.

"You mean he is not capable of love?"

"Do you know, Avdotya Romanovna, you are awfully like your brother, in everything, indeed!" he blurted out suddenly to his own surprise, but remembering at once what he had just before said of her brother, he turned as red as a crab and was overcome with confusion. Avdotya Romanovna couldn't help laughing when she looked at him.

"You may both be mistaken about Rodya," Pulcheria Alexandrovna remarked, slightly piqued. "I am not talking of our present difficulty, Dounia. What Pyotr Petrovitch writes in this letter and what you and I have supposed may be mistaken, but you can't imagine, Dmitri Prokofitch, how moody and, so to say, capricious he is. I never could depend on what he would do when he was only fifteen. And I am sure that he might do something now that nobody else would think of doing… Well, for instance, do you know how a year and a half ago he astounded me and gave me a shock that nearly killed me, when he had the idea of marrying that girl—what was her name—his landlady's daughter?"

"Did you hear about that affair?" asked Avdotya Romanovna.

"Do you suppose—" Pulcheria Alexandrovna continued warmly. "Do you suppose that my tears, my entreaties, my illness, my possible death from grief, our poverty would have made him pause? No, he would calmly have disregarded all obstacles. And yet it isn't that he doesn't love us!"

"He has never spoken a word of that affair to me," Razumihin answered cautiously. "But I did hear something from Praskovya Pavlovna herself, though she is by no means a gossip. And what I heard certainly was rather strange."

"And what did you hear?" both the ladies asked at once.

"Well, nothing very special. I only learned that the marriage, which only failed to take place through the girl's death, was not at all to Praskovya Pavlovna's liking. They say, too, the girl was not at all pretty, in fact I am told positively ugly… and such an invalid… and queer. But she seems to have had some good qualities. She must have had some good qualities or it's quite inexplicable…. She had no money either and he wouldn't have considered her money…. But it's always difficult to judge in such matters."

"I am sure she was a good girl," Avdotya Romanovna observed briefly.

"God forgive me, I simply rejoiced at her death. Though I don't know which of them would have caused most misery to the other—he to her or she to him," Pulcheria Alexandrovna concluded. Then she began tentatively questioning him about the scene on the previous day with Luzhin, hesitating and continually glancing at Dounia, obviously to the latter's annoyance. This incident more than all the rest evidently caused her uneasiness, even consternation. Razumihin described it in detail again, but this time he added his own conclusions: he openly blamed Raskolnikov for intentionally insulting Pyotr Petrovitch, not seeking to excuse him on the score of his illness.

"He had planned it before his illness," he added.

"I think so, too," Pulcheria Alexandrovna agreed with a dejected air. But she was very much surprised at hearing Razumihin express himself so carefully and even with a certain respect about Pyotr Petrovitch. Avdotya Romanovna, too, was struck by it.

"So this is your opinion of Pyotr Petrovitch?" Pulcheria Alexandrovna could not resist asking.

"I can have no other opinion of your daughter's future husband," Razumihin answered firmly and with warmth, "and I don't say it simply from vulgar politeness, but because… simply because Avdotya Romanovna has of her own free will deigned to accept this man. If I spoke so rudely of him last night, it was because I was disgustingly drunk and… mad besides; yes, mad, crazy, I lost my head completely… and this morning I am ashamed of it."

118

He crimsoned and ceased speaking. Avdotya Romanovna flushed, but did not break the silence. She had not uttered a word from the moment they began to speak of Luzhin.

Without her support Pulcheria Alexandrovna obviously did not know what to do. At last, faltering and continually glancing at her daughter, she confessed that she was exceedingly worried by one circumstance.

"You see, Dmitri Prokofitch," she began. "I'll be perfectly open with Dmitri Prokofitch, Dounia?"

"Of course, mother," said Avdotya Romanovna emphatically.

"This is what it is," she began in haste, as though the permission to speak of her trouble lifted a weight off her mind. "Very early this morning we got a note from Pyotr Petrovitch in reply to our letter announcing our arrival. He promised to meet us at the station, you know; instead of that he sent a servant to bring us the address of these lodgings and to show us the way; and he sent a message that he would be here himself this morning. But this morning this note came from him. You'd better read it yourself; there is one point in it which worries me very much... you will soon see what that is, and... tell me your candid opinion, Dmitri Prokofitch! You know Rodya's character better than anyone and no one can advise us better than you can. Dounia, I must tell you, made her decision at once, but I still don't feel sure how to act and I... I've been waiting for your opinion."

Razumihin opened the note which was dated the previous evening and read as follows:

"DEAR MADAM, PULCHERIA ALEXANDROVNA, I have the honour to inform you that owing to unforeseen obstacles I was rendered unable to meet you at the railway station; I sent a very competent person with the same object in view. I likewise shall be deprived of the honour of an interview with you tomorrow morning by business in the Senate that does not admit of delay, and also that I may not intrude on your family circle while you are meeting your son, and Avdotya Romanovna her brother. I shall have the honour of visiting you and paying you my respects at your lodgings not later than tomorrow evening at eight o'clock precisely, and herewith I venture to present my earnest and, I may add, imperative request that Rodion Romanovitch may not be present at our interview—as he offered me a gross and unprecedented affront on the occasion of my visit to him in his illness yesterday, and, moreover, since I desire from you personally an indispensable and circumstantial explanation upon a certain point, in regard to which I wish to learn your own interpretation. I have the honour to inform you, in anticipation, that if, in spite of my request, I meet Rodion Romanovitch, I shall be compelled to withdraw immediately and then you have only yourself to blame. I write on the assumption that Rodion Romanovitch who appeared so ill at my visit, suddenly recovered two hours later and so, being able to leave the house, may visit you also. I was confirmed in that belief by the testimony of my own eyes in the lodging of a drunken man who was run over and has since died, to whose daughter, a young woman of notorious behaviour, he gave twenty-five roubles on the pretext of the funeral, which gravely surprised me knowing what pains you were at to raise that sum. Herewith expressing my special respect to your estimable daughter, Avdotya Romanovna, I beg you to accept the respectful homage of

"Your humble servant,
"P. LUZHIN."

"What am I to do now, Dmitri Prokofitch?" began Pulcheria Alexandrovna, almost weeping. "How can I ask Rodya not to come? Yesterday he insisted so earnestly on our refusing Pyotr Petrovitch and now we are ordered not to receive Rodya! He will come on purpose if he knows, and... what will happen then?"

"Act on Avdotya Romanovna's decision," Razumihin answered calmly at once.

"Oh, dear me! She says... goodness knows what she says, she doesn't explain her object! She says that it would be best, at least, not that it would be best, but that it's absolutely necessary that Rodya should make a point of being here at eight o'clock and that they must meet.... I didn't want even to show him the letter, but to prevent him from coming by some stratagem with your help... because he is so irritable.... Besides I don't understand about that drunkard who died and that daughter, and how he could have given the daughter all the money... which..."

"Which cost you such sacrifice, mother," put in Avdotya Romanovna.

"He was not himself yesterday," Razumihin said thoughtfully, "if you only knew what he was up to in a restaurant yesterday, though there was sense in it too.... Hm! He did say something, as we were going home yesterday evening, about a dead man and a girl, but I didn't understand a word.... But last night, I myself..."

"The best thing, mother, will be for us to go to him ourselves and there I assure you we shall see at once what's to be done. Besides, it's getting late—good heavens, it's past ten," she cried looking at a splendid gold enamelled watch which hung round her neck on a thin Venetian chain, and looked entirely out of keeping with the rest of her dress. "A present from her fiancé," thought Razumihin.

"We must start, Dounia, we must start," her mother cried in a flutter. "He will be thinking we are still angry after yesterday, from our coming so late. Merciful heavens!"

While she said this she was hurriedly putting on her hat and mantle; Dounia, too, put on her things. Her gloves, as Razumihin noticed, were not merely shabby but had holes in them, and yet this evident poverty gave the two ladies an air of special dignity, which is always found in people who know how to wear poor clothes. Razumihin looked reverently at Dounia and felt proud of escorting her. "The queen who mended her stockings in prison," he thought, "must have looked then every inch a queen and even more a queen than at sumptuous banquets and *levées*."

"My God!" exclaimed Pulcheria Alexandrovna, "little did I think that I should ever fear seeing my son, my darling, darling Rodya! I am afraid, Dmitri Prokofitch," she added, glancing at him timidly.

"Don't be afraid, mother," said Dounia, kissing her, "better have faith in him."

"Oh, dear, I have faith in him, but I haven't slept all night," exclaimed the poor woman.

They came out into the street.

"Do you know, Dounia, when I dozed a little this morning I dreamed of Marfa Petrovna... she was all in white... she came up to me, took my hand, and shook her head at me, but so sternly as though she were blaming me.... Is that a good omen? Oh, dear me! You don't know, Dmitri Prokofitch, that Marfa Petrovna's dead!"

"No, I didn't know; who is Marfa Petrovna?"

"She died suddenly; and only fancy..."

"Afterwards, mamma," put in Dounia. "He doesn't know who Marfa Petrovna is."

"Ah, you don't know? And I was thinking that you knew all about us. Forgive me, Dmitri Prokofitch, I don't know what I am thinking about these last few days. I look upon you really as a providence for us, and so I took it for granted that you knew all about us. I look on you as a relation.... Don't be angry with me for saying so. Dear me, what's the matter with your right hand? Have you knocked it?"

"Yes, I bruised it," muttered Razumihin overjoyed.

"I sometimes speak too much from the heart, so that Dounia finds fault with me.... But, dear me, what a cupboard he lives in! I wonder whether he is awake? Does this woman, his landlady, consider it a room? Listen, you say he does not like to show his feelings, so perhaps I shall annoy him with my... weaknesses? Do advise me, Dmitri Prokofitch, how am I to treat him? I feel quite distracted, you know."

"Don't question him too much about anything if you see him frown; don't ask him too much about his health; he doesn't like that."

"Ah, Dmitri Prokofitch, how hard it is to be a mother! But here are the stairs.... What an awful staircase!"

"Mother, you are quite pale, don't distress yourself, darling," said Dounia caressing her, then with flashing eyes she added: "He ought to be happy at seeing you, and you are tormenting yourself so."

"Wait, I'll peep in and see whether he has waked up."

The ladies slowly followed Razumihin, who went on before, and when they reached the landlady's door on the fourth storey, they noticed that her door was a tiny crack open and that two keen black eyes were watching them from the darkness within. When their eyes met, the door was suddenly shut with such a slam that Pulcheria Alexandrovna almost cried out.

III

"He is well, quite well!" Zossimov cried cheerfully as they entered.

He had come in ten minutes earlier and was sitting in the same place as before, on the sofa. Raskolnikov was sitting in the opposite corner, fully dressed and carefully washed and combed, as he had not been for some time past. The room was immediately crowded, yet Nastasya managed to follow the visitors in and stayed to listen.

Raskolnikov really was almost well, as compared with his condition the day before, but he was still pale, listless, and sombre. He looked like a wounded man or one who has undergone some terrible physical suffering. His brows were knitted, his lips compressed, his eyes feverish. He spoke little and reluctantly, as though performing a duty, and there was a restlessness in his movements.

He only wanted a sling on his arm or a bandage on his finger to complete the impression of a man with a painful abscess or a broken arm. The pale, sombre face lighted up for a moment when his mother and sister entered, but this only gave it a look of more intense suffering, in place of its listless dejection. The light soon died away, but the look of suffering remained, and Zossimov, watching and studying his patient with all the zest of a young doctor beginning to practise, noticed in him no joy at the arrival of his mother and sister, but a sort of bitter, hidden determination to bear another hour or two of inevitable torture. He saw later that almost every word of the following conversation seemed to touch on some sore place and irritate it. But at the same time he marvelled at the power of controlling himself and hiding his feelings in a patient who the previous day had, like a monomaniac, fallen into a frenzy at the slightest word.

"Yes, I see myself now that I am almost well," said Raskolnikov, giving his mother and sister a kiss of welcome which made Pulcheria Alexandrovna radiant at once. "And I don't say this *as I did yesterday*," he said, addressing Razumihin, with a friendly pressure of his hand.

"Yes, indeed, I am quite surprised at him today," began Zossimov, much delighted at the ladies' entrance, for he had not succeeded in keeping up a conversation with his patient for ten minutes. "In another three or four days, if he goes on like this, he will be just as before, that is, as he was a month ago, or two... or perhaps even three. This has been coming on for a long while... eh? Confess, now, that it has been perhaps your own fault?" he added, with a tentative smile, as though still afraid of irritating him.

"It is very possible," answered Raskolnikov coldly.

"I should say, too," continued Zossimov with zest, "that your complete recovery depends solely on yourself. Now that one can talk to you, I should like to impress upon you that it is essential to avoid the elementary, so to speak, fundamental causes tending to produce your morbid condition: in that case you will be cured, if not, it will go from bad to worse. These fundamental causes I don't know, but they must be known to you. You are an intelligent man, and must have observed yourself, of course. I fancy the first stage of your derangement coincides with your leaving the university. You must not be left without occupation, and so, work and a definite aim set before you might, I fancy, be very beneficial."

"Yes, yes; you are perfectly right.... I will make haste and return to the university: and then everything will go smoothly...."

Zossimov, who had begun his sage advice partly to make an effect before the ladies, was certainly somewhat mystified, when, glancing at his patient, he observed unmistakable mockery on his face. This lasted an instant, however. Pulcheria Alexandrovna began at once thanking Zossimov, especially for his visit to their lodging the previous night.

"What! he saw you last night?" Raskolnikov asked, as though startled. "Then you have not slept either after your journey."

"Ach, Rodya, that was only till two o'clock. Dounia and I never go to bed before two at home."

"I don't know how to thank him either," Raskolnikov went on, suddenly frowning and looking down. "Setting aside the question of payment—forgive me for referring to it (he turned to Zossimov)—I really don't know what I have done to deserve such special attention from you! I simply don't understand it… and… and… it weighs upon me, indeed, because I don't understand it. I tell you so candidly."

"Don't be irritated." Zossimov forced himself to laugh. "Assume that you are my first patient—well—we fellows just beginning to practise love our first patients as if they were our children, and some almost fall in love with them. And, of course, I am not rich in patients."

"I say nothing about him," added Raskolnikov, pointing to Razumihin, "though he has had nothing from me either but insult and trouble."

"What nonsense he is talking! Why, you are in a sentimental mood today, are you?" shouted Razumihin.

If he had had more penetration he would have seen that there was no trace of sentimentality in him, but something indeed quite the opposite. But Avdotya Romanovna noticed it. She was intently and uneasily watching her brother.

"As for you, mother, I don't dare to speak," he went on, as though repeating a lesson learned by heart. "It is only today that I have been able to realise a little how distressed you must have been here yesterday, waiting for me to come back."

When he had said this, he suddenly held out his hand to his sister, smiling without a word. But in this smile there was a flash of real unfeigned feeling. Dounia caught it at once, and warmly pressed his hand, overjoyed and thankful. It was the first time he had addressed her since their dispute the previous day. The mother's face lighted up with ecstatic happiness at the sight of this conclusive unspoken reconciliation. "Yes, that is what I love him for," Razumihin, exaggerating it all, muttered to himself, with a vigorous turn in his chair. "He has these movements."

"And how well he does it all," the mother was thinking to herself. "What generous impulses he has, and how simply, how delicately he put an end to all the misunderstanding with his sister—simply by holding out his hand at the right minute and looking at her like that…. And what fine eyes he has, and how fine his whole face is!… He is even better looking than Dounia…. But, good heavens, what a suit—how terribly he's dressed!… Vasya, the messenger boy in Afanasy Ivanitch's shop, is better dressed! I could rush at him and hug him… weep over him—but I am afraid…. Oh, dear, he's so strange! He's talking kindly, but I'm afraid! Why, what am I afraid of?…"

"Oh, Rodya, you wouldn't believe," she began suddenly, in haste to answer his words to her, "how unhappy Dounia and I were yesterday! Now that it's all over and done with and we are quite happy again—I can tell you. Fancy, we ran here almost straight from the train to embrace you and that woman—ah, here she is! Good morning, Nastasya!… She told us at once that you were lying in a high fever and had just run away from the doctor in delirium, and they were looking for you in the streets. You can't imagine how we felt! I couldn't help thinking of the tragic end of Lieutenant Potanchikov, a friend of your father's—you can't remember him, Rodya—who ran out in the same way in a high fever and fell into the well in the courtyard and they couldn't pull him out till next day. Of course, we exaggerated things. We were on the point of rushing to find Pyotr Petrovitch to ask him to help…. Because we were alone, utterly alone," she said plaintively and stopped short, suddenly, recollecting it was still somewhat dangerous to speak of Pyotr Petrovitch, although "we are quite happy again."

"Yes, yes…. Of course it's very annoying…." Raskolnikov muttered in reply, but with such a preoccupied and inattentive air that Dounia gazed at him in perplexity.

"What else was it I wanted to say?" He went on trying to recollect. "Oh, yes; mother, and you too, Dounia, please don't think that I didn't mean to come and see you today and was waiting for you to come first."

"What are you saying, Rodya?" cried Pulcheria Alexandrovna. She, too, was surprised.

"Is he answering us as a duty?" Dounia wondered. "Is he being reconciled and asking forgiveness as though he were performing a rite or repeating a lesson?"

"I've only just waked up, and wanted to go to you, but was delayed owing to my clothes; I forgot yesterday to ask her... Nastasya... to wash out the blood... I've only just dressed."

"Blood! What blood?" Pulcheria Alexandrovna asked in alarm.

"Oh, nothing—don't be uneasy. It was when I was wandering about yesterday, rather delirious, I chanced upon a man who had been run over... a clerk..."

"Delirious? But you remember everything!" Razumihin interrupted.

"That's true," Raskolnikov answered with special carefulness. "I remember everything even to the slightest detail, and yet—why I did that and went there and said that, I can't clearly explain now."

"A familiar phenomenon," interposed Zossimov, "actions are sometimes performed in a masterly and most cunning way, while the direction of the actions is deranged and dependent on various morbid impressions—it's like a dream."

"Perhaps it's a good thing really that he should think me almost a madman," thought Raskolnikov.

"Why, people in perfect health act in the same way too," observed Dounia, looking uneasily at Zossimov.

"There is some truth in your observation," the latter replied. "In that sense we are certainly all not infrequently like madmen, but with the slight difference that the deranged are somewhat madder, for we must draw a line. A normal man, it is true, hardly exists. Among dozens—perhaps hundreds of thousands—hardly one is to be met with."

At the word "madman," carelessly dropped by Zossimov in his chatter on his favourite subject, everyone frowned.

Raskolnikov sat seeming not to pay attention, plunged in thought with a strange smile on his pale lips. He was still meditating on something.

"Well, what about the man who was run over? I interrupted you!" Razumihin cried hastily.

"What?" Raskolnikov seemed to wake up. "Oh... I got spattered with blood helping to carry him to his lodging. By the way, mamma, I did an unpardonable thing yesterday. I was literally out of my mind. I gave away all the money you sent me... to his wife for the funeral. She's a widow now, in consumption, a poor creature... three little children, starving... nothing in the house... there's a daughter, too... perhaps you'd have given it yourself if you'd seen them. But I had no right to do it I admit, especially as I knew how you needed the money yourself. To help others one must have the right to do it, or else *Crevez, chiens, si vous n'êtes pas contents.*" He laughed, "That's right, isn't it, Dounia?"

"No, it's not," answered Dounia firmly.

"Bah! you, too, have ideals," he muttered, looking at her almost with hatred, and smiling sarcastically. "I ought to have considered that.... Well, that's praiseworthy, and it's better for you... and if you reach a line you won't overstep, you will be unhappy... and if you overstep it, maybe you will be still unhappier.... But all that's nonsense," he added irritably, vexed at being carried away. "I only meant to say that I beg your forgiveness, mother," he concluded, shortly and abruptly.

"That's enough, Rodya, I am sure that everything you do is very good," said his mother, delighted.

"Don't be too sure," he answered, twisting his mouth into a smile.

A silence followed. There was a certain constraint in all this conversation, and in the silence, and in the reconciliation, and in the forgiveness, and all were feeling it.

"It is as though they were afraid of me," Raskolnikov was thinking to himself, looking askance at his mother and sister. Pulcheria Alexandrovna was indeed growing more timid the longer she kept silent.

"Yet in their absence I seemed to love them so much," flashed through his mind.

"Do you know, Rodya, Marfa Petrovna is dead," Pulcheria Alexandrovna suddenly blurted out.

"What Marfa Petrovna?"

"Oh, mercy on us—Marfa Petrovna Svidrigaïlov. I wrote you so much about her."

"A-a-h! Yes, I remember.... So she's dead! Oh, really?" he roused himself suddenly, as if waking up. "What did she die of?"

"Only imagine, quite suddenly," Pulcheria Alexandrovna answered hurriedly, encouraged by his curiosity. "On the very day I was sending you that letter! Would you believe it, that awful man seems to have been the cause of her death. They say he beat her dreadfully."

"Why, were they on such bad terms?" he asked, addressing his sister.

"Not at all. Quite the contrary indeed. With her, he was always very patient, considerate even. In fact, all those seven years of their married life he gave way to her, too much so indeed, in many cases. All of a sudden he seems to have lost patience."

"Then he could not have been so awful if he controlled himself for seven years? You seem to be defending him, Dounia?"

"No, no, he's an awful man! I can imagine nothing more awful!" Dounia answered, almost with a shudder, knitting her brows, and sinking into thought.

"That had happened in the morning," Pulcheria Alexandrovna went on hurriedly. "And directly afterwards she ordered the horses to be harnessed to drive to the town immediately after dinner. She always used to drive to the town in such cases. She ate a very good dinner, I am told...."

"After the beating?"

"That was always her... habit; and immediately after dinner, so as not to be late in starting, she went to the bathhouse.... You see, she was undergoing some treatment with baths. They have a cold spring there, and she used to bathe in it regularly every day, and no sooner had she got into the water when she suddenly had a stroke!"

"I should think so," said Zossimov.

"And did he beat her badly?"

"What does that matter!" put in Dounia.

"H'm! But I don't know why you want to tell us such gossip, mother," said Raskolnikov irritably, as it were in spite of himself.

"Ah, my dear, I don't know what to talk about," broke from Pulcheria Alexandrovna.

"Why, are you all afraid of me?" he asked, with a constrained smile.

"That's certainly true," said Dounia, looking directly and sternly at her brother. "Mother was crossing herself with terror as she came up the stairs."

His face worked, as though in convulsion.

"Ach, what are you saying, Dounia! Don't be angry, please, Rodya.... Why did you say that, Dounia?" Pulcheria Alexandrovna began, overwhelmed—"You see, coming here, I was dreaming all the way, in the train, how we should meet, how we should talk over everything together.... And I was so happy, I did not notice the journey! But what am I saying? I am happy now.... You should not, Dounia.... I am happy now—simply in seeing you, Rodya...."

"Hush, mother," he muttered in confusion, not looking at her, but pressing her hand. "We shall have time to speak freely of everything!"

As he said this, he was suddenly overwhelmed with confusion and turned pale. Again that awful sensation he had known of late passed with deadly chill over his soul. Again it became suddenly plain and perceptible to him that he had just told a fearful lie—that he would never now be able to speak freely of everything—that he would never again be able to *speak* of anything to anyone. The anguish of this thought was such that for a moment he almost forgot himself. He got up from his seat, and not looking at anyone walked towards the door.

"What are you about?" cried Razumihin, clutching him by the arm.

He sat down again, and began looking about him, in silence. They were all looking at him in perplexity.

"But what are you all so dull for?" he shouted, suddenly and quite unexpectedly. "Do say something! What's the use of sitting like this? Come, do speak. Let us talk.... We meet together and sit in silence.... Come, anything!"

"Thank God; I was afraid the same thing as yesterday was beginning again," said Pulcheria Alexandrovna, crossing herself.

125

"What is the matter, Rodya?" asked Avdotya Romanovna, distrustfully.

"Oh, nothing! I remembered something," he answered, and suddenly laughed.

"Well, if you remembered something; that's all right!... I was beginning to think..." muttered Zossimov, getting up from the sofa. "It is time for me to be off. I will look in again perhaps... if I can..." He made his bows, and went out.

"What an excellent man!" observed Pulcheria Alexandrovna.

"Yes, excellent, splendid, well-educated, intelligent," Raskolnikov began, suddenly speaking with surprising rapidity, and a liveliness he had not shown till then. "I can't remember where I met him before my illness.... I believe I have met him somewhere—... And this is a good man, too," he nodded at Razumihin. "Do you like him, Dounia?" he asked her; and suddenly, for some unknown reason, laughed.

"Very much," answered Dounia.

"Foo!—what a pig you are!" Razumihin protested, blushing in terrible confusion, and he got up from his chair. Pulcheria Alexandrovna smiled faintly, but Raskolnikov laughed aloud.

"Where are you off to?"

"I must go."

"You need not at all. Stay. Zossimov has gone, so you must. Don't go. What's the time? Is it twelve o'clock? What a pretty watch you have got, Dounia. But why are you all silent again? I do all the talking."

"It was a present from Marfa Petrovna," answered Dounia.

"And a very expensive one!" added Pulcheria Alexandrovna.

"A-ah! What a big one! Hardly like a lady's."

"I like that sort," said Dounia.

"So it is not a present from her fiancé," thought Razumihin, and was unreasonably delighted.

"I thought it was Luzhin's present," observed Raskolnikov.

"No, he has not made Dounia any presents yet."

"A-ah! And do you remember, mother, I was in love and wanted to get married?" he said suddenly, looking at his mother, who was disconcerted by the sudden change of subject and the way he spoke of it.

"Oh, yes, my dear."

Pulcheria Alexandrovna exchanged glances with Dounia and Razumihin.

"H'm, yes. What shall I tell you? I don't remember much indeed. She was such a sickly girl," he went on, growing dreamy and looking down again. "Quite an invalid. She was fond of giving alms to the poor, and was always dreaming of a nunnery, and once she burst into tears when she began talking to me about it. Yes, yes, I remember. I remember very well. She was an ugly little thing. I really don't know what drew me to her then—I think it was because she was always ill. If she had been lame or hunchback, I believe I should have liked her better still," he smiled dreamily. "Yes, it was a sort of spring delirium."

"No, it was not only spring delirium," said Dounia, with warm feeling.

He fixed a strained intent look on his sister, but did not hear or did not understand her words. Then, completely lost in thought, he got up, went up to his mother, kissed her, went back to his place and sat down.

"You love her even now?" said Pulcheria Alexandrovna, touched.

"Her? Now? Oh, yes.... You ask about her? No... that's all now, as it were, in another world... and so long ago. And indeed everything happening here seems somehow far away." He looked attentively at them. "You, now... I seem to be looking at you from a thousand miles away... but, goodness knows why we are talking of that! And what's the use of asking about it?" he added with annoyance, and biting his nails, fell into dreamy silence again.

"What a wretched lodging you have, Rodya! It's like a tomb," said Pulcheria Alexandrovna, suddenly breaking the oppressive silence. "I am sure it's quite half through your lodging you have become so melancholy."

"My lodging," he answered, listlessly. "Yes, the lodging had a great deal to do with it.... I thought that, too.... If only you knew, though, what a strange thing you said just now, mother," he said, laughing strangely.

A little more, and their companionship, this mother and this sister, with him after three years' absence, this intimate tone of conversation, in face of the utter impossibility of really speaking about anything, would have been beyond his power of endurance. But there was one urgent matter which must be settled one way or the other that day—so he had decided when he woke. Now he was glad to remember it, as a means of escape.

"Listen, Dounia," he began, gravely and drily, "of course I beg your pardon for yesterday, but I consider it my duty to tell you again that I do not withdraw from my chief point. It is me or Luzhin. If I am a scoundrel, you must not be. One is enough. If you marry Luzhin, I cease at once to look on you as a sister."

"Rodya, Rodya! It is the same as yesterday again," Pulcheria Alexandrovna cried, mournfully. "And why do you call yourself a scoundrel? I can't bear it. You said the same yesterday."

"Brother," Dounia answered firmly and with the same dryness. "In all this there is a mistake on your part. I thought it over at night, and found out the mistake. It is all because you seem to fancy I am sacrificing myself to someone and for someone. That is not the case at all. I am simply marrying for my own sake, because things are hard for me. Though, of course, I shall be glad if I succeed in being useful to my family. But that is not the chief motive for my decision...."

"She is lying," he thought to himself, biting his nails vindictively. "Proud creature! She won't admit she wants to do it out of charity! Too haughty! Oh, base characters! They even love as though they hate.... Oh, how I... hate them all!"

"In fact," continued Dounia, "I am marrying Pyotr Petrovitch because of two evils I choose the less. I intend to do honestly all he expects of me, so I am not deceiving him.... Why did you smile just now?" She, too, flushed, and there was a gleam of anger in her eyes.

"All?" he asked, with a malignant grin.

"Within certain limits. Both the manner and form of Pyotr Petrovitch's courtship showed me at once what he wanted. He may, of course, think too well of himself, but I hope he esteems me, too.... Why are you laughing again?"

"And why are you blushing again? You are lying, sister. You are intentionally lying, simply from feminine obstinacy, simply to hold your own against me.... You cannot respect Luzhin. I have seen him and talked with him. So you are selling yourself for money, and so in any case you are acting basely, and I am glad at least that you can blush for it."

"It is not true. I am not lying," cried Dounia, losing her composure. "I would not marry him if I were not convinced that he esteems me and thinks highly of me. I would not marry him if I were not firmly convinced that I can respect him. Fortunately, I can have convincing proof of it this very day... and such a marriage is not a vileness, as you say! And even if you were right, if I really had determined on a vile action, is it not merciless on your part to speak to me like that? Why do you demand of me a heroism that perhaps you have not either? It is despotism; it is tyranny. If I ruin anyone, it is only myself.... I am not committing a murder. Why do you look at me like that? Why are you so pale? Rodya, darling, what's the matter?"

"Good heavens! You have made him faint," cried Pulcheria Alexandrovna.

"No, no, nonsense! It's nothing. A little giddiness—not fainting. You have fainting on the brain. H'm, yes, what was I saying? Oh, yes. In what way will you get convincing proof today that you can respect him, and that he... esteems you, as you said. I think you said today?"

"Mother, show Rodya Pyotr Petrovitch's letter," said Dounia.

With trembling hands, Pulcheria Alexandrovna gave him the letter. He took it with great interest, but, before opening it, he suddenly looked with a sort of wonder at Dounia.

"It is strange," he said, slowly, as though struck by a new idea. "What am I making such a fuss for? What is it all about? Marry whom you like!"

He said this as though to himself, but said it aloud, and looked for some time at his sister, as though puzzled. He opened the letter at last, still with the same look of strange wonder on his face.

127

Then, slowly and attentively, he began reading, and read it through twice. Pulcheria Alexandrovna showed marked anxiety, and all indeed expected something particular.

"What surprises me," he began, after a short pause, handing the letter to his mother, but not addressing anyone in particular, "is that he is a business man, a lawyer, and his conversation is pretentious indeed, and yet he writes such an uneducated letter."

They all started. They had expected something quite different.

"But they all write like that, you know," Razumihin observed, abruptly.

"Have you read it?"

"Yes."

"We showed him, Rodya. We... consulted him just now," Pulcheria Alexandrovna began, embarrassed.

"That's just the jargon of the courts," Razumihin put in. "Legal documents are written like that to this day."

"Legal? Yes, it's just legal—business language—not so very uneducated, and not quite educated—business language!"

"Pyotr Petrovitch makes no secret of the fact that he had a cheap education, he is proud indeed of having made his own way," Avdotya Romanovna observed, somewhat offended by her brother's tone.

"Well, if he's proud of it, he has reason, I don't deny it. You seem to be offended, sister, at my making only such a frivolous criticism on the letter, and to think that I speak of such trifling matters on purpose to annoy you. It is quite the contrary, an observation apropos of the style occurred to me that is by no means irrelevant as things stand. There is one expression, 'blame yourselves,' put in very significantly and plainly, and there is besides a threat that he will go away at once if I am present. That threat to go away is equivalent to a threat to abandon you both if you are disobedient, and to abandon you now after summoning you to Petersburg. Well, what do you think? Can one resent such an expression from Luzhin, as we should if he" (he pointed to Razumihin) "had written it, or Zossimov, or one of us?"

"N-no," answered Dounia, with more animation. "I saw clearly that it was too naively expressed, and that perhaps he simply has no skill in writing... that is a true criticism, brother. I did not expect, indeed..."

"It is expressed in legal style, and sounds coarser than perhaps he intended. But I must disillusion you a little. There is one expression in the letter, one slander about me, and rather a contemptible one. I gave the money last night to the widow, a woman in consumption, crushed with trouble, and not 'on the pretext of the funeral,' but simply to pay for the funeral, and not to the daughter—a young woman, as he writes, of notorious behaviour (whom I saw last night for the first time in my life)—but to the widow. In all this I see a too hasty desire to slander me and to raise dissension between us. It is expressed again in legal jargon, that is to say, with a too obvious display of the aim, and with a very naive eagerness. He is a man of intelligence, but to act sensibly, intelligence is not enough. It all shows the man and... I don't think he has a great esteem for you. I tell you this simply to warn you, because I sincerely wish for your good..."

Dounia did not reply. Her resolution had been taken. She was only awaiting the evening.

"Then what is your decision, Rodya?" asked Pulcheria Alexandrovna, who was more uneasy than ever at the sudden, new businesslike tone of his talk.

"What decision?"

"You see Pyotr Petrovitch writes that you are not to be with us this evening, and that he will go away if you come. So will you... come?"

"That, of course, is not for me to decide, but for you first, if you are not offended by such a request; and secondly, by Dounia, if she, too, is not offended. I will do what you think best," he added, drily.

"Dounia has already decided, and I fully agree with her," Pulcheria Alexandrovna hastened to declare.

"I decided to ask you, Rodya, to urge you not to fail to be with us at this interview," said Dounia. "Will you come?"

"Yes."

"I will ask you, too, to be with us at eight o'clock," she said, addressing Razumihin. "Mother, I am inviting him, too."

"Quite right, Dounia. Well, since you have decided," added Pulcheria Alexandrovna, "so be it. I shall feel easier myself. I do not like concealment and deception. Better let us have the whole truth.... Pyotr Petrovitch may be angry or not, now!"

At that moment the door was softly opened, and a young girl walked into the room, looking timidly about her. Everyone turned towards her with surprise and curiosity. At first sight, Raskolnikov did not recognise her. It was Sofya Semyonovna Marmeladov. He had seen her yesterday for the first time, but at such a moment, in such surroundings and in such a dress, that his memory retained a very different image of her. Now she was a modestly and poorly-dressed young girl, very young, indeed, almost like a child, with a modest and refined manner, with a candid but somewhat frightened-looking face. She was wearing a very plain indoor dress, and had on a shabby old-fashioned hat, but she still carried a parasol. Unexpectedly finding the room full of people, she was not so much embarrassed as completely overwhelmed with shyness, like a little child. She was even about to retreat. "Oh... it's you!" said Raskolnikov, extremely astonished, and he, too, was confused. He at once recollected that his mother and sister knew through Luzhin's letter of "some young woman of notorious behaviour." He had only just been protesting against Luzhin's calumny and declaring that he had seen the girl last night for the first time, and suddenly she had walked in. He remembered, too, that he had not protested against the expression "of notorious behaviour." All this passed vaguely and fleetingly through his brain, but looking at her more intently, he saw that the humiliated creature was so humiliated that he felt suddenly sorry for her. When she made a movement to retreat in terror, it sent a pang to his heart.

"I did not expect you," he said, hurriedly, with a look that made her stop. "Please sit down. You come, no doubt, from Katerina Ivanovna. Allow me—not there. Sit here...."

At Sonia's entrance, Razumihin, who had been sitting on one of Raskolnikov's three chairs, close to the door, got up to allow her to enter. Raskolnikov had at first shown her the place on the sofa where Zossimov had been sitting, but feeling that the sofa which served him as a bed, was too *familiar* a place, he hurriedly motioned her to Razumihin's chair.

"You sit here," he said to Razumihin, putting him on the sofa.

Sonia sat down, almost shaking with terror, and looked timidly at the two ladies. It was evidently almost inconceivable to herself that she could sit down beside them. At the thought of it, she was so frightened that she hurriedly got up again, and in utter confusion addressed Raskolnikov.

"I... I... have come for one minute. Forgive me for disturbing you," she began falteringly. "I come from Katerina Ivanovna, and she had no one to send. Katerina Ivanovna told me to beg you... to be at the service... in the morning... at Mitrofanievsky... and then... to us... to her... to do her the honour... she told me to beg you..." Sonia stammered and ceased speaking.

"I will try, certainly, most certainly," answered Raskolnikov. He, too, stood up, and he, too, faltered and could not finish his sentence. "Please sit down," he said, suddenly. "I want to talk to you. You are perhaps in a hurry, but please, be so kind, spare me two minutes," and he drew up a chair for her.

Sonia sat down again, and again timidly she took a hurried, frightened look at the two ladies, and dropped her eyes. Raskolnikov's pale face flushed, a shudder passed over him, his eyes glowed.

"Mother," he said, firmly and insistently, "this is Sofya Semyonovna Marmeladov, the daughter of that unfortunate Mr. Marmeladov, who was run over yesterday before my eyes, and of whom I was just telling you."

Pulcheria Alexandrovna glanced at Sonia, and slightly screwed up her eyes. In spite of her embarrassment before Rodya's urgent and challenging look, she could not deny herself that satisfaction. Dounia gazed gravely and intently into the poor girl's face, and scrutinised her with perplexity. Sonia, hearing herself introduced, tried to raise her eyes again, but was more embarrassed than ever.

"I wanted to ask you," said Raskolnikov, hastily, "how things were arranged yesterday. You were not worried by the police, for instance?"

"No, that was all right... it was too evident, the cause of death... they did not worry us... only the lodgers are angry."

"Why?"

"At the body's remaining so long. You see it is hot now. So that, today, they will carry it to the cemetery, into the chapel, until tomorrow. At first Katerina Ivanovna was unwilling, but now she sees herself that it's necessary..."

"Today, then?"

"She begs you to do us the honour to be in the church tomorrow for the service, and then to be present at the funeral lunch."

"She is giving a funeral lunch?"

"Yes... just a little.... She told me to thank you very much for helping us yesterday. But for you, we should have had nothing for the funeral."

All at once her lips and chin began trembling, but, with an effort, she controlled herself, looking down again.

During the conversation, Raskolnikov watched her carefully. She had a thin, very thin, pale little face, rather irregular and angular, with a sharp little nose and chin. She could not have been called pretty, but her blue eyes were so clear, and when they lighted up, there was such a kindliness and simplicity in her expression that one could not help being attracted. Her face, and her whole figure indeed, had another peculiar characteristic. In spite of her eighteen years, she looked almost a little girl—almost a child. And in some of her gestures, this childishness seemed almost absurd.

"But has Katerina Ivanovna been able to manage with such small means? Does she even mean to have a funeral lunch?" Raskolnikov asked, persistently keeping up the conversation.

"The coffin will be plain, of course... and everything will be plain, so it won't cost much. Katerina Ivanovna and I have reckoned it all out, so that there will be enough left... and Katerina Ivanovna was very anxious it should be so. You know one can't... it's a comfort to her... she is like that, you know...."

"I understand, I understand... of course... why do you look at my room like that? My mother has just said it is like a tomb."

"You gave us everything yesterday," Sonia said suddenly, in reply, in a loud rapid whisper; and again she looked down in confusion. Her lips and chin were trembling once more. She had been struck at once by Raskolnikov's poor surroundings, and now these words broke out spontaneously. A silence followed. There was a light in Dounia's eyes, and even Pulcheria Alexandrovna looked kindly at Sonia.

"Rodya," she said, getting up, "we shall have dinner together, of course. Come, Dounia.... And you, Rodya, had better go for a little walk, and then rest and lie down before you come to see us.... I am afraid we have exhausted you...."

"Yes, yes, I'll come," he answered, getting up fussily. "But I have something to see to."

"But surely you will have dinner together?" cried Razumihin, looking in surprise at Raskolnikov. "What do you mean?"

"Yes, yes, I am coming... of course, of course! And you stay a minute. You do not want him just now, do you, mother? Or perhaps I am taking him from you?"

"Oh, no, no. And will you, Dmitri Prokofitch, do us the favour of dining with us?"

"Please do," added Dounia.

Razumihin bowed, positively radiant. For one moment, they were all strangely embarrassed.

"Goodbye, Rodya, that is till we meet. I do not like saying goodbye. Goodbye, Nastasya. Ah, I have said goodbye again."

Pulcheria Alexandrovna meant to greet Sonia, too; but it somehow failed to come off, and she went in a flutter out of the room.

But Avdotya Romanovna seemed to await her turn, and following her mother out, gave Sonia an attentive, courteous bow. Sonia, in confusion, gave a hurried, frightened curtsy. There was a look of poignant discomfort in her face, as though Avdotya Romanovna's courtesy and attention were oppressive and painful to her.

"Dounia, goodbye," called Raskolnikov, in the passage. "Give me your hand."

"Why, I did give it to you. Have you forgotten?" said Dounia, turning warmly and awkwardly to him.

"Never mind, give it to me again." And he squeezed her fingers warmly.

Dounia smiled, flushed, pulled her hand away, and went off quite happy.

"Come, that's capital," he said to Sonia, going back and looking brightly at her. "God give peace to the dead, the living have still to live. That is right, isn't it?"

Sonia looked surprised at the sudden brightness of his face. He looked at her for some moments in silence. The whole history of the dead father floated before his memory in those moments....

"Heavens, Dounia," Pulcheria Alexandrovna began, as soon as they were in the street, "I really feel relieved myself at coming away—more at ease. How little did I think yesterday in the train that I could ever be glad of that."

"I tell you again, mother, he is still very ill. Don't you see it? Perhaps worrying about us upset him. We must be patient, and much, much can be forgiven."

"Well, you were not very patient!" Pulcheria Alexandrovna caught her up, hotly and jealously. "Do you know, Dounia, I was looking at you two. You are the very portrait of him, and not so much in face as in soul. You are both melancholy, both morose and hot-tempered, both haughty and both generous.... Surely he can't be an egoist, Dounia. Eh? When I think of what is in store for us this evening, my heart sinks!"

"Don't be uneasy, mother. What must be, will be."

"Dounia, only think what a position we are in! What if Pyotr Petrovitch breaks it off?" poor Pulcheria Alexandrovna blurted out, incautiously.

"He won't be worth much if he does," answered Dounia, sharply and contemptuously.

"We did well to come away," Pulcheria Alexandrovna hurriedly broke in. "He was in a hurry about some business or other. If he gets out and has a breath of air... it is fearfully close in his room.... But where is one to get a breath of air here? The very streets here feel like shut-up rooms. Good heavens! what a town!... stay... this side... they will crush you—carrying something. Why, it is a piano they have got, I declare... how they push!... I am very much afraid of that young woman, too."

"What young woman, mother?

"Why, that Sofya Semyonovna, who was there just now."

"Why?"

"I have a presentiment, Dounia. Well, you may believe it or not, but as soon as she came in, that very minute, I felt that she was the chief cause of the trouble...."

"Nothing of the sort!" cried Dounia, in vexation. "What nonsense, with your presentiments, mother! He only made her acquaintance the evening before, and he did not know her when she came in."

"Well, you will see.... She worries me; but you will see, you will see! I was so frightened. She was gazing at me with those eyes. I could scarcely sit still in my chair when he began introducing her, do you remember? It seems so strange, but Pyotr Petrovitch writes like that about her, and he introduces her to us—to you! So he must think a great deal of her."

"People will write anything. We were talked about and written about, too. Have you forgotten? I am sure that she is a good girl, and that it is all nonsense."

"God grant it may be!"

"And Pyotr Petrovitch is a contemptible slanderer," Dounia snapped out, suddenly.

Pulcheria Alexandrovna was crushed; the conversation was not resumed.

"I will tell you what I want with you," said Raskolnikov, drawing Razumihin to the window.

"Then I will tell Katerina Ivanovna that you are coming," Sonia said hurriedly, preparing to depart.

"One minute, Sofya Semyonovna. We have no secrets. You are not in our way. I want to have another word or two with you. Listen!" he turned suddenly to Razumihin again. "You know that... what's his name... Porfiry Petrovitch?"

"I should think so! He is a relation. Why?" added the latter, with interest.

"Is not he managing that case... you know, about that murder?... You were speaking about it yesterday."

"Yes... well?" Razumihin's eyes opened wide.

"He was inquiring for people who had pawned things, and I have some pledges there, too—trifles—a ring my sister gave me as a keepsake when I left home, and my father's silver watch—they are only worth five or six roubles altogether... but I value them. So what am I to do now? I do not want to lose the things, especially the watch. I was quaking just now, for fear mother would ask to look at it, when we spoke of Dounia's watch. It is the only thing of father's left us. She would be ill if it were lost. You know what women are. So tell me what to do. I know I ought to have given notice at the police station, but would it not be better to go straight to Porfiry? Eh? What do you think? The matter might be settled more quickly. You see, mother may ask for it before dinner."

"Certainly not to the police station. Certainly to Porfiry," Razumihin shouted in extraordinary excitement. "Well, how glad I am. Let us go at once. It is a couple of steps. We shall be sure to find him."

"Very well, let us go."

"And he will be very, very glad to make your acquaintance. I have often talked to him of you at different times. I was speaking of you yesterday. Let us go. So you knew the old woman? So that's it! It is all turning out splendidly.... Oh, yes, Sofya Ivanovna..."

"Sofya Semyonovna," corrected Raskolnikov. "Sofya Semyonovna, this is my friend Razumihin, and he is a good man."

"If you have to go now," Sonia was beginning, not looking at Razumihin at all, and still more embarrassed.

"Let us go," decided Raskolnikov. "I will come to you today, Sofya Semyonovna. Only tell me where you live."

He was not exactly ill at ease, but seemed hurried, and avoided her eyes. Sonia gave her address, and flushed as she did so. They all went out together.

"Don't you lock up?" asked Razumihin, following him on to the stairs.

"Never," answered Raskolnikov. "I have been meaning to buy a lock for these two years. People are happy who have no need of locks," he said, laughing, to Sonia. They stood still in the gateway.

"Do you go to the right, Sofya Semyonovna? How did you find me, by the way?" he added, as though he wanted to say something quite different. He wanted to look at her soft clear eyes, but this was not easy.

"Why, you gave your address to Polenka yesterday."

133

"Polenka? Oh, yes; Polenka, that is the little girl. She is your sister? Did I give her the address?"

"Why, had you forgotten?"

"No, I remember."

"I had heard my father speak of you... only I did not know your name, and he did not know it. And now I came... and as I had learnt your name, I asked today, 'Where does Mr. Raskolnikov live?' I did not know you had only a room too.... Goodbye, I will tell Katerina Ivanovna."

She was extremely glad to escape at last; she went away looking down, hurrying to get out of sight as soon as possible, to walk the twenty steps to the turning on the right and to be at last alone, and then moving rapidly along, looking at no one, noticing nothing, to think, to remember, to meditate on every word, every detail. Never, never had she felt anything like this. Dimly and unconsciously a whole new world was opening before her. She remembered suddenly that Raskolnikov meant to come to her that day, perhaps at once!

"Only not today, please, not today!" she kept muttering with a sinking heart, as though entreating someone, like a frightened child. "Mercy! to me... to that room... he will see... oh, dear!"

She was not capable at that instant of noticing an unknown gentleman who was watching her and following at her heels. He had accompanied her from the gateway. At the moment when Razumihin, Raskolnikov, and she stood still at parting on the pavement, this gentleman, who was just passing, started on hearing Sonia's words: "and I asked where Mr. Raskolnikov lived?" He turned a rapid but attentive look upon all three, especially upon Raskolnikov, to whom Sonia was speaking; then looked back and noted the house. All this was done in an instant as he passed, and trying not to betray his interest, he walked on more slowly as though waiting for something. He was waiting for Sonia; he saw that they were parting, and that Sonia was going home.

"Home? Where? I've seen that face somewhere," he thought. "I must find out."

At the turning he crossed over, looked round, and saw Sonia coming the same way, noticing nothing. She turned the corner. He followed her on the other side. After about fifty paces he crossed over again, overtook her and kept two or three yards behind her.

He was a man about fifty, rather tall and thickly set, with broad high shoulders which made him look as though he stooped a little. He wore good and fashionable clothes, and looked like a gentleman of position. He carried a handsome cane, which he tapped on the pavement at each step; his gloves were spotless. He had a broad, rather pleasant face with high cheekbones and a fresh colour, not often seen in Petersburg. His flaxen hair was still abundant, and only touched here and there with grey, and his thick square beard was even lighter than his hair. His eyes were blue and had a cold and thoughtful look; his lips were crimson. He was a remarkably well-preserved man and looked much younger than his years.

When Sonia came out on the canal bank, they were the only two persons on the pavement. He observed her dreaminess and preoccupation. On reaching the house where she lodged, Sonia turned in at the gate; he followed her, seeming rather surprised. In the courtyard she turned to the right corner. "Bah!" muttered the unknown gentleman, and mounted the stairs behind her. Only then Sonia noticed him. She reached the third storey, turned down the passage, and rang at No. 9. On the door was inscribed in chalk, "Kapernaumov, Tailor." "Bah!" the stranger repeated again, wondering at the strange coincidence, and he rang next door, at No. 8. The doors were two or three yards apart.

"You lodge at Kapernaumov's," he said, looking at Sonia and laughing. "He altered a waistcoat for me yesterday. I am staying close here at Madame Resslich's. How odd!" Sonia looked at him attentively.

"We are neighbours," he went on gaily. "I only came to town the day before yesterday. Goodbye for the present."

Sonia made no reply; the door opened and she slipped in. She felt for some reason ashamed and uneasy.

On the way to Porfiry's, Razumihin was obviously excited.

"That's capital, brother," he repeated several times, "and I am glad! I am glad!"

"What are you glad about?" Raskolnikov thought to himself.

"I didn't know that you pledged things at the old woman's, too. And... was it long ago? I mean, was it long since you were there?"

"What a simple-hearted fool he is!"

"When was it?" Raskolnikov stopped still to recollect. "Two or three days before her death it must have been. But I am not going to redeem the things now," he put in with a sort of hurried and conspicuous solicitude about the things. "I've not more than a silver rouble left... after last night's accursed delirium!"

He laid special emphasis on the delirium.

"Yes, yes," Razumihin hastened to agree—with what was not clear. "Then that's why you... were stuck... partly... you know in your delirium you were continually mentioning some rings or chains! Yes, yes... that's clear, it's all clear now."

"Hullo! How that idea must have got about among them. Here this man will go to the stake for me, and I find him delighted at having *cleared up* why I spoke of rings in my delirium! What a hold the idea must have on all of them!"

"Shall we find him?" he asked suddenly.

"Oh, yes," Razumihin answered quickly. "He is a nice fellow, you will see, brother. Rather clumsy, that is to say, he is a man of polished manners, but I mean clumsy in a different sense. He is an intelligent fellow, very much so indeed, but he has his own range of ideas.... He is incredulous, sceptical, cynical... he likes to impose on people, or rather to make fun of them. His is the old, circumstantial method.... But he understands his work... thoroughly.... Last year he cleared up a case of murder in which the police had hardly a clue. He is very, very anxious to make your acquaintance!"

"On what grounds is he so anxious?"

"Oh, it's not exactly... you see, since you've been ill I happen to have mentioned you several times.... So, when he heard about you... about your being a law student and not able to finish your studies, he said, 'What a pity!' And so I concluded... from everything together, not only that; yesterday Zametov... you know, Rodya, I talked some nonsense on the way home to you yesterday, when I was drunk... I am afraid, brother, of your exaggerating it, you see."

"What? That they think I am a madman? Maybe they are right," he said with a constrained smile.

"Yes, yes.... That is, pooh, no!... But all that I said (and there was something else too) it was all nonsense, drunken nonsense."

"But why are you apologising? I am so sick of it all!" Raskolnikov cried with exaggerated irritability. It was partly assumed, however.

"I know, I know, I understand. Believe me, I understand. One's ashamed to speak of it."

"If you are ashamed, then don't speak of it."

Both were silent. Razumihin was more than ecstatic and Raskolnikov perceived it with repulsion. He was alarmed, too, by what Razumihin had just said about Porfiry.

"I shall have to pull a long face with him too," he thought, with a beating heart, and he turned white, "and do it naturally, too. But the most natural thing would be to do nothing at all. Carefully do nothing at all! No, *carefully* would not be natural again.... Oh, well, we shall see how it turns out.... We shall see... directly. Is it a good thing to go or not? The butterfly flies to the light. My heart is beating, that's what's bad!"

"In this grey house," said Razumihin.

"The most important thing, does Porfiry know that I was at the old hag's flat yesterday... and asked about the blood? I must find that out instantly, as soon as I go in, find out from his face; otherwise... I'll find out, if it's my ruin."

"I say, brother," he said suddenly, addressing Razumihin, with a sly smile, "I have been noticing all day that you seem to be curiously excited. Isn't it so?"

"Excited? Not a bit of it," said Razumihin, stung to the quick.

"Yes, brother, I assure you it's noticeable. Why, you sat on your chair in a way you never do sit, on the edge somehow, and you seemed to be writhing all the time. You kept jumping up for nothing. One moment you were angry, and the next your face looked like a sweetmeat. You even blushed; especially when you were invited to dinner, you blushed awfully."

"Nothing of the sort, nonsense! What do you mean?"

"But why are you wriggling out of it, like a schoolboy? By Jove, there he's blushing again."

"What a pig you are!"

"But why are you so shamefaced about it? Romeo! Stay, I'll tell of you today. Ha-ha-ha! I'll make mother laugh, and someone else, too..."

"Listen, listen, listen, this is serious.... What next, you fiend!" Razumihin was utterly overwhelmed, turning cold with horror. "What will you tell them? Come, brother... foo! what a pig you are!"

"You are like a summer rose. And if only you knew how it suits you; a Romeo over six foot high! And how you've washed today—you cleaned your nails, I declare. Eh? That's something unheard of! Why, I do believe you've got pomatum on your hair! Bend down."

"Pig!"

Raskolnikov laughed as though he could not restrain himself. So laughing, they entered Porfiry Petrovitch's flat. This is what Raskolnikov wanted: from within they could be heard laughing as they came in, still guffawing in the passage.

"Not a word here or I'll... brain you!" Razumihin whispered furiously, seizing Raskolnikov by the shoulder.

V

Raskolnikov was already entering the room. He came in looking as though he had the utmost difficulty not to burst out laughing again. Behind him Razumihin strode in gawky and awkward, shamefaced and red as a peony, with an utterly crestfallen and ferocious expression. His face and whole figure really were ridiculous at that moment and amply justified Raskolnikov's laughter. Raskolnikov, not waiting for an introduction, bowed to Porfiry Petrovitch, who stood in the middle of the room looking inquiringly at them. He held out his hand and shook hands, still apparently making desperate efforts to subdue his mirth and utter a few words to introduce himself. But he had no sooner succeeded in assuming a serious air and muttering something when he suddenly glanced again as though accidentally at Razumihin, and could no longer control himself: his stifled laughter broke out the more irresistibly the more he tried to restrain it. The extraordinary ferocity with which Razumihin received this "spontaneous" mirth gave the whole scene the appearance of most genuine fun and naturalness. Razumihin strengthened this impression as though on purpose.

"Fool! You fiend," he roared, waving his arm which at once struck a little round table with an empty tea-glass on it. Everything was sent flying and crashing.

"But why break chairs, gentlemen? You know it's a loss to the Crown," Porfiry Petrovitch quoted gaily.

Raskolnikov was still laughing, with his hand in Porfiry Petrovitch's, but anxious not to overdo it, awaited the right moment to put a natural end to it. Razumihin, completely put to confusion by upsetting the table and smashing the glass, gazed gloomily at the fragments, cursed and turned sharply to the window where he stood looking out with his back to the company with a fiercely scowling countenance, seeing nothing. Porfiry Petrovitch laughed and was ready to go on laughing, but obviously looked for explanations. Zametov had been sitting in the corner, but he rose at the visitors' entrance and was standing in expectation with a smile on his lips, though he looked with surprise and even it seemed incredulity at the whole scene and at Raskolnikov with a certain embarrassment. Zametov's unexpected presence struck Raskolnikov unpleasantly.

"I've got to think of that," he thought. "Excuse me, please," he began, affecting extreme embarrassment. "Raskolnikov."

"Not at all, very pleasant to see you... and how pleasantly you've come in.... Why, won't he even say good morning?" Porfiry Petrovitch nodded at Razumihin.

"Upon my honour I don't know why he is in such a rage with me. I only told him as we came along that he was like Romeo... and proved it. And that was all, I think!"

"Pig!" ejaculated Razumihin, without turning round.

"There must have been very grave grounds for it, if he is so furious at the word," Porfiry laughed.

"Oh, you sharp lawyer!... Damn you all!" snapped Razumihin, and suddenly bursting out laughing himself, he went up to Porfiry with a more cheerful face as though nothing had happened. "That'll do! We are all fools. To come to business. This is my friend Rodion Romanovitch Raskolnikov; in the first place he has heard of you and wants to make your acquaintance, and secondly, he has a little matter of business with you. Bah! Zametov, what brought you here? Have you met before? Have you known each other long?"

"What does this mean?" thought Raskolnikov uneasily.

Zametov seemed taken aback, but not very much so.

"Why, it was at your rooms we met yesterday," he said easily.

137

"Then I have been spared the trouble. All last week he was begging me to introduce him to you. Porfiry and you have sniffed each other out without me. Where is your tobacco?"

Porfiry Petrovitch was wearing a dressing-gown, very clean linen, and trodden-down slippers. He was a man of about five and thirty, short, stout even to corpulence, and clean shaven. He wore his hair cut short and had a large round head, particularly prominent at the back. His soft, round, rather snub-nosed face was of a sickly yellowish colour, but had a vigorous and rather ironical expression. It would have been good-natured except for a look in the eyes, which shone with a watery, mawkish light under almost white, blinking eyelashes. The expression of those eyes was strangely out of keeping with his somewhat womanish figure, and gave it something far more serious than could be guessed at first sight.

As soon as Porfiry Petrovitch heard that his visitor had a little matter of business with him, he begged him to sit down on the sofa and sat down himself on the other end, waiting for him to explain his business, with that careful and over-serious attention which is at once oppressive and embarrassing, especially to a stranger, and especially if what you are discussing is in your opinion of far too little importance for such exceptional solemnity. But in brief and coherent phrases Raskolnikov explained his business clearly and exactly, and was so well satisfied with himself that he even succeeded in taking a good look at Porfiry. Porfiry Petrovitch did not once take his eyes off him. Razumihin, sitting opposite at the same table, listened warmly and impatiently, looking from one to the other every moment with rather excessive interest.

"Fool," Raskolnikov swore to himself.

"You have to give information to the police," Porfiry replied, with a most businesslike air, "that having learnt of this incident, that is of the murder, you beg to inform the lawyer in charge of the case that such and such things belong to you, and that you desire to redeem them... or... but they will write to you."

"That's just the point, that at the present moment," Raskolnikov tried his utmost to feign embarrassment, "I am not quite in funds... and even this trifling sum is beyond me... I only wanted, you see, for the present to declare that the things are mine, and that when I have money...."

"That's no matter," answered Porfiry Petrovitch, receiving his explanation of his pecuniary position coldly, "but you can, if you prefer, write straight to me, to say, that having been informed of the matter, and claiming such and such as your property, you beg..."

"On an ordinary sheet of paper?" Raskolnikov interrupted eagerly, again interested in the financial side of the question.

"Oh, the most ordinary," and suddenly Porfiry Petrovitch looked with obvious irony at him, screwing up his eyes and, as it were, winking at him. But perhaps it was Raskolnikov's fancy, for it all lasted but a moment. There was certainly something of the sort, Raskolnikov could have sworn he winked at him, goodness knows why.

"He knows," flashed through his mind like lightning.

"Forgive my troubling you about such trifles," he went on, a little disconcerted, "the things are only worth five roubles, but I prize them particularly for the sake of those from whom they came to me, and I must confess that I was alarmed when I heard..."

"That's why you were so much struck when I mentioned to Zossimov that Porfiry was inquiring for everyone who had pledges!" Razumihin put in with obvious intention.

This was really unbearable. Raskolnikov could not help glancing at him with a flash of vindictive anger in his black eyes, but immediately recollected himself.

"You seem to be jeering at me, brother?" he said to him, with a well-feigned irritability. "I dare say I do seem to you absurdly anxious about such trash; but you mustn't think me selfish or grasping for that, and these two things may be anything but trash in my eyes. I told you just now that the silver watch, though it's not worth a cent, is the only thing left us of my father's. You may laugh at me, but my mother is here," he turned suddenly to Porfiry, "and if she knew," he turned again hurriedly to Razumihin, carefully making his voice tremble, "that the watch was lost, she would be in despair! You know what women are!"

"Not a bit of it! I didn't mean that at all! Quite the contrary!" shouted Razumihin distressed.

"Was it right? Was it natural? Did I overdo it?" Raskolnikov asked himself in a tremor. "Why did I say that about women?"

"Oh, your mother is with you?" Porfiry Petrovitch inquired.

"Yes."

"When did she come?"

"Last night."

Porfiry paused as though reflecting.

"Your things would not in any case be lost," he went on calmly and coldly. "I have been expecting you here for some time."

And as though that was a matter of no importance, he carefully offered the ashtray to Razumihin, who was ruthlessly scattering cigarette ash over the carpet. Raskolnikov shuddered, but Porfiry did not seem to be looking at him, and was still concerned with Razumihin's cigarette.

"What? Expecting him? Why, did you know that he had pledges *there*?" cried Razumihin.

Porfiry Petrovitch addressed himself to Raskolnikov.

"Your things, the ring and the watch, were wrapped up together, and on the paper your name was legibly written in pencil, together with the date on which you left them with her..."

"How observant you are!" Raskolnikov smiled awkwardly, doing his very utmost to look him straight in the face, but he failed, and suddenly added:

"I say that because I suppose there were a great many pledges... that it must be difficult to remember them all.... But you remember them all so clearly, and... and..."

"Stupid! Feeble!" he thought. "Why did I add that?"

"But we know all who had pledges, and you are the only one who hasn't come forward," Porfiry answered with hardly perceptible irony.

"I haven't been quite well."

"I heard that too. I heard, indeed, that you were in great distress about something. You look pale still."

"I am not pale at all.... No, I am quite well," Raskolnikov snapped out rudely and angrily, completely changing his tone. His anger was mounting, he could not repress it. "And in my anger I shall betray myself," flashed through his mind again. "Why are they torturing me?"

"Not quite well!" Razumihin caught him up. "What next! He was unconscious and delirious all yesterday. Would you believe, Porfiry, as soon as our backs were turned, he dressed, though he could hardly stand, and gave us the slip and went off on a spree somewhere till midnight, delirious all the time! Would you believe it! Extraordinary!"

"Really delirious? You don't say so!" Porfiry shook his head in a womanish way.

"Nonsense! Don't you believe it! But you don't believe it anyway," Raskolnikov let slip in his anger. But Porfiry Petrovitch did not seem to catch those strange words.

"But how could you have gone out if you hadn't been delirious?" Razumihin got hot suddenly. "What did you go out for? What was the object of it? And why on the sly? Were you in your senses when you did it? Now that all danger is over I can speak plainly."

"I was awfully sick of them yesterday." Raskolnikov addressed Porfiry suddenly with a smile of insolent defiance, "I ran away from them to take lodgings where they wouldn't find me, and took a lot of money with me. Mr. Zametov there saw it. I say, Mr. Zametov, was I sensible or delirious yesterday; settle our dispute."

He could have strangled Zametov at that moment, so hateful were his expression and his silence to him.

"In my opinion you talked sensibly and even artfully, but you were extremely irritable," Zametov pronounced dryly.

"And Nikodim Fomitch was telling me today," put in Porfiry Petrovitch, "that he met you very late last night in the lodging of a man who had been run over."

"And there," said Razumihin, "weren't you mad then? You gave your last penny to the widow for the funeral. If you wanted to help, give fifteen or twenty even, but keep three roubles for yourself at least, but he flung away all the twenty-five at once!"

"Maybe I found a treasure somewhere and you know nothing of it? So that's why I was liberal yesterday.... Mr. Zametov knows I've found a treasure! Excuse us, please, for disturbing you for half an hour with such trivialities," he said, turning to Porfiry Petrovitch, with trembling lips. "We are boring you, aren't we?"

"Oh no, quite the contrary, quite the contrary! If only you knew how you interest me! It's interesting to look on and listen... and I am really glad you have come forward at last."

"But you might give us some tea! My throat's dry," cried Razumihin.

"Capital idea! Perhaps we will all keep you company. Wouldn't you like... something more essential before tea?"

"Get along with you!"

Porfiry Petrovitch went out to order tea.

Raskolnikov's thoughts were in a whirl. He was in terrible exasperation.

"The worst of it is they don't disguise it; they don't care to stand on ceremony! And how if you didn't know me at all, did you come to talk to Nikodim Fomitch about me? So they don't care to hide that they are tracking me like a pack of dogs. They simply spit in my face." He was shaking with rage. "Come, strike me openly, don't play with me like a cat with a mouse. It's hardly civil, Porfiry Petrovitch, but perhaps I won't allow it! I shall get up and throw the whole truth in your ugly faces, and you'll see how I despise you." He could hardly breathe. "And what if it's only my fancy? What if I am mistaken, and through inexperience I get angry and don't keep up my nasty part? Perhaps it's all unintentional. All their phrases are the usual ones, but there is something about them.... It all might be said, but there is something. Why did he say bluntly, 'With her'? Why did Zametov add that I spoke artfully? Why do they speak in that tone? Yes, the tone.... Razumihin is sitting here, why does he see nothing? That innocent blockhead never does see anything! Feverish again! Did Porfiry wink at me just now? Of course it's nonsense! What could he wink for? Are they trying to upset my nerves or are they teasing me? Either it's ill fancy or they know! Even Zametov is rude.... Is Zametov rude? Zametov has changed his mind. I foresaw he would change his mind! He is at home here, while it's my first visit. Porfiry does not consider him a visitor; sits with his back to him. They're as thick as thieves, no doubt, over me! Not a doubt they were talking about me before we came. Do they know about the flat? If only they'd make haste! When I said that I ran away to take a flat he let it pass.... I put that in cleverly about a flat, it may be of use afterwards.... Delirious, indeed... ha-ha-ha! He knows all about last night! He didn't know of my mother's arrival! The hag had written the date on in pencil! You are wrong, you won't catch me! There are no facts... it's all supposition! You produce facts! The flat even isn't a fact but delirium. I know what to say to them.... Do they know about the flat? I won't go without finding out. What did I come for? But my being angry now, maybe is a fact! Fool, how irritable I am! Perhaps that's right; to play the invalid.... He is feeling me. He will try to catch me. Why did I come?"

All this flashed like lightning through his mind.

Porfiry Petrovitch returned quickly. He became suddenly more jovial.

"Your party yesterday, brother, has left my head rather.... And I am out of sorts altogether," he began in quite a different tone, laughing to Razumihin.

"Was it interesting? I left you yesterday at the most interesting point. Who got the best of it?"

"Oh, no one, of course. They got on to everlasting questions, floated off into space."

"Only fancy, Rodya, what we got on to yesterday. Whether there is such a thing as crime. I told you that we talked our heads off."

"What is there strange? It's an everyday social question," Raskolnikov answered casually.

"The question wasn't put quite like that," observed Porfiry.

"Not quite, that's true," Razumihin agreed at once, getting warm and hurried as usual. "Listen, Rodion, and tell us your opinion, I want to hear it. I was fighting tooth and nail with them and wanted you to help me. I told them you were coming.... It began with the socialist doctrine. You know their doctrine; crime is a protest against the abnormality of the social organisation and nothing more, and nothing more; no other causes admitted!..."

"You are wrong there," cried Porfiry Petrovitch; he was noticeably animated and kept laughing as he looked at Razumihin, which made him more excited than ever.

"Nothing is admitted," Razumihin interrupted with heat.

"I am not wrong. I'll show you their pamphlets. Everything with them is 'the influence of environment,' and nothing else. Their favourite phrase! From which it follows that, if society is normally organised, all crime will cease at once, since there will be nothing to protest against and all men will become righteous in one instant. Human nature is not taken into account, it is excluded, it's not supposed to exist! They don't recognise that humanity, developing by a historical living process, will become at last a normal society, but they believe that a social system that has come out of some mathematical brain is going to organise all humanity at once and make it just and sinless in an instant, quicker than any living process! That's why they instinctively dislike history, 'nothing but ugliness and stupidity in it,' and they explain it all as stupidity! That's why they so dislike the *living* process of life; they don't want a *living soul*! The living soul demands life, the soul won't obey the rules of mechanics, the soul is an object of suspicion, the soul is retrograde! But what they want though it smells of death and can be made of India-rubber, at least is not alive, has no will, is servile and won't revolt! And it comes in the end to their reducing everything to the building of walls and the planning of rooms and passages in a phalanstery! The phalanstery is ready, indeed, but your human nature is not ready for the phalanstery—it wants life, it hasn't completed its vital process, it's too soon for the graveyard! You can't skip over nature by logic. Logic presupposes three possibilities, but there are millions! Cut away a million, and reduce it all to the question of comfort! That's the easiest solution of the problem! It's seductively clear and you musn't think about it. That's the great thing, you mustn't think! The whole secret of life in two pages of print!"

"Now he is off, beating the drum! Catch hold of him, do!" laughed Porfiry. "Can you imagine," he turned to Raskolnikov, "six people holding forth like that last night, in one room, with punch as a preliminary! No, brother, you are wrong, environment accounts for a great deal in crime; I can assure you of that."

"Oh, I know it does, but just tell me: a man of forty violates a child of ten; was it environment drove him to it?"

"Well, strictly speaking, it did," Porfiry observed with noteworthy gravity; "a crime of that nature may be very well ascribed to the influence of environment."

Razumihin was almost in a frenzy. "Oh, if you like," he roared. "I'll prove to you that your white eyelashes may very well be ascribed to the Church of Ivan the Great's being two hundred and fifty feet high, and I will prove it clearly, exactly, progressively, and even with a Liberal tendency! I undertake to! Will you bet on it?"

"Done! Let's hear, please, how he will prove it!"

"He is always humbugging, confound him," cried Razumihin, jumping up and gesticulating. "What's the use of talking to you? He does all that on purpose; you don't know him, Rodion! He took their side yesterday, simply to make fools of them. And the things he said yesterday! And they were delighted! He can keep it up for a fortnight together. Last year he persuaded us that he was going into a monastery: he stuck to it for two months. Not long ago he took it into his head to declare he was going to get married, that he had everything ready for the wedding. He ordered new clothes indeed. We all began to congratulate him. There was no bride, nothing, all pure fantasy!"

"Ah, you are wrong! I got the clothes before. It was the new clothes in fact that made me think of taking you in."

"Are you such a good dissembler?" Raskolnikov asked carelessly.

"You wouldn't have supposed it, eh? Wait a bit, I shall take you in, too. Ha-ha-ha! No, I'll tell you the truth. All these questions about crime, environment, children, recall to my mind an article of yours which interested me at the time. 'On Crime'... or something of the sort, I forget the title, I read it with pleasure two months ago in the *Periodical Review*."

141

"My article? In the *Periodical Review*?" Raskolnikov asked in astonishment. "I certainly did write an article upon a book six months ago when I left the university, but I sent it to the *Weekly Review*."

"But it came out in the *Periodical*."

"And the *Weekly Review* ceased to exist, so that's why it wasn't printed at the time."

"That's true; but when it ceased to exist, the *Weekly Review* was amalgamated with the *Periodical*, and so your article appeared two months ago in the latter. Didn't you know?"

Raskolnikov had not known.

"Why, you might get some money out of them for the article! What a strange person you are! You lead such a solitary life that you know nothing of matters that concern you directly. It's a fact, I assure you."

"Bravo, Rodya! I knew nothing about it either!" cried Razumihin. "I'll run today to the reading-room and ask for the number. Two months ago? What was the date? It doesn't matter though, I will find it. Think of not telling us!"

"How did you find out that the article was mine? It's only signed with an initial."

"I only learnt it by chance, the other day. Through the editor; I know him.... I was very much interested."

"I analysed, if I remember, the psychology of a criminal before and after the crime."

"Yes, and you maintained that the perpetration of a crime is always accompanied by illness. Very, very original, but... it was not that part of your article that interested me so much, but an idea at the end of the article which I regret to say you merely suggested without working it out clearly. There is, if you recollect, a suggestion that there are certain persons who can... that is, not precisely are able to, but have a perfect right to commit breaches of morality and crimes, and that the law is not for them."

Raskolnikov smiled at the exaggerated and intentional distortion of his idea.

"What? What do you mean? A right to crime? But not because of the influence of environment?" Razumihin inquired with some alarm even.

"No, not exactly because of it," answered Porfiry. "In his article all men are divided into 'ordinary' and 'extraordinary.' Ordinary men have to live in submission, have no right to transgress the law, because, don't you see, they are ordinary. But extraordinary men have a right to commit any crime and to transgress the law in any way, just because they are extraordinary. That was your idea, if I am not mistaken?"

"What do you mean? That can't be right?" Razumihin muttered in bewilderment.

Raskolnikov smiled again. He saw the point at once, and knew where they wanted to drive him. He decided to take up the challenge.

"That wasn't quite my contention," he began simply and modestly. "Yet I admit that you have stated it almost correctly; perhaps, if you like, perfectly so." (It almost gave him pleasure to admit this.) "The only difference is that I don't contend that extraordinary people are always bound to commit breaches of morals, as you call it. In fact, I doubt whether such an argument could be published. I simply hinted that an 'extraordinary' man has the right... that is not an official right, but an inner right to decide in his own conscience to overstep... certain obstacles, and only in case it is essential for the practical fulfilment of his idea (sometimes, perhaps, of benefit to the whole of humanity). You say that my article isn't definite; I am ready to make it as clear as I can. Perhaps I am right in thinking you want me to; very well. I maintain that if the discoveries of Kepler and Newton could not have been made known except by sacrificing the lives of one, a dozen, a hundred, or more men, Newton would have had the right, would indeed have been in duty-bound... to *eliminate* the dozen or the hundred men for the sake of making his discoveries known to the whole of humanity. But it does not follow from that that Newton had a right to murder people right and left and to steal every day in the market. Then, I remember, I maintain in my article that all... well, legislators and leaders of men, such as Lycurgus, Solon, Mahomet, Napoleon, and so on, were all without exception criminals, from the very fact that, making a new law, they transgressed the ancient one, handed down from their ancestors and held sacred by the people, and they did not stop short at bloodshed either, if that bloodshed—often of innocent

142

persons fighting bravely in defence of ancient law—were of use to their cause. It's remarkable, in fact, that the majority, indeed, of these benefactors and leaders of humanity were guilty of terrible carnage. In short, I maintain that all great men or even men a little out of the common, that is to say capable of giving some new word, must from their very nature be criminals—more or less, of course. Otherwise it's hard for them to get out of the common rut; and to remain in the common rut is what they can't submit to, from their very nature again, and to my mind they ought not, indeed, to submit to it. You see that there is nothing particularly new in all that. The same thing has been printed and read a thousand times before. As for my division of people into ordinary and extraordinary, I acknowledge that it's somewhat arbitrary, but I don't insist upon exact numbers. I only believe in my leading idea that men are *in general* divided by a law of nature into two categories, inferior (ordinary), that is, so to say, material that serves only to reproduce its kind, and men who have the gift or the talent to utter *a new word*. There are, of course, innumerable subdivisions, but the distinguishing features of both categories are fairly well marked. The first category, generally speaking, are men conservative in temperament and law-abiding; they live under control and love to be controlled. To my thinking it is their duty to be controlled, because that's their vocation, and there is nothing humiliating in it for them. The second category all transgress the law; they are destroyers or disposed to destruction according to their capacities. The crimes of these men are of course relative and varied; for the most part they seek in very varied ways the destruction of the present for the sake of the better. But if such a one is forced for the sake of his idea to step over a corpse or wade through blood, he can, I maintain, find within himself, in his conscience, a sanction for wading through blood—that depends on the idea and its dimensions, note that. It's only in that sense I speak of their right to crime in my article (you remember it began with the legal question). There's no need for such anxiety, however; the masses will scarcely ever admit this right, they punish them or hang them (more or less), and in doing so fulfil quite justly their conservative vocation. But the same masses set these criminals on a pedestal in the next generation and worship them (more or less). The first category is always the man of the present, the second the man of the future. The first preserve the world and people it, the second move the world and lead it to its goal. Each class has an equal right to exist. In fact, all have equal rights with me—and *vive la guerre éternelle*—till the New Jerusalem, of course!"

"Then you believe in the New Jerusalem, do you?"

"I do," Raskolnikov answered firmly; as he said these words and during the whole preceding tirade he kept his eyes on one spot on the carpet.

"And... and do you believe in God? Excuse my curiosity."

"I do," repeated Raskolnikov, raising his eyes to Porfiry.

"And... do you believe in Lazarus' rising from the dead?"

"I... I do. Why do you ask all this?"

"You believe it literally?"

"Literally."

"You don't say so.... I asked from curiosity. Excuse me. But let us go back to the question; they are not always executed. Some, on the contrary..."

"Triumph in their lifetime? Oh, yes, some attain their ends in this life, and then..."

"They begin executing other people?"

"If it's necessary; indeed, for the most part they do. Your remark is very witty."

"Thank you. But tell me this: how do you distinguish those extraordinary people from the ordinary ones? Are there signs at their birth? I feel there ought to be more exactitude, more external definition. Excuse the natural anxiety of a practical law-abiding citizen, but couldn't they adopt a special uniform, for instance, couldn't they wear something, be branded in some way? For you know if confusion arises and a member of one category imagines that he belongs to the other, begins to 'eliminate obstacles' as you so happily expressed it, then..."

"Oh, that very often happens! That remark is wittier than the other."

"Thank you."

"No reason to; but take note that the mistake can only arise in the first category, that is among the ordinary people (as I perhaps unfortunately called them). In spite of their predisposition to obedience very many of them, through a playfulness of nature, sometimes vouchsafed even to the cow, like to imagine themselves advanced people, 'destroyers,' and to push themselves into the 'new movement,' and this quite sincerely. Meanwhile the really *new* people are very often unobserved by them, or even despised as reactionaries of grovelling tendencies. But I don't think there is any considerable danger here, and you really need not be uneasy for they never go very far. Of course, they might have a thrashing sometimes for letting their fancy run away with them and to teach them their place, but no more; in fact, even this isn't necessary as they castigate themselves, for they are very conscientious: some perform this service for one another and others chastise themselves with their own hands.... They will impose various public acts of penitence upon themselves with a beautiful and edifying effect; in fact you've nothing to be uneasy about.... It's a law of nature."

"Well, you have certainly set my mind more at rest on that score; but there's another thing worries me. Tell me, please, are there many people who have the right to kill others, these extraordinary people? I am ready to bow down to them, of course, but you must admit it's alarming if there are a great many of them, eh?"

"Oh, you needn't worry about that either," Raskolnikov went on in the same tone. "People with new ideas, people with the faintest capacity for saying something *new*, are extremely few in number, extraordinarily so in fact. One thing only is clear, that the appearance of all these grades and subdivisions of men must follow with unfailing regularity some law of nature. That law, of course, is unknown at present, but I am convinced that it exists, and one day may become known. The vast mass of mankind is mere material, and only exists in order by some great effort, by some mysterious process, by means of some crossing of races and stocks, to bring into the world at last perhaps one man out of a thousand with a spark of independence. One in ten thousand perhaps—I speak roughly, approximately—is born with some independence, and with still greater independence one in a hundred thousand. The man of genius is one of millions, and the great geniuses, the crown of humanity, appear on earth perhaps one in many thousand millions. In fact I have not peeped into the retort in which all this takes place. But there certainly is and must be a definite law, it cannot be a matter of chance."

"Why, are you both joking?" Razumihin cried at last. "There you sit, making fun of one another. Are you serious, Rodya?"

Raskolnikov raised his pale and almost mournful face and made no reply. And the unconcealed, persistent, nervous, and *discourteous* sarcasm of Porfiry seemed strange to Razumihin beside that quiet and mournful face.

"Well, brother, if you are really serious... You are right, of course, in saying that it's not new, that it's like what we've read and heard a thousand times already; but what is really original in all this, and is exclusively your own, to my horror, is that you sanction bloodshed *in the name of conscience*, and, excuse my saying so, with such fanaticism.... That, I take it, is the point of your article. But that sanction of bloodshed *by conscience* is to my mind... more terrible than the official, legal sanction of bloodshed...."

"You are quite right, it is more terrible," Porfiry agreed.

"Yes, you must have exaggerated! There is some mistake, I shall read it. You can't think that! I shall read it."

"All that is not in the article, there's only a hint of it," said Raskolnikov.

"Yes, yes." Porfiry couldn't sit still. "Your attitude to crime is pretty clear to me now, but... excuse me for my impertinence (I am really ashamed to be worrying you like this), you see, you've removed my anxiety as to the two grades getting mixed, but... there are various practical possibilities that make me uneasy! What if some man or youth imagines that he is a Lycurgus or Mahomet—a future one of course—and suppose he begins to remove all obstacles.... He has some great enterprise before him and needs money for it... and tries to get it... do you see?"

Zametov gave a sudden guffaw in his corner. Raskolnikov did not even raise his eyes to him.

"I must admit," he went on calmly, "that such cases certainly must arise. The vain and foolish are particularly apt to fall into that snare; young people especially."

"Yes, you see. Well then?"

"What then?" Raskolnikov smiled in reply; "that's not my fault. So it is and so it always will be. He said just now (he nodded at Razumihin) that I sanction bloodshed. Society is too well protected by prisons, banishment, criminal investigators, penal servitude. There's no need to be uneasy. You have but to catch the thief."

"And what if we do catch him?"

"Then he gets what he deserves."

"You are certainly logical. But what of his conscience?"

"Why do you care about that?"

"Simply from humanity."

"If he has a conscience he will suffer for his mistake. That will be his punishment—as well as the prison."

"But the real geniuses," asked Razumihin frowning, "those who have the right to murder? Oughtn't they to suffer at all even for the blood they've shed?"

"Why the word *ought*? It's not a matter of permission or prohibition. He will suffer if he is sorry for his victim. Pain and suffering are always inevitable for a large intelligence and a deep heart. The really great men must, I think, have great sadness on earth," he added dreamily, not in the tone of the conversation.

He raised his eyes, looked earnestly at them all, smiled, and took his cap. He was too quiet by comparison with his manner at his entrance, and he felt this. Everyone got up.

"Well, you may abuse me, be angry with me if you like," Porfiry Petrovitch began again, "but I can't resist. Allow me one little question (I know I am troubling you). There is just one little notion I want to express, simply that I may not forget it."

"Very good, tell me your little notion," Raskolnikov stood waiting, pale and grave before him.

"Well, you see... I really don't know how to express it properly.... It's a playful, psychological idea.... When you were writing your article, surely you couldn't have helped, he-he! fancying yourself... just a little, an 'extraordinary' man, uttering a *new word* in your sense.... That's so, isn't it?"

"Quite possibly," Raskolnikov answered contemptuously.

Razumihin made a movement.

"And, if so, could you bring yourself in case of worldly difficulties and hardship or for some service to humanity—to overstep obstacles?... For instance, to rob and murder?"

And again he winked with his left eye, and laughed noiselessly just as before.

"If I did I certainly should not tell you," Raskolnikov answered with defiant and haughty contempt.

"No, I was only interested on account of your article, from a literary point of view..."

"Foo! how obvious and insolent that is!" Raskolnikov thought with repulsion.

"Allow me to observe," he answered dryly, "that I don't consider myself a Mahomet or a Napoleon, nor any personage of that kind, and not being one of them I cannot tell you how I should act."

"Oh, come, don't we all think ourselves Napoleons now in Russia?" Porfiry Petrovitch said with alarming familiarity.

Something peculiar betrayed itself in the very intonation of his voice.

"Perhaps it was one of these future Napoleons who did for Alyona Ivanovna last week?" Zametov blurted out from the corner.

Raskolnikov did not speak, but looked firmly and intently at Porfiry. Razumihin was scowling gloomily. He seemed before this to be noticing something. He looked angrily around. There was a minute of gloomy silence. Raskolnikov turned to go.

"Are you going already?" Porfiry said amiably, holding out his hand with excessive politeness. "Very, very glad of your acquaintance. As for your request, have no uneasiness, write just as I told you, or, better still, come to me there yourself in a day or two... tomorrow, indeed. I shall be there at eleven o'clock for certain. We'll arrange it all; we'll have a talk. As one of the last to be *there*, you might perhaps be able to tell us something," he added with a most good-natured expression.

"You want to cross-examine me officially in due form?" Raskolnikov asked sharply.

"Oh, why? That's not necessary for the present. You misunderstand me. I lose no opportunity, you see, and... I've talked with all who had pledges.... I obtained evidence from some of them, and you are the last.... Yes, by the way," he cried, seemingly suddenly delighted, "I just remember, what was I thinking of?" he turned to Razumihin, "you were talking my ears off about that Nikolay... of course, I know, I know very well," he turned to Raskolnikov, "that the fellow is innocent, but what is one to do? We had to trouble Dmitri too.... This is the point, this is all: when you went up the stairs it was past seven, wasn't it?"

"Yes," answered Raskolnikov, with an unpleasant sensation at the very moment he spoke that he need not have said it.

"Then when you went upstairs between seven and eight, didn't you see in a flat that stood open on a second storey, do you remember? two workmen or at least one of them? They were painting there, didn't you notice them? It's very, very important for them."

"Painters? No, I didn't see them," Raskolnikov answered slowly, as though ransacking his memory, while at the same instant he was racking every nerve, almost swooning with anxiety to conjecture as quickly as possible where the trap lay and not to overlook anything. "No, I didn't see them, and I don't think I noticed a flat like that open.... But on the fourth storey" (he had mastered the trap now and was triumphant) "I remember now that someone was moving out of the flat opposite Alyona Ivanovna's.... I remember... I remember it clearly. Some porters were carrying out a sofa and they squeezed me against the wall. But painters... no, I don't remember that there were any painters, and I don't think that there was a flat open anywhere, no, there wasn't."

"What do you mean?" Razumihin shouted suddenly, as though he had reflected and realised. "Why, it was on the day of the murder the painters were at work, and he was there three days before? What are you asking?"

"Foo! I have muddled it!" Porfiry slapped himself on the forehead. "Deuce take it! This business is turning my brain!" he addressed Raskolnikov somewhat apologetically. "It would be such a great thing for us to find out whether anyone had seen them between seven and eight at the flat, so I fancied you could perhaps have told us something.... I quite muddled it."

"Then you should be more careful," Razumihin observed grimly.

The last words were uttered in the passage. Porfiry Petrovitch saw them to the door with excessive politeness.

They went out into the street gloomy and sullen, and for some steps they did not say a word. Raskolnikov drew a deep breath.

146

"I don't believe it, I can't believe it!" repeated Razumihin, trying in perplexity to refute Raskolnikov's arguments.

They were by now approaching Bakaleyev's lodgings, where Pulcheria Alexandrovna and Dounia had been expecting them a long while. Razumihin kept stopping on the way in the heat of discussion, confused and excited by the very fact that they were for the first time speaking openly about *it*.

"Don't believe it, then!" answered Raskolnikov, with a cold, careless smile. "You were noticing nothing as usual, but I was weighing every word."

"You are suspicious. That is why you weighed their words... h'm... certainly, I agree, Porfiry's tone was rather strange, and still more that wretch Zametov!... You are right, there was something about him—but why? Why?"

"He has changed his mind since last night."

"Quite the contrary! If they had that brainless idea, they would do their utmost to hide it, and conceal their cards, so as to catch you afterwards.... But it was all impudent and careless."

"If they had had facts—I mean, real facts—or at least grounds for suspicion, then they would certainly have tried to hide their game, in the hope of getting more (they would have made a search long ago besides). But they have no facts, not one. It is all mirage—all ambiguous. Simply a floating idea. So they try to throw me out by impudence. And perhaps, he was irritated at having no facts, and blurted it out in his vexation—or perhaps he has some plan... he seems an intelligent man. Perhaps he wanted to frighten me by pretending to know. They have a psychology of their own, brother. But it is loathsome explaining it all. Stop!"

"And it's insulting, insulting! I understand you. But... since we have spoken openly now (and it is an excellent thing that we have at last—I am glad) I will own now frankly that I noticed it in them long ago, this idea. Of course the merest hint only—an insinuation—but why an insinuation even? How dare they? What foundation have they? If only you knew how furious I have been. Think only! Simply because a poor student, unhinged by poverty and hypochondria, on the eve of a severe delirious illness (note that), suspicious, vain, proud, who has not seen a soul to speak to for six months, in rags and in boots without soles, has to face some wretched policemen and put up with their insolence; and the unexpected debt thrust under his nose, the IOU presented by Tchebarov, the new paint, thirty degrees Reaumur and a stifling atmosphere, a crowd of people, the talk about the murder of a person where he had been just before, and all that on an empty stomach—he might well have a fainting fit! And that, that is what they found it all on! Damn them! I understand how annoying it is, but in your place, Rodya, I would laugh at them, or better still, spit in their ugly faces, and spit a dozen times in all directions. I'd hit out in all directions, neatly too, and so I'd put an end to it. Damn them! Don't be downhearted. It's a shame!"

"He really has put it well, though," Raskolnikov thought.

"Damn them? But the cross-examination again, tomorrow?" he said with bitterness. "Must I really enter into explanations with them? I feel vexed as it is, that I condescended to speak to Zametov yesterday in the restaurant...."

"Damn it! I will go myself to Porfiry. I will squeeze it out of him, as one of the family: he must let me know the ins and outs of it all! And as for Zametov..."

"At last he sees through him!" thought Raskolnikov.

"Stay!" cried Razumihin, seizing him by the shoulder again. "Stay! you were wrong. I have thought it out. You are wrong! How was that a trap? You say that the question about the workmen was a trap. But if you had done *that*, could you have said you had seen them painting the flat... and the workmen? On the contrary, you would have seen nothing, even if you had seen it. Who would own it against himself?"

"If I had done *that thing*, I should certainly have said that I had seen the workmen and the flat," Raskolnikov answered, with reluctance and obvious disgust.

"But why speak against yourself?"

"Because only peasants, or the most inexperienced novices deny everything flatly at examinations. If a man is ever so little developed and experienced, he will certainly try to admit all the external facts that can't be avoided, but will seek other explanations of them, will introduce some special, unexpected turn, that will give them another significance and put them in another light. Porfiry might well reckon that I should be sure to answer so, and say I had seen them to give an air of truth, and then make some explanation."

"But he would have told you at once that the workmen could not have been there two days before, and that therefore you must have been there on the day of the murder at eight o'clock. And so he would have caught you over a detail."

"Yes, that is what he was reckoning on, that I should not have time to reflect, and should be in a hurry to make the most likely answer, and so would forget that the workmen could not have been there two days before."

"But how could you forget it?"

"Nothing easier. It is in just such stupid things clever people are most easily caught. The more cunning a man is, the less he suspects that he will be caught in a simple thing. The more cunning a man is, the simpler the trap he must be caught in. Porfiry is not such a fool as you think...."

"He is a knave then, if that is so!"

Raskolnikov could not help laughing. But at the very moment, he was struck by the strangeness of his own frankness, and the eagerness with which he had made this explanation, though he had kept up all the preceding conversation with gloomy repulsion, obviously with a motive, from necessity.

"I am getting a relish for certain aspects!" he thought to himself. But almost at the same instant he became suddenly uneasy, as though an unexpected and alarming idea had occurred to him. His uneasiness kept on increasing. They had just reached the entrance to Bakaleyev's.

"Go in alone!" said Raskolnikov suddenly. "I will be back directly."

"Where are you going? Why, we are just here."

"I can't help it.... I will come in half an hour. Tell them."

"Say what you like, I will come with you."

"You, too, want to torture me!" he screamed, with such bitter irritation, such despair in his eyes that Razumihin's hands dropped. He stood for some time on the steps, looking gloomily at Raskolnikov striding rapidly away in the direction of his lodging. At last, gritting his teeth and clenching his fist, he swore he would squeeze Porfiry like a lemon that very day, and went up the stairs to reassure Pulcheria Alexandrovna, who was by now alarmed at their long absence.

When Raskolnikov got home, his hair was soaked with sweat and he was breathing heavily. He went rapidly up the stairs, walked into his unlocked room and at once fastened the latch. Then in senseless terror he rushed to the corner, to that hole under the paper where he had put the things; put his hand in, and for some minutes felt carefully in the hole, in every crack and fold of the paper. Finding nothing, he got up and drew a deep breath. As he was reaching the steps of Bakaleyev's, he suddenly fancied that something, a chain, a stud or even a bit of paper in which they had been wrapped with the old woman's handwriting on it, might somehow have slipped out and been lost in some crack, and then might suddenly turn up as unexpected, conclusive evidence against him.

He stood as though lost in thought, and a strange, humiliated, half senseless smile strayed on his lips. He took his cap at last and went quietly out of the room. His ideas were all tangled. He went dreamily through the gateway.

"Here he is himself," shouted a loud voice.

He raised his head.

148

The porter was standing at the door of his little room and was pointing him out to a short man who looked like an artisan, wearing a long coat and a waistcoat, and looking at a distance remarkably like a woman. He stooped, and his head in a greasy cap hung forward. From his wrinkled flabby face he looked over fifty; his little eyes were lost in fat and they looked out grimly, sternly and discontentedly.

"What is it?" Raskolnikov asked, going up to the porter.

The man stole a look at him from under his brows and he looked at him attentively, deliberately; then he turned slowly and went out of the gate into the street without saying a word.

"What is it?" cried Raskolnikov.

"Why, he there was asking whether a student lived here, mentioned your name and whom you lodged with. I saw you coming and pointed you out and he went away. It's funny."

The porter too seemed rather puzzled, but not much so, and after wondering for a moment he turned and went back to his room.

Raskolnikov ran after the stranger, and at once caught sight of him walking along the other side of the street with the same even, deliberate step with his eyes fixed on the ground, as though in meditation. He soon overtook him, but for some time walked behind him. At last, moving on to a level with him, he looked at his face. The man noticed him at once, looked at him quickly, but dropped his eyes again; and so they walked for a minute side by side without uttering a word.

"You were inquiring for me... of the porter?" Raskolnikov said at last, but in a curiously quiet voice.

The man made no answer; he didn't even look at him. Again they were both silent.

"Why do you... come and ask for me... and say nothing.... What's the meaning of it?" Raskolnikov's voice broke and he seemed unable to articulate the words clearly.

The man raised his eyes this time and turned a gloomy sinister look at Raskolnikov.

"Murderer!" he said suddenly in a quiet but clear and distinct voice.

Raskolnikov went on walking beside him. His legs felt suddenly weak, a cold shiver ran down his spine, and his heart seemed to stand still for a moment, then suddenly began throbbing as though it were set free. So they walked for about a hundred paces, side by side in silence.

The man did not look at him.

"What do you mean... what is.... Who is a murderer?" muttered Raskolnikov hardly audibly.

"*You* are a murderer," the man answered still more articulately and emphatically, with a smile of triumphant hatred, and again he looked straight into Raskolnikov's pale face and stricken eyes.

They had just reached the crossroads. The man turned to the left without looking behind him. Raskolnikov remained standing, gazing after him. He saw him turn round fifty paces away and look back at him still standing there. Raskolnikov could not see clearly, but he fancied that he was again smiling the same smile of cold hatred and triumph.

With slow faltering steps, with shaking knees, Raskolnikov made his way back to his little garret, feeling chilled all over. He took off his cap and put it on the table, and for ten minutes he stood without moving. Then he sank exhausted on the sofa and with a weak moan of pain he stretched himself on it. So he lay for half an hour.

He thought of nothing. Some thoughts or fragments of thoughts, some images without order or coherence floated before his mind—faces of people he had seen in his childhood or met somewhere once, whom he would never have recalled, the belfry of the church at V——, the billiard table in a restaurant and some officers playing billiards, the smell of cigars in some underground tobacco shop, a tavern room, a back staircase quite dark, all sloppy with dirty water and strewn with eggshells, and the Sunday bells floating in from somewhere.... The images followed one another, whirling like a hurricane. Some of them he liked and tried to clutch at, but they faded and all the while there was an oppression within him, but it was not overwhelming, sometimes it was even pleasant.... The slight shivering still persisted, but that too was an almost pleasant sensation.

He heard the hurried footsteps of Razumihin; he closed his eyes and pretended to be asleep. Razumihin opened the door and stood for some time in the doorway as though hesitating, then he

149

stepped softly into the room and went cautiously to the sofa. Raskolnikov heard Nastasya's whisper:

"Don't disturb him! Let him sleep. He can have his dinner later."

"Quite so," answered Razumihin. Both withdrew carefully and closed the door. Another half-hour passed. Raskolnikov opened his eyes, turned on his back again, clasping his hands behind his head.

"Who is he? Who is that man who sprang out of the earth? Where was he, what did he see? He has seen it all, that's clear. Where was he then? And from where did he see? Why has he only now sprung out of the earth? And how could he see? Is it possible? Hm..." continued Raskolnikov, turning cold and shivering, "and the jewel case Nikolay found behind the door—was that possible? A clue? You miss an infinitesimal line and you can build it into a pyramid of evidence! A fly flew by and saw it! Is it possible?" He felt with sudden loathing how weak, how physically weak he had become. "I ought to have known it," he thought with a bitter smile. "And how dared I, knowing myself, knowing how I should be, take up an axe and shed blood! I ought to have known beforehand.... Ah, but I did know!" he whispered in despair. At times he came to a standstill at some thought.

"No, those men are not made so. The real *Master* to whom all is permitted storms Toulon, makes a massacre in Paris, *forgets* an army in Egypt, *wastes* half a million men in the Moscow expedition and gets off with a jest at Vilna. And altars are set up to him after his death, and so *all* is permitted. No, such people, it seems, are not of flesh but of bronze!"

One sudden irrelevant idea almost made him laugh. Napoleon, the pyramids, Waterloo, and a wretched skinny old woman, a pawnbroker with a red trunk under her bed—it's a nice hash for Porfiry Petrovitch to digest! How can they digest it! It's too inartistic. "A Napoleon creep under an old woman's bed! Ugh, how loathsome!"

At moments he felt he was raving. He sank into a state of feverish excitement. "The old woman is of no consequence," he thought, hotly and incoherently. "The old woman was a mistake perhaps, but she is not what matters! The old woman was only an illness.... I was in a hurry to overstep.... I didn't kill a human being, but a principle! I killed the principle, but I didn't overstep, I stopped on this side.... I was only capable of killing. And it seems I wasn't even capable of that... Principle? Why was that fool Razumihin abusing the socialists? They are industrious, commercial people; 'the happiness of all' is their case. No, life is only given to me once and I shall never have it again; I don't want to wait for 'the happiness of all.' I want to live myself, or else better not live at all. I simply couldn't pass by my mother starving, keeping my rouble in my pocket while I waited for the 'happiness of all.' I am putting my little brick into the happiness of all and so my heart is at peace. Ha-ha! Why have you let me slip? I only live once, I too want.... Ech, I am an aesthetic louse and nothing more," he added suddenly, laughing like a madman. "Yes, I am certainly a louse," he went on, clutching at the idea, gloating over it and playing with it with vindictive pleasure. "In the first place, because I can reason that I am one, and secondly, because for a month past I have been troubling benevolent Providence, calling it to witness that not for my own fleshly lusts did I undertake it, but with a grand and noble object—ha-ha! Thirdly, because I aimed at carrying it out as justly as possible, weighing, measuring and calculating. Of all the lice I picked out the most useless one and proposed to take from her only as much as I needed for the first step, no more nor less (so the rest would have gone to a monastery, according to her will, ha-ha!). And what shows that I am utterly a louse," he added, grinding his teeth, "is that I am perhaps viler and more loathsome than the louse I killed, and *I felt beforehand* that I should tell myself so *after* killing her. Can anything be compared with the horror of that? The vulgarity! The abjectness! I understand the 'prophet' with his sabre, on his steed: Allah commands and 'trembling' creation must obey! The 'prophet' is right, he is right when he sets a battery across the street and blows up the innocent and the guilty without deigning to explain! It's for you to obey, trembling creation, and not *to have desires*, for that's not for you!... I shall never, never forgive the old woman!"

His hair was soaked with sweat, his quivering lips were parched, his eyes were fixed on the ceiling.

150

"Mother, sister—how I loved them! Why do I hate them now? Yes, I hate them, I feel a physical hatred for them, I can't bear them near me.... I went up to my mother and kissed her, I remember.... To embrace her and think if she only knew... shall I tell her then? That's just what I might do.... *She* must be the same as I am," he added, straining himself to think, as it were struggling with delirium. "Ah, how I hate the old woman now! I feel I should kill her again if she came to life! Poor Lizaveta! Why did she come in?... It's strange though, why is it I scarcely ever think of her, as though I hadn't killed her? Lizaveta! Sonia! Poor gentle things, with gentle eyes.... Dear women! Why don't they weep? Why don't they moan? They give up everything... their eyes are soft and gentle.... Sonia, Sonia! Gentle Sonia!"

He lost consciousness; it seemed strange to him that he didn't remember how he got into the street. It was late evening. The twilight had fallen and the full moon was shining more and more brightly; but there was a peculiar breathlessness in the air. There were crowds of people in the street; workmen and business people were making their way home; other people had come out for a walk; there was a smell of mortar, dust and stagnant water. Raskolnikov walked along, mournful and anxious; he was distinctly aware of having come out with a purpose, of having to do something in a hurry, but what it was he had forgotten. Suddenly he stood still and saw a man standing on the other side of the street, beckoning to him. He crossed over to him, but at once the man turned and walked away with his head hanging, as though he had made no sign to him. "Stay, did he really beckon?" Raskolnikov wondered, but he tried to overtake him. When he was within ten paces he recognised him and was frightened; it was the same man with stooping shoulders in the long coat. Raskolnikov followed him at a distance; his heart was beating; they went down a turning; the man still did not look round. "Does he know I am following him?" thought Raskolnikov. The man went into the gateway of a big house. Raskolnikov hastened to the gate and looked in to see whether he would look round and sign to him. In the courtyard the man did turn round and again seemed to beckon him. Raskolnikov at once followed him into the yard, but the man was gone. He must have gone up the first staircase. Raskolnikov rushed after him. He heard slow measured steps two flights above. The staircase seemed strangely familiar. He reached the window on the first floor; the moon shone through the panes with a melancholy and mysterious light; then he reached the second floor. Bah! this is the flat where the painters were at work... but how was it he did not recognise it at once? The steps of the man above had died away. "So he must have stopped or hidden somewhere." He reached the third storey, should he go on? There was a stillness that was dreadful.... But he went on. The sound of his own footsteps scared and frightened him. How dark it was! The man must be hiding in some corner here. Ah! the flat was standing wide open, he hesitated and went in. It was very dark and empty in the passage, as though everything had been removed; he crept on tiptoe into the parlour which was flooded with moonlight. Everything there was as before, the chairs, the looking-glass, the yellow sofa and the pictures in the frames. A huge, round, copper-red moon looked in at the windows. "It's the moon that makes it so still, weaving some mystery," thought Raskolnikov. He stood and waited, waited a long while, and the more silent the moonlight, the more violently his heart beat, till it was painful. And still the same hush. Suddenly he heard a momentary sharp crack like the snapping of a splinter and all was still again. A fly flew up suddenly and struck the window pane with a plaintive buzz. At that moment he noticed in the corner between the window and the little cupboard something like a cloak hanging on the wall. "Why is that cloak here?" he thought, "it wasn't there before...." He went up to it quietly and felt that there was someone hiding behind it. He cautiously moved the cloak and saw, sitting on a chair in the corner, the old woman bent double so that he couldn't see her face; but it was she. He stood over her. "She is afraid," he thought. He stealthily took the axe from the noose and struck her one blow, then another on the skull. But strange to say she did not stir, as though she were made of wood. He was frightened, bent down nearer and tried to look at her; but she, too, bent her head lower. He bent right down to the ground and peeped up into her face from below, he peeped and turned cold with horror: the old woman was sitting and laughing, shaking with noiseless laughter, doing her utmost that he should not hear it. Suddenly he fancied that the door from the bedroom was opened a little and that there was laughter and whispering within. He was overcome with frenzy and he began hitting the old woman on the head with all his force, but at every blow of the axe the laughter and whispering from the bedroom grew louder and the old woman was simply shaking with mirth. He was rushing away, but the passage was full of people, the doors of the flats stood open and on the landing, on the stairs and everywhere below there were people, rows of heads, all looking, but huddled together in silence and expectation. Something gripped his heart, his legs were rooted to the spot, they would not move.... He tried to scream and woke up.

He drew a deep breath—but his dream seemed strangely to persist: his door was flung open and a man whom he had never seen stood in the doorway watching him intently.

Raskolnikov had hardly opened his eyes and he instantly closed them again. He lay on his back without stirring.

"Is it still a dream?" he wondered and again raised his eyelids hardly perceptibly; the stranger was standing in the same place, still watching him.

He stepped cautiously into the room, carefully closing the door after him, went up to the table, paused a moment, still keeping his eyes on Raskolnikov, and noiselessly seated himself on the chair by the sofa; he put his hat on the floor beside him and leaned his hands on his cane and his chin on his hands. It was evident that he was prepared to wait indefinitely. As far as Raskolnikov could make out from his stolen glances, he was a man no longer young, stout, with a full, fair, almost whitish beard.

Ten minutes passed. It was still light, but beginning to get dusk. There was complete stillness in the room. Not a sound came from the stairs. Only a big fly buzzed and fluttered against the window pane. It was unbearable at last. Raskolnikov suddenly got up and sat on the sofa.

"Come, tell me what you want."

"I knew you were not asleep, but only pretending," the stranger answered oddly, laughing calmly. "Arkady Ivanovitch Svidrigaïlov, allow me to introduce myself...."

"Can this be still a dream?" Raskolnikov thought once more.

He looked carefully and suspiciously at the unexpected visitor.

"Svidrigaïlov! What nonsense! It can't be!" he said at last aloud in bewilderment.

His visitor did not seem at all surprised at this exclamation.

"I've come to you for two reasons. In the first place, I wanted to make your personal acquaintance, as I have already heard a great deal about you that is interesting and flattering; secondly, I cherish the hope that you may not refuse to assist me in a matter directly concerning the welfare of your sister, Avdotya Romanovna. For without your support she might not let me come near her now, for she is prejudiced against me, but with your assistance I reckon on..."

"You reckon wrongly," interrupted Raskolnikov.

"They only arrived yesterday, may I ask you?"

Raskolnikov made no reply.

"It was yesterday, I know. I only arrived myself the day before. Well, let me tell you this, Rodion Romanovitch, I don't consider it necessary to justify myself, but kindly tell me what was there particularly criminal on my part in all this business, speaking without prejudice, with common sense?"

Raskolnikov continued to look at him in silence.

"That in my own house I persecuted a defenceless girl and 'insulted her with my infamous proposals'—is that it? (I am anticipating you.) But you've only to assume that I, too, am a man *et nihil humanum*... in a word, that I am capable of being attracted and falling in love (which does not depend on our will), then everything can be explained in the most natural manner. The question is, am I a monster, or am I myself a victim? And what if I am a victim? In proposing to the object of my passion to elope with me to America or Switzerland, I may have cherished the deepest respect for her and may have thought that I was promoting our mutual happiness! Reason is the slave of passion, you know; why, probably, I was doing more harm to myself than anyone!"

"But that's not the point," Raskolnikov interrupted with disgust. "It's simply that whether you are right or wrong, we dislike you. We don't want to have anything to do with you. We show you the door. Go out!"

Svidrigaïlov broke into a sudden laugh.

"But you're... but there's no getting round you," he said, laughing in the frankest way. "I hoped to get round you, but you took up the right line at once!"

"But you are trying to get round me still!"

"What of it? What of it?" cried Svidrigaïlov, laughing openly. "But this is what the French call *bonne guerre*, and the most innocent form of deception!... But still you have interrupted me; one way or another, I repeat again: there would never have been any unpleasantness except for what happened in the garden. Marfa Petrovna..."

"You have got rid of Marfa Petrovna, too, so they say?" Raskolnikov interrupted rudely.

"Oh, you've heard that, too, then? You'd be sure to, though.... But as for your question, I really don't know what to say, though my own conscience is quite at rest on that score. Don't suppose that I am in any apprehension about it. All was regular and in order; the medical inquiry diagnosed apoplexy due to bathing immediately after a heavy dinner and a bottle of wine, and indeed it could have proved nothing else. But I'll tell you what I have been thinking to myself of late, on my way here in the train, especially: didn't I contribute to all that... calamity, morally, in a way, by irritation or something of the sort. But I came to the conclusion that that, too, was quite out of the question."

Raskolnikov laughed.

"I wonder you trouble yourself about it!"

"But what are you laughing at? Only consider, I struck her just twice with a switch—there were no marks even... don't regard me as a cynic, please; I am perfectly aware how atrocious it was of me and all that; but I know for certain, too, that Marfa Petrovna was very likely pleased at my, so to say, warmth. The story of your sister had been wrung out to the last drop; for the last three days Marfa Petrovna had been forced to sit at home; she had nothing to show herself with in the town. Besides, she had bored them so with that letter (you heard about her reading the letter). And all of a sudden those two switches fell from heaven! Her first act was to order the carriage to be got out.... Not to speak of the fact that there are cases when women are very, very glad to be insulted in spite of all their show of indignation. There are instances of it with everyone; human beings in general, indeed, greatly love to be insulted, have you noticed that? But it's particularly so with women. One might even say it's their only amusement."

At one time Raskolnikov thought of getting up and walking out and so finishing the interview. But some curiosity and even a sort of prudence made him linger for a moment.

"You are fond of fighting?" he asked carelessly.

"No, not very," Svidrigaïlov answered, calmly. "And Marfa Petrovna and I scarcely ever fought. We lived very harmoniously, and she was always pleased with me. I only used the whip twice in all our seven years (not counting a third occasion of a very ambiguous character). The first time, two months after our marriage, immediately after we arrived in the country, and the last time was that of which we are speaking. Did you suppose I was such a monster, such a reactionary, such a slave driver? Ha, ha! By the way, do you remember, Rodion Romanovitch, how a few years ago, in those days of beneficent publicity, a nobleman, I've forgotten his name, was put to shame everywhere, in all the papers, for having thrashed a German woman in the railway train. You remember? It was in those days, that very year I believe, the 'disgraceful action of the *Age*' took place (you know, 'The Egyptian Nights,' that public reading, you remember? The dark eyes, you know! Ah, the golden days of our youth, where are they?). Well, as for the gentleman who thrashed the German, I feel no sympathy with him, because after all what need is there for sympathy? But I must say that there are sometimes such provoking 'Germans' that I don't believe there is a progressive who could quite answer for himself. No one looked at the subject from that point of view then, but that's the truly humane point of view, I assure you."

After saying this, Svidrigaïlov broke into a sudden laugh again. Raskolnikov saw clearly that this was a man with a firm purpose in his mind and able to keep it to himself.

"I expect you've not talked to anyone for some days?" he asked.

"Scarcely anyone. I suppose you are wondering at my being such an adaptable man?"

"No, I am only wondering at your being too adaptable a man."

"Because I am not offended at the rudeness of your questions? Is that it? But why take offence? As you asked, so I answered," he replied, with a surprising expression of simplicity. "You know, there's hardly anything I take interest in," he went on, as it were dreamily, "especially now, I've nothing to do.... You are quite at liberty to imagine though that I am making up to you with a motive, particularly as I told you I want to see your sister about something. But I'll confess frankly, I am very much bored. The last three days especially, so I am delighted to see you.... Don't be angry, Rodion Romanovitch, but you seem to be somehow awfully strange yourself. Say what you like, there's something wrong with you, and now, too... not this very minute, I mean, but now, generally.... Well, well, I won't, I won't, don't scowl! I am not such a bear, you know, as you think."

Raskolnikov looked gloomily at him.

"You are not a bear, perhaps, at all," he said. "I fancy indeed that you are a man of very good breeding, or at least know how on occasion to behave like one."

"I am not particularly interested in anyone's opinion," Svidrigaïlov answered, dryly and even with a shade of haughtiness, "and therefore why not be vulgar at times when vulgarity is such a convenient cloak for our climate... and especially if one has a natural propensity that way," he added, laughing again.

"But I've heard you have many friends here. You are, as they say, 'not without connections.' What can you want with me, then, unless you've some special object?"

"That's true that I have friends here," Svidrigaïlov admitted, not replying to the chief point. "I've met some already. I've been lounging about for the last three days, and I've seen them, or they've seen me. That's a matter of course. I am well dressed and reckoned not a poor man; the emancipation of the serfs hasn't affected me; my property consists chiefly of forests and water meadows. The revenue has not fallen off; but… I am not going to see them, I was sick of them long ago. I've been here three days and have called on no one…. What a town it is! How has it come into existence among us, tell me that? A town of officials and students of all sorts. Yes, there's a great deal I didn't notice when I was here eight years ago, kicking up my heels…. My only hope now is in anatomy, by Jove, it is!"

"Anatomy?"

"But as for these clubs, Dussauts, parades, or progress, indeed, maybe—well, all that can go on without me," he went on, again without noticing the question. "Besides, who wants to be a cardsharper?"

"Why, have you been a cardsharper then?"

"How could I help being? There was a regular set of us, men of the best society, eight years ago; we had a fine time. And all men of breeding, you know, poets, men of property. And indeed as a rule in our Russian society the best manners are found among those who've been thrashed, have you noticed that? I've deteriorated in the country. But I did get into prison for debt, through a low Greek who came from Nezhin. Then Marfa Petrovna turned up; she bargained with him and bought me off for thirty thousand silver pieces (I owed seventy thousand). We were united in lawful wedlock and she bore me off into the country like a treasure. You know she was five years older than I. She was very fond of me. For seven years I never left the country. And, take note, that all my life she held a document over me, the IOU for thirty thousand roubles, so if I were to elect to be restive about anything I should be trapped at once! And she would have done it! Women find nothing incompatible in that."

"If it hadn't been for that, would you have given her the slip?"

"I don't know what to say. It was scarcely the document restrained me. I didn't want to go anywhere else. Marfa Petrovna herself invited me to go abroad, seeing I was bored, but I've been abroad before, and always felt sick there. For no reason, but the sunrise, the bay of Naples, the sea—you look at them and it makes you sad. What's most revolting is that one is really sad! No, it's better at home. Here at least one blames others for everything and excuses oneself. I should have gone perhaps on an expedition to the North Pole, because *j'ai le vin mauvais* and hate drinking, and there's nothing left but wine. I have tried it. But, I say, I've been told Berg is going up in a great balloon next Sunday from the Yusupov Garden and will take up passengers at a fee. Is it true?"

"Why, would you go up?"

"I… No, oh, no," muttered Svidrigaïlov really seeming to be deep in thought.

"What does he mean? Is he in earnest?" Raskolnikov wondered.

"No, the document didn't restrain me," Svidrigaïlov went on, meditatively. "It was my own doing, not leaving the country, and nearly a year ago Marfa Petrovna gave me back the document on my name-day and made me a present of a considerable sum of money, too. She had a fortune, you know. 'You see how I trust you, Arkady Ivanovitch'—that was actually her expression. You don't believe she used it? But do you know I managed the estate quite decently, they know me in the neighbourhood. I ordered books, too. Marfa Petrovna at first approved, but afterwards she was afraid of my over-studying."

"You seem to be missing Marfa Petrovna very much?"

"Missing her? Perhaps. Really, perhaps I am. And, by the way, do you believe in ghosts?"

"What ghosts?"

"Why, ordinary ghosts."

"Do you believe in them?"

"Perhaps not, *pour vous plaire*…. I wouldn't say no exactly."

"Do you see them, then?"

Svidrigaïlov looked at him rather oddly.

156

"Marfa Petrovna is pleased to visit me," he said, twisting his mouth into a strange smile.

"How do you mean 'she is pleased to visit you'?"

"She has been three times. I saw her first on the very day of the funeral, an hour after she was buried. It was the day before I left to come here. The second time was the day before yesterday, at daybreak, on the journey at the station of Malaya Vishera, and the third time was two hours ago in the room where I am staying. I was alone."

"Were you awake?"

"Quite awake. I was wide awake every time. She comes, speaks to me for a minute and goes out at the door—always at the door. I can almost hear her."

"What made me think that something of the sort must be happening to you?" Raskolnikov said suddenly.

At the same moment he was surprised at having said it. He was much excited.

"What! Did you think so?" Svidrigaïlov asked in astonishment. "Did you really? Didn't I say that there was something in common between us, eh?"

"You never said so!" Raskolnikov cried sharply and with heat.

"Didn't I?"

"No!"

"I thought I did. When I came in and saw you lying with your eyes shut, pretending, I said to myself at once, 'Here's the man.'"

"What do you mean by 'the man?' What are you talking about?" cried Raskolnikov.

"What do I mean? I really don't know...." Svidrigaïlov muttered ingenuously, as though he, too, were puzzled.

For a minute they were silent. They stared in each other's faces.

"That's all nonsense!" Raskolnikov shouted with vexation. "What does she say when she comes to you?"

"She! Would you believe it, she talks of the silliest trifles and—man is a strange creature—it makes me angry. The first time she came in (I was tired you know: the funeral service, the funeral ceremony, the lunch afterwards. At last I was left alone in my study. I lighted a cigar and began to think), she came in at the door. 'You've been so busy today, Arkady Ivanovitch, you have forgotten to wind the dining-room clock,' she said. All those seven years I've wound that clock every week, and if I forgot it she would always remind me. The next day I set off on my way here. I got out at the station at daybreak; I'd been asleep, tired out, with my eyes half open, I was drinking some coffee. I looked up and there was suddenly Marfa Petrovna sitting beside me with a pack of cards in her hands. 'Shall I tell your fortune for the journey, Arkady Ivanovitch?' She was a great hand at telling fortunes. I shall never forgive myself for not asking her to. I ran away in a fright, and, besides, the bell rang. I was sitting today, feeling very heavy after a miserable dinner from a cookshop; I was sitting smoking, all of a sudden Marfa Petrovna again. She came in very smart in a new green silk dress with a long train. 'Good day, Arkady Ivanovitch! How do you like my dress? Aniska can't make like this.' (Aniska was a dressmaker in the country, one of our former serf girls who had been trained in Moscow, a pretty wench.) She stood turning round before me. I looked at the dress, and then I looked carefully, very carefully, at her face. 'I wonder you trouble to come to me about such trifles, Marfa Petrovna.' 'Good gracious, you won't let one disturb you about anything!' To tease her I said, 'I want to get married, Marfa Petrovna.' 'That's just like you, Arkady Ivanovitch; it does you very little credit to come looking for a bride when you've hardly buried your wife. And if you could make a good choice, at least, but I know it won't be for your happiness or hers, you will only be a laughingstock to all good people.' Then she went out and her train seemed to rustle. Isn't it nonsense, eh?"

"But perhaps you are telling lies?" Raskolnikov put in.

"I rarely lie," answered Svidrigaïlov thoughtfully, apparently not noticing the rudeness of the question.

"And in the past, have you ever seen ghosts before?"

"Y-yes, I have seen them, but only once in my life, six years ago. I had a serf, Filka; just after his burial I called out forgetting 'Filka, my pipe!' He came in and went to the cupboard where my

157

pipes were. I sat still and thought 'he is doing it out of revenge,' because we had a violent quarrel just before his death. 'How dare you come in with a hole in your elbow?' I said. 'Go away, you scamp!' He turned and went out, and never came again. I didn't tell Marfa Petrovna at the time. I wanted to have a service sung for him, but I was ashamed."

"You should go to a doctor."

"I know I am not well, without your telling me, though I don't know what's wrong; I believe I am five times as strong as you are. I didn't ask you whether you believe that ghosts are seen, but whether you believe that they exist."

"No, I won't believe it!" Raskolnikov cried, with positive anger.

"What do people generally say?" muttered Svidrigaïlov, as though speaking to himself, looking aside and bowing his head. "They say, 'You are ill, so what appears to you is only unreal fantasy.' But that's not strictly logical. I agree that ghosts only appear to the sick, but that only proves that they are unable to appear except to the sick, not that they don't exist."

"Nothing of the sort," Raskolnikov insisted irritably.

"No? You don't think so?" Svidrigaïlov went on, looking at him deliberately. "But what do you say to this argument (help me with it): ghosts are, as it were, shreds and fragments of other worlds, the beginning of them. A man in health has, of course, no reason to see them, because he is above all a man of this earth and is bound for the sake of completeness and order to live only in this life. But as soon as one is ill, as soon as the normal earthly order of the organism is broken, one begins to realise the possibility of another world; and the more seriously ill one is, the closer becomes one's contact with that other world, so that as soon as the man dies he steps straight into that world. I thought of that long ago. If you believe in a future life, you could believe in that, too."

"I don't believe in a future life," said Raskolnikov.

Svidrigaïlov sat lost in thought.

"And what if there are only spiders there, or something of that sort," he said suddenly.

"He is a madman," thought Raskolnikov.

"We always imagine eternity as something beyond our conception, something vast, vast! But why must it be vast? Instead of all that, what if it's one little room, like a bath house in the country, black and grimy and spiders in every corner, and that's all eternity is? I sometimes fancy it like that."

"Can it be you can imagine nothing juster and more comforting than that?" Raskolnikov cried, with a feeling of anguish.

"Juster? And how can we tell, perhaps that is just, and do you know it's what I would certainly have made it," answered Svidrigaïlov, with a vague smile.

This horrible answer sent a cold chill through Raskolnikov. Svidrigaïlov raised his head, looked at him, and suddenly began laughing.

"Only think," he cried, "half an hour ago we had never seen each other, we regarded each other as enemies; there is a matter unsettled between us; we've thrown it aside, and away we've gone into the abstract! Wasn't I right in saying that we were birds of a feather?"

"Kindly allow me," Raskolnikov went on irritably, "to ask you to explain why you have honoured me with your visit... and... and I am in a hurry, I have no time to waste. I want to go out."

"By all means, by all means. Your sister, Avdotya Romanovna, is going to be married to Mr. Luzhin, Pyotr Petrovitch?"

"Can you refrain from any question about my sister and from mentioning her name? I can't understand how you dare utter her name in my presence, if you really are Svidrigaïlov."

"Why, but I've come here to speak about her; how can I avoid mentioning her?"

"Very good, speak, but make haste."

"I am sure that you must have formed your own opinion of this Mr. Luzhin, who is a connection of mine through my wife, if you have only seen him for half an hour, or heard any facts about him. He is no match for Avdotya Romanovna. I believe Avdotya Romanovna is sacrificing herself generously and imprudently for the sake of... for the sake of her family. I fancied from all I had heard of you that you would be very glad if the match could be broken off without the sacrifice of worldly advantages. Now I know you personally, I am convinced of it."

"All this is very naive… excuse me, I should have said impudent on your part," said Raskolnikov.

"You mean to say that I am seeking my own ends. Don't be uneasy, Rodion Romanovitch, if I were working for my own advantage, I would not have spoken out so directly. I am not quite a fool. I will confess something psychologically curious about that: just now, defending my love for Avdotya Romanovna, I said I was myself the victim. Well, let me tell you that I've no feeling of love now, not the slightest, so that I wonder myself indeed, for I really did feel something…"

"Through idleness and depravity," Raskolnikov put in.

"I certainly am idle and depraved, but your sister has such qualities that even I could not help being impressed by them. But that's all nonsense, as I see myself now."

"Have you seen that long?"

"I began to be aware of it before, but was only perfectly sure of it the day before yesterday, almost at the moment I arrived in Petersburg. I still fancied in Moscow, though, that I was coming to try to get Avdotya Romanovna's hand and to cut out Mr. Luzhin."

"Excuse me for interrupting you; kindly be brief, and come to the object of your visit. I am in a hurry, I want to go out…"

"With the greatest pleasure. On arriving here and determining on a certain… journey, I should like to make some necessary preliminary arrangements. I left my children with an aunt; they are well provided for; and they have no need of me personally. And a nice father I should make, too! I have taken nothing but what Marfa Petrovna gave me a year ago. That's enough for me. Excuse me, I am just coming to the point. Before the journey which may come off, I want to settle Mr. Luzhin, too. It's not that I detest him so much, but it was through him I quarrelled with Marfa Petrovna when I learned that she had dished up this marriage. I want now to see Avdotya Romanovna through your mediation, and if you like in your presence, to explain to her that in the first place she will never gain anything but harm from Mr. Luzhin. Then, begging her pardon for all past unpleasantness, to make her a present of ten thousand roubles and so assist the rupture with Mr. Luzhin, a rupture to which I believe she is herself not disinclined, if she could see the way to it."

"You are certainly mad," cried Raskolnikov not so much angered as astonished. "How dare you talk like that!"

"I knew you would scream at me; but in the first place, though I am not rich, this ten thousand roubles is perfectly free; I have absolutely no need for it. If Avdotya Romanovna does not accept it, I shall waste it in some more foolish way. That's the first thing. Secondly, my conscience is perfectly easy; I make the offer with no ulterior motive. You may not believe it, but in the end Avdotya Romanovna and you will know. The point is, that I did actually cause your sister, whom I greatly respect, some trouble and unpleasantness, and so, sincerely regretting it, I want—not to compensate, not to repay her for the unpleasantness, but simply to do something to her advantage, to show that I am not, after all, privileged to do nothing but harm. If there were a millionth fraction of self-interest in my offer, I should not have made it so openly; and I should not have offered her ten thousand only, when five weeks ago I offered her more, Besides, I may, perhaps, very soon marry a young lady, and that alone ought to prevent suspicion of any design on Avdotya Romanovna. In conclusion, let me say that in marrying Mr. Luzhin, she is taking money just the same, only from another man. Don't be angry, Rodion Romanovitch, think it over coolly and quietly."

Svidrigaïlov himself was exceedingly cool and quiet as he was saying this.

"I beg you to say no more," said Raskolnikov. "In any case this is unpardonable impertinence."

"Not in the least. Then a man may do nothing but harm to his neighbour in this world, and is prevented from doing the tiniest bit of good by trivial conventional formalities. That's absurd. If I died, for instance, and left that sum to your sister in my will, surely she wouldn't refuse it?"

"Very likely she would."

"Oh, no, indeed. However, if you refuse it, so be it, though ten thousand roubles is a capital thing to have on occasion. In any case I beg you to repeat what I have said to Avdotya Romanovna."

"No, I won't."

"In that case, Rodion Romanovitch, I shall be obliged to try and see her myself and worry her by doing so."

"And if I do tell her, will you not try to see her?"

"I don't know really what to say. I should like very much to see her once more."

"Don't hope for it."

"I'm sorry. But you don't know me. Perhaps we may become better friends."

"You think we may become friends?"

"And why not?" Svidrigaïlov said, smiling. He stood up and took his hat. "I didn't quite intend to disturb you and I came here without reckoning on it... though I was very much struck by your face this morning."

"Where did you see me this morning?" Raskolnikov asked uneasily.

"I saw you by chance.... I kept fancying there is something about you like me.... But don't be uneasy. I am not intrusive; I used to get on all right with cardsharpers, and I never bored Prince Svirbey, a great personage who is a distant relation of mine, and I could write about Raphael's *Madonna* in Madam Prilukov's album, and I never left Marfa Petrovna's side for seven years, and I used to stay the night at Viazemsky's house in the Hay Market in the old days, and I may go up in a balloon with Berg, perhaps."

"Oh, all right. Are you starting soon on your travels, may I ask?"

"What travels?"

"Why, on that 'journey'; you spoke of it yourself."

"A journey? Oh, yes. I did speak of a journey. Well, that's a wide subject... if only you knew what you are asking," he added, and gave a sudden, loud, short laugh. "Perhaps I'll get married instead of the journey. They're making a match for me."

"Here?"

"Yes."

"How have you had time for that?"

"But I am very anxious to see Avdotya Romanovna once. I earnestly beg it. Well, goodbye for the present. Oh, yes. I have forgotten something. Tell your sister, Rodion Romanovitch, that Marfa Petrovna remembered her in her will and left her three thousand roubles. That's absolutely certain. Marfa Petrovna arranged it a week before her death, and it was done in my presence. Avdotya Romanovna will be able to receive the money in two or three weeks."

"Are you telling the truth?"

"Yes, tell her. Well, your servant. I am staying very near you."

As he went out, Svidrigaïlov ran up against Razumihin in the doorway.

II

It was nearly eight o'clock. The two young men hurried to Bakaleyev's, to arrive before Luzhin.

"Why, who was that?" asked Razumihin, as soon as they were in the street.

"It was Svidrigaïlov, that landowner in whose house my sister was insulted when she was their governess. Through his persecuting her with his attentions, she was turned out by his wife, Marfa Petrovna. This Marfa Petrovna begged Dounia's forgiveness afterwards, and she's just died suddenly. It was of her we were talking this morning. I don't know why I'm afraid of that man. He came here at once after his wife's funeral. He is very strange, and is determined on doing something.... We must guard Dounia from him... that's what I wanted to tell you, do you hear?"

"Guard her! What can he do to harm Avdotya Romanovna? Thank you, Rodya, for speaking to me like that.... We will, we will guard her. Where does he live?"

"I don't know."

"Why didn't you ask? What a pity! I'll find out, though."

"Did you see him?" asked Raskolnikov after a pause.

"Yes, I noticed him, I noticed him well."

"You did really see him? You saw him clearly?" Raskolnikov insisted.

"Yes, I remember him perfectly, I should know him in a thousand; I have a good memory for faces."

They were silent again.

"Hm!... that's all right," muttered Raskolnikov. "Do you know, I fancied... I keep thinking that it may have been an hallucination."

"What do you mean? I don't understand you."

"Well, you all say," Raskolnikov went on, twisting his mouth into a smile, "that I am mad. I thought just now that perhaps I really am mad, and have only seen a phantom."

"What do you mean?"

"Why, who can tell? Perhaps I am really mad, and perhaps everything that happened all these days may be only imagination."

"Ach, Rodya, you have been upset again!... But what did he say, what did he come for?"

Raskolnikov did not answer. Razumihin thought a minute.

"Now let me tell you my story," he began, "I came to you, you were asleep. Then we had dinner and then I went to Porfiry's, Zametov was still with him. I tried to begin, but it was no use. I couldn't speak in the right way. They don't seem to understand and can't understand, but are not a bit ashamed. I drew Porfiry to the window, and began talking to him, but it was still no use. He looked away and I looked away. At last I shook my fist in his ugly face, and told him as a cousin I'd brain him. He merely looked at me, I cursed and came away. That was all. It was very stupid. To Zametov I didn't say a word. But, you see, I thought I'd made a mess of it, but as I went downstairs a brilliant idea struck me: why should we trouble? Of course if you were in any danger or anything, but why need you care? You needn't care a hang for them. We shall have a laugh at them afterwards, and if I were in your place I'd mystify them more than ever. How ashamed they'll be afterwards! Hang them! We can thrash them afterwards, but let's laugh at them now!"

"To be sure," answered Raskolnikov. "But what will you say tomorrow?" he thought to himself. Strange to say, till that moment it had never occurred to him to wonder what Razumihin would think when he knew. As he thought it, Raskolnikov looked at him. Razumihin's account of his visit to Porfiry had very little interest for him, so much had come and gone since then.

In the corridor they came upon Luzhin; he had arrived punctually at eight, and was looking for the number, so that all three went in together without greeting or looking at one another. The young men walked in first, while Pyotr Petrovitch, for good manners, lingered a little in the passage, taking off his coat. Pulcheria Alexandrovna came forward at once to greet him in the doorway, Dounia was welcoming her brother. Pyotr Petrovitch walked in and quite amiably, though with redoubled dignity, bowed to the ladies. He looked, however, as though he were a little put out and could not yet recover himself. Pulcheria Alexandrovna, who seemed also a little embarrassed, hastened to make them all sit down at the round table where a samovar was boiling. Dounia and Luzhin were facing one another on opposite sides of the table. Razumihin and Raskolnikov were facing Pulcheria Alexandrovna, Razumihin was next to Luzhin and Raskolnikov was beside his sister.

A moment's silence followed. Pyotr Petrovitch deliberately drew out a cambric handkerchief reeking of scent and blew his nose with an air of a benevolent man who felt himself slighted, and was firmly resolved to insist on an explanation. In the passage the idea had occurred to him to keep on his overcoat and walk away, and so give the two ladies a sharp and emphatic lesson and make them feel the gravity of the position. But he could not bring himself to do this. Besides, he could not endure uncertainty, and he wanted an explanation: if his request had been so openly disobeyed, there was something behind it, and in that case it was better to find it out beforehand; it rested with him to punish them and there would always be time for that.

"I trust you had a favourable journey," he inquired officially of Pulcheria Alexandrovna.

"Oh, very, Pyotr Petrovitch."

"I am gratified to hear it. And Avdotya Romanovna is not overfatigued either?"

"I am young and strong, I don't get tired, but it was a great strain for mother," answered Dounia.

"That's unavoidable! our national railways are of terrible length. 'Mother Russia,' as they say, is a vast country.... In spite of all my desire to do so, I was unable to meet you yesterday. But I trust all passed off without inconvenience?"

"Oh, no, Pyotr Petrovitch, it was all terribly disheartening," Pulcheria Alexandrovna hastened to declare with peculiar intonation, "and if Dmitri Prokofitch had not been sent us, I really believe by God Himself, we should have been utterly lost. Here, he is! Dmitri Prokofitch Razumihin," she added, introducing him to Luzhin.

"I had the pleasure... yesterday," muttered Pyotr Petrovitch with a hostile glance sidelong at Razumihin; then he scowled and was silent.

Pyotr Petrovitch belonged to that class of persons, on the surface very polite in society, who make a great point of punctiliousness, but who, directly they are crossed in anything, are completely disconcerted, and become more like sacks of flour than elegant and lively men of society. Again all was silent; Raskolnikov was obstinately mute, Avdotya Romanovna was unwilling to open the conversation too soon. Razumihin had nothing to say, so Pulcheria Alexandrovna was anxious again.

"Marfa Petrovna is dead, have you heard?" she began having recourse to her leading item of conversation.

"To be sure, I heard so. I was immediately informed, and I have come to make you acquainted with the fact that Arkady Ivanovitch Svidrigaïlov set off in haste for Petersburg immediately after his wife's funeral. So at least I have excellent authority for believing."

"To Petersburg? here?" Dounia asked in alarm and looked at her mother.

"Yes, indeed, and doubtless not without some design, having in view the rapidity of his departure, and all the circumstances preceding it."

"Good heavens! won't he leave Dounia in peace even here?" cried Pulcheria Alexandrovna.

"I imagine that neither you nor Avdotya Romanovna have any grounds for uneasiness, unless, of course, you are yourselves desirous of getting into communication with him. For my part I am on my guard, and am now discovering where he is lodging."

"Oh, Pyotr Petrovitch, you would not believe what a fright you have given me," Pulcheria Alexandrovna went on: "I've only seen him twice, but I thought him terrible, terrible! I am convinced that he was the cause of Marfa Petrovna's death."

"It's impossible to be certain about that. I have precise information. I do not dispute that he may have contributed to accelerate the course of events by the moral influence, so to say, of the affront; but as to the general conduct and moral characteristics of that personage, I am in agreement with you. I do not know whether he is well off now, and precisely what Marfa Petrovna left him; this will be known to me within a very short period; but no doubt here in Petersburg, if he has any pecuniary resources, he will relapse at once into his old ways. He is the most depraved, and abjectly vicious specimen of that class of men. I have considerable reason to believe that Marfa Petrovna, who was so unfortunate as to fall in love with him and to pay his debts eight years ago, was of service to him also in another way. Solely by her exertions and sacrifices, a criminal charge, involving an element of fantastic and homicidal brutality for which he might well have been sentenced to Siberia, was hushed up. That's the sort of man he is, if you care to know."

"Good heavens!" cried Pulcheria Alexandrovna. Raskolnikov listened attentively.

"Are you speaking the truth when you say that you have good evidence of this?" Dounia asked sternly and emphatically.

"I only repeat what I was told in secret by Marfa Petrovna. I must observe that from the legal point of view the case was far from clear. There was, and I believe still is, living here a woman called Resslich, a foreigner, who lent small sums of money at interest, and did other commissions, and with this woman Svidrigaïlov had for a long while close and mysterious relations. She had a relation, a niece I believe, living with her, a deaf and dumb girl of fifteen, or perhaps not more than fourteen. Resslich hated this girl, and grudged her every crust; she used to beat her mercilessly. One day the girl was found hanging in the garret. At the inquest the verdict was suicide. After the usual proceedings the matter ended, but, later on, information was given that the child had been… cruelly outraged by Svidrigaïlov. It is true, this was not clearly established, the information was given by another German woman of loose character whose word could not be trusted; no statement was actually made to the police, thanks to Marfa Petrovna's money and exertions; it did not get beyond gossip. And yet the story is a very significant one. You heard, no doubt, Avdotya Romanovna, when you were with them the story of the servant Philip who died of ill treatment he received six years ago, before the abolition of serfdom."

"I heard, on the contrary, that this Philip hanged himself."

"Quite so, but what drove him, or rather perhaps disposed him, to suicide was the systematic persecution and severity of Mr. Svidrigaïlov."

"I don't know that," answered Dounia, dryly. "I only heard a queer story that Philip was a sort of hypochondriac, a sort of domestic philosopher, the servants used to say, 'he read himself silly,' and that he hanged himself partly on account of Mr. Svidrigaïlov's mockery of him and not his blows. When I was there he behaved well to the servants, and they were actually fond of him, though they certainly did blame him for Philip's death."

"I perceive, Avdotya Romanovna, that you seem disposed to undertake his defence all of a sudden," Luzhin observed, twisting his lips into an ambiguous smile, "there's no doubt that he is an astute man, and insinuating where ladies are concerned, of which Marfa Petrovna, who has died so strangely, is a terrible instance. My only desire has been to be of service to you and your mother with my advice, in view of the renewed efforts which may certainly be anticipated from him. For my part it's my firm conviction, that he will end in a debtor's prison again. Marfa Petrovna had not the slightest intention of settling anything substantial on him, having regard for his children's interests, and, if she left him anything, it would only be the merest sufficiency, something insignificant and ephemeral, which would not last a year for a man of his habits."

"Pyotr Petrovitch, I beg you," said Dounia, "say no more of Mr. Svidrigaïlov. It makes me miserable."

"He has just been to see me," said Raskolnikov, breaking his silence for the first time.

There were exclamations from all, and they all turned to him. Even Pyotr Petrovitch was roused.

"An hour and a half ago, he came in when I was asleep, waked me, and introduced himself," Raskolnikov continued. "He was fairly cheerful and at ease, and quite hopes that we shall become friends. He is particularly anxious, by the way, Dounia, for an interview with you, at which he asked me to assist. He has a proposition to make to you, and he told me about it. He told me, too, that a week before her death Marfa Petrovna left you three thousand roubles in her will, Dounia, and that you can receive the money very shortly."

"Thank God!" cried Pulcheria Alexandrovna, crossing herself. "Pray for her soul, Dounia!"

"It's a fact!" broke from Luzhin.

"Tell us, what more?" Dounia urged Raskolnikov.

"Then he said that he wasn't rich and all the estate was left to his children who are now with an aunt, then that he was staying somewhere not far from me, but where, I don't know, I didn't ask...."

"But what, what does he want to propose to Dounia?" cried Pulcheria Alexandrovna in a fright. "Did he tell you?"

"Yes."

"What was it?"

"I'll tell you afterwards."

Raskolnikov ceased speaking and turned his attention to his tea.

Pyotr Petrovitch looked at his watch.

"I am compelled to keep a business engagement, and so I shall not be in your way," he added with an air of some pique and he began getting up.

"Don't go, Pyotr Petrovitch," said Dounia, "you intended to spend the evening. Besides, you wrote yourself that you wanted to have an explanation with mother."

"Precisely so, Avdotya Romanovna," Pyotr Petrovitch answered impressively, sitting down again, but still holding his hat. "I certainly desired an explanation with you and your honoured mother upon a very important point indeed. But as your brother cannot speak openly in my presence of some proposals of Mr. Svidrigaïlov, I, too, do not desire and am not able to speak openly... in the presence of others... of certain matters of the greatest gravity. Moreover, my most weighty and urgent request has been disregarded...."

Assuming an aggrieved air, Luzhin relapsed into dignified silence.

"Your request that my brother should not be present at our meeting was disregarded solely at my insistance," said Dounia. "You wrote that you had been insulted by my brother; I think that this must be explained at once, and you must be reconciled. And if Rodya really has insulted you, then he *should* and *will* apologise."

Pyotr Petrovitch took a stronger line.

"There are insults, Avdotya Romanovna, which no goodwill can make us forget. There is a line in everything which it is dangerous to overstep; and when it has been overstepped, there is no return."

"That wasn't what I was speaking of exactly, Pyotr Petrovitch," Dounia interrupted with some impatience. "Please understand that our whole future depends now on whether all this is explained and set right as soon as possible. I tell you frankly at the start that I cannot look at it in any other light, and if you have the least regard for me, all this business must be ended today, however hard that may be. I repeat that if my brother is to blame he will ask your forgiveness."

"I am surprised at your putting the question like that," said Luzhin, getting more and more irritated. "Esteeming, and so to say, adoring you, I may at the same time, very well indeed, be able to dislike some member of your family. Though I lay claim to the happiness of your hand, I cannot accept duties incompatible with..."

"Ah, don't be so ready to take offence, Pyotr Petrovitch," Dounia interrupted with feeling, "and be the sensible and generous man I have always considered, and wish to consider, you to be. I've given you a great promise, I am your betrothed. Trust me in this matter and, believe me, I shall be capable of judging impartially. My assuming the part of judge is as much a surprise for my brother as for you. When I insisted on his coming to our interview today after your letter, I told him nothing of what I meant to do. Understand that, if you are not reconciled, I must choose

164

between you—it must be either you or he. That is how the question rests on your side and on his. I don't want to be mistaken in my choice, and I must not be. For your sake I must break off with my brother, for my brother's sake I must break off with you. I can find out for certain now whether he is a brother to me, and I want to know it; and of you, whether I am dear to you, whether you esteem me, whether you are the husband for me."

"Avdotya Romanovna," Luzhin declared huffily, "your words are of too much consequence to me; I will say more, they are offensive in view of the position I have the honour to occupy in relation to you. To say nothing of your strange and offensive setting me on a level with an impertinent boy, you admit the possibility of breaking your promise to me. You say 'you or he,' showing thereby of how little consequence I am in your eyes... I cannot let this pass considering the relationship and... the obligations existing between us."

"What!" cried Dounia, flushing. "I set your interest beside all that has hitherto been most precious in my life, what has made up the *whole* of my life, and here you are offended at my making too *little* account of you."

Raskolnikov smiled sarcastically, Razumihin fidgeted, but Pyotr Petrovitch did not accept the reproof; on the contrary, at every word he became more persistent and irritable, as though he relished it.

"Love for the future partner of your life, for your husband, ought to outweigh your love for your brother," he pronounced sententiously, "and in any case I cannot be put on the same level.... Although I said so emphatically that I would not speak openly in your brother's presence, nevertheless, I intend now to ask your honoured mother for a necessary explanation on a point of great importance closely affecting my dignity. Your son," he turned to Pulcheria Alexandrovna, "yesterday in the presence of Mr. Razsudkin (or... I think that's it? excuse me I have forgotten your surname)" (he bowed politely to Razumihin) "insulted me by misrepresenting the idea I expressed to you in a private conversation, drinking coffee, that is, that marriage with a poor girl who has had experience of trouble is more advantageous from the conjugal point of view than with one who has lived in luxury, since it is more profitable for the moral character. Your son intentionally exaggerated the significance of my words and made them ridiculous, accusing me of malicious intentions, and, as far as I could see, relied upon your correspondence with him. I shall consider myself happy, Pulcheria Alexandrovna, if it is possible for you to convince me of an opposite conclusion, and thereby considerately reassure me. Kindly let me know in what terms precisely you repeated my words in your letter to Rodion Romanovitch."

"I don't remember," faltered Pulcheria Alexandrovna. "I repeated them as I understood them. I don't know how Rodya repeated them to you, perhaps he exaggerated."

"He could not have exaggerated them, except at your instigation."

"Pyotr Petrovitch," Pulcheria Alexandrovna declared with dignity, "the proof that Dounia and I did not take your words in a very bad sense is the fact that we are here."

"Good, mother," said Dounia approvingly.

"Then this is my fault again," said Luzhin, aggrieved.

"Well, Pyotr Petrovitch, you keep blaming Rodion, but you yourself have just written what was false about him," Pulcheria Alexandrovna added, gaining courage.

"I don't remember writing anything false."

"You wrote," Raskolnikov said sharply, not turning to Luzhin, "that I gave money yesterday not to the widow of the man who was killed, as was the fact, but to his daughter (whom I had never seen till yesterday). You wrote this to make dissension between me and my family, and for that object added coarse expressions about the conduct of a girl whom you don't know. All that is mean slander."

"Excuse me, sir," said Luzhin, quivering with fury. "I enlarged upon your qualities and conduct in my letter solely in response to your sister's and mother's inquiries, how I found you, and what impression you made on me. As for what you've alluded to in my letter, be so good as to point out one word of falsehood, show, that is, that you didn't throw away your money, and that there are not worthless persons in that family, however unfortunate."

"To my thinking, you, with all your virtues, are not worth the little finger of that unfortunate girl at whom you throw stones."

"Would you go so far then as to let her associate with your mother and sister?"

"I have done so already, if you care to know. I made her sit down today with mother and Dounia."

"Rodya!" cried Pulcheria Alexandrovna. Dounia crimsoned, Razumihin knitted his brows. Luzhin smiled with lofty sarcasm.

"You may see for yourself, Avdotya Romanovna," he said, "whether it is possible for us to agree. I hope now that this question is at an end, once and for all. I will withdraw, that I may not hinder the pleasures of family intimacy, and the discussion of secrets." He got up from his chair and took his hat. "But in withdrawing, I venture to request that for the future I may be spared similar meetings, and, so to say, compromises. I appeal particularly to you, honoured Pulcheria Alexandrovna, on this subject, the more as my letter was addressed to you and to no one else."

Pulcheria Alexandrovna was a little offended.

"You seem to think we are completely under your authority, Pyotr Petrovitch. Dounia has told you the reason your desire was disregarded, she had the best intentions. And indeed you write as though you were laying commands upon me. Are we to consider every desire of yours as a command? Let me tell you on the contrary that you ought to show particular delicacy and consideration for us now, because we have thrown up everything, and have come here relying on you, and so we are in any case in a sense in your hands."

"That is not quite true, Pulcheria Alexandrovna, especially at the present moment, when the news has come of Marfa Petrovna's legacy, which seems indeed very apropos, judging from the new tone you take to me," he added sarcastically.

"Judging from that remark, we may certainly presume that you were reckoning on our helplessness," Dounia observed irritably.

"But now in any case I cannot reckon on it, and I particularly desire not to hinder your discussion of the secret proposals of Arkady Ivanovitch Svidrigaïlov, which he has entrusted to your brother and which have, I perceive, a great and possibly a very agreeable interest for you."

"Good heavens!" cried Pulcheria Alexandrovna.

Razumihin could not sit still on his chair.

"Aren't you ashamed now, sister?" asked Raskolnikov.

"I am ashamed, Rodya," said Dounia. "Pyotr Petrovitch, go away," she turned to him, white with anger.

Pyotr Petrovitch had apparently not at all expected such a conclusion. He had too much confidence in himself, in his power and in the helplessness of his victims. He could not believe it even now. He turned pale, and his lips quivered.

"Avdotya Romanovna, if I go out of this door now, after such a dismissal, then, you may reckon on it, I will never come back. Consider what you are doing. My word is not to be shaken."

"What insolence!" cried Dounia, springing up from her seat. "I don't want you to come back again."

"What! So that's how it stands!" cried Luzhin, utterly unable to the last moment to believe in the rupture and so completely thrown out of his reckoning now. "So that's how it stands! But do you know, Avdotya Romanovna, that I might protest?"

"What right have you to speak to her like that?" Pulcheria Alexandrovna intervened hotly. "And what can you protest about? What rights have you? Am I to give my Dounia to a man like you? Go away, leave us altogether! We are to blame for having agreed to a wrong action, and I above all...."

"But you have bound me, Pulcheria Alexandrovna," Luzhin stormed in a frenzy, "by your promise, and now you deny it and... besides... I have been led on account of that into expenses...."

This last complaint was so characteristic of Pyotr Petrovitch, that Raskolnikov, pale with anger and with the effort of restraining it, could not help breaking into laughter. But Pulcheria Alexandrovna was furious.

166

"Expenses? What expenses? Are you speaking of our trunk? But the conductor brought it for nothing for you. Mercy on us, we have bound you! What are you thinking about, Pyotr Petrovitch, it was you bound us, hand and foot, not we!"

"Enough, mother, no more please," Avdotya Romanovna implored. "Pyotr Petrovitch, do be kind and go!"

"I am going, but one last word," he said, quite unable to control himself. "Your mamma seems to have entirely forgotten that I made up my mind to take you, so to speak, after the gossip of the town had spread all over the district in regard to your reputation. Disregarding public opinion for your sake and reinstating your reputation, I certainly might very well reckon on a fitting return, and might indeed look for gratitude on your part. And my eyes have only now been opened! I see myself that I may have acted very, very recklessly in disregarding the universal verdict...."

"Does the fellow want his head smashed?" cried Razumihin, jumping up.

"You are a mean and spiteful man!" cried Dounia.

"Not a word! Not a movement!" cried Raskolnikov, holding Razumihin back; then going close up to Luzhin, "Kindly leave the room!" he said quietly and distinctly, "and not a word more or…"

Pyotr Petrovitch gazed at him for some seconds with a pale face that worked with anger, then he turned, went out, and rarely has any man carried away in his heart such vindictive hatred as he felt against Raskolnikov. Him, and him alone, he blamed for everything. It is noteworthy that as he went downstairs he still imagined that his case was perhaps not utterly lost, and that, so far as the ladies were concerned, all might "very well indeed" be set right again.

167

The fact was that up to the last moment he had never expected such an ending; he had been overbearing to the last degree, never dreaming that two destitute and defenceless women could escape from his control. This conviction was strengthened by his vanity and conceit, a conceit to the point of fatuity. Pyotr Petrovitch, who had made his way up from insignificance, was morbidly given to self-admiration, had the highest opinion of his intelligence and capacities, and sometimes even gloated in solitude over his image in the glass. But what he loved and valued above all was the money he had amassed by his labour, and by all sorts of devices: that money made him the equal of all who had been his superiors.

When he had bitterly reminded Dounia that he had decided to take her in spite of evil report, Pyotr Petrovitch had spoken with perfect sincerity and had, indeed, felt genuinely indignant at such "black ingratitude." And yet, when he made Dounia his offer, he was fully aware of the groundlessness of all the gossip. The story had been everywhere contradicted by Marfa Petrovna, and was by then disbelieved by all the townspeople, who were warm in Dounia'a defence. And he would not have denied that he knew all that at the time. Yet he still thought highly of his own resolution in lifting Dounia to his level and regarded it as something heroic. In speaking of it to Dounia, he had let out the secret feeling he cherished and admired, and he could not understand that others should fail to admire it too. He had called on Raskolnikov with the feelings of a benefactor who is about to reap the fruits of his good deeds and to hear agreeable flattery. And as he went downstairs now, he considered himself most undeservedly injured and unrecognised.

Dounia was simply essential to him; to do without her was unthinkable. For many years he had had voluptuous dreams of marriage, but he had gone on waiting and amassing money. He brooded with relish, in profound secret, over the image of a girl—virtuous, poor (she must be poor), very young, very pretty, of good birth and education, very timid, one who had suffered much, and was completely humbled before him, one who would all her life look on him as her saviour, worship him, admire him and only him. How many scenes, how many amorous episodes he had imagined on this seductive and playful theme, when his work was over! And, behold, the dream of so many years was all but realised; the beauty and education of Avdotya Romanovna had impressed him; her helpless position had been a great allurement; in her he had found even more than he dreamed of. Here was a girl of pride, character, virtue, of education and breeding superior to his own (he felt that), and this creature would be slavishly grateful all her life for his heroic condescension, and would humble herself in the dust before him, and he would have absolute, unbounded power over her! ... Not long before, he had, too, after long reflection and hesitation, made an important change in his career and was now entering on a wider circle of business. With this change his cherished dreams of rising into a higher class of society seemed likely to be realised.... He was, in fact, determined to try his fortune in Petersburg. He knew that women could do a very great deal. The fascination of a charming, virtuous, highly educated woman might make his way easier, might do wonders in attracting people to him, throwing an aureole round him, and now everything was in ruins! This sudden horrible rupture affected him like a clap of thunder; it was like a hideous joke, an absurdity. He had only been a tiny bit masterful, had not even time to speak out, had simply made a joke, been carried away—and it had ended so seriously. And, of course, too, he did love Dounia in his own way; he already possessed her in his dreams—and all at once! No! The next day, the very next day, it must all be set right, smoothed over, settled. Above all he must crush that conceited milksop who was the cause of it all. With a sick feeling he could not help recalling Razumihin too, but, he soon reassured himself on that score; as though a fellow like that could be put on a level with him! The man he really dreaded in earnest was Svidrigaïlov.... He had, in short, a great deal to attend to....

"No, I, I am more to blame than anyone!" said Dounia, kissing and embracing her mother. "I was tempted by his money, but on my honour, brother, I had no idea he was such a base man. If I had seen through him before, nothing would have tempted me! Don't blame me, brother!"

"God has delivered us! God has delivered us!" Pulcheria Alexandrovna muttered, but half consciously, as though scarcely able to realise what had happened.

They were all relieved, and in five minutes they were laughing. Only now and then Dounia turned white and frowned, remembering what had passed. Pulcheria Alexandrovna was surprised to find that she, too, was glad: she had only that morning thought rupture with Luzhin a terrible misfortune. Razumihin was delighted. He did not yet dare to express his joy fully, but he was in a fever of excitement as though a ton-weight had fallen off his heart. Now he had the right to devote his life to them, to serve them.... Anything might happen now! But he felt afraid to think of further possibilities and dared not let his imagination range. But Raskolnikov sat still in the same place, almost sullen and indifferent. Though he had been the most insistent on getting rid of Luzhin, he seemed now the least concerned at what had happened. Dounia could not help thinking that he was still angry with her, and Pulcheria Alexandrovna watched him timidly.

"What did Svidrigaïlov say to you?" said Dounia, approaching him.

"Yes, yes!" cried Pulcheria Alexandrovna.

Raskolnikov raised his head.

"He wants to make you a present of ten thousand roubles and he desires to see you once in my presence."

"See her! On no account!" cried Pulcheria Alexandrovna. "And how dare he offer her money!"

Then Raskolnikov repeated (rather dryly) his conversation with Svidrigaïlov, omitting his account of the ghostly visitations of Marfa Petrovna, wishing to avoid all unnecessary talk.

"What answer did you give him?" asked Dounia.

"At first I said I would not take any message to you. Then he said that he would do his utmost to obtain an interview with you without my help. He assured me that his passion for you was a passing infatuation, now he has no feeling for you. He doesn't want you to marry Luzhin.... His talk was altogether rather muddled."

"How do you explain him to yourself, Rodya? How did he strike you?"

"I must confess I don't quite understand him. He offers you ten thousand, and yet says he is not well off. He says he is going away, and in ten minutes he forgets he has said it. Then he says he is going to be married and has already fixed on the girl.... No doubt he has a motive, and probably a bad one. But it's odd that he should be so clumsy about it if he had any designs against you.... Of course, I refused this money on your account, once for all. Altogether, I thought him very strange.... One might almost think he was mad. But I may be mistaken; that may only be the part he assumes. The death of Marfa Petrovna seems to have made a great impression on him."

"God rest her soul," exclaimed Pulcheria Alexandrovna. "I shall always, always pray for her! Where should we be now, Dounia, without this three thousand! It's as though it had fallen from heaven! Why, Rodya, this morning we had only three roubles in our pocket and Dounia and I were just planning to pawn her watch, so as to avoid borrowing from that man until he offered help."

Dounia seemed strangely impressed by Svidrigaïlov's offer. She still stood meditating.

"He has got some terrible plan," she said in a half whisper to herself, almost shuddering.

Raskolnikov noticed this disproportionate terror.

"I fancy I shall have to see him more than once again," he said to Dounia.

169

"We will watch him! I will track him out!" cried Razumihin, vigorously. "I won't lose sight of him. Rodya has given me leave. He said to me himself just now. 'Take care of my sister.' Will you give me leave, too, Avdotya Romanovna?"

Dounia smiled and held out her hand, but the look of anxiety did not leave her face. Pulcheria Alexandrovna gazed at her timidly, but the three thousand roubles had obviously a soothing effect on her.

A quarter of an hour later, they were all engaged in a lively conversation. Even Raskolnikov listened attentively for some time, though he did not talk. Razumihin was the speaker.

"And why, why should you go away?" he flowed on ecstatically. "And what are you to do in a little town? The great thing is, you are all here together and you need one another—you do need one another, believe me. For a time, anyway.... Take me into partnership, and I assure you we'll plan a capital enterprise. Listen! I'll explain it all in detail to you, the whole project! It all flashed into my head this morning, before anything had happened... I tell you what; I have an uncle, I must introduce him to you (a most accommodating and respectable old man). This uncle has got a capital of a thousand roubles, and he lives on his pension and has no need of that money. For the last two years he has been bothering me to borrow it from him and pay him six percent interest. I know what that means; he simply wants to help me. Last year I had no need of it, but this year I resolved to borrow it as soon as he arrived. Then you lend me another thousand of your three and we have enough for a start, so we'll go into partnership, and what are we going to do?"

Then Razumihin began to unfold his project, and he explained at length that almost all our publishers and booksellers know nothing at all of what they are selling, and for that reason they are usually bad publishers, and that any decent publications pay as a rule and give a profit, sometimes a considerable one. Razumihin had, indeed, been dreaming of setting up as a publisher. For the last two years he had been working in publishers' offices, and knew three European languages well, though he had told Raskolnikov six days before that he was "*schwach*" in German with an object of persuading him to take half his translation and half the payment for it. He had told a lie then, and Raskolnikov knew he was lying.

"Why, why should we let our chance slip when we have one of the chief means of success— money of our own!" cried Razumihin warmly. "Of course there will be a lot of work, but we will work, you, Avdotya Romanovna, I, Rodion.... You get a splendid profit on some books nowadays! And the great point of the business is that we shall know just what wants translating, and we shall be translating, publishing, learning all at once. I can be of use because I have experience. For nearly two years I've been scuttling about among the publishers, and now I know every detail of their business. You need not be a saint to make pots, believe me! And why, why should we let our chance slip! Why, I know—and I kept the secret—two or three books which one might get a hundred roubles simply for thinking of translating and publishing. Indeed, and I would not take five hundred for the very idea of one of them. And what do you think? If I were to tell a publisher, I dare say he'd hesitate—they are such blockheads! And as for the business side, printing, paper, selling, you trust to me, I know my way about. We'll begin in a small way and go on to a large. In any case it will get us our living and we shall get back our capital."

Dounia's eyes shone.

"I like what you are saying, Dmitri Prokofitch!" she said.

"I know nothing about it, of course," put in Pulcheria Alexandrovna, "it may be a good idea, but again God knows. It's new and untried. Of course, we must remain here at least for a time." She looked at Rodya.

"What do you think, brother?" said Dounia.

"I think he's got a very good idea," he answered. "Of course, it's too soon to dream of a publishing firm, but we certainly might bring out five or six books and be sure of success. I know of one book myself which would be sure to go well. And as for his being able to manage it, there's no doubt about that either. He knows the business.... But we can talk it over later...."

"Hurrah!" cried Razumihin. "Now, stay, there's a flat here in this house, belonging to the same owner. It's a special flat apart, not communicating with these lodgings. It's furnished, rent moderate, three rooms. Suppose you take them to begin with. I'll pawn your watch tomorrow and bring you the money, and everything can be arranged then. You can all three live together, and Rodya will be with you. But where are you off to, Rodya?"

"What, Rodya, you are going already?" Pulcheria Alexandrovna asked in dismay.

"At such a minute?" cried Razumihin.

Dounia looked at her brother with incredulous wonder. He held his cap in his hand, he was preparing to leave them.

"One would think you were burying me or saying goodbye forever," he said somewhat oddly. He attempted to smile, but it did not turn out a smile. "But who knows, perhaps it is the last time we shall see each other..." he let slip accidentally. It was what he was thinking, and it somehow was uttered aloud.

"What is the matter with you?" cried his mother.

"Where are you going, Rodya?" asked Dounia rather strangely.

"Oh, I'm quite obliged to..." he answered vaguely, as though hesitating what he would say. But there was a look of sharp determination in his white face.

"I meant to say... as I was coming here... I meant to tell you, mother, and you, Dounia, that it would be better for us to part for a time. I feel ill, I am not at peace.... I will come afterwards, I will come of myself... when it's possible. I remember you and love you.... Leave me, leave me alone. I decided this even before... I'm absolutely resolved on it. Whatever may come to me, whether I come to ruin or not, I want to be alone. Forget me altogether, it's better. Don't inquire about me. When I can, I'll come of myself or... I'll come of myself. Perhaps it will all come back, but now if you love me, give me up... else I shall begin to hate you, I feel it.... Goodbye!"

"Good God!" cried Pulcheria Alexandrovna. Both his mother and his sister were terribly alarmed. Razumihin was also.

"Rodya, Rodya, be reconciled with us! Let us be as before!" cried his poor mother.

He turned slowly to the door and slowly went out of the room. Dounia overtook him.

"Brother, what are you doing to mother?" she whispered, her eyes flashing with indignation.

He looked dully at her.

"No matter, I shall come.... I'm coming," he muttered in an undertone, as though not fully conscious of what he was saying, and he went out of the room.

"Wicked, heartless egoist!" cried Dounia.

"He is insane, but not heartless. He is mad! Don't you see it? You're heartless after that!" Razumihin whispered in her ear, squeezing her hand tightly. "I shall be back directly," he shouted to the horror-stricken mother, and he ran out of the room.

Raskolnikov was waiting for him at the end of the passage.

"I knew you would run after me," he said. "Go back to them—be with them... be with them tomorrow and always.... I... perhaps I shall come... if I can. Goodbye."

And without holding out his hand he walked away.

"But where are you going? What are you doing? What's the matter with you? How can you go on like this?" Razumihin muttered, at his wits' end.

Raskolnikov stopped once more.

"Once for all, never ask me about anything. I have nothing to tell you. Don't come to see me. Maybe I'll come here.... Leave me, but *don't leave* them. Do you understand me?"

It was dark in the corridor, they were standing near the lamp. For a minute they were looking at one another in silence. Razumihin remembered that minute all his life. Raskolnikov's burning and intent eyes grew more penetrating every moment, piercing into his soul, into his consciousness. Suddenly Razumihin started. Something strange, as it were, passed between them.... Some idea, some hint, as it were, slipped, something awful, hideous, and suddenly understood on both sides.... Razumihin turned pale.

"Do you understand now?" said Raskolnikov, his face twitching nervously. "Go back, go to them," he said suddenly, and turning quickly, he went out of the house.

I will not attempt to describe how Razumihin went back to the ladies, how he soothed them, how he protested that Rodya needed rest in his illness, protested that Rodya was sure to come, that he would come every day, that he was very, very much upset, that he must not be irritated, that he,

Razumihin, would watch over him, would get him a doctor, the best doctor, a consultation.... In fact from that evening Razumihin took his place with them as a son and a brother.

Raskolnikov went straight to the house on the canal bank where Sonia lived. It was an old green house of three storeys. He found the porter and obtained from him vague directions as to the whereabouts of Kapernaumov, the tailor. Having found in the corner of the courtyard the entrance to the dark and narrow staircase, he mounted to the second floor and came out into a gallery that ran round the whole second storey over the yard. While he was wandering in the darkness, uncertain where to turn for Kapernaumov's door, a door opened three paces from him; he mechanically took hold of it.

"Who is there?" a woman's voice asked uneasily.

"It's I... come to see you," answered Raskolnikov, and he walked into the tiny entry.

On a broken chair stood a candle in a battered copper candlestick.

"It's you! Good heavens!" cried Sonia weakly, and she stood rooted to the spot.

"Which is your room? This way?" and Raskolnikov, trying not to look at her, hastened in.

A minute later Sonia, too, came in with the candle, set down the candlestick and, completely disconcerted, stood before him inexpressibly agitated and apparently frightened by his unexpected visit. The colour rushed suddenly to her pale face and tears came into her eyes... She felt sick and ashamed and happy, too.... Raskolnikov turned away quickly and sat on a chair by the table. He scanned the room in a rapid glance.

It was a large but exceedingly low-pitched room, the only one let by the Kapernaumovs, to whose rooms a closed door led in the wall on the left. In the opposite side on the right hand wall was another door, always kept locked. That led to the next flat, which formed a separate lodging. Sonia's room looked like a barn; it was a very irregular quadrangle and this gave it a grotesque appearance. A wall with three windows looking out on to the canal ran aslant so that one corner formed a very acute angle, and it was difficult to see in it without very strong light. The other corner was disproportionately obtuse. There was scarcely any furniture in the big room: in the corner on the right was a bedstead, beside it, nearest the door, a chair. A plain, deal table covered by a blue cloth stood against the same wall, close to the door into the other flat. Two rush-bottom chairs stood by the table. On the opposite wall near the acute angle stood a small plain wooden chest of drawers looking, as it were, lost in a desert. That was all there was in the room. The yellow, scratched and shabby wallpaper was black in the corners. It must have been damp and full of fumes in the winter. There was every sign of poverty; even the bedstead had no curtain.

Sonia looked in silence at her visitor, who was so attentively and unceremoniously scrutinising her room, and even began at last to tremble with terror, as though she was standing before her judge and the arbiter of her destinies.

"I am late.... It's eleven, isn't it?" he asked, still not lifting his eyes.

"Yes," muttered Sonia, "oh yes, it is," she added, hastily, as though in that lay her means of escape. "My landlady's clock has just struck... I heard it myself...."

"I've come to you for the last time," Raskolnikov went on gloomily, although this was the first time. "I may perhaps not see you again..."

"Are you... going away?"

"I don't know... tomorrow...."

"Then you are not coming to Katerina Ivanovna tomorrow?" Sonia's voice shook.

"I don't know. I shall know tomorrow morning.... Never mind that: I've come to say one word...."

He raised his brooding eyes to her and suddenly noticed that he was sitting down while she was all the while standing before him.

"Why are you standing? Sit down," he said in a changed voice, gentle and friendly.

She sat down. He looked kindly and almost compassionately at her.

"How thin you are! What a hand! Quite transparent, like a dead hand."

He took her hand. Sonia smiled faintly.

"I have always been like that," she said.

"Even when you lived at home?"

"Yes."

"Of course, you were," he added abruptly and the expression of his face and the sound of his voice changed again suddenly.

He looked round him once more.

"You rent this room from the Kapernaumovs?"

"Yes...."

"They live there, through that door?"

"Yes.... They have another room like this."

"All in one room?"

"Yes."

"I should be afraid in your room at night," he observed gloomily.

"They are very good people, very kind," answered Sonia, who still seemed bewildered, "and all the furniture, everything... everything is theirs. And they are very kind and the children, too, often come to see me."

"They all stammer, don't they?"

"Yes.... He stammers and he's lame. And his wife, too.... It's not exactly that she stammers, but she can't speak plainly. She is a very kind woman. And he used to be a house serf. And there are seven children... and it's only the eldest one that stammers and the others are simply ill... but they don't stammer.... But where did you hear about them?" she added with some surprise.

"Your father told me, then. He told me all about you.... And how you went out at six o'clock and came back at nine and how Katerina Ivanovna knelt down by your bed."

Sonia was confused.

"I fancied I saw him today," she whispered hesitatingly.

"Whom?"

"Father. I was walking in the street, out there at the corner, about ten o'clock and he seemed to be walking in front. It looked just like him. I wanted to go to Katerina Ivanovna...."

"You were walking in the streets?"

"Yes," Sonia whispered abruptly, again overcome with confusion and looking down.

"Katerina Ivanovna used to beat you, I dare say?"

"Oh no, what are you saying? No!" Sonia looked at him almost with dismay.

"You love her, then?"

"Love her? Of course!" said Sonia with plaintive emphasis, and she clasped her hands in distress. "Ah, you don't.... If you only knew! You see, she is quite like a child.... Her mind is quite unhinged, you see... from sorrow. And how clever she used to be... how generous... how kind! Ah, you don't understand, you don't understand!"

Sonia said this as though in despair, wringing her hands in excitement and distress. Her pale cheeks flushed, there was a look of anguish in her eyes. It was clear that she was stirred to the very depths, that she was longing to speak, to champion, to express something. A sort of *insatiable* compassion, if one may so express it, was reflected in every feature of her face.

"Beat me! how can you? Good heavens, beat me! And if she did beat me, what then? What of it? You know nothing, nothing about it.... She is so unhappy... ah, how unhappy! And ill.... She is seeking righteousness, she is pure. She has such faith that there must be righteousness everywhere and she expects it.... And if you were to torture her, she wouldn't do wrong. She doesn't see that it's impossible for people to be righteous and she is angry at it. Like a child, like a child. She is good!"

174

"And what will happen to you?"

Sonia looked at him inquiringly.

"They are left on your hands, you see. They were all on your hands before, though. . . . And your father came to you to beg for drink. Well, how will it be now?"

"I don't know," Sonia articulated mournfully.

"Will they stay there?"

"I don't know. . . . They are in debt for the lodging, but the landlady, I hear, said today that she wanted to get rid of them, and Katerina Ivanovna says that she won't stay another minute."

"How is it she is so bold? She relies upon you?"

"Oh, no, don't talk like that. . . . We are one, we live like one." Sonia was agitated again and even angry, as though a canary or some other little bird were to be angry. "And what could she do? What, what could she do?" she persisted, getting hot and excited. "And how she cried today! Her mind is unhinged, haven't you noticed it? At one minute she is worrying like a child that everything should be right tomorrow, the lunch and all that. . . . Then she is wringing her hands, spitting blood, weeping, and all at once she will begin knocking her head against the wall, in despair. Then she will be comforted again. She builds all her hopes on you; she says that you will help her now and that she will borrow a little money somewhere and go to her native town with me and set up a boarding school for the daughters of gentlemen and take me to superintend it, and we will begin a new splendid life. And she kisses and hugs me, comforts me, and you know she has such faith, such faith in her fancies! One can't contradict her. And all the day long she has been washing, cleaning, mending. She dragged the wash tub into the room with her feeble hands and sank on the bed, gasping for breath. We went this morning to the shops to buy shoes for Polenka and Lida for theirs are quite worn out. Only the money we'd reckoned wasn't enough, not nearly enough. And she picked out such dear little boots, for she has taste, you don't know. And there in the shop she burst out crying before the shopmen because she hadn't enough. . . . Ah, it was sad to see her. . . ."

"Well, after that I can understand your living like this," Raskolnikov said with a bitter smile.

"And aren't you sorry for them? Aren't you sorry?" Sonia flew at him again. "Why, I know, you gave your last penny yourself, though you'd seen nothing of it, and if you'd seen everything, oh dear! And how often, how often I've brought her to tears! Only last week! Yes, I! Only a week before his death. I was cruel! And how often I've done it! Ah, I've been wretched at the thought of it all day!"

Sonia wrung her hands as she spoke at the pain of remembering it.

"You were cruel?"

"Yes, I—I. I went to see them," she went on, weeping, "and father said, 'read me something, Sonia, my head aches, read to me, here's a book.' He had a book he had got from Andrey Semyonovitch Lebeziatnikov, he lives there, he always used to get hold of such funny books. And I said, 'I can't stay,' as I didn't want to read, and I'd gone in chiefly to show Katerina Ivanovna some collars. Lizaveta, the pedlar, sold me some collars and cuffs cheap, pretty, new, embroidered ones. Katerina Ivanovna liked them very much; she put them on and looked at herself in the glass and was delighted with them. 'Make me a present of them, Sonia,' she said, 'please do.' '*Please do*,' she said, she wanted them so much. And when could she wear them? They just reminded her of her old happy days. She looked at herself in the glass, admired herself, and she has no clothes at all, no things of her own, hasn't had all these years! And she never asks anyone for anything; she is proud, she'd sooner give away everything. And these she asked for, she liked them so much. And I was sorry to give them. 'What use are they to you, Katerina Ivanovna?' I said. I spoke like that to her, I ought not to have said that! She gave me such a look. And she was so grieved, so grieved at my refusing her. And it was so sad to see. . . . And she was not grieved for the collars, but for my refusing, I saw that. Ah, if only I could bring it all back, change it, take back those words! Ah, if I . . . but it's nothing to you!"

"Did you know Lizaveta, the pedlar?"

"Yes. . . . Did you know her?" Sonia asked with some surprise.

175

"Katerina Ivanovna is in consumption, rapid consumption; she will soon die," said Raskolnikov after a pause, without answering her question.

"Oh, no, no, no!"

And Sonia unconsciously clutched both his hands, as though imploring that she should not.

"But it will be better if she does die."

"No, not better, not at all better!" Sonia unconsciously repeated in dismay.

"And the children? What can you do except take them to live with you?"

"Oh, I don't know," cried Sonia, almost in despair, and she put her hands to her head.

It was evident that that idea had very often occurred to her before and he had only roused it again.

"And, what, if even now, while Katerina Ivanovna is alive, you get ill and are taken to the hospital, what will happen then?" he persisted pitilessly.

"How can you? That cannot be!"

And Sonia's face worked with awful terror.

"Cannot be?" Raskolnikov went on with a harsh smile. "You are not insured against it, are you? What will happen to them then? They will be in the street, all of them, she will cough and beg and knock her head against some wall, as she did today, and the children will cry.... Then she will fall down, be taken to the police station and to the hospital, she will die, and the children..."

"Oh, no.... God will not let it be!" broke at last from Sonia's overburdened bosom.

She listened, looking imploringly at him, clasping her hands in dumb entreaty, as though it all depended upon him.

Raskolnikov got up and began to walk about the room. A minute passed. Sonia was standing with her hands and her head hanging in terrible dejection.

"And can't you save? Put by for a rainy day?" he asked, stopping suddenly before her.

"No," whispered Sonia.

"Of course not. Have you tried?" he added almost ironically.

"Yes."

"And it didn't come off! Of course not! No need to ask."

And again he paced the room. Another minute passed.

"You don't get money every day?"

Sonia was more confused than ever and colour rushed into her face again.

"No," she whispered with a painful effort.

"It will be the same with Polenka, no doubt," he said suddenly.

"No, no! It can't be, no!" Sonia cried aloud in desperation, as though she had been stabbed. "God would not allow anything so awful!"

"He lets others come to it."

"No, no! God will protect her, God!" she repeated beside herself.

"But, perhaps, there is no God at all," Raskolnikov answered with a sort of malignance, laughed and looked at her.

Sonia's face suddenly changed; a tremor passed over it. She looked at him with unutterable reproach, tried to say something, but could not speak and broke into bitter, bitter sobs, hiding her face in her hands.

"You say Katerina Ivanovna's mind is unhinged; your own mind is unhinged," he said after a brief silence.

Five minutes passed. He still paced up and down the room in silence, not looking at her. At last he went up to her; his eyes glittered. He put his two hands on her shoulders and looked straight into her tearful face. His eyes were hard, feverish and piercing, his lips were twitching. All at once he bent down quickly and dropping to the ground, kissed her foot. Sonia drew back from him as from a madman. And certainly he looked like a madman.

"What are you doing to me?" she muttered, turning pale, and a sudden anguish clutched at her heart.

He stood up at once.

"I did not bow down to you, I bowed down to all the suffering of humanity," he said wildly and walked away to the window. "Listen," he added, turning to her a minute later. "I said just now to an insolent man that he was not worth your little finger... and that I did my sister honour making her sit beside you."

"Ach, you said that to them! And in her presence?" cried Sonia, frightened. "Sit down with me! An honour! Why, I'm... dishonourable.... Ah, why did you say that?"

"It was not because of your dishonour and your sin I said that of you, but because of your great suffering. But you are a great sinner, that's true," he added almost solemnly, "and your worst sin is that you have destroyed and betrayed yourself *for nothing*. Isn't that fearful? Isn't it fearful that you are living in this filth which you loathe so, and at the same time you know yourself (you've only to open your eyes) that you are not helping anyone by it, not saving anyone from anything? Tell me," he went on almost in a frenzy, "how this shame and degradation can exist in you side by side with other, opposite, holy feelings? It would be better, a thousand times better and wiser to leap into the water and end it all!"

"But what would become of them?" Sonia asked faintly, gazing at him with eyes of anguish, but not seeming surprised at his suggestion.

Raskolnikov looked strangely at her. He read it all in her face; so she must have had that thought already, perhaps many times, and earnestly she had thought out in her despair how to end it and so earnestly, that now she scarcely wondered at his suggestion. She had not even noticed the cruelty of his words. (The significance of his reproaches and his peculiar attitude to her shame she had, of course, not noticed either, and that, too, was clear to him.) But he saw how monstrously the thought of her disgraceful, shameful position was torturing her and had long tortured her. "What, what," he thought, "could hitherto have hindered her from putting an end to it?" Only then he realised what those poor little orphan children and that pitiful half-crazy Katerina Ivanovna, knocking her head against the wall in her consumption, meant for Sonia.

But, nevertheless, it was clear to him again that with her character and the amount of education she had after all received, she could not in any case remain so. He was still confronted by the question, how could she have remained so long in that position without going out of her mind, since she could not bring herself to jump into the water? Of course he knew that Sonia's position was an exceptional case, though unhappily not unique and not infrequent, indeed; but that very exceptionalness, her tinge of education, her previous life might, one would have thought, have killed her at the first step on that revolting path. What held her up—surely not depravity? All that infamy had obviously only touched her mechanically, not one drop of real depravity had penetrated to her heart; he saw that. He saw through her as she stood before him....

"There are three ways before her," he thought, "the canal, the madhouse, or... at last to sink into depravity which obscures the mind and turns the heart to stone."

The last idea was the most revolting, but he was a sceptic, he was young, abstract, and therefore cruel, and so he could not help believing that the last end was the most likely.

"But can that be true?" he cried to himself. "Can that creature who has still preserved the purity of her spirit be consciously drawn at last into that sink of filth and iniquity? Can the process already have begun? Can it be that she has only been able to bear it till now, because vice has begun to be less loathsome to her? No, no, that cannot be!" he cried, as Sonia had just before. "No, what has kept her from the canal till now is the idea of sin and they, the children.... And if she has not gone out of her mind... but who says she has not gone out of her mind? Is she in her senses? Can one talk, can one reason as she does? How can she sit on the edge of the abyss of loathsomeness into which she is slipping and refuse to listen when she is told of danger? Does she expect a miracle? No doubt she does. Doesn't that all mean madness?"

He stayed obstinately at that thought. He liked that explanation indeed better than any other. He began looking more intently at her.

"So you pray to God a great deal, Sonia?" he asked her.

Sonia did not speak; he stood beside her waiting for an answer.

"What should I be without God?" she whispered rapidly, forcibly, glancing at him with suddenly flashing eyes, and squeezing his hand.

"Ah, so that is it!" he thought.

"And what does God do for you?" he asked, probing her further.

Sonia was silent a long while, as though she could not answer. Her weak chest kept heaving with emotion.

"Be silent! Don't ask! You don't deserve!" she cried suddenly, looking sternly and wrathfully at him.

"That's it, that's it," he repeated to himself.

"He does everything," she whispered quickly, looking down again.

"That's the way out! That's the explanation," he decided, scrutinising her with eager curiosity, with a new, strange, almost morbid feeling. He gazed at that pale, thin, irregular, angular little face, those soft blue eyes, which could flash with such fire, such stern energy, that little body still shaking with indignation and anger—and it all seemed to him more and more strange, almost impossible. "She is a religious maniac!" he repeated to himself.

There was a book lying on the chest of drawers. He had noticed it every time he paced up and down the room. Now he took it up and looked at it. It was the New Testament in the Russian translation. It was bound in leather, old and worn.

"Where did you get that?" he called to her across the room.

She was still standing in the same place, three steps from the table.

"It was brought me," she answered, as it were unwillingly, not looking at him.

"Who brought it?"

"Lizaveta, I asked her for it."

"Lizaveta! strange!" he thought.

Everything about Sonia seemed to him stranger and more wonderful every moment. He carried the book to the candle and began to turn over the pages.

"Where is the story of Lazarus?" he asked suddenly.

Sonia looked obstinately at the ground and would not answer. She was standing sideways to the table.

"Where is the raising of Lazarus? Find it for me, Sonia."

She stole a glance at him.

"You are not looking in the right place.... It's in the fourth gospel," she whispered sternly, without looking at him.

"Find it and read it to me," he said. He sat down with his elbow on the table, leaned his head on his hand and looked away sullenly, prepared to listen.

"In three weeks' time they'll welcome me in the madhouse! I shall be there if I am not in a worse place," he muttered to himself.

Sonia heard Raskolnikov's request distrustfully and moved hesitatingly to the table. She took the book however.

"Haven't you read it?" she asked, looking up at him across the table.

Her voice became sterner and sterner.

"Long ago.... When I was at school. Read!"

"And haven't you heard it in church?"

"I... haven't been. Do you often go?"

"N-no," whispered Sonia.

Raskolnikov smiled.

"I understand.... And you won't go to your father's funeral tomorrow?"

"Yes, I shall. I was at church last week, too... I had a requiem service."

"For whom?"

"For Lizaveta. She was killed with an axe."

His nerves were more and more strained. His head began to go round.

"Were you friends with Lizaveta?"

"Yes.... She was good... she used to come... not often... she couldn't.... We used to read together and... talk. She will see God."

The last phrase sounded strange in his ears. And here was something new again: the mysterious meetings with Lizaveta and both of them—religious maniacs.

"I shall be a religious maniac myself soon! It's infectious!"

"Read!" he cried irritably and insistently.

Sonia still hesitated. Her heart was throbbing. She hardly dared to read to him. He looked almost with exasperation at the "unhappy lunatic."

"What for? You don't believe?..." she whispered softly and as it were breathlessly.

"Read! I want you to," he persisted. "You used to read to Lizaveta."

Sonia opened the book and found the place. Her hands were shaking, her voice failed her. Twice she tried to begin and could not bring out the first syllable.

"Now a certain man was sick named Lazarus of Bethany..." she forced herself at last to read, but at the third word her voice broke like an overstrained string. There was a catch in her breath.

Raskolnikov saw in part why Sonia could not bring herself to read to him and the more he saw this, the more roughly and irritably he insisted on her doing so. He understood only too well how painful it was for her to betray and unveil all that was her *own*. He understood that these feelings really were her *secret treasure*, which she had kept perhaps for years, perhaps from childhood, while she lived with an unhappy father and a distracted stepmother crazed by grief, in the midst of starving children and unseemly abuse and reproaches. But at the same time he knew now and knew for certain that, although it filled her with dread and suffering, yet she had a tormenting desire to read and to read to *him* that he might hear it, and to read *now* whatever might come of it!... He read this in her eyes, he could see it in her intense emotion. She mastered herself, controlled the spasm in her throat and went on reading the eleventh chapter of St. John. She went on to the nineteenth verse:

"And many of the Jews came to Martha and Mary to comfort them concerning their brother.

"Then Martha as soon as she heard that Jesus was coming went and met Him: but Mary sat still in the house.

"Then said Martha unto Jesus, Lord, if Thou hadst been here, my brother had not died.

"But I know that even now whatsoever Thou wilt ask of God, God will give it Thee...."

Then she stopped again with a shamefaced feeling that her voice would quiver and break again.

"Jesus said unto her, thy brother shall rise again.

"Martha saith unto Him, I know that he shall rise again in the resurrection, at the last day.

"Jesus said unto her, I am the resurrection and the life: he that believeth in Me though he were dead, yet shall he live.

"And whosoever liveth and believeth in Me shall never die. Believest thou this?

"She saith unto Him,"

(And drawing a painful breath, Sonia read distinctly and forcibly as though she were making a public confession of faith.)

"Yea, Lord: I believe that Thou art the Christ, the Son of God Which should come into the world."

She stopped and looked up quickly at him, but controlling herself went on reading. Raskolnikov sat without moving, his elbows on the table and his eyes turned away. She read to the thirty-second verse.

"Then when Mary was come where Jesus was and saw Him, she fell down at His feet, saying unto Him, Lord if Thou hadst been here, my brother had not died.

"When Jesus therefore saw her weeping, and the Jews also weeping which came with her, He groaned in the spirit and was troubled,

"And said, Where have ye laid him? They said unto Him, Lord, come and see.

"Jesus wept.

"Then said the Jews, behold how He loved him!

"And some of them said, could not this Man which opened the eyes of the blind, have caused that even this man should not have died?"

Raskolnikov turned and looked at her with emotion. Yes, he had known it! She was trembling in a real physical fever. He had expected it. She was getting near the story of the greatest miracle and a feeling of immense triumph came over her. Her voice rang out like a bell; triumph and joy gave it power. The lines danced before her eyes, but she knew what she was reading by heart. At the last verse, "Could not this Man which opened the eyes of the blind…" dropping her voice she passionately reproduced the doubt, the reproach and censure of the blind disbelieving Jews, who in another moment would fall at His feet as though struck by thunder, sobbing and believing.… "And *he, he*—too, is blinded and unbelieving, he, too, will hear, he, too, will believe, yes, yes! At once, now," was what she was dreaming, and she was quivering with happy anticipation.

"Jesus therefore again groaning in Himself cometh to the grave. It was a cave, and a stone lay upon it.

"Jesus said, Take ye away the stone. Martha, the sister of him that was dead, saith unto Him, Lord by this time he stinketh: for he hath been dead four days."

She laid emphasis on the word *four*.

"Jesus saith unto her, Said I not unto thee that if thou wouldest believe, thou shouldest see the glory of God?

"Then they took away the stone from the place where the dead was laid. And Jesus lifted up His eyes and said, Father, I thank Thee that Thou hast heard Me.

"And I knew that Thou hearest Me always; but because of the people which stand by I said it, that they may believe that Thou hast sent Me.

"And when He thus had spoken, He cried with a loud voice, Lazarus, come forth.

"And he that was dead came forth."

(She read loudly, cold and trembling with ecstasy, as though she were seeing it before her eyes.)

"Bound hand and foot with graveclothes; and his face was bound about with a napkin. Jesus saith unto them, Loose him and let him go.

"Then many of the Jews which came to Mary and had seen the things which Jesus did believed on Him."

She could read no more, closed the book and got up from her chair quickly.

"That is all about the raising of Lazarus," she whispered severely and abruptly, and turning away she stood motionless, not daring to raise her eyes to him. She still trembled feverishly. The candle-end was flickering out in the battered candlestick, dimly lighting up in the poverty-stricken room the murderer and the harlot who had so strangely been reading together the eternal book. Five minutes or more passed.

"I came to speak of something," Raskolnikov said aloud, frowning. He got up and went to Sonia. She lifted her eyes to him in silence. His face was particularly stern and there was a sort of savage determination in it.

"I have abandoned my family today," he said, "my mother and sister. I am not going to see them. I've broken with them completely."

"What for?" asked Sonia amazed. Her recent meeting with his mother and sister had left a great impression which she could not analyse. She heard his news almost with horror.

"I have only you now," he added. "Let us go together.… I've come to you, we are both accursed, let us go our way together!"

His eyes glittered "as though he were mad," Sonia thought, in her turn.

"Go where?" she asked in alarm and she involuntarily stepped back.

"How do I know? I only know it's the same road, I know that and nothing more. It's the same goal!"

She looked at him and understood nothing. She knew only that he was terribly, infinitely unhappy.

"No one of them will understand, if you tell them, but I have understood. I need you, that is why I have come to you."

"I don't understand," whispered Sonia.

"You'll understand later. Haven't you done the same? You, too, have transgressed… have had the strength to transgress. You have laid hands on yourself, you have destroyed a life… *your own* (it's all the same!). You might have lived in spirit and understanding, but you'll end in the Hay

Market.... But you won't be able to stand it, and if you remain alone you'll go out of your mind like me. You are like a mad creature already. So we must go together on the same road! Let us go!"

"What for? What's all this for?" said Sonia, strangely and violently agitated by his words.

"What for? Because you can't remain like this, that's why! You must look things straight in the face at last, and not weep like a child and cry that God won't allow it. What will happen, if you should really be taken to the hospital tomorrow? She is mad and in consumption, she'll soon die and the children? Do you mean to tell me Polenka won't come to grief? Haven't you seen children here at the street corners sent out by their mothers to beg? I've found out where those mothers live and in what surroundings. Children can't remain children there! At seven the child is vicious and a thief. Yet children, you know, are the image of Christ: 'theirs is the kingdom of Heaven.' He bade us honour and love them, they are the humanity of the future...."

"What's to be done, what's to be done?" repeated Sonia, weeping hysterically and wringing her hands.

"What's to be done? Break what must be broken, once for all, that's all, and take the suffering on oneself. What, you don't understand? You'll understand later.... Freedom and power, and above all, power! Over all trembling creation and all the ant-heap!... That's the goal, remember that! That's my farewell message. Perhaps it's the last time I shall speak to you. If I don't come tomorrow, you'll hear of it all, and then remember these words. And some day later on, in years to come, you'll understand perhaps what they meant. If I come tomorrow, I'll tell you who killed Lizaveta.... Goodbye."

Sonia started with terror.

"Why, do you know who killed her?" she asked, chilled with horror, looking wildly at him.

"I know and will tell... you, only you. I have chosen you out. I'm not coming to you to ask forgiveness, but simply to tell you. I chose you out long ago to hear this, when your father talked of you and when Lizaveta was alive, I thought of it. Goodbye, don't shake hands. Tomorrow!"

He went out. Sonia gazed at him as at a madman. But she herself was like one insane and felt it. Her head was going round.

"Good heavens, how does he know who killed Lizaveta? What did those words mean? It's awful!" But at the same time *the idea* did not enter her head, not for a moment! "Oh, he must be terribly unhappy!... He has abandoned his mother and sister.... What for? What has happened? And what had he in his mind? What did he say to her? He had kissed her foot and said... said (yes, he had said it clearly) that he could not live without her.... Oh, merciful heavens!"

Sonia spent the whole night feverish and delirious. She jumped up from time to time, wept and wrung her hands, then sank again into feverish sleep and dreamt of Polenka, Katerina Ivanovna and Lizaveta, of reading the gospel and him... him with pale face, with burning eyes... kissing her feet, weeping.

On the other side of the door on the right, which divided Sonia's room from Madame Resslich's flat, was a room which had long stood empty. A card was fixed on the gate and a notice stuck in the windows over the canal advertising it to let. Sonia had long been accustomed to the room's being uninhabited. But all that time Mr. Svidrigaïlov had been standing, listening at the door of the empty room. When Raskolnikov went out he stood still, thought a moment, went on tiptoe to his own room which adjoined the empty one, brought a chair and noiselessly carried it to the door that led to Sonia's room. The conversation had struck him as interesting and remarkable, and he had greatly enjoyed it—so much so that he brought a chair that he might not in the future, tomorrow, for instance, have to endure the inconvenience of standing a whole hour, but might listen in comfort.

When next morning at eleven o'clock punctually Raskolnikov went into the department of the investigation of criminal causes and sent his name in to Porfiry Petrovitch, he was surprised at being kept waiting so long: it was at least ten minutes before he was summoned. He had expected that they would pounce upon him. But he stood in the waiting-room, and people, who apparently had nothing to do with him, were continually passing to and fro before him. In the next room which looked like an office, several clerks were sitting writing and obviously they had no notion who or what Raskolnikov might be. He looked uneasily and suspiciously about him to see whether there was not some guard, some mysterious watch being kept on him to prevent his escape. But there was nothing of the sort: he saw only the faces of clerks absorbed in petty details, then other people, no one seemed to have any concern with him. He might go where he liked for them. The conviction grew stronger in him that if that enigmatic man of yesterday, that phantom sprung out of the earth, had seen everything, they would not have let him stand and wait like that. And would they have waited till he elected to appear at eleven? Either the man had not yet given information, or... or simply he knew nothing, had seen nothing (and how could he have seen anything?) and so all that had happened to him the day before was again a phantom exaggerated by his sick and overstrained imagination. This conjecture had begun to grow strong the day before, in the midst of all his alarm and despair. Thinking it all over now and preparing for a fresh conflict, he was suddenly aware that he was trembling—and he felt a rush of indignation at the thought that he was trembling with fear at facing that hateful Porfiry Petrovitch. What he dreaded above all was meeting that man again; he hated him with an intense, unmitigated hatred and was afraid his hatred might betray him. His indignation was such that he ceased trembling at once; he made ready to go in with a cold and arrogant bearing and vowed to himself to keep as silent as possible, to watch and listen and for once at least to control his overstrained nerves. At that moment he was summoned to Porfiry Petrovitch.

He found Porfiry Petrovitch alone in his study. His study was a room neither large nor small, furnished with a large writing-table, that stood before a sofa, upholstered in checked material, a bureau, a bookcase in the corner and several chairs—all government furniture, of polished yellow wood. In the further wall there was a closed door, beyond it there were no doubt other rooms. On Raskolnikov's entrance Porfiry Petrovitch had at once closed the door by which he had come in and they remained alone. He met his visitor with an apparently genial and good-tempered air, and it was only after a few minutes that Raskolnikov saw signs of a certain awkwardness in him, as though he had been thrown out of his reckoning or caught in something very secret.

"Ah, my dear fellow! Here you are... in our domain"... began Porfiry, holding out both hands to him. "Come, sit down, old man... or perhaps you don't like to be called 'my dear fellow' and 'old man!'—*tout court*? Please don't think it too familiar.... Here, on the sofa."

Raskolnikov sat down, keeping his eyes fixed on him. "In our domain," the apologies for familiarity, the French phrase *tout court*, were all characteristic signs.

"He held out both hands to me, but he did not give me one—he drew it back in time," struck him suspiciously. Both were watching each other, but when their eyes met, quick as lightning they looked away.

"I brought you this paper... about the watch. Here it is. Is it all right or shall I copy it again?"

"What? A paper? Yes, yes, don't be uneasy, it's all right," Porfiry Petrovitch said as though in haste, and after he had said it he took the paper and looked at it. "Yes, it's all right. Nothing more is needed," he declared with the same rapidity and he laid the paper on the table.

A minute later when he was talking of something else he took it from the table and put it on his bureau.

"I believe you said yesterday you would like to question me... formally... about my acquaintance with the murdered woman?" Raskolnikov was beginning again. "Why did I put in 'I believe'" passed through his mind in a flash. "Why am I so uneasy at having put in that '*I believe*'?" came in a second flash. And he suddenly felt that his uneasiness at the mere contact with Porfiry, at the first words, at the first looks, had grown in an instant to monstrous proportions, and that this was fearfully dangerous. His nerves were quivering, his emotion was increasing. "It's bad, it's bad! I shall say too much again."

"Yes, yes, yes! There's no hurry, there's no hurry," muttered Porfiry Petrovitch, moving to and fro about the table without any apparent aim, as it were making dashes towards the window, the bureau and the table, at one moment avoiding Raskolnikov's suspicious glance, then again standing still and looking him straight in the face.

His fat round little figure looked very strange, like a ball rolling from one side to the other and rebounding back.

"We've plenty of time. Do you smoke? have you your own? Here, a cigarette!" he went on, offering his visitor a cigarette. "You know I am receiving you here, but my own quarters are through there, you know, my government quarters. But I am living outside for the time, I had to have some repairs done here. It's almost finished now.... Government quarters, you know, are a capital thing. Eh, what do you think?"

"Yes, a capital thing," answered Raskolnikov, looking at him almost ironically.

"A capital thing, a capital thing," repeated Porfiry Petrovitch, as though he had just thought of something quite different. "Yes, a capital thing," he almost shouted at last, suddenly staring at Raskolnikov and stopping short two steps from him.

This stupid repetition was too incongruous in its ineptitude with the serious, brooding and enigmatic glance he turned upon his visitor.

But this stirred Raskolnikov's spleen more than ever and he could not resist an ironical and rather incautious challenge.

"Tell me, please," he asked suddenly, looking almost insolently at him and taking a kind of pleasure in his own insolence. "I believe it's a sort of legal rule, a sort of legal tradition—for all investigating lawyers—to begin their attack from afar, with a trivial, or at least an irrelevant subject, so as to encourage, or rather, to divert the man they are cross-examining, to disarm his caution and then all at once to give him an unexpected knockdown blow with some fatal question. Isn't that so? It's a sacred tradition, mentioned, I fancy, in all the manuals of the art?"

"Yes, yes.... Why, do you imagine that was why I spoke about government quarters... eh?"

And as he said this Porfiry Petrovitch screwed up his eyes and winked; a good-humoured, crafty look passed over his face. The wrinkles on his forehead were smoothed out, his eyes contracted, his features broadened and he suddenly went off into a nervous prolonged laugh, shaking all over and looking Raskolnikov straight in the face. The latter forced himself to laugh, too, but when Porfiry, seeing that he was laughing, broke into such a guffaw that he turned almost crimson, Raskolnikov's repulsion overcame all precaution; he left off laughing, scowled and stared with hatred at Porfiry, keeping his eyes fixed on him while his intentionally prolonged laughter lasted. There was lack of precaution on both sides, however, for Porfiry Petrovitch seemed to be laughing in his visitor's face and to be very little disturbed at the annoyance with which the visitor received it. The latter fact was very significant in Raskolnikov's eyes: he saw that Porfiry Petrovitch had not been embarrassed just before either, but that he, Raskolnikov, had perhaps fallen into a trap; that there must be something, some motive here unknown to him; that, perhaps, everything was in readiness and in another moment would break upon him...

He went straight to the point at once, rose from his seat and took his cap.

"Porfiry Petrovitch," he began resolutely, though with considerable irritation, "yesterday you expressed a desire that I should come to you for some inquiries" (he laid special stress on the word "inquiries"). "I have come and if you have anything to ask me, ask it, and if not, allow me to withdraw. I have no time to spare.... I have to be at the funeral of that man who was run over, of

183

whom you… know also," he added, feeling angry at once at having made this addition and more irritated at his anger. "I am sick of it all, do you hear? and have long been. It's partly what made me ill. In short," he shouted, feeling that the phrase about his illness was still more out of place, "in short, kindly examine me or let me go, at once. And if you must examine me, do so in the proper form! I will not allow you to do so otherwise, and so meanwhile, goodbye, as we have evidently nothing to keep us now."

"Good heavens! What do you mean? What shall I question you about?" cackled Porfiry Petrovitch with a change of tone, instantly leaving off laughing. "Please don't disturb yourself," he began fidgeting from place to place and fussily making Raskolnikov sit down. "There's no hurry, there's no hurry, it's all nonsense. Oh, no, I'm very glad you've come to see me at last… I look upon you simply as a visitor. And as for my confounded laughter, please excuse it, Rodion Romanovitch. Rodion Romanovitch? That is your name?… It's my nerves, you tickled me so with your witty observation; I assure you, sometimes I shake with laughter like an india-rubber ball for half an hour at a time…. I'm often afraid of an attack of paralysis. Do sit down. Please do, or I shall think you are angry…"

Raskolnikov did not speak; he listened, watching him, still frowning angrily. He did sit down, but still held his cap.

"I must tell you one thing about myself, my dear Rodion Romanovitch," Porfiry Petrovitch continued, moving about the room and again avoiding his visitor's eyes. "You see, I'm a bachelor, a man of no consequence and not used to society; besides, I have nothing before me, I'm set, I'm running to seed and… and have you noticed, Rodion Romanovitch, that in our Petersburg circles, if two clever men meet who are not intimate, but respect each other, like you and me, it takes them half an hour before they can find a subject for conversation—they are dumb, they sit opposite each other and feel awkward. Everyone has subjects of conversation, ladies for instance… people in high society always have their subjects of conversation, *c'est de rigueur*, but people of the middle sort like us, thinking people that is, are always tongue-tied and awkward. What is the reason of it? Whether it is the lack of public interest, or whether it is we are so honest we don't want to deceive one another, I don't know. What do you think? Do put down your cap, it looks as if you were just going, it makes me uncomfortable… I am so delighted…"

Raskolnikov put down his cap and continued listening in silence with a serious frowning face to the vague and empty chatter of Porfiry Petrovitch. "Does he really want to distract my attention with his silly babble?"

"I can't offer you coffee here; but why not spend five minutes with a friend?" Porfiry pattered on, "and you know all these official duties… please don't mind my running up and down, excuse it, my dear fellow, I am very much afraid of offending you, but exercise is absolutely indispensable for me. I'm always sitting and so glad to be moving about for five minutes… I suffer from my sedentary life… I always intend to join a gymnasium; they say that officials of all ranks, even Privy Councillors, may be seen skipping gaily there; there you have it, modern science… yes, yes…. But as for my duties here, inquiries and all such formalities… you mentioned inquiries yourself just now… I assure you these interrogations are sometimes more embarrassing for the interrogator than for the interrogated…. You made the observation yourself just now very aptly and wittily." (Raskolnikov had made no observation of the kind.) "One gets into a muddle! A regular muddle! One keeps harping on the same note, like a drum! There is to be a reform and we shall be called by a different name, at least, he-he-he! And as for our legal tradition, as you so wittily called it, I thoroughly agree with you. Every prisoner on trial, even the rudest peasant, knows that they begin by disarming him with irrelevant questions (as you so happily put it) and then deal him a knockdown blow, he-he-he!—your felicitous comparison, he-he! So you really imagined that I meant by 'government quarters'… he-he! You are an ironical person. Come. I won't go on! Ah, by the way, yes! One word leads to another. You spoke of formality just now, apropos of the inquiry, you know. But what's the use of formality? In many cases it's nonsense. Sometimes one has a friendly chat and gets a good deal more out of it. One can always fall back on formality, allow me to assure you. And after all, what does it amount to?

An examining lawyer cannot be bounded by formality at every step. The work of investigation is, so to speak, a free art in its own way, he-he-he!"

Porfiry Petrovitch took breath a moment. He had simply babbled on uttering empty phrases, letting slip a few enigmatic words and again reverting to incoherence. He was almost running about the room, moving his fat little legs quicker and quicker, looking at the ground, with his right hand behind his back, while with his left making gesticulations that were extraordinarily incongruous with his words. Raskolnikov suddenly noticed that as he ran about the room he seemed twice to stop for a moment near the door, as though he were listening.

"Is he expecting anything?"

"You are certainly quite right about it," Porfiry began gaily, looking with extraordinary simplicity at Raskolnikov (which startled him and instantly put him on his guard); "certainly quite right in laughing so wittily at our legal forms, he-he! Some of these elaborate psychological methods are exceedingly ridiculous and perhaps useless, if one adheres too closely to the forms. Yes... I am talking of forms again. Well, if I recognise, or more strictly speaking, if I suspect someone or other to be a criminal in any case entrusted to me... you're reading for the law, of course, Rodion Romanovitch?"

"Yes, I was..."

"Well, then it is a precedent for you for the future—though don't suppose I should venture to instruct you after the articles you publish about crime! No, I simply make bold to state it by way of fact, if I took this man or that for a criminal, why, I ask, should I worry him prematurely, even though I had evidence against him? In one case I may be bound, for instance, to arrest a man at once, but another may be in quite a different position, you know, so why shouldn't I let him walk about the town a bit? he-he-he! But I see you don't quite understand, so I'll give you a clearer example. If I put him in prison too soon, I may very likely give him, so to speak, moral support, he-he! You're laughing?"

Raskolnikov had no idea of laughing. He was sitting with compressed lips, his feverish eyes fixed on Porfiry Petrovitch's.

"Yet that is the case, with some types especially, for men are so different. You say 'evidence.' Well, there may be evidence. But evidence, you know, can generally be taken two ways. I am an examining lawyer and a weak man, I confess it. I should like to make a proof, so to say, mathematically clear. I should like to make a chain of evidence such as twice two are four, it ought to be a direct, irrefutable proof! And if I shut him up too soon—even though I might be convinced *he* was the man, I should very likely be depriving myself of the means of getting further evidence against him. And how? By giving him, so to speak, a definite position, I shall put him out of suspense and set his mind at rest, so that he will retreat into his shell. They say that at Sevastopol, soon after Alma, the clever people were in a terrible fright that the enemy would attack openly and take Sevastopol at once. But when they saw that the enemy preferred a regular siege, they were delighted, I am told and reassured, for the thing would drag on for two months at least. You're laughing, you don't believe me again? Of course, you're right, too. You're right, you're right. These are special cases, I admit. But you must observe this, my dear Rodion Romanovitch, the general case, the case for which all legal forms and rules are intended, for which they are calculated and laid down in books, does not exist at all, for the reason that every case, every crime, for instance, so soon as it actually occurs, at once becomes a thoroughly special case and sometimes a case unlike any that's gone before. Very comic cases of that sort sometimes occur. If I leave one man quite alone, if I don't touch him and don't worry him, but let him know or at least suspect every moment that I know all about it and am watching him day and night, and if he is in continual suspicion and terror, he'll be bound to lose his head. He'll come of himself, or maybe do something which will make it as plain as twice two are four—it's delightful. It may be so with a simple peasant, but with one of our sort, an intelligent man cultivated on a certain side, it's a dead certainty. For, my dear fellow, it's a very important matter to know on what side a man is cultivated. And then there are nerves, there are nerves, you have overlooked them! Why, they are all sick, nervous and irritable!... And then how they all suffer from spleen! That I assure you is a regular goldmine for us. And it's no anxiety to me, his running about the town free! Let him, let him walk about for a bit! I know well enough that I've caught him and that he won't escape me. Where could he escape to, he-he? Abroad, perhaps? A Pole will escape abroad, but not here, especially as I am watching and have taken measures. Will he escape into the depths of the country perhaps? But you know, peasants live there, real rude Russian peasants. A modern cultivated man would prefer prison to living with such strangers as our peasants. He-he! But that's all nonsense, and on the surface. It's not merely that he has nowhere to run to, he is *psychologically* unable to escape me, he-he! What an expression! Through a law of nature he can't escape me if he had anywhere to go. Have you seen a butterfly round a candle? That's how he will keep circling and circling round me. Freedom will lose its attractions. He'll begin to brood, he'll weave a tangle round himself, he'll worry himself to death! What's more he will provide me with a mathematical proof—if I only give him long enough interval.... And he'll keep circling round me, getting nearer and nearer and then—flop! He'll fly straight into my mouth and I'll swallow him, and that will be very amusing, he-he-he! You don't believe me?"

Raskolnikov made no reply; he sat pale and motionless, still gazing with the same intensity into Porfiry's face.

"It's a lesson," he thought, turning cold. "This is beyond the cat playing with a mouse, like yesterday. He can't be showing off his power with no motive... prompting me; he is far too clever for that... he must have another object. What is it? It's all nonsense, my friend, you are pretending, to scare me! You've no proofs and the man I saw had no real existence. You simply want to make me lose my head, to work me up beforehand and so to crush me. But you are wrong, you won't do it! But why give me such a hint? Is he reckoning on my shattered nerves? No, my friend, you are wrong, you won't do it even though you have some trap for me... let us see what you have in store for me."

And he braced himself to face a terrible and unknown ordeal. At times he longed to fall on Porfiry and strangle him. This anger was what he dreaded from the beginning. He felt that his parched lips were flecked with foam, his heart was throbbing. But he was still determined not to speak till the right moment. He realised that this was the best policy in his position, because instead of saying too much he would be irritating his enemy by his silence and provoking him into speaking too freely. Anyhow, this was what he hoped for.

"No, I see you don't believe me, you think I am playing a harmless joke on you," Porfiry began again, getting more and more lively, chuckling at every instant and again pacing round the room. "And to be sure you're right: God has given me a figure that can awaken none but comic ideas in other people; a buffoon; but let me tell you, and I repeat it, excuse an old man, my dear Rodion Romanovitch, you are a man still young, so to say, in your first youth and so you put intellect above everything, like all young people. Playful wit and abstract arguments fascinate you and that's for all the world like the old Austrian *Hof-kriegsrath*, as far as I can judge of military matters, that is: on paper they'd beaten Napoleon and taken him prisoner, and there in their study they worked it all out in the cleverest fashion, but look you, General Mack surrendered with all his army, he-he-he! I see, I see, Rodion Romanovitch, you are laughing at a civilian like me, taking examples out of military history! But I can't help it, it's my weakness. I am fond of military science. And I'm ever so fond of reading all military histories. I've certainly missed my proper career. I ought to have been in the army, upon my word I ought. I shouldn't have been a Napoleon, but I might have been a major, he-he! Well, I'll tell you the whole truth, my dear fellow, about this *special case*, I mean: actual fact and a man's temperament, my dear sir, are weighty matters and it's astonishing how they sometimes deceive the sharpest calculation! I—listen to an old man—am speaking seriously, Rodion Romanovitch" (as he said this Porfiry Petrovitch, who was scarcely five-and-thirty, actually seemed to have grown old; even his voice changed and he seemed to shrink together) "Moreover, I'm a candid man... am I a candid man or not? What do you say? I fancy I really am: I tell you these things for nothing and don't even expect a reward for it, he-he! Well, to proceed, wit in my opinion is a splendid thing, it is, so to say, an adornment of nature and a consolation of life, and what tricks it can play! So that it sometimes is hard for a poor examining lawyer to know where he is, especially when he's liable to be carried away by his own fancy, too, for you know he is a man after all! But the poor fellow

186

is saved by the criminal's temperament, worse luck for him! But young people carried away by their own wit don't think of that 'when they overstep all obstacles,' as you wittily and cleverly expressed it yesterday. He will lie—that is, the man who is a *special case*, the incognito, and he will lie well, in the cleverest fashion; you might think he would triumph and enjoy the fruits of his wit, but at the most interesting, the most flagrant moment he will faint. Of course there may be illness and a stuffy room as well, but anyway! Anyway he's given us the idea! He lied incomparably, but he didn't reckon on his temperament. That's what betrays him! Another time he will be carried away by his playful wit into making fun of the man who suspects him, he will turn pale as it were on purpose to mislead, but his paleness will be *too natural*, too much like the real thing, again he has given us an idea! Though his questioner may be deceived at first, he will think differently next day if he is not a fool, and, of course, it is like that at every step! He puts himself forward where he is not wanted, speaks continually when he ought to keep silent, brings in all sorts of allegorical allusions, he-he! Comes and asks why didn't you take me long ago? he-he-he! And that can happen, you know, with the cleverest man, the psychologist, the literary man. The temperament reflects everything like a mirror! Gaze into it and admire what you see! But why are you so pale, Rodion Romanovitch? Is the room stuffy? Shall I open the window?"

"Oh, don't trouble, please," cried Raskolnikov and he suddenly broke into a laugh. "Please don't trouble."

Porfiry stood facing him, paused a moment and suddenly he too laughed. Raskolnikov got up from the sofa, abruptly checking his hysterical laughter.

"Porfiry Petrovitch," he began, speaking loudly and distinctly, though his legs trembled and he could scarcely stand. "I see clearly at last that you actually suspect me of murdering that old woman and her sister Lizaveta. Let me tell you for my part that I am sick of this. If you find that you have a right to prosecute me legally, to arrest me, then prosecute me, arrest me. But I will not let myself be jeered at to my face and worried…"

His lips trembled, his eyes glowed with fury and he could not restrain his voice.

"I won't allow it!" he shouted, bringing his fist down on the table. "Do you hear that, Porfiry Petrovitch? I won't allow it."

"Good heavens! What does it mean?" cried Porfiry Petrovitch, apparently quite frightened. "Rodion Romanovitch, my dear fellow, what is the matter with you?"

"I won't allow it," Raskolnikov shouted again.

"Hush, my dear man! They'll hear and come in. Just think, what could we say to them?" Porfiry Petrovitch whispered in horror, bringing his face close to Raskolnikov's.

"I won't allow it, I won't allow it," Raskolnikov repeated mechanically, but he too spoke in a sudden whisper.

Porfiry turned quickly and ran to open the window.

"Some fresh air! And you must have some water, my dear fellow. You're ill!" and he was running to the door to call for some when he found a decanter of water in the corner. "Come, drink a little," he whispered, rushing up to him with the decanter. "It will be sure to do you good."

Porfiry Petrovitch's alarm and sympathy were so natural that Raskolnikov was silent and began looking at him with wild curiosity. He did not take the water, however.

"Rodion Romanovitch, my dear fellow, you'll drive yourself out of your mind, I assure you, ach, ach! Have some water, do drink a little."

He forced him to take the glass. Raskolnikov raised it mechanically to his lips, but set it on the table again with disgust.

"Yes, you've had a little attack! You'll bring back your illness again, my dear fellow," Porfiry Petrovitch cackled with friendly sympathy, though he still looked rather disconcerted. "Good heavens, you must take more care of yourself! Dmitri Prokofitch was here, came to see me yesterday—I know, I know, I've a nasty, ironical temper, but what they made of it!… Good heavens, he came yesterday after you'd been. We dined and he talked and talked away, and I could only throw up my hands in despair! Did he come from you? But do sit down, for mercy's sake, sit down!"

187

"No, not from me, but I knew he went to you and why he went," Raskolnikov answered sharply.

"You knew?"

"I knew. What of it?"

"Why this, Rodion Romanovitch, that I know more than that about you; I know about everything. I know how you went *to take a flat* at night when it was dark and how you rang the bell and asked about the blood, so that the workmen and the porter did not know what to make of it. Yes, I understand your state of mind at that time… but you'll drive yourself mad like that, upon my word! You'll lose your head! You're full of generous indignation at the wrongs you've received, first from destiny, and then from the police officers, and so you rush from one thing to another to force them to speak out and make an end of it all, because you are sick of all this suspicion and foolishness. That's so, isn't it? I have guessed how you feel, haven't I? Only in that way you'll lose your head and Razumihin's, too; he's too *good* a man for such a position, you must know that. You are ill and he is good and your illness is infectious for him… I'll tell you about it when you are more yourself…. But do sit down, for goodness' sake. Please rest, you look shocking, do sit down."

Raskolnikov sat down; he no longer shivered, he was hot all over. In amazement he listened with strained attention to Porfiry Petrovitch who still seemed frightened as he looked after him with friendly solicitude. But he did not believe a word he said, though he felt a strange inclination to believe. Porfiry's unexpected words about the flat had utterly overwhelmed him. "How can it be, he knows about the flat then," he thought suddenly, "and he tells it me himself!"

"Yes, in our legal practice there was a case almost exactly similar, a case of morbid psychology," Porfiry went on quickly. "A man confessed to murder and how he kept it up! It was a regular hallucination; he brought forward facts, he imposed upon everyone and why? He had been partly, but only partly, unintentionally the cause of a murder and when he knew that he had given the murderers the opportunity, he sank into dejection, it got on his mind and turned his brain, he began imagining things and he persuaded himself that he was the murderer. But at last the High Court of Appeal went into it and the poor fellow was acquitted and put under proper care. Thanks to the Court of Appeal! Tut-tut-tut! Why, my dear fellow, you may drive yourself into delirium if you have the impulse to work upon your nerves, to go ringing bells at night and asking about blood! I've studied all this morbid psychology in my practice. A man is sometimes tempted to jump out of a window or from a belfry. Just the same with bell-ringing…. It's all illness, Rodion Romanovitch! You have begun to neglect your illness. You should consult an experienced doctor, what's the good of that fat fellow? You are lightheaded! You were delirious when you did all this!"

For a moment Raskolnikov felt everything going round.

"Is it possible, is it possible," flashed through his mind, "that he is still lying? He can't be, he can't be." He rejected that idea, feeling to what a degree of fury it might drive him, feeling that that fury might drive him mad.

"I was not delirious. I knew what I was doing," he cried, straining every faculty to penetrate Porfiry's game, "I was quite myself, do you hear?"

"Yes, I hear and understand. You said yesterday you were not delirious, you were particularly emphatic about it! I understand all you can tell me! A-ach!… Listen, Rodion Romanovitch, my dear fellow. If you were actually a criminal, or were somehow mixed up in this damnable business, would you insist that you were not delirious but in full possession of your faculties? And so emphatically and persistently? Would it be possible? Quite impossible, to my thinking. If you had anything on your conscience, you certainly ought to insist that you were delirious. That's so, isn't it?"

There was a note of slyness in this inquiry. Raskolnikov drew back on the sofa as Porfiry bent over him and stared in silent perplexity at him.

"Another thing about Razumihin—you certainly ought to have said that he came of his own accord, to have concealed your part in it! But you don't conceal it! You lay stress on his coming at your instigation."

Raskolnikov had not done so. A chill went down his back.

"You keep telling lies," he said slowly and weakly, twisting his lips into a sickly smile, "you are trying again to show that you know all my game, that you know all I shall say beforehand," he said, conscious himself that he was not weighing his words as he ought. "You want to frighten me... or you are simply laughing at me..."

He still stared at him as he said this and again there was a light of intense hatred in his eyes.

"You keep lying," he said. "You know perfectly well that the best policy for the criminal is to tell the truth as nearly as possible... to conceal as little as possible. I don't believe you!"

"What a wily person you are!" Porfiry tittered, "there's no catching you; you've a perfect monomania. So you don't believe me? But still you do believe me, you believe a quarter; I'll soon make you believe the whole, because I have a sincere liking for you and genuinely wish you good."

Raskolnikov's lips trembled.

"Yes, I do," went on Porfiry, touching Raskolnikov's arm genially, "you must take care of your illness. Besides, your mother and sister are here now; you must think of them. You must soothe and comfort them and you do nothing but frighten them..."

"What has that to do with you? How do you know it? What concern is it of yours? You are keeping watch on me and want to let me know it?"

"Good heavens! Why, I learnt it all from you yourself! You don't notice that in your excitement you tell me and others everything. From Razumihin, too, I learnt a number of interesting details yesterday. No, you interrupted me, but I must tell you that, for all your wit, your suspiciousness makes you lose the commonsense view of things. To return to bell-ringing, for instance. I, an examining lawyer, have betrayed a precious thing like that, a real fact (for it is a fact worth having), and you see nothing in it! Why, if I had the slightest suspicion of you, should I have acted like that? No, I should first have disarmed your suspicions and not let you see I knew of that fact, should have diverted your attention and suddenly have dealt you a knockdown blow (your expression) saying: 'And what were you doing, sir, pray, at ten or nearly eleven at the murdered woman's flat and why did you ring the bell and why did you ask about blood? And why did you invite the porters to go with you to the police station, to the lieutenant?' That's how I ought to have acted if I had a grain of suspicion of you. I ought to have taken your evidence in due form, searched your lodging and perhaps have arrested you, too... so I have no suspicion of you, since I have not done that! But you can't look at it normally and you see nothing, I say again."

Raskolnikov started so that Porfiry Petrovitch could not fail to perceive it.

"You are lying all the while," he cried, "I don't know your object, but you are lying. You did not speak like that just now and I cannot be mistaken!"

"I am lying?" Porfiry repeated, apparently incensed, but preserving a good-humoured and ironical face, as though he were not in the least concerned at Raskolnikov's opinion of him. "I am lying... but how did I treat you just now, I, the examining lawyer? Prompting you and giving you every means for your defence; illness, I said, delirium, injury, melancholy and the police officers and all the rest of it? Ah! He-he-he! Though, indeed, all those psychological means of defence are not very reliable and cut both ways: illness, delirium, I don't remember—that's all right, but why, my good sir, in your illness and in your delirium were you haunted by just those delusions and not by any others? There may have been others, eh? He-he-he!"

Raskolnikov looked haughtily and contemptuously at him.

"Briefly," he said loudly and imperiously, rising to his feet and in so doing pushing Porfiry back a little, "briefly, I want to know, do you acknowledge me perfectly free from suspicion or not? Tell me, Porfiry Petrovitch, tell me once for all and make haste!"

"What a business I'm having with you!" cried Porfiry with a perfectly good-humoured, sly and composed face. "And why do you want to know, why do you want to know so much, since they haven't begun to worry you? Why, you are like a child asking for matches! And why are you so uneasy? Why do you force yourself upon us, eh? He-he-he!"

"I repeat," Raskolnikov cried furiously, "that I can't put up with it!"

"With what? Uncertainty?" interrupted Porfiry.

189

"Don't jeer at me! I won't have it! I tell you I won't have it. I can't and I won't, do you hear, do you hear?" he shouted, bringing his fist down on the table again.

"Hush! Hush! They'll overhear! I warn you seriously, take care of yourself. I am not joking," Porfiry whispered, but this time there was not the look of old womanish good nature and alarm in his face. Now he was peremptory, stern, frowning and for once laying aside all mystification.

But this was only for an instant. Raskolnikov, bewildered, suddenly fell into actual frenzy, but, strange to say, he again obeyed the command to speak quietly, though he was in a perfect paroxysm of fury.

"I will not allow myself to be tortured," he whispered, instantly recognising with hatred that he could not help obeying the command and driven to even greater fury by the thought. "Arrest me, search me, but kindly act in due form and don't play with me! Don't dare!"

"Don't worry about the form," Porfiry interrupted with the same sly smile, as it were, gloating with enjoyment over Raskolnikov. "I invited you to see me quite in a friendly way."

"I don't want your friendship and I spit on it! Do you hear? And, here, I take my cap and go. What will you say now if you mean to arrest me?"

He took up his cap and went to the door.

"And won't you see my little surprise?" chuckled Porfiry, again taking him by the arm and stopping him at the door.

He seemed to become more playful and good-humoured, which maddened Raskolnikov.

"What surprise?" he asked, standing still and looking at Porfiry in alarm.

"My little surprise, it's sitting there behind the door, he-he-he!" (He pointed to the locked door.) "I locked him in that he should not escape."

"What is it? Where? What?…"

Raskolnikov walked to the door and would have opened it, but it was locked.

"It's locked, here is the key!"

And he brought a key out of his pocket.

"You are lying," roared Raskolnikov without restraint, "you lie, you damned punchinello!" and he rushed at Porfiry who retreated to the other door, not at all alarmed.

"I understand it all! You are lying and mocking so that I may betray myself to you…"

"Why, you could not betray yourself any further, my dear Rodion Romanovitch. You are in a passion. Don't shout, I shall call the clerks."

"You are lying! Call the clerks! You knew I was ill and tried to work me into a frenzy to make me betray myself, that was your object! Produce your facts! I understand it all. You've no evidence, you have only wretched rubbishly suspicions like Zametov's! You knew my character, you wanted to drive me to fury and then to knock me down with priests and deputies…. Are you waiting for them? eh! What are you waiting for? Where are they? Produce them?"

"Why deputies, my good man? What things people will imagine! And to do so would not be acting in form as you say, you don't know the business, my dear fellow…. And there's no escaping form, as you see," Porfiry muttered, listening at the door through which a noise could be heard.

"Ah, they're coming," cried Raskolnikov. "You've sent for them! You expected them! Well, produce them all: your deputies, your witnesses, what you like!… I am ready!"

But at this moment a strange incident occurred, something so unexpected that neither Raskolnikov nor Porfiry Petrovitch could have looked for such a conclusion to their interview.

When he remembered the scene afterwards, this is how Raskolnikov saw it.

The noise behind the door increased, and suddenly the door was opened a little.

"What is it?" cried Porfiry Petrovitch, annoyed. "Why, I gave orders..."

For an instant there was no answer, but it was evident that there were several persons at the door, and that they were apparently pushing somebody back.

"What is it?" Porfiry Petrovitch repeated, uneasily.

"The prisoner Nikolay has been brought," someone answered.

"He is not wanted! Take him away! Let him wait! What's he doing here? How irregular!" cried Porfiry, rushing to the door.

"But he..." began the same voice, and suddenly ceased.

Two seconds, not more, were spent in actual struggle, then someone gave a violent shove, and then a man, very pale, strode into the room.

This man's appearance was at first sight very strange. He stared straight before him, as though seeing nothing. There was a determined gleam in his eyes; at the same time there was a deathly pallor in his face, as though he were being led to the scaffold. His white lips were faintly twitching.

He was dressed like a workman and was of medium height, very young, slim, his hair cut in round crop, with thin spare features. The man whom he had thrust back followed him into the room and succeeded in seizing him by the shoulder; he was a warder; but Nikolay pulled his arm away.

Several persons crowded inquisitively into the doorway. Some of them tried to get in. All this took place almost instantaneously.

"Go away, it's too soon! Wait till you are sent for!... Why have you brought him so soon?" Porfiry Petrovitch muttered, extremely annoyed, and as it were thrown out of his reckoning.

But Nikolay suddenly knelt down.

"What's the matter?" cried Porfiry, surprised.

"I am guilty! Mine is the sin! I am the murderer," Nikolay articulated suddenly, rather breathless, but speaking fairly loudly.

For ten seconds there was silence as though all had been struck dumb; even the warder stepped back, mechanically retreated to the door, and stood immovable.

"What is it?" cried Porfiry Petrovitch, recovering from his momentary stupefaction.

"I... am the murderer," repeated Nikolay, after a brief pause.

"What... you... what... whom did you kill?" Porfiry Petrovitch was obviously bewildered.

Nikolay again was silent for a moment.

"Alyona Ivanovna and her sister Lizaveta Ivanovna, I... killed... with an axe. Darkness came over me," he added suddenly, and was again silent.

He still remained on his knees. Porfiry Petrovitch stood for some moments as though meditating, but suddenly roused himself and waved back the uninvited spectators. They instantly vanished and closed the door. Then he looked towards Raskolnikov, who was standing in the corner, staring wildly at Nikolay and moved towards him, but stopped short, looked from Nikolay to Raskolnikov and then again at Nikolay, and seeming unable to restrain himself darted at the latter.

"You're in too great a hurry," he shouted at him, almost angrily. "I didn't ask you what came over you.... Speak, did you kill them?"

"I am the murderer.... I want to give evidence," Nikolay pronounced.

"Ach! What did you kill them with?"

"An axe. I had it ready."

"Ach, he is in a hurry! Alone?"

Nikolay did not understand the question.

"Did you do it alone?"

"Yes, alone. And Mitka is not guilty and had no share in it."

"Don't be in a hurry about Mitka! A-ach! How was it you ran downstairs like that at the time? The porters met you both!"

"It was to put them off the scent... I ran after Mitka," Nikolay replied hurriedly, as though he had prepared the answer.

"I knew it!" cried Porfiry, with vexation. "It's not his own tale he is telling," he muttered as though to himself, and suddenly his eyes rested on Raskolnikov again.

He was apparently so taken up with Nikolay that for a moment he had forgotten Raskolnikov. He was a little taken aback.

"My dear Rodion Romanovitch, excuse me!" he flew up to him, "this won't do; I'm afraid you must go... it's no good your staying... I will... you see, what a surprise!... Goodbye!"

And taking him by the arm, he showed him to the door.

"I suppose you didn't expect it?" said Raskolnikov who, though he had not yet fully grasped the situation, had regained his courage.

"You did not expect it either, my friend. See how your hand is trembling! He-he!"

"You're trembling, too, Porfiry Petrovitch!"

"Yes, I am; I didn't expect it."

They were already at the door; Porfiry was impatient for Raskolnikov to be gone.

"And your little surprise, aren't you going to show it to me?" Raskolnikov said, sarcastically.

"Why, his teeth are chattering as he asks, he-he! You are an ironical person! Come, till we meet!"

"I believe we can say *goodbye*!"

"That's in God's hands," muttered Porfiry, with an unnatural smile.

As he walked through the office, Raskolnikov noticed that many people were looking at him. Among them he saw the two porters from *the* house, whom he had invited that night to the police station. They stood there waiting. But he was no sooner on the stairs than he heard the voice of Porfiry Petrovitch behind him. Turning round, he saw the latter running after him, out of breath.

"One word, Rodion Romanovitch; as to all the rest, it's in God's hands, but as a matter of form there are some questions I shall have to ask you... so we shall meet again, shan't we?"

And Porfiry stood still, facing him with a smile.

"Shan't we?" he added again.

He seemed to want to say something more, but could not speak out.

"You must forgive me, Porfiry Petrovitch, for what has just passed... I lost my temper," began Raskolnikov, who had so far regained his courage that he felt irresistibly inclined to display his coolness.

"Don't mention it, don't mention it," Porfiry replied, almost gleefully. "I myself, too... I have a wicked temper, I admit it! But we shall meet again. If it's God's will, we may see a great deal of one another."

"And will get to know each other through and through?" added Raskolnikov.

"Yes; know each other through and through," assented Porfiry Petrovitch, and he screwed up his eyes, looking earnestly at Raskolnikov. "Now you're going to a birthday party?"

"To a funeral."

"Of course, the funeral! Take care of yourself, and get well."

"I don't know what to wish you," said Raskolnikov, who had begun to descend the stairs, but looked back again. "I should like to wish you success, but your office is such a comical one."

"Why comical?" Porfiry Petrovitch had turned to go, but he seemed to prick up his ears at this.

192

"Why, how you must have been torturing and harassing that poor Nikolay psychologically, after your fashion, till he confessed! You must have been at him day and night, proving to him that he was the murderer, and now that he has confessed, you'll begin vivisecting him again. 'You are lying,' you'll say. 'You are not the murderer! You can't be! It's not your own tale you are telling!' You must admit it's a comical business!"

"He-he-he! You noticed then that I said to Nikolay just now that it was not his own tale he was telling?"

"How could I help noticing it!"

"He-he! You are quick-witted. You notice everything! You've really a playful mind! And you always fasten on the comic side... he-he! They say that was the marked characteristic of Gogol, among the writers."

"Yes, of Gogol."

"Yes, of Gogol.... I shall look forward to meeting you."

"So shall I."

Raskolnikov walked straight home. He was so muddled and bewildered that on getting home he sat for a quarter of an hour on the sofa, trying to collect his thoughts. He did not attempt to think about Nikolay; he was stupefied; he felt that his confession was something inexplicable, amazing—something beyond his understanding. But Nikolay's confession was an actual fact. The consequences of this fact were clear to him at once, its falsehood could not fail to be discovered, and then they would be after him again. Till then, at least, he was free and must do something for himself, for the danger was imminent.

But how imminent? His position gradually became clear to him. Remembering, sketchily, the main outlines of his recent scene with Porfiry, he could not help shuddering again with horror. Of course, he did not yet know all Porfiry's aims, he could not see into all his calculations. But he had already partly shown his hand, and no one knew better than Raskolnikov how terrible Porfiry's "lead" had been for him. A little more and he *might* have given himself away completely, circumstantially. Knowing his nervous temperament and from the first glance seeing through him, Porfiry, though playing a bold game, was bound to win. There's no denying that Raskolnikov had compromised himself seriously, but no *facts* had come to light as yet; there was nothing positive. But was he taking a true view of the position? Wasn't he mistaken? What had Porfiry been trying to get at? Had he really some surprise prepared for him? And what was it? Had he really been expecting something or not? How would they have parted if it had not been for the unexpected appearance of Nikolay?

Porfiry had shown almost all his cards—of course, he had risked something in showing them— and if he had really had anything up his sleeve (Raskolnikov reflected), he would have shown that, too. What was that "surprise"? Was it a joke? Had it meant anything? Could it have concealed anything like a fact, a piece of positive evidence? His yesterday's visitor? What had become of him? Where was he today? If Porfiry really had any evidence, it must be connected with him....

He sat on the sofa with his elbows on his knees and his face hidden in his hands. He was still shivering nervously. At last he got up, took his cap, thought a minute, and went to the door.

He had a sort of presentiment that for today, at least, he might consider himself out of danger. He had a sudden sense almost of joy; he wanted to make haste to Katerina Ivanovna's. He would be too late for the funeral, of course, but he would be in time for the memorial dinner, and there at once he would see Sonia.

He stood still, thought a moment, and a suffering smile came for a moment on to his lips.

"Today! Today," he repeated to himself. "Yes, today! So it must be...."

But as he was about to open the door, it began opening of itself. He started and moved back. The door opened gently and slowly, and there suddenly appeared a figure—yesterday's visitor *from underground.*

The man stood in the doorway, looked at Raskolnikov without speaking, and took a step forward into the room. He was exactly the same as yesterday; the same figure, the same dress, but there was a great change in his face; he looked dejected and sighed deeply. If he had only put his hand up to his cheek and leaned his head on one side he would have looked exactly like a peasant woman.

"What do you want?" asked Raskolnikov, numb with terror. The man was still silent, but suddenly he bowed down almost to the ground, touching it with his finger.

"What is it?" cried Raskolnikov.

"I have sinned," the man articulated softly.

"How?"

"By evil thoughts."

They looked at one another.

"I was vexed. When you came, perhaps in drink, and bade the porters go to the police station and asked about the blood, I was vexed that they let you go and took you for drunken. I was so vexed that I lost my sleep. And remembering the address we came here yesterday and asked for you...."

"Who came?" Raskolnikov interrupted, instantly beginning to recollect.

"I did, I've wronged you."

"Then you come from that house?"

"I was standing at the gate with them... don't you remember? We have carried on our trade in that house for years past. We cure and prepare hides, we take work home... most of all I was vexed...."

And the whole scene of the day before yesterday in the gateway came clearly before Raskolnikov's mind; he recollected that there had been several people there besides the porters, women among them. He remembered one voice had suggested taking him straight to the police-station. He could not recall the face of the speaker, and even now he did not recognise it, but he remembered that he had turned round and made him some answer....

So this was the solution of yesterday's horror. The most awful thought was that he had been actually almost lost, had almost done for himself on account of such a *trivial* circumstance. So this man could tell nothing except his asking about the flat and the blood stains. So Porfiry, too, had nothing but that *delirium*, no facts but this *psychology* which *cuts both ways*, nothing positive. So if no more facts come to light (and they must not, they must not!) then... then what can they do to him? How can they convict him, even if they arrest him? And Porfiry then had only just heard about the flat and had not known about it before.

"Was it you who told Porfiry... that I'd been there?" he cried, struck by a sudden idea.

"What Porfiry?"

"The head of the detective department?"

"Yes. The porters did not go there, but I went."

"Today?"

"I got there two minutes before you. And I heard, I heard it all, how he worried you."

"Where? What? When?"

"Why, in the next room. I was sitting there all the time."

"What? Why, then you were the surprise? But how could it happen? Upon my word!"

"I saw that the porters did not want to do what I said," began the man; "for it's too late, said they, and maybe he'll be angry that we did not come at the time. I was vexed and I lost my sleep, and I began making inquiries. And finding out yesterday where to go, I went today. The first time I went he wasn't there, when I came an hour later he couldn't see me. I went the third time, and they showed me in. I informed him of everything, just as it happened, and he began skipping about the room and punching himself on the chest. 'What do you scoundrels mean by it? If I'd known about it I should have arrested him!' Then he ran out, called somebody and began talking to him in the corner, then he turned to me, scolding and questioning me. He scolded me a great deal; and I told him everything, and I told him that you didn't dare to say a word in answer to me yesterday and that you didn't recognise me. And he fell to running about again and kept hitting himself on the chest, and getting angry and running about, and when you were announced he told me to go into the next room. 'Sit there a bit,' he said. 'Don't move, whatever you may hear.' And he set a chair there for me and locked me in. 'Perhaps,' he said, 'I may call you.' And when

194

Nikolay'd been brought he let me out as soon as you were gone. 'I shall send for you again and question you,' he said."

"And did he question Nikolay while you were there?"

"He got rid of me as he did of you, before he spoke to Nikolay."

The man stood still, and again suddenly bowed down, touching the ground with his finger.

"Forgive me for my evil thoughts, and my slander."

"May God forgive you," answered Raskolnikov.

And as he said this, the man bowed down again, but not to the ground, turned slowly and went out of the room.

"It all cuts both ways, now it all cuts both ways," repeated Raskolnikov, and he went out more confident than ever.

"Now we'll make a fight for it," he said, with a malicious smile, as he went down the stairs. His malice was aimed at himself; with shame and contempt he recollected his "cowardice."

The morning that followed the fateful interview with Dounia and her mother brought sobering influences to bear on Pyotr Petrovitch. Intensely unpleasant as it was, he was forced little by little to accept as a fact beyond recall what had seemed to him only the day before fantastic and incredible. The black snake of wounded vanity had been gnawing at his heart all night. When he got out of bed, Pyotr Petrovitch immediately looked in the looking-glass. He was afraid that he had jaundice. However his health seemed unimpaired so far, and looking at his noble, clear-skinned countenance which had grown fattish of late, Pyotr Petrovitch for an instant was positively comforted in the conviction that he would find another bride and, perhaps, even a better one. But coming back to the sense of his present position, he turned aside and spat vigorously, which excited a sarcastic smile in Andrey Semyonovitch Lebeziatnikov, the young friend with whom he was staying. That smile Pyotr Petrovitch noticed, and at once set it down against his young friend's account. He had set down a good many points against him of late. His anger was redoubled when he reflected that he ought not to have told Andrey Semyonovitch about the result of yesterday's interview. That was the second mistake he had made in temper, through impulsiveness and irritability.... Moreover, all that morning one unpleasantness followed another. He even found a hitch awaiting him in his legal case in the senate. He was particularly irritated by the owner of the flat which had been taken in view of his approaching marriage and was being redecorated at his own expense; the owner, a rich German tradesman, would not entertain the idea of breaking the contract which had just been signed and insisted on the full forfeit money, though Pyotr Petrovitch would be giving him back the flat practically redecorated. In the same way the upholsterers refused to return a single rouble of the instalment paid for the furniture purchased but not yet removed to the flat.

"Am I to get married simply for the sake of the furniture?" Pyotr Petrovitch ground his teeth and at the same time once more he had a gleam of desperate hope. "Can all that be really so irrevocably over? Is it no use to make another effort?" The thought of Dounia sent a voluptuous pang through his heart. He endured anguish at that moment, and if it had been possible to slay Raskolnikov instantly by wishing it, Pyotr Petrovitch would promptly have uttered the wish.

"It was my mistake, too, not to have given them money," he thought, as he returned dejectedly to Lebeziatnikov's room, "and why on earth was I such a Jew? It was false economy! I meant to keep them without a penny so that they should turn to me as their providence, and look at them! foo! If I'd spent some fifteen hundred roubles on them for the trousseau and presents, on knickknacks, dressing-cases, jewellery, materials, and all that sort of trash from Knopp's and the English shop, my position would have been better and... stronger! They could not have refused me so easily! They are the sort of people that would feel bound to return money and presents if they broke it off; and they would find it hard to do it! And their conscience would prick them: how can we dismiss a man who has hitherto been so generous and delicate?... H'm! I've made a blunder."

And grinding his teeth again, Pyotr Petrovitch called himself a fool—but not aloud, of course.

He returned home, twice as irritated and angry as before. The preparations for the funeral dinner at Katerina Ivanovna's excited his curiosity as he passed. He had heard about it the day before; he fancied, indeed, that he had been invited, but absorbed in his own cares he had paid no attention. Inquiring of Madame Lippevechsel who was busy laying the table while Katerina Ivanovna was away at the cemetery, he heard that the entertainment was to be a great affair, that all the lodgers had been invited, among them some who had not known the dead man, that even Andrey Semyonovitch Lebeziatnikov was invited in spite of his previous quarrel with Katerina Ivanovna, that he, Pyotr Petrovitch, was not only invited, but was eagerly expected as he was the most important of the lodgers. Amalia Ivanovna herself had been invited with great ceremony in spite of the recent unpleasantness, and so she was very busy with preparations and was taking a positive pleasure in them; she was moreover dressed up to the nines, all in new black silk, and she was proud of it. All this suggested an idea to Pyotr Petrovitch and he went into his room, or rather Lebeziatnikov's, somewhat thoughtful. He had learnt that Raskolnikov was to be one of the guests.

Andrey Semyonovitch had been at home all the morning. The attitude of Pyotr Petrovitch to this gentleman was strange, though perhaps natural. Pyotr Petrovitch had despised and hated him from the day he came to stay with him and at the same time he seemed somewhat afraid of him. He had not come to stay with him on his arrival in Petersburg simply from parsimony, though that had been perhaps his chief object. He had heard of Andrey Semyonovitch, who had once been his ward, as a leading young progressive who was taking an important part in certain interesting circles, the doings of which were a legend in the provinces. It had impressed Pyotr Petrovitch. These powerful omniscient circles who despised everyone and showed everyone up had long inspired in him a peculiar but quite vague alarm. He had not, of course, been able to form even an approximate notion of what they meant. He, like everyone, had heard that there were, especially in Petersburg, progressives of some sort, nihilists and so on, and, like many people, he exaggerated and distorted the significance of those words to an absurd degree. What for many years past he had feared more than anything was *being shown up* and this was the chief ground for his continual uneasiness at the thought of transferring his business to Petersburg. He was afraid of this as little children are sometimes panic-stricken. Some years before, when he was just entering on his own career, he had come upon two cases in which rather important personages in the province, patrons of his, had been cruelly shown up. One instance had ended in great scandal for the person attacked and the other had very nearly ended in serious trouble. For this reason Pyotr Petrovitch intended to go into the subject as soon as he reached Petersburg and, if necessary, to anticipate contingencies by seeking the favour of "our younger generation." He relied on Andrey Semyonovitch for this and before his visit to Raskolnikov he had succeeded in picking up some current phrases. He soon discovered that Andrey Semyonovitch was a commonplace simpleton, but that by no means reassured Pyotr Petrovitch. Even if he had been certain that all the progressives were fools like him, it would not have allayed his uneasiness. All the doctrines, the ideas, the systems, with which Andrey Semyonovitch pestered him had no interest for him. He had his own object—he simply wanted to find out at once what was happening *here*. Had these people any power or not? Had he anything to fear from them? Would they expose any enterprise of his? And what precisely was now the object of their attacks? Could he somehow make up to them and get round them if they really were powerful? Was this the thing to do or not? Couldn't he gain something through them? In fact hundreds of questions presented themselves.

Andrey Semyonovitch was an anæmic, scrofulous little man, with strangely flaxen mutton-chop whiskers of which he was very proud. He was a clerk and had almost always something wrong with his eyes. He was rather softhearted, but self-confident and sometimes extremely conceited in speech, which had an absurd effect, incongruous with his little figure. He was one of the lodgers most respected by Amalia Ivanovna, for he did not get drunk and paid regularly for his lodgings. Andrey Semyonovitch really was rather stupid; he attached himself to the cause of progress and "our younger generation" from enthusiasm. He was one of the numerous and varied legion of dullards, of half-animate abortions, conceited, half-educated coxcombs, who attach themselves to the idea most in fashion only to vulgarise it and who caricature every cause they serve, however sincerely.

Though Lebeziatnikov was so good-natured, he, too, was beginning to dislike Pyotr Petrovitch. This happened on both sides unconsciously. However simple Andrey Semyonovitch might be, he began to see that Pyotr Petrovitch was duping him and secretly despising him, and that "he was not the right sort of man." He had tried expounding to him the system of Fourier and the Darwinian theory, but of late Pyotr Petrovitch began to listen too sarcastically and even to be rude. The fact was he had begun instinctively to guess that Lebeziatnikov was not merely a commonplace simpleton, but, perhaps, a liar, too, and that he had no connections of any consequence even in his own circle, but had simply picked things up third-hand; and that very likely he did not even know much about his own work of propaganda, for he was in too great a muddle. A fine person he would be to show anyone up! It must be noted, by the way, that Pyotr Petrovitch had during those ten days eagerly accepted the strangest praise from Andrey Semyonovitch; he had not protested, for instance, when Andrey Semyonovitch belauded him for being ready to contribute to the establishment of the new "commune," or to abstain from christening his future children, or to acquiesce if Dounia were to take a lover a month after marriage, and so on. Pyotr Petrovitch so enjoyed hearing his own praises that he did not disdain even such virtues when they were attributed to him.

Pyotr Petrovitch had had occasion that morning to realise some five-percent bonds and now he sat down to the table and counted over bundles of notes. Andrey Semyonovitch who hardly ever had any money walked about the room pretending to himself to look at all those bank notes with indifference and even contempt. Nothing would have convinced Pyotr Petrovitch that Andrey Semyonovitch could really look on the money unmoved, and the latter, on his side, kept thinking bitterly that Pyotr Petrovitch was capable of entertaining such an idea about him and was, perhaps, glad of the opportunity of teasing his young friend by reminding him of his inferiority and the great difference between them.

He found him incredibly inattentive and irritable, though he, Andrey Semyonovitch, began enlarging on his favourite subject, the foundation of a new special "commune." The brief remarks that dropped from Pyotr Petrovitch between the clicking of the beads on the reckoning frame betrayed unmistakable and discourteous irony. But the "humane" Andrey Semyonovitch ascribed Pyotr Petrovitch's ill-humour to his recent breach with Dounia and he was burning with impatience to discourse on that theme. He had something progressive to say on the subject which might console his worthy friend and "could not fail" to promote his development.

"There is some sort of festivity being prepared at that… at the widow's, isn't there?" Pyotr Petrovitch asked suddenly, interrupting Andrey Semyonovitch at the most interesting passage.

"Why, don't you know? Why, I was telling you last night what I think about all such ceremonies. And she invited you too, I heard. You were talking to her yesterday…"

"I should never have expected that beggarly fool would have spent on this feast all the money she got from that other fool, Raskolnikov. I was surprised just now as I came through at the preparations there, the wines! Several people are invited. It's beyond everything!" continued Pyotr Petrovitch, who seemed to have some object in pursuing the conversation. "What? You say I am asked too? When was that? I don't remember. But I shan't go. Why should I? I only said a word to her in passing yesterday of the possibility of her obtaining a year's salary as a destitute widow of a government clerk. I suppose she has invited me on that account, hasn't she? He-he-he!"

"I don't intend to go either," said Lebeziatnikov.

"I should think not, after giving her a thrashing! You might well hesitate, he-he!"

"Who thrashed? Whom?" cried Lebeziatnikov, flustered and blushing.

"Why, you thrashed Katerina Ivanovna a month ago. I heard so yesterday… so that's what your convictions amount to… and the woman question, too, wasn't quite sound, he-he-he!" and Pyotr Petrovitch, as though comforted, went back to clicking his beads.

"It's all slander and nonsense!" cried Lebeziatnikov, who was always afraid of allusions to the subject. "It was not like that at all, it was quite different. You've heard it wrong; it's a libel. I was simply defending myself. She rushed at me first with her nails, she pulled out all my whiskers…. It's permissable for anyone, I should hope, to defend himself and I never allow anyone to use violence to me on principle, for it's an act of despotism. What was I to do? I simply pushed her back."

"He-he-he!" Luzhin went on laughing maliciously.

"You keep on like that because you are out of humour yourself…. But that's nonsense and it has nothing, nothing whatever to do with the woman question! You don't understand; I used to think, indeed, that if women are equal to men in all respects, even in strength (as is maintained now) there ought to be equality in that, too. Of course, I reflected afterwards that such a question ought not really to arise, for there ought not to be fighting and in the future society fighting is unthinkable… and that it would be a queer thing to seek for equality in fighting. I am not so stupid… though, of course, there is fighting… there won't be later, but at present there is…

confound it! How muddled one gets with you! It's not on that account that I am not going. I am not going on principle, not to take part in the revolting convention of memorial dinners, that's why! Though, of course, one might go to laugh at it.... I am sorry there won't be any priests at it. I should certainly go if there were."

"Then you would sit down at another man's table and insult it and those who invited you. Eh?"

"Certainly not insult, but protest. I should do it with a good object. I might indirectly assist the cause of enlightenment and propaganda. It's a duty of every man to work for enlightenment and propaganda and the more harshly, perhaps, the better. I might drop a seed, an idea.... And something might grow up from that seed. How should I be insulting them? They might be offended at first, but afterwards they'd see I'd done them a service. You know, Terebyeva (who is in the community now) was blamed because when she left her family and... devoted... herself, she wrote to her father and mother that she wouldn't go on living conventionally and was entering on a free marriage and it was said that that was too harsh, that she might have spared them and have written more kindly. I think that's all nonsense and there's no need of softness; on the contrary, what's wanted is protest. Varents had been married seven years, she abandoned her two children, she told her husband straight out in a letter: 'I have realised that I cannot be happy with you. I can never forgive you that you have deceived me by concealing from me that there is another organisation of society by means of the communities. I have only lately learned it from a greathearted man to whom I have given myself and with whom I am establishing a community. I speak plainly because I consider it dishonest to deceive you. Do as you think best. Do not hope to get me back, you are too late. I hope you will be happy.' That's how letters like that ought to be written!"

"Is that Terebyeva the one you said had made a third free marriage?"

"No, it's only the second, really! But what if it were the fourth, what if it were the fifteenth, that's all nonsense! And if ever I regretted the death of my father and mother, it is now, and I sometimes think if my parents were living what a protest I would have aimed at them! I would have done something on purpose... I would have shown them! I would have astonished them! I am really sorry there is no one!"

"To surprise! He-he! Well, be that as you will," Pyotr Petrovitch interrupted, "but tell me this; do you know the dead man's daughter, the delicate-looking little thing? It's true what they say about her, isn't it?"

"What of it? I think, that is, it is my own personal conviction that this is the normal condition of women. Why not? I mean, *distinguons*. In our present society it is not altogether normal, because it is compulsory, but in the future society it will be perfectly normal, because it will be voluntary. Even as it is, she was quite right: she was suffering and that was her asset, so to speak, her capital which she had a perfect right to dispose of. Of course, in the future society there will be no need of assets, but her part will have another significance, rational and in harmony with her environment. As to Sofya Semyonovna personally, I regard her action as a vigorous protest against the organisation of society, and I respect her deeply for it; I rejoice indeed when I look at her!"

"I was told that you got her turned out of these lodgings."

Lebeziatnikov was enraged.

"That's another slander," he yelled. "It was not so at all! That was all Katerina Ivanovna's invention, for she did not understand! And I never made love to Sofya Semyonovna! I was simply developing her, entirely disinterestedly, trying to rouse her to protest.... All I wanted was her protest and Sofya Semyonovna could not have remained here anyway!"

"Have you asked her to join your community?"

"You keep on laughing and very inappropriately, allow me to tell you. You don't understand! There is no such role in a community. The community is established that there should be no such roles. In a community, such a role is essentially transformed and what is stupid here is sensible there, what, under present conditions, is unnatural becomes perfectly natural in the community. It all depends on the environment. It's all the environment and man himself is nothing. And I am on good terms with Sofya Semyonovna to this day, which is a proof that she never regarded me as having wronged her. I am trying now to attract her to the community, but on quite, quite a different footing. What are you laughing at? We are trying to establish a community of our own, a special one, on a broader basis. We have gone further in our convictions. We reject more! And meanwhile I'm still developing Sofya Semyonovna. She has a beautiful, beautiful character!"

"And you take advantage of her fine character, eh? He-he!"

"No, no! Oh, no! On the contrary."

"Oh, on the contrary! He-he-he! A queer thing to say!"

"Believe me! Why should I disguise it? In fact, I feel it strange myself how timid, chaste and modern she is with me!"

"And you, of course, are developing her... he-he! trying to prove to her that all that modesty is nonsense?"

"Not at all, not at all! How coarsely, how stupidly—excuse me saying so—you misunderstand the word development! Good heavens, how... crude you still are! We are striving for the freedom of women and you have only one idea in your head.... Setting aside the general question of chastity and feminine modesty as useless in themselves and indeed prejudices, I fully accept her chastity with me, because that's for her to decide. Of course if she were to tell me herself that she wanted me, I should think myself very lucky, because I like the girl very much; but as it is, no one has ever treated her more courteously than I, with more respect for her dignity... I wait in hopes, that's all!"

"You had much better make her a present of something. I bet you never thought of that."

"You don't understand, as I've told you already! Of course, she is in such a position, but it's another question. Quite another question! You simply despise her. Seeing a fact which you mistakenly consider deserving of contempt, you refuse to take a humane view of a fellow creature. You don't know what a character she is! I am only sorry that of late she has quite given up reading and borrowing books. I used to lend them to her. I am sorry, too, that with all the energy and resolution in protesting—which she has already shown once—she has little self-reliance, little, so to say, independence, so as to break free from certain prejudices and certain foolish ideas. Yet she thoroughly understands some questions, for instance about kissing of hands, that is, that it's an insult to a woman for a man to kiss her hand, because it's a sign of inequality. We had a debate about it and I described it to her. She listened attentively to an account of the workmen's associations in France, too. Now I am explaining the question of coming into the room in the future society."

"And what's that, pray?"

"We had a debate lately on the question: Has a member of the community the right to enter another member's room, whether man or woman, at any time... and we decided that he has!"

"It might be at an inconvenient moment, he-he!"

Lebeziatnikov was really angry.

"You are always thinking of something unpleasant," he cried with aversion. "Tfoo! How vexed I am that when I was expounding our system, I referred prematurely to the question of personal privacy! It's always a stumbling-block to people like you, they turn it into ridicule before they understand it. And how proud they are of it, too! Tfoo! I've often maintained that that question should not be approached by a novice till he has a firm faith in the system. And tell me, please, what do you find so shameful even in cesspools? I should be the first to be ready to clean out any cesspool you like. And it's not a question of self-sacrifice, it's simply work, honourable, useful work which is as good as any other and much better than the work of a Raphael and a Pushkin, because it is more useful."

"And more honourable, more honourable, he-he-he!"

"What do you mean by 'more honourable'? I don't understand such expressions to describe human activity. 'More honourable,' 'nobler'—all those are old-fashioned prejudices which I reject. Everything which is *of use* to mankind is honourable. I only understand one word: *useful*! You can snigger as much as you like, but that's so!"

Pyotr Petrovitch laughed heartily. He had finished counting the money and was putting it away. But some of the notes he left on the table. The "cesspool question" had already been a subject of dispute between them. What was absurd was that it made Lebeziatnikov really angry, while it amused Luzhin and at that moment he particularly wanted to anger his young friend.

"It's your ill-luck yesterday that makes you so ill-humoured and annoying," blurted out Lebeziatnikov, who in spite of his "independence" and his "protests" did not venture to oppose Pyotr Petrovitch and still behaved to him with some of the respect habitual in earlier years.

"You'd better tell me this," Pyotr Petrovitch interrupted with haughty displeasure, "can you... or rather are you really friendly enough with that young person to ask her to step in here for a minute? I think they've all come back from the cemetery... I heard the sound of steps... I want to see her, that young person."

"What for?" Lebeziatnikov asked with surprise.

"Oh, I want to. I am leaving here today or tomorrow and therefore I wanted to speak to her about... However, you may be present during the interview. It's better you should be, indeed. For there's no knowing what you might imagine."

"I shan't imagine anything. I only asked and, if you've anything to say to her, nothing is easier than to call her in. I'll go directly and you may be sure I won't be in your way."

Five minutes later Lebeziatnikov came in with Sonia. She came in very much surprised and overcome with shyness as usual. She was always shy in such circumstances and was always afraid of new people, she had been as a child and was even more so now.... Pyotr Petrovitch met her "politely and affably," but with a certain shade of bantering familiarity which in his opinion was suitable for a man of his respectability and weight in dealing with a creature so young and so *interesting* as she. He hastened to "reassure" her and made her sit down facing him at the table. Sonia sat down, looked about her—at Lebeziatnikov, at the notes lying on the table and then again at Pyotr Petrovitch and her eyes remained riveted on him. Lebeziatnikov was moving to the door. Pyotr Petrovitch signed to Sonia to remain seated and stopped Lebeziatnikov.

"Is Raskolnikov in there? Has he come?" he asked him in a whisper.

"Raskolnikov? Yes. Why? Yes, he is there. I saw him just come in.... Why?"

"Well, I particularly beg you to remain here with us and not to leave me alone with this... young woman. I only want a few words with her, but God knows what they may make of it. I shouldn't like Raskolnikov to repeat anything.... You understand what I mean?"

"I understand!" Lebeziatnikov saw the point. "Yes, you are right.... Of course, I am convinced personally that you have no reason to be uneasy, but... still, you are right. Certainly I'll stay. I'll stand here at the window and not be in your way... I think you are right..."

Pyotr Petrovitch returned to the sofa, sat down opposite Sonia, looked attentively at her and assumed an extremely dignified, even severe expression, as much as to say, "don't you make any mistake, madam." Sonia was overwhelmed with embarrassment.

"In the first place, Sofya Semyonovna, will you make my excuses to your respected mamma.... That's right, isn't it? Katerina Ivanovna stands in the place of a mother to you?" Pyotr Petrovitch began with great dignity, though affably.

It was evident that his intentions were friendly.

"Quite so, yes; the place of a mother," Sonia answered, timidly and hurriedly.

"Then will you make my apologies to her? Through inevitable circumstances I am forced to be absent and shall not be at the dinner in spite of your mamma's kind invitation."

"Yes... I'll tell her... at once."

And Sonia hastily jumped up from her seat.

"Wait, that's not all," Pyotr Petrovitch detained her, smiling at her simplicity and ignorance of good manners, "and you know me little, my dear Sofya Semyonovna, if you suppose I would have ventured to trouble a person like you for a matter of so little consequence affecting myself only. I have another object."

Sonia sat down hurriedly. Her eyes rested again for an instant on the grey-and-rainbow-coloured notes that remained on the table, but she quickly looked away and fixed her eyes on Pyotr Petrovitch. She felt it horribly indecorous, especially for *her*, to look at another person's money. She stared at the gold eyeglass which Pyotr Petrovitch held in his left hand and at the massive and extremely handsome ring with a yellow stone on his middle finger. But suddenly she looked away and, not knowing where to turn, ended by staring Pyotr Petrovitch again straight in the face. After a pause of still greater dignity he continued.

"I chanced yesterday in passing to exchange a couple of words with Katerina Ivanovna, poor woman. That was sufficient to enable me to ascertain that she is in a position—preternatural, if one may so express it."

"Yes... preternatural..." Sonia hurriedly assented.

"Or it would be simpler and more comprehensible to say, ill."

"Yes, simpler and more comprehen... yes, ill."

"Quite so. So then from a feeling of humanity and so to speak compassion, I should be glad to be of service to her in any way, foreseeing her unfortunate position. I believe the whole of this poverty-stricken family depends now entirely on you?"

"Allow me to ask," Sonia rose to her feet, "did you say something to her yesterday of the possibility of a pension? Because she told me you had undertaken to get her one. Was that true?"

"Not in the slightest, and indeed it's an absurdity! I merely hinted at her obtaining temporary assistance as the widow of an official who had died in the service—if only she has patronage... but apparently your late parent had not served his full term and had not indeed been in the service at all of late. In fact, if there could be any hope, it would be very ephemeral, because there would be no claim for assistance in that case, far from it.... And she is dreaming of a pension already, he-he-he!... A go-ahead lady!"

"Yes, she is. For she is credulous and good-hearted, and she believes everything from the goodness of her heart and... and... and she is like that... yes... You must excuse her," said Sonia, and again she got up to go.

"But you haven't heard what I have to say."

"No, I haven't heard," muttered Sonia.

"Then sit down." She was terribly confused; she sat down again a third time.

"Seeing her position with her unfortunate little ones, I should be glad, as I have said before, so far as lies in my power, to be of service, that is, so far as is in my power, not more. One might for instance get up a subscription for her, or a lottery, something of the sort, such as is always arranged in such cases by friends or even outsiders desirous of assisting people. It was of that I intended to speak to you; it might be done."

"Yes, yes... God will repay you for it," faltered Sonia, gazing intently at Pyotr Petrovitch.

"It might be, but we will talk of it later. We might begin it today, we will talk it over this evening and lay the foundation so to speak. Come to me at seven o'clock. Mr. Lebeziatnikov, I hope, will assist us. But there is one circumstance of which I ought to warn you beforehand and for which I venture to trouble you, Sofya Semyonovna, to come here. In my opinion money cannot be, indeed it's unsafe to put it into Katerina Ivanovna's own hands. The dinner today is a proof of that. Though she has not, so to speak, a crust of bread for tomorrow and... well, boots or shoes, or anything; she has bought today Jamaica rum, and even, I believe, Madeira and... and coffee. I saw it as I passed through. Tomorrow it will all fall upon you again, they won't have a crust of bread. It's absurd, really, and so, to my thinking, a subscription ought to be raised so that the unhappy widow should not know of the money, but only you, for instance. Am I right?"

"I don't know... this is only today, once in her life.... She was so anxious to do honour, to celebrate the memory.... And she is very sensible... but just as you think and I shall be very, very... they will all be... and God will reward... and the orphans..."

Sonia burst into tears.

"Very well, then, keep it in mind; and now will you accept for the benefit of your relation the small sum that I am able to spare, from me personally. I am very anxious that my name should not be mentioned in connection with it. Here... having so to speak anxieties of my own, I cannot do more..."

And Pyotr Petrovitch held out to Sonia a ten-rouble note carefully unfolded. Sonia took it, flushed crimson, jumped up, muttered something and began taking leave. Pyotr Petrovitch accompanied her ceremoniously to the door. She got out of the room at last, agitated and distressed, and returned to Katerina Ivanovna, overwhelmed with confusion.

All this time Lebeziatnikov had stood at the window or walked about the room, anxious not to interrupt the conversation; when Sonia had gone he walked up to Pyotr Petrovitch and solemnly held out his hand.

"I heard and *saw* everything," he said, laying stress on the last verb. "That is honourable, I mean to say, it's humane! You wanted to avoid gratitude, I saw! And although I cannot, I confess, in principle sympathise with private charity, for it not only fails to eradicate the evil but even promotes it, yet I must admit that I saw your action with pleasure—yes, yes, I like it."

"That's all nonsense," muttered Pyotr Petrovitch, somewhat disconcerted, looking carefully at Lebeziatnikov.

"No, it's not nonsense! A man who has suffered distress and annoyance as you did yesterday and who yet can sympathise with the misery of others, such a man... even though he is making a social mistake—is still deserving of respect! I did not expect it indeed of you, Pyotr Petrovitch, especially as according to your ideas... oh, what a drawback your ideas are to you! How distressed you are for instance by your ill-luck yesterday," cried the simple-hearted Lebeziatnikov, who felt a return of affection for Pyotr Petrovitch. "And, what do you want with marriage, with *legal* marriage, my dear, noble Pyotr Petrovitch? Why do you cling to this *legality* of marriage? Well, you may beat me if you like, but I am glad, positively glad it hasn't come off, that you are free, that you are not quite lost for humanity... you see, I've spoken my mind!"

"Because I don't want in your free marriage to be made a fool of and to bring up another man's children, that's why I want legal marriage," Luzhin replied in order to make some answer.

He seemed preoccupied by something.

"Children? You referred to children," Lebeziatnikov started off like a warhorse at the trumpet call. "Children are a social question and a question of first importance, I agree; but the question of children has another solution. Some refuse to have children altogether, because they suggest the institution of the family. We'll speak of children later, but now as to the question of honour, I confess that's my weak point. That horrid, military, Pushkin expression is unthinkable in the dictionary of the future. What does it mean indeed? It's nonsense, there will be no deception in a free marriage! That is only the natural consequence of a legal marriage, so to say, its corrective, a protest. So that indeed it's not humiliating... and if I ever, to suppose an absurdity, were to be legally married, I should be positively glad of it. I should say to my wife: 'My dear, hitherto I have loved you, now I respect you, for you've shown you can protest!' You laugh! That's because you are incapable of getting away from prejudices. Confound it all! I understand now where the unpleasantness is of being deceived in a legal marriage, but it's simply a despicable consequence of a despicable position in which both are humiliated. When the deception is open, as in a free marriage, then it does not exist, it's unthinkable. Your wife will only prove how she respects you by considering you incapable of opposing her happiness and avenging yourself on her for her new husband. Damn it all! I sometimes dream if I were to be married, pfoo! I mean if I were to marry, legally or not, it's just the same, I should present my wife with a lover if she had not found one for herself. 'My dear,' I should say, 'I love you, but even more than that I desire you to respect me. See!' Am I not right?"

Pyotr Petrovitch sniggered as he listened, but without much merriment. He hardly heard it indeed. He was preoccupied with something else and even Lebeziatnikov at last noticed it. Pyotr Petrovitch seemed excited and rubbed his hands. Lebeziatnikov remembered all this and reflected upon it afterwards.

It would be difficult to explain exactly what could have originated the idea of that senseless dinner in Katerina Ivanovna's disordered brain. Nearly ten of the twenty roubles, given by Raskolnikov for Marmeladov's funeral, were wasted upon it. Possibly Katerina Ivanovna felt obliged to honour the memory of the deceased "suitably," that all the lodgers, and still more Amalia Ivanovna, might know "that he was in no way their inferior, and perhaps very much their superior," and that no one had the right "to turn up his nose at him." Perhaps the chief element was that peculiar "poor man's pride," which compels many poor people to spend their last savings on some traditional social ceremony, simply in order to do "like other people," and not to "be looked down upon." It is very probable, too, that Katerina Ivanovna longed on this occasion, at the moment when she seemed to be abandoned by everyone, to show those "wretched contemptible lodgers" that she knew "how to do things, how to entertain" and that she had been brought up "in a genteel, she might almost say aristocratic colonel's family" and had not been meant for sweeping floors and washing the children's rags at night. Even the poorest and most broken-spirited people are sometimes liable to these paroxysms of pride and vanity which take the form of an irresistible nervous craving. And Katerina Ivanovna was not broken-spirited; she might have been killed by circumstance, but her spirit could not have been broken, that is, she could not have been intimidated, her will could not be crushed. Moreover Sonia had said with good reason that her mind was unhinged. She could not be said to be insane, but for a year past she had been so harassed that her mind might well be overstrained. The later stages of consumption are apt, doctors tell us, to affect the intellect.

There was no great variety of wines, nor was there Madeira; but wine there was. There was vodka, rum and Lisbon wine, all of the poorest quality but in sufficient quantity. Besides the traditional rice and honey, there were three or four dishes, one of which consisted of pancakes, all prepared in Amalia Ivanovna's kitchen. Two samovars were boiling, that tea and punch might be offered after dinner. Katerina Ivanovna had herself seen to purchasing the provisions, with the help of one of the lodgers, an unfortunate little Pole who had somehow been stranded at Madame Lippevechsel's. He promptly put himself at Katerina Ivanovna's disposal and had been all that morning and all the day before running about as fast as his legs could carry him, and very anxious that everyone should be aware of it. For every trifle he ran to Katerina Ivanovna, even hunting her out at the bazaar, at every instant called her "*Pani*." She was heartily sick of him before the end, though she had declared at first that she could not have got on without this "serviceable and magnanimous man." It was one of Katerina Ivanovna's characteristics to paint everyone she met in the most glowing colours. Her praises were so exaggerated as sometimes to be embarrassing; she would invent various circumstances to the credit of her new acquaintance and quite genuinely believe in their reality. Then all of a sudden she would be disillusioned and would rudely and contemptuously repulse the person she had only a few hours before been literally adoring. She was naturally of a gay, lively and peace-loving disposition, but from continual failures and misfortunes she had come to desire so *keenly* that all should live in peace and joy and should not *dare* to break the peace, that the slightest jar, the smallest disaster reduced her almost to frenzy, and she would pass in an instant from the brightest hopes and fancies to cursing her fate and raving, and knocking her head against the wall.

Amalia Ivanovna, too, suddenly acquired extraordinary importance in Katerina Ivanovna's eyes and was treated by her with extraordinary respect, probably only because Amalia Ivanovna had thrown herself heart and soul into the preparations. She had undertaken to lay the table, to provide the linen, crockery, etc., and to cook the dishes in her kitchen, and Katerina Ivanovna had left it all in her hands and gone herself to the cemetery. Everything had been well done. Even the tablecloth was nearly clean; the crockery, knives, forks and glasses were, of course, of all shapes and patterns, lent by different lodgers, but the table was properly laid at the time fixed, and Amalia Ivanovna, feeling she had done her work well, had put on a black silk dress and a cap with new mourning ribbons and met the returning party with some pride. This pride, though justifiable, displeased Katerina Ivanovna for some reason: "as though the table could not have been laid except by Amalia Ivanovna!" She disliked the cap with new ribbons, too. "Could she be stuck up, the stupid German, because she was mistress of the house, and had consented as a favour to help her poor lodgers! As a favour! Fancy that! Katerina Ivanovna's father who had been a colonel and almost a governor had sometimes had the table set for forty persons, and then anyone like Amalia Ivanovna, or rather Ludwigovna, would not have been allowed into the kitchen."

Katerina Ivanovna, however, put off expressing her feelings for the time and contented herself with treating her coldly, though she decided inwardly that she would certainly have to put Amalia Ivanovna down and set her in her proper place, for goodness only knew what she was fancying herself. Katerina Ivanovna was irritated too by the fact that hardly any of the lodgers invited had come to the funeral, except the Pole who had just managed to run into the cemetery, while to the memorial dinner the poorest and most insignificant of them had turned up, the wretched creatures, many of them not quite sober. The older and more respectable of them all, as if by common consent, stayed away. Pyotr Petrovitch Luzhin, for instance, who might be said to be the most respectable of all the lodgers, did not appear, though Katerina Ivanovna had the evening before told all the world, that is Amalia Ivanovna, Polenka, Sonia and the Pole, that he was the most generous, noble-hearted man with a large property and vast connections, who had been a friend of her first husband's, and a guest in her father's house, and that he had promised to use all his influence to secure her a considerable pension. It must be noted that when Katerina Ivanovna exalted anyone's connections and fortune, it was without any ulterior motive, quite disinterestedly, for the mere pleasure of adding to the consequence of the person praised. Probably "taking his cue" from Luzhin, "that contemptible wretch Lebeziatnikov had not turned up either. What did he fancy himself? He was only asked out of kindness and because he was sharing the same room with Pyotr Petrovitch and was a friend of his, so that it would have been awkward not to invite him."

Among those who failed to appear were "the genteel lady and her old-maidish daughter," who had only been lodgers in the house for the last fortnight, but had several times complained of the noise and uproar in Katerina Ivanovna's room, especially when Marmeladov had come back drunk. Katerina Ivanovna heard this from Amalia Ivanovna who, quarrelling with Katerina Ivanovna, and threatening to turn the whole family out of doors, had shouted at her that they "were not worth the foot" of the honourable lodgers whom they were disturbing. Katerina Ivanovna determined now to invite this lady and her daughter, "whose foot she was not worth," and who had turned away haughtily when she casually met them, so that they might know that "she was more noble in her thoughts and feelings and did not harbour malice," and might see that she was not accustomed to her way of living. She had proposed to make this clear to them at dinner with allusions to her late father's governorship, and also at the same time to hint that it was exceedingly stupid of them to turn away on meeting her. The fat colonel-major (he was really a discharged officer of low rank) was also absent, but it appeared that he had been "not himself" for the last two days. The party consisted of the Pole, a wretched looking clerk with a spotty face and a greasy coat, who had not a word to say for himself, and smelt abominably, a deaf and almost blind old man who had once been in the post office and who had been from immemorial ages maintained by someone at Amalia Ivanovna's.

A retired clerk of the commissariat department came, too; he was drunk, had a loud and most unseemly laugh and only fancy—was without a waistcoat! One of the visitors sat straight down to the table without even greeting Katerina Ivanovna. Finally one person having no suit appeared in his dressing-gown, but this was too much, and the efforts of Amalia Ivanovna and the Pole succeeded in removing him. The Pole brought with him, however, two other Poles who did not live at Amalia Ivanovna's and whom no one had seen here before. All this irritated Katerina

Ivanovna intensely. "For whom had they made all these preparations then?" To make room for the visitors the children had not even been laid for at the table; but the two little ones were sitting on a bench in the furthest corner with their dinner laid on a box, while Polenka as a big girl had to look after them, feed them, and keep their noses wiped like well-bred children's.

Katerina Ivanovna, in fact, could hardly help meeting her guests with increased dignity, and even haughtiness. She stared at some of them with special severity, and loftily invited them to take their seats. Rushing to the conclusion that Amalia Ivanovna must be responsible for those who were absent, she began treating her with extreme nonchalance, which the latter promptly observed and resented. Such a beginning was no good omen for the end. All were seated at last.

Raskolnikov came in almost at the moment of their return from the cemetery. Katerina Ivanovna was greatly delighted to see him, in the first place, because he was the one "educated visitor, and, as everyone knew, was in two years to take a professorship in the university," and secondly because he immediately and respectfully apologised for having been unable to be at the funeral. She positively pounced upon him, and made him sit on her left hand (Amalia Ivanovna was on her right). In spite of her continual anxiety that the dishes should be passed round correctly and that everyone should taste them, in spite of the agonising cough which interrupted her every minute and seemed to have grown worse during the last few days, she hastened to pour out in a half whisper to Raskolnikov all her suppressed feelings and her just indignation at the failure of the dinner, interspersing her remarks with lively and uncontrollable laughter at the expense of her visitors and especially of her landlady.

"It's all that cuckoo's fault! You know whom I mean? Her, her!" Katerina Ivanovna nodded towards the landlady. "Look at her, she's making round eyes, she feels that we are talking about her and can't understand. Pfoo, the owl! Ha-ha! (*Cough-cough-cough.*) And what does she put on that cap for? (*Cough-cough-cough.*) Have you noticed that she wants everyone to consider that she is patronising me and doing me an honour by being here? I asked her like a sensible woman to invite people, especially those who knew my late husband, and look at the set of fools she has brought! The sweeps! Look at that one with the spotty face. And those wretched Poles, ha-ha-ha! (*Cough-cough-cough.*) Not one of them has ever poked his nose in here, I've never set eyes on them. What have they come here for, I ask you? There they sit in a row. Hey, *pan!*" she cried suddenly to one of them, "have you tasted the pancakes? Take some more! Have some beer! Won't you have some vodka? Look, he's jumped up and is making his bows, they must be quite starved, poor things. Never mind, let them eat! They don't make a noise, anyway, though I'm really afraid for our landlady's silver spoons... Amalia Ivanovna!" she addressed her suddenly, almost aloud, "if your spoons should happen to be stolen, I won't be responsible, I warn you! Ha-ha-ha!" She laughed turning to Raskolnikov, and again nodding towards the landlady, in high glee at her sally. "She didn't understand, she didn't understand again! Look how she sits with her mouth open! An owl, a real owl! An owl in new ribbons, ha-ha-ha!"

Here her laugh turned again to an insufferable fit of coughing that lasted five minutes. Drops of perspiration stood out on her forehead and her handkerchief was stained with blood. She showed Raskolnikov the blood in silence, and as soon as she could get her breath began whispering to him again with extreme animation and a hectic flush on her cheeks.

"Do you know, I gave her the most delicate instructions, so to speak, for inviting that lady and her daughter, you understand of whom I am speaking? It needed the utmost delicacy, the greatest nicety, but she has managed things so that that fool, that conceited baggage, that provincial nonentity, simply because she is the widow of a major, and has come to try and get a pension and to fray out her skirts in the government offices, because at fifty she paints her face (everybody knows it)... a creature like that did not think fit to come, and has not even answered the invitation, which the most ordinary good manners required! I can't understand why Pyotr Petrovitch has not come? But where's Sonia? Where has she gone? Ah, there she is at last! what is it, Sonia, where have you been? It's odd that even at your father's funeral you should be so unpunctual. Rodion Romanovitch, make room for her beside you. That's your place, Sonia... take what you like. Have some of the cold entrée with jelly, that's the best. They'll bring the pancakes directly. Have they given the children some? Polenka, have you got everything? (*Cough-cough-cough.*) That's all right. Be a good girl, Lida, and, Kolya, don't fidget with your feet; sit like a little gentleman. What are you saying, Sonia?"

Sonia hastened to give her Pyotr Petrovitch's apologies, trying to speak loud enough for everyone to hear and carefully choosing the most respectful phrases which she attributed to Pyotr Petrovitch. She added that Pyotr Petrovitch had particularly told her to say that, as soon as he possibly could, he would come immediately to discuss *business* alone with her and to consider what could be done for her, etc., etc.

Sonia knew that this would comfort Katerina Ivanovna, would flatter her and gratify her pride. She sat down beside Raskolnikov; she made him a hurried bow, glancing curiously at him. But for the rest of the time she seemed to avoid looking at him or speaking to him. She seemed absentminded, though she kept looking at Katerina Ivanovna, trying to please her. Neither she nor Katerina Ivanovna had been able to get mourning; Sonia was wearing dark brown, and Katerina Ivanovna had on her only dress, a dark striped cotton one.

The message from Pyotr Petrovitch was very successful. Listening to Sonia with dignity, Katerina Ivanovna inquired with equal dignity how Pyotr Petrovitch was, then at once whispered almost aloud to Raskolnikov that it certainly would have been strange for a man of Pyotr Petrovitch's position and standing to find himself in such "extraordinary company," in spite of his devotion to her family and his old friendship with her father.

"That's why I am so grateful to you, Rodion Romanovitch, that you have not disdained my hospitality, even in such surroundings," she added almost aloud. "But I am sure that it was only your special affection for my poor husband that has made you keep your promise."

Then once more with pride and dignity she scanned her visitors, and suddenly inquired aloud across the table of the deaf man: "Wouldn't he have some more meat, and had he been given some wine?" The old man made no answer and for a long while could not understand what he was asked, though his neighbours amused themselves by poking and shaking him. He simply gazed about him with his mouth open, which only increased the general mirth.

"What an imbecile! Look, look! Why was he brought? But as to Pyotr Petrovitch, I always had confidence in him," Katerina Ivanovna continued, "and, of course, he is not like..." with an extremely stern face she addressed Amalia Ivanovna so sharply and loudly that the latter was quite disconcerted, "not like your dressed up draggletails whom my father would not have taken as cooks into his kitchen, and my late husband would have done them honour if he had invited them in the goodness of his heart."

"Yes, he was fond of drink, he was fond of it, he did drink!" cried the commissariat clerk, gulping down his twelfth glass of vodka.

"My late husband certainly had that weakness, and everyone knows it," Katerina Ivanovna attacked him at once, "but he was a kind and honourable man, who loved and respected his family. The worst of it was his good nature made him trust all sorts of disreputable people, and he drank with fellows who were not worth the sole of his shoe. Would you believe it, Rodion Romanovitch, they found a gingerbread cock in his pocket; he was dead drunk, but he did not forget the children!"

"A cock? Did you say a cock?" shouted the commissariat clerk.

Katerina Ivanovna did not vouchsafe a reply. She sighed, lost in thought.

"No doubt you think, like everyone, that I was too severe with him," she went on, addressing Raskolnikov. "But that's not so! He respected me, he respected me very much! He was a kindhearted man! And how sorry I was for him sometimes! He would sit in a corner and look at me, I used to feel so sorry for him, I used to want to be kind to him and then would think to myself: 'Be kind to him and he will drink again,' it was only by severity that you could keep him within bounds."

"Yes, he used to get his hair pulled pretty often," roared the commissariat clerk again, swallowing another glass of vodka.

"Some fools would be the better for a good drubbing, as well as having their hair pulled. I am not talking of my late husband now!" Katerina Ivanovna snapped at him.

The flush on her cheeks grew more and more marked, her chest heaved. In another minute she would have been ready to make a scene. Many of the visitors were sniggering, evidently delighted. They began poking the commissariat clerk and whispering something to him. They were evidently trying to egg him on.

"Allow me to ask what are you alluding to," began the clerk, "that is to say, whose… about whom… did you say just now… But I don't care! That's nonsense! Widow! I forgive you…. Pass!"

And he took another drink of vodka.

Raskolnikov sat in silence, listening with disgust. He only ate from politeness, just tasting the food that Katerina Ivanovna was continually putting on his plate, to avoid hurting her feelings. He watched Sonia intently. But Sonia became more and more anxious and distressed; she, too, foresaw that the dinner would not end peaceably, and saw with terror Katerina Ivanovna's growing irritation. She knew that she, Sonia, was the chief reason for the "genteel" ladies' contemptuous treatment of Katerina Ivanovna's invitation. She had heard from Amalia Ivanovna that the mother was positively offended at the invitation and had asked the question: "How could she let her daughter sit down beside *that young person*?" Sonia had a feeling that Katerina Ivanovna had already heard this and an insult to Sonia meant more to Katerina Ivanovna than an insult to herself, her children, or her father, Sonia knew that Katerina Ivanovna would not be satisfied now, "till she had shown those draggletails that they were both…" To make matters worse someone passed Sonia, from the other end of the table, a plate with two hearts pierced with an arrow, cut out of black bread. Katerina Ivanovna flushed crimson and at once said aloud across the table that the man who sent it was "a drunken ass!"

Amalia Ivanovna was foreseeing something amiss, and at the same time deeply wounded by Katerina Ivanovna's haughtiness, and to restore the good-humour of the company and raise herself in their esteem she began, apropos of nothing, telling a story about an acquaintance of hers "Karl from the chemist's," who was driving one night in a cab, and that "the cabman wanted him to kill, and Karl very much begged him not to kill, and wept and clasped hands, and frightened and from fear pierced his heart." Though Katerina Ivanovna smiled, she observed at once that Amalia Ivanovna ought not to tell anecdotes in Russian; the latter was still more offended, and she retorted that her "*Vater aus Berlin* was a very important man, and always went with his hands in pockets." Katerina Ivanovna could not restrain herself and laughed so much that Amalia Ivanovna lost patience and could scarcely control herself.

"Listen to the owl!" Katerina Ivanovna whispered at once, her good-humour almost restored, "she meant to say he kept his hands in his pockets, but she said he put his hands in people's pockets. (*Cough-cough.*) And have you noticed, Rodion Romanovitch, that all these Petersburg foreigners, the Germans especially, are all stupider than we! Can you fancy anyone of us telling how 'Karl from the chemist's' 'pierced his heart from fear' and that the idiot, instead of punishing the cabman, 'clasped his hands and wept, and much begged.' Ah, the fool! And you know she fancies it's very touching and does not suspect how stupid she is! To my thinking that drunken commissariat clerk is a great deal cleverer, anyway one can see that he has addled his brains with drink, but you know, these foreigners are always so well behaved and serious…. Look how she sits glaring! She is angry, ha-ha! (*Cough-cough-cough.*)"

Regaining her good-humour, Katerina Ivanovna began at once telling Raskolnikov that when she had obtained her pension, she intended to open a school for the daughters of gentlemen in her native town T——. This was the first time she had spoken to him of the project, and she launched out into the most alluring details. It suddenly appeared that Katerina Ivanovna had in her hands the very certificate of honour of which Marmeladov had spoken to Raskolnikov in the tavern, when he told him that Katerina Ivanovna, his wife, had danced the shawl dance before the governor and other great personages on leaving school. This certificate of honour was obviously intended now to prove Katerina Ivanovna's right to open a boarding-school; but she had armed herself with it chiefly with the object of overwhelming "those two stuck-up draggletails" if they came to the dinner, and proving incontestably that Katerina Ivanovna was of the most noble, "she might even say aristocratic family, a colonel's daughter and was far superior to certain

209

adventuresses who have been so much to the fore of late." The certificate of honour immediately passed into the hands of the drunken guests, and Katerina Ivanovna did not try to retain it, for it actually contained the statement *en toutes lettres*, that her father was of the rank of a major, and also a companion of an order, so that she really was almost the daughter of a colonel.

Warming up, Katerina Ivanovna proceeded to enlarge on the peaceful and happy life they would lead in T——, on the gymnasium teachers whom she would engage to give lessons in her boarding-school, one a most respectable old Frenchman, one Mangot, who had taught Katerina Ivanovna herself in old days and was still living in T——, and would no doubt teach in her school on moderate terms. Next she spoke of Sonia who would go with her to T—— and help her in all her plans. At this someone at the further end of the table gave a sudden guffaw.

Though Katerina Ivanovna tried to appear to be disdainfully unaware of it, she raised her voice and began at once speaking with conviction of Sonia's undoubted ability to assist her, of "her gentleness, patience, devotion, generosity and good education," tapping Sonia on the cheek and kissing her warmly twice. Sonia flushed crimson, and Katerina Ivanovna suddenly burst into tears, immediately observing that she was "nervous and silly, that she was too much upset, that it was time to finish, and as the dinner was over, it was time to hand round the tea."

At that moment, Amalia Ivanovna, deeply aggrieved at taking no part in the conversation, and not being listened to, made one last effort, and with secret misgivings ventured on an exceedingly deep and weighty observation, that "in the future boarding-school she would have to pay particular attention to *die Wäsche*, and that there certainly must be a good *dame* to look after the linen, and secondly that the young ladies must not novels at night read."

Katerina Ivanovna, who certainly was upset and very tired, as well as heartily sick of the dinner, at once cut short Amalia Ivanovna, saying "she knew nothing about it and was talking nonsense, that it was the business of the laundry maid, and not of the directress of a high-class boarding-school to look after *die Wäsche*, and as for novel-reading, that was simply rudeness, and she begged her to be silent." Amalia Ivanovna fired up and getting angry observed that she only "meant her good," and that "she had meant her very good," and that "it was long since she had paid her *gold* for the lodgings."

Katerina Ivanovna at once "set her down," saying that it was a lie to say she wished her good, because only yesterday when her dead husband was lying on the table, she had worried her about the lodgings. To this Amalia Ivanovna very appropriately observed that she had invited those ladies, but "those ladies had not come, because those ladies *are* ladies and cannot come to a lady who is not a lady." Katerina Ivanovna at once pointed out to her, that as she was a slut she could not judge what made one really a lady. Amalia Ivanovna at once declared that her "*Vater aus Berlin* was a very, very important man, and both hands in pockets went, and always used to say: 'Poof! poof!'" and she leapt up from the table to represent her father, sticking her hands in her pockets, puffing her cheeks, and uttering vague sounds resembling "poof! poof!" amid loud laughter from all the lodgers, who purposely encouraged Amalia Ivanovna, hoping for a fight.

But this was too much for Katerina Ivanovna, and she at once declared, so that all could hear, that Amalia Ivanovna probably never had a father, but was simply a drunken Petersburg Finn, and had certainly once been a cook and probably something worse. Amalia Ivanovna turned as red as a lobster and squealed that perhaps Katerina Ivanovna never had a father, "but she had a *Vater aus Berlin* and that he wore a long coat and always said poof-poof-poof!"

Katerina Ivanovna observed contemptuously that all knew what her family was and that on that very certificate of honour it was stated in print that her father was a colonel, while Amalia Ivanovna's father—if she really had one—was probably some Finnish milkman, but that probably she never had a father at all, since it was still uncertain whether her name was Amalia Ivanovna or Amalia Ludwigovna.

At this Amalia Ivanovna, lashed to fury, struck the table with her fist, and shrieked that she was Amalia Ivanovna, and not Ludwigovna, "that her *Vater* was named Johann and that he was a burgomeister, and that Katerina Ivanovna's *Vater* was quite never a burgomeister." Katerina Ivanovna rose from her chair, and with a stern and apparently calm voice (though she was pale and her chest was heaving) observed that "if she dared for one moment to set her contemptible wretch of a father on a level with her papa, she, Katerina Ivanovna, would tear her cap off her head and trample it under foot." Amalia Ivanovna ran about the room, shouting at the top of her voice, that she was mistress of the house and that Katerina Ivanovna should leave the lodgings that minute; then she rushed for some reason to collect the silver spoons from the table. There was a great outcry and uproar, the children began crying. Sonia ran to restrain Katerina Ivanovna, but when Amalia Ivanovna shouted something about "the yellow ticket," Katerina Ivanovna pushed Sonia away, and rushed at the landlady to carry out her threat.

At that minute the door opened, and Pyotr Petrovitch Luzhin appeared on the threshold. He stood scanning the party with severe and vigilant eyes. Katerina Ivanovna rushed to him.

"Pyotr Petrovitch," she cried, "protect me... you at least! Make this foolish woman understand that she can't behave like this to a lady in misfortune... that there is a law for such things.... I'll go to the governor-general himself.... She shall answer for it.... Remembering my father's hospitality protect these orphans."

"Allow me, madam.... Allow me." Pyotr Petrovitch waved her off. "Your papa as you are well aware I had not the honour of knowing" (someone laughed aloud) "and I do not intend to take part in your everlasting squabbles with Amalia Ivanovna.... I have come here to speak of my own affairs... and I want to have a word with your stepdaughter, Sofya... Ivanovna, I think it is? Allow me to pass."

Pyotr Petrovitch, edging by her, went to the opposite corner where Sonia was.

Katerina Ivanovna remained standing where she was, as though thunderstruck. She could not understand how Pyotr Petrovitch could deny having enjoyed her father's hospitality. Though she had invented it herself, she believed in it firmly by this time. She was struck too by the businesslike, dry and even contemptuous menacing tone of Pyotr Petrovitch. All the clamour gradually died away at his entrance. Not only was this "serious business man" strikingly incongruous with the rest of the party, but it was evident, too, that he had come upon some matter of consequence, that some exceptional cause must have brought him and that therefore something was going to happen. Raskolnikov, standing beside Sonia, moved aside to let him pass; Pyotr Petrovitch did not seem to notice him. A minute later Lebeziatnikov, too, appeared in the doorway; he did not come in, but stood still, listening with marked interest, almost wonder, and seemed for a time perplexed.

"Excuse me for possibly interrupting you, but it's a matter of some importance," Pyotr Petrovitch observed, addressing the company generally. "I am glad indeed to find other persons present. Amalia Ivanovna, I humbly beg you as mistress of the house to pay careful attention to what I have to say to Sofya Ivanovna. Sofya Ivanovna," he went on, addressing Sonia, who was very much surprised and already alarmed, "immediately after your visit I found that a hundred-rouble note was missing from my table, in the room of my friend Mr. Lebeziatnikov. If in any way whatever you know and will tell us where it is now, I assure you on my word of honour and call all present to witness that the matter shall end there. In the opposite case I shall be compelled to have recourse to very serious measures and then... you must blame yourself."

Complete silence reigned in the room. Even the crying children were still. Sonia stood deadly pale, staring at Luzhin and unable to say a word. She seemed not to understand. Some seconds passed.

"Well, how is it to be then?" asked Luzhin, looking intently at her.

"I don't know.... I know nothing about it," Sonia articulated faintly at last.

"No, you know nothing?" Luzhin repeated and again he paused for some seconds. "Think a moment, mademoiselle," he began severely, but still, as it were, admonishing her. "Reflect, I am prepared to give you time for consideration. Kindly observe this: if I were not so entirely convinced I should not, you may be sure, with my experience venture to accuse you so directly. Seeing that for such direct accusation before witnesses, if false or even mistaken, I should myself in a certain sense be made responsible, I am aware of that. This morning I changed for my own purposes several five-percent securities for the sum of approximately three thousand roubles. The account is noted down in my pocketbook. On my return home I proceeded to count the money— as Mr. Lebeziatnikov will bear witness—and after counting two thousand three hundred roubles I put the rest in my pocketbook in my coat pocket. About five hundred roubles remained on the table and among them three notes of a hundred roubles each. At that moment you entered (at my invitation)—and all the time you were present you were exceedingly embarrassed; so that three times you jumped up in the middle of the conversation and tried to make off. Mr. Lebeziatnikov can bear witness to this. You yourself, mademoiselle, probably will not refuse to confirm my statement that I invited you through Mr. Lebeziatnikov, solely in order to discuss with you the hopeless and destitute position of your relative, Katerina Ivanovna (whose dinner I was unable to attend), and the advisability of getting up something of the nature of a subscription, lottery or the like, for her benefit. You thanked me and even shed tears. I describe all this as it took place, primarily to recall it to your mind and secondly to show you that not the slightest detail has escaped my recollection. Then I took a ten-rouble note from the table and handed it to you by way of first instalment on my part for the benefit of your relative. Mr. Lebeziatnikov saw all this. Then I accompanied you to the door—you being still in the same state of embarrassment—after which, being left alone with Mr. Lebeziatnikov I talked to him for ten minutes—then Mr. Lebeziatnikov went out and I returned to the table with the money lying on it, intending to count it and to put it aside, as I proposed doing before. To my surprise one hundred-rouble note had disappeared. Kindly consider the position. Mr. Lebeziatnikov I cannot suspect. I am ashamed to allude to such a supposition. I cannot have made a mistake in my reckoning, for the minute before your entrance I had finished my accounts and found the total correct. You will admit that recollecting your embarrassment, your eagerness to get away and the fact that you kept your hands for some time on the table, and taking into consideration your social position and the habits associated with it, I was, so to say, with horror and positively against my will, *compelled* to entertain a suspicion—a cruel, but justifiable suspicion! I will add further and repeat that in spite of my positive conviction, I realise that I run a certain risk in making this accusation, but as you see, I could not let it pass. I have taken action and I will tell you why: solely, madam, solely, owing to your black ingratitude! Why! I invite you for the benefit of your destitute relative, I present you with my donation of ten roubles and you, on the spot, repay me for all that with such an action. It is too bad! You need a lesson. Reflect! Moreover, like a true friend I beg you—and you could have no better friend at this moment—think what you are doing, otherwise I shall be immovable! Well, what do you say?"

"I have taken nothing," Sonia whispered in terror, "you gave me ten roubles, here it is, take it."

Sonia pulled her handkerchief out of her pocket, untied a corner of it, took out the ten-rouble note and gave it to Luzhin.

"And the hundred roubles you do not confess to taking?" he insisted reproachfully, not taking the note.

Sonia looked about her. All were looking at her with such awful, stern, ironical, hostile eyes. She looked at Raskolnikov... he stood against the wall, with his arms crossed, looking at her with glowing eyes.

"Good God!" broke from Sonia.

"Amalia Ivanovna, we shall have to send word to the police and therefore I humbly beg you meanwhile to send for the house porter," Luzhin said softly and even kindly.

"*Gott der Barmherzige!* I knew she was the thief," cried Amalia Ivanovna, throwing up her hands.

"You knew it?" Luzhin caught her up, "then I suppose you had some reason before this for thinking so. I beg you, worthy Amalia Ivanovna, to remember your words which have been uttered before witnesses."

There was a buzz of loud conversation on all sides. All were in movement.

"What!" cried Katerina Ivanovna, suddenly realising the position, and she rushed at Luzhin. "What! You accuse her of stealing? Sonia? Ah, the wretches, the wretches!"

And running to Sonia she flung her wasted arms round her and held her as in a vise.

"Sonia! how dared you take ten roubles from him? Foolish girl! Give it to me! Give me the ten roubles at once—here!"

And snatching the note from Sonia, Katerina Ivanovna crumpled it up and flung it straight into Luzhin's face. It hit him in the eye and fell on the ground. Amalia Ivanovna hastened to pick it up. Pyotr Petrovitch lost his temper.

"Hold that mad woman!" he shouted.

At that moment several other persons, besides Lebeziatnikov, appeared in the doorway, among them the two ladies.

"What! Mad? Am I mad? Idiot!" shrieked Katerina Ivanovna. "You are an idiot yourself, pettifogging lawyer, base man! Sonia, Sonia take his money! Sonia a thief! Why, she'd give away her last penny!" and Katerina Ivanovna broke into hysterical laughter. "Did you ever see such an idiot?" she turned from side to side. "And you too?" she suddenly saw the landlady, "and you too, sausage eater, you declare that she is a thief, you trashy Prussian hen's leg in a crinoline! She hasn't been out of this room: she came straight from you, you wretch, and sat down beside me, everyone saw her. She sat here, by Rodion Romanovitch. Search her! Since she's not left the room, the money would have to be on her! Search her, search her! But if you don't find it, then excuse me, my dear fellow, you'll answer for it! I'll go to our Sovereign, to our Sovereign, to our gracious Tsar himself, and throw myself at his feet, today, this minute! I am alone in the world! They would let me in! Do you think they wouldn't? You're wrong, I will get in! I will get in! You reckoned on her meekness! You relied upon that! But I am not so submissive, let me tell you! You've gone too far yourself. Search her, search her!"

And Katerina Ivanovna in a frenzy shook Luzhin and dragged him towards Sonia.

"I am ready, I'll be responsible... but calm yourself, madam, calm yourself. I see that you are not so submissive!... Well, well, but as to that..." Luzhin muttered, "that ought to be before the police... though indeed there are witnesses enough as it is.... I am ready.... But in any case it's difficult for a man... on account of her sex.... But with the help of Amalia Ivanovna... though, of course, it's not the way to do things.... How is it to be done?"

"As you will! Let anyone who likes search her!" cried Katerina Ivanovna. "Sonia, turn out your pockets! See! Look, monster, the pocket is empty, here was her handkerchief! Here is the other pocket, look! D'you see, d'you see?"

And Katerina Ivanovna turned—or rather snatched—both pockets inside out. But from the right pocket a piece of paper flew out and describing a parabola in the air fell at Luzhin's feet. Everyone saw it, several cried out. Pyotr Petrovitch stooped down, picked up the paper in two fingers, lifted it where all could see it and opened it. It was a hundred-rouble note folded in eight. Pyotr Petrovitch held up the note showing it to everyone.

"Thief! Out of my lodging. Police, police!" yelled Amalia Ivanovna. "They must to Siberia be sent! Away!"

Exclamations arose on all sides. Raskolnikov was silent, keeping his eyes fixed on Sonia, except for an occasional rapid glance at Luzhin. Sonia stood still, as though unconscious. She was hardly able to feel surprise. Suddenly the colour rushed to her cheeks; she uttered a cry and hid her face in her hands.

"No, it wasn't I! I didn't take it! I know nothing about it," she cried with a heartrending wail, and she ran to Katerina Ivanovna, who clasped her tightly in her arms, as though she would shelter her from all the world.

"Sonia! Sonia! I don't believe it! You see, I don't believe it!" she cried in the face of the obvious fact, swaying her to and fro in her arms like a baby, kissing her face continually, then snatching at her hands and kissing them, too, "you took it! How stupid these people are! Oh dear! You are fools, fools," she cried, addressing the whole room, "you don't know, you don't know what a heart she has, what a girl she is! She take it, she? She'd sell her last rag, she'd go barefoot to help you if you needed it, that's what she is! She has the yellow passport because my children were starving, she sold herself for us! Ah, husband, husband! Do you see? Do you see? What a memorial dinner for you! Merciful heavens! Defend her, why are you all standing still? Rodion Romanovitch, why don't you stand up for her? Do you believe it, too? You are not worth her little finger, all of you together! Good God! Defend her now, at least!"

The wail of the poor, consumptive, helpless woman seemed to produce a great effect on her audience. The agonised, wasted, consumptive face, the parched bloodstained lips, the hoarse voice, the tears unrestrained as a child's, the trustful, childish and yet despairing prayer for help were so piteous that everyone seemed to feel for her. Pyotr Petrovitch at any rate was at once moved to *compassion.*

"Madam, madam, this incident does not reflect upon you!" he cried impressively, "no one would take upon himself to accuse you of being an instigator or even an accomplice in it, especially as you have proved her guilt by turning out her pockets, showing that you had no previous idea of it. I am most ready, most ready to show compassion, if poverty, so to speak, drove Sofya Semyonovna to it, but why did you refuse to confess, mademoiselle? Were you afraid of the disgrace? The first step? You lost your head, perhaps? One can quite understand it.... But how could you have lowered yourself to such an action? Gentlemen," he addressed the whole company, "gentlemen! Compassionate and, so to say, commiserating these people, I am ready to overlook it even now in spite of the personal insult lavished upon me! And may this disgrace be a lesson to you for the future," he said, addressing Sonia, "and I will carry the matter no further. Enough!"

Pyotr Petrovitch stole a glance at Raskolnikov. Their eyes met, and the fire in Raskolnikov's seemed ready to reduce him to ashes. Meanwhile Katerina Ivanovna apparently heard nothing. She was kissing and hugging Sonia like a madwoman. The children, too, were embracing Sonia on all sides, and Polenka—though she did not fully understand what was wrong—was drowned in tears and shaking with sobs, as she hid her pretty little face, swollen with weeping, on Sonia's shoulder.

"How vile!" a loud voice cried suddenly in the doorway.

Pyotr Petrovitch looked round quickly.

"What vileness!" Lebeziatnikov repeated, staring him straight in the face.

Pyotr Petrovitch gave a positive start—all noticed it and recalled it afterwards. Lebeziatnikov strode into the room.

"And you dared to call me as witness?" he said, going up to Pyotr Petrovitch.

"What do you mean? What are you talking about?" muttered Luzhin.

"I mean that you ... are a slanderer, that's what my words mean!" Lebeziatnikov said hotly, looking sternly at him with his shortsighted eyes.

He was extremely angry. Raskolnikov gazed intently at him, as though seizing and weighing each word. Again there was a silence. Pyotr Petrovitch indeed seemed almost dumbfounded for the first moment.

"If you mean that for me,..." he began, stammering. "But what's the matter with you? Are you out of your mind?"

"I'm in my mind, but you are a scoundrel! Ah, how vile! I have heard everything. I kept waiting on purpose to understand it, for I must own even now it is not quite logical.... What you have done it all for I can't understand."

"Why, what have I done then? Give over talking in your nonsensical riddles! Or maybe you are drunk!"

"You may be a drunkard, perhaps, vile man, but I am not! I never touch vodka, for it's against my convictions. Would you believe it, he, he himself, with his own hands gave Sofya Semyonovna that hundred-rouble note—I saw it, I was a witness, I'll take my oath! He did it, he!" repeated Lebeziatnikov, addressing all.

"Are you crazy, milksop?" squealed Luzhin. "She is herself before you—she herself here declared just now before everyone that I gave her only ten roubles. How could I have given it to her?"

"I saw it, I saw it," Lebeziatnikov repeated, "and though it is against my principles, I am ready this very minute to take any oath you like before the court, for I saw how you slipped it in her pocket. Only like a fool I thought you did it out of kindness! When you were saying goodbye to her at the door, while you held her hand in one hand, with the other, the left, you slipped the note into her pocket. I saw it, I saw it!"

Luzhin turned pale.

"What lies!" he cried impudently, "why, how could you, standing by the window, see the note? You fancied it with your shortsighted eyes. You are raving!"

"No, I didn't fancy it. And though I was standing some way off, I saw it all. And though it certainly would be hard to distinguish a note from the window——that's true——I knew for certain that it was a hundred-rouble note, because, when you were going to give Sofya Semyonovna ten roubles, you took up from the table a hundred-rouble note (I saw it because I was standing near then, and an idea struck me at once, so that I did not forget you had it in your hand). You folded it and kept it in your hand all the time. I didn't think of it again until, when you were getting up, you changed it from your right hand to your left and nearly dropped it! I noticed it because the same idea struck me again, that you meant to do her a kindness without my seeing. You can fancy how I watched you and I saw how you succeeded in slipping it into her pocket. I saw it, I saw it, I'll take my oath."

Lebeziatnikov was almost breathless. Exclamations arose on all hands chiefly expressive of wonder, but some were menacing in tone. They all crowded round Pyotr Petrovitch. Katerina Ivanovna flew to Lebeziatnikov.

"I was mistaken in you! Protect her! You are the only one to take her part! She is an orphan. God has sent you!"

Katerina Ivanovna, hardly knowing what she was doing, sank on her knees before him.

"A pack of nonsense!" yelled Luzhin, roused to fury, "it's all nonsense you've been talking! 'An idea struck you, you didn't think, you noticed'——what does it amount to? So I gave it to her on the sly on purpose? What for? With what object? What have I to do with this…?"

"What for? That's what I can't understand, but that what I am telling you is the fact, that's certain! So far from my being mistaken, you infamous criminal man, I remember how, on account of it, a question occurred to me at once, just when I was thanking you and pressing your hand. What made you put it secretly in her pocket? Why you did it secretly, I mean? Could it be simply to conceal it from me, knowing that my convictions are opposed to yours and that I do not approve of private benevolence, which effects no radical cure? Well, I decided that you really were ashamed of giving such a large sum before me. Perhaps, too, I thought, he wants to give her a surprise, when she finds a whole hundred-rouble note in her pocket. (For I know, some benevolent people are very fond of decking out their charitable actions in that way.) Then the idea struck me, too, that you wanted to test her, to see whether, when she found it, she would come to thank you. Then, too, that you wanted to avoid thanks and that, as the saying is, your right hand should not know… something of that sort, in fact. I thought of so many possibilities that I put off considering it, but still thought it indelicate to show you that I knew your secret. But another idea struck me again that Sofya Semyonovna might easily lose the money before she noticed it, that was why I decided to come in here to call her out of the room and to tell her that you put a hundred roubles in her pocket. But on my way I went first to Madame Kobilatnikov's to take them the *General Treatise on the Positive Method* and especially to recommend Piderit's article (and also Wagner's); then I come on here and what a state of things I find! Now could I, could I, have all these ideas and reflections if I had not seen you put the hundred-rouble note in her pocket?"

When Lebeziatnikov finished his long-winded harangue with the logical deduction at the end, he was quite tired, and the perspiration streamed from his face. He could not, alas, even express himself correctly in Russian, though he knew no other language, so that he was quite exhausted, almost emaciated after this heroic exploit. But his speech produced a powerful effect. He had spoken with such vehemence, with such conviction that everyone obviously believed him. Pyotr Petrovitch felt that things were going badly with him.

"What is it to do with me if silly ideas did occur to you?" he shouted, "that's no evidence. You may have dreamt it, that's all! And I tell you, you are lying, sir. You are lying and slandering from some spite against me, simply from pique, because I did not agree with your freethinking, godless, social propositions!"

But this retort did not benefit Pyotr Petrovitch. Murmurs of disapproval were heard on all sides.

"Ah, that's your line now, is it!" cried Lebeziatnikov, "that's nonsense! Call the police and I'll take my oath! There's only one thing I can't understand: what made him risk such a contemptible action. Oh, pitiful, despicable man!"

"I can explain why he risked such an action, and if necessary, I, too, will swear to it," Raskolnikov said at last in a firm voice, and he stepped forward.

He appeared to be firm and composed. Everyone felt clearly, from the very look of him that he really knew about it and that the mystery would be solved.

"Now I can explain it all to myself," said Raskolnikov, addressing Lebeziatnikov. "From the very beginning of the business, I suspected that there was some scoundrelly intrigue at the bottom of it. I began to suspect it from some special circumstances known to me only, which I will explain at once to everyone: they account for everything. Your valuable evidence has finally made everything clear to me. I beg all, all to listen. This gentleman (he pointed to Luzhin) was recently engaged to be married to a young lady—my sister, Avdotya Romanovna Raskolnikov. But coming to Petersburg he quarrelled with me, the day before yesterday, at our first meeting and I drove him out of my room—I have two witnesses to prove it. He is a very spiteful man.... The day before yesterday I did not know that he was staying here, in your room, and that consequently on the very day we quarrelled—the day before yesterday—he saw me give Katerina Ivanovna some money for the funeral, as a friend of the late Mr. Marmeladov. He at once wrote a note to my mother and informed her that I had given away all my money, not to Katerina Ivanovna but to Sofya Semyonovna, and referred in a most contemptible way to the... character of Sofya Semyonovna, that is, hinted at the character of my attitude to Sofya Semyonovna. All this you understand was with the object of dividing me from my mother and sister, by insinuating that I was squandering on unworthy objects the money which they had sent me and which was all they had. Yesterday evening, before my mother and sister and in his presence, I declared that I had given the money to Katerina Ivanovna for the funeral and not to Sofya Semyonovna and that I had no acquaintance with Sofya Semyonovna and had never seen her before, indeed. At the same time I added that he, Pyotr Petrovitch Luzhin, with all his virtues, was not worth Sofya Semyonovna's little finger, though he spoke so ill of her. To his question—would I let Sofya Semyonovna sit down beside my sister, I answered that I had already done so that day. Irritated that my mother and sister were unwilling to quarrel with me at his insinuations, he gradually began being unpardonably rude to them. A final rupture took place and he was turned out of the house. All this happened yesterday evening. Now I beg your special attention: consider: if he had now succeeded in proving that Sofya Semyonovna was a thief, he would have shown to my mother and sister that he was almost right in his suspicions, that he had reason to be angry at my putting my sister on a level with Sofya Semyonovna, that, in attacking me, he was protecting and preserving the honour of my sister, his betrothed. In fact he might even, through all this, have been able to estrange me from my family, and no doubt he hoped to be restored to favour with them; to say nothing of revenging himself on me personally, for he has grounds for supposing that the honour and happiness of Sofya Semyonovna are very precious to me. That was what he was working for! That's how I understand it. That's the whole reason for it and there can be no other!"

It was like this, or somewhat like this, that Raskolnikov wound up his speech which was followed very attentively, though often interrupted by exclamations from his audience. But in spite of interruptions he spoke clearly, calmly, exactly, firmly. His decisive voice, his tone of conviction and his stern face made a great impression on everyone.

"Yes, yes, that's it," Lebeziatnikov assented gleefully, "that must be it, for he asked me, as soon as Sofya Semyonovna came into our room, whether you were here, whether I had seen you among Katerina Ivanovna's guests. He called me aside to the window and asked me in secret. It was essential for him that you should be here! That's it, that's it!"

Luzhin smiled contemptuously and did not speak. But he was very pale. He seemed to be deliberating on some means of escape. Perhaps he would have been glad to give up everything and get away, but at the moment this was scarcely possible. It would have implied admitting the truth of the accusations brought against him. Moreover, the company, which had already been excited by drink, was now too much stirred to allow it. The commissariat clerk, though indeed he had not grasped the whole position, was shouting louder than anyone and was making some suggestions very unpleasant to Luzhin. But not all those present were drunk; lodgers came in from all the rooms. The three Poles were tremendously excited and were continually shouting at him: "The *pan* is a *lajdak*!" and muttering threats in Polish. Sonia had been listening with strained attention, though she too seemed unable to grasp it all; she seemed as though she had just returned to consciousness. She did not take her eyes off Raskolnikov, feeling that all her safety lay in him. Katerina Ivanovna breathed hard and painfully and seemed fearfully exhausted. Amalia Ivanovna stood looking more stupid than anyone, with her mouth wide open, unable to make out what had happened. She only saw that Pyotr Petrovitch had somehow come to grief.

Raskolnikov was attempting to speak again, but they did not let him. Everyone was crowding round Luzhin with threats and shouts of abuse. But Pyotr Petrovitch was not intimidated. Seeing that his accusation of Sonia had completely failed, he had recourse to insolence:

"Allow me, gentlemen, allow me! Don't squeeze, let me pass!" he said, making his way through the crowd. "And no threats, if you please! I assure you it will be useless, you will gain nothing by it. On the contrary, you'll have to answer, gentlemen, for violently obstructing the course of justice. The thief has been more than unmasked, and I shall prosecute. Our judges are not so blind and... not so drunk, and will not believe the testimony of two notorious infidels, agitators, and atheists, who accuse me from motives of personal revenge which they are foolish enough to admit.... Yes, allow me to pass!"

"Don't let me find a trace of you in my room! Kindly leave at once, and everything is at an end between us! When I think of the trouble I've been taking, the way I've been expounding... all this fortnight!"

"I told you myself today that I was going, when you tried to keep me; now I will simply add that you are a fool. I advise you to see a doctor for your brains and your short sight. Let me pass, gentlemen!"

He forced his way through. But the commissariat clerk was unwilling to let him off so easily: he picked up a glass from the table, brandished it in the air and flung it at Pyotr Petrovitch; but the glass flew straight at Amalia Ivanovna. She screamed, and the clerk, overbalancing, fell heavily under the table. Pyotr Petrovitch made his way to his room and half an hour later had left the house. Sonia, timid by nature, had felt before that day that she could be ill-treated more easily than anyone, and that she could be wronged with impunity. Yet till that moment she had fancied that she might escape misfortune by care, gentleness and submissiveness before everyone. Her disappointment was too great. She could, of course, bear with patience and almost without murmur anything, even this. But for the first minute she felt it too bitter. In spite of her triumph and her justification—when her first terror and stupefaction had passed and she could understand it all clearly—the feeling of her helplessness and of the wrong done to her made her heart throb with anguish and she was overcome with hysterical weeping. At last, unable to bear any more, she rushed out of the room and ran home, almost immediately after Luzhin's departure. When amidst loud laughter the glass flew at Amalia Ivanovna, it was more than the landlady could endure. With a shriek she rushed like a fury at Katerina Ivanovna, considering her to blame for everything.

"Out of my lodgings! At once! Quick march!"

And with these words she began snatching up everything she could lay her hands on that belonged to Katerina Ivanovna, and throwing it on the floor. Katerina Ivanovna, pale, almost fainting, and gasping for breath, jumped up from the bed where she had sunk in exhaustion and darted at Amalia Ivanovna. But the battle was too unequal: the landlady waved her away like a feather.

"What! As though that godless calumny was not enough—this vile creature attacks me! What! On the day of my husband's funeral I am turned out of my lodging! After eating my bread and salt she turns me into the street, with my orphans! Where am I to go?" wailed the poor woman, sobbing and gasping. "Good God!" she cried with flashing eyes, "is there no justice upon earth? Whom should you protect if not us orphans? We shall see! There is law and justice on earth, there is, I will find it! Wait a bit, godless creature! Polenka, stay with the children, I'll come back. Wait for me, if you have to wait in the street. We will see whether there is justice on earth!"

218

And throwing over her head that green shawl which Marmeladov had mentioned to Raskolnikov, Katerina Ivanovna squeezed her way through the disorderly and drunken crowd of lodgers who still filled the room, and, wailing and tearful, she ran into the street—with a vague intention of going at once somewhere to find justice. Polenka with the two little ones in her arms crouched, terrified, on the trunk in the corner of the room, where she waited trembling for her mother to come back. Amalia Ivanovna raged about the room, shrieking, lamenting and throwing everything she came across on the floor. The lodgers talked incoherently, some commented to the best of their ability on what had happened, others quarrelled and swore at one another, while others struck up a song....

"Now it's time for me to go," thought Raskolnikov. "Well, Sofya Semyonovna, we shall see what you'll say now!"

And he set off in the direction of Sonia's lodgings.

Raskolnikov had been a vigorous and active champion of Sonia against Luzhin, although he had such a load of horror and anguish in his own heart. But having gone through so much in the morning, he found a sort of relief in a change of sensations, apart from the strong personal feeling which impelled him to defend Sonia. He was agitated too, especially at some moments, by the thought of his approaching interview with Sonia: he *had* to tell her who had killed Lizaveta. He knew the terrible suffering it would be to him and, as it were, brushed away the thought of it. So when he cried as he left Katerina Ivanovna's, "Well, Sofya Semyonovna, we shall see what you'll say now!" he was still superficially excited, still vigorous and defiant from his triumph over Luzhin. But, strange to say, by the time he reached Sonia's lodging, he felt a sudden impotence and fear. He stood still in hesitation at the door, asking himself the strange question: "Must he tell her who killed Lizaveta?" It was a strange question because he felt at the very time not only that he could not help telling her, but also that he could not put off the telling. He did not yet know why it must be so, he only *felt* it, and the agonising sense of his impotence before the inevitable almost crushed him. To cut short his hesitation and suffering, he quickly opened the door and looked at Sonia from the doorway. She was sitting with her elbows on the table and her face in her hands, but seeing Raskolnikov she got up at once and came to meet him as though she were expecting him.

"What would have become of me but for you?" she said quickly, meeting him in the middle of the room.

Evidently she was in haste to say this to him. It was what she had been waiting for.

Raskolnikov went to the table and sat down on the chair from which she had only just risen. She stood facing him, two steps away, just as she had done the day before.

"Well, Sonia?" he said, and felt that his voice was trembling, "it was all due to 'your social position and the habits associated with it.' Did you understand that just now?"

Her face showed her distress.

"Only don't talk to me as you did yesterday," she interrupted him. "Please don't begin it. There is misery enough without that."

She made haste to smile, afraid that he might not like the reproach.

"I was silly to come away from there. What is happening there now? I wanted to go back directly, but I kept thinking that... you would come."

He told her that Amalia Ivanovna was turning them out of their lodging and that Katerina Ivanovna had run off somewhere "to seek justice."

"My God!" cried Sonia, "let's go at once...."

And she snatched up her cape.

"It's everlastingly the same thing!" said Raskolnikov, irritably. "You've no thought except for them! Stay a little with me."

"But... Katerina Ivanovna?"

"You won't lose Katerina Ivanovna, you may be sure, she'll come to you herself since she has run out," he added peevishly. "If she doesn't find you here, you'll be blamed for it...."

Sonia sat down in painful suspense. Raskolnikov was silent, gazing at the floor and deliberating.

"This time Luzhin did not want to prosecute you," he began, not looking at Sonia, "but if he had wanted to, if it had suited his plans, he would have sent you to prison if it had not been for Lebeziatnikov and me. Ah?"

"Yes," she assented in a faint voice. "Yes," she repeated, preoccupied and distressed.

"But I might easily not have been there. And it was quite an accident Lebeziatnikov's turning up."

Sonia was silent.

"And if you'd gone to prison, what then? Do you remember what I said yesterday?"

Again she did not answer. He waited.

"I thought you would cry out again 'don't speak of it, leave off.'" Raskolnikov gave a laugh, but rather a forced one. "What, silence again?" he asked a minute later. "We must talk about something, you know. It would be interesting for me to know how you would decide a certain 'problem' as Lebeziatnikov would say." (He was beginning to lose the thread.) "No, really, I am serious. Imagine, Sonia, that you had known all Luzhin's intentions beforehand. Known, that is, for a fact, that they would be the ruin of Katerina Ivanovna and the children and yourself thrown in—since you don't count yourself for anything—Polenka too... for she'll go the same way. Well, if suddenly it all depended on your decision whether he or they should go on living, that is whether Luzhin should go on living and doing wicked things, or Katerina Ivanovna should die? How would you decide which of them was to die? I ask you?"

Sonia looked uneasily at him. There was something peculiar in this hesitating question, which seemed approaching something in a roundabout way.

"I felt that you were going to ask some question like that," she said, looking inquisitively at him.

"I dare say you did. But how is it to be answered?"

"Why do you ask about what could not happen?" said Sonia reluctantly.

"Then it would be better for Luzhin to go on living and doing wicked things? You haven't dared to decide even that!"

"But I can't know the Divine Providence.... And why do you ask what can't be answered? What's the use of such foolish questions? How could it happen that it should depend on my decision—who has made me a judge to decide who is to live and who is not to live?"

"Oh, if the Divine Providence is to be mixed up in it, there is no doing anything," Raskolnikov grumbled morosely.

"You'd better say straight out what you want!" Sonia cried in distress. "You are leading up to something again.... Can you have come simply to torture me?"

She could not control herself and began crying bitterly. He looked at her in gloomy misery. Five minutes passed.

"Of course you're right, Sonia," he said softly at last. He was suddenly changed. His tone of assumed arrogance and helpless defiance was gone. Even his voice was suddenly weak. "I told you yesterday that I was not coming to ask forgiveness and almost the first thing I've said is to ask forgiveness.... I said that about Luzhin and Providence for my own sake. I was asking forgiveness, Sonia...."

He tried to smile, but there was something helpless and incomplete in his pale smile. He bowed his head and hid his face in his hands.

And suddenly a strange, surprising sensation of a sort of bitter hatred for Sonia passed through his heart. As it were wondering and frightened of this sensation, he raised his head and looked intently at her; but he met her uneasy and painfully anxious eyes fixed on him; there was love in them; his hatred vanished like a phantom. It was not the real feeling; he had taken the one feeling for the other. It only meant that *that* minute had come.

He hid his face in his hands again and bowed his head. Suddenly he turned pale, got up from his chair, looked at Sonia, and without uttering a word sat down mechanically on her bed.

His sensations that moment were terribly like the moment when he had stood over the old woman with the axe in his hand and felt that "he must not lose another minute."

"What's the matter?" asked Sonia, dreadfully frightened.

He could not utter a word. This was not at all, not at all the way he had intended to "tell" and he did not understand what was happening to him now. She went up to him, softly, sat down on the bed beside him and waited, not taking her eyes off him. Her heart throbbed and sank. It was unendurable; he turned his deadly pale face to her. His lips worked, helplessly struggling to utter something. A pang of terror passed through Sonia's heart.

"What's the matter?" she repeated, drawing a little away from him.

"Nothing, Sonia, don't be frightened.... It's nonsense. It really is nonsense, if you think of it," he muttered, like a man in delirium. "Why have I come to torture you?" he added suddenly, looking at her. "Why, really? I keep asking myself that question, Sonia...."

He had perhaps been asking himself that question a quarter of an hour before, but now he spoke helplessly, hardly knowing what he said and feeling a continual tremor all over.

"Oh, how you are suffering!" she muttered in distress, looking intently at him.

"It's all nonsense.... Listen, Sonia." He suddenly smiled, a pale helpless smile for two seconds. "You remember what I meant to tell you yesterday?"

Sonia waited uneasily.

"I said as I went away that perhaps I was saying goodbye forever, but that if I came today I would tell you who... who killed Lizaveta."

She began trembling all over.

"Well, here I've come to tell you."

"Then you really meant it yesterday?" she whispered with difficulty. "How do you know?" she asked quickly, as though suddenly regaining her reason.

Sonia's face grew paler and paler, and she breathed painfully.

"I know."

She paused a minute.

"Have they found him?" she asked timidly.

"No."

"Then how do you know about *it*?" she asked again, hardly audibly and again after a minute's pause.

He turned to her and looked very intently at her.

"Guess," he said, with the same distorted helpless smile.

A shudder passed over her.

"But you... why do you frighten me like this?" she said, smiling like a child.

"I must be a great friend of *his*... since I know," Raskolnikov went on, still gazing into her face, as though he could not turn his eyes away. "He... did not mean to kill that Lizaveta... he... killed her accidentally.... He meant to kill the old woman when she was alone and he went there... and then Lizaveta came in... he killed her too."

Another awful moment passed. Both still gazed at one another.

"You can't guess, then?" he asked suddenly, feeling as though he were flinging himself down from a steeple.

"N-no..." whispered Sonia.

"Take a good look."

As soon as he had said this again, the same familiar sensation froze his heart. He looked at her and all at once seemed to see in her face the face of Lizaveta. He remembered clearly the expression in Lizaveta's face, when he approached her with the axe and she stepped back to the wall, putting out her hand, with childish terror in her face, looking as little children do when they begin to be frightened of something, looking intently and uneasily at what frightens them, shrinking back and holding out their little hands on the point of crying. Almost the same thing happened now to Sonia. With the same helplessness and the same terror, she looked at him for a while and, suddenly putting out her left hand, pressed her fingers faintly against his breast and slowly began to get up from the bed, moving further from him and keeping her eyes fixed even more immovably on him. Her terror infected him. The same fear showed itself on his face. In the same way he stared at her and almost with the same *childish* smile.

"Have you guessed?" he whispered at last.

"Good God!" broke in an awful wail from her bosom.

She sank helplessly on the bed with her face in the pillows, but a moment later she got up, moved quickly to him, seized both his hands and, gripping them tight in her thin fingers, began looking into his face again with the same intent stare. In this last desperate look she tried to look into him and catch some last hope. But there was no hope; there was no doubt remaining; it was all true! Later on, indeed, when she recalled that moment, she thought it strange and wondered why she had seen at once that there was no doubt. She could not have said, for instance, that she had foreseen something of the sort—and yet now, as soon as he told her, she suddenly fancied that she had really foreseen this very thing.

"Stop, Sonia, enough! don't torture me," he begged her miserably.

It was not at all, not at all like this he had thought of telling her, but this is how it happened.

She jumped up, seeming not to know what she was doing, and, wringing her hands, walked into the middle of the room; but quickly went back and sat down again beside him, her shoulder almost touching his. All of a sudden she started as though she had been stabbed, uttered a cry and fell on her knees before him, she did not know why.

"What have you done—what have you done to yourself?" she said in despair, and, jumping up, she flung herself on his neck, threw her arms round him, and held him tightly.

Raskolnikov drew back and looked at her with a mournful smile.

"You are a strange girl, Sonia—you kiss me and hug me when I tell you about that.... You don't think what you are doing."

"There is no one—no one in the whole world now so unhappy as you!" she cried in a frenzy, not hearing what he said, and she suddenly broke into violent hysterical weeping.

A feeling long unfamiliar to him flooded his heart and softened it at once. He did not struggle against it. Two tears started into his eyes and hung on his eyelashes.

"Then you won't leave me, Sonia?" he said, looking at her almost with hope.

"No, no, never, nowhere!" cried Sonia. "I will follow you, I will follow you everywhere. Oh, my God! Oh, how miserable I am!... Why, why didn't I know you before! Why didn't you come before? Oh, dear!"

"Here I have come."

"Yes, now! What's to be done now?... Together, together!" she repeated as it were unconsciously, and she hugged him again. "I'll follow you to Siberia!"

He recoiled at this, and the same hostile, almost haughty smile came to his lips.

"Perhaps I don't want to go to Siberia yet, Sonia," he said.

Sonia looked at him quickly.

Again after her first passionate, agonising sympathy for the unhappy man the terrible idea of the murder overwhelmed her. In his changed tone she seemed to hear the murderer speaking. She looked at him bewildered. She knew nothing as yet, why, how, with what object it had been. Now all these questions rushed at once into her mind. And again she could not believe it: "He, he is a murderer! Could it be true?"

"What's the meaning of it? Where am I?" she said in complete bewilderment, as though still unable to recover herself. "How could you, you, a man like you.... How could you bring yourself to it?... What does it mean?"

"Oh, well—to plunder. Leave off, Sonia," he answered wearily, almost with vexation.

Sonia stood as though struck dumb, but suddenly she cried:

"You were hungry! It was... to help your mother? Yes?"

"No, Sonia, no," he muttered, turning away and hanging his head. "I was not so hungry.... I certainly did want to help my mother, but... that's not the real thing either.... Don't torture me, Sonia."

Sonia clasped her hands.

"Could it, could it all be true? Good God, what a truth! Who could believe it? And how could you give away your last farthing and yet rob and murder! Ah," she cried suddenly, "that money you gave Katerina Ivanovna... that money.... Can that money..."

"No, Sonia," he broke in hurriedly, "that money was not it. Don't worry yourself! That money my mother sent me and it came when I was ill, the day I gave it to you.... Razumihin saw it... he received it for me.... That money was mine—my own."

Sonia listened to him in bewilderment and did her utmost to comprehend.

223

"And *that* money.... I don't even know really whether there was any money," he added softly, as though reflecting. "I took a purse off her neck, made of chamois leather... a purse stuffed full of something... but I didn't look in it; I suppose I hadn't time.... And the things—chains and trinkets—I buried under a stone with the purse next morning in a yard off the V—— Prospect. They are all there now...."

Sonia strained every nerve to listen.

"Then why... why, you said you did it to rob, but you took nothing?" she asked quickly, catching at a straw.

"I don't know.... I haven't yet decided whether to take that money or not," he said, musing again; and, seeming to wake up with a start, he gave a brief ironical smile. "Ach, what silly stuff I am talking, eh?"

The thought flashed through Sonia's mind, wasn't he mad? But she dismissed it at once. "No, it was something else." She could make nothing of it, nothing.

"Do you know, Sonia," he said suddenly with conviction, "let me tell you: if I'd simply killed because I was hungry," laying stress on every word and looking enigmatically but sincerely at her, "I should be *happy* now. You must believe that! What would it matter to you," he cried a moment later with a sort of despair, "what would it matter to you if I were to confess that I did wrong? What do you gain by such a stupid triumph over me? Ah, Sonia, was it for that I've come to you today?"

Again Sonia tried to say something, but did not speak.

"I asked you to go with me yesterday because you are all I have left."

"Go where?" asked Sonia timidly.

"Not to steal and not to murder, don't be anxious," he smiled bitterly. "We are so different.... And you know, Sonia, it's only now, only this moment that I understand *where* I asked you to go with me yesterday! Yesterday when I said it I did not know where. I asked you for one thing, I came to you for one thing—not to leave me. You won't leave me, Sonia?"

She squeezed his hand.

"And why, why did I tell her? Why did I let her know?" he cried a minute later in despair, looking with infinite anguish at her. "Here you expect an explanation from me, Sonia; you are sitting and waiting for it, I see that. But what can I tell you? You won't understand and will only suffer misery... on my account! Well, you are crying and embracing me again. Why do you do it? Because I couldn't bear my burden and have come to throw it on another: you suffer too, and I shall feel better! And can you love such a mean wretch?"

"But aren't you suffering, too?" cried Sonia.

Again a wave of the same feeling surged into his heart, and again for an instant softened it.

"Sonia, I have a bad heart, take note of that. It may explain a great deal. I have come because I am bad. There are men who wouldn't have come. But I am a coward and... a mean wretch. But... never mind! That's not the point. I must speak now, but I don't know how to begin."

He paused and sank into thought.

"Ach, we are so different," he cried again, "we are not alike. And why, why did I come? I shall never forgive myself that."

"No, no, it was a good thing you came," cried Sonia. "It's better I should know, far better!"

He looked at her with anguish.

"What if it were really that?" he said, as though reaching a conclusion. "Yes, that's what it was! I wanted to become a Napoleon, that is why I killed her.... Do you understand now?"

"N-no," Sonia whispered naively and timidly. "Only speak, speak, I shall understand, I shall understand *in myself*!" she kept begging him.

"You'll understand? Very well, we shall see!" He paused and was for some time lost in meditation.

"It was like this: I asked myself one day this question—what if Napoleon, for instance, had happened to be in my place, and if he had not had Toulon nor Egypt nor the passage of Mont Blanc to begin his career with, but instead of all those picturesque and monumental things, there had simply been some ridiculous old hag, a pawnbroker, who had to be murdered too to get

224

money from her trunk (for his career, you understand). Well, would he have brought himself to that if there had been no other means? Wouldn't he have felt a pang at its being so far from monumental and... and sinful, too? Well, I must tell you that I worried myself fearfully over that 'question' so that I was awfully ashamed when I guessed at last (all of a sudden, somehow) that it would not have given him the least pang, that it would not even have struck him that it was not monumental... that he would not have seen that there was anything in it to pause over, and that, if he had had no other way, he would have strangled her in a minute without thinking about it! Well, I too... left off thinking about it... murdered her, following his example. And that's exactly how it was! Do you think it funny? Yes, Sonia, the funniest thing of all is that perhaps that's just how it was."

Sonia did not think it at all funny.

"You had better tell me straight out... without examples," she begged, still more timidly and scarcely audibly.

He turned to her, looked sadly at her and took her hands.

"You are right again, Sonia. Of course that's all nonsense, it's almost all talk! You see, you know of course that my mother has scarcely anything, my sister happened to have a good education and was condemned to drudge as a governess. All their hopes were centered on me. I was a student, but I couldn't keep myself at the university and was forced for a time to leave it. Even if I had lingered on like that, in ten or twelve years I might (with luck) hope to be some sort of teacher or clerk with a salary of a thousand roubles" (he repeated it as though it were a lesson) "and by that time my mother would be worn out with grief and anxiety and I could not succeed in keeping her in comfort while my sister... well, my sister might well have fared worse! And it's a hard thing to pass everything by all one's life, to turn one's back upon everything, to forget one's mother and decorously accept the insults inflicted on one's sister. Why should one? When one has buried them to burden oneself with others—wife and children—and to leave them again without a farthing? So I resolved to gain possession of the old woman's money and to use it for my first years without worrying my mother, to keep myself at the university and for a little while after leaving it—and to do this all on a broad, thorough scale, so as to build up a completely new career and enter upon a new life of independence.... Well... that's all.... Well, of course in killing the old woman I did wrong.... Well, that's enough."

He struggled to the end of his speech in exhaustion and let his head sink.

"Oh, that's not it, that's not it," Sonia cried in distress. "How could one... no, that's not right, not right."

"You see yourself that it's not right. But I've spoken truly, it's the truth."

"As though that could be the truth! Good God!"

"I've only killed a louse, Sonia, a useless, loathsome, harmful creature."

"A human being—a louse!"

"I too know it wasn't a louse," he answered, looking strangely at her. "But I am talking nonsense, Sonia," he added. "I've been talking nonsense a long time.... That's not it, you are right there. There were quite, quite other causes for it! I haven't talked to anyone for so long, Sonia.... My head aches dreadfully now."

His eyes shone with feverish brilliance. He was almost delirious; an uneasy smile strayed on his lips. His terrible exhaustion could be seen through his excitement. Sonia saw how he was suffering. She too was growing dizzy. And he talked so strangely; it seemed somehow comprehensible, but yet... "But how, how! Good God!" And she wrung her hands in despair.

"No, Sonia, that's not it," he began again suddenly, raising his head, as though a new and sudden train of thought had struck and as it were roused him—"that's not it! Better... imagine— yes, it's certainly better—imagine that I am vain, envious, malicious, base, vindictive and... well, perhaps with a tendency to insanity. (Let's have it all out at once! They've talked of madness already, I noticed.) I told you just now I could not keep myself at the university. But do you know that perhaps I might have done? My mother would have sent me what I needed for the fees and I could have earned enough for clothes, boots and food, no doubt. Lessons had turned up at half a rouble. Razumihin works! But I turned sulky and wouldn't. (Yes, sulkiness, that's the right word for it!) I sat in my room like a spider. You've been in my den, you've seen it.... And do you know, Sonia, that low ceilings and tiny rooms cramp the soul and the mind? Ah, how I hated that garret! And yet I wouldn't go out of it! I wouldn't on purpose! I didn't go out for days together, and I wouldn't work, I wouldn't even eat, I just lay there doing nothing. If Nastasya brought me anything, I ate it, if she didn't, I went all day without; I wouldn't ask, on purpose, from sulkiness! At night I had no light, I lay in the dark and I wouldn't earn money for candles. I ought to have studied, but I sold my books; and the dust lies an inch thick on the notebooks on my table. I preferred lying still and thinking. And I kept thinking.... And I had dreams all the time, strange dreams of all sorts, no need to describe! Only then I began to fancy that... No, that's not it! Again I am telling you wrong! You see I kept asking myself then: why am I so stupid that if others are stupid—and I know they are—yet I won't be wiser? Then I saw, Sonia, that if one waits for everyone to get wiser it will take too long.... Afterwards I understood that that would never come to pass, that men won't change and that nobody can alter it and that it's not worth wasting effort over it. Yes, that's so. That's the law of their nature, Sonia,... that's so!... And I know now, Sonia, that whoever is strong in mind and spirit will have power over them. Anyone who is greatly daring is right in their eyes. He who despises most things will be a lawgiver among them and he who dares most of all will be most in the right! So it has been till now and so it will always be. A man must be blind not to see it!"

Though Raskolnikov looked at Sonia as he said this, he no longer cared whether she understood or not. The fever had complete hold of him; he was in a sort of gloomy ecstasy (he certainly had been too long without talking to anyone). Sonia felt that his gloomy creed had become his faith and code.

"I divined then, Sonia," he went on eagerly, "that power is only vouchsafed to the man who dares to stoop and pick it up. There is only one thing, one thing needful: one has only to dare! Then for the first time in my life an idea took shape in my mind which no one had ever thought of before me, no one! I saw clear as daylight how strange it is that not a single person living in this mad world has had the daring to go straight for it all and send it flying to the devil! I... I wanted *to have the daring*... and I killed her. I only wanted to have the daring, Sonia! That was the whole cause of it!"

"Oh hush, hush," cried Sonia, clasping her hands. "You turned away from God and God has smitten you, has given you over to the devil!"

"Then Sonia, when I used to lie there in the dark and all this became clear to me, was it a temptation of the devil, eh?"

"Hush, don't laugh, blasphemer! You don't understand, you don't understand! Oh God! He won't understand!"

"Hush, Sonia! I am not laughing. I know myself that it was the devil leading me. Hush, Sonia, hush!" he repeated with gloomy insistence. "I know it all, I have thought it all over and over and whispered it all over to myself, lying there in the dark.... I've argued it all over with myself, every point of it, and I know it all, all! And how sick, how sick I was then of going over it all! I have kept wanting to forget it and make a new beginning, Sonia, and leave off thinking. And you don't suppose that I went into it headlong like a fool? I went into it like a wise man, and that was just my destruction. And you mustn't suppose that I didn't know, for instance, that if I began to question myself whether I had the right to gain power—I certainly hadn't the right—or that if I asked myself whether a human being is a louse it proved that it wasn't so for me, though it might be for a man who would go straight to his goal without asking questions.... If I worried myself all those days, wondering whether Napoleon would have done it or not, I felt clearly of course that I wasn't Napoleon. I had to endure all the agony of that battle of ideas, Sonia, and I longed to throw it off: I wanted to murder without casuistry, to murder for my own sake, for myself alone! I didn't want to lie about it even to myself. It wasn't to help my mother I did the murder—that's nonsense—I didn't do the murder to gain wealth and power and to become a benefactor of mankind. Nonsense! I simply did it; I did the murder for myself, for myself alone, and whether I became a benefactor to others, or spent my life like a spider catching men in my web and sucking the life out of men, I couldn't have cared at that moment.... And it was not the money I wanted,

Sonia, when I did it. It was not so much the money I wanted, but something else.... I know it all now.... Understand me! Perhaps I should never have committed a murder again. I wanted to find out something else; it was something else led me on. I wanted to find out then and quickly whether I was a louse like everybody else or a man. Whether I can step over barriers or not, whether I dare stoop to pick up or not, whether I am a trembling creature or whether I have the *right*..."

"To kill? Have the right to kill?" Sonia clasped her hands.

"Ach, Sonia!" he cried irritably and seemed about to make some retort, but was contemptuously silent. "Don't interrupt me, Sonia. I want to prove one thing only, that the devil led me on then and he has shown me since that I had not the right to take that path, because I am just such a louse as all the rest. He was mocking me and here I've come to you now! Welcome your guest! If I were not a louse, should I have come to you? Listen: when I went then to the old woman's I only went to *try*.... You may be sure of that!"

"And you murdered her!"

"But how did I murder her? Is that how men do murders? Do men go to commit a murder as I went then? I will tell you some day how I went! Did I murder the old woman? I murdered myself, not her! I crushed myself once for all, forever.... But it was the devil that killed that old woman, not I. Enough, enough, Sonia, enough! Let me be!" he cried in a sudden spasm of agony, "let me be!"

He leaned his elbows on his knees and squeezed his head in his hands as in a vise.

"What suffering!" A wail of anguish broke from Sonia.

"Well, what am I to do now?" he asked, suddenly raising his head and looking at her with a face hideously distorted by despair.

"What are you to do?" she cried, jumping up, and her eyes that had been full of tears suddenly began to shine. "Stand up!" (She seized him by the shoulder, he got up, looking at her almost bewildered.) "Go at once, this very minute, stand at the crossroads, bow down, first kiss the earth which you have defiled and then bow down to all the world and say to all men aloud, 'I am a murderer!' Then God will send you life again. Will you go, will you go?" she asked him, trembling all over, snatching his two hands, squeezing them tight in hers and gazing at him with eyes full of fire.

He was amazed at her sudden ecstasy.

"You mean Siberia, Sonia? I must give myself up?" he asked gloomily.

"Suffer and expiate your sin by it, that's what you must do."

"No! I am not going to them, Sonia!"

"But how will you go on living? What will you live for?" cried Sonia, "how is it possible now? Why, how can you talk to your mother? (Oh, what will become of them now?) But what am I saying? You have abandoned your mother and your sister already. He has abandoned them already! Oh, God!" she cried, "why, he knows it all himself. How, how can he live by himself! What will become of you now?"

"Don't be a child, Sonia," he said softly. "What wrong have I done them? Why should I go to them? What should I say to them? That's only a phantom.... They destroy men by millions themselves and look on it as a virtue. They are knaves and scoundrels, Sonia! I am not going to them. And what should I say to them—that I murdered her, but did not dare to take the money and hid it under a stone?" he added with a bitter smile. "Why, they would laugh at me, and would call me a fool for not getting it. A coward and a fool! They wouldn't understand and they don't deserve to understand. Why should I go to them? I won't. Don't be a child, Sonia...."

"It will be too much for you to bear, too much!" she repeated, holding out her hands in despairing supplication.

"Perhaps I've been unfair to myself," he observed gloomily, pondering, "perhaps after all I am a man and not a louse and I've been in too great a hurry to condemn myself. I'll make another fight for it."

A haughty smile appeared on his lips.

"What a burden to bear! And your whole life, your whole life!"

227

"I shall get used to it," he said grimly and thoughtfully. "Listen," he began a minute later, "stop crying, it's time to talk of the facts: I've come to tell you that the police are after me, on my track...."

"Ach!" Sonia cried in terror.

"Well, why do you cry out? You want me to go to Siberia and now you are frightened? But let me tell you: I shall not give myself up. I shall make a struggle for it and they won't do anything to me. They've no real evidence. Yesterday I was in great danger and believed I was lost; but today things are going better. All the facts they know can be explained two ways, that's to say I can turn their accusations to my credit, do you understand? And I shall, for I've learnt my lesson. But they will certainly arrest me. If it had not been for something that happened, they would have done so today for certain; perhaps even now they will arrest me today.... But that's no matter, Sonia; they'll let me out again... for there isn't any real proof against me, and there won't be, I give you my word for it. And they can't convict a man on what they have against me. Enough.... I only tell you that you may know.... I will try to manage somehow to put it to my mother and sister so that they won't be frightened.... My sister's future is secure, however, now, I believe... and my mother's must be too.... Well, that's all. Be careful, though. Will you come and see me in prison when I am there?"

"Oh, I will, I will."

They sat side by side, both mournful and dejected, as though they had been cast up by the tempest alone on some deserted shore. He looked at Sonia and felt how great was her love for him, and strange to say he felt it suddenly burdensome and painful to be so loved. Yes, it was a strange and awful sensation! On his way to see Sonia he had felt that all his hopes rested on her; he expected to be rid of at least part of his suffering, and now, when all her heart turned towards him, he suddenly felt that he was immeasurably unhappier than before.

"Sonia," he said, "you'd better not come and see me when I am in prison."

Sonia did not answer, she was crying. Several minutes passed.

"Have you a cross on you?" she asked, as though suddenly thinking of it.

He did not at first understand the question.

"No, of course not. Here, take this one, of cypress wood. I have another, a copper one that belonged to Lizaveta. I changed with Lizaveta: she gave me her cross and I gave her my little icon. I will wear Lizaveta's now and give you this. Take it... it's mine! It's mine, you know," she begged him. "We will go to suffer together, and together we will bear our cross!"

"Give it me," said Raskolnikov.

He did not want to hurt her feelings. But immediately he drew back the hand he held out for the cross.

"Not now, Sonia. Better later," he added to comfort her.

"Yes, yes, better," she repeated with conviction, "when you go to meet your suffering, then put it on. You will come to me, I'll put it on you, we will pray and go together."

At that moment someone knocked three times at the door.

"Sofya Semyonovna, may I come in?" they heard in a very familiar and polite voice.

Sonia rushed to the door in a fright. The flaxen head of Mr. Lebeziatnikov appeared at the door.

228

Lebeziatnikov looked perturbed.

"I've come to you, Sofya Semyonovna," he began. "Excuse me... I thought I should find you," he said, addressing Raskolnikov suddenly, "that is, I didn't mean anything... of that sort... But I just thought... Katerina Ivanovna has gone out of her mind," he blurted out suddenly, turning from Raskolnikov to Sonia.

Sonia screamed.

"At least it seems so. But... we don't know what to do, you see! She came back—she seems to have been turned out somewhere, perhaps beaten.... So it seems at least,... She had run to your father's former chief, she didn't find him at home: he was dining at some other general's.... Only fancy, she rushed off there, to the other general's, and, imagine, she was so persistent that she managed to get the chief to see her, had him fetched out from dinner, it seems. You can imagine what happened. She was turned out, of course; but, according to her own story, she abused him and threw something at him. One may well believe it.... How it is she wasn't taken up, I can't understand! Now she is telling everyone, including Amalia Ivanovna; but it's difficult to understand her, she is screaming and flinging herself about.... Oh yes, she shouts that since everyone has abandoned her, she will take the children and go into the street with a barrel-organ, and the children will sing and dance, and she too, and collect money, and will go every day under the general's window... 'to let everyone see wellborn children, whose father was an official, begging in the street.' She keeps beating the children and they are all crying. She is teaching Lida to sing 'My Village,' the boy to dance, Polenka the same. She is tearing up all the clothes, and making them little caps like actors; she means to carry a tin basin and make it tinkle, instead of music.... She won't listen to anything.... Imagine the state of things! It's beyond anything!"

Lebeziatnikov would have gone on, but Sonia, who had heard him almost breathless, snatched up her cloak and hat, and ran out of the room, putting on her things as she went. Raskolnikov followed her and Lebeziatnikov came after him.

"She has certainly gone mad!" he said to Raskolnikov, as they went out into the street. "I didn't want to frighten Sofya Semyonovna, so I said 'it seemed like it,' but there isn't a doubt of it. They say that in consumption the tubercles sometimes occur in the brain; it's a pity I know nothing of medicine. I did try to persuade her, but she wouldn't listen."

"Did you talk to her about the tubercles?"

"Not precisely of the tubercles. Besides, she wouldn't have understood! But what I say is, that if you convince a person logically that he has nothing to cry about, he'll stop crying. That's clear. Is it your conviction that he won't?"

"Life would be too easy if it were so," answered Raskolnikov.

"Excuse me, excuse me; of course it would be rather difficult for Katerina Ivanovna to understand, but do you know that in Paris they have been conducting serious experiments as to the possibility of curing the insane, simply by logical argument? One professor there, a scientific man of standing, lately dead, believed in the possibility of such treatment. His idea was that there's nothing really wrong with the physical organism of the insane, and that insanity is, so to say, a logical mistake, an error of judgment, an incorrect view of things. He gradually showed the madman his error and, would you believe it, they say he was successful? But as he made use of douches too, how far success was due to that treatment remains uncertain.... So it seems at least."

Raskolnikov had long ceased to listen. Reaching the house where he lived, he nodded to Lebeziatnikov and went in at the gate. Lebeziatnikov woke up with a start, looked about him and hurried on.

Raskolnikov went into his little room and stood still in the middle of it. Why had he come back here? He looked at the yellow and tattered paper, at the dust, at his sofa.... From the yard came a loud continuous knocking; someone seemed to be hammering... He went to the window, rose on tiptoe and looked out into the yard for a long time with an air of absorbed attention. But the yard was empty and he could not see who was hammering. In the house on the left he saw some open windows; on the windowsills were pots of sickly-looking geraniums. Linen was hung out of the windows... He knew it all by heart. He turned away and sat down on the sofa.

Never, never had he felt himself so fearfully alone!

Yes, he felt once more that he would perhaps come to hate Sonia, now that he had made her more miserable.

"Why had he gone to her to beg for her tears? What need had he to poison her life? Oh, the meanness of it!"

"I will remain alone," he said resolutely, "and she shall not come to the prison!"

Five minutes later he raised his head with a strange smile. That was a strange thought.

"Perhaps it really would be better in Siberia," he thought suddenly.

He could not have said how long he sat there with vague thoughts surging through his mind. All at once the door opened and Dounia came in. At first she stood still and looked at him from the doorway, just as he had done at Sonia; then she came in and sat down in the same place as yesterday, on the chair facing him. He looked silently and almost vacantly at her.

"Don't be angry, brother; I've only come for one minute," said Dounia.

Her face looked thoughtful but not stern. Her eyes were bright and soft. He saw that she too had come to him with love.

"Brother, now I know all, *all*. Dmitri Prokofitch has explained and told me everything. They are worrying and persecuting you through a stupid and contemptible suspicion.... Dmitri Prokofitch told me that there is no danger, and that you are wrong in looking upon it with such horror. I don't think so, and I fully understand how indignant you must be, and that that indignation may have a permanent effect on you. That's what I am afraid of. As for your cutting yourself off from us, I don't judge you, I don't venture to judge you, and forgive me for having blamed you for it. I feel that I too, if I had so great a trouble, should keep away from everyone. I shall tell mother nothing *of this*, but I shall talk about you continually and shall tell her from you that you will come very soon. Don't worry about her; *I* will set her mind at rest; but don't you try her too much—come once at least; remember that she is your mother. And now I have come simply to say" (Dounia began to get up) "that if you should need me or should need... all my life or anything... call me, and I'll come. Goodbye!"

She turned abruptly and went towards the door.

"Dounia!" Raskolnikov stopped her and went towards her. "That Razumihin, Dmitri Prokofitch, is a very good fellow."

Dounia flushed slightly.

"Well?" she asked, waiting a moment.

"He is competent, hardworking, honest and capable of real love.... Goodbye, Dounia."

Dounia flushed crimson, then suddenly she took alarm.

"But what does it mean, brother? Are we really parting forever that you... give me such a parting message?"

"Never mind.... Goodbye."

He turned away, and walked to the window. She stood a moment, looked at him uneasily, and went out troubled.

No, he was not cold to her. There was an instant (the very last one) when he had longed to take her in his arms and *say goodbye* to her, and even *to tell* her, but he had not dared even to touch her hand.

230

"Afterwards she may shudder when she remembers that I embraced her, and will feel that I stole her kiss."

"And would *she* stand that test?" he went on a few minutes later to himself. "No, she wouldn't; girls like that can't stand things! They never do."

And he thought of Sonia.

There was a breath of fresh air from the window. The daylight was fading. He took up his cap and went out.

He could not, of course, and would not consider how ill he was. But all this continual anxiety and agony of mind could not but affect him. And if he were not lying in high fever it was perhaps just because this continual inner strain helped to keep him on his legs and in possession of his faculties. But this artificial excitement could not last long.

He wandered aimlessly. The sun was setting. A special form of misery had begun to oppress him of late. There was nothing poignant, nothing acute about it; but there was a feeling of permanence, of eternity about it; it brought a foretaste of hopeless years of this cold leaden misery, a foretaste of an eternity "on a square yard of space." Towards evening this sensation usually began to weigh on him more heavily.

"With this idiotic, purely physical weakness, depending on the sunset or something, one can't help doing something stupid! You'll go to Dounia, as well as to Sonia," he muttered bitterly.

He heard his name called. He looked round. Lebeziatnikov rushed up to him.

"Only fancy, I've been to your room looking for you. Only fancy, she's carried out her plan, and taken away the children. Sofya Semyonovna and I have had a job to find them. She is rapping on a frying-pan and making the children dance. The children are crying. They keep stopping at the crossroads and in front of shops; there's a crowd of fools running after them. Come along!"

"And Sonia?" Raskolnikov asked anxiously, hurrying after Lebeziatnikov.

"Simply frantic. That is, it's not Sofya Semyonovna's frantic, but Katerina Ivanovna, though Sofya Semyonova's frantic too. But Katerina Ivanovna is absolutely frantic. I tell you she is quite mad. They'll be taken to the police. You can fancy what an effect that will have.... They are on the canal bank, near the bridge now, not far from Sofya Semyonovna's, quite close."

On the canal bank near the bridge and not two houses away from the one where Sonia lodged, there was a crowd of people, consisting principally of gutter children. The hoarse broken voice of Katerina Ivanovna could be heard from the bridge, and it certainly was a strange spectacle likely to attract a street crowd. Katerina Ivanovna in her old dress with the green shawl, wearing a torn straw hat, crushed in a hideous way on one side, was really frantic. She was exhausted and breathless. Her wasted consumptive face looked more suffering than ever, and indeed out of doors in the sunshine a consumptive always looks worse than at home. But her excitement did not flag, and every moment her irritation grew more intense. She rushed at the children, shouted at them, coaxed them, told them before the crowd how to dance and what to sing, began explaining to them why it was necessary, and driven to desperation by their not understanding, beat them.... Then she would make a rush at the crowd; if she noticed any decently dressed person stopping to look, she immediately appealed to him to see what these children "from a genteel, one may say aristocratic, house" had been brought to. If she heard laughter or jeering in the crowd, she would rush at once at the scoffers and begin squabbling with them. Some people laughed, others shook their heads, but everyone felt curious at the sight of the madwoman with the frightened children. The frying-pan of which Lebeziatnikov had spoken was not there, at least Raskolnikov did not see it. But instead of rapping on the pan, Katerina Ivanovna began clapping her wasted hands, when she made Lida and Kolya dance and Polenka sing. She too joined in the singing, but broke down at the second note with a fearful cough, which made her curse in despair and even shed tears. What made her most furious was the weeping and terror of Kolya and Lida. Some effort had been made to dress the children up as street singers are dressed. The boy had on a turban made of something red and white to look like a Turk. There had been no costume for Lida; she simply had a red knitted cap, or rather a night cap that had belonged to Marmeladov, decorated with a broken piece of white ostrich feather, which had been Katerina Ivanovna's grandmother's and had been preserved as a family possession. Polenka was in her everyday dress; she looked in timid

231

perplexity at her mother, and kept at her side, hiding her tears. She dimly realised her mother's condition, and looked uneasily about her. She was terribly frightened of the street and the crowd. Sonia followed Katerina Ivanovna, weeping and beseeching her to return home, but Katerina Ivanovna was not to be persuaded.

"Leave off, Sonia, leave off," she shouted, speaking fast, panting and coughing. "You don't know what you ask; you are like a child! I've told you before that I am not coming back to that drunken German. Let everyone, let all Petersburg see the children begging in the streets, though their father was an honourable man who served all his life in truth and fidelity, and one may say died in the service." (Katerina Ivanovna had by now invented this fantastic story and thoroughly believed it.) "Let that wretch of a general see it! And you are silly, Sonia: what have we to eat? Tell me that. We have worried you enough, I won't go on so! Ah, Rodion Romanovitch, is that you?" she cried, seeing Raskolnikov and rushing up to him. "Explain to this silly girl, please, that nothing better could be done! Even organ-grinders earn their living, and everyone will see at once that we are different, that we are an honourable and bereaved family reduced to beggary. And that general will lose his post, you'll see! We shall perform under his windows every day, and if the Tsar drives by, I'll fall on my knees, put the children before me, show them to him, and say 'Defend us father.' He is the father of the fatherless, he is merciful, he'll protect us, you'll see, and that wretch of a general.... Lida, *tenez vous droite*! Kolya, you'll dance again. Why are you whimpering? Whimpering again! What are you afraid of, stupid? Goodness, what am I to do with them, Rodion Romanovitch? If you only knew how stupid they are! What's one to do with such children?"

And she, almost crying herself—which did not stop her uninterrupted, rapid flow of talk— pointed to the crying children. Raskolnikov tried to persuade her to go home, and even said, hoping to work on her vanity, that it was unseemly for her to be wandering about the streets like an organ-grinder, as she was intending to become the principal of a boarding-school.

"A boarding-school, ha-ha-ha! A castle in the air," cried Katerina Ivanovna, her laugh ending in a cough. "No, Rodion Romanovitch, that dream is over! All have forsaken us!... And that general.... You know, Rodion Romanovitch, I threw an inkpot at him—it happened to be standing in the waiting-room by the paper where you sign your name. I wrote my name, threw it at him and ran away. Oh, the scoundrels, the scoundrels! But enough of them, now I'll provide for the children myself, I won't bow down to anybody! She has had to bear enough for us!" she pointed to Sonia. "Polenka, how much have you got? Show me! What, only two farthings! Oh, the mean wretches! They give us nothing, only run after us, putting their tongues out. There, what is that blockhead laughing at?" (She pointed to a man in the crowd.) "It's all because Kolya here is so stupid; I have such a bother with him. What do you want, Polenka? Tell me in French, *parlez-moi français*. Why, I've taught you, you know some phrases. Else how are you to show that you are of good family, well brought-up children, and not at all like other organ-grinders? We aren't going to have a Punch and Judy show in the street, but to sing a genteel song.... Ah, yes,... What are we to sing? You keep putting me out, but we... you see, we are standing here, Rodion Romanovitch, to find something to sing and get money, something Kolya can dance to.... For, as you can fancy, our performance is all impromptu.... We must talk it over and rehearse it all thoroughly, and then we shall go to Nevsky, where there are far more people of good society, and we shall be noticed at once. Lida knows 'My Village' only, nothing but 'My Village,' and everyone sings that. We must sing something far more genteel.... Well, have you thought of anything, Polenka? If only you'd help your mother! My memory's quite gone, or I should have thought of something. We really can't sing 'An Hussar.' Ah, let us sing in French, 'Cinq sous,' I have taught it you, I have taught it you. And as it is in French, people will see at once that you are children of good family, and that will be much more touching.... You might sing 'Marlborough s'en va-t-en guerre,' for that's quite a child's song and is sung as a lullaby in all the aristocratic houses.

"*Marlborough s'en va-t-en guerre*

Ne sait quand reviendra ..."

she began singing. "But no, better sing 'Cinq sous.' Now, Kolya, your hands on your hips, make haste, and you, Lida, keep turning the other way, and Polenka and I will sing and clap our hands!
"*Cinq sous, cinq sous*

Pour monter notre ménage."

(*Cough-cough-cough!*) "Set your dress straight, Polenka, it's slipped down on your shoulders," she observed, panting from coughing. "Now it's particularly necessary to behave nicely and genteelly, that all may see that you are wellborn children. I said at the time that the bodice should be cut longer, and made of two widths. It was your fault, Sonia, with your advice to make it shorter, and now you see the child is quite deformed by it.... Why, you're all crying again! What's the matter, stupids? Come, Kolya, begin. Make haste, make haste! Oh, what an unbearable child!

"*Cinq sous, cinq sous.*

"A policeman again! What do you want?"

A policeman was indeed forcing his way through the crowd. But at that moment a gentleman in civilian uniform and an overcoat—a solid-looking official of about fifty with a decoration on his neck (which delighted Katerina Ivanovna and had its effect on the policeman)—approached and without a word handed her a green three-rouble note. His face wore a look of genuine sympathy. Katerina Ivanovna took it and gave him a polite, even ceremonious, bow.

"I thank you, honoured sir," she began loftily. "The causes that have induced us (take the money, Polenka: you see there are generous and honourable people who are ready to help a poor gentlewoman in distress). You see, honoured sir, these orphans of good family—I might even say of aristocratic connections—and that wretch of a general sat eating grouse... and stamped at my disturbing him. 'Your excellency,' I said, 'protect the orphans, for you knew my late husband, Semyon Zaharovitch, and on the very day of his death the basest of scoundrels slandered his only daughter.'... That policeman again! Protect me," she cried to the official. "Why is that policeman edging up to me? We have only just run away from one of them. What do you want, fool?"

"It's forbidden in the streets. You mustn't make a disturbance."

"It's you're making a disturbance. It's just the same as if I were grinding an organ. What business is it of yours?"

"You have to get a licence for an organ, and you haven't got one, and in that way you collect a crowd. Where do you lodge?"

"What, a license?" wailed Katerina Ivanovna. "I buried my husband today. What need of a license?"

"Calm yourself, madam, calm yourself," began the official. "Come along; I will escort you.... This is no place for you in the crowd. You are ill."

"Honoured sir, honoured sir, you don't know," screamed Katerina Ivanovna. "We are going to the Nevsky.... Sonia, Sonia! Where is she? She is crying too! What's the matter with you all? Kolya, Lida, where are you going?" she cried suddenly in alarm. "Oh, silly children! Kolya, Lida, where are they off to?..."

Kolya and Lida, scared out of their wits by the crowd, and their mother's mad pranks, suddenly seized each other by the hand, and ran off at the sight of the policeman who wanted to take them away somewhere. Weeping and wailing, poor Katerina Ivanovna ran after them. She was a piteous and unseemly spectacle, as she ran, weeping and panting for breath. Sonia and Polenka rushed after them.

"Bring them back, bring them back, Sonia! Oh stupid, ungrateful children!... Polenka! catch them.... It's for your sakes I..."

She stumbled as she ran and fell down.

"She's cut herself, she's bleeding! Oh, dear!" cried Sonia, bending over her.

All ran up and crowded around. Raskolnikov and Lebeziatnikov were the first at her side, the official too hastened up, and behind him the policeman who muttered, "Bother!" with a gesture of impatience, feeling that the job was going to be a troublesome one.

"Pass on! Pass on!" he said to the crowd that pressed forward.

233

"She's dying," someone shouted.

"She's gone out of her mind," said another.

"Lord have mercy upon us," said a woman, crossing herself. "Have they caught the little girl and the boy? They're being brought back, the elder one's got them.... Ah, the naughty imps!"

When they examined Katerina Ivanovna carefully, they saw that she had not cut herself against a stone, as Sonia thought, but that the blood that stained the pavement red was from her chest.

"I've seen that before," muttered the official to Raskolnikov and Lebeziatnikov; "that's consumption; the blood flows and chokes the patient. I saw the same thing with a relative of my own not long ago... nearly a pint of blood, all in a minute.... What's to be done though? She is dying."

"This way, this way, to my room!" Sonia implored. "I live here!... See, that house, the second from here.... Come to me, make haste," she turned from one to the other. "Send for the doctor! Oh, dear!"

Thanks to the official's efforts, this plan was adopted, the policeman even helping to carry Katerina Ivanovna. She was carried to Sonia's room, almost unconscious, and laid on the bed. The blood was still flowing, but she seemed to be coming to herself. Raskolnikov, Lebeziatnikov, and the official accompanied Sonia into the room and were followed by the policeman, who first drove back the crowd which followed to the very door. Polenka came in holding Kolya and Lida, who were trembling and weeping. Several persons came in too from the Kapernaumovs' room; the landlord, a lame one-eyed man of strange appearance with whiskers and hair that stood up like a brush, his wife, a woman with an everlastingly scared expression, and several open-mouthed children with wonder-struck faces. Among these, Svidrigaïlov suddenly made his appearance. Raskolnikov looked at him with surprise, not understanding where he had come from and not having noticed him in the crowd. A doctor and priest wore spoken of. The official whispered to Raskolnikov that he thought it was too late now for the doctor, but he ordered him to be sent for. Kapernaumov ran himself.

Meanwhile Katerina Ivanovna had regained her breath. The bleeding ceased for a time. She looked with sick but intent and penetrating eyes at Sonia, who stood pale and trembling, wiping the sweat from her brow with a handkerchief. At last she asked to be raised. They sat her up on the bed, supporting her on both sides.

"Where are the children?" she said in a faint voice. "You've brought them, Polenka? Oh the sillies! Why did you run away.... Och!"

Once more her parched lips were covered with blood. She moved her eyes, looking about her.

"So that's how you live, Sonia! Never once have I been in your room."

She looked at her with a face of suffering.

"We have been your ruin, Sonia. Polenka, Lida, Kolya, come here! Well, here they are, Sonia, take them all! I hand them over to you, I've had enough! The ball is over." (Cough!) "Lay me down, let me die in peace."

They laid her back on the pillow.

"What, the priest? I don't want him. You haven't got a rouble to spare. I have no sins. God must forgive me without that. He knows how I have suffered.... And if He won't forgive me, I don't care!"

She sank more and more into uneasy delirium. At times she shuddered, turned her eyes from side to side, recognised everyone for a minute, but at once sank into delirium again. Her breathing was hoarse and difficult, there was a sort of rattle in her throat.

"I said to him, your excellency," she ejaculated, gasping after each word. "That Amalia Ludwigovna, ah! Lida, Kolya, hands on your hips, make haste! Glissez, glissez! pas de basque! Tap with your heels, be a graceful child!

"Du hast Diamanten und Perlen

"What next? That's the thing to sing.

"Du hast die schönsten Augen,

Mädchen, was willst du mehr?

"What an idea! *Was willst du mehr?* What things the fool invents! Ah, yes!
"In the heat of midday in the vale of Dagestan.

"Ah, how I loved it! I loved that song to distraction, Polenka! Your father, you know, used to sing it when we were engaged.... Oh those days! Oh that's the thing for us to sing! How does it go? I've forgotten. Remind me! How was it?"

She was violently excited and tried to sit up. At last, in a horribly hoarse, broken voice, she began, shrieking and gasping at every word, with a look of growing terror.
"In the heat of midday!... in the vale!... of Dagestan!...

With lead in my breast!..."

"Your excellency!" she wailed suddenly with a heartrending scream and a flood of tears, "protect the orphans! You have been their father's guest... one may say aristocratic...." She started, regaining consciousness, and gazed at all with a sort of terror, but at once recognised Sonia.

"Sonia, Sonia!" she articulated softly and caressingly, as though surprised to find her there. "Sonia darling, are you here, too?"

They lifted her up again.

"Enough! It's over! Farewell, poor thing! I am done for! I am broken!" she cried with vindictive despair, and her head fell heavily back on the pillow.

She sank into unconsciousness again, but this time it did not last long. Her pale, yellow, wasted face dropped back, her mouth fell open, her leg moved convulsively, she gave a deep, deep sigh and died.

Sonia fell upon her, flung her arms about her, and remained motionless with her head pressed to the dead woman's wasted bosom. Polenka threw herself at her mother's feet, kissing them and weeping violently. Though Kolya and Lida did not understand what had happened, they had a feeling that it was something terrible; they put their hands on each other's little shoulders, stared straight at one another and both at once opened their mouths and began screaming. They were both still in their fancy dress; one in a turban, the other in the cap with the ostrich feather.

And how did "the certificate of merit" come to be on the bed beside Katerina Ivanovna? It lay there by the pillow; Raskolnikov saw it.

He walked away to the window. Lebeziatnikov skipped up to him.

"She is dead," he said.

"Rodion Romanovitch, I must have two words with you," said Svidrigaïlov, coming up to them.

Lebeziatnikov at once made room for him and delicately withdrew. Svidrigaïlov drew Raskolnikov further away.

"I will undertake all the arrangements, the funeral and that. You know it's a question of money and, as I told you, I have plenty to spare. I will put those two little ones and Polenka into some good orphan asylum, and I will settle fifteen hundred roubles to be paid to each on coming of age, so that Sofya Semyonovna need have no anxiety about them. And I will pull her out of the mud too, for she is a good girl, isn't she? So tell Avdotya Romanovna that that is how I am spending her ten thousand."

"What is your motive for such benevolence?" asked Raskolnikov.

"Ah! you sceptical person!" laughed Svidrigaïlov. "I told you I had no need of that money. Won't you admit that it's simply done from humanity? She wasn't 'a louse,' you know" (he pointed to the corner where the dead woman lay), "was she, like some old pawnbroker woman? Come, you'll agree, is Luzhin to go on living, and doing wicked things or is she to die? And if I didn't help them, Polenka would go the same way."

He said this with an air of a sort of gay winking slyness, keeping his eyes fixed on Raskolnikov, who turned white and cold, hearing his own phrases, spoken to Sonia. He quickly stepped back and looked wildly at Svidrigaïlov.

"How do you know?" he whispered, hardly able to breathe.

"Why, I lodge here at Madame Resslich's, the other side of the wall. Here is Kapernaumov, and there lives Madame Resslich, an old and devoted friend of mine. I am a neighbour."

"You?"

"Yes," continued Svidrigaïlov, shaking with laughter. "I assure you on my honour, dear Rodion Romanovitch, that you have interested me enormously. I told you we should become friends, I foretold it. Well, here we have. And you will see what an accommodating person I am. You'll see that you can get on with me!"

PART VI

237

A strange period began for Raskolnikov: it was as though a fog had fallen upon him and wrapped him in a dreary solitude from which there was no escape. Recalling that period long after, he believed that his mind had been clouded at times, and that it had continued so, with intervals, till the final catastrophe. He was convinced that he had been mistaken about many things at that time, for instance as to the date of certain events. Anyway, when he tried later on to piece his recollections together, he learnt a great deal about himself from what other people told him. He had mixed up incidents and had explained events as due to circumstances which existed only in his imagination. At times he was a prey to agonies of morbid uneasiness, amounting sometimes to panic. But he remembered, too, moments, hours, perhaps whole days, of complete apathy, which came upon him as a reaction from his previous terror and might be compared with the abnormal insensibility, sometimes seen in the dying. He seemed to be trying in that latter stage to escape from a full and clear understanding of his position. Certain essential facts which required immediate consideration were particularly irksome to him. How glad he would have been to be free from some cares, the neglect of which would have threatened him with complete, inevitable ruin.

He was particularly worried about Svidrigaïlov, he might be said to be permanently thinking of Svidrigaïlov. From the time of Svidrigaïlov's too menacing and unmistakable words in Sonia's room at the moment of Katerina Ivanovna's death, the normal working of his mind seemed to break down. But although this new fact caused him extreme uneasiness, Raskolnikov was in no hurry for an explanation of it. At times, finding himself in a solitary and remote part of the town, in some wretched eating-house, sitting alone lost in thought, hardly knowing how he had come there, he suddenly thought of Svidrigaïlov. He recognised suddenly, clearly, and with dismay that he ought at once to come to an understanding with that man and to make what terms he could. Walking outside the city gates one day, he positively fancied that they had fixed a meeting there, that he was waiting for Svidrigaïlov. Another time he woke up before daybreak lying on the ground under some bushes and could not at first understand how he had come there.

But during the two or three days after Katerina Ivanovna's death, he had two or three times met Svidrigaïlov at Sonia's lodging, where he had gone aimlessly for a moment. They exchanged a few words and made no reference to the vital subject, as though they were tacitly agreed not to speak of it for a time.

Katerina Ivanovna's body was still lying in the coffin, Svidrigaïlov was busy making arrangements for the funeral. Sonia too was very busy. At their last meeting Svidrigaïlov informed Raskolnikov that he had made an arrangement, and a very satisfactory one, for Katerina Ivanovna's children; that he had, through certain connections, succeeded in getting hold of certain personages by whose help the three orphans could be at once placed in very suitable institutions; that the money he had settled on them had been of great assistance, as it is much easier to place orphans with some property than destitute ones. He said something too about Sonia and promised to come himself in a day or two to see Raskolnikov, mentioning that "he would like to consult with him, that there were things they must talk over...."

This conversation took place in the passage on the stairs. Svidrigaïlov looked intently at Raskolnikov and suddenly, after a brief pause, dropping his voice, asked: "But how is it, Rodion Romanovitch; you don't seem yourself? You look and you listen, but you don't seem to understand. Cheer up! We'll talk things over; I am only sorry, I've so much to do of my own business and other people's. Ah, Rodion Romanovitch," he added suddenly, "what all men need is fresh air, fresh air... more than anything!"

He moved to one side to make way for the priest and server, who were coming up the stairs. They had come for the requiem service. By Svidrigaïlov's orders it was sung twice a day punctually. Svidrigaïlov went his way. Raskolnikov stood still a moment, thought, and followed the priest into Sonia's room. He stood at the door. They began quietly, slowly and mournfully singing the service. From his childhood the thought of death and the presence of death had something oppressive and mysteriously awful; and it was long since he had heard the requiem service. And there was something else here as well, too awful and disturbing. He looked at the children: they were all kneeling by the coffin; Polenka was weeping. Behind them Sonia prayed, softly and, as it were, timidly weeping.

"These last two days she hasn't said a word to me, she hasn't glanced at me," Raskolnikov thought suddenly. The sunlight was bright in the room; the incense rose in clouds; the priest read, "Give rest, oh Lord...." Raskolnikov stayed all through the service. As he blessed them and took his leave, the priest looked round strangely. After the service, Raskolnikov went up to Sonia. She took both his hands and let her head sink on his shoulder. This slight friendly gesture bewildered Raskolnikov. It seemed strange to him that there was no trace of repugnance, no trace of disgust, no tremor in her hand. It was the furthest limit of self-abnegation, at least so he interpreted it.

Sonia said nothing. Raskolnikov pressed her hand and went out. He felt very miserable. If it had been possible to escape to some solitude, he would have thought himself lucky, even if he had to spend his whole life there. But although he had almost always been by himself of late, he had never been able to feel alone. Sometimes he walked out of the town on to the high road, once he had even reached a little wood, but the lonelier the place was, the more he seemed to be aware of an uneasy presence near him. It did not frighten him, but greatly annoyed him, so that he made haste to return to the town, to mingle with the crowd, to enter restaurants and taverns, to walk in busy thoroughfares. There he felt easier and even more solitary. One day at dusk he sat for an hour listening to songs in a tavern and he remembered that he positively enjoyed it. But at last he had suddenly felt the same uneasiness again, as though his conscience smote him. "Here I sit listening to singing, is that what I ought to be doing?" he thought. Yet he felt at once that that was not the only cause of his uneasiness; there was something requiring immediate decision, but it was something he could not clearly understand or put into words. It was a hopeless tangle. "No, better the struggle again! Better Porfiry again... or Svidrigaïlov.... Better some challenge again... some attack. Yes, yes!" he thought. He went out of the tavern and rushed away almost at a run. The thought of Dounia and his mother suddenly reduced him almost to a panic. That night he woke up before morning among some bushes in Krestovsky Island, trembling all over with fever; he walked home, and it was early morning when he arrived. After some hours' sleep the fever left him, but he woke up late, two o'clock in the afternoon.

He remembered that Katerina Ivanovna's funeral had been fixed for that day, and was glad that he was not present at it. Nastasya brought him some food; he ate and drank with appetite, almost with greediness. His head was fresher and he was calmer than he had been for the last three days. He even felt a passing wonder at his previous attacks of panic.

The door opened and Razumihin came in.

"Ah, he's eating, then he's not ill," said Razumihin. He took a chair and sat down at the table opposite Raskolnikov.

He was troubled and did not attempt to conceal it. He spoke with evident annoyance, but without hurry or raising his voice. He looked as though he had some special fixed determination.

"Listen," he began resolutely. "As far as I am concerned, you may all go to hell, but from what I see, it's clear to me that I can't make head or tail of it; please don't think I've come to ask you questions. I don't want to know, hang it! If you begin telling me your secrets, I dare say I shouldn't stay to listen, I should go away cursing. I have only come to find out once for all whether it's a fact that you are mad? There is a conviction in the air that you are mad or very nearly so. I admit I've been disposed to that opinion myself, judging from your stupid, repulsive and quite inexplicable actions, and from your recent behavior to your mother and sister. Only a monster or a madman could treat them as you have; so you must be mad."

"When did you see them last?"

"Just now. Haven't you seen them since then? What have you been doing with yourself? Tell me, please. I've been to you three times already. Your mother has been seriously ill since yesterday. She had made up her mind to come to you; Avdotya Romanovna tried to prevent her;

she wouldn't hear a word. 'If he is ill, if his mind is giving way, who can look after him like his mother?' she said. We all came here together, we couldn't let her come alone all the way. We kept begging her to be calm. We came in, you weren't here; she sat down, and stayed ten minutes, while we stood waiting in silence. She got up and said: 'If he's gone out, that is, if he is well, and has forgotten his mother, it's humiliating and unseemly for his mother to stand at his door begging for kindness.' She returned home and took to her bed; now she is in a fever. 'I see,' she said, 'that he has time for *his girl*.' She means by *your girl* Sofya Semyonovna, your betrothed or your mistress, I don't know. I went at once to Sofya Semyonovna's, for I wanted to know what was going on. I looked round, I saw the coffin, the children crying, and Sofya Semyonovna trying them on mourning dresses. No sign of you. I apologised, came away, and reported to Avdotya Romanovna. So that's all nonsense and you haven't got a girl; the most likely thing is that you are mad. But here you sit, guzzling boiled beef as though you'd not had a bite for three days. Though as far as that goes, madmen eat too, but though you have not said a word to me yet… you are not mad! That I'd swear! Above all, you are not mad! So you may go to hell, all of you, for there's some mystery, some secret about it, and I don't intend to worry my brains over your secrets. So I've simply come to swear at you," he finished, getting up, "to relieve my mind. And I know what to do now."

"What do you mean to do now?"

"What business is it of yours what I mean to do?"

"You are going in for a drinking bout."

"How… how did you know?"

"Why, it's pretty plain."

Razumihin paused for a minute.

"You always have been a very rational person and you've never been mad, never," he observed suddenly with warmth. "You're right: I shall drink. Goodbye!"

And he moved to go out.

"I was talking with my sister—the day before yesterday, I think it was—about you, Razumihin."

"About me! But… where can you have seen her the day before yesterday?" Razumihin stopped short and even turned a little pale.

One could see that his heart was throbbing slowly and violently.

"She came here by herself, sat there and talked to me."

"She did!"

"Yes."

"What did you say to her… I mean, about me?"

"I told her you were a very good, honest, and industrious man. I didn't tell her you love her, because she knows that herself."

"She knows that herself?"

"Well, it's pretty plain. Wherever I might go, whatever happened to me, you would remain to look after them. I, so to speak, give them into your keeping, Razumihin. I say this because I know quite well how you love her, and am convinced of the purity of your heart. I know that she too may love you and perhaps does love you already. Now decide for yourself, as you know best, whether you need go in for a drinking bout or not."

"Rodya! You see… well…. Ach, damn it! But where do you mean to go? Of course, if it's all a secret, never mind…. But I… I shall find out the secret… and I am sure that it must be some ridiculous nonsense and that you've made it all up. Anyway you are a capital fellow, a capital fellow!…"

"That was just what I wanted to add, only you interrupted, that that was a very good decision of yours not to find out these secrets. Leave it to time, don't worry about it. You'll know it all in time when it must be. Yesterday a man said to me that what a man needs is fresh air, fresh air, fresh air. I mean to go to him directly to find out what he meant by that."

Razumihin stood lost in thought and excitement, making a silent conclusion.

240

"He's a political conspirator! He must be. And he's on the eve of some desperate step, that's certain. It can only be that! And... and Dounia knows," he thought suddenly.

"So Avdotya Romanovna comes to see you," he said, weighing each syllable, "and you're going to see a man who says we need more air, and so of course that letter... that too must have something to do with it," he concluded to himself.

"What letter?"

"She got a letter today. It upset her very much—very much indeed. Too much so. I began speaking of you, she begged me not to. Then... then she said that perhaps we should very soon have to part... then she began warmly thanking me for something; then she went to her room and locked herself in."

"She got a letter?" Raskolnikov asked thoughtfully.

"Yes, and you didn't know? hm..."

They were both silent.

"Goodbye, Rodion. There was a time, brother, when I.... Never mind, goodbye. You see, there was a time.... Well, goodbye! I must be off too. I am not going to drink. There's no need now.... That's all stuff!"

He hurried out; but when he had almost closed the door behind him, he suddenly opened it again, and said, looking away:

"Oh, by the way, do you remember that murder, you know Porfiry's, that old woman? Do you know the murderer has been found, he has confessed and given the proofs. It's one of those very workmen, the painter, only fancy! Do you remember I defended them here? Would you believe it, all that scene of fighting and laughing with his companions on the stairs while the porter and the two witnesses were going up, he got up on purpose to disarm suspicion. The cunning, the presence of mind of the young dog! One can hardly credit it; but it's his own explanation, he has confessed it all. And what a fool I was about it! Well, he's simply a genius of hypocrisy and resourcefulness in disarming the suspicions of the lawyers—so there's nothing much to wonder at, I suppose! Of course people like that are always possible. And the fact that he couldn't keep up the character, but confessed, makes him easier to believe in. But what a fool I was! I was frantic on their side!"

"Tell me, please, from whom did you hear that, and why does it interest you so?" Raskolnikov asked with unmistakable agitation.

"What next? You ask me why it interests me!... Well, I heard it from Porfiry, among others... It was from him I heard almost all about it."

"From Porfiry?"

"From Porfiry."

"What... what did he say?" Raskolnikov asked in dismay.

"He gave me a capital explanation of it. Psychologically, after his fashion."

"He explained it? Explained it himself?"

"Yes, yes; goodbye. I'll tell you all about it another time, but now I'm busy. There was a time when I fancied... But no matter, another time!... What need is there for me to drink now? You have made me drunk without wine. I am drunk, Rodya! Goodbye, I'm going. I'll come again very soon."

He went out.

"He's a political conspirator, there's not a doubt about it," Razumihin decided, as he slowly descended the stairs. "And he's drawn his sister in; that's quite, quite in keeping with Avdotya Romanovna's character. There are interviews between them!... She hinted at it too... So many of her words... and hints... bear that meaning! And how else can all this tangle be explained? Hm! And I was almost thinking... Good heavens, what I thought! Yes, I took leave of my senses and I wronged him! It was his doing, under the lamp in the corridor that day. Pfoo! What a crude, nasty, vile idea on my part! Nikolay is a brick, for confessing.... And how clear it all is now! His illness then, all his strange actions... before this, in the university, how morose he used to be, how gloomy.... But what's the meaning now of that letter? There's something in that, too, perhaps. Whom was it from? I suspect...! No, I must find out!"

He thought of Dounia, realising all he had heard and his heart throbbed, and he suddenly broke into a run.

As soon as Razumihin went out, Raskolnikov got up, turned to the window, walked into one corner and then into another, as though forgetting the smallness of his room, and sat down again on the sofa. He felt, so to speak, renewed; again the struggle, so a means of escape had come.

"Yes, a means of escape had come! It had been too stifling, too cramping, the burden had been too agonising. A lethargy had come upon him at times. From the moment of the scene with Nikolay at Porfiry's he had been suffocating, penned in without hope of escape. After Nikolay's confession, on that very day had come the scene with Sonia; his behaviour and his last words had been utterly unlike anything he could have imagined beforehand; he had grown feebler, instantly and fundamentally! And he had agreed at the time with Sonia, he had agreed in his heart he could not go on living alone with such a thing on his mind!

"And Svidrigaïlov was a riddle... He worried him, that was true, but somehow not on the same point. He might still have a struggle to come with Svidrigaïlov. Svidrigaïlov, too, might be a means of escape; but Porfiry was a different matter.

"And so Porfiry himself had explained it to Razumihin, had explained it *psychologically*. He had begun bringing in his damned psychology again! Porfiry? But to think that Porfiry should for one moment believe that Nikolay was guilty, after what had passed between them before Nikolay's appearance, after that tête-à-tête interview, which could have only *one* explanation? (During those days Raskolnikov had often recalled passages in that scene with Porfiry; he could not bear to let his mind rest on it.) Such words, such gestures had passed between them, they had exchanged such glances, things had been said in such a tone and had reached such a pass, that Nikolay, whom Porfiry had seen through at the first word, at the first gesture, could not have shaken his conviction.

"And to think that even Razumihin had begun to suspect! The scene in the corridor under the lamp had produced its effect then. He had rushed to Porfiry.... But what had induced the latter to receive him like that? What had been his object in putting Razumihin off with Nikolay? He must have some plan; there was some design, but what was it? It was true that a long time had passed since that morning—too long a time—and no sight nor sound of Porfiry. Well, that was a bad sign...."

Raskolnikov took his cap and went out of the room, still pondering. It was the first time for a long while that he had felt clear in his mind, at least. "I must settle Svidrigaïlov," he thought, "and as soon as possible; he, too, seems to be waiting for me to come to him of my own accord." And at that moment there was such a rush of hate in his weary heart that he might have killed either of those two—Porfiry or Svidrigaïlov. At least he felt that he would be capable of doing it later, if not now.

"We shall see, we shall see," he repeated to himself.

But no sooner had he opened the door than he stumbled upon Porfiry himself in the passage. He was coming in to see him. Raskolnikov was dumbfounded for a minute, but only for one minute. Strange to say, he was not very much astonished at seeing Porfiry and scarcely afraid of him. He was simply startled, but was quickly, instantly, on his guard. "Perhaps this will mean the end? But how could Porfiry have approached so quietly, like a cat, so that he had heard nothing? Could he have been listening at the door?"

"You didn't expect a visitor, Rodion Romanovitch," Porfiry explained, laughing. "I've been meaning to look in a long time; I was passing by and thought why not go in for five minutes. Are you going out? I won't keep you long. Just let me have one cigarette."

"Sit down, Porfiry Petrovitch, sit down." Raskolnikov gave his visitor a seat with so pleased and friendly an expression that he would have marvelled at himself, if he could have seen it.

The last moment had come, the last drops had to be drained! So a man will sometimes go through half an hour of mortal terror with a brigand, yet when the knife is at his throat at last, he feels no fear.

Raskolnikov seated himself directly facing Porfiry, and looked at him without flinching. Porfiry screwed up his eyes and began lighting a cigarette.

242

"Speak, speak," seemed as though it would burst from Raskolnikov's heart. "Come, why don't you speak?"

"Ah these cigarettes!" Porfiry Petrovitch ejaculated at last, having lighted one. "They are pernicious, positively pernicious, and yet I can't give them up! I cough, I begin to have tickling in my throat and a difficulty in breathing. You know I am a coward, I went lately to Dr. B——n; he always gives at least half an hour to each patient. He positively laughed looking at me; he sounded me: 'Tobacco's bad for you,' he said, 'your lungs are affected.' But how am I to give it up? What is there to take its place? I don't drink, that's the mischief, he-he-he, that I don't. Everything is relative, Rodion Romanovitch, everything is relative!"

"Why, he's playing his professional tricks again," Raskolnikov thought with disgust. All the circumstances of their last interview suddenly came back to him, and he felt a rush of the feeling that had come upon him then.

"I came to see you the day before yesterday, in the evening; you didn't know?" Porfiry Petrovitch went on, looking round the room. "I came into this very room. I was passing by, just as I did today, and I thought I'd return your call. I walked in as your door was wide open, I looked round, waited and went out without leaving my name with your servant. Don't you lock your door?"

Raskolnikov's face grew more and more gloomy. Porfiry seemed to guess his state of mind.

"I've come to have it out with you, Rodion Romanovitch, my dear fellow! I owe you an explanation and must give it to you," he continued with a slight smile, just patting Raskolnikov's knee.

But almost at the same instant a serious and careworn look came into his face; to his surprise Raskolnikov saw a touch of sadness in it. He had never seen and never suspected such an expression in his face.

"A strange scene passed between us last time we met, Rodion Romanovitch. Our first interview, too, was a strange one; but then... and one thing after another! This is the point: I have perhaps acted unfairly to you; I feel it. Do you remember how we parted? Your nerves were unhinged and your knees were shaking and so were mine. And, you know, our behaviour was unseemly, even ungentlemanly. And yet we are gentlemen, above all, in any case, gentlemen; that must be understood. Do you remember what we came to?... and it was quite indecorous."

"What is he up to, what does he take me for?" Raskolnikov asked himself in amazement, raising his head and looking with open eyes on Porfiry.

"I've decided openness is better between us," Porfiry Petrovitch went on, turning his head away and dropping his eyes, as though unwilling to disconcert his former victim and as though disdaining his former wiles. "Yes, such suspicions and such scenes cannot continue for long. Nikolay put a stop to it, or I don't know what we might not have come to. That damned workman was sitting at the time in the next room—can you realise that? You know that, of course; and I am aware that he came to you afterwards. But what you supposed then was not true: I had not sent for anyone, I had made no kind of arrangements. You ask why I hadn't? What shall I say to you? it had all come upon me so suddenly. I had scarcely sent for the porters (you noticed them as you went out, I dare say). An idea flashed upon me; I was firmly convinced at the time, you see, Rodion Romanovitch. Come, I thought—even if I let one thing slip for a time, I shall get hold of something else—I shan't lose what I want, anyway. You are nervously irritable, Rodion Romanovitch, by temperament; it's out of proportion with other qualities of your heart and character, which I flatter myself I have to some extent divined. Of course I did reflect even then that it does not always happen that a man gets up and blurts out his whole story. It does happen sometimes, if you make a man lose all patience, though even then it's rare. I was capable of realising that. If I only had a fact, I thought, the least little fact to go upon, something I could lay hold of, something tangible, not merely psychological. For if a man is guilty, you must be able to get something substantial out of him; one may reckon upon most surprising results indeed. I was reckoning on your temperament, Rodion Romanovitch, on your temperament above all things! I had great hopes of you at that time."

"But what are you driving at now?" Raskolnikov muttered at last, asking the question without thinking.

"What is he talking about?" he wondered distractedly, "does he really take me to be innocent?"

"What am I driving at? I've come to explain myself, I consider it my duty, so to speak. I want to make clear to you how the whole business, the whole misunderstanding arose. I've caused you a great deal of suffering, Rodion Romanovitch. I am not a monster. I understand what it must mean for a man who has been unfortunate, but who is proud, imperious and above all, impatient, to have to bear such treatment! I regard you in any case as a man of noble character and not without elements of magnanimity, though I don't agree with all your convictions. I wanted to tell you this first, frankly and quite sincerely, for above all I don't want to deceive you. When I made your acquaintance, I felt attracted by you. Perhaps you will laugh at my saying so. You have a right to. I know you disliked me from the first and indeed you've no reason to like me. You may think what you like, but I desire now to do all I can to efface that impression and to show that I am a man of heart and conscience. I speak sincerely."

Porfiry Petrovitch made a dignified pause. Raskolnikov felt a rush of renewed alarm. The thought that Porfiry believed him to be innocent began to make him uneasy.

"It's scarcely necessary to go over everything in detail," Porfiry Petrovitch went on. "Indeed, I could scarcely attempt it. To begin with there were rumours. Through whom, how, and when those rumours came to me… and how they affected you, I need not go into. My suspicions were aroused by a complete accident, which might just as easily not have happened. What was it? Hm! I believe there is no need to go into that either. Those rumours and that accident led to one idea in my mind. I admit it openly—for one may as well make a clean breast of it—I was the first to pitch on you. The old woman's notes on the pledges and the rest of it—that all came to nothing. Yours was one of a hundred. I happened, too, to hear of the scene at the office, from a man who described it capitally, unconsciously reproducing the scene with great vividness. It was just one thing after another, Rodion Romanovitch, my dear fellow! How could I avoid being brought to certain ideas? From a hundred rabbits you can't make a horse, a hundred suspicions don't make a proof, as the English proverb says, but that's only from the rational point of view—you can't help being partial, for after all a lawyer is only human. I thought, too, of your article in that journal, do you remember, on your first visit we talked of it? I jeered at you at the time, but that was only to lead you on. I repeat, Rodion Romanovitch, you are ill and impatient. That you were bold, headstrong, in earnest and… had felt a great deal I recognised long before. I, too, have felt the same, so that your article seemed familiar to me. It was conceived on sleepless nights, with a throbbing heart, in ecstasy and suppressed enthusiasm. And that proud suppressed enthusiasm in young people is dangerous! I jeered at you then, but let me tell you that, as a literary amateur, I am awfully fond of such first essays, full of the heat of youth. There is a mistiness and a chord vibrating in the mist. Your article is absurd and fantastic, but there's a transparent sincerity, a youthful incorruptible pride and the daring of despair in it. It's a gloomy article, but that's what's fine in it. I read your article and put it aside, thinking as I did so 'that man won't go the common way.' Well, I ask you, after that as a preliminary, how could I help being carried away by what followed? Oh, dear, I am not saying anything, I am not making any statement now. I simply noted it at the time. What is there in it? I reflected. There's nothing in it, that is really nothing and perhaps absolutely nothing. And it's not at all the thing for the prosecutor to let himself be carried away by notions: here I have Nikolay on my hands with actual evidence against him—you may think what you like of it, but it's evidence. He brings in his psychology, too; one has to consider him, too, for it's a matter of life and death. Why am I explaining this to you? That you may understand, and not blame my malicious behaviour on that occasion. It was not malicious, I assure

245

you, he-he! Do you suppose I didn't come to search your room at the time? I did, I did, he-he! I was here when you were lying ill in bed, not officially, not in my own person, but I was here. Your room was searched to the last thread at the first suspicion; but *umsonst*! I thought to myself, now that man will come, will come of himself and quickly, too; if he's guilty, he's sure to come. Another man wouldn't, but he will. And you remember how Mr. Razumihin began discussing the subject with you? We arranged that to excite you, so we purposely spread rumours, that he might discuss the case with you, and Razumihin is not a man to restrain his indignation. Mr. Zametov was tremendously struck by your anger and your open daring. Think of blurting out in a restaurant 'I killed her.' It was too daring, too reckless. I thought so myself, if he is guilty he will be a formidable opponent. That was what I thought at the time. I was expecting you. But you simply bowled Zametov over and... well, you see, it all lies in this—that this damnable psychology can be taken two ways! Well, I kept expecting you, and so it was, you came! My heart was fairly throbbing. Ach!

"Now, why need you have come? Your laughter, too, as you came in, do you remember? I saw it all plain as daylight, but if I hadn't expected you so specially, I should not have noticed anything in your laughter. You see what influence a mood has! Mr. Razumihin then—ah, that stone, that stone under which the things were hidden! I seem to see it somewhere in a kitchen garden. It was in a kitchen garden, you told Zametov and afterwards you repeated that in my office? And when we began picking your article to pieces, how you explained it! One could take every word of yours in two senses, as though there were another meaning hidden.

"So in this way, Rodion Romanovitch, I reached the furthest limit, and knocking my head against a post, I pulled myself up, asking myself what I was about. After all, I said, you can take it all in another sense if you like, and it's more natural so, indeed. I couldn't help admitting it was more natural. I was bothered! 'No, I'd better get hold of some little fact' I said. So when I heard of the bell-ringing, I held my breath and was all in a tremor. 'Here is my little fact,' thought I, and I didn't think it over, I simply wouldn't. I would have given a thousand roubles at that minute to have seen you with my own eyes, when you walked a hundred paces beside that workman, after he had called you murderer to your face, and you did not dare to ask him a question all the way. And then what about your trembling, what about your bell-ringing in your illness, in semi-delirium?

"And so, Rodion Romanovitch, can you wonder that I played such pranks on you? And what made you come at that very minute? Someone seemed to have sent you, by Jove! And if Nikolay had not parted us... and do you remember Nikolay at the time? Do you remember him clearly? It was a thunderbolt, a regular thunderbolt! And how I met him! I didn't believe in the thunderbolt, not for a minute. You could see it for yourself; and how could I? Even afterwards, when you had gone and he began making very, very plausible answers on certain points, so that I was surprised at him myself, even then I didn't believe his story! You see what it is to be as firm as a rock! No, thought I, *Morgenfrüh*. What has Nikolay got to do with it!"

"Razumihin told me just now that you think Nikolay guilty and had yourself assured him of it...."

His voice failed him, and he broke off. He had been listening in indescribable agitation, as this man who had seen through and through him, went back upon himself. He was afraid of believing it and did not believe it. In those still ambiguous words he kept eagerly looking for something more definite and conclusive.

"Mr. Razumihin!" cried Porfiry Petrovitch, seeming glad of a question from Raskolnikov, who had till then been silent. "He-he-he! But I had to put Mr. Razumihin off; two is company, three is none. Mr. Razumihin is not the right man, besides he is an outsider. He came running to me with a pale face.... But never mind him, why bring him in? To return to Nikolay, would you like to know what sort of a type he is, how I understand him, that is? To begin with, he is still a child and not exactly a coward, but something by way of an artist. Really, don't laugh at my describing him so. He is innocent and responsive to influence. He has a heart, and is a fantastic fellow. He sings and dances, he tells stories, they say, so that people come from other villages to hear him. He attends school too, and laughs till he cries if you hold up a finger to him; he will drink himself

246

senseless—not as a regular vice, but at times, when people treat him, like a child. And he stole, too, then, without knowing it himself, for 'How can it be stealing, if one picks it up?' And do you know he is an Old Believer, or rather a dissenter? There have been Wanderers[2] in his family, and he was for two years in his village under the spiritual guidance of a certain elder. I learnt all this from Nikolay and from his fellow villagers. And what's more, he wanted to run into the wilderness! He was full of fervour, prayed at night, read the old books, 'the true' ones, and read himself crazy.

"Petersburg had a great effect upon him, especially the women and the wine. He responds to everything and he forgot the elder and all that. I learnt that an artist here took a fancy to him, and used to go and see him, and now this business came upon him.

"Well, he was frightened, he tried to hang himself! He ran away! How can one get over the idea the people have of Russian legal proceedings? The very word 'trial' frightens some of them. Whose fault is it? We shall see what the new juries will do. God grant they do good! Well, in prison, it seems, he remembered the venerable elder; the Bible, too, made its appearance again. Do you know, Rodion Romanovitch, the force of the word 'suffering' among some of these people! It's not a question of suffering for someone's benefit, but simply, 'one must suffer.' If they suffer at the hands of the authorities, so much the better. In my time there was a very meek and mild prisoner who spent a whole year in prison always reading his Bible on the stove at night and he read himself crazy, and so crazy, do you know, that one day, apropos of nothing, he seized a brick and flung it at the governor; though he had done him no harm. And the way he threw it too: aimed it a yard on one side on purpose, for fear of hurting him. Well, we know what happens to a prisoner who assaults an officer with a weapon. So 'he took his suffering.'

"So I suspect now that Nikolay wants to take his suffering or something of the sort. I know it for certain from facts, indeed. Only he doesn't know that I know. What, you don't admit that there are such fantastic people among the peasants? Lots of them. The elder now has begun influencing him, especially since he tried to hang himself. But he'll come and tell me all himself. You think he'll hold out? Wait a bit, he'll take his words back. I am waiting from hour to hour for him to come and abjure his evidence. I have come to like that Nikolay and am studying him in detail. And what do you think? He-he! He answered me very plausibly on some points, he obviously had collected some evidence and prepared himself cleverly. But on other points he is simply at sea, knows nothing and doesn't even suspect that he doesn't know!

"No, Rodion Romanovitch, Nikolay doesn't come in! This is a fantastic, gloomy business, a modern case, an incident of today when the heart of man is troubled, when the phrase is quoted that blood 'renews,' when comfort is preached as the aim of life. Here we have bookish dreams, a heart unhinged by theories. Here we see resolution in the first stage, but resolution of a special kind: he resolved to do it like jumping over a precipice or from a bell tower and his legs shook as he went to the crime. He forgot to shut the door after him, and murdered two people for a theory. He committed the murder and couldn't take the money, and what he did manage to snatch up he hid under a stone. It wasn't enough for him to suffer agony behind the door while they battered at the door and rung the bell, no, he had to go to the empty lodging, half delirious, to recall the bell-ringing, he wanted to feel the cold shiver over again.... Well, that we grant, was through illness, but consider this: he is a murderer, but looks upon himself as an honest man, despises others, poses as injured innocence. No, that's not the work of a Nikolay, my dear Rodion Romanovitch!"

All that had been said before had sounded so like a recantation that these words were too great a shock. Raskolnikov shuddered as though he had been stabbed.

"Then... who then... is the murderer?" he asked in a breathless voice, unable to restrain himself.

Porfiry Petrovitch sank back in his chair, as though he were amazed at the question.

"Who is the murderer?" he repeated, as though unable to believe his ears. "Why, *you*, Rodion Romanovitch! You are the murderer," he added, almost in a whisper, in a voice of genuine conviction.

Raskolnikov leapt from the sofa, stood up for a few seconds and sat down again without uttering a word. His face twitched convulsively.

"Your lip is twitching just as it did before," Porfiry Petrovitch observed almost sympathetically. "You've been misunderstanding me, I think, Rodion Romanovitch," he added after a brief pause, "that's why you are so surprised. I came on purpose to tell you everything and deal openly with you."

"It was not I murdered her," Raskolnikov whispered like a frightened child caught in the act.

"No, it was you, you Rodion Romanovitch, and no one else," Porfiry whispered sternly, with conviction.

They were both silent and the silence lasted strangely long, about ten minutes. Raskolnikov put his elbow on the table and passed his fingers through his hair. Porfiry Petrovitch sat quietly waiting. Suddenly Raskolnikov looked scornfully at Porfiry.

"You are at your old tricks again, Porfiry Petrovitch! Your old method again. I wonder you don't get sick of it!"

"Oh, stop that, what does that matter now? It would be a different matter if there were witnesses present, but we are whispering alone. You see yourself that I have not come to chase and capture you like a hare. Whether you confess it or not is nothing to me now; for myself, I am convinced without it."

"If so, what did you come for?" Raskolnikov asked irritably. "I ask you the same question again: if you consider me guilty, why don't you take me to prison?"

"Oh, that's your question! I will answer you, point for point. In the first place, to arrest you so directly is not to my interest."

"How so? If you are convinced you ought...."

"Ach, what if I am convinced? That's only my dream for the time. Why should I put you in safety? You know that's it, since you ask me to do it. If I confront you with that workman for instance and you say to him 'were you drunk or not? Who saw me with you? I simply took you to be drunk, and you were drunk, too.' Well, what could I answer, especially as your story is a more likely one than his? for there's nothing but psychology to support his evidence—that's almost unseemly with his ugly mug, while you hit the mark exactly, for the rascal is an inveterate drunkard and notoriously so. And I have myself admitted candidly several times already that that psychology can be taken in two ways and that the second way is stronger and looks far more probable, and that apart from that I have as yet nothing against you. And though I shall put you in prison and indeed have come—quite contrary to etiquette—to inform you of it beforehand, yet I tell you frankly, also contrary to etiquette, that it won't be to my advantage. Well, secondly, I've come to you because ..."

"Yes, yes, secondly?" Raskolnikov was listening breathless.

"Because, as I told you just now, I consider I owe you an explanation. I don't want you to look upon me as a monster, as I have a genuine liking for you, you may believe me or not. And in the third place I've come to you with a direct and open proposition—that you should surrender and confess. It will be infinitely more to your advantage and to my advantage too, for my task will be done. Well, is this open on my part or not?"

Raskolnikov thought a minute.

"Listen, Porfiry Petrovitch. You said just now you have nothing but psychology to go on, yet now you've gone on mathematics. Well, what if you are mistaken yourself, now?"

"No, Rodion Romanovitch, I am not mistaken. I have a little fact even then, Providence sent it me."

"What little fact?"

"I won't tell you what, Rodion Romanovitch. And in any case, I haven't the right to put it off any longer, I must arrest you. So think it over: it makes no difference to me *now* and so I speak only for your sake. Believe me, it will be better, Rodion Romanovitch."

Raskolnikov smiled malignantly.

"That's not simply ridiculous, it's positively shameless. Why, even if I were guilty, which I don't admit, what reason should I have to confess, when you tell me yourself that I shall be in greater safety in prison?"

"Ah, Rodion Romanovitch, don't put too much faith in words, perhaps prison will not be altogether a restful place. That's only theory and my theory, and what authority am I for you? Perhaps, too, even now I am hiding something from you? I can't lay bare everything, he-he! And how can you ask what advantage? Don't you know how it would lessen your sentence? You would be confessing at a moment when another man has taken the crime on himself and so has muddled the whole case. Consider that! I swear before God that I will so arrange that your confession shall come as a complete surprise. We will make a clean sweep of all these psychological points, of a suspicion against you, so that your crime will appear to have been something like an aberration, for in truth it was an aberration. I am an honest man, Rodion Romanovitch, and will keep my word."

Raskolnikov maintained a mournful silence and let his head sink dejectedly. He pondered a long while and at last smiled again, but his smile was sad and gentle.

"No!" he said, apparently abandoning all attempt to keep up appearances with Porfiry, "it's not worth it, I don't care about lessening the sentence!"

"That's just what I was afraid of!" Porfiry cried warmly and, as it seemed, involuntarily. "That's just what I feared, that you wouldn't care about the mitigation of sentence."

Raskolnikov looked sadly and expressively at him.

"Ah, don't disdain life!" Porfiry went on. "You have a great deal of it still before you. How can you say you don't want a mitigation of sentence? You are an impatient fellow!"

"A great deal of what lies before me?"

"Of life. What sort of prophet are you, do you know much about it? Seek and ye shall find. This may be God's means for bringing you to Him. And it's not forever, the bondage...."

"The time will be shortened," laughed Raskolnikov.

"Why, is it the bourgeois disgrace you are afraid of? It may be that you are afraid of it without knowing it, because you are young! But anyway *you* shouldn't be afraid of giving yourself up and confessing."

"Ach, hang it!" Raskolnikov whispered with loathing and contempt, as though he did not want to speak aloud.

He got up again as though he meant to go away, but sat down again in evident despair.

"Hang it, if you like! You've lost faith and you think that I am grossly flattering you; but how long has your life been? How much do you understand? You made up a theory and then were ashamed that it broke down and turned out to be not at all original! It turned out something base, that's true, but you are not hopelessly base. By no means so base! At least you didn't deceive yourself for long, you went straight to the furthest point at one bound. How do I regard you? I regard you as one of those men who would stand and smile at their torturer while he cuts their entrails out, if only they have found faith or God. Find it and you will live. You have long needed a change of air. Suffering, too, is a good thing. Suffer! Maybe Nikolay is right in wanting to suffer. I know you don't believe in it—but don't be over-wise; fling yourself straight into life, without deliberation; don't be afraid—the flood will bear you to the bank and set you safe on your feet again. What bank? How can I tell? I only believe that you have long life before you. I know that you take all my words now for a set speech prepared beforehand, but maybe you will remember them after. They may be of use some time. That's why I speak. It's as well that you only killed the old woman. If you'd invented another theory you might perhaps have done something a thousand times more hideous. You ought to thank God, perhaps. How do you know? Perhaps God is saving you for something. But keep a good heart and have less fear! Are you afraid of the great expiation before you? No, it would be shameful to be afraid of it. Since you have taken such a step, you must harden your heart. There is justice in it. You must fulfil the demands of justice. I know that you don't believe it, but indeed, life will bring you through. You will live it down in time. What you need now is fresh air, fresh air, fresh air!"

Raskolnikov positively started.

"But who are you? what prophet are you? From the height of what majestic calm do you proclaim these words of wisdom?"

"Who am I? I am a man with nothing to hope for, that's all. A man perhaps of feeling and sympathy, maybe of some knowledge too, but my day is over. But you are a different matter, there is life waiting for you. Though, who knows? maybe your life, too, will pass off in smoke and come to nothing. Come, what does it matter, that you will pass into another class of men? It's not comfort you regret, with your heart! What of it that perhaps no one will see you for so long? It's not time, but yourself that will decide that. Be the sun and all will see you. The sun has before all to be the sun. Why are you smiling again? At my being such a Schiller? I bet you're imagining that I am trying to get round you by flattery. Well, perhaps I am, he-he-he! Perhaps you'd better not believe my word, perhaps you'd better never believe it altogether—I'm made that way, I confess it. But let me add, you can judge for yourself, I think, how far I am a base sort of man and how far I am honest."

"When do you mean to arrest me?"

"Well, I can let you walk about another day or two. Think it over, my dear fellow, and pray to God. It's more in your interest, believe me."

"And what if I run away?" asked Raskolnikov with a strange smile.

"No, you won't run away. A peasant would run away, a fashionable dissenter would run away, the flunkey of another man's thought, for you've only to show him the end of your little finger and he'll be ready to believe in anything for the rest of his life. But you've ceased to believe in your theory already, what will you run away with? And what would you do in hiding? It would be hateful and difficult for you, and what you need more than anything in life is a definite position, an atmosphere to suit you. And what sort of atmosphere would you have? If you ran away, you'd come back to yourself. *You can't get on without us.* And if I put you in prison—say you've been there a month, or two, or three—remember my word, you'll confess of yourself and perhaps to your own surprise. You won't know an hour beforehand that you are coming with a confession. I am convinced that you will decide, 'to take your suffering.' You don't believe my words now, but you'll come to it of yourself. For suffering, Rodion Romanovitch, is a great thing. Never mind my having grown fat, I know all the same. Don't laugh at it, there's an idea in suffering, Nikolay is right. No, you won't run away, Rodion Romanovitch."

Raskolnikov got up and took his cap. Porfiry Petrovitch also rose.

"Are you going for a walk? The evening will be fine, if only we don't have a storm. Though it would be a good thing to freshen the air."

He, too, took his cap.

"Porfiry Petrovitch, please don't take up the notion that I have confessed to you today," Raskolnikov pronounced with sullen insistence. "You're a strange man and I have listened to you from simple curiosity. But I have admitted nothing, remember that!"

"Oh, I know that, I'll remember. Look at him, he's trembling! Don't be uneasy, my dear fellow, have it your own way. Walk about a bit, you won't be able to walk too far. If anything happens, I have one request to make of you," he added, dropping his voice. "It's an awkward one, but important. If anything were to happen (though indeed I don't believe in it and think you quite incapable of it), yet in case you were taken during these forty or fifty hours with the notion of putting an end to the business in some other way, in some fantastic fashion—laying hands on yourself—(it's an absurd proposition, but you must forgive me for it) do leave a brief but precise note, only two lines, and mention the stone. It will be more generous. Come, till we meet! Good thoughts and sound decisions to you!"

Porfiry went out, stooping and avoiding looking at Raskolnikov. The latter went to the window and waited with irritable impatience till he calculated that Porfiry had reached the street and moved away. Then he too went hurriedly out of the room.

250

He hurried to Svidrigaïlov's. What he had to hope from that man he did not know. But that man had some hidden power over him. Having once recognised this, he could not rest, and now the time had come.

On the way, one question particularly worried him: had Svidrigaïlov been to Porfiry's?

As far as he could judge, he would swear to it, that he had not. He pondered again and again, went over Porfiry's visit; no, he hadn't been, of course he hadn't.

But if he had not been yet, would he go? Meanwhile, for the present he fancied he couldn't. Why? He could not have explained, but if he could, he would not have wasted much thought over it at the moment. It all worried him and at the same time he could not attend to it. Strange to say, none would have believed it perhaps, but he only felt a faint vague anxiety about his immediate future. Another, much more important anxiety tormented him—it concerned himself, but in a different, more vital way. Moreover, he was conscious of immense moral fatigue, though his mind was working better that morning than it had done of late.

And was it worth while, after all that had happened, to contend with these new trivial difficulties? Was it worth while, for instance, to manoeuvre that Svidrigaïlov should not go to Porfiry's? Was it worth while to investigate, to ascertain the facts, to waste time over anyone like Svidrigaïlov?

Oh, how sick he was of it all!

And yet he was hastening to Svidrigaïlov; could he be expecting something *new* from him, information, or means of escape? Men will catch at straws! Was it destiny or some instinct bringing them together? Perhaps it was only fatigue, despair; perhaps it was not Svidrigaïlov but some other whom he needed, and Svidrigaïlov had simply presented himself by chance. Sonia? But what should he go to Sonia for now? To beg her tears again? He was afraid of Sonia, too. Sonia stood before him as an irrevocable sentence. He must go his own way or hers. At that moment especially he did not feel equal to seeing her. No, would it not be better to try Svidrigaïlov? And he could not help inwardly owning that he had long felt that he must see him for some reason.

But what could they have in common? Their very evildoing could not be of the same kind. The man, moreover, was very unpleasant, evidently depraved, undoubtedly cunning and deceitful, possibly malignant. Such stories were told about him. It is true he was befriending Katerina Ivanovna's children, but who could tell with what motive and what it meant? The man always had some design, some project.

There was another thought which had been continually hovering of late about Raskolnikov's mind, and causing him great uneasiness. It was so painful that he made distinct efforts to get rid of it. He sometimes thought that Svidrigaïlov was dogging his footsteps. Svidrigaïlov had found out his secret and had had designs on Dounia. What if he had them still? Wasn't it practically certain that he had? And what if, having learnt his secret and so having gained power over him, he were to use it as a weapon against Dounia?

This idea sometimes even tormented his dreams, but it had never presented itself so vividly to him as on his way to Svidrigaïlov. The very thought moved him to gloomy rage. To begin with, this would transform everything, even his own position; he would have at once to confess his secret to Dounia. Would he have to give himself up perhaps to prevent Dounia from taking some rash step? The letter? This morning Dounia had received a letter. From whom could she get letters in Petersburg? Luzhin, perhaps? It's true Razumihin was there to protect her, but Razumihin knew nothing of the position. Perhaps it was his duty to tell Razumihin? He thought of it with repugnance.

In any case he must see Svidrigaïlov as soon as possible, he decided finally. Thank God, the details of the interview were of little consequence, if only he could get at the root of the matter; but if Svidrigaïlov were capable... if he were intriguing against Dounia—then...

Raskolnikov was so exhausted by what he had passed through that month that he could only decide such questions in one way; "then I shall kill him," he thought in cold despair.

A sudden anguish oppressed his heart, he stood still in the middle of the street and began looking about to see where he was and which way he was going. He found himself in X—— Prospect, thirty or forty paces from the Hay Market, through which he had come. The whole second storey of the house on the left was used as a tavern. All the windows were wide open; judging from the figures moving at the windows, the rooms were full to overflowing. There were sounds of singing, of clarionet and violin, and the boom of a Turkish drum. He could hear women shrieking. He was about to turn back wondering why he had come to the X—— Prospect, when suddenly at one of the end windows he saw Svidrigaïlov, sitting at a tea-table right in the open window with a pipe in his mouth. Raskolnikov was dreadfully taken aback, almost terrified. Svidrigaïlov was silently watching and scrutinising him and, what struck Raskolnikov at once, seemed to be meaning to get up and slip away unobserved. Raskolnikov at once pretended not to have seen him, but to be looking absentmindedly away, while he watched him out of the corner of his eye. His heart was beating violently. Yet, it was evident that Svidrigaïlov did not want to be seen. He took the pipe out of his mouth and was on the point of concealing himself, but as he got up and moved back his chair, he seemed to have become suddenly aware that Raskolnikov had seen him, and was watching him. What had passed between them was much the same as what happened at their first meeting in Raskolnikov's room. A sly smile came into Svidrigaïlov's face and grew broader and broader. Each knew that he was seen and watched by the other. At last Svidrigaïlov broke into a loud laugh.

"Well, well, come in if you want me; I am here!" he shouted from the window.

Raskolnikov went up into the tavern. He found Svidrigaïlov in a tiny back room, adjoining the saloon in which merchants, clerks and numbers of people of all sorts were drinking tea at twenty little tables to the desperate bawling of a chorus of singers. The click of billiard balls could be heard in the distance. On the table before Svidrigaïlov stood an open bottle and a glass half full of champagne. In the room he found also a boy with a little hand organ, a healthy-looking red-cheeked girl of eighteen, wearing a tucked-up striped skirt, and a Tyrolese hat with ribbons. In spite of the chorus in the other room, she was singing some servants' hall song in a rather husky contralto, to the accompaniment of the organ.

"Come, that's enough," Svidrigaïlov stopped her at Raskolnikov's entrance. The girl at once broke off and stood waiting respectfully. She had sung her guttural rhymes, too, with a serious and respectful expression in her face.

"Hey, Philip, a glass!" shouted Svidrigaïlov.

"I won't drink anything," said Raskolnikov.

"As you like, I didn't mean it for you. Drink, Katia! I don't want anything more today, you can go." He poured her out a full glass, and laid down a yellow note.

Katia drank off her glass of wine, as women do, without putting it down, in twenty gulps, took the note and kissed Svidrigaïlov's hand, which he allowed quite seriously. She went out of the room and the boy trailed after her with the organ. Both had been brought in from the street. Svidrigaïlov had not been a week in Petersburg, but everything about him was already, so to speak, on a patriarchal footing; the waiter, Philip, was by now an old friend and very obsequious.

The door leading to the saloon had a lock on it. Svidrigaïlov was at home in this room and perhaps spent whole days in it. The tavern was dirty and wretched, not even second-rate.

"I was going to see you and looking for you," Raskolnikov began, "but I don't know what made me turn from the Hay Market into the X—— Prospect just now. I never take this turning. I turn to the right from the Hay Market. And this isn't the way to you. I simply turned and here you are. It is strange!"

"Why don't you say at once 'it's a miracle'?"

"Because it may be only chance."

"Oh, that's the way with all you folk," laughed Svidrigaïlov. "You won't admit it, even if you do inwardly believe it a miracle! Here you say that it may be only chance. And what cowards they all are here, about having an opinion of their own, you can't fancy, Rodion Romanovitch. I don't mean you, you have an opinion of your own and are not afraid to have it. That's how it was you attracted my curiosity."

"Nothing else?"

"Well, that's enough, you know," Svidrigaïlov was obviously exhilarated, but only slightly so, he had not had more than half a glass of wine.

"I fancy you came to see me before you knew that I was capable of having what you call an opinion of my own," observed Raskolnikov.

"Oh, well, it was a different matter. Everyone has his own plans. And apropos of the miracle let me tell you that I think you have been asleep for the last two or three days. I told you of this tavern myself, there is no miracle in your coming straight here. I explained the way myself, told you where it was, and the hours you could find me here. Do you remember?"

"I don't remember," answered Raskolnikov with surprise.

"I believe you. I told you twice. The address has been stamped mechanically on your memory. You turned this way mechanically and yet precisely according to the direction, though you are not aware of it. When I told you then, I hardly hoped you understood me. You give yourself away too much, Rodion Romanovitch. And another thing, I'm convinced there are lots of people in Petersburg who talk to themselves as they walk. This is a town of crazy people. If only we had scientific men, doctors, lawyers and philosophers might make most valuable investigations in Petersburg each in his own line. There are few places where there are so many gloomy, strong and queer influences on the soul of man as in Petersburg. The mere influences of climate mean so much. And it's the administrative centre of all Russia and its character must be reflected on the whole country. But that is neither here nor there now. The point is that I have several times watched you. You walk out of your house—holding your head high—twenty paces from home you let it sink, and fold your hands behind your back. You look and evidently see nothing before nor beside you. At last you begin moving your lips and talking to yourself, and sometimes you wave one hand and declaim, and at last stand still in the middle of the road. That's not at all the thing. Someone may be watching you besides me, and it won't do you any good. It's nothing really to do with me and I can't cure you, but, of course, you understand me."

"Do you know that I am being followed?" asked Raskolnikov, looking inquisitively at him.

"No, I know nothing about it," said Svidrigaïlov, seeming surprised.

"Well, then, let us leave me alone," Raskolnikov muttered, frowning.

"Very good, let us leave you alone."

"You had better tell me, if you come here to drink, and directed me twice to come here to you, why did you hide, and try to get away just now when I looked at the window from the street? I saw it."

"He-he! And why was it you lay on your sofa with closed eyes and pretended to be asleep, though you were wide awake while I stood in your doorway? I saw it."

"I may have had… reasons. You know that yourself."

"And I may have had my reasons, though you don't know them."

Raskolnikov dropped his right elbow on the table, leaned his chin in the fingers of his right hand, and stared intently at Svidrigaïlov. For a full minute he scrutinised his face, which had impressed him before. It was a strange face, like a mask; white and red, with bright red lips, with a flaxen beard, and still thick flaxen hair. His eyes were somehow too blue and their expression somehow too heavy and fixed. There was something awfully unpleasant in that handsome face, which looked so wonderfully young for his age. Svidrigaïlov was smartly dressed in light summer clothes and was particularly dainty in his linen. He wore a huge ring with a precious stone in it.

"Have I got to bother myself about you, too, now?" said Raskolnikov suddenly, coming with nervous impatience straight to the point. "Even though perhaps you are the most dangerous man if

253

you care to injure me, I don't want to put myself out any more. I will show you at once that I don't prize myself as you probably think I do. I've come to tell you at once that if you keep to your former intentions with regard to my sister and if you think to derive any benefit in that direction from what has been discovered of late, I will kill you before you get me locked up. You can reckon on my word. You know that I can keep it. And in the second place if you want to tell me anything—for I keep fancying all this time that you have something to tell me—make haste and tell it, for time is precious and very likely it will soon be too late."

"Why in such haste?" asked Svidrigaïlov, looking at him curiously.

"Everyone has his plans," Raskolnikov answered gloomily and impatiently.

"You urged me yourself to frankness just now, and at the first question you refuse to answer," Svidrigaïlov observed with a smile. "You keep fancying that I have aims of my own and so you look at me with suspicion. Of course it's perfectly natural in your position. But though I should like to be friends with you, I shan't trouble myself to convince you of the contrary. The game isn't worth the candle and I wasn't intending to talk to you about anything special."

"What did you want me, for, then? It was you who came hanging about me."

"Why, simply as an interesting subject for observation. I liked the fantastic nature of your position—that's what it was! Besides you are the brother of a person who greatly interested me, and from that person I had in the past heard a very great deal about you, from which I gathered that you had a great influence over her; isn't that enough? Ha-ha-ha! Still I must admit that your question is rather complex, and is difficult for me to answer. Here, you, for instance, have come to me not only for a definite object, but for the sake of hearing something new. Isn't that so? Isn't that so?" persisted Svidrigaïlov with a sly smile. "Well, can't you fancy then that I, too, on my way here in the train was reckoning on you, on your telling me something new, and on my making some profit out of you! You see what rich men we are!"

"What profit could you make?"

"How can I tell you? How do I know? You see in what a tavern I spend all my time and it's my enjoyment, that's to say it's no great enjoyment, but one must sit somewhere; that poor Katia now—you saw her?… If only I had been a glutton now, a club gourmand, but you see I can eat this."

He pointed to a little table in the corner where the remnants of a terrible-looking beefsteak and potatoes lay on a tin dish.

"Have you dined, by the way? I've had something and want nothing more. I don't drink, for instance, at all. Except for champagne I never touch anything, and not more than a glass of that all the evening, and even that is enough to make my head ache. I ordered it just now to wind myself up, for I am just going off somewhere and you see me in a peculiar state of mind. That was why I hid myself just now like a schoolboy, for I was afraid you would hinder me. But I believe," he pulled out his watch, "I can spend an hour with you. It's half-past four now. If only I'd been something, a landowner, a father, a cavalry officer, a photographer, a journalist… I am nothing, no specialty, and sometimes I am positively bored. I really thought you would tell me something new."

"But what are you, and why have you come here?"

"What am I? You know, a gentleman, I served for two years in the cavalry, then I knocked about here in Petersburg, then I married Marfa Petrovna and lived in the country. There you have my biography!"

"You are a gambler, I believe?"

"No, a poor sort of gambler. A cardsharper—not a gambler."

"You have been a cardsharper then?"

"Yes, I've been a cardsharper too."

"Didn't you get thrashed sometimes?"

"It did happen. Why?"

"Why, you might have challenged them… altogether it must have been lively."

"I won't contradict you, and besides I am no hand at philosophy. I confess that I hastened here for the sake of the women."

254

"As soon as you buried Marfa Petrovna?"

"Quite so," Svidrigaïlov smiled with engaging candour. "What of it? You seem to find something wrong in my speaking like that about women?"

"You ask whether I find anything wrong in vice?"

"Vice! Oh, that's what you are after! But I'll answer you in order, first about women in general; you know I am fond of talking. Tell me, what should I restrain myself for? Why should I give up women, since I have a passion for them? It's an occupation, anyway."

"So you hope for nothing here but vice?"

"Oh, very well, for vice then. You insist on its being vice. But anyway I like a direct question. In this vice at least there is something permanent, founded indeed upon nature and not dependent on fantasy, something present in the blood like an ever-burning ember, forever setting one on fire and, maybe, not to be quickly extinguished, even with years. You'll agree it's an occupation of a sort."

"That's nothing to rejoice at, it's a disease and a dangerous one."

"Oh, that's what you think, is it! I agree, that it is a disease like everything that exceeds moderation. And, of course, in this one must exceed moderation. But in the first place, everybody does so in one way or another, and in the second place, of course, one ought to be moderate and prudent, however mean it may be, but what am I to do? If I hadn't this, I might have to shoot myself. I am ready to admit that a decent man ought to put up with being bored, but yet..."

"And could you shoot yourself?"

"Oh, come!" Svidrigaïlov parried with disgust. "Please don't speak of it," he added hurriedly and with none of the bragging tone he had shown in all the previous conversation. His face quite changed. "I admit it's an unpardonable weakness, but I can't help it. I am afraid of death and I dislike its being talked of. Do you know that I am to a certain extent a mystic?"

"Ah, the apparitions of Marfa Petrovna! Do they still go on visiting you?"

"Oh, don't talk of them; there have been no more in Petersburg, confound them!" he cried with an air of irritation. "Let's rather talk of that... though... H'm! I have not much time, and can't stay long with you, it's a pity! I should have found plenty to tell you."

"What's your engagement, a woman?"

"Yes, a woman, a casual incident.... No, that's not what I want to talk of."

"And the hideousness, the filthiness of all your surroundings, doesn't that affect you? Have you lost the strength to stop yourself?"

"And do you pretend to strength, too? He-he-he! You surprised me just now, Rodion Romanovitch, though I knew beforehand it would be so. You preach to me about vice and aesthetics! You—a Schiller, you—an idealist! Of course that's all as it should be and it would be surprising if it were not so, yet it is strange in reality.... Ah, what a pity I have no time, for you're a most interesting type! And, by the way, are you fond of Schiller? I am awfully fond of him."

"But what a braggart you are," Raskolnikov said with some disgust.

"Upon my word, I am not," answered Svidrigaïlov laughing. "However, I won't dispute it, let me be a braggart, why not brag, if it hurts no one? I spent seven years in the country with Marfa Petrovna, so now when I come across an intelligent person like you—intelligent and highly interesting—I am simply glad to talk and, besides, I've drunk that half-glass of champagne and it's gone to my head a little. And besides, there's a certain fact that has wound me up tremendously, but about that I... will keep quiet. Where are you off to?" he asked in alarm.

Raskolnikov had begun getting up. He felt oppressed and stifled and, as it were, ill at ease at having come here. He felt convinced that Svidrigaïlov was the most worthless scoundrel on the face of the earth.

"A-ach! Sit down, stay a little!" Svidrigaïlov begged. "Let them bring you some tea, anyway. Stay a little, I won't talk nonsense, about myself, I mean. I'll tell you something. If you like I'll tell you how a woman tried 'to save' me, as you would call it? It will be an answer to your first question indeed, for the woman was your sister. May I tell you? It will help to spend the time."

"Tell me, but I trust that you..."

"Oh, don't be uneasy. Besides, even in a worthless low fellow like me, Avdotya Romanovna can only excite the deepest respect."

IV

"You know perhaps—yes, I told you myself," began Svidrigaïlov, "that I was in the debtors' prison here, for an immense sum, and had not any expectation of being able to pay it. There's no need to go into particulars how Marfa Petrovna bought me out; do you know to what a point of insanity a woman can sometimes love? She was an honest woman, and very sensible, although completely uneducated. Would you believe that this honest and jealous woman, after many scenes of hysterics and reproaches, condescended to enter into a kind of contract with me which she kept throughout our married life? She was considerably older than I, and besides, she always kept a clove or something in her mouth. There was so much swinishness in my soul and honesty too, of a sort, as to tell her straight out that I couldn't be absolutely faithful to her. This confession drove her to frenzy, but yet she seems in a way to have liked my brutal frankness. She thought it showed I was unwilling to deceive her if I warned her like this beforehand and for a jealous woman, you know, that's the first consideration. After many tears an unwritten contract was drawn up between us: first, that I would never leave Marfa Petrovna and would always be her husband; secondly, that I would never absent myself without her permission; thirdly, that I would never set up a permanent mistress; fourthly, in return for this, Marfa Petrovna gave me a free hand with the maidservants, but only with her secret knowledge; fifthly, God forbid my falling in love with a woman of our class; sixthly, in case I—which God forbid—should be visited by a great serious passion I was bound to reveal it to Marfa Petrovna. On this last score, however, Marfa Petrovna was fairly at ease. She was a sensible woman and so she could not help looking upon me as a dissolute profligate incapable of real love. But a sensible woman and a jealous woman are two very different things, and that's where the trouble came in. But to judge some people impartially we must renounce certain preconceived opinions and our habitual attitude to the ordinary people about us. I have reason to have faith in your judgment rather than in anyone's. Perhaps you have already heard a great deal that was ridiculous and absurd about Marfa Petrovna. She certainly had some very ridiculous ways, but I tell you frankly that I feel really sorry for the innumerable woes of which I was the cause. Well, and that's enough, I think, by way of a decorous *oraison funèbre* for the most tender wife of a most tender husband. When we quarrelled, I usually held my tongue and did not irritate her and that gentlemanly conduct rarely failed to attain its object, it influenced her, it pleased her, indeed. These were times when she was positively proud of me. But your sister she couldn't put up with, anyway. And however she came to risk taking such a beautiful creature into her house as a governess. My explanation is that Marfa Petrovna was an ardent and impressionable woman and simply fell in love herself—literally fell in love—with your sister. Well, little wonder—look at Avdotya Romanovna! I saw the danger at the first glance and what do you think, I resolved not to look at her even. But Avdotya Romanovna herself made the first step, would you believe it? Would you believe it too that Marfa Petrovna was positively angry with me at first for my persistent silence about your sister, for my careless reception of her continual adoring praises of Avdotya Romanovna. I don't know what it was she wanted! Well, of course, Marfa Petrovna told Avdotya Romanovna every detail about me. She had the unfortunate habit of telling literally everyone all our family secrets and continually complaining of me; how could she fail to confide in such a delightful new friend? I expect they talked of nothing else but me and no doubt Avdotya Romanovna heard all those dark mysterious rumours that were current about me.... I don't mind betting that you too have heard something of the sort already?"

"I have. Luzhin charged you with having caused the death of a child. Is that true?"

"Don't refer to those vulgar tales, I beg," said Svidrigaïlov with disgust and annoyance. "If you insist on wanting to know about all that idiocy, I will tell you one day, but now…"

"I was told too about some footman of yours in the country whom you treated badly."

"I beg you to drop the subject," Svidrigaïlov interrupted again with obvious impatience.

"Was that the footman who came to you after death to fill your pipe?… you told me about it yourself." Raskolnikov felt more and more irritated.

Svidrigaïlov looked at him attentively and Raskolnikov fancied he caught a flash of spiteful mockery in that look. But Svidrigaïlov restrained himself and answered very civilly:

"Yes, it was. I see that you, too, are extremely interested and shall feel it my duty to satisfy your curiosity at the first opportunity. Upon my soul! I see that I really might pass for a romantic figure with some people. Judge how grateful I must be to Marfa Petrovna for having repeated to Avdotya Romanovna such mysterious and interesting gossip about me. I dare not guess what impression it made on her, but in any case it worked in my interests. With all Avdotya Romanovna's natural aversion and in spite of my invariably gloomy and repellent aspect—she did at least feel pity for me, pity for a lost soul. And if once a girl's heart is moved to *pity*, it's more dangerous than anything. She is bound to want to 'save him,' to bring him to his senses, and lift him up and draw him to nobler aims, and restore him to new life and usefulness—well, we all know how far such dreams can go. I saw at once that the bird was flying into the cage of herself. And I too made ready. I think you are frowning, Rodion Romanovitch? There's no need. As you know, it all ended in smoke. (Hang it all, what a lot I am drinking!) Do you know, I always, from the very beginning, regretted that it wasn't your sister's fate to be born in the second or third century AD, as the daughter of a reigning prince or some governor or proconsul in Asia Minor. She would undoubtedly have been one of those who would endure martyrdom and would have smiled when they branded her bosom with hot pincers. And she would have gone to it of herself. And in the fourth or fifth century she would have walked away into the Egyptian desert and would have stayed there thirty years living on roots and ecstasies and visions. She is simply thirsting to face some torture for someone, and if she can't get her torture, she'll throw herself out of a window. I've heard something of a Mr. Razumihin—he's said to be a sensible fellow; his surname suggests it, indeed. He's probably a divinity student. Well, he'd better look after your sister! I believe I understand her, and I am proud of it. But at the beginning of an acquaintance, as you know, one is apt to be more heedless and stupid. One doesn't see clearly. Hang it all, why is she so handsome? It's not my fault. In fact, it began on my side with a most irresistible physical desire. Avdotya Romanovna is awfully chaste, incredibly and phenomenally so. Take note, I tell you this about your sister as a fact. She is almost morbidly chaste, in spite of her broad intelligence, and it will stand in her way. There happened to be a girl in the house then, Parasha, a black-eyed wench, whom I had never seen before—she had just come from another village—very pretty, but incredibly stupid: she burst into tears, wailed so that she could be heard all over the place and caused scandal. One day after dinner Avdotya Romanovna followed me into an avenue in the garden and with flashing eyes *insisted* on my leaving poor Parasha alone. It was almost our first conversation by ourselves. I, of course, was only too pleased to obey her wishes, tried to appear disconcerted, embarrassed, in fact played my part not badly. Then came interviews, mysterious conversations, exhortations, entreaties, supplications, even tears—would you believe it, even tears? Think what the passion for propaganda will bring some girls to! I, of course, threw it all on my destiny, posed as hungering and thirsting for light, and finally resorted to the most powerful weapon in the subjection of the female heart, a weapon which never fails one. It's the well-known resource—flattery. Nothing in the world is harder than speaking the truth and nothing easier than flattery. If there's the hundredth part of a false note in speaking the truth, it leads to a discord, and that leads to trouble. But if all, to the last note, is false in flattery, it is just as agreeable, and is heard not without satisfaction. It may be a coarse satisfaction, but still a satisfaction. And however coarse the flattery, at least half will be sure to seem true. That's so for all stages of development and classes of society. A vestal virgin might be seduced by flattery. I can never remember without laughter how I once seduced a lady who was devoted to her husband, her children, and her principles. What fun it was and how little trouble! And the lady really had

258

principles—of her own, anyway. All my tactics lay in simply being utterly annihilated and prostrate before her purity. I flattered her shamelessly, and as soon as I succeeded in getting a pressure of the hand, even a glance from her, I would reproach myself for having snatched it by force, and would declare that she had resisted, so that I could never have gained anything but for my being so unprincipled. I maintained that she was so innocent that she could not foresee my treachery, and yielded to me unconsciously, unawares, and so on. In fact, I triumphed, while my lady remained firmly convinced that she was innocent, chaste, and faithful to all her duties and obligations and had succumbed quite by accident. And how angry she was with me when I explained to her at last that it was my sincere conviction that she was just as eager as I. Poor Marfa Petrovna was awfully weak on the side of flattery, and if I had only cared to, I might have had all her property settled on me during her lifetime. (I am drinking an awful lot of wine now and talking too much.) I hope you won't be angry if I mention now that I was beginning to produce the same effect on Avdotya Romanovna. But I was stupid and impatient and spoiled it all. Avdotya Romanovna had several times—and one time in particular—been greatly displeased by the expression of my eyes, would you believe it? There was sometimes a light in them which frightened her and grew stronger and stronger and more unguarded till it was hateful to her. No need to go into detail, but we parted. There I acted stupidly again. I fell to jeering in the coarsest way at all such propaganda and efforts to convert me; Parasha came on to the scene again, and not she alone; in fact there was a tremendous to-do. Ah, Rodion Romanovitch, if you could only see how your sister's eyes can flash sometimes! Never mind my being drunk at this moment and having had a whole glass of wine. I am speaking the truth. I assure you that this glance has haunted my dreams; the very rustle of her dress was more than I could stand at last. I really began to think that I might become epileptic. I could never have believed that I could be moved to such a frenzy. It was essential, indeed, to be reconciled, but by then it was impossible. And imagine what I did then! To what a pitch of stupidity a man can be brought by frenzy! Never undertake anything in a frenzy, Rodion Romanovitch. I reflected that Avdotya Romanovna was after all a beggar (ach, excuse me, that's not the word… but does it matter if it expresses the meaning?), that she lived by her work, that she had her mother and you to keep (ach, hang it, you are frowning again), and I resolved to offer her all my money—thirty thousand roubles I could have realised then—if she would run away with me here, to Petersburg. Of course I should have vowed eternal love, rapture, and so on. Do you know, I was so wild about her at that time that if she had told me to poison Marfa Petrovna or to cut her throat and to marry herself, it would have been done at once! But it ended in the catastrophe of which you know already. You can fancy how frantic I was when I heard that Marfa Petrovna had got hold of that scoundrelly attorney, Luzhin, and had almost made a match between them—which would really have been just the same thing as I was proposing. Wouldn't it? Wouldn't it? I notice that you've begun to be very attentive… you interesting young man…."

Svidrigaïlov struck the table with his fist impatiently. He was flushed. Raskolnikov saw clearly that the glass or glass and a half of champagne that he had sipped almost unconsciously was affecting him—and he resolved to take advantage of the opportunity. He felt very suspicious of Svidrigaïlov.

"Well, after what you have said, I am fully convinced that you have come to Petersburg with designs on my sister," he said directly to Svidrigaïlov, in order to irritate him further.

"Oh, nonsense," said Svidrigaïlov, seeming to rouse himself. "Why, I told you… besides your sister can't endure me."

"Yes, I am certain that she can't, but that's not the point."

"Are you so sure that she can't?" Svidrigaïlov screwed up his eyes and smiled mockingly. "You are right, she doesn't love me, but you can never be sure of what has passed between husband and wife or lover and mistress. There's always a little corner which remains a secret to the world and is only known to those two. Will you answer for it that Avdotya Romanovna regarded me with aversion?"

"From some words you've dropped, I notice that you still have designs—and of course evil ones—on Dounia and mean to carry them out promptly."

"What, have I dropped words like that?" Svidrigaïlov asked in naive dismay, taking not the slightest notice of the epithet bestowed on his designs.

"Why, you are dropping them even now. Why are you so frightened? What are you so afraid of now?"

"Me—afraid? Afraid of you? You have rather to be afraid of me, *cher ami*. But what nonsense.... I've drunk too much though, I see that. I was almost saying too much again. Damn the wine! Hi! there, water!"

He snatched up the champagne bottle and flung it without ceremony out of the window. Philip brought the water.

"That's all nonsense!" said Svidrigaïlov, wetting a towel and putting it to his head. "But I can answer you in one word and annihilate all your suspicions. Do you know that I am going to get married?"

"You told me so before."

"Did I? I've forgotten. But I couldn't have told you so for certain for I had not even seen my betrothed; I only meant to. But now I really have a betrothed and it's a settled thing, and if it weren't that I have business that can't be put off, I would have taken you to see them at once, for I should like to ask your advice. Ach, hang it, only ten minutes left! See, look at the watch. But I must tell you, for it's an interesting story, my marriage, in its own way. Where are you off to? Going again?"

"No, I'm not going away now."

"Not at all? We shall see. I'll take you there, I'll show you my betrothed, only not now. For you'll soon have to be off. You have to go to the right and I to the left. Do you know that Madame Resslich, the woman I am lodging with now, eh? I know what you're thinking, that she's the woman whose girl they say drowned herself in the winter. Come, are you listening? She arranged it all for me. You're bored, she said, you want something to fill up your time. For, you know, I am a gloomy, depressed person. Do you think I'm lighthearted? No, I'm gloomy. I do no harm, but sit in a corner without speaking a word for three days at a time. And that Resslich is a sly hussy, I tell you. I know what she has got in her mind; she thinks I shall get sick of it, abandon my wife and depart, and she'll get hold of her and make a profit out of her—in our class, of course, or higher. She told me the father was a broken-down retired official, who has been sitting in a chair for the last three years with his legs paralysed. The mamma, she said, was a sensible woman. There is a son serving in the provinces, but he doesn't help; there is a daughter, who is married, but she doesn't visit them. And they've two little nephews on their hands, as though their own children were not enough, and they've taken from school their youngest daughter, a girl who'll be sixteen in another month, so that then she can be married. She was for me. We went there. How funny it was! I present myself—a landowner, a widower, of a well-known name, with connections, with a fortune. What if I am fifty and she is not sixteen? Who thinks of that? But it's fascinating, isn't it? It is fascinating, ha-ha! You should have seen how I talked to the papa and mamma. It was worth paying to have seen me at that moment. She comes in, curtseys, you can fancy, still in a short frock—an unopened bud! Flushing like a sunset—she had been told, no doubt. I don't know how you feel about female faces, but to my mind these sixteen years, these childish eyes, shyness and tears of bashfulness are better than beauty; and she is a perfect little picture, too. Fair hair in little curls, like a lamb's, full little rosy lips, tiny feet, a charmer!... Well, we made friends. I told them I was in a hurry owing to domestic circumstances, and the next day, that is the day before yesterday, we were betrothed. When I go now I take her on my knee at once and keep her there.... Well, she flushes like a sunset and I kiss her every minute. Her mamma of course impresses on her that this is her husband and that this must be so. It's simply delicious! The present betrothed condition is perhaps better than marriage. Here you have what is called *la nature et la vérité*, ha-ha! I've talked to her twice, she is far from a fool. Sometimes she steals a look at me that positively scorches me. Her face is like Raphael's Madonna. You know, the Sistine Madonna's face has something fantastic in it, the face of mournful religious ecstasy. Haven't you noticed it? Well, she's something in that line. The day after we'd been betrothed, I bought her presents to the value of fifteen hundred roubles—a set of diamonds and another of pearls and a silver dressing-

260

case as large as this, with all sorts of things in it, so that even my Madonna's face glowed. I sat her on my knee, yesterday, and I suppose rather too unceremoniously—she flushed crimson and the tears started, but she didn't want to show it. We were left alone, she suddenly flung herself on my neck (for the first time of her own accord), put her little arms round me, kissed me, and vowed that she would be an obedient, faithful, and good wife, would make me happy, would devote all her life, every minute of her life, would sacrifice everything, everything, and that all she asks in return is my *respect*, and that she wants 'nothing, nothing more from me, no presents.' You'll admit that to hear such a confession, alone, from an angel of sixteen in a muslin frock, with little curls, with a flush of maiden shyness in her cheeks and tears of enthusiasm in her eyes is rather fascinating! Isn't it fascinating? It's worth paying for, isn't it? Well… listen, we'll go to see my betrothed, only not just now!"

"The fact is this monstrous difference in age and development excites your sensuality! Will you really make such a marriage?"

"Why, of course. Everyone thinks of himself, and he lives most gaily who knows best how to deceive himself. Ha-ha! But why are you so keen about virtue? Have mercy on me, my good friend. I am a sinful man. Ha-ha-ha!"

"But you have provided for the children of Katerina Ivanovna. Though… though you had your own reasons…. I understand it all now."

"I am always fond of children, very fond of them," laughed Svidrigaïlov. "I can tell you one curious instance of it. The first day I came here I visited various haunts, after seven years I simply rushed at them. You probably notice that I am not in a hurry to renew acquaintance with my old friends. I shall do without them as long as I can. Do you know, when I was with Marfa Petrovna in the country, I was haunted by the thought of these places where anyone who knows his way about can find a great deal. Yes, upon my soul! The peasants have vodka, the educated young people, shut out from activity, waste themselves in impossible dreams and visions and are crippled by theories; Jews have sprung up and are amassing money, and all the rest give themselves up to debauchery. From the first hour the town reeked of its familiar odours. I chanced to be in a frightful den—I like my dens dirty—it was a dance, so called, and there was a cancan such as I never saw in my day. Yes, there you have progress. All of a sudden I saw a little girl of thirteen, nicely dressed, dancing with a specialist in that line, with another one vis-à-vis. Her mother was sitting on a chair by the wall. You can't fancy what a cancan that was! The girl was ashamed, blushed, at last felt insulted, and began to cry. Her partner seized her and began whirling her round and performing before her; everyone laughed and—I like your public, even the cancan public—they laughed and shouted, 'Serves her right—serves her right! Shouldn't bring children!' Well, it's not my business whether that consoling reflection was logical or not. I at once fixed on my plan, sat down by the mother, and began by saying that I too was a stranger and that people here were ill-bred and that they couldn't distinguish decent folks and treat them with respect, gave her to understand that I had plenty of money, offered to take them home in my carriage. I took them home and got to know them. They were lodging in a miserable little hole and had only just arrived from the country. She told me that she and her daughter could only regard my acquaintance as an honour. I found out that they had nothing of their own and had come to town upon some legal business. I proffered my services and money. I learnt that they had gone to the dancing saloon by mistake, believing that it was a genuine dancing class. I offered to assist in the young girl's education in French and dancing. My offer was accepted with enthusiasm as an honour—and we are still friendly…. If you like, we'll go and see them, only not just now."

"Stop! Enough of your vile, nasty anecdotes, depraved vile, sensual man!"

"Schiller, you are a regular Schiller! *O la vertu va-t-elle se nicher?* But you know I shall tell you these things on purpose, for the pleasure of hearing your outcries!"

"I dare say. I can see I am ridiculous myself," muttered Raskolnikov angrily.

Svidrigaïlov laughed heartily; finally he called Philip, paid his bill, and began getting up.

"I say, but I am drunk, *assez causé*," he said. "It's been a pleasure."

"I should rather think it must be a pleasure!" cried Raskolnikov, getting up. "No doubt it is a pleasure for a worn-out profligate to describe such adventures with a monstrous project of the same sort in his mind—especially under such circumstances and to such a man as me.... It's stimulating!"

"Well, if you come to that," Svidrigaïlov answered, scrutinising Raskolnikov with some surprise, "if you come to that, you are a thorough cynic yourself. You've plenty to make you so, anyway. You can understand a great deal... and you can do a great deal too. But enough. I sincerely regret not having had more talk with you, but I shan't lose sight of you.... Only wait a bit."

Svidrigaïlov walked out of the restaurant. Raskolnikov walked out after him. Svidrigaïlov was not however very drunk, the wine had affected him for a moment, but it was passing off every minute. He was preoccupied with something of importance and was frowning. He was apparently excited and uneasy in anticipation of something. His manner to Raskolnikov had changed during the last few minutes, and he was ruder and more sneering every moment. Raskolnikov noticed all this, and he too was uneasy. He became very suspicious of Svidrigaïlov and resolved to follow him.

They came out on to the pavement.

"You go to the right, and I to the left, or if you like, the other way. Only *adieu, mon plaisir*, may we meet again."

And he walked to the right towards the Hay Market.

Raskolnikov walked after him.

"What's this?" cried Svidrigaïlov turning round, "I thought I said ..."

"It means that I am not going to lose sight of you now."

"What?"

Both stood still and gazed at one another, as though measuring their strength.

"From all your half tipsy stories," Raskolnikov observed harshly, "I am *positive* that you have not given up your designs on my sister, but are pursuing them more actively than ever. I have learnt that my sister received a letter this morning. You have hardly been able to sit still all this time.... You may have unearthed a wife on the way, but that means nothing. I should like to make certain myself."

Raskolnikov could hardly have said himself what he wanted and of what he wished to make certain.

"Upon my word! I'll call the police!"

"Call away!"

Again they stood for a minute facing each other. At last Svidrigaïlov's face changed. Having satisfied himself that Raskolnikov was not frightened at his threat, he assumed a mirthful and friendly air.

"What a fellow! I purposely refrained from referring to your affair, though I am devoured by curiosity. It's a fantastic affair. I've put it off till another time, but you're enough to rouse the dead.... Well, let us go, only I warn you beforehand I am only going home for a moment, to get some money; then I shall lock up the flat, take a cab and go to spend the evening at the Islands. Now, now are you going to follow me?"

"I'm coming to your lodgings, not to see you but Sofya Semyonovna, to say I'm sorry not to have been at the funeral."

"That's as you like, but Sofya Semyonovna is not at home. She has taken the three children to an old lady of high rank, the patroness of some orphan asylums, whom I used to know years ago. I charmed the old lady by depositing a sum of money with her to provide for the three children of Katerina Ivanovna and subscribing to the institution as well. I told her too the story of Sofya Semyonovna in full detail, suppressing nothing. It produced an indescribable effect on her. That's why Sofya Semyonovna has been invited to call today at the X—— Hotel where the lady is staying for the time."

"No matter, I'll come all the same."

"As you like, it's nothing to me, but I won't come with you; here we are at home. By the way, I am convinced that you regard me with suspicion just because I have shown such delicacy and have not so far troubled you with questions ... you understand? It struck you as extraordinary; I don't mind betting it's that. Well, it teaches one to show delicacy!"

"And to listen at doors!"

"Ah, that's it, is it?" laughed Svidrigaïlov. "Yes, I should have been surprised if you had let that pass after all that has happened. Ha-ha! Though I did understand something of the pranks you had been up to and were telling Sofya Semyonovna about, what was the meaning of it? Perhaps I am quite behind the times and can't understand. For goodness' sake, explain it, my dear boy. Expound the latest theories!"

"You couldn't have heard anything. You're making it all up!"

"But I'm not talking about that (though I did hear something). No, I'm talking of the way you keep sighing and groaning now. The Schiller in you is in revolt every moment, and now you tell me not to listen at doors. If that's how you feel, go and inform the police that you had this mischance: you made a little mistake in your theory. But if you are convinced that one mustn't listen at doors, but one may murder old women at one's pleasure, you'd better be off to America and make haste. Run, young man! There may still be time. I'm speaking sincerely. Haven't you the money? I'll give you the fare."

"I'm not thinking of that at all," Raskolnikov interrupted with disgust.

"I understand (but don't put yourself out, don't discuss it if you don't want to). I understand the questions you are worrying over—moral ones, aren't they? Duties of citizen and man? Lay them all aside. They are nothing to you now, ha-ha! You'll say you are still a man and a citizen. If so you ought not to have got into this coil. It's no use taking up a job you are not fit for. Well, you'd better shoot yourself, or don't you want to?"

"You seem trying to enrage me, to make me leave you."

"What a queer fellow! But here we are. Welcome to the staircase. You see, that's the way to Sofya Semyonovna. Look, there is no one at home. Don't you believe me? Ask Kapernaumov. She leaves the key with him. Here is Madame de Kapernaumov herself. Hey, what? She is rather deaf. Has she gone out? Where? Did you hear? She is not in and won't be till late in the evening probably. Well, come to my room; you wanted to come and see me, didn't you? Here we are. Madame Resslich's not at home. She is a woman who is always busy, an excellent woman I assure you.... She might have been of use to you if you had been a little more sensible. Now, see! I take this five-percent bond out of the bureau—see what a lot I've got of them still—this one will be turned into cash today. I mustn't waste any more time. The bureau is locked, the flat is locked, and here we are again on the stairs. Shall we take a cab? I'm going to the Islands. Would you like a lift? I'll take this carriage. Ah, you refuse? You are tired of it! Come for a drive! I believe it will come on to rain. Never mind, we'll put down the hood...."

Svidrigaïlov was already in the carriage. Raskolnikov decided that his suspicions were at least for that moment unjust. Without answering a word he turned and walked back towards the Hay Market. If he had only turned round on his way he might have seen Svidrigaïlov get out not a hundred paces off, dismiss the cab and walk along the pavement. But he had turned the corner and could see nothing. Intense disgust drew him away from Svidrigaïlov.

"To think that I could for one instant have looked for help from that coarse brute, that depraved sensualist and blackguard!" he cried.

Raskolnikov's judgment was uttered too lightly and hastily: there was something about Svidrigaïlov which gave him a certain original, even a mysterious character. As concerned his sister, Raskolnikov was convinced that Svidrigaïlov would not leave her in peace. But it was too tiresome and unbearable to go on thinking and thinking about this.

When he was alone, he had not gone twenty paces before he sank, as usual, into deep thought. On the bridge he stood by the railing and began gazing at the water. And his sister was standing close by him.

He met her at the entrance to the bridge, but passed by without seeing her. Dounia had never met him like this in the street before and was struck with dismay. She stood still and did not know whether to call to him or not. Suddenly she saw Svidrigaïlov coming quickly from the direction of the Hay Market.

He seemed to be approaching cautiously. He did not go on to the bridge, but stood aside on the pavement, doing all he could to avoid Raskolnikov's seeing him. He had observed Dounia for some time and had been making signs to her. She fancied he was signalling to beg her not to speak to her brother, but to come to him.

That was what Dounia did. She stole by her brother and went up to Svidrigaïlov.

"Let us make haste away," Svidrigaïlov whispered to her, "I don't want Rodion Romanovitch to know of our meeting. I must tell you I've been sitting with him in the restaurant close by, where he looked me up and I had great difficulty in getting rid of him. He has somehow heard of my letter to you and suspects something. It wasn't you who told him, of course, but if not you, who then?"

"Well, we've turned the corner now," Dounia interrupted, "and my brother won't see us. I have to tell you that I am going no further with you. Speak to me here. You can tell it all in the street."

"In the first place, I can't say it in the street; secondly, you must hear Sofya Semyonovna too; and, thirdly, I will show you some papers.... Oh well, if you won't agree to come with me, I shall refuse to give any explanation and go away at once. But I beg you not to forget that a very curious secret of your beloved brother's is entirely in my keeping."

Dounia stood still, hesitating, and looked at Svidrigaïlov with searching eyes.

"What are you afraid of?" he observed quietly. "The town is not the country. And even in the country you did me more harm than I did you."

"Have you prepared Sofya Semyonovna?"

"No, I have not said a word to her and am not quite certain whether she is at home now. But most likely she is. She has buried her stepmother today: she is not likely to go visiting on such a day. For the time I don't want to speak to anyone about it and I half regret having spoken to you. The slightest indiscretion is as bad as betrayal in a thing like this. I live there in that house, we are coming to it. That's the porter of our house—he knows me very well; you see, he's bowing; he sees I'm coming with a lady and no doubt he has noticed your face already and you will be glad of that if you are afraid of me and suspicious. Excuse my putting things so coarsely. I haven't a flat to myself; Sofya Semyonovna's room is next to mine—she lodges in the next flat. The whole floor is let out in lodgings. Why are you frightened like a child? Am I really so terrible?"

Svidrigaïlov's lips were twisted in a condescending smile; but he was in no smiling mood. His heart was throbbing and he could scarcely breathe. He spoke rather loud to cover his growing excitement. But Dounia did not notice this peculiar excitement, she was so irritated by his remark that she was frightened of him like a child and that he was so terrible to her.

"Though I know that you are not a man... of honour, I am not in the least afraid of you. Lead the way," she said with apparent composure, but her face was very pale.

Svidrigaïlov stopped at Sonia's room.

"Allow me to inquire whether she is at home.... She is not. How unfortunate! But I know she may come quite soon. If she's gone out, it can only be to see a lady about the orphans. Their mother is dead.... I've been meddling and making arrangements for them. If Sofya Semyonovna does not come back in ten minutes, I will send her to you, today if you like. This is my flat. These are my two rooms. Madame Resslich, my landlady, has the next room. Now, look this way. I will show you my chief piece of evidence: this door from my bedroom leads into two perfectly empty rooms, which are to let. Here they are... You must look into them with some attention."

Svidrigaïlov occupied two fairly large furnished rooms. Dounia was looking about her mistrustfully, but saw nothing special in the furniture or position of the rooms. Yet there was something to observe, for instance, that Svidrigaïlov's flat was exactly between two sets of almost uninhabited apartments. His rooms were not entered directly from the passage, but through the landlady's two almost empty rooms. Unlocking a door leading out of his bedroom, Svidrigaïlov showed Dounia the two empty rooms that were to let. Dounia stopped in the doorway, not knowing what she was called to look upon, but Svidrigaïlov hastened to explain.

"Look here, at this second large room. Notice that door, it's locked. By the door stands a chair, the only one in the two rooms. I brought it from my rooms so as to listen more conveniently. Just the other side of the door is Sofya Semyonovna's table; she sat there talking to Rodion Romanovitch. And I sat here listening on two successive evenings, for two hours each time—and of course I was able to learn something, what do you think?"

"You listened?"

"Yes, I did. Now come back to my room; we can't sit down here."

He brought Avdotya Romanovna back into his sitting-room and offered her a chair. He sat down at the opposite side of the table, at least seven feet from her, but probably there was the same glow in his eyes which had once frightened Dounia so much. She shuddered and once more looked about her distrustfully. It was an involuntary gesture; she evidently did not wish to betray her uneasiness. But the secluded position of Svidrigaïlov's lodging had suddenly struck her. She wanted to ask whether his landlady at least were at home, but pride kept her from asking. Moreover, she had another trouble in her heart incomparably greater than fear for herself. She was in great distress.

"Here is your letter," she said, laying it on the table. "Can it be true what you write? You hint at a crime committed, you say, by my brother. You hint at it too clearly; you daren't deny it now. I must tell you that I'd heard of this stupid story before you wrote and don't believe a word of it. It's a disgusting and ridiculous suspicion. I know the story and why and how it was invented. You can have no proofs. You promised to prove it. Speak! But let me warn you that I don't believe you! I don't believe you!"

Dounia said this, speaking hurriedly, and for an instant the colour rushed to her face.

"If you didn't believe it, how could you risk coming alone to my rooms? Why have you come? Simply from curiosity?"

"Don't torment me. Speak, speak!"

"There's no denying that you are a brave girl. Upon my word, I thought you would have asked Mr. Razumihin to escort you here. But he was not with you nor anywhere near. I was on the lookout. It's spirited of you, it proves you wanted to spare Rodion Romanovitch. But everything is divine in you.... About your brother, what am I to say to you? You've just seen him yourself. What did you think of him?"

"Surely that's not the only thing you are building on?"

"No, not on that, but on his own words. He came here on two successive evenings to see Sofya Semyonovna. I've shown you where they sat. He made a full confession to her. He is a murderer. He killed an old woman, a pawnbroker, with whom he had pawned things himself. He killed her sister too, a pedlar woman called Lizaveta, who happened to come in while he was murdering her sister. He killed them with an axe he brought with him. He murdered them to rob them and he did rob them. He took money and various things.... He told all this, word for word, to Sofya Semyonovna, the only person who knows his secret. But she has had no share by word or deed in the murder; she was as horrified at it as you are now. Don't be anxious, she won't betray him."

"It cannot be," muttered Dounia, with white lips. She gasped for breath. "It cannot be. There was not the slightest cause, no sort of ground.... It's a lie, a lie!"

"He robbed her, that was the cause, he took money and things. It's true that by his own admission he made no use of the money or things, but hid them under a stone, where they are now. But that was because he dared not make use of them."

"But how could he steal, rob? How could he dream of it?" cried Dounia, and she jumped up from the chair. "Why, you know him, and you've seen him, can he be a thief?"

She seemed to be imploring Svidrigaïlov; she had entirely forgotten her fear.

"There are thousands and millions of combinations and possibilities, Avdotya Romanovna. A thief steals and knows he is a scoundrel, but I've heard of a gentleman who broke open the mail. Who knows, very likely he thought he was doing a gentlemanly thing! Of course I should not have believed it myself if I'd been told of it as you have, but I believe my own ears. He explained all the causes of it to Sofya Semyonovna too, but she did not believe her ears at first, yet she believed her own eyes at last."

"What... were the causes?"

"It's a long story, Avdotya Romanovna. Here's... how shall I tell you?—A theory of a sort, the same one by which I for instance consider that a single misdeed is permissible if the principal aim is right, a solitary wrongdoing and hundreds of good deeds! It's galling too, of course, for a young man of gifts and overweening pride to know that if he had, for instance, a paltry three thousand, his whole career, his whole future would be differently shaped and yet not to have that three thousand. Add to that, nervous irritability from hunger, from lodging in a hole, from rags, from a vivid sense of the charm of his social position and his sister's and mother's position too. Above all, vanity, pride and vanity, though goodness knows he may have good qualities too.... I am not blaming him, please don't think it; besides, it's not my business. A special little theory came in too—a theory of a sort—dividing mankind, you see, into material and superior persons, that is

266

persons to whom the law does not apply owing to their superiority, who make laws for the rest of mankind, the material, that is. It's all right as a theory, *une théorie comme une autre*. Napoleon attracted him tremendously, that is, what affected him was that a great many men of genius have not hesitated at wrongdoing, but have overstepped the law without thinking about it. He seems to have fancied that he was a genius too—that is, he was convinced of it for a time. He has suffered a great deal and is still suffering from the idea that he could make a theory, but was incapable of boldly overstepping the law, and so he is not a man of genius. And that's humiliating for a young man of any pride, in our day especially...."

"But remorse? You deny him any moral feeling then? Is he like that?"

"Ah, Avdotya Romanovna, everything is in a muddle now; not that it was ever in very good order. Russians in general are broad in their ideas, Avdotya Romanovna, broad like their land and exceedingly disposed to the fantastic, the chaotic. But it's a misfortune to be broad without a special genius. Do you remember what a lot of talk we had together on this subject, sitting in the evenings on the terrace after supper? Why, you used to reproach me with breadth! Who knows, perhaps we were talking at the very time when he was lying here thinking over his plan. There are no sacred traditions amongst us, especially in the educated class, Avdotya Romanovna. At the best someone will make them up somehow for himself out of books or from some old chronicle. But those are for the most part the learned and all old fogeys, so that it would be almost ill-bred in a man of society. You know my opinions in general, though. I never blame anyone. I do nothing at all, I persevere in that. But we've talked of this more than once before. I was so happy indeed as to interest you in my opinions.... You are very pale, Avdotya Romanovna."

"I know his theory. I read that article of his about men to whom all is permitted. Razumihin brought it to me."

"Mr. Razumihin? Your brother's article? In a magazine? Is there such an article? I didn't know. It must be interesting. But where are you going, Avdotya Romanovna?"

"I want to see Sofya Semyonovna," Dounia articulated faintly. "How do I go to her? She has come in, perhaps. I must see her at once. Perhaps she..."

Avdotya Romanovna could not finish. Her breath literally failed her.

"Sofya Semyonovna will not be back till night, at least I believe not. She was to have been back at once, but if not, then she will not be in till quite late."

"Ah, then you are lying! I see... you were lying... lying all the time.... I don't believe you! I don't believe you!" cried Dounia, completely losing her head.

Almost fainting, she sank on to a chair which Svidrigaïlov made haste to give her.

"Avdotya Romanovna, what is it? Control yourself! Here is some water. Drink a little...."

He sprinkled some water over her. Dounia shuddered and came to herself.

"It has acted violently," Svidrigaïlov muttered to himself, frowning. "Avdotya Romanovna, calm yourself! Believe me, he has friends. We will save him. Would you like me to take him abroad? I have money, I can get a ticket in three days. And as for the murder, he will do all sorts of good deeds yet, to atone for it. Calm yourself. He may become a great man yet. Well, how are you? How do you feel?"

"Cruel man! To be able to jeer at it! Let me go..."

"Where are you going?"

"To him. Where is he? Do you know? Why is this door locked? We came in at that door and now it is locked. When did you manage to lock it?"

"We couldn't be shouting all over the flat on such a subject. I am far from jeering; it's simply that I'm sick of talking like this. But how can you go in such a state? Do you want to betray him? You will drive him to fury, and he will give himself up. Let me tell you, he is already being watched; they are already on his track. You will simply be giving him away. Wait a little: I saw him and was talking to him just now. He can still be saved. Wait a bit, sit down; let us think it over together. I asked you to come in order to discuss it alone with you and to consider it thoroughly. But do sit down!"

"How can you save him? Can he really be saved?"

Dounia sat down. Svidrigaïlov sat down beside her.

"It all depends on you, on you, on you alone," he began with glowing eyes, almost in a whisper and hardly able to utter the words for emotion.

Dounia drew back from him in alarm. He too was trembling all over.

"You... one word from you, and he is saved. I... I'll save him. I have money and friends. I'll send him away at once. I'll get a passport, two passports, one for him and one for me. I have friends... capable people.... If you like, I'll take a passport for you... for your mother.... What do you want with Razumihin? I love you too.... I love you beyond everything.... Let me kiss the hem of your dress, let me, let me.... The very rustle of it is too much for me. Tell me, 'do that,' and I'll do it. I'll do everything. I will do the impossible. What you believe, I will believe. I'll do anything—anything! Don't, don't look at me like that. Do you know that you are killing me?..."

He was almost beginning to rave.... Something seemed suddenly to go to his head. Dounia jumped up and rushed to the door.

"Open it! Open it!" she called, shaking the door. "Open it! Is there no one there?"

Svidrigaïlov got up and came to himself. His still trembling lips slowly broke into an angry mocking smile.

"There is no one at home," he said quietly and emphatically. "The landlady has gone out, and it's waste of time to shout like that. You are only exciting yourself uselessly."

"Where is the key? Open the door at once, at once, base man!"

"I have lost the key and cannot find it."

"This is an outrage," cried Dounia, turning pale as death. She rushed to the furthest corner, where she made haste to barricade herself with a little table.

She did not scream, but she fixed her eyes on her tormentor and watched every movement he made.

Svidrigaïlov remained standing at the other end of the room facing her. He was positively composed, at least in appearance, but his face was pale as before. The mocking smile did not leave his face.

"You spoke of outrage just now, Avdotya Romanovna. In that case you may be sure I've taken measures. Sofya Semyonovna is not at home. The Kapernaumovs are far away—there are five locked rooms between. I am at least twice as strong as you are and I have nothing to fear, besides. For you could not complain afterwards. You surely would not be willing actually to betray your brother? Besides, no one would believe you. How should a girl have come alone to visit a solitary man in his lodgings? So that even if you do sacrifice your brother, you could prove nothing. It is very difficult to prove an assault, Avdotya Romanovna."

"Scoundrel!" whispered Dounia indignantly.

"As you like, but observe I was only speaking by way of a general proposition. It's my personal conviction that you are perfectly right—violence is hateful. I only spoke to show you that you need have no remorse even if... you were willing to save your brother of your own accord, as I suggest to you. You would be simply submitting to circumstances, to violence, in fact, if we must use that word. Think about it. Your brother's and your mother's fate are in your hands. I will be your slave... all my life... I will wait here."

Svidrigaïlov sat down on the sofa about eight steps from Dounia. She had not the slightest doubt now of his unbending determination. Besides, she knew him. Suddenly she pulled out of her pocket a revolver, cocked it and laid it in her hand on the table. Svidrigaïlov jumped up.

"Aha! So that's it, is it?" he cried, surprised but smiling maliciously. "Well, that completely alters the aspect of affairs. You've made things wonderfully easier for me, Avdotya Romanovna. But where did you get the revolver? Was it Mr. Razumihin? Why, it's my revolver, an old friend! And how I've hunted for it! The shooting lessons I've given you in the country have not been thrown away."

"It's not your revolver, it belonged to Marfa Petrovna, whom you killed, wretch! There was nothing of yours in her house. I took it when I began to suspect what you were capable of. If you dare to advance one step, I swear I'll kill you." She was frantic.

"But your brother? I ask from curiosity," said Svidrigaïlov, still standing where he was.

"Inform, if you want to! Don't stir! Don't come nearer! I'll shoot! You poisoned your wife, I know; you are a murderer yourself!" She held the revolver ready.

"Are you so positive I poisoned Marfa Petrovna?"

"You did! You hinted it yourself; you talked to me of poison.... I know you went to get it... you had it in readiness.... It was your doing.... It must have been your doing.... Scoundrel!"

"Even if that were true, it would have been for your sake... you would have been the cause."

"You are lying! I hated you always, always...."

"Oho, Avdotya Romanovna! You seem to have forgotten how you softened to me in the heat of propaganda. I saw it in your eyes. Do you remember that moonlight night, when the nightingale was singing?"

"That's a lie," there was a flash of fury in Dounia's eyes, "that's a lie and a libel!"

"A lie? Well, if you like, it's a lie. I made it up. Women ought not to be reminded of such things," he smiled. "I know you will shoot, you pretty wild creature. Well, shoot away!"

Dounia raised the revolver, and deadly pale, gazed at him, measuring the distance and awaiting the first movement on his part. Her lower lip was white and quivering and her big black eyes flashed like fire. He had never seen her so handsome. The fire glowing in her eyes at the moment she raised the revolver seemed to kindle him and there was a pang of anguish in his heart. He took a step forward and a shot rang out. The bullet grazed his hair and flew into the wall behind. He stood still and laughed softly.

"The wasp has stung me. She aimed straight at my head. What's this? Blood?" he pulled out his handkerchief to wipe the blood, which flowed in a thin stream down his right temple. The bullet seemed to have just grazed the skin.

Dounia lowered the revolver and looked at Svidrigaïlov not so much in terror as in a sort of wild amazement. She seemed not to understand what she was doing and what was going on.

"Well, you missed! Fire again, I'll wait," said Svidrigaïlov softly, still smiling, but gloomily. "If you go on like that, I shall have time to seize you before you cock again."

Dounia started, quickly cocked the pistol and again raised it.

"Let me be," she cried in despair. "I swear I'll shoot again. I... I'll kill you."

"Well... at three paces you can hardly help it. But if you don't... then." His eyes flashed and he took two steps forward. Dounia shot again: it missed fire.

"You haven't loaded it properly. Never mind, you have another charge there. Get it ready, I'll wait."

He stood facing her, two paces away, waiting and gazing at her with wild determination, with feverishly passionate, stubborn, set eyes. Dounia saw that he would sooner die than let her go. "And... now, of course she would kill him, at two paces!" Suddenly she flung away the revolver.

"She's dropped it!" said Svidrigaïlov with surprise, and he drew a deep breath. A weight seemed to have rolled from his heart—perhaps not only the fear of death; indeed he may scarcely have felt it at that moment. It was the deliverance from another feeling, darker and more bitter, which he could not himself have defined.

He went to Dounia and gently put his arm round her waist. She did not resist, but, trembling like a leaf, looked at him with suppliant eyes. He tried to say something, but his lips moved without being able to utter a sound.

"Let me go," Dounia implored. Svidrigaïlov shuddered. Her voice now was quite different.

"Then you don't love me?" he asked softly. Dounia shook her head.

"And... and you can't? Never?" he whispered in despair.

"Never!"

There followed a moment of terrible, dumb struggle in the heart of Svidrigaïlov. He looked at her with an indescribable gaze. Suddenly he withdrew his arm, turned quickly to the window and stood facing it. Another moment passed.

"Here's the key."

He took it out of the left pocket of his coat and laid it on the table behind him, without turning or looking at Dounia.

"Take it! Make haste!"

269

He looked stubbornly out of the window. Dounia went up to the table to take the key.

"Make haste! Make haste!" repeated Svidrigaïlov, still without turning or moving. But there seemed a terrible significance in the tone of that "make haste."

Dounia understood it, snatched up the key, flew to the door, unlocked it quickly and rushed out of the room. A minute later, beside herself, she ran out on to the canal bank in the direction of X—— Bridge.

Svidrigaïlov remained three minutes standing at the window. At last he slowly turned, looked about him and passed his hand over his forehead. A strange smile contorted his face, a pitiful, sad, weak smile, a smile of despair. The blood, which was already getting dry, smeared his hand. He looked angrily at it, then wetted a towel and washed his temple. The revolver which Dounia had flung away lay near the door and suddenly caught his eye. He picked it up and examined it. It was a little pocket three-barrel revolver of old-fashioned construction. There were still two charges and one capsule left in it. It could be fired again. He thought a little, put the revolver in his pocket, took his hat and went out.

He spent that evening till ten o'clock going from one low haunt to another. Katia too turned up and sang another gutter song, how a certain
"villain and tyrant,

began kissing Katia."
Svidrigaïlov treated Katia and the organ-grinder and some singers and the waiters and two little clerks. He was particularly drawn to these clerks by the fact that they both had crooked noses, one bent to the left and the other to the right. They took him finally to a pleasure garden, where he paid for their entrance. There was one lanky three-year-old pine-tree and three bushes in the garden, besides a "Vauxhall," which was in reality a drinking-bar where tea too was served, and there were a few green tables and chairs standing round it. A chorus of wretched singers and a drunken but exceedingly depressed German clown from Munich with a red nose entertained the public. The clerks quarrelled with some other clerks and a fight seemed imminent. Svidrigaïlov was chosen to decide the dispute. He listened to them for a quarter of an hour, but they shouted so loud that there was no possibility of understanding them. The only fact that seemed certain was that one of them had stolen something and had even succeeded in selling it on the spot to a Jew, but would not share the spoil with his companion. Finally it appeared that the stolen object was a teaspoon belonging to the Vauxhall. It was missed and the affair began to seem troublesome. Svidrigaïlov paid for the spoon, got up, and walked out of the garden. It was about six o'clock. He had not drunk a drop of wine all this time and had ordered tea more for the sake of appearances than anything.

It was a dark and stifling evening. Threatening storm-clouds came over the sky about ten o'clock. There was a clap of thunder, and the rain came down like a waterfall. The water fell not in drops, but beat on the earth in streams. There were flashes of lightning every minute and each flash lasted while one could count five.

Drenched to the skin, he went home, locked himself in, opened the bureau, took out all his money and tore up two or three papers. Then, putting the money in his pocket, he was about to change his clothes, but, looking out of the window and listening to the thunder and the rain, he gave up the idea, took up his hat and went out of the room without locking the door. He went straight to Sonia. She was at home.

She was not alone: the four Kapernaumov children were with her. She was giving them tea. She received Svidrigaïlov in respectful silence, looking wonderingly at his soaking clothes. The children all ran away at once in indescribable terror.

Svidrigaïlov sat down at the table and asked Sonia to sit beside him. She timidly prepared to listen.

"I may be going to America, Sofya Semyonovna," said Svidrigaïlov, "and as I am probably seeing you for the last time, I have come to make some arrangements. Well, did you see the lady today? I know what she said to you, you need not tell me." (Sonia made a movement and blushed.) "Those people have their own way of doing things. As to your sisters and your brother, they are really provided for and the money assigned to them I've put into safe keeping and have received acknowledgments. You had better take charge of the receipts, in case anything happens. Here, take them! Well now, that's settled. Here are three five-percent bonds to the value of three thousand roubles. Take those for yourself, entirely for yourself, and let that be strictly between ourselves, so that no one knows of it, whatever you hear. You will need the money, for to go on living in the old way, Sofya Semyonovna, is bad, and besides there is no need for it now."

"I am so much indebted to you, and so are the children and my stepmother," said Sonia hurriedly, "and if I've said so little… please don't consider…"

"That's enough! that's enough!"

"But as for the money, Arkady Ivanovitch, I am very grateful to you, but I don't need it now. I can always earn my own living. Don't think me ungrateful. If you are so charitable, that money…."

"It's for you, for you, Sofya Semyonovna, and please don't waste words over it. I haven't time for it. You will want it. Rodion Romanovitch has two alternatives: a bullet in the brain or Siberia." (Sonia looked wildly at him, and started.) "Don't be uneasy, I know all about it from himself and I am not a gossip; I won't tell anyone. It was good advice when you told him to give himself up and confess. It would be much better for him. Well, if it turns out to be Siberia, he will go and you will follow him. That's so, isn't it? And if so, you'll need money. You'll need it for him, do you understand? Giving it to you is the same as my giving it to him. Besides, you promised Amalia Ivanovna to pay what's owing. I heard you. How can you undertake such obligations so heedlessly, Sofya Semyonovna? It was Katerina Ivanovna's debt and not yours, so you ought not to have taken any notice of the German woman. You can't get through the world like that. If you are ever questioned about me—tomorrow or the day after you will be asked—don't say anything about my coming to see you now and don't show the money to anyone or say a word about it. Well, now goodbye." (He got up.) "My greetings to Rodion Romanovitch. By the way, you'd better put the money for the present in Mr. Razumihin's keeping. You know Mr. Razumihin? Of course you do. He's not a bad fellow. Take it to him tomorrow or… when the time comes. And till then, hide it carefully."

Sonia too jumped up from her chair and looked in dismay at Svidrigaïlov. She longed to speak, to ask a question, but for the first moments she did not dare and did not know how to begin.

"How can you… how can you be going now, in such rain?"

"Why, be starting for America, and be stopped by rain! Ha, ha! Goodbye, Sofya Semyonovna, my dear! Live and live long, you will be of use to others. By the way… tell Mr. Razumihin I send my greetings to him. Tell him Arkady Ivanovitch Svidrigaïlov sends his greetings. Be sure to."

He went out, leaving Sonia in a state of wondering anxiety and vague apprehension.

It appeared afterwards that on the same evening, at twenty past eleven, he made another very eccentric and unexpected visit. The rain still persisted. Drenched to the skin, he walked into the little flat where the parents of his betrothed lived, in Third Street in Vassilyevsky Island. He knocked some time before he was admitted, and his visit at first caused great perturbation; but Svidrigaïlov could be very fascinating when he liked, so that the first, and indeed very intelligent surmise of the sensible parents that Svidrigaïlov had probably had so much to drink that he did not know what he was doing vanished immediately. The decrepit father was wheeled in to see Svidrigaïlov by the tender and sensible mother, who as usual began the conversation with various irrelevant questions. She never asked a direct question, but began by smiling and rubbing her hands and then, if she were obliged to ascertain something—for instance, when Svidrigaïlov would like to have the wedding—she would begin by interested and almost eager questions about Paris and the court life there, and only by degrees brought the conversation round to Third Street. On other occasions this had of course been very impressive, but this time Arkady Ivanovitch seemed particularly impatient, and insisted on seeing his betrothed at once, though he had been informed, to begin with, that she had already gone to bed. The girl of course appeared.

Svidrigaïlov informed her at once that he was obliged by very important affairs to leave Petersburg for a time, and therefore brought her fifteen thousand roubles and begged her accept them as a present from him, as he had long been intending to make her this trifling present before their wedding. The logical connection of the present with his immediate departure and the absolute necessity of visiting them for that purpose in pouring rain at midnight was not made clear. But it all went off very well; even the inevitable ejaculations of wonder and regret, the inevitable questions were extraordinarily few and restrained. On the other hand, the gratitude expressed was most glowing and was reinforced by tears from the most sensible of mothers. Svidrigaïlov got up, laughed, kissed his betrothed, patted her cheek, declared he would soon come back, and noticing in her eyes, together with childish curiosity, a sort of earnest dumb inquiry, reflected and kissed her again, though he felt sincere anger inwardly at the thought that his present would be immediately locked up in the keeping of the most sensible of mothers. He went away, leaving them all in a state of extraordinary excitement, but the tender mamma, speaking quietly in a half whisper, settled some of the most important of their doubts, concluding that Svidrigaïlov was a great man, a man of great affairs and connections and of great wealth—there was no knowing what he had in his mind. He would start off on a journey and give away money just as the fancy took him, so that there was nothing surprising about it. Of course it was strange that he was wet through, but Englishmen, for instance, are even more eccentric, and all these people of high society didn't think of what was said of them and didn't stand on ceremony. Possibly, indeed, he came like that on purpose to show that he was not afraid of anyone. Above all, not a word should be said about it, for God knows what might come of it, and the money must be locked up, and it was most fortunate that Fedosya, the cook, had not left the kitchen. And above all not a word must be said to that old cat, Madame Resslich, and so on and so on. They sat up whispering till two o'clock, but the girl went to bed much earlier, amazed and rather sorrowful.

Svidrigaïlov meanwhile, exactly at midnight, crossed the bridge on the way back to the mainland. The rain had ceased and there was a roaring wind. He began shivering, and for one moment he gazed at the black waters of the Little Neva with a look of special interest, even inquiry. But he soon felt it very cold, standing by the water; he turned and went towards Y——— Prospect. He walked along that endless street for a long time, almost half an hour, more than once stumbling in the dark on the wooden pavement, but continually looking for something on the right side of the street. He had noticed passing through this street lately that there was a hotel somewhere towards the end, built of wood, but fairly large, and its name he remembered was something like Adrianople. He was not mistaken: the hotel was so conspicuous in that Godforsaken place that he could not fail to see it even in the dark. It was a long, blackened wooden building, and in spite of the late hour there were lights in the windows and signs of life within. He went in and asked a ragged fellow who met him in the corridor for a room. The latter, scanning Svidrigaïlov, pulled himself together and led him at once to a close and tiny room in the distance, at the end of the corridor, under the stairs. There was no other, all were occupied. The ragged fellow looked inquiringly.

"Is there tea?" asked Svidrigaïlov.

"Yes, sir."

"What else is there?"

"Veal, vodka, savouries."

"Bring me tea and veal."

"And you want nothing else?" he asked with apparent surprise.

"Nothing, nothing."

The ragged man went away, completely disillusioned.

"It must be a nice place," thought Svidrigaïlov. "How was it I didn't know it? I expect I look as if I came from a *café chantant* and have had some adventure on the way. It would be interesting to know who stayed here?"

He lighted the candle and looked at the room more carefully. It was a room so low-pitched that Svidrigaïlov could only just stand up in it; it had one window; the bed, which was very dirty, and the plain-stained chair and table almost filled it up. The walls looked as though they were made of planks, covered with shabby paper, so torn and dusty that the pattern was indistinguishable, though the general colour—yellow—could still be made out. One of the walls was cut short by the sloping ceiling, though the room was not an attic but just under the stairs.

Svidrigaïlov set down the candle, sat down on the bed and sank into thought. But a strange persistent murmur which sometimes rose to a shout in the next room attracted his attention. The murmur had not ceased from the moment he entered the room. He listened: someone was upbraiding and almost tearfully scolding, but he heard only one voice.

273

Svidrigaïlov got up, shaded the light with his hand and at once he saw light through a crack in the wall; he went up and peeped through. The room, which was somewhat larger than his, had two occupants. One of them, a very curly-headed man with a red inflamed face, was standing in the pose of an orator, without his coat, with his legs wide apart to preserve his balance, and smiting himself on the breast. He reproached the other with being a beggar, with having no standing whatever. He declared that he had taken the other out of the gutter and he could turn him out when he liked, and that only the finger of Providence sees it all. The object of his reproaches was sitting in a chair, and had the air of a man who wants dreadfully to sneeze, but can't. He sometimes turned sheepish and befogged eyes on the speaker, but obviously had not the slightest idea what he was talking about and scarcely heard it. A candle was burning down on the table; there were wineglasses, a nearly empty bottle of vodka, bread and cucumber, and glasses with the dregs of stale tea. After gazing attentively at this, Svidrigaïlov turned away indifferently and sat down on the bed.

The ragged attendant, returning with the tea, could not resist asking him again whether he didn't want anything more, and again receiving a negative reply, finally withdrew. Svidrigaïlov made haste to drink a glass of tea to warm himself, but could not eat anything. He began to feel feverish. He took off his coat and, wrapping himself in the blanket, lay down on the bed. He was annoyed. "It would have been better to be well for the occasion," he thought with a smile. The room was close, the candle burnt dimly, the wind was roaring outside, he heard a mouse scratching in the corner and the room smelt of mice and of leather. He lay in a sort of reverie: one thought followed another. He felt a longing to fix his imagination on something. "It must be a garden under the window," he thought. "There's a sound of trees. How I dislike the sound of trees on a stormy night, in the dark! They give one a horrid feeling." He remembered how he had disliked it when he passed Petrovsky Park just now. This reminded him of the bridge over the Little Neva and he felt cold again as he had when standing there. "I never have liked water," he thought, "even in a landscape," and he suddenly smiled again at a strange idea: "Surely now all these questions of taste and comfort ought not to matter, but I've become more particular, like an animal that picks out a special place... for such an occasion. I ought to have gone into the Petrovsky Park! I suppose it seemed dark, cold, ha-ha! As though I were seeking pleasant sensations!... By the way, why haven't I put out the candle?" he blew it out. "They've gone to bed next door," he thought, not seeing the light at the crack. "Well, now, Marfa Petrovna, now is the time for you to turn up; it's dark, and the very time and place for you. But now you won't come!"

He suddenly recalled how, an hour before carrying out his design on Dounia, he had recommended Raskolnikov to trust her to Razumihin's keeping. "I suppose I really did say it, as Raskolnikov guessed, to tease myself. But what a rogue that Raskolnikov is! He's gone through a good deal. He may be a successful rogue in time when he's got over his nonsense. But now he's *too* eager for life. These young men are contemptible on that point. But, hang the fellow! Let him please himself, it's nothing to do with me."

He could not get to sleep. By degrees Dounia's image rose before him, and a shudder ran over him. "No, I must give up all that now," he thought, rousing himself. "I must think of something else. It's queer and funny. I never had a great hatred for anyone, I never particularly desired to avenge myself even, and that's a bad sign, a bad sign, a bad sign. I never liked quarrelling either, and never lost my temper—that's a bad sign too. And the promises I made her just now, too—Damnation! But—who knows?—perhaps she would have made a new man of me somehow...."

He ground his teeth and sank into silence again. Again Dounia's image rose before him, just as she was when, after shooting the first time, she had lowered the revolver in terror and gazed blankly at him, so that he might have seized her twice over and she would not have lifted a hand to defend herself if he had not reminded her. He recalled how at that instant he felt almost sorry for her, how he had felt a pang at his heart...

"Aïe! Damnation, these thoughts again! I must put it away!"

He was dozing off; the feverish shiver had ceased, when suddenly something seemed to run over his arm and leg under the bedclothes. He started. "Ugh! hang it! I believe it's a mouse," he thought, "that's the veal I left on the table." He felt fearfully disinclined to pull off the blanket, get up, get cold, but all at once something unpleasant ran over his leg again. He pulled off the blanket and lighted the candle. Shaking with feverish chill he bent down to examine the bed: there was nothing. He shook the blanket and suddenly a mouse jumped out on the sheet. He tried to catch it, but the mouse ran to and fro in zigzags without leaving the bed, slipped between his fingers, ran over his hand and suddenly darted under the pillow. He threw down the pillow, but in one instant felt something leap on his chest and dart over his body and down his back under his shirt. He trembled nervously and woke up.

The room was dark. He was lying on the bed and wrapped up in the blanket as before. The wind was howling under the window. "How disgusting," he thought with annoyance.

He got up and sat on the edge of the bedstead with his back to the window. "It's better not to sleep at all," he decided. There was a cold damp draught from the window, however; without getting up he drew the blanket over him and wrapped himself in it. He was not thinking of anything and did not want to think. But one image rose after another, incoherent scraps of thought without beginning or end passed through his mind. He sank into drowsiness. Perhaps the cold, or the dampness, or the dark, or the wind that howled under the window and tossed the trees roused a sort of persistent craving for the fantastic. He kept dwelling on images of flowers, he fancied a charming flower garden, a bright, warm, almost hot day, a holiday—Trinity day. A fine, sumptuous country cottage in the English taste overgrown with fragrant flowers, with flower beds going round the house; the porch, wreathed in climbers, was surrounded with beds of roses. A light, cool staircase, carpeted with rich rugs, was decorated with rare plants in china pots. He noticed particularly in the windows nosegays of tender, white, heavily fragrant narcissus bending over their bright, green, thick long stalks. He was reluctant to move away from them, but he went up the stairs and came into a large, high drawing-room and again everywhere—at the windows, the doors on to the balcony, and on the balcony itself—were flowers. The floors were strewn with freshly-cut fragrant hay, the windows were open, a fresh, cool, light air came into the room. The birds were chirruping under the window, and in the middle of the room, on a table covered with a white satin shroud, stood a coffin. The coffin was covered with white silk and edged with a thick white frill; wreaths of flowers surrounded it on all sides. Among the flowers lay a girl in a white muslin dress, with her arms crossed and pressed on her bosom, as though carved out of marble. But her loose fair hair was wet; there was a wreath of roses on her head. The stern and already rigid profile of her face looked as though chiselled of marble too, and the smile on her pale lips was full of an immense unchildish misery and sorrowful appeal. Svidrigaïlov knew that girl; there was no holy image, no burning candle beside the coffin; no sound of prayers: the girl had drowned herself. She was only fourteen, but her heart was broken. And she had destroyed herself, crushed by an insult that had appalled and amazed that childish soul, had smirched that angel purity with unmerited disgrace and torn from her a last scream of despair, unheeded and brutally disregarded, on a dark night in the cold and wet while the wind howled. ...

Svidrigaïlov came to himself, got up from the bed and went to the window. He felt for the latch and opened it. The wind lashed furiously into the little room and stung his face and his chest, only covered with his shirt, as though with frost. Under the window there must have been something like a garden, and apparently a pleasure garden. There, too, probably there were tea-tables and singing in the daytime. Now drops of rain flew in at the window from the trees and bushes; it was dark as in a cellar, so that he could only just make out some dark blurs of objects. Svidrigaïlov, bending down with elbows on the windowsill, gazed for five minutes into the darkness; the boom of a cannon, followed by a second one, resounded in the darkness of the night. "Ah, the signal! The river is overflowing," he thought. "By morning it will be swirling down the street in the lower parts, flooding the basements and cellars. The cellar rats will swim out, and men will curse in the rain and wind as they drag their rubbish to their upper storeys. What time is it now?" And he had hardly thought it when, somewhere near, a clock on the wall, ticking away hurriedly, struck three.

"Aha! It will be light in an hour! Why wait? I'll go out at once straight to the park. I'll choose a great bush there drenched with rain, so that as soon as one's shoulder touches it, millions of drops drip on one's head."

275

He moved away from the window, shut it, lighted the candle, put on his waistcoat, his overcoat and his hat and went out, carrying the candle, into the passage to look for the ragged attendant who would be asleep somewhere in the midst of candle-ends and all sorts of rubbish, to pay him for the room and leave the hotel. "It's the best minute; I couldn't choose a better."

He walked for some time through a long narrow corridor without finding anyone and was just going to call out, when suddenly in a dark corner between an old cupboard and the door he caught sight of a strange object which seemed to be alive. He bent down with the candle and saw a little girl, not more than five years old, shivering and crying, with her clothes as wet as a soaking house-flannel. She did not seem afraid of Svidrigaïlov, but looked at him with blank amazement out of her big black eyes. Now and then she sobbed as children do when they have been crying a long time, but are beginning to be comforted. The child's face was pale and tired, she was numb with cold. "How can she have come here? She must have hidden here and not slept all night." He began questioning her. The child suddenly becoming animated, chattered away in her baby language, something about "mammy" and that "mammy would beat her," and about some cup that she had "bwoken." The child chattered on without stopping. He could only guess from what she said that she was a neglected child, whose mother, probably a drunken cook, in the service of the hotel, whipped and frightened her; that the child had broken a cup of her mother's and was so frightened that she had run away the evening before, had hidden for a long while somewhere outside in the rain, at last had made her way in here, hidden behind the cupboard and spent the night there, crying and trembling from the damp, the darkness and the fear that she would be badly beaten for it. He took her in his arms, went back to his room, sat her on the bed, and began undressing her. The torn shoes which she had on her stockingless feet were as wet as if they had been standing in a puddle all night. When he had undressed her, he put her on the bed, covered her up and wrapped her in the blanket from her head downwards. She fell asleep at once. Then he sank into dreary musing again.

"What folly to trouble myself," he decided suddenly with an oppressive feeling of annoyance. "What idiocy!" In vexation he took up the candle to go and look for the ragged attendant again and make haste to go away. "Damn the child!" he thought as he opened the door, but he turned again to see whether the child was asleep. He raised the blanket carefully. The child was sleeping soundly, she had got warm under the blanket, and her pale cheeks were flushed. But strange to say that flush seemed brighter and coarser than the rosy cheeks of childhood. "It's a flush of fever," thought Svidrigaïlov. It was like the flush from drinking, as though she had been given a full glass to drink. Her crimson lips were hot and glowing; but what was this? He suddenly fancied that her long black eyelashes were quivering, as though the lids were opening and a sly crafty eye peeped out with an unchildlike wink, as though the little girl were not asleep, but pretending. Yes, it was so. Her lips parted in a smile. The corners of her mouth quivered, as though she were trying to control them. But now she quite gave up all effort, now it was a grin, a broad grin; there was something shameless, provocative in that quite unchildish face; it was depravity, it was the face of a harlot, the shameless face of a French harlot. Now both eyes opened wide; they turned a glowing, shameless glance upon him; they laughed, invited him.... There was something infinitely hideous and shocking in that laugh, in those eyes, in such nastiness in the face of a child. "What, at five years old?" Svidrigaïlov muttered in genuine horror. "What does it mean?" And now she turned to him, her little face all aglow, holding out her arms.... "Accursed child!" Svidrigaïlov cried, raising his hand to strike her, but at that moment he woke up.

He was in the same bed, still wrapped in the blanket. The candle had not been lighted, and daylight was streaming in at the windows.

"I've had nightmare all night!" He got up angrily, feeling utterly shattered; his bones ached. There was a thick mist outside and he could see nothing. It was nearly five. He had overslept himself! He got up, put on his still damp jacket and overcoat. Feeling the revolver in his pocket, he took it out and then he sat down, took a notebook out of his pocket and in the most conspicuous place on the title page wrote a few lines in large letters. Reading them over, he sank into thought with his elbows on the table. The revolver and the notebook lay beside him. Some flies woke up and settled on the untouched veal, which was still on the table. He stared at them and at last with his free right hand began trying to catch one. He tried till he was tired, but could not catch it. At last, realising that he was engaged in this interesting pursuit, he started, got up and walked resolutely out of the room. A minute later he was in the street.

A thick milky mist hung over the town. Svidrigaïlov walked along the slippery dirty wooden pavement towards the Little Neva. He was picturing the waters of the Little Neva swollen in the night, Petrovsky Island, the wet paths, the wet grass, the wet trees and bushes and at last the bush.... He began ill-humouredly staring at the houses, trying to think of something else. There was not a cabman or a passerby in the street. The bright yellow, wooden, little houses looked dirty and dejected with their closed shutters. The cold and damp penetrated his whole body and he began to shiver. From time to time he came across shop signs and read each carefully. At last he reached the end of the wooden pavement and came to a big stone house. A dirty, shivering dog crossed his path with its tail between its legs. A man in a greatcoat lay face downwards; dead drunk, across the pavement. He looked at him and went on. A high tower stood up on the left. "Bah!" he shouted, "here is a place. Why should it be Petrovsky? It will be in the presence of an official witness anyway...."

He almost smiled at this new thought and turned into the street where there was the big house with the tower. At the great closed gates of the house, a little man stood with his shoulder leaning against them, wrapped in a grey soldier's coat, with a copper Achilles helmet on his head. He cast a drowsy and indifferent glance at Svidrigaïlov. His face wore that perpetual look of peevish dejection, which is so sourly printed on all faces of Jewish race without exception. They both, Svidrigaïlov and Achilles, stared at each other for a few minutes without speaking. At last it struck Achilles as irregular for a man not drunk to be standing three steps from him, staring and not saying a word.

"What do you want here?" he said, without moving or changing his position.

"Nothing, brother, good morning," answered Svidrigaïlov.

"This isn't the place."

"I am going to foreign parts, brother."

"To foreign parts?"

"To America."

"America."

Svidrigaïlov took out the revolver and cocked it. Achilles raised his eyebrows.

"I say, this is not the place for such jokes!"

"Why shouldn't it be the place?"

"Because it isn't."

"Well, brother, I don't mind that. It's a good place. When you are asked, you just say he was going, he said, to America."

He put the revolver to his right temple.

"You can't do it here, it's not the place," cried Achilles, rousing himself, his eyes growing bigger and bigger.

Svidrigaïlov pulled the trigger.

The same day, about seven o'clock in the evening, Raskolnikov was on his way to his mother's and sister's lodging—the lodging in Bakaleyev's house which Razumihin had found for them. The stairs went up from the street. Raskolnikov walked with lagging steps, as though still hesitating whether to go or not. But nothing would have turned him back: his decision was taken.

"Besides, it doesn't matter, they still know nothing," he thought, "and they are used to thinking of me as eccentric."

He was appallingly dressed: his clothes torn and dirty, soaked with a night's rain. His face was almost distorted from fatigue, exposure, the inward conflict that had lasted for twenty-four hours. He had spent all the previous night alone, God knows where. But anyway he had reached a decision.

He knocked at the door which was opened by his mother. Dounia was not at home. Even the servant happened to be out. At first Pulcheria Alexandrovna was speechless with joy and surprise; then she took him by the hand and drew him into the room.

"Here you are!" she began, faltering with joy. "Don't be angry with me, Rodya, for welcoming you so foolishly with tears: I am laughing not crying. Did you think I was crying? No, I am delighted, but I've got into such a stupid habit of shedding tears. I've been like that ever since your father's death. I cry for anything. Sit down, dear boy, you must be tired; I see you are. Ah, how muddy you are."

"I was in the rain yesterday, mother...." Raskolnikov began.

"No, no," Pulcheria Alexandrovna hurriedly interrupted, "you thought I was going to cross-question you in the womanish way I used to; don't be anxious, I understand, I understand it all: now I've learned the ways here and truly I see for myself that they are better. I've made up my mind once for all: how could I understand your plans and expect you to give an account of them? God knows what concerns and plans you may have, or what ideas you are hatching; so it's not for me to keep nudging your elbow, asking you what you are thinking about? But, my goodness! why am I running to and fro as though I were crazy...? I am reading your article in the magazine for the third time, Rodya. Dmitri Prokofitch brought it to me. Directly I saw it I cried out to myself: 'There, foolish one,' I thought, 'that's what he is busy about; that's the solution of the mystery! Learned people are always like that. He may have some new ideas in his head just now; he is thinking them over and I worry him and upset him.' I read it, my dear, and of course there was a great deal I did not understand; but that's only natural—how should I?"

"Show me, mother."

Raskolnikov took the magazine and glanced at his article. Incongruous as it was with his mood and his circumstances, he felt that strange and bitter sweet sensation that every author experiences the first time he sees himself in print; besides, he was only twenty-three. It lasted only a moment. After reading a few lines he frowned and his heart throbbed with anguish. He recalled all the inward conflict of the preceding months. He flung the article on the table with disgust and anger.

"But, however foolish I may be, Rodya, I can see for myself that you will very soon be one of the leading—if not the leading man—in the world of Russian thought. And they dared to think you were mad! You don't know, but they really thought that. Ah, the despicable creatures, how could they understand genius! And Dounia, Dounia was all but believing it—what do you say to that? Your father sent twice to magazines—the first time poems (I've got the manuscript and will show you) and the second time a whole novel (I begged him to let me copy it out) and how we prayed that they should be taken—they weren't! I was breaking my heart, Rodya, six or seven days ago over your food and your clothes and the way you are living. But now I see again how foolish I was, for you can attain any position you like by your intellect and talent. No doubt you don't care about that for the present and you are occupied with much more important matters...."

"Dounia's not at home, mother?"

"No, Rodya. I often don't see her; she leaves me alone. Dmitri Prokofitch comes to see me, it's so good of him, and he always talks about you. He loves you and respects you, my dear. I don't say that Dounia is very wanting in consideration. I am not complaining. She has her ways and I have mine; she seems to have got some secrets of late and I never have any secrets from you two. Of course, I am sure that Dounia has far too much sense, and besides she loves you and me... but I don't know what it will all lead to. You've made me so happy by coming now, Rodya, but she has missed you by going out; when she comes in I'll tell her: 'Your brother came in while you were out. Where have you been all this time?' You mustn't spoil me, Rodya, you know; come when you can, but if you can't, it doesn't matter, I can wait. I shall know, anyway, that you are fond of me, that will be enough for me. I shall read what you write, I shall hear about you from everyone, and sometimes you'll come yourself to see me. What could be better? Here you've come now to comfort your mother, I see that."

Here Pulcheria Alexandrovna began to cry.

"Here I am again! Don't mind my foolishness. My goodness, why am I sitting here?" she cried, jumping up. "There is coffee and I don't offer you any. Ah, that's the selfishness of old age. I'll get it at once!"

"Mother, don't trouble, I am going at once. I haven't come for that. Please listen to me."

Pulcheria Alexandrovna went up to him timidly.

"Mother, whatever happens, whatever you hear about me, whatever you are told about me, will you always love me as you do now?" he asked suddenly from the fullness of his heart, as though not thinking of his words and not weighing them.

"Rodya, Rodya, what is the matter? How can you ask me such a question? Why, who will tell me anything about you? Besides, I shouldn't believe anyone, I should refuse to listen."

"I've come to assure you that I've always loved you and I am glad that we are alone, even glad Dounia is out," he went on with the same impulse. "I have come to tell you that though you will be unhappy, you must believe that your son loves you now more than himself, and that all you thought about me, that I was cruel and didn't care about you, was all a mistake. I shall never cease to love you.... Well, that's enough: I thought I must do this and begin with this...."

Pulcheria Alexandrovna embraced him in silence, pressing him to her bosom and weeping gently.

"I don't know what is wrong with you, Rodya," she said at last. "I've been thinking all this time that we were simply boring you and now I see that there is a great sorrow in store for you, and that's why you are miserable. I've foreseen it a long time, Rodya. Forgive me for speaking about it. I keep thinking about it and lie awake at nights. Your sister lay talking in her sleep all last night, talking of nothing but you. I caught something, but I couldn't make it out. I felt all the morning as though I were going to be hanged, waiting for something, expecting something, and now it has come! Rodya, Rodya, where are you going? You are going away somewhere?"

"Yes."

"That's what I thought! I can come with you, you know, if you need me. And Dounia, too; she loves you, she loves you dearly—and Sofya Semyonovna may come with us if you like. You see, I am glad to look upon her as a daughter even... Dmitri Prokofitch will help us to go together. But... where... are you going?"

"Goodbye, mother."

"What, today?" she cried, as though losing him forever.

"I can't stay, I must go now...."

"And can't I come with you?"

"No, but kneel down and pray to God for me. Your prayer perhaps will reach Him."

"Let me bless you and sign you with the cross. That's right, that's right. Oh, God, what are we doing?"

Yes, he was glad, he was very glad that there was no one there, that he was alone with his mother. For the first time after all those awful months his heart was softened. He fell down before her, he kissed her feet and both wept, embracing. And she was not surprised and did not question him this time. For some days she had realised that something awful was happening to her son and that now some terrible minute had come for him.

"Rodya, my darling, my first born," she said sobbing, "now you are just as when you were little. You would run like this to me and hug me and kiss me. When your father was living and we were poor, you comforted us simply by being with us and when I buried your father, how often we wept together at his grave and embraced, as now. And if I've been crying lately, it's that my mother's heart had a foreboding of trouble. The first time I saw you, that evening, you remember, as soon as we arrived here, I guessed simply from your eyes. My heart sank at once, and today when I opened the door and looked at you, I thought the fatal hour had come. Rodya, Rodya, you are not going away today?"

"No!"

"You'll come again?"

"Yes... I'll come."

"Rodya, don't be angry, I don't dare to question you. I know I mustn't. Only say two words to me—is it far where you are going?"

"Very far."

"What is awaiting you there? Some post or career for you?"

"What God sends... only pray for me." Raskolnikov went to the door, but she clutched him and gazed despairingly into his eyes. Her face worked with terror.

"Enough, mother," said Raskolnikov, deeply regretting that he had come.

"Not forever, it's not yet forever? You'll come, you'll come tomorrow?"

"I will, I will, goodbye." He tore himself away at last.

It was a warm, fresh, bright evening; it had cleared up in the morning. Raskolnikov went to his lodgings; he made haste. He wanted to finish all before sunset. He did not want to meet anyone till then. Going up the stairs he noticed that Nastasya rushed from the samovar to watch him intently. "Can anyone have come to see me?" he wondered. He had a disgusted vision of Porfiry. But opening his door he saw Dounia. She was sitting alone, plunged in deep thought, and looked as though she had been waiting a long time. He stopped short in the doorway. She rose from the sofa in dismay and stood up facing him. Her eyes, fixed upon him, betrayed horror and infinite grief. And from those eyes alone he saw at once that she knew.

"Am I to come in or go away?" he asked uncertainly.

"I've been all day with Sofya Semyonovna. We were both waiting for you. We thought that you would be sure to come there."

Raskolnikov went into the room and sank exhausted on a chair.

"I feel weak, Dounia, I am very tired; and I should have liked at this moment to be able to control myself."

He glanced at her mistrustfully.

"Where were you all night?"

"I don't remember clearly. You see, sister, I wanted to make up my mind once for all, and several times I walked by the Neva, I remember that I wanted to end it all there, but... I couldn't make up my mind," he whispered, looking at her mistrustfully again.

"Thank God! That was just what we were afraid of, Sofya Semyonovna and I. Then you still have faith in life? Thank God, thank God!"

Raskolnikov smiled bitterly.

"I haven't faith, but I have just been weeping in mother's arms; I haven't faith, but I have just asked her to pray for me. I don't know how it is, Dounia, I don't understand it."

"Have you been at mother's? Have you told her?" cried Dounia, horror-stricken. "Surely you haven't done that?"

"No, I didn't tell her… in words; but she understood a great deal. She heard you talking in your sleep. I am sure she half understands it already. Perhaps I did wrong in going to see her. I don't know why I did go. I am a contemptible person, Dounia."

"A contemptible person, but ready to face suffering! You are, aren't you?"

"Yes, I am going. At once. Yes, to escape the disgrace I thought of drowning myself, Dounia, but as I looked into the water, I thought that if I had considered myself strong till now I'd better not be afraid of disgrace," he said, hurrying on. "It's pride, Dounia."

"Pride, Rodya."

There was a gleam of fire in his lustreless eyes; he seemed to be glad to think that he was still proud.

"You don't think, sister, that I was simply afraid of the water?" he asked, looking into her face with a sinister smile.

"Oh, Rodya, hush!" cried Dounia bitterly. Silence lasted for two minutes. He sat with his eyes fixed on the floor; Dounia stood at the other end of the table and looked at him with anguish. Suddenly he got up.

"It's late, it's time to go! I am going at once to give myself up. But I don't know why I am going to give myself up."

Big tears fell down her cheeks.

"You are crying, sister, but can you hold out your hand to me?"

"You doubted it?"

She threw her arms round him.

"Aren't you half expiating your crime by facing the suffering?" she cried, holding him close and kissing him.

"Crime? What crime?" he cried in sudden fury. "That I killed a vile noxious insect, an old pawnbroker woman, of use to no one!… Killing her was atonement for forty sins. She was sucking the life out of poor people. Was that a crime? I am not thinking of it and I am not thinking of expiating it, and why are you all rubbing it in on all sides? 'A crime! a crime!' Only now I see clearly the imbecility of my cowardice, now that I have decided to face this superfluous disgrace. It's simply because I am contemptible and have nothing in me that I have decided to, perhaps too for my advantage, as that… Porfiry… suggested!"

"Brother, brother, what are you saying? Why, you have shed blood?" cried Dounia in despair.

"Which all men shed," he put in almost frantically, "which flows and has always flowed in streams, which is spilt like champagne, and for which men are crowned in the Capitol and are called afterwards benefactors of mankind. Look into it more carefully and understand it! I too wanted to do good to men and would have done hundreds, thousands of good deeds to make up for that one piece of stupidity, not stupidity even, simply clumsiness, for the idea was by no means so stupid as it seems now that it has failed…. (Everything seems stupid when it fails.) By that stupidity I only wanted to put myself into an independent position, to take the first step, to obtain means, and then everything would have been smoothed over by benefits immeasurable in comparison…. But I… I couldn't carry out even the first step, because I am contemptible, that's what's the matter! And yet I won't look at it as you do. If I had succeeded I should have been crowned with glory, but now I'm trapped."

"But that's not so, not so! Brother, what are you saying?"

"Ah, it's not picturesque, not aesthetically attractive! I fail to understand why bombarding people by regular siege is more honourable. The fear of appearances is the first symptom of impotence. I've never, never recognised this more clearly than now, and I am further than ever from seeing that what I did was a crime. I've never, never been stronger and more convinced than now."

The colour had rushed into his pale exhausted face, but as he uttered his last explanation, he happened to meet Dounia's eyes and he saw such anguish in them that he could not help being checked. He felt that he had, anyway, made these two poor women miserable, that he was, anyway, the cause…

281

"Dounia darling, if I am guilty forgive me (though I cannot be forgiven if I am guilty). Goodbye! We won't dispute. It's time, high time to go. Don't follow me, I beseech you, I have somewhere else to go.... But you go at once and sit with mother. I entreat you to! It's my last request of you. Don't leave her at all; I left her in a state of anxiety, that she is not fit to bear; she will die or go out of her mind. Be with her! Razumihin will be with you. I've been talking to him.... Don't cry about me: I'll try to be honest and manly all my life, even if I am a murderer. Perhaps I shall some day make a name. I won't disgrace you, you will see; I'll still show.... Now goodbye for the present," he concluded hurriedly, noticing again a strange expression in Dounia's eyes at his last words and promises. "Why are you crying? Don't cry, don't cry: we are not parting forever! Ah, yes! Wait a minute, I'd forgotten!"

He went to the table, took up a thick dusty book, opened it and took from between the pages a little watercolour portrait on ivory. It was the portrait of his landlady's daughter, who had died of fever, that strange girl who had wanted to be a nun. For a minute he gazed at the delicate expressive face of his betrothed, kissed the portrait and gave it to Dounia.

"I used to talk a great deal about it to her, only to her," he said thoughtfully. "To her heart I confided much of what has since been so hideously realised. Don't be uneasy," he returned to Dounia, "she was as much opposed to it as you, and I am glad that she is gone. The great point is that everything now is going to be different, is going to be broken in two," he cried, suddenly returning to his dejection. "Everything, everything, and am I prepared for it? Do I want it myself? They say it is necessary for me to suffer! What's the object of these senseless sufferings? shall I know any better what they are for, when I am crushed by hardships and idiocy, and weak as an old man after twenty years' penal servitude? And what shall I have to live for then? Why am I consenting to that life now? Oh, I knew I was contemptible when I stood looking at the Neva at daybreak today!"

At last they both went out. It was hard for Dounia, but she loved him. She walked away, but after going fifty paces she turned round to look at him again. He was still in sight. At the corner he too turned and for the last time their eyes met; but noticing that she was looking at him, he motioned her away with impatience and even vexation, and turned the corner abruptly.

"I am wicked, I see that," he thought to himself, feeling ashamed a moment later of his angry gesture to Dounia. "But why are they so fond of me if I don't deserve it? Oh, if only I were alone and no one loved me and I too had never loved anyone! *Nothing of all this would have happened.* But I wonder shall I in those fifteen or twenty years grow so meek that I shall humble myself before people and whimper at every word that I am a criminal? Yes, that's it, that's it, that's what they are sending me there for, that's what they want. Look at them running to and fro about the streets, every one of them a scoundrel and a criminal at heart and, worse still, an idiot. But try to get me off and they'd be wild with righteous indignation. Oh, how I hate them all!"

He fell to musing by what process it could come to pass, that he could be humbled before all of them, indiscriminately—humbled by conviction. And yet why not? It must be so. Would not twenty years of continual bondage crush him utterly? Water wears out a stone. And why, why should he live after that? Why should he go now when he knew that it would be so? It was the hundredth time perhaps that he had asked himself that question since the previous evening, but still he went.

VIII

When he went into Sonia's room, it was already getting dark. All day Sonia had been waiting for him in terrible anxiety. Dounia had been waiting with her. She had come to her that morning, remembering Svidrigaïlov's words that Sonia knew. We will not describe the conversation and tears of the two girls, and how friendly they became. Dounia gained one comfort at least from that interview, that her brother would not be alone. He had gone to her, Sonia, first with his confession; he had gone to her for human fellowship when he needed it; she would go with him wherever fate might send him. Dounia did not ask, but she knew it was so. She looked at Sonia almost with reverence and at first almost embarrassed her by it. Sonia was almost on the point of tears. She felt herself, on the contrary, hardly worthy to look at Dounia. Dounia's gracious image when she had bowed to her so attentively and respectfully at their first meeting in Raskolnikov's room had remained in her mind as one of the fairest visions of her life.

Dounia at last became impatient and, leaving Sonia, went to her brother's room to await him there; she kept thinking that he would come there first. When she had gone, Sonia began to be tortured by the dread of his committing suicide, and Dounia too feared it. But they had spent the day trying to persuade each other that that could not be, and both were less anxious while they were together. As soon as they parted, each thought of nothing else. Sonia remembered how Svidrigaïlov had said to her the day before that Raskolnikov had two alternatives—Siberia or... Besides she knew his vanity, his pride and his lack of faith.

"Is it possible that he has nothing but cowardice and fear of death to make him live?" she thought at last in despair.

Meanwhile the sun was setting. Sonia was standing in dejection, looking intently out of the window, but from it she could see nothing but the unwhitewashed blank wall of the next house. At last when she began to feel sure of his death—he walked into the room.

She gave a cry of joy, but looking carefully into his face she turned pale.

"Yes," said Raskolnikov, smiling. "I have come for your cross, Sonia. It was you told me to go to the crossroads; why is it you are frightened now it's come to that?"

Sonia gazed at him astonished. His tone seemed strange to her; a cold shiver ran over her, but in a moment she guessed that the tone and the words were a mask. He spoke to her looking away, as though to avoid meeting her eyes.

"You see, Sonia, I've decided that it will be better so. There is one fact.... But it's a long story and there's no need to discuss it. But do you know what angers me? It annoys me that all those stupid brutish faces will be gaping at me directly, pestering me with their stupid questions, which I shall have to answer—they'll point their fingers at me.... Tfoo! You know I am not going to Porfiry, I am sick of him. I'd rather go to my friend, the Explosive Lieutenant; how I shall surprise him, what a sensation I shall make! But I must be cooler; I've become too irritable of late. You know I was nearly shaking my fist at my sister just now, because she turned to take a last look at me. It's a brutal state to be in! Ah! what am I coming to! Well, where are the crosses?"

He seemed hardly to know what he was doing. He could not stay still or concentrate his attention on anything; his ideas seemed to gallop after one another, he talked incoherently, his hands trembled slightly.

Without a word Sonia took out of the drawer two crosses, one of cypress wood and one of copper. She made the sign of the cross over herself and over him, and put the wooden cross on his neck.

"It's the symbol of my taking up the cross," he laughed. "As though I had not suffered much till now! The wooden cross, that is the peasant one; the copper one, that is Lizaveta's—you will wear yourself, show me! So she had it on... at that moment? I remember two things like these too, a silver one and a little icon. I threw them back on the old woman's neck. Those would be appropriate now, really, those are what I ought to put on now.... But I am talking nonsense and forgetting what matters; I'm somehow forgetful.... You see I have come to warn you, Sonia, so that you might know... that's all—that's all I came for. But I thought I had more to say. You wanted me to go yourself. Well, now I am going to prison and you'll have your wish. Well, what are you crying for? You too? Don't. Leave off! Oh, how I hate it all!"

But his feeling was stirred; his heart ached, as he looked at her. "Why is she grieving too?" he thought to himself. "What am I to her? Why does she weep? Why is she looking after me, like my mother or Dounia? She'll be my nurse."

"Cross yourself, say at least one prayer," Sonia begged in a timid broken voice.

"Oh certainly, as much as you like! And sincerely, Sonia, sincerely...."

But he wanted to say something quite different.

He crossed himself several times. Sonia took up her shawl and put it over her head. It was the green *drap de dames* shawl of which Marmeladov had spoken, "the family shawl." Raskolnikov thought of that looking at it, but he did not ask. He began to feel himself that he was certainly forgetting things and was disgustingly agitated. He was frightened at this. He was suddenly struck too by the thought that Sonia meant to go with him.

"What are you doing? Where are you going? Stay here, stay! I'll go alone," he cried in cowardly vexation, and almost resentful, he moved towards the door. "What's the use of going in procession?" he muttered going out.

Sonia remained standing in the middle of the room. He had not even said goodbye to her; he had forgotten her. A poignant and rebellious doubt surged in his heart.

"Was it right, was it right, all this?" he thought again as he went down the stairs. "Couldn't he stop and retract it all... and not go?"

But still he went. He felt suddenly once for all that he mustn't ask himself questions. As he turned into the street he remembered that he had not said goodbye to Sonia, that he had left her in the middle of the room in her green shawl, not daring to stir after he had shouted at her, and he stopped short for a moment. At the same instant, another thought dawned upon him, as though it had been lying in wait to strike him then.

"Why, with what object did I go to her just now? I told her—on business; on what business? I had no sort of business! To tell her I was *going*; but where was the need? Do I love her? No, no, I drove her away just now like a dog. Did I want her crosses? Oh, how low I've sunk! No, I wanted her tears, I wanted to see her terror, to see how her heart ached! I had to have something to cling to, something to delay me, some friendly face to see! And I dared to believe in myself, to dream of what I would do! I am a beggarly contemptible wretch, contemptible!"

He walked along the canal bank, and he had not much further to go. But on reaching the bridge he stopped and turning out of his way along it went to the Hay Market.

He looked eagerly to right and left, gazed intently at every object and could not fix his attention on anything; everything slipped away. "In another week, another month I shall be driven in a prison van over this bridge, how shall I look at the canal then? I should like to remember this!" slipped into his mind. "Look at this sign! How shall I read those letters then? It's written here 'Campany,' that's a thing to remember, that letter *a*, and to look at it again in a month—how shall I look at it then? What shall I be feeling and thinking then?... How trivial it all must be, what I am fretting about now! Of course it must all be interesting... in its way... (Ha-ha-ha! What am I thinking about?) I am becoming a baby, I am showing off to myself; why am I ashamed? Foo! how people shove! that fat man—a German he must be—who pushed against me, does he know whom he pushed? There's a peasant woman with a baby, begging. It's curious that she thinks me happier than she is. I might give her something, for the incongruity of it. Here's a five kopeck piece left in my pocket, where did I get it? Here, here... take it, my good woman!"

"God bless you," the beggar chanted in a lachrymose voice.

284

He went into the Hay Market. It was distasteful, very distasteful to be in a crowd, but he walked just where he saw most people. He would have given anything in the world to be alone; but he knew himself that he would not have remained alone for a moment. There was a man drunk and disorderly in the crowd; he kept trying to dance and falling down. There was a ring round him. Raskolnikov squeezed his way through the crowd, stared for some minutes at the drunken man and suddenly gave a short jerky laugh. A minute later he had forgotten him and did not see him, though he still stared. He moved away at last, not remembering where he was; but when he got into the middle of the square an emotion suddenly came over him, overwhelming him body and mind.

He suddenly recalled Sonia's words, "Go to the crossroads, bow down to the people, kiss the earth, for you have sinned against it too, and say aloud to the whole world, 'I am a murderer.'" He trembled, remembering that. And the hopeless misery and anxiety of all that time, especially of the last hours, had weighed so heavily upon him that he positively clutched at the chance of this new unmixed, complete sensation. It came over him like a fit; it was like a single spark kindled in his soul and spreading fire through him. Everything in him softened at once and the tears started into his eyes. He fell to the earth on the spot....

He knelt down in the middle of the square, bowed down to the earth, and kissed that filthy earth with bliss and rapture. He got up and bowed down a second time.

"He's boozed," a youth near him observed.

There was a roar of laughter.

"He's going to Jerusalem, brothers, and saying goodbye to his children and his country. He's bowing down to all the world and kissing the great city of St. Petersburg and its pavement," added a workman who was a little drunk.

"Quite a young man, too!" observed a third.

"And a gentleman," someone observed soberly.

"There's no knowing who's a gentleman and who isn't nowadays."

These exclamations and remarks checked Raskolnikov, and the words, "I am a murderer," which were perhaps on the point of dropping from his lips, died away. He bore these remarks quietly, however, and, without looking round, he turned down a street leading to the police office. He had a glimpse of something on the way which did not surprise him; he had felt that it must be so. The second time he bowed down in the Hay Market he saw, standing fifty paces from him on the left, Sonia. She was hiding from him behind one of the wooden shanties in the marketplace. She had followed him then on his painful way! Raskolnikov at that moment felt and knew once for all that Sonia was with him forever and would follow him to the ends of the earth, wherever fate might take him. It wrung his heart... but he was just reaching the fatal place.

He went into the yard fairly resolutely. He had to mount to the third storey. "I shall be some time going up," he thought. He felt as though the fateful moment was still far off, as though he had plenty of time left for consideration.

Again the same rubbish, the same eggshells lying about on the spiral stairs, again the open doors of the flats, again the same kitchens and the same fumes and stench coming from them. Raskolnikov had not been here since that day. His legs were numb and gave way under him, but still they moved forward. He stopped for a moment to take breath, to collect himself, so as to enter *like a man*. "But why? what for?" he wondered, reflecting. "If I must drink the cup what difference does it make? The more revolting the better." He imagined for an instant the figure of the "explosive lieutenant," Ilya Petrovitch. Was he actually going to him? Couldn't he go to someone else? To Nikodim Fomitch? Couldn't he turn back and go straight to Nikodim Fomitch's lodgings? At least then it would be done privately.... No, no! To the "explosive lieutenant"! If he must drink it, drink it off at once.

Turning cold and hardly conscious, he opened the door of the office. There were very few people in it this time—only a house porter and a peasant. The doorkeeper did not even peep out from behind his screen. Raskolnikov walked into the next room. "Perhaps I still need not speak," passed through his mind. Some sort of clerk not wearing a uniform was settling himself at a bureau to write. In a corner another clerk was seating himself. Zametov was not there, nor, of course, Nikodim Fomitch.

"No one in?" Raskolnikov asked, addressing the person at the bureau.

"Whom do you want?"

"A-ah! Not a sound was heard, not a sight was seen, but I scent the Russian... how does it go on in the fairy tale... I've forgotten! 'At your service!'" a familiar voice cried suddenly.

Raskolnikov shuddered. The Explosive Lieutenant stood before him. He had just come in from the third room. "It is the hand of fate," thought Raskolnikov. "Why is he here?"

"You've come to see us? What about?" cried Ilya Petrovitch. He was obviously in an exceedingly good humour and perhaps a trifle exhilarated. "If it's on business you are rather early.[3] It's only a chance that I am here... however I'll do what I can. I must admit, I... what is it, what is it? Excuse me...."

"Raskolnikov."

"Of course, Raskolnikov. You didn't imagine I'd forgotten? Don't think I am like that... Rodion Ro—Ro—Rodionovitch, that's it, isn't it?"

"Rodion Romanovitch."

"Yes, yes, of course, Rodion Romanovitch! I was just getting at it. I made many inquiries about you. I assure you I've been genuinely grieved since that... since I behaved like that... it was explained to me afterwards that you were a literary man... and a learned one too... and so to say the first steps... Mercy on us! What literary or scientific man does not begin by some originality of conduct! My wife and I have the greatest respect for literature, in my wife it's a genuine passion! Literature and art! If only a man is a gentleman, all the rest can be gained by talents, learning, good sense, genius. As for a hat—well, what does a hat matter? I can buy a hat as easily as I can a bun; but what's under the hat, what the hat covers, I can't buy that! I was even meaning to come and apologise to you, but thought maybe you'd... But I am forgetting to ask you, is there anything you want really? I hear your family have come?"

"Yes, my mother and sister."

"I've even had the honour and happiness of meeting your sister—a highly cultivated and charming person. I confess I was sorry I got so hot with you. There it is! But as for my looking suspiciously at your fainting fit—that affair has been cleared up splendidly! Bigotry and fanaticism! I understand your indignation. Perhaps you are changing your lodging on account of your family's arriving?"

"No, I only looked in... I came to ask... I thought that I should find Zametov here."

"Oh, yes! Of course, you've made friends, I heard. Well, no, Zametov is not here. Yes, we've lost Zametov. He's not been here since yesterday... he quarrelled with everyone on leaving... in the rudest way. He is a feather-headed youngster, that's all; one might have expected something from him, but there, you know what they are, our brilliant young men. He wanted to go in for some examination, but it's only to talk and boast about it, it will go no further than that. Of course it's a very different matter with you or Mr. Razumihin there, your friend. Your career is an intellectual one and you won't be deterred by failure. For you, one may say, all the attractions of life *nihil est*—you are an ascetic, a monk, a hermit!... A book, a pen behind your ear, a learned research—that's where your spirit soars! I am the same way myself.... Have you read *Livingstone's Travels?*"

"No."

"Oh, I have. There are a great many Nihilists about nowadays, you know, and indeed it is not to be wondered at. What sort of days are they? I ask you. But we thought... you are not a Nihilist of course? Answer me openly, openly!"

"N-no..."

"Believe me, you can speak openly to me as you would to yourself! Official duty is one thing but... you are thinking I meant to say *friendship* is quite another? No, you're wrong! It's not friendship, but the feeling of a man and a citizen, the feeling of humanity and of love for the Almighty. I may be an official, but I am always bound to feel myself a man and a citizen.... You were asking about Zametov. Zametov will make a scandal in the French style in a house of bad reputation, over a glass of champagne... that's all your Zametov is good for! While I'm perhaps, so to speak, burning with devotion and lofty feelings, and besides I have rank, consequence, a post! I am married and have children, I fulfil the duties of a man and a citizen, but who is he, may I ask? I appeal to you as a man ennobled by education... Then these midwives, too, have become extraordinarily numerous."

Raskolnikov raised his eyebrows inquiringly. The words of Ilya Petrovitch, who had obviously been dining, were for the most part a stream of empty sounds for him. But some of them he understood. He looked at him inquiringly, not knowing how it would end.

"I mean those crop-headed wenches," the talkative Ilya Petrovitch continued. "Midwives is my name for them. I think it a very satisfactory one, ha-ha! They go to the Academy, study anatomy. If I fall ill, am I to send for a young lady to treat me? What do you say? Ha-ha!" Ilya Petrovitch laughed, quite pleased with his own wit. "It's an immoderate zeal for education, but once you're educated, that's enough. Why abuse it? Why insult honourable people, as that scoundrel Zametov does? Why did he insult me, I ask you? Look at these suicides, too, how common they are, you can't fancy! People spend their last halfpenny and kill themselves, boys and girls and old people. Only this morning we heard about a gentleman who had just come to town. Nil Pavlitch, I say, what was the name of that gentleman who shot himself?"

"Svidrigaïlov," someone answered from the other room with drowsy listlessness.

Raskolnikov started.

"Svidrigaïlov! Svidrigaïlov has shot himself!" he cried.

"What, do you know Svidrigaïlov?"

"Yes... I knew him.... He hadn't been here long."

"Yes, that's so. He had lost his wife, was a man of reckless habits and all of a sudden shot himself, and in such a shocking way.... He left in his notebook a few words: that he dies in full possession of his faculties and that no one is to blame for his death. He had money, they say. How did you come to know him?"

"I... was acquainted... my sister was governess in his family."

"Bah-bah-bah! Then no doubt you can tell us something about him. You had no suspicion?"

"I saw him yesterday... he... was drinking wine; I knew nothing."

Raskolnikov felt as though something had fallen on him and was stifling him.

"You've turned pale again. It's so stuffy here..."

"Yes, I must go," muttered Raskolnikov. "Excuse my troubling you...."

"Oh, not at all, as often as you like. It's a pleasure to see you and I am glad to say so."

Ilya Petrovitch held out his hand.

"I only wanted... I came to see Zametov."

"I understand, I understand, and it's a pleasure to see you."

"I... am very glad... goodbye," Raskolnikov smiled.

He went out; he reeled, he was overtaken with giddiness and did not know what he was doing. He began going down the stairs, supporting himself with his right hand against the wall. He fancied that a porter pushed past him on his way upstairs to the police office, that a dog in the lower storey kept up a shrill barking and that a woman flung a rolling-pin at it and shouted. He went down and out into the yard. There, not far from the entrance, stood Sonia, pale and horror-stricken. She looked wildly at him. He stood still before her. There was a look of poignant agony, of despair, in her face. She clasped her hands. His lips worked in an ugly, meaningless smile. He stood still a minute, grinned and went back to the police office.

Ilya Petrovitch had sat down and was rummaging among some papers. Before him stood the same peasant who had pushed by on the stairs.

"Hulloa! Back again! have you left something behind? What's the matter?"

Raskolnikov, with white lips and staring eyes, came slowly nearer. He walked right to the table, leaned his hand on it, tried to say something, but could not; only incoherent sounds were audible.

"You are feeling ill, a chair! Here, sit down! Some water!"

Raskolnikov dropped on to a chair, but he kept his eyes fixed on the face of Ilya Petrovitch, which expressed unpleasant surprise. Both looked at one another for a minute and waited. Water was brought.

"It was I..." began Raskolnikov.

"Drink some water."

Raskolnikov refused the water with his hand, and softly and brokenly, but distinctly said:

"*It was I killed the old pawnbroker woman and her sister Lizaveta with an axe and robbed them.*"

Ilya Petrovitch opened his mouth. People ran up on all sides.

Raskolnikov repeated his statement.

EPILOGUE

I

Siberia. On the banks of a broad solitary river stands a town, one of the administrative centres of Russia; in the town there is a fortress, in the fortress there is a prison. In the prison the second-class convict Rodion Raskolnikov has been confined for nine months. Almost a year and a half has passed since his crime.

There had been little difficulty about his trial. The criminal adhered exactly, firmly, and clearly to his statement. He did not confuse nor misrepresent the facts, nor soften them in his own interest, nor omit the smallest detail. He explained every incident of the murder, the secret of *the pledge* (the piece of wood with a strip of metal) which was found in the murdered woman's hand. He described minutely how he had taken her keys, what they were like, as well as the chest and its contents; he explained the mystery of Lizaveta's murder; described how Koch and, after him, the student knocked, and repeated all they had said to one another; how he afterwards had run downstairs and heard Nikolay and Dmitri shouting; how he had hidden in the empty flat and afterwards gone home. He ended by indicating the stone in the yard off the Voznesensky Prospect under which the purse and the trinkets were found. The whole thing, in fact, was perfectly clear. The lawyers and the judges were very much struck, among other things, by the fact that he had hidden the trinkets and the purse under a stone, without making use of them, and that, what was more, he did not now remember what the trinkets were like, or even how many there were. The fact that he had never opened the purse and did not even know how much was in it seemed incredible. There turned out to be in the purse three hundred and seventeen roubles and sixty kopecks. From being so long under the stone, some of the most valuable notes lying uppermost had suffered from the damp. They were a long while trying to discover why the accused man should tell a lie about this, when about everything else he had made a truthful and straightforward confession. Finally some of the lawyers more versed in psychology admitted that it was possible he had really not looked into the purse, and so didn't know what was in it when he hid it under the stone. But they immediately drew the deduction that the crime could only have been committed through temporary mental derangement, through homicidal mania, without object or the pursuit of gain. This fell in with the most recent fashionable theory of temporary insanity, so often applied in our days in criminal cases. Moreover Raskolnikov's hypochondriacal condition was proved by many witnesses, by Dr. Zossimov, his former fellow students, his landlady and her servant. All this pointed strongly to the conclusion that Raskolnikov was not quite like an ordinary murderer and robber, but that there was another element in the case.

To the intense annoyance of those who maintained this opinion, the criminal scarcely attempted to defend himself. To the decisive question as to what motive impelled him to the murder and the robbery, he answered very clearly with the coarsest frankness that the cause was his miserable position, his poverty and helplessness, and his desire to provide for his first steps in life by the help of the three thousand roubles he had reckoned on finding. He had been led to the murder through his shallow and cowardly nature, exasperated moreover by privation and failure. To the question what led him to confess, he answered that it was his heartfelt repentance. All this was almost coarse....

289

The sentence however was more merciful than could have been expected, perhaps partly because the criminal had not tried to justify himself, but had rather shown a desire to exaggerate his guilt. All the strange and peculiar circumstances of the crime were taken into consideration. There could be no doubt of the abnormal and poverty-stricken condition of the criminal at the time. The fact that he had made no use of what he had stolen was put down partly to the effect of remorse, partly to his abnormal mental condition at the time of the crime. Incidentally the murder of Lizaveta served indeed to confirm the last hypothesis: a man commits two murders and forgets that the door is open! Finally, the confession, at the very moment when the case was hopelessly muddled by the false evidence given by Nikolay through melancholy and fanaticism, and when, moreover, there were no proofs against the real criminal, no suspicions even (Porfiry Petrovitch fully kept his word)—all this did much to soften the sentence. Other circumstances, too, in the prisoner's favour came out quite unexpectedly. Razumihin somehow discovered and proved that while Raskolnikov was at the university he had helped a poor consumptive fellow student and had spent his last penny on supporting him for six months, and when this student died, leaving a decrepit old father whom he had maintained almost from his thirteenth year, Raskolnikov had got the old man into a hospital and paid for his funeral when he died. Raskolnikov's landlady bore witness, too, that when they had lived in another house at Five Corners, Raskolnikov had rescued two little children from a house on fire and was burnt in doing so. This was investigated and fairly well confirmed by many witnesses. These facts made an impression in his favour.

And in the end the criminal was, in consideration of extenuating circumstances, condemned to penal servitude in the second class for a term of eight years only.

At the very beginning of the trial Raskolnikov's mother fell ill. Dounia and Razumihin found it possible to get her out of Petersburg during the trial. Razumihin chose a town on the railway not far from Petersburg, so as to be able to follow every step of the trial and at the same time to see Avdotya Romanovna as often as possible. Pulcheria Alexandrovna's illness was a strange nervous one and was accompanied by a partial derangement of her intellect.

When Dounia returned from her last interview with her brother, she had found her mother already ill, in feverish delirium. That evening Razumihin and she agreed what answers they must make to her mother's questions about Raskolnikov and made up a complete story for her mother's benefit of his having to go away to a distant part of Russia on a business commission, which would bring him in the end money and reputation.

But they were struck by the fact that Pulcheria Alexandrovna never asked them anything on the subject, neither then nor thereafter. On the contrary, she had her own version of her son's sudden departure; she told them with tears how he had come to say goodbye to her, hinting that she alone knew many mysterious and important facts, and that Rodya had many very powerful enemies, so that it was necessary for him to be in hiding. As for his future career, she had no doubt that it would be brilliant when certain sinister influences could be removed. She assured Razumihin that her son would be one day a great statesman, that his article and brilliant literary talent proved it. This article she was continually reading, she even read it aloud, almost took it to bed with her, but scarcely asked where Rodya was, though the subject was obviously avoided by the others, which might have been enough to awaken her suspicions.

They began to be frightened at last at Pulcheria Alexandrovna's strange silence on certain subjects. She did not, for instance, complain of getting no letters from him, though in previous years she had only lived on the hope of letters from her beloved Rodya. This was the cause of great uneasiness to Dounia; the idea occurred to her that her mother suspected that there was something terrible in her son's fate and was afraid to ask, for fear of hearing something still more awful. In any case, Dounia saw clearly that her mother was not in full possession of her faculties.

It happened once or twice, however, that Pulcheria Alexandrovna gave such a turn to the conversation that it was impossible to answer her without mentioning where Rodya was, and on receiving unsatisfactory and suspicious answers she became at once gloomy and silent, and this mood lasted for a long time. Dounia saw at last that it was hard to deceive her and came to the conclusion that it was better to be absolutely silent on certain points; but it became more and more evident that the poor mother suspected something terrible. Dounia remembered her brother's telling her that her mother had overheard her talking in her sleep on the night after her interview with Svidrigaïlov and before the fatal day of the confession: had not she made out something from that? Sometimes days and even weeks of gloomy silence and tears would be succeeded by a period of hysterical animation, and the invalid would begin to talk almost incessantly of her son, of her hopes of his future.... Her fancies were sometimes very strange. They humoured her, pretended to agree with her (she saw perhaps that they were pretending), but she still went on talking.

Five months after Raskolnikov's confession, he was sentenced. Razumihin and Sonia saw him in prison as often as it was possible. At last the moment of separation came. Dounia swore to her brother that the separation should not be for ever, Razumihin did the same. Razumihin, in his youthful ardour, had firmly resolved to lay the foundations at least of a secure livelihood during the next three or four years, and saving up a certain sum, to emigrate to Siberia, a country rich in every natural resource and in need of workers, active men and capital. There they would settle in the town where Rodya was and all together would begin a new life. They all wept at parting.

Raskolnikov had been very dreamy for a few days before. He asked a great deal about his mother and was constantly anxious about her. He worried so much about her that it alarmed Dounia. When he heard about his mother's illness he became very gloomy. With Sonia he was particularly reserved all the time. With the help of the money left to her by Svidrigaïlov, Sonia had long ago made her preparations to follow the party of convicts in which he was despatched to Siberia. Not a word passed between Raskolnikov and her on the subject, but both knew it would be so. At the final leave-taking he smiled strangely at his sister's and Razumihin's fervent anticipations of their happy future together when he should come out of prison. He predicted that their mother's illness would soon have a fatal ending. Sonia and he at last set off.

Two months later Dounia was married to Razumihin. It was a quiet and sorrowful wedding; Porfiry Petrovitch and Zossimov were invited however. During all this period Razumihin wore an air of resolute determination. Dounia put implicit faith in his carrying out his plans and indeed she could not but believe in him. He displayed a rare strength of will. Among other things he began attending university lectures again in order to take his degree. They were continually making plans for the future; both counted on settling in Siberia within five years at least. Till then they rested their hopes on Sonia.

Pulcheria Alexandrovna was delighted to give her blessing to Dounia's marriage with Razumihin; but after the marriage she became even more melancholy and anxious. To give her pleasure Razumihin told her how Raskolnikov had looked after the poor student and his decrepit father and how a year ago he had been burnt and injured in rescuing two little children from a fire. These two pieces of news excited Pulcheria Alexandrovna's disordered imagination almost to ecstasy. She was continually talking about them, even entering into conversation with strangers in the street, though Dounia always accompanied her. In public conveyances and shops, wherever she could capture a listener, she would begin the discourse about her son, his article, how he had helped the student, how he had been burnt at the fire, and so on! Dounia did not know how to restrain her. Apart from the danger of her morbid excitement, there was the risk of someone's recalling Raskolnikov's name and speaking of the recent trial. Pulcheria Alexandrovna found out the address of the mother of the two children her son had saved and insisted on going to see her.

At last her restlessness reached an extreme point. She would sometimes begin to cry suddenly and was often ill and feverishly delirious. One morning she declared that by her reckoning Rodya ought soon to be home, that she remembered when he said goodbye to her he said that they must expect him back in nine months. She began to prepare for his coming, began to do up her room for him, to clean the furniture, to wash and put up new hangings and so on. Dounia was anxious, but said nothing and helped her to arrange the room. After a fatiguing day spent in continual fancies, in joyful daydreams and tears, Pulcheria Alexandrovna was taken ill in the night and by morning she was feverish and delirious. It was brain fever. She died within a fortnight. In her delirium she dropped words which showed that she knew a great deal more about her son's terrible fate than they had supposed.

For a long time Raskolnikov did not know of his mother's death, though a regular correspondence had been maintained from the time he reached Siberia. It was carried on by means of Sonia, who wrote every month to the Razumihins and received an answer with unfailing regularity. At first they found Sonia's letters dry and unsatisfactory, but later on they came to the conclusion that the letters could not be better, for from these letters they received a complete picture of their unfortunate brother's life. Sonia's letters were full of the most matter-of-fact detail, the simplest and clearest description of all Raskolnikov's surroundings as a convict. There was no word of her own hopes, no conjecture as to the future, no description of her feelings. Instead of any attempt to interpret his state of mind and inner life, she gave the simple facts—that is, his own words, an exact account of his health, what he asked for at their interviews, what commission he gave her and so on. All these facts she gave with extraordinary minuteness. The picture of their unhappy brother stood out at last with great clearness and precision. There could be no mistake, because nothing was given but facts.

But Dounia and her husband could get little comfort out of the news, especially at first. Sonia wrote that he was constantly sullen and not ready to talk, that he scarcely seemed interested in the news she gave him from their letters, that he sometimes asked after his mother and that when, seeing that he had guessed the truth, she told him at last of her death, she was surprised to find that he did not seem greatly affected by it, not externally at any rate. She told them that, although he seemed so wrapped up in himself and, as it were, shut himself off from everyone—he took a very direct and simple view of his new life; that he understood his position, expected nothing better for the time, had no ill-founded hopes (as is so common in his position) and scarcely seemed surprised at anything in his surroundings, so unlike anything he had known before. She wrote that his health was satisfactory; he did his work without shirking or seeking to do more; he was almost indifferent about food, but except on Sundays and holidays the food was so bad that at last he had been glad to accept some money from her, Sonia, to have his own tea every day. He begged her not to trouble about anything else, declaring that all this fuss about him only annoyed him. Sonia wrote further that in prison he shared the same room with the rest, that she had not seen the inside of their barracks, but concluded that they were crowded, miserable and unhealthy; that he slept on a plank bed with a rug under him and was unwilling to make any other arrangement. But that he lived so poorly and roughly, not from any plan or design, but simply from inattention and indifference.

Sonia wrote simply that he had at first shown no interest in her visits, had almost been vexed with her indeed for coming, unwilling to talk and rude to her. But that in the end these visits had become a habit and almost a necessity for him, so that he was positively distressed when she was ill for some days and could not visit him. She used to see him on holidays at the prison gates or in the guardroom, to which he was brought for a few minutes to see her. On working days she would go to see him at work either at the workshops or at the brick kilns, or at the sheds on the banks of the Irtish.

About herself, Sonia wrote that she had succeeded in making some acquaintances in the town, that she did sewing, and, as there was scarcely a dressmaker in the town, she was looked upon as an indispensable person in many houses. But she did not mention that the authorities were, through her, interested in Raskolnikov; that his task was lightened and so on.

At last the news came (Dounia had indeed noticed signs of alarm and uneasiness in the preceding letters) that he held aloof from everyone, that his fellow prisoners did not like him, that he kept silent for days at a time and was becoming very pale. In the last letter Sonia wrote that he had been taken very seriously ill and was in the convict ward of the hospital.

He was ill a long time. But it was not the horrors of prison life, not the hard labour, the bad food, the shaven head, or the patched clothes that crushed him. What did he care for all those trials and hardships! he was even glad of the hard work. Physically exhausted, he could at least reckon on a few hours of quiet sleep. And what was the food to him—the thin cabbage soup with beetles floating in it? In the past as a student he had often not had even that. His clothes were warm and suited to his manner of life. He did not even feel the fetters. Was he ashamed of his shaven head and particoloured coat? Before whom? Before Sonia? Sonia was afraid of him, how could he be ashamed before her? And yet he was ashamed even before Sonia, whom he tortured because of it with his contemptuous rough manner. But it was not his shaven head and his fetters he was ashamed of: his pride had been stung to the quick. It was wounded pride that made him ill. Oh, how happy he would have been if he could have blamed himself! He could have borne anything then, even shame and disgrace. But he judged himself severely, and his exasperated conscience found no particularly terrible fault in his past, except a simple *blunder* which might happen to anyone. He was ashamed just because he, Raskolnikov, had so hopelessly, stupidly come to grief through some decree of blind fate, and must humble himself and submit to "the idiocy" of a sentence, if he were anyhow to be at peace.

Vague and objectless anxiety in the present, and in the future a continual sacrifice leading to nothing—that was all that lay before him. And what comfort was it to him that at the end of eight years he would only be thirty-two and able to begin a new life! What had he to live for? What had he to look forward to? Why should he strive? To live in order to exist? Why, he had been ready a thousand times before to give up existence for the sake of an idea, for a hope, even for a fancy. Mere existence had always been too little for him; he had always wanted more. Perhaps it was just because of the strength of his desires that he had thought himself a man to whom more was permissible than to others.

And if only fate would have sent him repentance—burning repentance that would have torn his heart and robbed him of sleep, that repentance, the awful agony of which brings visions of hanging or drowning! Oh, he would have been glad of it! Tears and agonies would at least have been life. But he did not repent of his crime.

At least he might have found relief in raging at his stupidity, as he had raged at the grotesque blunders that had brought him to prison. But now in prison, *in freedom*, he thought over and criticised all his actions again and by no means found them so blundering and so grotesque as they had seemed at the fatal time.

"In what way," he asked himself, "was my theory stupider than others that have swarmed and clashed from the beginning of the world? One has only to look at the thing quite independently, broadly, and uninfluenced by commonplace ideas, and my idea will by no means seem so... strange. Oh, sceptics and halfpenny philosophers, why do you halt halfway!

"Why does my action strike them as so horrible?" he said to himself. "Is it because it was a crime? What is meant by crime? My conscience is at rest. Of course, it was a legal crime, of course, the letter of the law was broken and blood was shed. Well, punish me for the letter of the law... and that's enough. Of course, in that case many of the benefactors of mankind who snatched power for themselves instead of inheriting it ought to have been punished at their first steps. But those men succeeded and so *they were right*, and I didn't, and so I had no right to have taken that step."

It was only in that that he recognised his criminality, only in the fact that he had been unsuccessful and had confessed it.

He suffered too from the question: why had he not killed himself? Why had he stood looking at the river and preferred to confess? Was the desire to live so strong and was it so hard to overcome it? Had not Svidrigaïlov overcome it, although he was afraid of death?

In misery he asked himself this question, and could not understand that, at the very time he had been standing looking into the river, he had perhaps been dimly conscious of the fundamental falsity in himself and his convictions. He didn't understand that that consciousness might be the promise of a future crisis, of a new view of life and of his future resurrection.

He preferred to attribute it to the dead weight of instinct which he could not step over, again through weakness and meanness. He looked at his fellow prisoners and was amazed to see how they all loved life and prized it. It seemed to him that they loved and valued life more in prison than in freedom. What terrible agonies and privations some of them, the tramps for instance, had endured! Could they care so much for a ray of sunshine, for the primeval forest, the cold spring hidden away in some unseen spot, which the tramp had marked three years before, and longed to see again, as he might to see his sweetheart, dreaming of the green grass round it and the bird singing in the bush? As he went on he saw still more inexplicable examples.

In prison, of course, there was a great deal he did not see and did not want to see; he lived as it were with downcast eyes. It was loathsome and unbearable for him to look. But in the end there was much that surprised him and he began, as it were involuntarily, to notice much that he had not suspected before. What surprised him most of all was the terrible impossible gulf that lay between him and all the rest. They seemed to be a different species, and he looked at them and they at him with distrust and hostility. He felt and knew the reasons of his isolation, but he would never have admitted till then that those reasons were so deep and strong. There were some Polish exiles, political prisoners, among them. They simply looked down upon all the rest as ignorant churls; but Raskolnikov could not look upon them like that. He saw that these ignorant men were in many respects far wiser than the Poles. There were some Russians who were just as contemptuous, a former officer and two seminarists. Raskolnikov saw their mistake as clearly. He was disliked and avoided by everyone; they even began to hate him at last—why, he could not tell. Men who had been far more guilty despised and laughed at his crime.

"You're a gentleman," they used to say. "You shouldn't hack about with an axe; that's not a gentleman's work."

The second week in Lent, his turn came to take the sacrament with his gang. He went to church and prayed with the others. A quarrel broke out one day, he did not know how. All fell on him at once in a fury.

"You're an infidel! You don't believe in God," they shouted. "You ought to be killed."

He had never talked to them about God nor his belief, but they wanted to kill him as an infidel. He said nothing. One of the prisoners rushed at him in a perfect frenzy. Raskolnikov awaited him calmly and silently; his eyebrows did not quiver, his face did not flinch. The guard succeeded in intervening between him and his assailant, or there would have been bloodshed.

There was another question he could not decide: why were they all so fond of Sonia? She did not try to win their favour; she rarely met them, sometimes only she came to see him at work for a moment. And yet everybody knew her, they knew that she had come out to follow *him*, knew how and where she lived. She never gave them money, did them no particular services. Only once at Christmas she sent them all presents of pies and rolls. But by degrees closer relations sprang up between them and Sonia. She would write and post letters for them to their relations. Relations of the prisoners who visited the town, at their instructions, left with Sonia presents and money for them. Their wives and sweethearts knew her and used to visit her. And when she visited Raskolnikov at work, or met a party of the prisoners on the road, they all took off their hats to her. "Little mother Sofya Semyonovna, you are our dear, good little mother," coarse branded criminals said to that frail little creature. She would smile and bow to them and everyone was delighted when she smiled. They even admired her gait and turned round to watch her walking; they admired her too for being so little, and, in fact, did not know what to admire her most for. They even came to her for help in their illnesses.

He was in the hospital from the middle of Lent till after Easter. When he was better, he remembered the dreams he had had while he was feverish and delirious. He dreamt that the whole world was condemned to a terrible new strange plague that had come to Europe from the depths of Asia. All were to be destroyed except a very few chosen. Some new sorts of microbes were

294

attacking the bodies of men, but these microbes were endowed with intelligence and will. Men attacked by them became at once mad and furious. But never had men considered themselves so intellectual and so completely in possession of the truth as these sufferers, never had they considered their decisions, their scientific conclusions, their moral convictions so infallible. Whole villages, whole towns and peoples went mad from the infection. All were excited and did not understand one another. Each thought that he alone had the truth and was wretched looking at the others, beat himself on the breast, wept, and wrung his hands. They did not know how to judge and could not agree what to consider evil and what good; they did not know whom to blame, whom to justify. Men killed each other in a sort of senseless spite. They gathered together in armies against one another, but even on the march the armies would begin attacking each other, the ranks would be broken and the soldiers would fall on each other, stabbing and cutting, biting and devouring each other. The alarm bell was ringing all day long in the towns; men rushed together, but why they were summoned and who was summoning them no one knew. The most ordinary trades were abandoned, because everyone proposed his own ideas, his own improvements, and they could not agree. The land too was abandoned. Men met in groups, agreed on something, swore to keep together, but at once began on something quite different from what they had proposed. They accused one another, fought and killed each other. There were conflagrations and famine. All men and all things were involved in destruction. The plague spread and moved further and further. Only a few men could be saved in the whole world. They were a pure chosen people, destined to found a new race and a new life, to renew and purify the earth, but no one had seen these men, no one had heard their words and their voices.

Raskolnikov was worried that this senseless dream haunted his memory so miserably, the impression of this feverish delirium persisted so long. The second week after Easter had come. There were warm bright spring days; in the prison ward the grating windows under which the sentinel paced were opened. Sonia had only been able to visit him twice during his illness; each time she had to obtain permission, and it was difficult. But she often used to come to the hospital yard, especially in the evening, sometimes only to stand a minute and look up at the windows of the ward.

One evening, when he was almost well again, Raskolnikov fell asleep. On waking up he chanced to go to the window, and at once saw Sonia in the distance at the hospital gate. She seemed to be waiting for someone. Something stabbed him to the heart at that minute. He shuddered and moved away from the window. Next day Sonia did not come, nor the day after; he noticed that he was expecting her uneasily. At last he was discharged. On reaching the prison he learnt from the convicts that Sofya Semyonovna was lying ill at home and was unable to go out.

He was very uneasy and sent to inquire after her; he soon learnt that her illness was not dangerous. Hearing that he was anxious about her, Sonia sent him a pencilled note, telling him that she was much better, that she had a slight cold and that she would soon, very soon come and see him at his work. His heart throbbed painfully as he read it.

Again it was a warm bright day. Early in the morning, at six o'clock, he went off to work on the river bank, where they used to pound alabaster and where there was a kiln for baking it in a shed. There were only three of them sent. One of the convicts went with the guard to the fortress to fetch a tool; the other began getting the wood ready and laying it in the kiln. Raskolnikov came out of the shed on to the river bank, sat down on a heap of logs by the shed and began gazing at the wide deserted river. From the high bank a broad landscape opened before him, the sound of singing floated faintly audible from the other bank. In the vast steppe, bathed in sunshine, he could just see, like black specks, the nomads' tents. There there was freedom, there other men were living, utterly unlike those here; there time itself seemed to stand still, as though the age of Abraham and his flocks had not passed. Raskolnikov sat gazing, his thoughts passed into daydreams, into contemplation; he thought of nothing, but a vague restlessness excited and troubled him. Suddenly he found Sonia beside him; she had come up noiselessly and sat down at his side. It was still quite early; the morning chill was still keen. She wore her poor old burnous and the green shawl; her face still showed signs of illness, it was thinner and paler. She gave him a joyful smile of welcome, but held out her hand with her usual timidity. She was always timid of holding out her hand to him and sometimes did not offer it at all, as though afraid he would repel it. He always took her hand as though with repugnance, always seemed vexed to meet her and was sometimes obstinately silent throughout her visit. Sometimes she trembled before him and went away deeply grieved. But now their hands did not part. He stole a rapid glance at her and dropped his eyes on the ground without speaking. They were alone, no one had seen them. The guard had turned away for the time.

How it happened he did not know. But all at once something seemed to seize him and fling him at her feet. He wept and threw his arms round her knees. For the first instant she was terribly frightened and she turned pale. She jumped up and looked at him trembling. But at the same moment she understood, and a light of infinite happiness came into her eyes. She knew and had no doubt that he loved her beyond everything and that at last the moment had come....

They wanted to speak, but could not; tears stood in their eyes. They were both pale and thin; but those sick pale faces were bright with the dawn of a new future, of a full resurrection into a new life. They were renewed by love; the heart of each held infinite sources of life for the heart of the other.

They resolved to wait and be patient. They had another seven years to wait, and what terrible suffering and what infinite happiness before them! But he had risen again and he knew it and felt it in all his being, while she—she only lived in his life.

On the evening of the same day, when the barracks were locked, Raskolnikov lay on his plank bed and thought of her. He had even fancied that day that all the convicts who had been his enemies looked at him differently; he had even entered into talk with them and they answered him in a friendly way. He remembered that now, and thought it was bound to be so. Wasn't everything now bound to be changed?

He thought of her. He remembered how continually he had tormented her and wounded her heart. He remembered her pale and thin little face. But these recollections scarcely troubled him now; he knew with what infinite love he would now repay all her sufferings. And what were all, *all* the agonies of the past! Everything, even his crime, his sentence and imprisonment, seemed to him now in the first rush of feeling an external, strange fact with which he had no concern. But he could not think for long together of anything that evening, and he could not have analysed anything consciously; he was simply feeling. Life had stepped into the place of theory and something quite different would work itself out in his mind.

Under his pillow lay the New Testament. He took it up mechanically. The book belonged to Sonia; it was the one from which she had read the raising of Lazarus to him. At first he was afraid that she would worry him about religion, would talk about the gospel and pester him with books. But to his great surprise she had not once approached the subject and had not even offered him the Testament. He had asked her for it himself not long before his illness and she brought him the book without a word. Till now he had not opened it.

He did not open it now, but one thought passed through his mind: "Can her convictions not be mine now? Her feelings, her aspirations at least...."

She too had been greatly agitated that day, and at night she was taken ill again. But she was so happy—and so unexpectedly happy—that she was almost frightened of her happiness. Seven years, *only* seven years! At the beginning of their happiness at some moments they were both ready to look on those seven years as though they were seven days. He did not know that the new life would not be given him for nothing, that he would have to pay dearly for it, that it would cost him great striving, great suffering.

But that is the beginning of a new story—the story of the gradual renewal of a man, the story of his gradual regeneration, of his passing from one world into another, of his initiation into a new unknown life. That might be the subject of a new story, but our present story is ended.

Made in the USA
Monee, IL
15 December 2021